Broken Benevolence

Dr. Naomi Alexander, Book 3

S.F. Powell

NIB KARATASI
PRESS

©ACT3 ENTERPRISES LLC

Nib Karatasi Press, Upper Marlboro, MD

For permission requests, write to the publisher, addressed "Attention: Permissions Coordinator," at this address: ACT3 Enterprises, LLC – Nib Karatasi Press, PO Box 4726, Upper Marlboro, MD 20775

Online contact: visit www.sfpowell.com

Publisher's Note: This is a work of fiction. Names, characters, places, and incidents are a product of the author's imagination. Locales and public names are sometimes used for atmospheric purposes. Any resemblance to actual people, living or dead, or to businesses, companies, events, institutions, or locales is completely coincidental. The author is not a doctor. This work of fiction is for entertainment only and is not intended as a substitute for the medical advice of real physicians. The reader should regularly consult a licensed physician in matters relating to their mental/ physical health.

Broken Benevolence / S.F. Powell

Library of Congress Control Number: 2023906793

ISBNs: 978-1-7327224-6-0 / 978-1-7327224-7-7 / 978-1-7327224-8-4

Book Cover Design by ebooklaunch.com

Author photograph by Vicki Kelliebrew

Also By S.F. Powell

Like Sweet Buttermilk
Obscure Boundaries

Acknowledgments

Forever grateful to the Creator, for all of it. We're doing the thing.

Thanks to:
My "Front Pew" Crew (you know who you are)
Greg Prather
Aileen Atcherson

And always: Momma

To:
Pam – whose strength inspires without meaning to.
Debbie – whose perseverance is (no longer) her best kept secret.

"This above all: to thine own self be true."

—William Shakespeare, *Hamlet*

Prologue

"A White Christmas" (Two Years Ago)

G ingerbread.

That's what this smells like.

And pine. And burned bacon. Blood. Urine. Holly.

But oddly, mainly, this horror smells like...gingerbread.

Everything happened so fast. And now, time moved at a glacial pace.

Why... Why does blood smell metallic? Like...licking a rusty nail?

"Ma?!" That was followed by a heavy moan: Chelsea.

Marcus made no sound, but she could help no one.

Metal. And gingerbread. And pine, and urine, and...

Pain was everywhere and nowhere. She couldn't isolate where she hurt worst or even hurt exactly—uncertain if that was good or bad.

Does it smell and taste so metallic because of the iron in it? The copper, maybe? And did someone turn the air conditioner on?

The thirty degrees outside slinked inside. Growing colder by the second, she wondered why she'd be pondering such unimportant things when the pain in her ribs and the subtle but continuous feeling of draining away throughout her everything else told her not to mind such trivialities: she'd be dead soon.

"Ma?! Please! Someb—!" Chelsea again; her moan an almost rallying cry of painful hopelessness.

Rustling movement and footsteps overhead.

Someone dropped their keys; they landed next to a crushed gingerbread square. In the glow of the twinkling Christmas tree lights, she saw letters on a maroon crescent-moon keychain before a glove-holding brown hand (a Masonic ring askew on the pinky) picked them up. The ring had tape for a better fit. The carpet, soggy now with bodily fluids from her and others, squelched as Carhartt work boots passed her. Mesmerizing hues of red, yellow, and green bounced off the odd-shaped scuff on the left boot before it disappeared from view.

The devil's in the details.

She wanted to laugh at that. And why was Marcus so quiet? She stared at the Christmas tree (the twinkling colors offering their support) and tried to remember if they fried more bacon after burning the first round. She tried to rise, but pain (crisp, sharp, and unforgiving) halted everything.

Staring at the Christmas tree lights was better.

Repeated clicking and beams preceded distinct buzz-whir sounds. Distinct...but she couldn't place it.

Larimore popped into her mind and was gone just as quickly.

"Is the bitch dead?" A sadly familiar voice asked this question with such hopeful anticipation; she experienced pain having nothing to do with her plethora of physical injuries. Familiar, too, was the staid cologne scent now mingling with the blood and urine and pine and gingerbread.

"Lickety-split," came the answer in a voice that might have been familiar (the phrasing peculiar) if the gingerbread and blood and pine and urine smells (and the fading-away sensation) didn't keep interfering.

No response to Mr. Lickety-Split.

A trained swimmer back in the day, she still had skill with holding her breath and used it now. She stared straight, moved no muscle, and made no sound for fear of having the question answered with force in the absolute affirmative.

She thought she heard Chelsea moan again, but pain throughout her own body was in furious debate with the fading-away sensation, the winner yet to be determined.

No fading, Cecily. Focus on the lights...and pray.

Red (closer to a pinkish) and blue and white and green and yellow...

Much better.

Someone cleared away the condoms.

Another of them then cleared the duct tape from over her mouth, snatching it off with unfounded, unnecessary, and confounding malice, creating a new source of pain spanning the front of her face—but she could breathe so much better now, breathe over and around the blood in her nasal passages (suffocation probability: reduced).

"White Christmas" by the Drifters played on and on from the CD player in the kitchen, adding a note of seasonal cheer. Thinking she heard sirens, she prayed within as she focused on the lights, thanking God for her many blessings, praying for the well-being of her children, and—

Is... Is that blood dripping from the bulbs? From the tree? My *blood?!*

She laughed then. Laughed through the pain, not caring if she was heard, and helped along to her doom (a much better relief compared to this).

She laughed and worried for her children as the pain began losing the debate with her consciousness.

Cecily laughed as she faded, thoughts of the Gingerbread Man dancing in her pained head...

He didn't know what the fuck was so funny.

How could she be...*laughing?*

Her laughter died as emergency responders arrived, sirens blaring.

Dammit. Who called the—?

Chest burning and stinging inside and out, he reclined, resuming the position, and waited.

He fumed over the turn of events but began planning anew.

Chapter One

Southern Belle in the North

S he liked the cold. And the quiet. And right now, each endeavored to make her feel welcomed. The cold made you go inside yourself for warmth. The quiet? Well, nothing to do in the quiet but think.

Cecily slowed her already slow walking pace.

No hurry to get home. Not today. Not on the anniversary of—

There were anniversaries of births and marriages and career service achievements. And anniversaries...of other things.

"It doesn't feel like two years." She startled at the sound of her voice breaking through and against the thirty-nine-degree day. The temperature was above-freezing but didn't feel like it. MIA for two days now, the sun allowed an uncharitable pall to cast upon the withering lawns and chilly sidewalks. The air itself was...gray.

She was a Southern belle in the north: Cleveland didn't get cold like this. Cecily pulled her handkerchief from her coat pocket and dabbed her tearing-from-the-cold eyes.

Two *years*? The question (both asked and answered) sat in her throat, threatening to choke her with the realization that, yes, although it didn't feel like it, it had been two years since the home invasion.

And yet, another winter of discontent.

Cecily sent her gaze forward: about a mile before reaching home.

Oscar called her a nut for getting off the bus so far from home. Said she was a nut for taking the bus back and forth to work—especially with an Infinity Q70, a Nissan Maxima, and a newly restored 1967 Cadillac Deville convertible parked at home. Oscar called her a nut (and other names, too) for a lot of things.

The Deville was hers, however. To do (or not do) with as she pleased. Even Oscar didn't have the keys—and that felt good. It was her piece of happiness.

"Larimore's gonna love it." She whispered the words as if she weren't alone on the street, and gumminess formed behind her eyelids as her heart sank. She was far from home (and not the home waiting at the end of her walk). Cleveland, Mississippi: *that* was home. Or it used to be.

As small as it was, she missed her family. She needed to call Kyle, too. Only older by two years, he sometimes acted like he was her father. And although Daddy died when she was 18, Kyle was 20, and Larimore was 16, their father (and Mama, too) did a fine job raising them to that point. At 44, she didn't need Kyle's guidance. Cecily grinned against the cold; maybe it was time to visit him.

Kyle wasn't visiting her. Not while she was married to Oscar. Kyle loved Roland. But Roland...was gone.

Fighting tears (it was just too cold to cry), Cecily wished for a hat (although she wouldn't wear it for fear of messing up her hair and pissing Oscar off), and her stupid contact lenses irritated (although she could see fine without them).

Besides, tears would not bring her dead husband back.

She shifted thoughts to her Deville and her younger brother's utter joy once he laid eyes on it (*if* he ever laid eyes on it). Larimore was up for parole soon; there was hope.

She sat on the bench in the mini park, taking her usual time to prepare for going home. She did her best to forget what day it was, but she wasn't one of the lucky ones—and an elephant never forgets.

Two years. Or was it just yesterday?

Refusing to allow tears to freeze on her cheeks, Cecily wanted her parents in a way she hadn't wanted (or needed) them since she was a child. But a train wreck left that option defunct.

Why are you harping on all this stuff? Because it's the anniversary?

She focused on a sparrow, pondering the answer.

His eye is on the sparrow...

Cecily startled as the bird took flight. She needed to get home.

Wonder what's happening at the Ellis? The Arts and Jazz Festival's coming this spring...

Her mind here, there, and everywhere, she didn't feel good; feeling much like one of her "episodes" (as Oscar called them) coming on. She dreaded them but couldn't help them, either. The episodes left her drained and confused, and so...*angry.*

Not this time. I don't care what day it is; I won't this time.

Her grandson's tiny, innocent giggle filled her head, and Cecily smiled despite the cold. Maybe she could get away for a little while, visit Marcus and her grandson (named Roland after his grandfather). She missed her son, but like her brother, Marcus wanted no part of her marriage to Oscar. And after being beaten and shot when those men invaded their home two years ago (today), he also imposed and expressed his protest by moving away and staying away. Oscar wasn't his father, and he didn't like him, her son often told her, so there was no need in faking the funk. And, embracing his adulthood at 22, Marcus faked no funks. He and his Uncle Kyle got along splendidly. Marcus's dislike of Oscar aside, Cecily missed her son.

Chelsea (now 20) left the house after her rape and assault two years ago and never looked back. And although she sided with her brother on many of his views about Oscar, Chelsea was less expressive with her protest, displayed more tolerance and understanding. Still, she stayed away—and Cecily missed her daughter, too.

She once worried Oscar had somehow abused them, but Marcus and Chelsea were adamant he hadn't. She reassured them their inheritance was safe, couldn't be touched by anyone but them. Marcus and Chelsea weren't concerned about the money, either; they had complete faith in her and the handling of their financial affairs. They simply didn't like Oscar, didn't like her with him.

Her children were adults, couldn't be convinced of Oscar's merits, so discussions about him didn't happen. Oscar had good qualities. He did. Although her children disagreed, marrying Oscar benefited her. In the end, Oscar had her best interests at heart.

No one else would want her, anyway.

Oscar had his fair share of trials, of failures and successes. He tried hard, too. You didn't just walk away from that. Oscar wasn't always the nicest person and could be downright mean sometimes, but she wasn't perfect, either. You take the good and bad in marriage. After six years of marriage, taking more of the bad was presumable.

You didn't have it bad with Roland.

She didn't have it bad now, either (did she?). Cecily sighed. She didn't feel good: anxious and headachy.

Two years.

The case had grown cold. Although they had DNA samples, nothing more had come of it. It surprised and saddened her: despite advances in forensic and crime-solving technology, cases still went unsolved.

Despair threatened to surface, and Cecily almost went with it. It was a daily struggle *not* to give in. Not to just run into the waiting arms of Miss Madness and find a bizarre peace and solace only she could give. But there were her children to consider, and her grandson, and Oscar.

Go home, Cecily. Just go home.

She should, and she would.

Your flowers can't be out here like this, Cecily. Take them inside.

Cecily glanced down at her fingers curled around the green foil paper enclosing fresh flowers. She'd forgotten she had them. They could be fickle with her (sometimes lasting weeks, other times, just days), but she liked fresh flowers, no matter the season.

Flowers are perfect for acknowledging anniversaries.

Cecily shut her eyes. When she opened them again, she watched a squirrel scurry across the street, another following, right on its tail. Perhaps they were hurrying to get out of the cold.

She'd given the police what she remembered: the keychain, the scuff on the boot, the missing brooch (a high school graduation gift from her mother; it was the only thing they took, but one of the many things that hurt). But it wasn't much, so they couldn't do much with it. Oscar even reported a name he thought he heard them call out as they moved about the house that night, but again: nothing.

And she was left with nothing, too: nothing but the pain of what happened to her family, nothing but...episodes.

Cecily sat, missing her home in Cleveland, missing Marcus and Chelsea, missing Roland.

Sadness, intense and full, stabbed her middle with thoughts of her dead husband. She'd spent sixteen loving years with Roland "RC" Cooper, bore him two children, and then...brain cancer gave them *in sickness and in health* before finally opting for *till death do us part*. He'd been gone almost ten years now, and while her memories of him softened with time, her love for Roland and the sadness over losing him didn't.

"Oh, Roland..." Cecily watched the condensation of her breath in the cold air disappear—much like Roland did from her life.

It was cold. Just downright, no-wind-chill cold, *stiff* cold (unusual for early December). Sitting still on a park bench made it even colder.

Cecily didn't move. She breathed in the frosty gray air, gazed into the gray day, and didn't move. This wasn't her usual quiet moment of respite taken before doing something. Today, this anniversary day, sitting on the bench was different. She so didn't feel good.

Maybe I'll stop in to see Janyce first.

Janyce (with a "Y," not an "I") was the closest thing she had to a friend up here, so Cecily guessed Janyce was her best friend (although, at 44, do you have "best" friends anymore?). She met Janyce Mabry soon after she and Oscar and the kids moved into the neighborhood (and befriended her soon after that).

Cecily liked Janyce because she was loud and materialistic. Janyce wasn't a good listener, but she was an excellent distraction, so the tradeoff was fair enough. Janyce's husband, "Hank" (his real name was Carson, and although curious, Cecily never asked why he had such an odd nickname), was a quiet soul much like herself, with this bass of a voice making people take pause sometimes when he spoke. He was such a sweet guy, and Cecily, for the life of her, couldn't figure out why he ended up (or even stayed) with Janyce. But she said nothing: to each his own and all that.

The Mabrys were childless, and Cecily sensed that while Hank would've welcomed a son or daughter (or both), Janyce wasn't interested—because she didn't want to share. Being a parent meant sharing your blessings with them such that, if you could, you one day afforded them a life better than your own. But Janyce liked her things and her Hank: sharing either would be problematic for her.

Oscar wasn't interested in having children, either, having abandoned his parental rights to his daughter, Keisha. Keisha was grown, living in Germany, but Cecily ensured the lines of communication remained open. Oscar couldn't have cared less. He said he was too old to have children, but in the deepest parts of herself, Cecily believed he didn't want to share, either.

Advances in medicine made it possible for women, even in their 50s, to have healthy babies, but Cecily was far past the baby-having stage of her life. With Oscar six years her senior, given his view of age and having children, he was way past. It mattered not. And when she interacted with that deepest part of herself? It was all for the best.

If Janyce's silver Mercedes sat in the driveway, she would visit and extend her respite. She could sit with Janyce and listen to her tales of shopping adventures and merchandise returns, of upcoming travel plans and holiday party plans...and lose herself long enough to forget (if only temporarily) what today was.

Cecily doubted Janyce remembered what this day was; she too often suggested Cecily forget what happened, leave all that in the past.

Headachy sensation frolicked at her temples, and nausea wanted to play, too, flitting around to tease her stomach. The gray cold introduced itself to her bones as she sat on the park bench, but Cecily stayed put. Even the promise of warmth inside the Mabry home couldn't get her moving.

Not yet. She liked the cold.

All this mind-wandering interfered with a memory trying to surface. A memory the police could do something with. A memory to free her...

Cecily focused, trying to obliterate thoughts of Cleveland and Kyle and Larimore and train wrecks and Roland and Chelsea and Marcus and little Roland and Oscar and Janyce (and even "Hank"), to allow the memory to burst through.

It wouldn't.

It was there; Cecily sensed it circulating her subconscious. But it was cold, and she didn't feel good. Frustrated and fed up with her unsuccessful attempts to release it, the memory turned tail on her, moving in the opposite direction, burrowing deeper in her mind.

Desperate, Cecily willed the memory forward, wanting it to stop messing with her already and illuminate the darkness, *her* darkness. "Please...?"

A tiny puff of condensation winked at her before vanishing into the gray cold.

Not to be cajoled, the memory stayed put in the recesses of her mind.

Cecily stayed put, too, thinking of nothing and no one in particular, just wanting to feel better. The no-wind-chill cold added a mild breeze to its fun, sending wafts of pine to her nostrils. Sometimes the whiff of pine gave her the creeps, made her afraid and weary.

Times like now.

Janyce's house.

"Yes!" Cecily got moving.

Alas, the temporary asylum of the Mabrys' family room (or kitchen) wasn't available: although her car was in her driveway, Janyce wasn't home. Cecily's disappointment numbed her; she couldn't move at first. Her legs stubborn and uncooperative, she stood on the Mabry porch.

Today just wasn't her day.

Or maybe it was precisely her day.

Legs finally working, Cecily made her way the few houses down to her own home. She gripped the wrapped stems of her flowers tighter, thinking of playing a little Nina Simone to quell her nerves, maybe listen to "Mississippi Goddam" on repeat—it was a violent protest song, sometimes soothing her when it didn't...ignite her.

She paused in her driveway, feeling better as she ran a hand over her "Devin," once more hopeful her younger brother would get to see it soon.

The 1967 Cadillac Deville convertible pushed its interesting blue against the hateful grayness of the day (its paint wasn't royal-blue or cyan or a sky-blue, but a combination such that only "interesting blue" sufficed). Cecily took her keys out of her bag (Marcus had the other set) and got inside, relishing the new-leather smell. She worked hard to restore the car and had a ball doing it. "Devin" (her improvised derivative of Deville) was auto-show ready, but having the car finished also meant the distraction was over.

Take it for a spin. Don't go in there yet.

"Saturday," Cecily promised herself (and the steering wheel). Now having something to look forward to, she nodded with excitement and confirmation, thinking of riding with the top down in the bitter cold. "I need to get you in the garage, though, boy; this isn't cutting it." She got out, leaving Devin to sit and chill (literally) in the driveway. No, her car wasn't a "girl," and Cecily liked it that way.

Why doesn't Oscar have a set of keys?

"You know why." Cecily headed for her front door, entertaining it no further.

She entered the house, the alarm beeping to announce her presence—and then everything went wrong.

The music: wrong. And the smells: all very, very bad and wrong. Oscar smiled at her as he approached from their kitchen, a plate of gingerbread squares in his hand.

And then everything (the whole awful lot of it) was happening again.

Cecily didn't remember going into the closet, but there she was (the coattails brushing against her said so), and she wasn't leaving. She didn't bother to turn on the light, preferring the dark. She wasn't going out there. Out there with the wrong music and the wrong...*smells*. "White Christmas" by the Drifters insisted on traveling through her covered ears. She thought she screamed for the music to stop, but wasn't sure. Oscar talked to her through the door, asking what was wrong, asking if she was okay. She screamed for him not to open the door, not to let those things (the music and smells) in with her.

Pine and holly and burned bacon and urine and gingerbread and...blood.

... She'd just finished putting the leftovers away, trying to figure out the best way to get the odor of burned bacon out of her home, when a loud bang from the front of the house sent her that way, fear knotting her insides. She had time to see her front door hanging open, to wonder why the alarm didn't sound, to see someone in a ski mask and wearing dark-blue heading through their living room, when white pain crashed through the back of her head.

...Screams. Chelsea. Those screams cut short. Cecily's eyes fluttered open. Her head felt the size of a pumpkin and had the pain to go with it. Someone was on top of her, grunting and breathing gingerbread breath on her; an erection hurried in and out of her passage. Her screams bounced against the duct tape covering her mouth and ricocheted into her throat; the binding plastic ties dug into her wrists. More men took turns with her in the rape-train, saying such vulgar, unnecessary things. She checked out, sending her mind somewhere, *anywhere* else...

...Rustling from somewhere upstairs, a gunshot, and then another. Chelsea?! Marcus?! Oscar? The last man finished his business, pulled away, and then a boot (black and just big) rammed *into her torso from her left. Another slammed into her head from the right. And then...nothing.*

"Please..." Cecily pleaded into the dark closet, wanting everything to stop. The headache teasing her temples as she sat on the bench earlier now exploded in her head, threatening to take up permanent residence. The tang of bile surrounded her, but the putrid stink didn't add to her distress. It wasn't a bad smell. Not like those others. "Please..." On her knees, Cecily rocked in place.

...*Sharp, vicious, critical pain seared her abdomen, bringing her around in time* to see the blade leaving her body. Her face throbbed in atrocious magnitude. She'd also voided her bladder at some point. In a haze of pain-filled vision, she observed several soiled condoms around her. *Several!?* The cold from outdoors flooded in from the busted front door, but it was warm compared to the iciness filling her body. Nothing from Marcus. Faint moans from Chelsea.

Staring at the Christmas tree, *Cecily faded again;...the darkness much better than this.*

The closet door opened despite her protests, and although the music stopped, Cecily could still hear it, still smell, not just the gingerbread Oscar made, but the pine, and holly, and—

"Ma'am?"

Curled into a ball on the floor, Cecily didn't move or speak.

"Just help her, man!" Oscar liked to bark orders when he was impatient (or bored).

"Sir, if you'd step back."

Oscar scoffed, but Cecily sensed him stepping back.

A hand touched her shoulder. It was a kind hand, but she cringed away from it still.

The hand left her.

Images from that night wouldn't let her go, but she couldn't keep company with the wrong music, bad smells, and depraved people. Help was here, just like it was back then.

Wasn't it?

"Ma'am? ...Cecily?"

"...Yes."

"Cecily,...can I help you up?" This voice was soft and caring but distinctly male.

Cecily felt herself nodding.

"I'm going to touch your arm now. Is that all right?"

Cecily allowed the gentleman to help her stand, but she wouldn't open her eyes.

"Ma'am, are you ill?" A woman's voice: caring but also annoyed.

"What th—? She's got vomit all down her clothes and on the floor. Of course, she's ill."

"Sir..." The tone (from the man) implored Oscar to shut up.

Cecily opened her eyes, wavering some with the light hitting them, but Mr. EMT held her steady at the elbow.

"Take it easy, ma'am," Miss EMT cautioned. She was tall and slender, her hair in a tight bun at the top which arched her eyebrows.

Cecily shifted her gaze to Oscar.

He had that look: the one appearing concerned and nervous, but with eyes reading the opposite. His mustache twitched with disapproval.

She may pay for this later. This was her third episode in as many weeks. They came more frequently since Thanksgiving, but Cecily didn't know how to help that.

Her flowers lay on the floor, delicate petals scattered, some crushed. Where was her bag?

Cecily looked at Mr. EMT (cute, late 20s, mediocre nose). "I'm okay now. Just need some water..." But she trembled still, and something in her eyes must have told Mr. EMT she wasn't okay at all.

He shook his head. "Ma'am— Cecily, I'd like to check your vitals."

"Len...?"

"Len" eyed Miss EMT (her badge read: "Donella") and nodded.

Hours later, Cecily lay in a hospital bed, trying to follow the documentary on television (a fascinating exposition on the Hershey company), doing her best to fight the effects of whatever sedative they administered. She failed miserably (and didn't dream at all).

She awoke, surprised to find it was the next day. The day *after*. The anniversary was gone.

She should've felt better.

Cecily signaled for her nurse.

It was mid-afternoon by the time she could freshen, eat (not much), and have her consult with Dr. Englewood.

Possessing a suitable bedside manner, he was a tall beanpole of a man with a slender, pinched, weak nose. He reminded her of Ichabod Crane. She and Oscar listened as Englewood recapped her medical condition (physically healthy but underweight) and prescribed alternatives to help her mental state.

Oscar went on his rant about her having seen a psychiatrist before, how nothing helped, how doctors get paid much money for a bunch of *I-don't-knows* as diagnoses and not helping people.

Cecily said nothing, in part agreeing with her husband. She'd spent months under the psychiatric care of Dr. Lewis, resulting in little more than a few venting exercises and several prescriptions for drugs with names most couldn't pronounce, and she had never filled. She was none the worse for it, but none the better, either: the "episodes" continued.

Dr. Englewood listened to Oscar's doctors-are-quacks tirade with only the tiniest hint of annoyance in his brown eyes before he nodded acceptance of Oscar's right to have an opinion. Englewood continued his task, asking her questions before entering something in her chart. He understood when she couldn't remember much of what happened while in that closet yesterday, let alone what happened two years ago.

She kept the things she did remember to herself: it was all too muddled to make sense—and she had enough people thinking she was crazy. In the end, Dr. Englewood couldn't force her to do anything. She was of sound mind (essentially) and not a threat to anyone (thus far).

When Oscar left the room to take a call, Dr. Englewood placed a brochure on her side table and a business card in her hand. "Sometimes, the *second* time's the charm," he'd said, his eyes imploring her to take his medical advice.

Cecily nodded, unsure what she was going to do (if anything).

Dr. Englewood and Oscar passed each other in the doorway, the doctor offering Oscar a customary parting shake of his hand.

Oscar didn't stay long (or *couldn't stay*), but Cecily chilled, allowing her mind the rest it needed. She called the office and informed Josh she'd be out a few days. She talked with Chelsea and Marcus and updated them (only half-listening to Marcus's leave-Oscar speech) before enjoying the delightful babble of her toddler grandson on the phone.

It was quiet, and she wasn't doing anything other than completing another page of the Jumbo Word-Find book a nurse kindly offered, when Cecily put her pencil down and reached for the brochure and card she'd placed on the side table without giving much additional thought. Joshua's "Get Well Soon" balloon and his flowers rested on the table, too, and a wisp of breath bottled inside her chest with her upturned lips at them.

Setting the card aside, Cecily reviewed the brochure first.

The brochure was for a psychiatric facility in Virginia, with pages of copy full of soothing words and marketing jargon to get you to sign right up. Cecily put it down, uninterested. She picked up the business card.

She expected more information than that provided.

Dr. Lewis's card was Crayola-blue with white lettering (tiny swirls and curly-cues in each corner)—and a neat little three-line tag about his services on the back. Cecily remembered his card being rather busy, so she expected more of the same from the card in her hand.

But looking at it, Cecily guessed the essentials were all that mattered. Cream-colored with black sans-serif lettering, the card provided rank and file: name, occupation, office address, phone number. No sales copy on the back to convince you to call, no tagline with calming, cajoling words to persuade you. The only flourish (if you could call it that) was the psychiatry symbol in the upper-left corner. Not with the Greek symbol for Psi and the infamous caduceus down the middle, but with Psi and the Rod of Asclepius down the center instead.

People commonly recognized the caduceus (with its two snakes and wings) as the symbol for medicine, but the Rod was the correct symbol. She didn't know why she kept track of such trivia in her head, but it was sometimes useful—like now.

Cecily stared alternately at the name on the card and the Rod of Asclepius (with its single snake winding a staff—no wings). This card was for another psychiatrist: this one female.

The name?

Dr. Naomi E.M. Alexander.

Chapter Two

The Best-Laid Plans

(of Game Show Contestants)

H e called her "Cicely" instead of "Cecily" by honest mistake.

But she corrected him (who cares if rightfully so?), and he was determined to break her. Determined to break her little uppity, Southern-hick ass and leave no doubt. He grew to love her, too, but the breaking,...*that* had to come first.

She was from Cleveland, Mississippi. Who the fuck knew? The only Cleveland he knew belonged to Ohio. Average height, slender, nice butt, small but shapely tits, hair she forever wore in a ponytail—until he broke her of that, too. She was one of those bright, intelligent, speak-softly-and-carry-a-big-stick types of women—until he put a dent in that line of thinking, reminding her: the only "big stick" she needed be concerned about was his. Her first husband ("Roland": such a sissy name) was a punk for letting her get away with such nonsense.

Didn't matter he was dead: a punk's a punk, dead or alive.

She brought some of that Mississippi up to the DMV with her.

That accent still fluttered through her speech (when untouched by an occasional stutter), driving him crazy. He couldn't stand it but tolerated it because Cecily was a catch. Her pretty face and nice bod made her a hot catch. Degrees in two majors from Delta State University made her an intelligent catch (he planned to finish and get his associate degree soon).

But the kicker? The bomb-ass motherfucking kicker? Her financial bottom line: $17.2 million and growing. He didn't know that soft-spoken, bright, funny, pretty, Southern hick carried the motherlode—until he snooped and peeped her financial statements while she went to the store. They weren't three months into the relationship when he discovered that delicious tidbit. Smart girls sometimes did stupid things: like leaving their information readily available. Well, it wasn't all that readily available, but one should take extra precautions: you never know whom you're dealing with.

Oscar slunk further into the cushions of his recliner.

A rerun of one of his favorite shows, *Housewives of Atlanta*, was on, and he was missing all the cleavage and trash-talk. That's the only reason he watched: the cleavage, booties, and the trash-talking—but foremost, the abundance of cleavage. Women being women.

But he was missing it on account of being annoyed—because something went wrong two years ago. Science and luck joined forces against him. The angle of the knife penetrated deep, yet missed every major artery and only nicked some organs. Cecily was a slender woman: there couldn't have been much room to miss anything. She'd even had bleeding on the brain from Carl's and Brickey's kicks to her head, but she pulled through it all—just fine. Chelsea and Marcus, too. What the hell? He didn't understand it; the plan was perfect. Home invasions were up in their neighborhood then; it should've been a lock.

Not getting his usual thrill watching Atlanta tits-and-ass, he switched to the Game Show Network (GSN); he liked a good game show. Except for *Jeopardy!* That show was for pompous assholes with nothing else to do but know trivia about shit like seventeenth-century dynasties and European geography. He rarely got an answer (Oh, excuse me, *question*) right on that lame-ass show (had to be rigged); no point watching it.

Oscar shifted in his seat.

He should be at work (Cecily returned to work days ago). But he used the excuse of his wife being in the hospital for all it was worth. It was only seasonal work, and he didn't have paid time off, so his check would be lighter come payday. That was okay: they didn't need the money—Cecily had plenty. His wife was a nut for working when she didn't have to, but the more she earned, the more there was in the kitty.

She said working was fulfilling or some other women's lib bullshit, but he didn't ride her about it. Let her work, shit; it also kept her out of his hair. He only worked the little he did to keep up appearances.

That's all women needed: appearances. Times they gave you the finger-wave-and-neck-roll full of attitude (something Cecily never did; it wasn't her style): you beefed up said appearances to make it seem like their views mattered, to appease them. Simple.

All that mattered was keeping them quiet and the pussy coming.

Oscar wasn't a fan of *Deal of the Century*, but it was on, so he watched it. The show schedule during this part of the day was whack; the good stuff came on later. He had his lineup for programs of interest: cop shows, game shows, reality TV (the Black ones because they always gave up the T&A), and shows with judges named Judy. He got a kick out of that one, especially. Got a kick out of seeing how the woman believed her views of life (accented with a Yiddish expression or two) were universal, almost biblical. She was a joke—and the joke was on her; she had to use toilet paper like anybody else. He couldn't imagine her playing hide-the-sausage; it just didn't compute. She made bank, though; he'd give her that. Yeah, he saved time to watch the shows with judges named Judy.

He had other interests besides television, had some things going on. He had a few network marketing opportunities in operation. Those were lucrative if you worked them right; he hadn't found the formula to make it work for him. It was only a matter of time. People enrolled in his downline—he just didn't know what it took to get them to make him money. He sent them to the local meetings for that motivation jazz but still had little to show for it: a couple hundred dollars here and there. It had been five years; another three to five should have him set.

He also planned to get those last few courses behind him for his associate degree. He could knock them out, but hadn't been in the scholarly frame of mind.

Anyway, he had some things cooking; he was moving and shaking. Everything just needed to gel.

Thirsty, Oscar went to his fridge, grabbed a Corona, and drained it, standing before the cool air of the opened fridge cooling the basement's sixty-seven-degree warmth. He used the empty bottle to close the refrigerator door and tossed the bottle into Cecily's stupid recycle-bin (getting full). He'll take the container upstairs later. Oscar spat a loogie into his spittoon (which Cecily hated, and he enjoyed because she hated it so much) and went to his desk.

He kept his desk neat because order and organization were important. Even if those two things failed him two years ago, Oscar believed nothing good came from disorganization and chaos. His desk stayed neat to detect anything out of place. He wasn't worried about Cecily (she knew better), but that son of hers...

He didn't keep the good stuff near his desk (that would be stupid), but in the utility room: in a cashbox in the hole of their sump pump where he'd affixed a tiny shelf in there special. It was perfect; no one was sticking their hands down there. Floorboards and air vents and ceiling tiles, sure, but not sump pump holes.

Oscar retrieved the cashbox. At his desk, he examined the contents as *Deal of the Century* ended and an episode from the original *Family Feud* aired: time for a block of that Hatfields-McCoys game show with the hillbilly theme song. That Richard Dawson was a trip: getting his jollies kissing every female contestant. That irritated him sometimes, but he held no grudge; *Family Feud* ranked suitable entertainment: he always came up with the top five survey answers.

Oscar stared at the contents of his box: wads of cash, the To-Do list, Polaroid shots from the event (he still jerked-off to them sometimes), and samples of Cecily's handwriting. He stared at the To-Do list: a folded sheet of yellow legal pad paper, portions of the edges frayed and discolored with blood (*red and yellow make orange!*). He unfolded it, giving a cursory review and rundown, trying to see if he missed something. Nothing. Nothing missed. Except for the part where somebody called 9-1-1. *That* he hadn't counted on.

Annoyed, he refolded the list and returned it to its spot. Holding on to this stuff was stupid, but he couldn't let it go. Not yet. Otherwise, he'd been careful not to slip up. It was why the case went unsolved to this day. They had some DNA, but matches weren't in their databases—and wouldn't be. His men walked the straight-and-narrow, not so much as a parking ticket. They were smart men, patient. They knew what was at stake; Oscar didn't have to worry about any weak link.

Yeah, it was the best-laid plan, almost perfect, but *almost* didn't cut it, didn't give him what he needed. The perfect plan would've ended differently. They did a good job, though. Almost too good. He still had the scar from the bullet wound; they just missed his carrot artery. So, not a complete job, but a good one, and all would get paid well for it.

Oscar watched a commercial for a holiday auto show, images of classic cars whizzing by. He scoffed, thinking of Cecily's car. It was show-ready, but *he* couldn't show it. Cecily could, Marcus could, but he couldn't. That was one area he had yet to break her, but he'd let her have that little piece. She cared for that car better than she did him most times, but what the fuck: you had to give them something to make them think they had everything under control. He had his year-old Nissan Maxima, access to the Q70. He didn't press the issue over the Deville because it would *all* be his one day.

Well, not everything. Cecily's jerk of a son had a baby now (a son named after his punk granddaddy), so Marcus's money would go to him. Nothing to be done about that. It irritated him to no end, but whatever. Cecily's children didn't have access to their money until age 25; there was still time, motive, and opportunity (he watched a bunch of crime shows, too) to accomplish his goals.

He'd already convinced Cecily to have the papers drawn up, naming him powerful attorney in case of her death or mental incapacitation. He likely already had that right as her husband, but he didn't want to leave anything to chance. Cecily's asshole brother, Kyle, was always in her ear, trying to foil his plans, but ultimately the papers were drawn, signed, and delivered (Cecily took care of it herself). *So, fuck you, Kyle.* He had Cecily good and primed, so he wasn't worried; he didn't even bother reading all that mess.

There was also a special little something called life insurance; in effect since close to the day of their marriage and thus vested some years ago, the date of incontestability long passed. All that was needed was working the new plan carefully.

None of this is love, man.

Oscar sent that nattering little whiny bitch voice away with a scoff. He loved Cecily, but he needed to move on (he wasn't the family man he made himself out to be), and he wasn't leaving all that money behind. Bitching-up now only made matters worse, leaving room for mistakes. He did love her. But things were different now.

Besides, Cecily knew none of this. He kept Cecily under control, but he was good to her. Good to her, for appearance's sake (although he meant a good deal of it). It was too complicated to think about too much. Bottom line: his dear wife had to go.

Physically or mentally: made him no difference.

A picture of Cecily rested on his desk, and Oscar flipped it over, rubbing his chest to soothe the uncomfortable full feeling there.

He'd spotted Cecily at different times over several weeks before meeting her face-to-face in the laundry-item aisle of Walmart. He liked her looks from jump, but she always had her teenagers with her. They belonged to her; he knew that. The boy (a handsome young man) looked like her, and the girl (a hottie already) favored her mother, too. Since single women loved Walmart, he made Walmart his "shopping" grounds as well. Delia had just kicked his ass out and to the curb (there was no breaking that one, after all), and he'd suddenly found himself on the desperate side (something he loathed). He had an apartment again (month-to-month) using some of the money he filched from Delia and the bit of savings he accumulated working seasonal gigs, but that money wouldn't last forever. He could've stayed with some buddies, but to catch another female, he needed to have his own place—at least starting off. Appearances were everything.

Prettier than Delia, the woman also seemed to have a desperation about her as she shopped, but he couldn't be sure. He couldn't have been sure about anything unless he talked to her. The teenagers left their mother to shop elsewhere, so Oscar took his chance. He usually shopped for *single* without the *mother*, but they were teenagers and almost grown, so practically the same thing. He didn't do toddlers and preteens: they needed too much of your time, needed too much...of *you*. It was why he made no slip-ups in *that* department. Well, there was the *one* slip-up: a daughter, Keisha. But she was grown now and living in Germany, last he heard. The baby mama knew better than to expect child support from him, and so handled all that on her own. He was okay with it. Kids weren't for everyone. And, at his age, kids surely weren't for him.

He wasn't one of the tall ones, but for all intense purposes, he wasn't bad looking (enough women confirmed that much for him). He could stand to lose a few pounds (he had a Corona-belly forming but not yet full-grown), but he wasn't fat. Delia always said he had a "talk to me" face (whatever that meant), so once he saw the teenagers leave the lady by her lonesome, he approached, watching her browsing the fabric softeners. He'd nodded his hello, she smiled back, and he saw that maybe *desperation* wasn't right, but *vulnerable* came close.

One month later, he moved into her townhouse. It was only a matter of weeks before he had her thinking she was madly in love.

Another month and he discovered the motherlode.

They were married five, six months after that. He'd changed his life (for the much better) in as little as seven months.

A few months into the marriage, she corrected his accidental mispronunciation of her name.

Breaking her didn't require violence (not intense violence), but a perfectly timed expression of something unexpected, unusual, and okay, with a dash of violence thrown in, did the damage necessary. He'd already drawn her in by then, worked on many of her vulnerabilities, so when his words rolled off his tongue with slithery precision to bring her uppity, hick-ass down, words emphasized with a severe, prolonged pinch to her side, the shift in their relationship solidified (point: Oscar).

When he hit her, he used punches sparingly—and never to her face.

"I think that's when that sometimes-stutter started." Oscar nodded. Yeah, he was pretty sure that's when it began. Or soon after another good pinching bruise or two.

She wasn't in love with him. He knew that. Cecily probably didn't know or realize it, but he did. But breaking her and owning her didn't require that. It only required having enough love to nurture the appearance of being in love. Cecily loved him. He loved her. That was all you needed right there. Just enough.

Her love for her children, that maternal crap to protect them, kept her from revealing the real to them. Cecily took part in keeping up a few appearances herself. They never liked him; he knew that, too. Chelsea liked him maybe a little (and he found he wanted her approval on some level), but the son: no happenings. But Marcus and Chelsea were teenagers then, involved in many teenaged activities, preoccupations, and distractions, so Oscar managed the situation well.

"She actually called out that punk's name." Cashbox in hand, he reclaimed his seat, remembering how Cecily called for Roland while she was in that closet, going through whatever the fuck crazy shit she was going through in there. Oscar seethed with the memory, but just as quickly, he grinned. He didn't expect the gingerbread to send her over like that. He expected something, hoped for something (she'd been showing signs), but not to *that extent*. Oscar chuckled as Richard Dawson explained the dollar values were doubled.

He planned to continue messing with her now-fragile mind, keep her unsure, unfocused, and...unhinged. Marcus and Chelsea stayed in her ear, but since they pretty much abandoned their mother after the invasion, Oscar could work his magic to his benefit. He didn't drive her over the edge hard and fast; these things had to be done delicately. Cecily going over the deep end full throttle didn't have the right look; it didn't show well.

Appearances were everything.

Movement from upstairs: Cecily.

"Os-Oscar?"

He muted the sound on the television. "Yeah. What's up?"

"Nothing. J-Just wanted to remind y-you to call Odessa b-back. I'm headed out, r-run a f-few errands. G-Get some flowers."

Her and those damned fresh flowers she insisted on setting in a vase on the kitchen table. He wondered if he should "water" these, then decided not. He'll get the next bunch.

"N-Need anything?"

He sometimes made her specify where she was going, but not this time. The trick to it all was keeping her unsure of when they had to play that *other* game. "Nah. But...feel like making Crepe Suzette?"

Oscar grinned with the ensuing pause; no, she didn't feel like it.

"That's fine, sure."

"A'ight. Then I'm good."

"Oscar, d-don't forget your appointment w-with Doctor Halim's c-coming up."

He didn't forget, and he dreaded it: bad news sometimes came in ones. "Yeah, I remembered. Be careful."

"O-Okay. Shouldn't be m-more than a few hours: b-back by five-thirty at the l-latest."

Oscar grinned again. He didn't ask for a time frame this time, either, but her cooperation was appreciated—and expected.

"Cigarettes?" she asked as if hoping the answer was no; she'd been trying to get him to quit for years.

He had quit for this last week—because he had that appointment with Halim. "Nah, I'm good."

"All right." She closed the basement door.

He turned the volume back on just as Dickey Dawson asked them to "put another twenty seconds on the clock, please."

A few minutes later, he heard the alarm setting and then the Deville starting up; she was gone.

"I should've gotten 'going out' approval, though." He sometimes made her get prior hair-and-clothing approval before she went out alone; a show of control he exercised more in the early part of their relationship but still did from time to time. He made it appear rooted in love for her and making sure she looked good (which made him look good).

She mentioned calling Odessa back.

He'd rather not call his sister back. They were just going to argue-without-arguing again. It was the core of their relationship, and he wasn't in the mood. Let her do that mess with their baby brother.

Odessa didn't like him, anyway; he was hard-pressed to believe she loved him. The only emotion he sensed from his sister was disappointment. But even that was better than what his little brother broadcast toward him: contained distaste. Otis went so far as telling him that, as an older brother, he was nothing to look up to.

Instead of using his family nickname, "OJ" (for Oscar Jerome), Otis changed the meaning to "Old Joke," having good laughs at Oscar's expense. Since the OJ trials of 1995, Oscar dispensed with the nickname altogether, preferring people stick with "Oscar." Otis, however, still called him "OJ" sometimes when he was in one of his moods.

His siblings didn't respect him in the least. These days, he barely talked to them, let alone saw them. And maybe all that hurt somewhere inside, but Oscar didn't dwell.

Odessa and Otis thought they were better because they had college degrees, some status in their communities, and always got their snide digs in to remind him of his lesser status. He was the oldest, yet he carried no weight with his siblings (Otis even made it a point to ensure visits to their parents down in Florida didn't overlap by more than a day). It got to the point he and Cecily stopped going to family get-togethers because he couldn't afford the damage to the finely tuned appearance of a different persona he'd refined to land Cecily (and all the others). And besides, Odessa liked to correct him too much: correct his grammar, his word usage. He didn't have a bachelor's degree, but he had gone to college (he planned to get that associate degree next semester, maybe); she didn't have to show him up so much.

No, he wasn't calling Odie back anytime soon.

What about you stealing from them? Totaling Otis's car? And that four-thousand dollar "investment" Odessa and your parents couldn't afford but afforded you? How about—?

"Shut up. Whatever, man. Okay!?" He hated thinking about his family. A lot of that wasn't his fault. Oscar rubbed his chest, grumbling, "Shoulda been a policeman," to the dark basement (smelling faintly of the fading ocean-breeze air freshener Cecily plugged in last month). Policeman, detective; *that* would've had some miles on it: the uniform, becoming detective, knowing about cases and shit on local crimes, the life-risk factor. He'd been a security guard for some years; he would've been a cinch to make officer.

Being the black sheep of the family, he didn't have his family's love and support (they didn't even care about his recent heart problems), but once he had Cecily's money, Oscar knew all that would change. Blood was thicker than water, and money couldn't buy love, but what money could buy (and influence) was sometimes just as good—even if only the appearance of it. All he had to do was stick with the plan.

Plan A didn't pan out, so he was on Plan B. And if Plan B didn't work out... Well, there were twenty-six letters in the alphabet.

Plan A morphed into Plan B; the mental-incapacity angle was less messy. Dr. Lewis's sessions, because they didn't help, only gave Cecily a deeper sense of despair, which worked in Oscar's favor. The notion she was incurable reinforced the idea something was seriously wrong with her. When she stopped going to Dr. Lewis, Oscar stepped in to help. The little things were enough: like a plateful of innocently baked gingerbread squares.

So now, here they were, getting ready to do the whole psychiatrist-bit again. It fell in line with his alternate, less-violent plan, so he would go through with it—for appearance's sake. However, he didn't have the most comfortable feeling in his gut for this go-round. He couldn't put his finger on it, but something about this next go-round made his insides all watery and jittery.

It wasn't because this Dr. Alexander was female; that mattered least to him. Women were women. She had the same weak spots as all the other split-tails, and he'd exploit those weak points. She could be broken (most could). But (and he didn't know why exactly) he didn't feel good about going to her. They could always change doctors.

You should leave this all alone, man. Think of your health.

Oscar shook his head in answer to himself; he was too far in it now. And although he didn't take those pills Halim put him on (like he was supposed to), he was fine, felt good (today, anyway). And well, aspects of these plans for Cecily amused him. Aspects...aroused him.

For the tiniest moments, Oscar wondered if he was okay, if he was sane. But before any deeper consideration, his attention shifted to give the fifth most popular survey answer, his anxiety over meeting Dr. Alexander all but forgotten.

Chapter Three

Christmas Presents

R elying on the use of her right hand put her in a weird mood, but given the pain in her left wrist (even with the brace on), Dr. Naomi Alexander realized she'd have to manage.

She'd manage because part of her was also excited. There were big plans for this afternoon. She also had to read up on a new patient scheduled for next week, but that was later.

Adjusting to the awkwardness of using her right hand as she held James Baldwin's *Go Tell It on the Mountain*, she read a few passages to a group of elderly residents at Garden Meadows, a senior-citizen facility in Laurel, Maryland. She usually volunteered her services here every other Tuesday, but today was Friday.

Naomi read to her audience, scanning them as the words flowed and wondering if any instances of her auric sight or visionary abilities would ignite. She'd termed these talents *aura-flickers* and *flashes of truth*, respectively. Her flashes of truth manifested as acute hunches (sometimes with imagery) somehow, someway, grounded in truth.

As she read, she saw traces of reflection in the men's eyes, as if relating to the tale of John Grimes in Baldwin's semi-autobiographical novel. The women, too, wore soft, thoughtful smiles as she read, nodding at certain parts. So much history in the room. So much wisdom and experience (albeit touched by the effects of age and illness). Filled with pride over her audience, Naomi sat straighter, read with more conviction.

Still and attentive, a few of their auras soon flickered for her at random, some in tandem. Most of those few flickered in solid shades of teal, fuchsia, or pumpkin-orange (Christmas season be damned), and some... Well, some of those auras were quite faded. Fading auras were a sad occurrence, but Naomi didn't tarry.

Garden Meadows was an older, more rundown facility, but the staff kept the place clean and airy and, as the Christmas holiday approached, quite festive. Mistletoe, garland, and twinkling lights hung throughout the rooms reserved for social activities; the aromas of pine and cookie dough commingled in the early morning holiday atmosphere. In the kitchen: homemade cookies baked in preparation for the upcoming Christmas party.

Along with the aura-flickers, Naomi experienced a flash of truth about one of the staff. In it, she saw staff aide, "Jontavious" (oh, these names), wearing a lab coat and performing lab duties. She didn't know Jontavious well, but in her flash, he chuckled while working in earnest with a coworker, and Naomi was pleased for him. Jontavious wouldn't be working for Garden Meadows much longer.

The thirty-degree range chill in the air last week had warmed to a comfortable fifty-nine degrees, but that didn't detract from the cozy holiday feeling of the room. Naomi sat in front of the most enormous Christmas tree she'd ever had the pleasure of sitting in front of. The tree was massive: just big and green and colorful.

She exercised caution using the fingers of her left hand to push her glasses up the bridge of her nose and read more of Baldwin's prose. She finished the selection for today's reading, to the soft claps and words of praise for her reading style and appreciation for taking the time to read to them. They looked forward to her visits—as much as Naomi looked forward to visiting.

The alternate Tuesdays she worked with the crew at Hardluck Rebound, feeding the homeless. Years ago, she left Hardluck Rebound and switched to Abiding Ways for her charitable efforts. But she didn't like the vibe at Abiding Ways and much liked the people volunteering with Hardluck Rebound, so she returned to them and never looked back. Reading to the elderly at Garden Meadows was her solo charitable gig. Money was fine to give, but people didn't realize their time was just as valuable (if not more).

Naomi exchanged hugs with some of her reading group members (holding in a grimace of pain every time someone bumped against her brace). She said her goodbyes, breathing in the varying and sometimes competing redolences of perfumes, colognes, soiled incontinence pads, and analgesic creams. She'd next see them the Tuesday after New Year's when she resumed reading *Go Tell It on the Mountain*.

Before she left, they presented her with a gift-tin of York Peppermint Patties, along with two woolen hats (likely inspired to keep her head warm in the winter months). During her visits, many of the senior ladies commented on her short hair, fretting she'd catch her death of cold. Common colds came from viruses, not cold weather per se, but you didn't debate with history, wisdom, and experience. Little did they know, her hair was longer than it had been in years.

While heading to her car, the excitement returned, making her stomach fluttery with anticipation. She had a few errands to run to keep her mind occupied, including calling Mark to confirm execution of the plan.

She had four hours to fill.

The wait was going to be torturous.

Naomi drove with composure despite her desire to test the limits of her new BMW 540i and speed to her destination. Reluctant to let go of her beloved X5, she traded it for a new silver X5 and bought a metallic-blue 540i sedan to meet her other driving needs. She sometimes missed her first X5, but the new one handled better (more power) and looked good.

However, driving with her less-dominant hand didn't allow for much sport-driving indulgence. Her left wrist throbbed its painful protest at being unable to steer the vehicle, so Naomi readjusted its position next to her (she needed to loosen the brace some). She drove her 540i above all, using the X5 for travel with over three passengers—as in, when in the car with both Leslie and Viv, or with Leslie and Leslie's mentor, Joy Giles, or when out on dates with Kevin, who preferred driving the X5 whenever they went out.

That last, she didn't have to worry about. She wasn't going out with Kevin; not now...or soon.

She listened to J.C. Bach's Symphony No. 1 in G major, Op. 6, letting the violins lift her spirits, deflating with thoughts of her situation (or lack thereof) with Kevin. The ride to her destination was uneventful but took forever when she finally approached and turned onto Bard O' Avon Court.

Interestingly, strains of the Supremes' "Someday We'll Be Together" drifted through the door as she rang the bell. The music stopped. Seconds later, the front door opened, and Naomi couldn't help smiling ear-to-ear.

"Hey, lady." Viv Phillips pulled the door open further as she stepped back, allowing Naomi's entry.

"Hi, Viv. Ready?" Naomi hugged Viv and headed for the open space of the Phillipses' kitchen-family-sunroom area. Viv's body oil, with elements of cloves, roses, vanilla, and hints of musk, wafted with her.

"Yep. Where're we going? It's your turn to pick. I don't mind a ride if you're wanting authentic B-more coddies." Viv followed, the steady click of her heels marking her progress on the hardwood floor.

Naomi settled onto her customary barstool, watching her friend open the refrigerator and grab a bottled water. Viv looked stunning in a fitted forest-green dress and matching heels with lace accents. As usual, she wore her illusion necklace: Rick's wedding band suspended in her suprasternal notch. Viv thumbed toward the refrigerator, asking with her eyes if she could get Naomi anything. Her aura flickered this dull yellowish-gray before disappearing: depressed, low emotional energy.

"Well, a trek to Baltimore is in order, but not for coddies." Naomi shook her head before grinning with a hedging smirk. "Thought we'd do Manje Trankil."

Viv locked eyes with her.

Manje Trankil (Haitian-Creole for "tranquil dining") was one of the new restaurants at Baltimore's Inner Harbor (*new* meaning open less than three years). The restaurant, featuring a bar and dancefloor, played slow to mid-tempo R&B, Soul, and Haitian music. Even with the dance-floor, they rarely played fast beats, keeping things tranquil. She and Viv hadn't eaten at Manje for several months, so it was ideal for their monthly lunch date. She got together with Viv more often than monthly, but one day a month, they made it a point to make a federal case of going out and sitting down to eat. Naomi didn't make a federal case out of much of anything, but she made exceptions. However, Viv locked eyes with her because Manje Trankil had also developed a unique association for Viv.

Viv smiled, her black eyes trying to sparkle in opposition to the sadness in them. "That's fine. It is Christmas." She sipped her water.

Naomi carried her gaze around the Phillips home, around the spacious open-concept kitchen-family-sunroom area. Viv repainted the kitchen last year (one of her mini-distraction projects), and the giant wooden spoon was on the wall (another of Viv's distraction projects), but that was it: not one piece of garland or holly, not one stocking, not one shred of tinsel or any Christmas decoration. Naomi put on a dazzling smile, wanting her smile to help brighten Viv's. She chuckled. "Looking around here, you wouldn't know it. But it is, Viv."

Viv's gaze turned curious, suspicious. "What's up with you?"

"What?"

Viv shrugged. "I don't know. You're all..."

"I'm all...?"

Viv's gaze steadied on her. "All non-Naomi-like."

Naomi scoffed. "What? Because I'm smiling? I smile, Viv."

Viv returned an odd look as she nodded her agreement. She shifted her attention to Naomi's brace, giving a nod to indicate it. "Carpal still got you on the injured-reserve list, huh?"

"A bitch and a pain, yeah." She jerked her head toward the family room where the silenced "Someday We'll Be Together" waited. "Was that your version of Christmas music I heard earlier?"

Viv smiled again, and this time the sparkle pushed forth more. Not much, but a little. "You can say that. Playing that helps me cope, reminds me better days are coming."

"I see. And the non-Christmas atmosphere yet again?"

Viv grew somber. "I know. I may put something up on Christmas Eve. The tree, maybe. We'll see."

It was just pitiful, but Naomi understood. "Alna and RJ cool with this again, sweetie?"

Viv bobbed her head. "RJ's two, so he's fine, but Al's been with me on this, Naomi. She gets it."

Naomi watched her friend. The woman was gorgeous, but her eyes projected a dull distance of dejection, conveying a depth of loneliness for Rick bordering painful.

Viv held her bottle of water, staring into the empty sink. "She's twelve, but she gets it."

"The tree. Christmas Eve, Viv."

Viv turned to her. "Yes, ma'am."

"Presents?"

"RJ's too young to care about the Santa-thing, and Al's long over it, so..." Viv looked at Naomi, those eyes firing defiance—a sad, coal-black defiance. "It may not be 'Christmassy' around here, but my babies have presents, yes." She recapped her water and put it back in the fridge.

"Good. Now, one more play of the song, and then let's go." Naomi raised her braced wrist, holding in a wince. "You're driving."

With a smile brighter but somehow still melancholy, Viv grabbed the remote from the counter and aimed it toward the entertainment center in her family room.

Forty-five minutes later, they were in Rick's black Range Rover, well on the John Hanson Highway, gabbing while traveling toward Annapolis, when "Can't Hide Love" by Earth, Wind & Fire came on the radio.

"Nope." Viv changed the station to one featuring smooth jazz.

"Okay..." Naomi watched and held in a chuckle as a man in a neighboring vehicle barely held his lane for his frequent glances over at Viv.

"Sorry. Can't do slow jams or anything by EWF these days."

"So, I've noticed." Naomi kept eyes on the man in the car as he stared hard some additional seconds before pulling ahead in his blue Honda Civic. He had to be in his 20s. *You go, Viv.*

"I can't listen to anything by Earth, Wind and Fire; Frankie Beverly and Maze; Gil Scott Heron; Dave Koz; Marvin Gaye; David Sanborn; L.T.D.; War; the Dramatics; Sam Cooke; New Birth; Jeffrey Osborne; the Isley Brothers; the Dells; the O'Jays; Blue Magic; Phil Collins; Enchantment; Donny Hathaway; Prince; the Spinners; Grover Washington; Boney James; the Delfonics; Friends of Distinction; the Stylistics; the Beatles; Keiko Matsui; Anthony Hamilton; the Commodores; Jill Scott; Pieces of a Dream; Bruno Mars; the Roots; Parliament Funkadelic; the Originals; Kenny G; Bob Marley; Stevie Wonder; the Ohio Players; Norman Connors; Art Tatum; Paul Hardcastle; Frank Sinatra; Andraé Crouch; Joe Sample; George Benson; or the AWB right now."

"That's quite a list." Hearing the Beatles or Ol' Blue Eyes on it didn't surprise her, but she almost laughed at how Viv rattled those artists off. "Sure you didn't leave anyone off?"

"Heavy D; Jerry Butler; Rick James; Tupac; Wes Montgomery; the Soul Stirrers; Incognito; Kem; Maxwell; Lauryn Hill; the Fugees; Alex Bugnon; Fourplay; Peter Tosh; Ramsey Lewis; Nat King Cole; Sister Rosetta Tharpe; Mighty Clouds of Joy; the Swan Silvertones; Jaheim; David Sanborn; the Persuasions; James Cleveland; Curtis Salgado; Ray Charles; the Canton Spirituals—"

This time, Naomi did laugh.

Viv chuckled but then gave a pensive nod.

"A few of those are more current."

Viv changed lanes. "True. They have strong old-school vibes, though. I can't listen to his key faves without imagining him stopping at a certain point in a song and pointing out some special element, or just memories of him with the music, period."

Although she liked EWF, too, Naomi listened to the smooth jazz without qualms. "So, what about you? I know Phyllis Hyman is in there."

"Of course. Pretty much the same as Rick. We also like: Roy Ayers; Sarah Vaughan; Aretha Franklin; Sly and the Family Stone; Elton John; Teena Marie; James Brown; Lalah Hathaway; Yolanda Adams; Gladys Knight; Al Green; Najee; Maysa; D'Angelo; George Duke; Mother's Finest; Dorothy Norwood; the Emotions; Luther Vandross; Burning Spear; Gerald Albright; Peabo Bryson; Diana Krall; the Davis Sisters; Angela Bofill; Kim Waters; Dinah Washington; Jean Carne; Al Jarreau; Joni Mitchell; Joan Baez; James Taylor; Sadé; Meshell Ndegeocello; Nina Simone; Jimmy Cliff; Kirk Whalum; Natalie Cole; Bob James; the Marsalis brothers; Celine Dion; the Jackson Southernaires; Gospel Harmonettes; Mary J. Blige; Otis Redding; Kenny Lattimore; Narada Michael Walden; Curtis Mayfield..."

Their list covered the gamut for hers.

"I miss the other station, though." Viv sucked her teeth. "Their re-vamped format blows."

"So, what's your go-to now?"

"Depends. I listen to WMMJ or WHUR often. They don't play as much music from the sixties and seventies anymore during the day, but it'll do. Now, stuff from the nineties is classic."

"Time waits for no one."

"I guess." A pained expression crossed Viv's features as she checked the rearview mirror. "Know what I'm missing most right now, Naomi?"

"Not specifically, no."

"The way he can look at me sometimes. When I can *see* he loves me, how much in love with me he is."

"Okay."

"Rick lets me see it, Naomi. Just puts his heart right there in his beautiful, molten-fire eyes, and lets me *see* it. ...God, I miss him."

They rode in silence a spell: Viv watching the road, Naomi watching the scenery.

"I keep smelling him everywhere, too. Smelling the scents from our history together: his Guerlain Vetiver, Eau Sauvage, or his Creed Green. Or, girl, his Hermès Terre d'Hermès. Is... Is that crazy?"

It wasn't crazy. Viv missed her husband—especially with the holiday season upon them. Naomi still missed Tyson sometimes (and Kevin).

They drew closer to Manje Trankil, and Naomi's chest lightened with each passing mile. This was going to be so good.

"Naomi, do you realize that in two months, apart from brief sporadic periods, I will not have had unsupervised interaction with my husband for one thousand days? I mean, no true intimacy with Rick whatsoever?"

Moderately shocked, Naomi didn't speak at first. She considered how long Rick Phillips had been in prison, translated that into approximated days, and was stunned. Many people, many Black men, had been in prison for much longer, but she didn't know those people; those men weren't...family. "Never looked at it like that, Viv, no."

"I know." She turned the music down, speaking in a hush. "A near thousand days." Viv reached for the dash. "I will listen to this some-times..." A few clicks later, Aretha Franklin's "Ain't Nothing Like the Real Thing" floated into the car's interior.

They listened, then were silent for the time to reach the city, both women lost in their respective thoughts. Viv silenced the music after the song played, but with Viv, it was always a comfortable quiet; Naomi felt no pressure to fill the silence.

They came to a stoplight. "If I could hold him, Naomi. That would be my Christmas. Just put my arms around his neck for solid seconds, with-out restriction or eyes monitoring, and *hold* my baby. Laugh privately with him about the stuff *we* find funny: Merry Christmas to me. Rick's my buddy. Intimacy isn't restricted to sex."

"You're right, sweetie. You don't laugh when you visit?"

"A chuckle here and there, sure. But the atmosphere isn't conducive to the kind of laughter I'm talking about. In there: very little is funny."

"You have a point. So, unsupervised holding and genuine laughter at a good private joke: Merry Christmas."

Viv bared a tepid grin. "Yes. But now, a *Merry*, Merry Christmas?" She closed her eyes with emotion and shivered. "Tasting his tongue while one of his sexy hands squeezes one of my tit— and I'm feeling those deliciously mild twinges inside from him thrusting his thick, porn-worthy, practically ni—" Viv swallowed and went quiet.

"...Light's green, Viv."

"Thanks." Viv pulled off, resuming the journey to Manje.

Naomi had to swallow herself. Given the context of her statement, Viv saying "practically ni—" before cutting her sentence indicated Rick's erection size: practically nine inches. Naomi filled in the obvious blank: fully erect, the man was a solid eight-and-a-half *at least*. Apparently, those *practically ni—* inches were thick, too (and, ahem, "porn-worthy"). Interesting.

And, contrary to popular belief, decidedly out of the norm.

Tall men sometimes worked with smaller-than-average penises, shorter men possibly worked with larger-than-average penises, but those, too, were along a broad spectrum. It had nothing to do with shoe-size, thumb-size, or nose proportions. The only indicator of a man's erection size in sooth was a ruler. Nature didn't discriminate, didn't favor, even so, the norm was *well below* eight inches (let alone nine). Rick is likely longer and thicker when his arousal's amplified, edging him closer to—

Well, well.

Naomi swallowed again.

Viv glimpsed her with a twinkle in her eyes. "I'll reiterate: that man handles his business, Naomi." Viv checked the traffic ahead of her and then glimpsed Naomi again. "Handles it and leaves the matter *settled*; you hear me?" She resumed watching the road, releasing a low, shuddery breath of "Jesus."

"I hear you, Viv," Naomi chuckled.

After a moment, Viv did, too. She then shook her head with a touch of sadness. "Anyway, Rick's been in a funk. Doesn't even want us visiting him for the holidays. Says it's too hard. That it'll be better for him after New Year's. He said it was up to me, but..." She bounced a shoulder.

"That's just a few more weeks, Viv. You can do it."

"Yeah, I'll get through. But I miss me some Richard A. Phillips Senior, girl. I do; even if it is 'supervised.'"

"You mean, Richard A. *S.* Phillips Senior, don't you?"

Viv adopted an odd expression, her eyes sending a joking but mildly serious warning. "Girl, don't you mention Rick's full middle names around him. I guess all the legal stuff revealed that tidbit. But, girl, he hates it. Acts like it doesn't exist and, as such, so do I."

People were funny. "I like 'Stannis.'"

"I do, too. But Rick hates it. He doesn't consider 'Stannis' a part of his name with anything other than necessary legalities."

"That why he was shooting for RJ to have a different name?"

"Somewhat. Part of it had to do with Jonathan. But I made *that* executive decision."

"You did. And you weren't hurt Rick wanted genetic testing on RJ?"

Viv shook her head. "I knew RJ was Rick's, but Rick wanted to be sure for reasons other than pride. If he were possibly raising Jonathan's son, we would've needed Jonathan's medical history, etcetera."

Naomi nodded her understanding, her respect for Rick elevating. Listening to Fourplay on the radio, she had a question she'd wanted to ask for years, but either the timing failed her, her courage, or a combination of both. "...So, how're you handling your desires, Viv?"

Viv rendered a light laugh. "Took you long enough. You've wanted to ask that for years, I know."

Naomi grinned, surprised at Viv's insight.

"Miss Shoot-from-the-Hip couldn't be so straightforward, huh?"

"I use discretion, Viv."

"I know you do. But you and I are past that, Naomi, don't you think? Past that hesitancy circling honest dialogue. I mean, just saying what it is should be SOP for us now. No holds barred and no penalty of friendship for that honesty."

"True." And it was. She and Viv were very like-minded.

"Okay then."

"So...?"

Viv smirked as she drove, the traffic getting heavier as they moved closer to the harbor. "Well, Rick and I can get some jail-nookie in if either Clinton or, I think his name is 'Jason,' are there. They like Rick, so they work out a privilege or two for my baby. But it's not a guaranteed thing, and more of a rushed quickie when it happens. If not, then...I use my toys: either after talking with him, reading one of his letters,...or while watching a home video with him in it."

"I see."

"One of my favorites is from summer a few years ago. We spent a week with Patrice and Garrett at their timeshare at Hilton Head. Lou and Tim were there, too. The kids were asleep, so it was grown-folks' time. We were hanging, oldies playing in the background, everyone sipping, puffing, singing, talking, having a mini talent show. Passing the bottle, the joints, or video camera around. It was a hot summer night, but we were having a ball. There're natural shots of my baby talking, smiling, laughing. Just looking *good*, Naomi. And then there's this part where Rick is singing 'Be Ever Wonderful.' His shirt is off..."

The image of a shirtless Rick singing the ballad stirred an inkling of Viv's certain arousal.

"Of course, later that night—"

"And I can fill in the rest. That's enough 'saying what it is' for today."

They laughed (Viv's laugh nowhere near as full).

Viv grew reflective. "Yeah. There's also this home video of him singing gospel songs with Papa Phillips and David at our wedding reception. His uncles and male cousins join in, too. Rick's a young man in the video, early twenties, but he sings so soulfully..." She exhaled a wistful-sounding breath. "The toys and quickies provide a physical release, Naomi. But that emotional connection with Rick, releasing our surges of raw, deep emotion communicated through words, with looks, and through touch as we're being intimate: *that* I don't get to experience now. Feels like I'm going crazy sometimes."

Sensing her friend's sadness growing, Naomi changed the subject, if only partially. "I'd like to see the video of him singing with his family. See Rick as a young man."

"Oh, okay. I can make a copy for you. Yeah, check him out from back in the day." She tittered some, and that was better.

"I'll be looking at you, too."

"I know, right?! My hair was pinned-up, but some of the hairstyles of our guests!" Viv laughed harder this time, and that was much better.

They approached the parking garage.

"...Thanks, Naomi."

"No problem."

Still with their coats on, they stood in the subdued lighting of Manje Trankil's waiting area chatting, listening for "Alexander, party of two" for all of three minutes, when Naomi spotted her co-conspirator, who caught her eye with a subtle nod and wink. When he turned to rejoin the bar conversation, Naomi tapped Viv's shoulder.

"Is... Isn't that Mark? Mark Dilworth?" The butterflies in Naomi's stomach flitted, making her tummy flutter. She pointed toward the bar.

Viv turned, sending her gaze toward the bar area. "Where...? I don't—? Yes! That's him. What in the world?"

"My thoughts exactly. Wanna say hello?"

Viv grinned at her (trace of sadness in it). "But of course. Come on."

After brief confirmation with the attendant, they headed for the bar, Naomi's stomach doing somersaults of anticipation.

Rick's former coworker, Mark Dilworth, was one of the most admirable White men Naomi had the pleasure of knowing. He may have even been *the* coolest and nicest man of Caucasian persuasion in that personal category. He and his wife, Barbara, didn't miss any of Rick's court proceedings, offering Rick and Viv a level of support that surprised Viv and that she truly needed. Naomi got to know Mark and Barbara Dilworth well. Between Naomi's contacts and Mark's, both were able to influence the outcome of Rick's case and avoid the *excessive* due process often befalling men of color.

It was an option she wished many Black men serving undue time in prison had.

Mark sat at the bar, drink in hand, laughing with a blond-haired gentleman on his right at something the bartender said. The blond gentleman was loud, so the bartender gestured for him to keep it down.

Manje wasn't packed, but it wasn't sparse attendance, either. A sizable crowd ruled standard at Manje Trankil. Good for them.

Walking in front of Viv, Naomi approached Mark from his right (being careful not to bump her brace). Mark smiled and talked and held his drink, ignoring their approach.

"Get you, ladies, anything?" With his penny-brown linebacker physique, the bartender looked more like a bouncer. He handed the blond gentleman another lager as he pulled a now-empty glass away. Blondie (his complexion good and pink from his lager consumption) reminded Naomi of a young David Soul of *Starsky and Hutch* fame.

"We'll wait, thanks," Naomi replied, and then Mark Dilworth did a double take.

His gray eyes widened. "What?! Viv? Naomi?!" He stood and shifted in front of her, his stocky frame taking up much of the space between him and her.

He didn't hug her (he knew better), but he laughed and shook his sandy-brown hair out of his eyes as he leaned around Naomi to hug Viv and kiss her cheek.

Viv leaned back from their hug, frowning at Mark with a semi-smile. "Mark, what're you doing up here? Where's Barb? She here?" Viv looked toward the ladies' room as if expecting her to appear from that direction.

"Yeah, Mark. What're you doing in my neck of the woods?"

Mark presented a tilted smile. "Baltimore isn't your neck of the woods anymore."

Naomi chuckled with a teasing shake of her head at Mark as the blond gentleman ("Hutch") talked baseball with the bartender. She liked Mark. "Oh, it is, my friend. Always will be."

Mark answered Viv: "Barb's home. I'm having a business lunch in a half-hour. Hadn't been here before: wanted to get the lay of the land."

Viv tilted her head in understanding. "Oh, okay."

His brows furrowed. "Sure, you don't want anything?"

Viv conferred with Naomi.

Mark spoke before Naomi could reply. "I'm buying."

"Oh, well, in that case..." Naomi sprung a half-crooked smile.

Chuckling, Mark signaled the bartender. He put a hand on Viv's shoulder, then issued an I'm-so-forgetful smack to his forehead. "Oh, dag! Pardon my rudeness. I'm just— Anyway, I'm here with a buddy of mine. Viv, Naomi, this is..." Mark shifted, unblocking the view of the patrons behind him to introduce his buddy.

He'd barely moved when Viv gasped, a hand covering her mouth.

Rick Phillips sat at the bar wearing this hesitant smile that would've been murderously beautiful had it fully formed. Without fully forming, this smile was just regular beautiful.

The gentleman behind Rick leaned closer to him. "That her?"

Rick nodded, his eyes on Viv.

The crowd in the bar section went about their business, but the four people involved in this reunion, and the three innocent-bystanding witnesses, were quiet. Naomi, Mark, the bartender, Hutch, and Rick's "buddy" scarcely moved and didn't speak, all eyes on Viv.

The hand Viv still held at her mouth trembled now. She turned to Naomi. "Oh, my God."

Naomi nodded, her eyes stinging. "Merry Christmas, Viv."

Understanding Naomi was in on it dawned in Viv's eyes, but the shock of seeing her husband kept her from absorbing everything on a normal scale; she nodded her thanks absentmindedly, then focused on one man sitting at the bar (still wearing that adorably hesitant smile). "Ricky...?"

Naomi looked at Mark. They hadn't rehearsed any of that, just discussed the highlights of the game plan. They couldn't rehearse it (Viv's interaction was an unknown variable), so they winged it—to splendid results.

A shade rosier in his face, Mark winked at her with a smile expressing his happiness at a plan coming together.

Just as tickled, Naomi nodded at her co-conspirator and turned back to watch the magic unfold.

Viv stared at her husband, hand trembling at her mouth, and shook her head as if telling herself this wasn't real. Oh, but those black eyes of hers drank her husband in, hoping it was so. "...Rick?"

Rick saluted her with a gentle head tip. "Lady Blue." He opened his arms to Viv and waited.

Viv startled upon hearing his affectionate name for her. With another soft gasp, she handed Naomi her purse and then eased toward Rick, moving between his parted legs and into his arms.

Naomi (and she guessed Mark, and their unintended cohorts, too) expected a wild tongue-thrashing, expected Viv to rush into his arms and virtually rape the man in the middle of Manje, but neither happened. The couple bowed their heads (foreheads touching) and prayed. Whispered pockets of the Lord's Prayer traveled to Naomi's ears. Their quiet prayer finished, the couple went still, breathing each other's air.

Rick closed his eyes, drawing Viv closer. "All I want, is to hold you."

Rick's buddy looked on, his eyes darting from Rick to Viv and back, waiting. Even with her distance from him, Naomi determined he was tipsy. The bartender cleaned a wine glass, wearing a soft, admiring smile as he watched the couple. "David Soul" (over the initial surprise) eyeballed his phone while Mark Dilworth looked over at Rick and Viv as if just about to pop with excited joy for his friends.

Forehead still to Rick's, Viv shifted a hand to Rick's hair and caressed it. She sniffed. "...Welcome home."

A tear trailed Rick's cheek. "Thank you."

"God bless, you two." Hutch tossed a twenty-dollar bill on top of the bar, then stepped away with a wave and parting nod to Mark.

Now Rick sniffed (crybabies both). "I live you, Vivian."

Viv pecked his lips. "I live you, boy." She pulled back some and beheld her husband. Tears stained both their faces. There was a time when Viv didn't allow herself to cry. But oh, so much had happened since then.

Naomi shifted her position, moving closer.

With her view of Rick unobstructed now, Naomi took in the sole object of Viv's desire as he gazed into his wife's eyes. He wore a lead-gray Tom Ford three-piece herringbone suit. A tie striped with shades of yellow accented Rick's signature crisp, white shirt. His pocket square was a solid firefly-yellow with an easy straight fold and no points.

His choice to wear something with his wife's favorite color touched Naomi—and was so Rick Phillips. He varied his tie knots; today, he wore the True Love knot. Wearing a striped tie was perfect for this knot: the stripes created a flawless pinwheel effect. His shoes were classic: black leather cap-toe oxford lace-ups sans brogueing.

Gazing at Rick on that barstool, everything looked sublime. Yes, it did.

When he was a patient three years ago, he was slender; slender but muscular. He'd gained little weight since then, but he was slightly heavier now—in all the best ways there were to be slightly heavier.

Viv reached for Rick's face, her fingers touching lightly. She gazed at him with wonder, her head moving slowly with the same.

Although Naomi knew Rick didn't meet the man until within the past hour, Rick's buddy leaned toward the couple with suggested familiarity. His tipsy eyes focused on Viv. "Uh, Miss, he's real. You're not dreaming. Would you want *me* in your dream if you were?"

Viv laughed (they all did) and wrapped Rick in her embrace, holding him tight. The expected tongue-thrashing still hadn't happened, only tight hugs, gentle touches, and quiet prayers: all quite telling.

The mild December day didn't negate the need for outerwear, but not here. "Take your coat off, sweetie."

"Yeah, come on..." Rick stood, rising to his six feet two-plus inches.

A shade over five-nine in her stocking feet, even with her three-inch heels on, Viv looked up at him. Time stopped... And then Viv Phillips smiled. She smiled this smile Naomi hadn't seen before. The broad smile lit up Viv's face, and now those dark irises sparkled and shone with such loving glee, Naomi teared up all over again.

Rick smiled back. He pecked Viv's lips and then guided her in a turn away from him, removing her coat by sliding it off her shoulders.

She sensed the men looking at Viv, but Naomi focused on Rick.

Rick watched the slow reveal of Viv in that dress, taking his time to move his eyes over her form. Viv was shapely: end of discussion. Rick closed his eyes with a tiny wince, his gaze over Viv saying everything within seconds as he blindly handed her coat out to someone (anyone) who would take it.

Mark did the honors, accepting the coat from Rick's outstretched hand. A gentleman, Mark then came over to Naomi and assisted with removing hers, being careful of her brace. He smelled of an aftershave (with traces of cedar) she wasn't familiar with. After Naomi voiced her thanks, Mark draped both coats across his arm and moved back to his original standing spot, an abundant smile creasing his face, his gray eyes dancing as he watched the couple.

Naomi relished her catbird view to see it all. Some nice R&B or Soul or Haitian-Creole music likely played overhead, but who heard it with all this going on? Rick and Viv were glorious fun to watch.

Looking at Rick, the bartender uttered a low chortle. "I feel you, man."

Rick's "buddy" (Naomi still waited on a name) shook his head with a soft whistle. "I'm with you, Rodney. She's... Daaamn..."

So, the bartender's name was Rodney. And the buddy's?

"Stay respectful, Dwight," Rodney cautioned (answering the question).

"I'm chill, man. But you started it."

Rodney just shook his head.

Rick cleared his throat. "You're beautiful, Viv."

She was.

Quivering (still in mild shock), Viv blushed and whispered her thanks. Her eyes fell on Naomi's, thanking her again, too.

Naomi nodded and smiled, trying to send calming vibes Viv's way.

Rick bit his bottom lip and turned Viv back to him as he sat, holding her at the waist. The entire exchange, from Rick removing Viv's coat to turning her to face him, only took seconds but suspended time.

"Here it comes," Mark said.

And Naomi saw it coming, too. "I believe so."

Finished cleaning the wine glass, Rodney set it down. "Oh, yeah."

With something sounding part gasp, part whimper, Viv pressed against her husband's body and kissed him, making Rick moan. Their kiss wasn't the wild-tonguing Naomi expected, but the passionate intensity behind it was still evident in an otherwise tender moment.

A smile jotted across Naomi's lips. "Get 'im, Viv."

When Viv pulled back, the two gazed into each other's eyes, silent dialogue passing between them. Rick smiled and nodded at something gone unspoken, and they commenced with soft, slow pecks to the lips.

Naomi believed Viv was prepared to throw caution to the wind and have sex with Rick mid-Manje, but then Rick whispered in her ear.

Viv sent him an impish smirk, shaking her head at a teasing pace.

Now it was Rick's turn to blush.

Viv's expression changed to something mixing blush and arousal.

"Ready to get at him, huh, Viv?" Dwight apparently considered himself on a nickname basis.

Using her thumb to wipe a trace of lip-gloss transfer from her husband's bottom lip, Viv's expression intensified in indirect answer to Dwight's question.

Rodney offered warning number two. "Chill, Dwight."

Dwight raised an apologetic hand more to Rodney than anyone else. "Sorry. Didn't mean no disrespect. I'm just happy for 'em. Gotta be happy 'bout somethin' around here."

Rick's and Viv's gazes entwined, communicating without words, manifest in their facial expressions and head movements suggesting conversation, and ending with Viv pecking Rick's lips and him nodding.

"Did you two, like, have a conversation and shit without speaking?" Dwight scoffed his awe.

Oblivious to Dwight (and Rodney's third warning), the couple engaged in a tasteful kiss, barely using tongues.

A gentleman farther down the bar (two empty shot glasses in front of him) offered his opinion. "Get a room."

Drunkenly upset, Dwight (balding and looking like he could use a sandwich or two) rounded on the man and went into a mini tirade, filling the man in on what Rick filled Dwight in on hours ago, his nose and eyes flaring while explaining how the couple hadn't been together in three years. Rick and Viv paused their slow-peck kissing, watching their defender with amused grins. Dwight ended by telling the man he was hating on others because he *wished* he needed to get a room.

Rodney did what he could to keep Dwight calm and the situation from escalating (as a few heads at neighboring tables turned their way). But Dwight wasn't having it as he pleaded the couple's case, telling Rodney that if Rodney was under the same circumstances, Rodney knew he'd have his lady bent over the bar by now.

Everyone's ensuing light chuckle helped defuse the situation.

When the chuckles died down, no one spoke.

Mark looked annoyed, sending his own frown at the "get a room" gentleman infringing on his plan-coming-together joy.

Naomi found herself sending the man a look of unhappy, feeling a tad infringed upon, too.

"Cut 'em some slack, man. You heard the story, and they're not being disruptive." Rodney sent a shot glass full of brown down to the gentleman as peace offering.

The gentleman gazed at Rick and Viv. He nodded his apology and extended a hand toward Rick across the two barstools separating them.

Eyes turned to Rick.

Rick stared in the gentleman's direction, the grin gone, his jaw muscles working (he sometimes gritted his teeth when angry).

His jaw unclenched with Viv's soothing rub over his head, the anger leaving his face with her gentle peck to his temple. With a curt nod and semi-smile, Rick extended his hand to the man, squashing the mini-beef, and there was an actual collective sigh of relief.

The gentleman turned back, getting down to short business with his shot glass. He extended it toward the couple with a toast of "To reunions."

Rick gestured at his wedding ring on Viv's illusion necklace. "That for anyone special?"

With the biggest smile accompanying new tears springing, Viv tried snatching the ring off, but the necklace wouldn't break. After lowering her lids with a composing sigh, she unclasped the necklace. She removed Rick's wedding band and placed it on his finger.

The small crew clapped discreetly.

When the couple kissed this time, it entailed a sample of that tongue-thrashing expected earlier, but it was still low-key and in good taste. Viv sent a hand to Rick's hair, gripping it.

Dwight whistled low. "Aww yeah. Get it y'all!"

Rick's hair was longer than it was months ago; his former blended-fade was now a short two-inch 'fro, sheared-off and tapered on the corners. The style showed off the slightly coiled texture of his hair, giving his haircut subtle nuance of contour and class.

Viv's soft whimper into Rick's mouth broke Naomi's heart but also stirred some internal glee. She also grew a bit too interested in watching them kiss, getting glimpses of Rick's tongue in and out of Viv's mouth as he held her waist, adding these gentle nips to her lips as he kissed her. An inkling of missing Kevin surfaced. Naomi shifted her attention to those also focused on the kiss.

Rodney, Dwight, Mark, and even Get-A-Room watched the couple; their attention directed lower—to the general area of Viv's behind in that dress. Her dress wasn't tight and ill-fitting but curved effectively over her female form.

Leaning forward with lips parted, the men appeared as if waiting with bated breath for Rick to send his hands down from Viv's waist to exercise his right to grab onto something else. But Rick didn't reach lower. He ended the kiss (leaving his boys hanging).

Postures straightened and mouths closed with varied clearings of throats.

Naomi held in a scoff.

Men. If it wouldn't hurt her wrist further, she would've given each a bonk on the head with her brace.

Rick extended a warm, soft smile to his wife. "Kisses don't lie, Vivian."

Viv played in his hair. She shook her head, her eyes boring into Rick's. "No, they don't."

"Kiss her again!" Dwight glanced at Rodney, fearing warning four.

Rodney said nothing.

Rick kept eyes on Viv. "Oh, I will, but later. Got someone else here I want to say hello to."

"I'm sure you're gonna do more than kiss 'er, man." Rodney voiced another hushed chortle.

Naomi expected Rick to reply with his "Damn skippy," but he only smirked as he trailed a pondering gaze over his wife with a musing nod. "Oh, that's a given. Basic math." His fingers at Viv's waist seemed to tighten on her with anticipation of that given, and then he stood, giving Viv's lips a peck. He interlocked his hand with Viv's, and the two navigated the tables and chairs as they headed for Mark.

Rodney gathered the remaining empty glasses from the bar: an old-fashioned (Rick's) and a highball (Mark's).

Rick extended Mark Dilworth a power-handshake and one-armed embrace as if Mark had as much melanin in his skin as he did. "Thanks, man. This went well."

Mark's grin lit his face. "It did, didn't it?"

Viv leaned close, kissing Mark's cheek. "It did, sweetie. Thank you. I'm talking: Best. Christmas. *E-ver!*"

They laughed, but Mark grew earnest. "Anything for you two."

Rick nodded his appreciation. "Coming back at you, Dil." Still holding his wife's hand, he started in Naomi's direction, wearing a genial smile. When he reached her, he released Viv's hand and gathered Naomi in a bear hug. "And you, Sis..."

Unable to help it, Naomi stiffened but then allowed herself to be hugged, hugging back as Viv retrieved her purse.

Rick held on to her, and she breathed in a delicate, intoxicating blend of citrus, rosemary, basil, and vetiver: Christian Dior Eau Sauvage (a classic fragrance Naomi now knew was a pertinent part of his history with Viv). Her hug back also allowed her to feel the muscles rippling under his Tom Ford attire.

Their relationship blossomed and deepened over the years in unexpected ways. Rick considered her family, his "little big sister," because, although diminutive, she was seven years older than he. She considered Rick and Viv family, too.

Rick settled her to her feet, then lowered his posture to hold her at the waist and peck her lips. "Thank you. Thank you. Thank you." He straightened his posture with another smile, sending the full (murderous) power of it to Naomi's core.

Lord have mercy.

Still feeling remnants of the sensation of his soft lips and the brush of his mustache, his Eau Sauvage now on her somehow, Naomi smiled up at her big little brother. "Buy me a drink, and we'll call it even."

Low laughter drifted from the others.

"Nope. I'm buying, remember?" Mark still held their coats.

Naomi shrugged, eyes on Rick. "Guess that's it then. We're even."

Rick's golden-auburn eyes shimmered at her, and she was in his embrace again. Viv had a hand to Rick's back with a kindhearted nod.

When Rick released her this time, he reached for Viv's hand, interlocking their fingers again, and settled his gaze on Naomi. "I won't ever be able to thank you fully, but I'm go'n give it my best." Guiding Viv to stand beside him, he focused on Naomi's brace. He peered at her with empathy before focusing on her brace again with a headshake. "That looks painful, Sis. And annoying, troublesome. I feel you."

Naomi inclined her head with appreciation. Rick did "feel her," understood in a way the others didn't—because he was left-handed, too.

Mark stepped up. "Come on, let's get a table." He raised an inquiring eyebrow at her. "You're good with that, right?" In his question, he was also asking if she was ready to continue the reunion fun.

Naomi grinned. "Of course."

"I got you, folks." Rodney raised a hand and snapped his fingers.

Parting words to Rodney and Dwight behind them, the four sat at a table near a window with prime view of the harbor. Their attendant, Alaina (late 20s, Creole accent), inquired if she could get anyone drinks.

Knowing his audience, Mark ordered: Belvedere vodka tonic for Naomi, Southern Comfort with a lemon wedge for Viv, Jack & Coke for himself. He paused before ordering for Rick. "Got Pappy Van Family Reserve or Elijah Craig?"

Alaina nodded. "We have Pappy FR fifteen and Elijah twelve and twenty-three, sir."

Mark glanced at Rick. "Make it EC twenty-three: neat. Thanks."

She'd long ago learned Rick was a bourbon man. And with discriminating tastes: Pappy Van and Elijah Craig held quality status. She already had something for him for Christmas, but now she had an idea for a little something else.

They chatted while awaiting their drinks, Mark, Naomi, and Rick filling Viv in on the details of Rick's early release and the subsequent plan coming together. When the menus and drinks arrived, everyone acknowledged Mark's forty-third birthday the previous week. She and Mark then toasted their friends, and Viv grew teary-eyed.

Alaina returned for their food order, and Mark also handled that, adding humor. "And we'll have a plate full of all your featured veggies for my man, here..." Mark pointed at Rick.

Everyone hollered, leaving Alaina confused at not getting the joke: Rick "hated" vegetables.

They resumed conversation while waiting for their food, chatting it up right through its arrival.

Bright light from the sunny day poured into Manje's. Naomi sat next to Mark, facing into the restaurant, while Rick and Viv faced them and a view of the harbor. The couple engaged in low-key interplay with their hands as conversation flowed. Naomi sat diagonally from Rick, taking subtle inventory of the man looking nothing close to his 40 years. She hadn't seen Rick in several months. And in that time, she hadn't forgotten his looks, but looking at him now, up close and personal like this, it still amazed her how beautiful the man was.

Smooth, cinnamon-brown skin covered him. The short boxed beard he wore three years ago was gone; he now sported the Hipster, the hairs low and trimmed to his face. His irises (with that strange mix of reds and dark golds) shimmered and glowed with fire-like hues as he laughed and talked with everyone. His eye color—complemented by girlishly-long lashes—was peculiar, striking.

Rick's happiness at being with Viv again (unmistakable in his devastating smile with the peekaboo dimples) infused everyone at the table. The scar running along the top of the cartilage of his right ear added a dose of character to break up (if not enhance) all the prettiness. Rick's chiseled features (that cleft in his chin too much) necessitated several camera-clicks or a magazine spread; *handsome* sold the man short. Naomi noted the disappointed looks of two women looking on as Rick laughed and flirted with his wife.

She hadn't forgotten his looks, but as he laughed and chatted, her ears reacquainted themselves with his faint Southern accent. Some of his words carried traces of Virginian dialect. Rick's parents were from way below the Mason Dixon, so his learned speech pattern and dialect carried bits of Georgia and Alabama, creating a distinct Virginian-Georgian-Alabamian mix. During discussion, Rick used many phrases of excitement and agreement—except one. Naomi eagerly anticipated his use of "Damn skippy" and was disappointed at having not yet heard it.

Still maintaining her contributions to the conversation, Naomi shifted attention to the woman Rick smiled at incessantly. Viv (42) could be taken for any of Hollywood's hottest actresses. Her creamy butterscotch-caramel complexion appeared flush with excitement at being with Rick again. Earlier, she'd freshened her shaded lip gloss, and now her lips closed and parted with a shade of some warm, dark berry. Eyebrows (thick and shaped with a gentle arch) rose and fell with her responses to the conversation.

The tasteful, eye-catching forest-green dress provided pleasing contrast to the rich chestnut and auburn teased spirals of her hair, giving Viv a touch of wildness that turned a few admiring heads, both male and female.

Viv's sultry eyes (the irises an unrelenting jet-black) sparkled with delight. Viv's smiles no longer carried deep sadness, but Naomi recognized traces of skepticism: as if she expected at any moment to be awakened from this dream and so was hesitant to invest in its occurrence. But it wasn't a dream (ask Dwight). Viv also, at times, stared at Rick as everyone talked, again appearing in disbelief.

Viewing the couple sitting side-by-side was goodness. The chemistry between them crackled even during laughing moments, and there were still times when the couple spoke to each other without uttering a word;

that, too, was special to watch. It wasn't just a look of understanding between them; the two exchanged dialogue without parting their lips.

Complementary platinum-and-diamond wedding bands gleamed in the sunlight with the hand movements accompanying their light hand play and chatter.

Cinnamon and butterscotch: an excellent combination.

During conversation, Naomi learned Rick was proficient with a yo-yo. The billiard room on the other side of Manje Trankil drew the couple's attention often; they enjoyed playing sometimes.

Rick was in the middle of explaining his views on the differences between music by Earth, Wind & Fire, and that by War, when Mark chuckled. "Viv: stop staring at him so hard. He's not—"

"Dil, come on." Rick grinned. "A gorgeous woman is staring at me, giving 'let's play' signals, and you're killing the mood, wrecking the flow. Shut up, man."

All but Viv laughed.

Viv quasi-smiled but continued staring at Rick.

Rick's expression sobered. "Nah, but let her stare, man." He rested his eyes on Viv and interlocked their hands before shifting his gaze to Mark. "Let her stare. Let her do whatever the fuck she wants."

Mark nodded his understanding. "You got it. Just teasing." He sent Viv and Naomi a mischievous look. "Let's *all* stare at Rick!"

Naomi joined in the fun, widening her eyes and leaning over the table toward Rick, staring at him. Mark did the same. Viv, laughing some now, leaned closer to Rick, widening her eyes with a stare, too. Still holding his wife's hand, Rick hollered, and everyone howled, all four having a good time.

Mark ordered another round, and the conversation kept on rocking.

As they talked, Naomi noticed a change in how Viv held Rick's hand. Viv stroked Rick's palm with her middle finger, an old-time gesture for interest in sex Naomi hadn't seen in decades. Biting her bottom lip, Viv loosened Rick's tie knot. Viv bit her bottom lip for either of two purposes: suppressing rage or desire. This lip-biting: suppressed desire. Naomi expected to see more of Viv's lip-biting for years to come.

Naomi brought the issue forward. "You okay, Viv?"

Viv sent a soft smirk her way. "Girl, no. I am sliding around in this chair." She caressed Rick's hair, adding a soft grip into it. "I'm feening for him like you wouldn't believe. If this is a dream, then dammit, I'm going to dream it up and get it in!" She raised an eyebrow. "How's that?"

Naomi smiled, expecting nothing less.

Viv winked and turned back to Rick, kissing his cheek. "So, I hope you're ready to stay *up*, and I don't mean 'awake.' It's going to be you and me...for several rounds. It's time for you to come all the way *home*. The end."

Mark turned a shade pinker as he sipped his second Jack and Coke.

Rick swallowed and cleared his throat, lashes lowering with his blush.

Viv played in Rick's hair as she fixed Naomi with a look: "I want FedEx out the gate."

Naomi released two notes of a chuckle.

The fellas issued puzzled, inquiring glances, but Naomi and Viv didn't elaborate.

Alaina stopped by their table. "Everything okay? Need anything?"

Viv sat taller with an inquiring smile. "Can I get a box of your OOTW Butter Peanut Butter cookies to go?"

"We have them in small bags, too, ma'am."

Viv looked at Rick and then back to Alaina. "I know, but uh, we're going to need the box, so..."

Making no assumptions, Alaina grinned, sending her gaze around to everyone. "So, who likes peanut butter?"

All eyes fell on Rick.

Alaina inspected Rick with a smile. "I see. Well, I'll pass on to Chef Malen and his wife, Chef Galena, that they have more fans; it's her special recipe. Let me know when you're getting ready to leave. I'll make sure you get a warm batch." The smile and look in her eyes held part flirt with Rick, but she wasn't offensive about it. She left.

Rick frowned. "OOTW?"

Naomi clarified: "Out of this world. And they are. You're going to be pleased, sweetie."

Rick shifted his attention to Viv, gazing at her with such a mixture of love and desire, cookies were the last thing he cared about. "Sounds good."

Mark, seeming uncomfortable with the sexual energy brewing across the table, coughed.

Naomi shook her head, holding in laughter.

Viv grinned at her husband; she was the same, but so different. "Yes. They're buttery and very peanut-buttery—just like you like. With this creamy cookie texture keeping them moist even when exposed to air."

Rick's lips turned with a gentle smirk. "I see."

Viv looked downward. "The past couple years,...I've come here to get one on your birthd—" She shook her head with a sigh.

Naomi knew about Viv's trip to Manje every June for the past two years to honor her husband's birthday while he was away. Rick didn't want Viv visiting him for birthdays and holidays, except Christmas, because it hurt too much, so Viv coped in small ways; getting something with her husband's favorite food on his birthday was one of them. Viv told no one else about doing that until just now.

Rick took Viv's hand and leaned closer, waiting for her to look at him.

Viv lifted her eyes.

"Sounds good, Lady Blue. We'll take those cookies and celebrate more than just my missed birthdays. Over and over again. Okay?" Looking at him, it was clear: the only *cookie* Rick was interested in right now...was Viv's.

Viv's nod back was steady.

The couple locked eyes, and Naomi knew Viv couldn't and didn't want to help herself when she replied: "I...am going...to fuck you so good, Richard, Senior. *So good.* I live you." Viv glanced their way. "Sorry."

Mark shrugged with a headshake. "Understandable. And we're all well over twenty-one. No apologies necessary."

Naomi thumbed in Mark's direction. "Ditto Mark."

Rick sustained an ardent smirk at his wife, but there was something else in his gaze Naomi couldn't read specifically but had the gist of: no doubt he planned to return the favor.

Rick and Viv ordered dishes (Rick: broiled seafood, Viv: white-sauce pasta) but hadn't eaten much at all: food was the last thing on their minds. Naomi discovered the same outcome when she checked Mark's surf-and-turf plate and her light-fare sampler: no one had eaten much of anything. Doggie bags all around, please.

Rick gazed out the window, his attention directed toward the sky. "Closing in on two o'clock: 'bout one forty-five."

Mark shook his head. "You still do that, man?"

Viv grinned, sending her chin high. "Isn't it the best?"

Naomi nodded and grinned back. Her friend was gone over her husband, just gone.

Mark gestured toward Rick's torso. "So, what's the point of the pocket watch?"

Rick sipped his water, giving Mark a smirking shrug.

Viv chimed in: "For overcast days, or if he's indoors with no view outside, and he's unable to read the sky for the time." She was just gone. It was the cutest thing. Naomi didn't blame her one bit.

Mark rolled his eyes upward with a playful scoff. "Okay, Viv."

Rick set his glass down with a glance at his wife. He pulled a silver vintage pocket watch from its place for humorous emphasis and slipped it back with a sigh. "So, folks..."

Naomi pointed toward the empty dancefloor. "Why don't you take advantage of the dancefloor first? I'm sure something apropos will play soon."

Rick and Viv sent her bewildered looks.

Naomi gazed back plainly.

Rick smirked with a headshake. "Okay, Sis." He offered Viv his hand. "Care to dance?"

Blushing, Viv accepted his hand.

After Rick removed his suit jacket, the couple went to the dancefloor, falling into the Bop to some slow-to-mid-tempo Haitian groove. Rick said something to Viv. Moments later, Viv closed her eyes. Even with Viv's eyes closed, the two danced effortlessly, as if three years apart meant nothing.

Naomi decided what she wanted to do with her extra tickets to the charity gala next month. She usually pawned them off on some unsuspecting soul. Not this year.

The song ended, and Viv opened her eyes. As Rick took Viv's hand, sporadic rounds of applause sounded from other Manje patrons. On their way back to the table, Atlantic Starr's "Am I Dreaming" floated into the room. The couple paused and looked over at her.

Naomi nodded confirmation the song was for them, gesturing for them to return to the dancefloor. She and Mark coordinated with Manje Trankil's manager and sous-chef (and Chef Malen's wife), Galena Quimby, to play "Am I Dreaming" whenever Rick and Viv came to the dancefloor (Mark having given details of the setup beforehand, so the deejay would recognize Rick and Viv). The warm feeling in her belly had little to do with Mr. Belvedere (for a change) and much more to do with this reunion coming off without a hitch.

Naomi and her co-conspirator went quiet as Rick guided Viv close to slow dance with her. They watched the reunited couple.

Mark finished his drink. "They're something, huh? Special."

"They really are."

"Yeah. That's good love right there. It's nice seeing the fairytale can exist for some people. And I can't think of two people more deserving."

Naomi turned to Mark with a grin. "We did good, didn't we?"

Mark issued a chuckling nod. "That we did. How 'bout you? Care to dance? Celebrate our surprise-reunion joint-venture?"

Naomi looked at him.

"Hey, I can do my thang. Don't let the lack of melanin fool you."

Naomi sounded a low, amused hoot. "I like you, Mark." She shook her head. "But no, I want to enjoy watching them. Thank you, though."

"No problem. Well, how about...?"

Naomi paused her gaze on him, waiting.

"Fist bump? Blow it up?"

Naomi laughed again. "That's fine."

Mark held his fist toward her.

Naomi touched her fist to his, and they made soft explosion sounds, simulating their fists "exploding" upon impact: a celebration of sorts. She found it irritatingly odd how folk of European descent often adopted many gestures and expressions originating from people of color yet had the nerve to have racist impulses, but she said nothing; she liked Mark and believed him an exception to the rule.

They laughed at themselves and resumed watching Rick and Viv on the dancefloor. The two looked so in love: singing some of the lyrics to each other, talking, and sometimes pecking lips as they danced.

Mark cleared his throat.

Naomi turned to him.

"He's my brother." Mark glanced at her sideways.

Naomi was sure he expected her to argue the point based on race, but Naomi imparted a relaxed smile. "And you're his."

Mark gawked her way, surprise in his gray eyes. "Think so? I mean..."

Naomi just looked at him.

Mark grinned. "Thanks." He shifted his attention to Mr. and Mrs. Phillips. "...And, while I can tell it matters not to you, I like you, too."

Naomi grinned with a soft nod. It didn't matter, but it was still nice to hear. People need people.

"They don't know it yet, but Barb and I are having them over for some holiday fun: a little 'welcome home' shindig for Rick we're including as part New Year's celebration."

"I'm sure Viv will love that."

He fingered a shock of his brownish-blond hair away from his eyes. "Yeah. Nothing extravagant, but it should be nice. Planning to invite Louise and Tim. I'd like you to come, Naomi. You and your family are welcome to join us."

Naomi hesitated. People needed people, but Naomi's people list wasn't long. She liked it that way. "Maybe. Give me the details. Les and I might stop through."

Mark grinned hard, his gray eyes shining with something Naomi couldn't pin down.

She signaled Alaina over and requested the warm peanut butter cookies to go as Rick and Viv returned to the table, hands interlocked.

"Thanks for that, guys," Viv gleamed. "You were right, Naomi: the song—very apropos. This does feel like a dream."

"Yeah. Truly..." Rick gazed at his wife, "on point."

Viv lowered her eyes before shifting her attention to them. "Only now, I'm like, *really* ready to get out of here—*if* you know what I mean."

Naomi hollered. She'd never seen Viv blush so much.

"No kidding! Meaning quite clear." Mark laughed, too.

Rick shook his head, frowning with mock confusion. "I'm sorry. I don't know what you mean. Is there a problem?"

Viv trailed her gaze over him and then looked in his eyes. "Oh yeah. Big Problem. Big, three-year-old Problem. And you have a Big-ass Solution, honey. Yes, Lord. It's time to go."

Viv's double-meaning drifted around them, and Naomi wished the couple's auras would flicker for her.

Rick blushed hard with lowered eyes and some throat-clearing. After a beat, he pinned his gaze on them, too. "It's time to go. Basic math."

Naomi and Mark chuckled.

Mark nipped a cold fry. "You kids go 'head. We got it."

Viv's gaze, alternating between Naomi and Mark, turned sincere. "I cannot thank you enough for this."

Naomi shrugged. "Probably can't, but Mark and I will put our heads together, devise ways you can start."

Mark grinned and nodded his agreement while rubbing his hands together in exaggerated suggested anticipation. "Many, many ways to start, my dear child." He added a mocking evil laugh for good measure, making everyone chuckle. "Oh!" Mark glanced at her.

Naomi dipped her chin in affirmation.

Mark reached into his jacket pocket.

Viv's brows dented with trepidatious inquiry. "What now?"

"Yeah, I was in on the front end of this, but now..." Rick's frown mirrored Viv's.

Mark extended a small envelope toward Rick.

Rick released Viv's hand and accepted the envelope from Mark, wearing a curious smirk. He peered inside, his fingers moving within the interior. After a glance at Viv, he frowned again without revealing the contents and stared at Mark.

Nodding with chest puffed out, Mark grinned, showing his love for Rick and Viv. "Tickets to the Spirit of Baltimore...and keycards to the Smithson Fifth hotel."

Viv drew a hand to cover her mouth yet again.

Rick studied Mark for seconds, his expression hard to read. Goodness! That man was a sight for *all* eyes.

Viv lowered her hand. "The Smithson... With the shoulder-deep whirlpool baths..." She locked eyes with her husband as both reflected on a time they stayed at the Smithson, doing something in hot, shoulder-deep water. Naomi wondered whose shoulders Viv was referring to.

Mark jounced his shoulders. "You'd know better than I would; I've never been. I know it's a fave spot for you two, so... Suite nine-seventeen. Have two nights together—on us."

Rick raised an eyebrow. "That's not cheap, man."

Mark grinned, shaking his head. "No, but split several ways, it's more than manageable. Raid that minibar."

Now, Viv raised an eyebrow. "'Several'?"

"Yes: you have quite a few benefactors." Naomi sipped some water. "Now, mind your business and enjoy the Smithson. Merry Christmas."

The couple gazed at each other in awe, shaking their heads. They shifted their attention back to Naomi and Mark, looking happily stunned.

Naomi winked at them. "Close your mouth, sweetie. I've already talked with Louise. Babysitting: done."

Viv reclaimed Rick's hand and bowed her head. Rick pocketed the envelope and followed suit. Seconds later, their small prayer finished, the couple lifted their heads with smiles and released hands.

"Thank you so much." Viv took a calming sip of water.

Rick shook Mark's hand in thanks and reached for Viv's coat. "And on that note..." He held her coat open as Viv slipped into it.

"See you on the thirteenth, Rick."

Rick nodded at Mark.

Viv searched their faces. "What? Something related to his release?"

Mark shook his head. "Nothing like that. DMG Inc. wants him back, Viv. The firm lost several major clients because Rick wasn't managing their accounts. Rick starts mid-January. He'll be starting at middle management, but it's Rick: he'll be back at the top in no time."

Rick gave Mark a curt nod. "Preciate the vote of confidence, man."

Mark returned an amiable wave of his hand, keeping eyes on Viv.

Viv blinked at them; mouth parted again. She likely didn't expect her husband to be employed from jump street.

Naomi imbued her smile with warmth. "Merry Christmas, Viv."

Rick kissed Viv's cheek. "Come on, baby. I'll tell you more about it on the way." He looked at Mark. "The thirteenth. Eight-seventeen in the AM."

Mark chuckled. "Yeah, bring that back, man: those weird time frames of yours."

Rick shook his head. "Not 'weird,' just—"

"Non-standard," Viv and Mark chimed in answer.

"Because it helps..." Rick eyed Viv and Mark, prompting them to finish if they were so smart.

Mark and Viv were so smart. "People remember better."

Rick smirked at them. "Long as you know." Grinning, he stepped away from his wife and approached Naomi. "A'ight, Sis, gimme my hug."

Naomi pushed her chair back and stood to say goodbye-for-now to her "brother."

Being careful of her brace, Rick scooped her up in a tight hug, kissed her cheek (his Eau Sauvage speaking sexily to her), and put her down. "Peace, love, and blessings, lady." Fingertips to her waist, he pecked her lips, and Naomi (although fleeting) wanted Rick in a way she shouldn't have, wanted him to put her up against the wall and deliver the package. FedEx was fine; she didn't care—it would still be UPS.

"Back at you, little brother." She looked over at Mark and Viv.

Viv held on to Mark Dilworth for quiet seconds. She said something in his ear that made him nod and chuckle before giving her a parting kiss to her cheek as Alaina returned with a box of OOTW Butter Peanut Butter cookies, warm from the oven.

The couple switched off, Rick extending a hand to Mark for another power-handshake embrace.

Viv shook her head at Naomi as she stepped up. "I'm going to get you. Don't know how yet, but oh yeah." She laughed softly then; a pleasant sound emanating from the woman's soul.

"Oh, you'll be too busy for plots and plans. I'm not worried."

"Mark driving you back?"

Naomi shook her head. "Leslie and Trevor picked up my car from your house; they should be along soon."

Viv's eyes narrowed. "So, 'several' were in on this abundance of Christmas presents, huh?"

"Perhaps. FYI, you have a packed bag in the cargo area."

Slowly shaking her head, Viv's eyes filled with curious wonder. "Who—? What—? When...?"

"Let the devil mind the details. God's got the endgame."

Viv extended her arms for a hug. "Thank you, Naomi. I'm grateful."

"I know you are." She hugged Viv tight, breathing in the warm scents of her body oil, as the men joked about something holding notes of being men-only. Viv kissed her cheek as they parted, reminding Naomi just how much people needed people.

Rick shrugged back into his suit jacket before coming over to Viv. He took her hand, locking eyes with her. "You ready?"

A beat of underlying meaning passed between them.

"I am." Viv smiled and picked up the box of cookies, this odd but pleasant look on her face hinting her excited anticipation of being alone with her husband—completely unsupervised.

With parting smiles and waves, they headed away.

Naomi sat. She glanced at her glass: Belvedere had left the building. She pondered ordering another.

Mark hollered after them. "Call me in a few days, Rick."

Rick released Viv's hand, placing it at the small of her back as she walked before him. He looked back at Mark with a nod.

Lord have mercy.

Mark sat and joined Naomi in watching the Phillipses leave. They both chuckled as Dwight came up to the couple with some probably drunken parting words, Rodney nowhere near to give his warnings.

The couple resumed their exit from Manje Trankil.

"So,...what do you think's going to be happening with them tonight, tomorrow...?"

Naomi laughed. "Not much: just a lengthy, in-depth discussion of Viv's problem and Rick's demonstrations of his ideas for potential solutions." According to Viv, Rick had excellent problem-solving skills.

"Yeah. With slides and props and everything!"

Naomi laughed with Mark Dilworth, appreciating him dearly.

She watched the couple leave, believing, if Viv had to do it all again, she would. If it meant having the level of connection with her husband, born out of suffering, that she had with Rick now, she would do all of it (except the Jonathan part)...again.

Naomi turned to Mark. "One for the road?" She'd had two drinks, but she felt fine. How you felt had nothing to do with driving after drinking, but...

Mark smiled. "You bet." He signaled Alaina, then ordered refills of their drinks, bringing Belvedere back for a return engagement.

She laughed and talked with Mark (about his job, Barbara, about Rick and Viv) for a good twenty minutes, enjoying his company until Leslie and Trevor arrived. Before she left, Mark handed her a formal invitation to the Dilworths' welcome home gathering for Rick. Inside, he included a personal note of sincere elegance.

Unable to resist, she picked up some coddies before leaving Baltimore; more to go with her Trankil leftovers. Leslie loved them, too, so it was all good.

Driving home ("Shine On Me" by the Davis Sisters playing on low), Naomi noticed herself smiling often.

Taking part in Viv and Rick's reunion was one of the finest moments she ever remembered being a part of.

Reuniting the Phillipses was fun, uplifting. But now she had homework to do. With a new patient scheduled next week, preparation was in order—using the delivered, thick manila file folder on her desk.

She stared at the folder, classical music playing in the background, an old-fashioned glass containing Hennessy X.O. in her right hand.

Naomi didn't like going into anything blind if she could help it, and with new patients, she could help it. Completed preliminary question-naires, brief medical histories, and a good internet search were usually all she needed to get a feel for what she was walking into, for who was walking into her office. In two hours, she'd gleaned insight and details far exceeding the basics, but the basics were fine for appointment one next week.

Cecily Edana Jamison, 44, was born in Cleveland, Mississippi, the second of three children born to Bennett and Yolanda Jamison. She has an older brother (by two years), Kyle, and a younger brother (by eighteen months), Larimore. When Cecily was 18, her parents were killed in a cargo train derailment accident. From this, the Jamison children won a settlement exceeding forty million dollars.

While a junior at Delta State, Cecily married her college sweetheart, Roland "RC" Cooper. She graduated magna cum laude with degrees in finance and business administration, while Roland finished cum laude with a degree in accounting. The couple had two children: Marcus and Chelsea. After fifteen years of marriage, Cecily lost Roland to brain cancer. In her grief, she and her children moved to the Washington DC Metropolitan area for a fresh start.

Cecily met Oscar "OJ" Brooks a year or so later.

Naomi didn't focus on Oscar's information as much as she did Cecily's (she was the patient, the one experiencing accelerating post-traumatic stress disorder (PTSD) occurrences, after all), but she absorbed the gist.

Oscar Jerome Brooks, 50, was the firstborn son of Walter and Nancy Brooks and lived in the DMV area all his life. He has two siblings: a sister, Odessa, and baby brother, Otis. Everything suggested a normal and uneventful childhood, but Naomi sensed competition with his siblings. With a high school diploma and some college credits at Southern College of Maryland Community College, he was partial to seasonal work, having held jobs as a data processor, security guard, and inventory clerk. Still, Naomi saw nothing years-long continuous. From what she ascertained, Oscar's "working" translated as more of a boondoggle.

December, two years ago, Cecily, Marcus, and Chelsea (and Oscar) suffered severe injury and trauma during a home invasion. Physical recovery complete, Marcus and Chelsea (and Oscar) recovered mentally as well, leading normal lives.

Having suffered the most severe injuries, Cecily's recovery took longer. Her body was healed; Cecily's mind awaited its turn.

After reading Dr. Lewis's summary findings from a year ago, Naomi already had ideas about her treatment approach.

Tired (but knowing little sleep awaited her), Naomi closed the folder and turned off her computer. She finished the fingerful of Hennessy and turned on her desk lamp (her wrist sending a sharp reminder all was not yet well in the carpal tunnel). She turned off the ceiling fan light. The violins of Johannes Brahms' Ein deutsches Requiem, Op. 45, floated into her office on low, sounding louder in the low lighting.

Naomi closed the door, leaving Brahms to it.

As she headed upstairs to her bedroom, Naomi pictured Oscar (having no clue what he looked like) frowning at her preliminary questionnaire, and she let out a gentle puff of a laugh.

Her questions went beyond demographics, requesting responses to questions seemingly unrelated to anything. The questions were both linear and random but held purpose.

The questions alone presented one story.

But the answers...

They told a tale all themselves.

Chapter Four

Broken Compasses

December could be such a fickle month. It had an image problem: mostly a fall month often categorized as winter.

Naomi stared out her office window, trying to reconcile this morning's icicles with last week's mild temperatures. Winter had advised Autumn of its impending descent, making Autumn hightail it. She'd be back, though; winter in the days of global warming didn't mean the same as it did twenty or even ten years ago. The cold came in brief spurts now, having most of its fun in late January and February.

And a *White* Christmas? Rare in the DC area.

All that had nothing to do with the twenty-nine-degree temperature outside and the odontoid icicles forming fangs outside her window, threatening to gobble her right up before Christmas Eve if she wasn't a good little girl. The icy roads had been well-treated: no issues commuting to the office. However, the weather made her unsure whether the Brooks family would show for their appointment.

You mean, Brooks couple, *don't you? Marcus and Chelsea are still Coopers, having little to no interest in being part of a Brooks "family."*

Naomi smirked, watching a delivery truck for Alan's Pastries pull up and approach the building's rear entrance. These days, *family* was a relative term (pardon the pun), so it had no ideal definition other than its core: a social unit of two or more persons having a shared commitment to some mutual relationship. Descendants of common ancestry anchored its traditional meaning, but people having no blood in common considered themselves family, while blood relatives could be deadly enemies.

The coming and going continued despite the cold. Naomi's thoughts centered on Cecily.

Any event shattering someone's comfortable existence, leaving them feeling hurt, helpless, and even hopeless, could result in someone experiencing PTSD: rape, assault, mode-of-transportation crashes, terrorist attacks, floods, hurricanes. It could be anything (attacks by kittens not excluded)—and anyone was susceptible. PTSD wasn't limited to the person actively experiencing trauma. It could occur in those who helped or witnessed it or affect persons close to the trauma victim.

Cecily's extended hospital stay likely delayed or altered her PTSD reaction, but life's stresses can awaken deep-rooted things; her recent PTSD occurrences were understood.

Based on Dr. Lewis's findings, Cecily exhibited symptoms specific to PTSD, displaying elements of reliving, avoidance, and arousal. She experienced recollections, other intrusive imagery, and emotions of despair and hopelessness. Dr. Lewis documented Cecily having difficulty concentrating in his sessions, along with some hyper-vigilance. Naomi hadn't yet witnessed these manifestations, but had nothing against this Dr. Lewis; she'd take his word for it for now.

People with PTSD tended to allow trauma to consume them; their lives often revolved around the traumatizing event. At some point, people suffer a tragedy or trauma (Dunkin' Donuts, anyone?), but not everyone develops PTSD behind it. Stress responses in such situations are natural—even the most extreme responses aren't necessarily pathological.

Protective mechanisms come into play for many life events: unwanted marriage; death of a loved one; hurricanes and tornadoes; terrorism. The key was ensuring the mechanism didn't persist and interfere with normal function.

The decision not to see a therapist wasn't denial of a problem—because there may not be one. Cecily's case is extreme (beating, rape, stabbing, son shot, daughter raped), but resilience is the rule, not the exception. Other factors complicated Cecily's case, thus requiring more professional help.

Some folk whizzed through a traumatic event, getting to the other side with little fanfare, while others struggled, developed PTSD. "Why" remained uncertain, but research showed it stemmed from a complex mix of the brain's regulation of hormones and chemicals released when stressed, responses to previous life experiences, and any inherited pre-dispositions—including personality.

The intercom buzzed. Naomi went to her desk. "Yes?"

"Doctor Alexander, Mister and Missus Brooks are here."

Naomi checked her seating area: notepad and recorder in place. The notepad was there by force of habit; the brace on her left wrist negated writing being an option. "I'm ready, Doctor Stewart." She collected her Cambridge mug full of cooling orange-spiced tea with a hint of lemon and sat in her counsel chair, ready to get to work.

She started the session timer and was off to a so-so start with Oscar as soon as he opened the door. He entered ahead of Cecily. He didn't hold the door open behind him or the door for her to enter before him. At 50 years old, Oscar's father taught him better. Naomi knew it. She didn't have antediluvian views of the roles of men and women by any means, but chivalry had its place—and certainly common courtesy did. But somewhere along his adulthood, he dispensed with gallantry (making his extension of related gestures toward a woman TLTB). His father may have taught him better, but Oscar was his own man now; holding doors open for a woman was a concept rejected in favor of... What, Naomi didn't know. Not holding the door open for his wife also revealed more about the man (and woman), lending credence to her initial impressions while reviewing their file last week.

Taller than Cecily but not tall at all, Oscar walked his five feet eight inches of false concern into the room, his eyes registering confusion and surprise as he ran them over her seating group. It was a false concern because she saw him purposely furrow his brow after adjusting to his confusion and shock. He then paused as if remembering what his facial expression was supposed to be and formed the "appropriate" one. What Oscar's passing confusion or surprise was rooted in, Naomi cared not.

Stop, Naomi. It hasn't been a minute, let alone two. Just give it a chance.

Sighing inside, Naomi set her mug down and stood, wearing a warm smile intended for at least *one* person entering her office.

Walking in behind Oscar, as she looked over the seating area, Cecily's eyes registered the same surprise and confusion Oscar's had. Still, she shrugged with a soft smile disappearing before reaching her entire face. Underneath her opened wool coat, she wore a tailored black pantsuit—making her overdressed for the occasion. Or perhaps Cecily's morbid attire expressed some internal view on the outcome of this session.

Cecily was slender. Shorter than Oscar but taller than her (most over 12 were), Cecily came in at about five-six, one-twenty-five. Her below-shoulder toffee-brown hair was camera-perfect with soft curl, and Naomi wondered if that was Cecily's preference or his.

With the freezing temperatures, her ensemble should have included a hat, scarf, and gloves. No makeup covered her tawny-brown complexion. The redness splotching her petite nose and cheeks showed telltale signs of rosacea (although mild), likely worsening with stress. The tiny mole just below Cecily's left eye drew Naomi's attention to her eyes and the non-natural hazel color of her irises: she wore contacts.

Even without the camera-perfect hair and contact lenses (prescription?), even with the rosacea, Cecily was quite pretty. During slavery, people of color looked worn and old by age 30. Nowadays, outside the influences of drugs and alcohol, it was unusual for a woman of color to look her actual age (by some abstract definition), but sometimes they did. Cecily, however, didn't look 44.

Black men tended not to look their age, but Naomi would place Oscar at 50 years. She could see he was a cutie in his younger years, however. Short with broad shoulders over a soft, non-muscular frame, balding wavy hair on his head, a friendly-muttonchops beard on his face, strands of gray in both, Oscar looked more tired than anything, especially around the eyes. Her medical training told her the man wasn't well. He didn't require emergency assistance, but Oscar wasn't feeling his best.

It didn't flicker, but Naomi imagined Oscar's aura casting off hues of charcoal mixed with a dark-red.

Skin the beigey-pink of flaked salmon, he had a wide nose but thin lips that now stretched in a smile around teeth needing cleaning; he was a smoker. Heavy coat across one arm, his attire was more casual with tan slacks and a mint-green polo shirt by Lacoste: dressed more for spring than winter. The mint-green against his light skin created a washed-out look, making him look even sicker. Naomi wondered why he wore a short-sleeved shirt in this weather. Every shirt button was unbuttoned, exposing his throat and upper chest area. Perhaps he overheated fast; the light perspiration dotting his forehead suggested as much.

Oscar extended a hand to her in greeting.

Still smiling at Cecily, Naomi accepted Oscar's sweaty palm and shook. She resisted the impulse to wipe her hand on her pants before shaking Cecily's (who likely knew the moisture came from her husband's hand). "Hi, Cecily."

"Hi." Cecily's expression blossomed with something close to hope before doubt and trepidation replaced it.

Naomi gestured to her seating group, giving them the option of loveseat, sofa, or each if they chose not to sit together. "Please."

Oscar moved to the sofa and sat. He didn't wait for Cecily to take her seat or even defer to her for her choice (considering she was the focus of this therapy). He tossed his coat across the sofa arm.

Naomi held in a grunt of disapproval. *This* dude.

As if everything was par for the course, Cecily removed her coat. She draped it over her folded arms and sat beside Oscar on his right, leaving a foot or two between them. Her position was closer to Naomi's chair.

Oscar crossed an ankle over his knee, sitting back expectantly.

Cecily placed folded hands atop her coat in her lap, waiting patiently.

Naomi took her seat. "It's up to you, but you don't have to hold on to your coats. You can hang them over there..." She pointed toward the varied coat hooks secured to the wall behind the entrance door.

He hesitated, but Oscar rose. He picked up his coat and Cecily's and hung them up, then returned and plopped on the sofa with a sigh. "So, where do we start first, Doc: the episodes? A prescription?"

Naomi kept eyes on Cecily, not appreciating him calling her "Doc."

Cecily shrugged with a nod. "Yeah. I mean, with Doctor Lewis—"

Naomi raised her left hand, cutting Cecily off.

Apology creased Cecily's features, and Naomi hated seeing it. She lowered her hand. "We're not jumping right into anything, okay?"

Cecily nodded.

Oscar gestured toward her brace. "Broke it, huh? Least it wasn't your good hand."

Naomi contrived a thin smile. "Yeah, lucky me." She turned to Cecily. "Before we begin, let's go over the rules and conditions of your therapy with me; give you a feel for how I roll..." Naomi started her recorder.

She wrapped it up directly, and the couple nodded concurrence, but Cecily gazed back, an odd look in her eyes. "Your business card has the Rod of Asclepius."

"It does."

Cecily shook her head with a quick hand-lift in apology. "I'm sorry. I don't know why I said that. Just..." She shook her head again and then lowered it.

Oscar rolled his eyes with a scoff.

"Cecily...?"

The woman lifted her eyes, sadness and trepidation permeating those contacts.

It took more effort, but having patients with colored contacts before, she'd become adept at reading expressions in them. "Do you want Oscar here?"

Cecily's eyes widened with a breath.

Oscar frowned and sat forward. "What?!"

Naomi focused on Cecily.

Cecily nodded vigorously. "I want him here, yes. He helps me." Her eyes, though, reflected something hinting quite the contrary.

Oscar sighed and sat back again. "Thanks, Cecily."

Cecily's eyes flitted, but she took Oscar's hand in solidarity.

Naomi glanced at their held hands before focusing on Cecily and pasting on a smile. "Okay then. Let's continue."

The couple bobbed their heads.

Silence followed.

Naomi began with bits from the preliminary questionnaire and other *safer* topics. "So, how's Kyle, Cecily? Larimore?" Discussing family was safe, and family farther away from home even safer. First, the safe stuff, then they could explore the less safe, the more...*sensitive* topics.

Interestingly, Cecily's eyes brightened and saddened in unison. But she released Oscar's hand and re-clasped hers in her lap. "Kyle's good. My two nieces are home for winter break, doing well. Glenda's doing well after her surgery."

Glenda was Kyle's second and current wife. "And Larimore?"

Oscar shook his head. "That loser."

Cecily ignored him instead of pleading her jailed brother's case, and Naomi saw a glimmer of hope in that. "Last we talked, he was doing well, too, considering." Her smile showed a kinship with her younger brother that she didn't have with Kyle. Cecily loved Kyle but had a stronger attachment to Larimore.

Naomi turned to a smirking Oscar. "And how about Odessa? Otis?"

"What—? What does any of this have to do with Cecily's episodes?" He rolled his eyes upward with irritation. He spoke nasally, as if suffering from chronic and perpetual sinus congestion.

Naomi didn't like how he said "episodes," as if it were something distasteful and contagious; it countered all that concern and sympathy he tried wearing on his face earlier. "It's all part of the warm-up; get everyone comfortable talking freely."

Oscar scoffed.

Cecily stared at her hands.

Naomi waited.

"My sister and brother are fine, I guess." Oscar glared at her, daring her to press him for more. His siblings were a sore spot for him.

"You wrote they live nearby. Spending the holidays with them, or are they coming to you and Cecily?" Naomi smiled. Daring her, even indirectly, was never a good thing.

"It... It hasn't been decided yet," Cecily offered. But Naomi recognized the fibnation; it had been decided—maybe years ago.

Oscar stared at a magazine on the center table. "If anything, it'll be at Odessa's. We'll stop through. That way..." He lifted his eyes from the magazine with a shrug.

Naomi didn't prompt him to finish, knowing what he started to say: that way, they could leave when Oscar's had his fill. She turned to Cecily. "Gonna visit Larimore?"

Cecily's eyes warmed. "Yes. Have a surprise for him." Her voice was soft, tempered: a signal of internal strength.

Naomi remarked: "Good for you, or rather, *him.*"

Cecily smiled, but when her husband scoffed, the smile withered, and her eyes grew desperate and sad again.

Naomi addressed Oscar. "I take it you have an issue with Larimore."

Oscar shook his head. "Never met 'im."

"Okay. But you say he's a 'loser.' Because he's in prison? Down on the convict, are you?" Her thoughts jumped to her "brother."

Cecily stared at her now, but the stare didn't fire challenge.

Oscar turned a hand upward in a partial shrug to make his next point. "I'm down on some of 'em, yeah. Depends. Serial killers, rapists, child molesters: nothing but losers. Stealing cuz you gotta eat and getting caught; I'm not down on that type of thing so much." He glanced Cecily's way. "But her brother got eleven years on aggravated assault because he was stupid enough to pistol-whip a former girlfriend's ex. *Former* girlfriend, mind you, not his girlfriend at the time, so he's getting locked up over some old mess. *Loser.* He got the extra time because he used a gun, which made them add deadly intent or force with a deadly weapon or something. *Loser.* To top it off, he lost most of his share of the settlement because the guy sued him. *Loser.* For all intense purposes, the guy who was his powerful attorney sucked on the legal end, so he hired a loser. *Two* losers. And...his name's 'Larimore': punk name if I ever heard one. *Loser.*"

So, Oscar never met the man he so detested, and Naomi had the feeling few names other than "Oscar" held non-punk status. It took her some seconds to understand his uses of *for all intense purposes* and *powerful attorney* were incorrect phrasings of *for all intents and purposes* and *power-of-attorney*. Okay. She glanced at Cecily: still staring at her but now semi-chewing her upper lip with what Naomi recognized as a mix of anxiety and withheld anger. Interesting. She liked seeing a bit of bitterness from Cecily; it meant she wasn't sleepwalking through what was happening to her. *She's feeling and reacting and has opinions.* A bit of anger said Cecily was *awake*.

Oscar placed his wife in his crosshairs. "Right or wrong?"

Cecily lowered her eyes, speaking in a dithering hush, "R-Right." She lifted her gaze back to Naomi.

If this were a personal setting, Naomi would've said something to Oscar about his treatment of Cecily, even if offhandedly. But this wasn't a nonprofessional setting. She needed to observe the dynamics of their relationship, see who they were as people *live and in color* and not solely on paper before she could begin helping the one needing treatment. She had to let this play out—to some extent.

Naomi wished she had effective use of her writing hand; Cecily stuttered her answer, and Naomi wasn't sure of its significance (if any). Legal pad steadfastly blank on her end table, she made mental note of it. Once she listened in playback, she'd be able to interpret it better.

"Cecily, what, if anything, about Doctor Lewis's treatment was most beneficial? Any part of his approach you feel you responded to best?"

Oscar scoffed and sat forward, reaching for the water pitcher on the center table. "No. He was a complete waste of time and mon—"

"Oscar, the question was Cecily's."

Oscar paused (pitcher held mid-pour) and glared at her again.

Naomi gazed back.

He shook his head and resumed getting some water.

Naomi smiled encouragement at Cecily for her to answer freely.

Cecily's brows furrowed and softened with her internal answer. She shrugged as Oscar sat back. "I don't know. I'm sorry."

Naomi nodded. "Fair enough. Now, what I'd like to do...," she checked her session clock (okay on time), "is have you tell me more about the spiritual side of yourselves. Something I like to call a 'spiritual compass,' if you will." She, at one time, considered dispensing with this aspect of her therapy, but old habits die hard.

Cecily nodded, her eyes considering, thoughtful.

Oscar gave a sighing eye-roll. "Come on, Doc. Dispense with the mystical mumbo-jumbo and just start helping her. Get that prescription pad out, do something concrete that'll get her better. Recommend a center for her to stay at. Something. Just..." He shook his head at Naomi.

Oh, the restraint doctors must use! "I understand you're impatient to have Cecily feeling better, Oscar. But let me go about it my way. Doctor Lewis left much to be desired, correct?"

Cecily bowed her head.

Oscar nodded grudgingly.

"Okay then. Just..." Naomi shook her head at Oscar, mimicking him, stopping short of mocking him. Spotting a trail of scar tissue over his clavicle, she used a head gesture to indicate it. "That from that night?"

Oscar's eyes softened, pleased to be the focus (if only momentarily), and then assumed a sad frown and headshake of pity as if on cue. "Yeah. Horrible night. Just...horrible. Bullet grazed my carrot artery. Didn't penetrate, though, thank God."

Naomi held in a chuckle and coughed to redirect the laugh threatening to destroy any progress she'd made with Cecily. *"Carrot" artery! And that scar's over his clavicle, not his carotid— I mean, "carrot."*

This dude.

Cecily frowned at her with concern. "You okay?"

Naomi gave a reassuring nod but spoke to Oscar. "Sorry to hear that."

Oscar returned a solemn nod and calming wave, letting her know he was all right.

Of that, Naomi was already sure. She looked at Cecily. Indeed, if Cecily knew *Rod of Asclepius*, she knew the correct term was *carotid* artery and not carrot artery (never mind his incorrect use of other phrases and terms). Was Oscar so dominant she couldn't even correct him from such embarrassment?

Cecily stared at her hands, wringing them.

Naomi reached for her tea. "Oscar?"

"Yeah?"

"For future reference, you want to say 'carotid' artery, not 'carrot.' Okay?" Since she couldn't see if the scar trailed further and where, if it did, Naomi stopped short of telling him his injury looked nowhere near his carotid—especially if the bullet didn't penetrate. She took a sip of her orange-spiced (hint of lemon).

And then Naomi saw why Cecily likely didn't correct Oscar; the man didn't like being corrected. His eyes and nose flared before he narrowed his eyes on her and formed a too-hard fake smile. "Okay, Doc. Got it." He drank some of his water.

Naomi now needed to address his calling her "Doc."

"I don't think sh-she likes that v-very m-much." Cecily could've been talking to her wringing hands: that's where her focus was.

Oscar frowned at her. "Who? Doesn't like what?"

Cecily's eyes wavered toward Naomi before lowering back to her lap, studying her squeezing, twisting hands again. "C-Calling her 'Doc.'"

That wasn't entirely true. Naomi didn't mind being called "Doc" in specific settings, by certain people, but it depended on the *person* using the sobriquet—and Oscar was not one of those persons. She noticed the stutter again.

Oscar turned his frown on her. "That bother you?"

"I'd appreciate 'Doctor Alexander' for now."

"What happened to everybody feeling comfortable?"

"The key word there is *everybody*, which includes me."

Oscar sucked his teeth with a headshake, and Naomi could see "Women!" in a dialogue bubble over his head. She held in another laugh.

He'd be all right—one way or another. He'd have to get over it, too. Or under it. Totally up to him.

"How much time is left?" Cecily stopped wringing her hands.

"There's time. Ready to end early?"

Cecily glanced in Oscar's direction. "Not necessarily, but..." she trailed off, but Naomi read her unvoiced answer: *Not necessarily, but Oscar's creating all this tension.*

"But this isn't getting us anywhere, is what she wants to say." He picked up a magazine from the table and thumbed through it. My, he was a fidgety one.

Knowing how to pick her battles (and so, biting her tongue), Naomi regarded Cecily. "Up to you..."

Cecily nodded and unclasped her hands, lifting one in Naomi's direction. "I'm sorry. Go ahead."

Naomi sipped more tea. "Okay. I want to talk about your spiritual compasses. Oscar, let's start with you—before you get too involved in one of those articles."

Oscar looked up from the magazine with a smirk. "Ha-ha."

Naomi extended a half-smile trying for genuine.

Oscar smiled back, and despite the condition of his teeth, this genuine smile was becoming. He placed the magazine down next to him. "So, what're you asking: what's my religion, or...if I believe in God, or...?"

"Yep. All of that. Expound however you wish."

Oscar's expression turned hedging. "And you want *total* honesty?"

"Or non-total honesty. Long as there's some level of truth-telling going on. It could be subtotal honesty—however you wanna spin it."

Cecily chuckled.

Oscar glanced at his wife and nudged her, but Naomi couldn't decipher its meaning, unable to tell if the nudge was friendly or a warning: Cecily's face revealed nothing. He cleared his throat. "Okay, well,...we don't do the church thing—"

"Oscar?"

He frowned his confusion at her. "What?"

"I'm not interested in the 'we' part as much as I am the 'I,' as in *you*, part of things. For now, anyway."

The frown vanished. "Oh. Gotcha. Well, *I* don't do the church thing."

"Ever?"

Oscar shook his head. "Not for a long time." He gestured toward his wife. "She goes on occasion, but it's not about her right now, I guess."

"You guessed right. Go on," Naomi replied.

"Well, I think it's all a big money-making racket. Invisible Dude in the Sky needs our money to build this building or buy this cathedral. You only hear about feeding the poor or visiting the elderly and stuff like that around the holidays or some other PR event, man."

"You could do your own goodwill-toward-men thing."

"True." But Oscar didn't speak further.

"Continue."

"It just seems all about the dollar to me. In church, on television... You give the money, only to hear you're still not good enough. Not that money's going to get you into heaven; even I know that. They preach about God's mercy but then make it seem like you're not gonna get it— It's just... I don't know. Not my thing."

"So, you believe in God, heaven?"

Oscar shrugged, looking uncomfortable now.

Naomi and Cecily waited.

"I...I believe there was a man named Jesus here thousands of years ago. The rest? I think men have just hyped it all up. Not saying some of those lessons weren't taught, that some of those 'miracles' didn't take place. But Old Testament, New Testament. It's *stories*. Just good, old-fashioned storytelling to me. Not that I've read 'em all, but I know a few of 'em. I mean, why write a New Testament if it doesn't replace the old one? And the New Testament has Matthew, Mark, Luke, John, and then a bunch of letters from Paul fussing at the Galatians, Ephesians, Colossians, Corinthians, or whoever.

"Plenty of people wrote letters and accounts about what they witnessed: maybe had different views on it. Why Paul's? Bunch of White men voted on what books would be in the Bible. '*Voted*' on it. On what the public would and wouldn't be exposed to. That says something to me right there. A lot of people don't know about that part of it. I mean, why isn't God speaking to us today, then? Me, you? Not just to people claiming to be 'preachers'...'spreading the Word.'"

He was getting uptight, using air quotes often and frowning his displeasure; seemed the dam had figuratively burst—he had quite the viewpoint on the matter.

Maybe his compass was broken and needed replacing.

Naomi let it ride, impressed with his knowledge (even if only high level). She actually agreed with a few of his points. "We give up our imaginary friends as children, only to gain a New One as adults, huh?"

Oscar nodded. "Invisible Dude in the Sky. Yeah."

"That's the Faith part," Cecily sighed.

Naomi smiled at her. "I agree."

Oscar scoffed. "Yeah, they tell you Faith and Prayer—and then hit you with the loopholes."

Naomi wasn't sure what that meant, but she was sure there was a valid point in there somewhere. "I take it you don't pray."

"Sometimes, I guess. But I mean, if all I gotta do, at the moment of my death, and I've heard this preached in church, is ask God's forgiveness, take the Oath, and I'm good, what's the rest of it all about?"

"I see." Although still fuzzy about his "loopholes," now she was curious about his "Oath" reference.

Oscar shook his head. "Too many people praying right this minute, for their loved one to live, for some 'miracle' cash. And you know what?"

Naomi sipped her tea; it was cool now but still good. "What?"

"That loved one's gonna die, and that debt'll still be due."

"Well, we're all gonna die, Oscar."

"Exactly." He sat back as if a professor proving his theorem.

"Exactly," Cecily whispered, her eyes on the fangs-of-ice outside the window. Naomi didn't think Oscar's jaded view rubbed off on Cecily completely, but as she watched her patient, she could see some of it did. She'd bet money Cecily's thoughts were of Roland.

Oscar gestured at his wife in a *See?* motion and expression, as if Cecily's one echoing word validated his entire diatribe.

Naomi didn't acknowledge his gesture; she sipped her tea. It grew quiet, Naomi giving Cecily a moment while giving Oscar a few seconds to gather his thoughts if he had more to say.

He exhaled. "Man, you can get a person worked up."

Naomi smirked at him as she set her mug down. "You got yourself worked up, buddy. I simply asked a question."

Oscar sent her an odd look and then laughed, the sound jolting considering the silence seconds ago. "You're right. Okay. Gotcha, Doc—tor Alexander." He caught himself and fixed it.

Naomi nodded her appreciation at him.

Cecily, however, didn't smile or even startle when Oscar laughed. She stared out the window as if hoping the icicle fangs would choose her for a snack—anything to remove her from this situation.

Naomi and Oscar focused on Cecily.

Oscar nudged her again, and this one, Naomi recognized as not friendly. "Come on, Cecily. What're you doing? You're gonna make this whole session a mute point, like those others with Doctor Lewis. This is important, Cecily, not negatory."

Annoyance and impatience laced his insincere compassion.

The incorrect use of *mute* for *moot*, always grated, and now, using *nugatory* (instead of *negatory*) may have been a better choice. Naomi didn't correct him, somehow realizing it would create problems for Cecily later. Oscar had issues with women, and one who corrected him (as his sister, a city councilwoman, likely did often) only made whatever that issue was for him worse. The internal grammar lesson prompted thoughts of Viv. Although a computer science professional, Viv had a thing for language, grammar, and English Literature. A bit of a wordsmith, that one.

"We can discuss your compass next session, Cecily."

Cecily pulled her eyes away from the icy teeth, gazing at Naomi. Her eyes were strange because they weren't her natural color, so Naomi also used facial tics and cues to detect emotion. "It's okay. I'm n-not having an e-episode or anything: just l-looking out the w-window."

Naomi nodded with a wan smile, not liking how Cecily said "episode," either. While Oscar's way held disdain, Cecily's held an acceptance that didn't sit well. "So, you have the same views as Oscar?"

Cecily shook her head.

Oscar went back to his magazine.

Naomi refrained from speaking.

"My views aren't the same in toto, but some of what he said makes sense to me."

"Okay."

"My family's Lutheran."

"And you?"

"Well, I pray and have faith, but I don't consider myself religious. And, I know I shouldn't, but sometimes I have doubts about parts of it."

"You mean, some concepts behind Christianity?"

Cecily hesitated before responding. "I'm sorry, but yeah. Sometimes my analytical mind wants to push through." Hints of her Mississippi roots pushed through, too, in her speaking.

Oscar shook his head while focusing on the magazine, but he intended that headshake for his wife and not whatever he wasn't reading.

"I'm sure you're not alone in that." Naomi noticed Cecily's stutter wasn't constant. She didn't know what to make of it. She wondered if that stutter would worsen as their sessions progressed, as the sessions grew more...intense. "Did you pray that night, Cecily?"

"Yeah."

But the affirmation sounded hollow. "Sure?"

Cecily stared at her. The handwringing resumed. Cecily's aura flickered in, and the planes of gray surrounding her didn't surprise Naomi.

Believing herself neither seer nor psychic, Naomi resisted the paranormal label regarding her abilities. She simply lived with them, continued learning what she could about them, and applied her own philosophies regarding whatever she was "seeing." Over the years, she'd determined: solely gray auras (not mixed with other colors) were more complicated, required special considerations.

Right now, those planes of gray told her Cecily was in some state of transition. Whether that transition was from dark to light or vice versa, Naomi didn't know; only additional work with Cecily would enlighten.

Oscar kept eyes on the magazine, but his eyes didn't move across the page, so he wasn't reading, just waiting. Like her picture window, wall-hangings, and bookcases, the periodicals on the table were another source for her patients' emotional refuge. They rarely read them: just used them for the mental distraction they needed before releasing inner thought, or, in Oscar's case, as a ruse for—

Cecily's eyes shifted back to the window. "You like the winter?"

"I do, yes."

Cecily returned a slow, contemplating nod. "...I ...I d-don't remember a l-lot about that n-night. So,...I don't know if I p-prayed or not, but..."

"But...?" Naomi prompted. Cecily still suffered post-traumatic amnesia; maybe this was a bit of a breakthrough.

Head down (suggesting absorption in the magazine), Oscar's eyes cut toward his wife.

Cecily squinted as if in pain.

Naomi leaned in her direction. "Cecily?"

The squint cleared, and now Cecily looked confused. "Just a phantom pain again. I...I get them sometimes. Sorry."

Oscar rolled his eyes with a sigh. "Not that again."

Cecily peered at Naomi, this time squinting with confused memory recall. "There was a crescent moon..."

Naomi nodded. "Yes...?"

"She's talking about the keychain. She thinks that's what she—"

"Saw that night. I know, Oscar, thank you. I'm familiar with a few of the details concerning that night."

Oscar, temporarily distracted from some unread article, sent her this piercing stare for seconds before he shrugged. "Oh, okay."

"We didn't h-have a storm d-door." Cecily stared out the window.

"That night, Cecily? You didn't have a storm door?" Random statements sometimes weren't random and often led to something more concrete, although seemingly unrelated.

Cecily stared out at the stiff December day. "Our neighbors had them. W-We have one n-now."

Oscar went back to his magazine scan; seems he only had patience for parts of the therapy involving him.

She could've encouraged his full participation (and maybe she should have), but Naomi didn't dwell on many shoulda-woulda-couldas—at least not in active therapy sessions; she didn't have the time. Naomi shifted her attention to the one most in need of her help.

Cecily concentrated on the sunless scene outside, when her eyes widened, and she took in a tiny breath.

Naomi shifted forward in her seat upon seeing sign of a memory surfacing then fading.

Cecily sighed, shook her head. The corners of her lips turned downward, then turned upward into something suggesting a smile. "The lights on the tree h-helped me f-forget the r-rest. And I prayed then. ...Yes. I like to m-meditate when I go running." So, Cecily's compass wasn't broken beyond repair; she just needed the needle re-magnetized.

Naomi sat back.

Oscar stared at his wife for long seconds before turning to Naomi. "I'm not a doctor, but she sounds like she needs to be fifty-one-fifty, ya know? Needs to be somewhere she can focus on nothing but getting well. Listen to her. She's rambling stuff together, can't keep her hands still, the episodes..." His expression became a conspiratorial hedge. "Sounds like a mental crisis. Come on, Doctor Alexander, don't waver like that Doctor Lewis did. You know it's best. She needs to be... You know..."

Naomi gazed at him. He seemed to be lobbying hard for his wife to be signed into a psychiatric facility. Seemed to be comfortably familiar with terms and jargon associated with mental health and involuntary hospitalization. "*Committed*? Is that the word you're looking for?"

After glancing at Cecily, Oscar looked at Naomi and nodded.

Cecily stared out the window, awaiting the icicle's bite, but she bobbed her head, too.

It pissed Naomi off seeing Cecily nod like that, but she kept calm. "Well, you're right, Oscar: you're not a doctor. And if there's going to be any involuntary anything, I'll cross that bridge when I get to it, but I'm not even on the road approaching that bridge. I will not be pressured regarding my treatment approach. Cecily wants you here, but I can change that arrangement if it's detrimental to either Cecily or me. You, of course, are welcome to choose a new physi—"

Oscar tipped his head forward. "Yeah, that might be bes—"

"No!" Cecily's hands weren't moving (she no longer wrung them), but the rest of her trembled as she remained riveted out the window.

Oscar frowned, this time with genuine concern. "Cecily?"

Cecily turned to Naomi, shaking her head. "No. It's too— I can't— I d-don't...w-want another doctor. I'm not changing."

Naomi gave her a genial nod. "Okay, Cecily." When Cecily, still trembling some, nodded and returned her gaze out the window, Naomi turned to Oscar. That answered that.

He sighed with a wan smile, raising his hands in suggested surrender. "Okay, okay. Sorry. I wasn't—" He shook his head and returned to his unread article.

Oh, but he was, and Naomi knew it. Oscar's grip on the magazine told her he wasn't pleased with the development, with Cecily putting her foot down (so to speak).

Naomi welcomed the ensuing silence, entertaining adding a splash of Henney to her tea next time.

"I'm... I'm sorry. I didn't m-mean to be r-rude."

Naomi shook her head at Cecily. "You have nothing to apologize for. I encourage spontaneous expression in here, okay?" Cecily apologized habitually. Under a different, non-medical arena, Naomi would find it nerve-racking.

Oscar stared at his article. He hadn't flipped a page since first opening the periodical.

Naomi gestured toward the water pitcher. "Would you care for some water, Cecily? Calm those nerves...?"

Cecily sighed, grinned, and appeared frightened in one expression. Nodding, she leaned to the table for her drink, her hands shaking as she poured. With each slow gulp, Naomi recognized it doing some good. When Cecily set her cup down, her trembles had ceased. "Thank you."

"You're welcome."

"I... I think Doctor Lewis helped with my ochlophobia."

"You have, or had, a fear of crowds?"

"Since the...thing. Yeah. But I think he helped with that."

Naomi sipped her tea (almost gone). "You've been around crowds since then with no issues?"

Oscar scoffed. "No."

Cecily looked embarrassed. "Well, no. But..."

Naomi lifted her brows. "Well, how do you know, sweetie?"

Oscar scoffed again. "Exactly."

Naomi ignored him and winked at Cecily. "Mind over matter?"

Cecily's grin was hesitant. "I think so, yes."

Naomi shrugged. "Works for you, works for me."

Cecily laughed then, and Naomi's focus became making sure she heard it from her again soon. If she could get Cecily to experience a moiety of happiness again in her office, that would be perfection.

Naomi's timer sounded, signaling the session's end. She set her Cambridge mug down (now devoid of delicious, orange-spiced tea) on her blank notepad and stopped the timer.

Cecily looked disappointed (a good sign).

With a heavy sigh, Oscar closed the magazine and placed it on the center table. "I guess that's it. Round one: Doc."

Naomi ignored his "Doc" reference and smirked at him. "You consider these sessions boxing matches?"

Oscar stood. "Time's up, Doc— tor Alexander." He was not happy.

Naomi looked up at him with an eased head-bob. "That it is. I'll take the point, but let's hope Cecily wins the remaining rounds."

Cecily made this soft gasping sound, something pitiful and sad. "Me?" Naomi winked at her.

"Yeah, let's." Oscar headed for their coats hanging behind the door.

Cecily was slow to stand, and Naomi wouldn't stand until she did.

Oscar returned. He stood by the sofa arm and waited, extending Cecily's coat toward her. "Here you go."

In a split-second flashback, Naomi saw Rick helping Viv with her coat as they prepared to leave Manje Trankil.

As if concluding the icicle fangs were giving her a pass after all, Cecily stood. She accepted her coat from her husband and put it on.

Naomi stood and stepped closer to the couple, extending her hand to Cecily. She was used to extending her right hand for handshakes with the majority right-handed folk she interacted with, but Cecily grasped her hand so tightly, Naomi worried she would need two braces (or a cast) before it was all over. Naomi smiled right through it. "See you Friday? I know that's only a few days, but I want to start some solid work before the holiday break."

Cecily nodded, her eyes searching Naomi's. "I want to keep that appointment, yes. See you then."

"What do you have in mind for 'real work,' Doctor Alexander: a lobotomy?" Oscar walked to the door, sounding an unpleasant chuckle.

"For you, maybe," Naomi answered somewhat jokingly (curious about his response to her reply).

There was a hiccup in his step. "Yeah, okay."

Cecily still held her hand, the grip less intense now. "So,...Friday?" Her grip started tightening again.

Nodding, Naomi gently removed her hand.

"Come on, Cecily. We're running on time. I'm already gonna hafta wait, but I don't want to be late to wait." He sucked his teeth with irritation directed at no one in particular. He gave her a narrow-eyed look. "You're the only doctor whose appointments start on time. Now I gotta go to this other—" He shook his head with a scoff of annoyance.

Cecily murmured. "We have Oscar's appointment after this one."

Naomi nodded.

"No need to tell my business, Home Skillet. Let's go. See you Friday, Doctor Alexander."

Naomi focused on Cecily, using her eyes to mean Cecily's head. "No hat or scarf? It's pretty cold out."

Cecily shook her head. "Nah. I'm a bit cryophilic."

Naomi nodded but didn't believe that was 100 percent true.

"I am," Cecily reassured, which, for Naomi, didn't reassure at all. "Okay."

"Cecily..." Oscar's call was slithery with impatience.

"B-Bye, Doctor Alexander. S-See you in a f-few." Cecily's smile was anything but bright.

Naomi nodded curtly (à la someone else). "Cool. Friday it is."

Cecily pulled her coat closed and turned away, heading for the door. The Brookses offered parting waves and left. As his voice traveled through her walls and closed door, Naomi heard Oscar saying something to her resident, adding "Home Skillet" in his address to her. *This* dude.

Naomi retrieved her mug and stopped the recorder, carrying the recorder to her desk for logging and other administrative tasks related to the session. She'd sit down with Veronica in a few to go over Veronica's related duties for this case, but first, she wanted to add her voice notes regarding the session.

She had a half-hour before her next appointment. A click of her remote toward her music player sent the oboes and strings of Bologne's Symphony No. 1 in G Major, Op.11, lilting into her office. She went to the window, mulling over the highlights of the session just ended.

For the average person, extreme responses to trauma were short-lived; the stress dealt with reasonably quickly in a matter of days or weeks. People with PTSD, however, experienced extended stress and extreme stressors, which didn't fade with time. Each day becomes a struggle to feel even a little better, or they may feel decidedly worse.

Cecily's flight-or-fight response was severely disrupted when those men broke into her home. Flight ended with that blow to her head—subsequently, so was her fight.

Flight-or-Fight in response to fear is natural, but when possibility of such a response is negated, the door for resulting PTSD is opened. The "after-stress" of the event lingers, creating fearful or frightened responses even when danger is minimal or nonexistent.

Like Mother Nature, PTSD didn't discriminate. It didn't belong solely to war veterans or victims of terrorism. It struck people of all ages and creeds, affecting anyone experiencing an intense or long-lasting trauma. If one experienced or had a family history of mental problems, like depression, they were more susceptible. Still, one having no mental stress before could suffer a trauma and find themselves pals with PTSD.

Sufferers experienced varying degrees of PTSD symptoms over time, the intensity fluctuating with the amount of PTSD triggers in their environment. It wasn't any healthier to avoid the triggers than to be around them constantly, so the trick was learning adaptive coping strategies that lessened or even negated a PTSD onset. Anything could be a trigger; it all depended on what rested in the victim's memories (that created reminders of the trauma). A person surviving a raging flood could, on a whim, freak out driving by a swimming pool, or maybe even seeing a broken tree branch could have devastating effects. You just never knew—and it wasn't always a rational tie.

The risk of developing PTSD, however, increased with the degree of trauma experienced: the more extreme or prolonged the event, the greater likelihood of PTSD. It was also more likely, depending on the extent the event was beyond the victim's control, how sudden it was, how unavoidable. In Cecily's case, her trauma was intentional and inflicted by multiple persons, thus more personal, as opposed to something traumatic but more impersonal, such as acts of God (like weather disasters or vehicular accidents). Intentional, personal harm, like the torture, rapes, and assaults suffered during the Brooks home invasion, increased the risk of developing PTSD. Cecily: textbook case if there ever was one.

Her medical background and knowledge of PTSD aside, anyone sitting with Mr. and Mrs. Brooks for longer than fifteen minutes could detect the disharmony. That, in and of itself, was bound to cause Cecily some anxiety. Cecily's trauma during the home invasion created deep psychological wounds, triggering numerous anxiety manifestations eliciting related defense mechanisms. Naomi suspected a mixture of denial, dissociation, some cognitive dissonance, repression, and rationalization, for starters.

Considering what happened to Cecily two years ago and the degree of stress and disharmony in the marriage, Naomi believed Cecily was in a precarious mental position. Oscar's attempts to guide the therapy (she sensed he wasn't done), being as seductive and manipulative as he could while emphasizing Cecily has problems (and not once acknowledging maybe *he* was the problem), was classic narcissistic personality.

She couldn't jump to conclusions regarding their relationship (although, being honest, she already had), so she needed to tread lightly to start. Once Cecily began getting comfortable in her therapy, and Naomi saw signs of healing and progression... Well, then, she'd go in for the kill. And maybe *kill* wasn't the best word; she was a physician, after all (a successful and well-respected one). Her methods weren't by the letter, but were by the book (mostly; it depended on what *book* you were reading). Her success with her patients spoke for itself.

Like the month of December, her flashes and flickers could be fickle. She hoped to see another aura-flicker (or two) from Cecily during her therapy course, but she may not, which was fine. Her training and skill as a psychiatrist were enough for all involved.

But first, Naomi needed to determine whether Cecily was happy or, at the very least, content (one didn't necessitate the other) in a male-dominant or controlling marriage. That determination required sleuthing Cecily's mind and emotions from common sense and psychiatric perspectives to deduce her true mental status. She couldn't assume Cecily wasn't happy or content, because there existed an anomaly group of women who didn't mind being in such relationships.

If Cecily wasn't happy, Naomi had to work her therapy to accomplish several goals—all with Oscar present.

Chapter Five

The Heart of the Matter

I t was all bullshit. This whole day so far: nothing but a bunch of bull.

First: the motherfucking cold. He got hot quickly, but there was no threat of that with today's temperature. It was too cold to be traipsing outdoors, going from one doctor's office to another—some bull. Maybe he should've let Cecily wear a hat and scarf today.

Second: the short doctor with the dyke haircut. She had to be gay. Had to be. And if she wasn't, she should have longer hair; short hair was for men. And what was up with that yellow furniture? Yellow: like huge plops of mustard. Dr. Lewis's office had normal brown furniture, maybe with a colored pillow or something, and books everywhere. His office looked just like those you saw in movies or television. This Dr. Alexander had the books on her shelves, but Oscar couldn't get past the yellow furniture; that crazy questionnaire she wanted them to complete before their session was bad enough. That "prudencesphere" mess threw him for a loop (it wasn't even a real place)—and proved she didn't have too much of that common sense she swore by. She had magazines on that table, though, and that was cool: gave him something to do while Cecily talked her drivel.

Dr. Alexander was on the cute side: short and brown with petite curves. He expected far different for a female psychiatrist, something more like a tall, beefy woman (like women from Germany or Russia). He didn't know why he expected that, but he did. Naomi was attractive, so a dress, maybe, and longer hair would've topped it off. He couldn't get with the short haircut *and* pantsuit.

The blood pressure cuff puffed and then tightened on his upper arm.

Her looks and that furniture aside, he didn't know what to make of the session with Dr. Alexander, couldn't get a fix on her. Yeah, she was female, but Oscar didn't think she had the same buttons to push, the same weak spots as all the others (sort of like Delia). She'd even had the nerve to ask Cecily if she wanted him there. Cecily said yes and took his hand, but Oscar sensed that doctor worked some secret purpose with the question, like opening some secret door she was only going to show Cecily the way through. He didn't like it. They needed to switch doctors. Dr. Alexander wasn't going to work (not for his purposes). But Cecily wasn't having it—and Oscar, for the first time, didn't think he'd be able to change her mind for her; he believed Dr. Alexander was the reason for that, too.

For such a small woman, that doctor had a lot of chutzpah (he learned that one from a judge named Judy): correcting him and shit (*carotid*, not carrot); nixing "Doc" and the first-name basis; asking about his family when she knew he didn't want to talk about them. Oh yeah, she had balls, that one. It wouldn't surprise him if she allowed Cecily to call her "Naomi," but not him; split-tails stuck together over the stupidest shit.

The nurse frowned with concern again. Iris frowned the first time she took his blood pressure but said nothing except she wanted to retake it. And now she was frowning again. She could frown all she wanted; he wasn't taking another damn pill. Prescriptions: that's where the doctors made their money. Oscar closed his eyes and tried to slow his breathing, hoping to help Frowning Iris feel better.

If there was anything about the session he liked, the spiritual compass stuff was interesting. He wasn't sure what her angle was with that one, but it let him get some things off his chest. Stuff he'd been trying to get through to his wife. It surprised him to hear Cecily agreed with some of it. However, when it was Cecily's turn, shit seemed shaky when she tried to recall whether she prayed the night of the invasion.

She'd paused like she remembered something, and Oscar suspected Dr. Alexander was up to some more secret shit. In his sessions, Dr. Lewis had also asked Cecily about that night, but Cecily shut him down, didn't want to pursue it—which worked in Oscar's favor. Cecily's pause in Dr. Alexander's office, though, generated concern. He needed Dr. Alexander to focus less on what happened then and deal with the here and now. Even if the then and now were related, these doctors knew how to make shit fit. He just had to guide this therapy, guide this Dr. Alexander. If they stayed with Dr. Alexander, that is. After that session, Cecily seemed to feel some misplaced empowerment, throwing a minor kink into the plans.

Meant he had to work things differently, that's all. When they were home, he'd counter whatever progress the lady doctor made in those sessions. Same as he did when Cecily was seeing Dr. Lewis. But he'd have to crank things up with this Dr. Alexander; she made him uneasy.

Iris wrote some shit down, said Halim would be in soon, and left.

So, the cold: bullshit, part one. Dr. Alexander: bullshit, part two. Part three of this bullshit day stemmed from another damn doctor: Dr. Halim. Oscar watched Cecily. She looked both professional and dainty as she flipped through a magazine. Sure, she could look through a magazine; they weren't visiting a cardiologist for *her* heart. This visit was important, but she appeared all nonchalant and shit.

"So, what do you think?"

She looked up from whatever article she was reading.

Oscar gestured toward the door. "The frowning."

Cecily closed the magazine (that was more like it). "Maybe your n-numbers were a b-bit high, or maybe Iris hasn't the f-first clue about what she's d-doing, and it troubled her."

She added that last for his benefit, and he appreciated it. Oscar chuckled with an agreeing scoff. "Yeah."

Cecily went back to her magazine article.

Oscar frowned himself now. They hadn't discussed the psych session, but Cecily talked little about anything since leaving Dr. Alexander's office. He could usually count on her to fill the silences with her prattling on about one topic or another. He paid attention to some of it, but most didn't have sticking power. This morning, she was more on the quiet side. More like...her old self (before the breaking). "Glad to see my health issues aren't affecting you."

She took three seconds too long to look up at him. If they weren't in this doctor's waiting room... But someone (Iris) might return before his message could hit home.

She closed the article again. "I'm sorry. There was an interesting write-up on the changing panel style for Marvel."

Comics? Fucking comic books? He's waiting to hear whatever the test results showed about his heart, and she's lost in some article about Spider-Bat or the X-Team or whatever. Unreal.

She collected the damn things: boxes of them in the smallest bedroom upstairs (boxes he sometimes helped himself to for a quick buck; that eBay was a beast). He noticed she didn't stutter *that* response, but that stuttering shit came and went. "Well, don't let me keep you." He wanted a cigarette so badly his mouth ached.

Cecily gazed at him. He could tell she was figuring what mood he was in—and how that affected her future. "You c-can't have anything yet, but I c-can get some w-water for you while we w-wait for Doctor Halim."

"Nah, don't worry about it. I'm fine."

She stood. "Sure?"

She just wanted to confirm how much trouble she was in. Very good. It was an unspoken language of theirs that kept the scales in balance. Oscar nodded; the trouble was minimal for now, so no, he didn't need any water, but thanks for finally coming correct.

Cecily nodded before she sat. The silence lingered.

"I hate this waiting!" He also hated Cecily not talking to fill the silence, but he couldn't let her know that. Asking her to keep him company with her nonsense chatter would make it seem like he *needed* her—and that's not how this works.

Cecily gazed in his general direction. She didn't pick up the magazine again, but she didn't say much, either—and that bothered him.

He reached into his pocket for a mint. He kept mints close these days; his breath began giving him trouble several months ago, brushing and mouthwash be damned. He didn't know if it was related, but it was another reason he needed to leave the cancer-sticks alone. He watched Cecily as he popped the mint in his mouth (not liking that preoccupied expression). "Why're you so quiet?"

She shrugged, and that bothered him more than the silence, adding to the bullshit factor of this day. "Just wondering what F-Friday's session is g-going to be about."

An image of a long, dark hall with a door at the far end popped into his head. The door was far away and murky but unmistakable. Subdued light filtered around its edges: Dr. Alexander's secret door for his wife. If Cecily found it, she'd better not walk through it; that's all he had to say. "She said, 'real work.' Maybe that means a prescription or setting you up for some inpatient stuff in a facility." He shrugged. "Who knows? You could do with something. These episodes of yours:...they're getting worse." That was only partly true, but the faltering look in Cecily's eyes made it completely true to her. It was enough. *Two can play this game, Dr. Alexan— Naomi.* "But I'm here for you, whatever goes down. You know that."

Cecily's hesitant smile traveled to replace the uncertainty in her eyes. "Yes, I know." She frowned at the closed door. "What is taking so long?" She turned to him, her smile less hesitant, the uncertainty all but gone. She was a pretty woman—even with that bit of red splotch across her face. "Your numbers must have b-been okay, Oscar. I think they w-would've been in here on the qu-quick if...you know..."

Oscar nodded. *On the quick* (a trace of twang on the word *on*) was something she brought up here from Mississippi; he wished she'd left down there.

Cecily checked her watch. "Wanna go to lunch after this? I'm off, so..." She grinned at him, giving him the attention she should've been giving all along (more like how things worked). "A good meal might cheer you up." Her tone was soft, modulated: showing how much the weaker sex she was.

"Think I'm going to need cheering?"

"I sure hope not." Her hazel eyes were on his when she spoke, and Oscar saw the love there, the sincerity. Cecily wasn't in love with him, but she loved him enough not to want harm to come his way. "And I'm here for you, too."

Oscar nodded his appreciation. That comment canceled the surprise punch to her kidneys he'd planned for later. Nice save. "I am getting hungry."

"Well, there you go. Lunch then. Got a taste for anything?"

Oscar liked Cecily. He did. He loved her, too. But... "Nothing comes to mi—"

Three quick raps on the door, and it opened without answer as Dr. Halim whooshed in. A brown man of medium height, he had the whitest teeth Oscar had ever seen. "My apologies."

Cecily smiled at Dr. Halim. "We were about to blow this joint." She always found a kind word or expression, even when annoyed—that ability of hers annoyed *him* sometimes.

Dr. Halim pushed his glasses up his nose with an inquiring smile, not getting the joke. "No need for that," he tapped his folder, "we're ready to proceed."

"Good news, I hope." She looked hopeful.

When Dr. Halim turned to Oscar, he smiled. But his eyes weren't hopeful at all. "Ah yes: the man of the hour. How're you feeling, Oscar? Done with the smoking, yes?"

Oscar nodded at his doctor, focusing on his grave eyes contradicting his smiling lips. He then listened as Halim hemmed and hawed with a lot of reading of this level and that level on his charts, adding a bunch of medical jargon with words only someone paid over some quarter-million dollars a year would care to pronounce instead of getting to the point. Oscar looked at Cecily often, wanting to see if she was getting any of this. Seemed she was: her facial expressions changed with Dr. Halim's words as if she understood his longwinded gobbledygook.

There was a pause. Dr. Halim looked at them. "Let's take this to my office..." He turned for the door and led the way.

Oscar glanced at his wife, who was glancing at him. Their eyes expressed the same thing: *oh, shit.*

The door to Dr. Halim's office was no secret, only down the hall and around the corner. But the trip there felt long.

PAH: severe Pulmonary Arterial Hypertension (PAH). That's what all that gobbledygook Halim spouted boiled down to. Some rare shit with his lungs and heart he was the lucky one to get. PAH should've stood for "Punk-Ass Heart." That's the gist of what Halim told him was his condition.

He said something about it being a rare progressive lung disease affecting the pulmonary arteries carrying oxygen-rich blood from his heart to his lungs. The small arteries narrowed, restricting blood flow, and putting severe strain on his heart because his body can't get the oxygen it needs. Said it was why he experienced bouts of fatigue, short-ness of breath, sweating, and uncomfortable feelings in his chest. There was no cure for the shit.

When Cecily took his hand and asked for the prognosis, Oscar thought she was in on it. But that was just his crazy mind reaching out for the insanity wanting to claim him along with the PAH. He knew better: Cecily couldn't be in on it. Could she?

Halim informed them: once PAH was discovered, the average life ex-pectancy was between one and five years. Solid rest, proper medication, and surgery could extend his life expectancy by several more years. And he had to give up the cancer-sticks for good, forever.

Today: nothing but pure, unadulterated bullshit. Fuck it all.

As part of that solid rest, Dr. Halim advised him to restrict sexual activity until his health regimen was established and stabilized. Oscar laughed his ass off at that one and told him that would be *no*. And he knew Dr. Halim understood where he was coming from. If he had a dick, he understood perfectly. But who knew who had what these days? He wasn't feeling the surge like he used to, anyway, but when it hit—oh, he wasn't denying himself that pleasure, hell no.

Surgery was out. Next to prescriptions, that was their other big mon-ey-maker. He didn't trust surgery, didn't trust doctors, so one and one was two. He'd gone all this time without going under the knife, and Dr. Halim said the medication seemed to be working. Oscar sighed to himself; he just had to be better about taking it regularly.

This PAH shit tossed one hellafied monkey wrench into his planned operations. Even if shit went how it was supposed to with Cecily, and he got her committed, how long would he have to enjoy it? They should've been hearing this news about Cecily, not him. Weren't heart problems a women's disease?

The whole thing, the complete bullshit of this day, pissed him off.

He needed a cigarette.

If things had gone as planned two years ago...

If someone (Mr. or Mrs. Anonymous) hadn't called the damn cops.

Cecily asked some more questions, and Halim replied with more of his gobbledygook, but Oscar barely heard them. He was too pissed to care. He was sure anger didn't help him none, but he was too pissed to care about that, either.

She didn't immediately write a prescription, and her furniture was...yellow. Those two thoughts circled Cecily's brain since ending her session with Dr. Alexander. Cecily didn't know what to make of the bright color contrasting the dreary blue-gray outside Dr. Alexander's office window, but the shock of it surprised her in a good way, made her want to chuckle.

Dr. Alexander was a small woman. That surprised her, too. Cecily couldn't tell Dr. Alexander's height when she looked the doctor up online (she had some excellent credentials), but she still somehow expected...taller. Her haircut was nice. Longer than the haircut shown online, the tapered pixie with short bangs fit her face and was ideal for Dr. Alexander's short stature. Cecily sometimes pondered getting hers cut into something sassy and funky, but, well, that was out.

The session itself had its ups and downs, but the ups outnumbered the downs—so different from her sessions with Dr. Lewis.

Naomi (Cecily reckoned *she* could call her that) even talked about the spiritual aspects of life. God never entered the picture when she sat with Dr. Lewis. Hearing Oscar's side on religion and spirituality was interesting, not because she hadn't heard it before, but because his whole demeanor was different as he relayed his thoughts on the matter; it was a side of him she thought she could like more, maybe even love.

She'd also remembered something from the night of the invasion. During the session, she'd said she didn't remember anything, but...she did. But she needed to keep it to herself (for now, at least). Because she didn't trust her thoughts as much as she used to, let alone her memories, she needed to be sure she remembered, well, what she remembered. She'd made an internal memo, planning to put it to paper once she got home. Maybe put it away and bring it out later. Read the words, and hopefully, more of it will fill in (if it was an actual memory).

If another episode threatened from reading the words and thinking on the memory (much like it did in Dr. Alexander's office), Cecily would let it take her. She'd suffer through the bad smells, music, and abstract pain (felt real to her, though) and let it do what it would with her. If it meant getting some answers, she'd welcome another one. Or so she thought. The episodes made her ill with dread and hopelessness, nauseated, and just...*unwell*.

When Naomi (sitting firm and proper in that rather cool yet unusual mustard-yellow tufted barrel chair) asked if she wanted Oscar to stay, the question unnerved her. She took Oscar's hand in response and told her she wanted him there, but Dr. Alexander asking it to begin with, made Cecily wonder if she'd made the right choice. These were her problems, not Oscar's, so maybe she needed to work through them with her doctor alone. But Oscar was her anchor. Even when he was mean to her, a part of her still felt sorry for him. They'd been through a lot together. Cecily imagined they'd get through this, too. There was nothing wrong with Oscar pushing for her to be hospitalized for the episodes. She understood where he was coming from; it put a strain on things—on everything. But she wanted to believe she could overcome the episodes on her own, in time, and just maybe, with help from the doctor with that yellow furniture.

There was something about her Cecily liked. Maybe it was her re-served-yet-welcoming persona. Perhaps it was the quality of authority coming from her. Naomi was petite, but she wasn't a petite life-force. Dr. Lewis had been both patronizing and condescending, nosy, and even impatient. He was never rude and always professional, but Dr. Lewis was still an easy read.

Dr. Alexander wasn't an easy read, but Cecily didn't detect any bad juju from her. Cecily detected *heart* behind her doctor's aloof-ness—Naomi wasn't the Tinman. If anything, she was like a gumshoe of her mental stresses (of which there were many): asking questions Cecily knew held some secondary hidden purpose, scrutinizing body language,...and getting under Oscar's skin.

She had to admit she was happy Naomi pissed Oscar off a few times. Oscar didn't show it, but Cecily knew. Married to him and under his reign for six years, she knew what irritated him. Cecily dared not correct Oscar saying "carrot" for *carotid*, so when Dr. Alexander called him on it, Cecily's whole body tingled with several things all at once: relief at someone finally bringing that faux pas to his attention, a bit of happy at Oscar's displeasure at being corrected, and anxiety over how his annoyance might play out later.

Then there was the issue about him calling her "Doc."

Naomi didn't show her displeasure with that address (she wasn't an easy read), but Cecily sensed it and pointed it out. She didn't believe Naomi would take any irritation out on her, but Cecily wanted her sessions to be as stress-free as possible. Oscar being there with his suggestions and suspicions was enough. There were periods of tension as her husband had to realign his thinking on what he could get away with in Dr. Alexander's office, but he'd come around; crisis over for the time being.

He'd try again, though. Oscar would try his best to get under Dr. Alexander's skin and disrupt her flow. Being contrary suffused his blood. He didn't like doctors. He recognized the need for them, but didn't like them; always thought they were paid too much to end up saying "I/We don't know" eight times out of ten. That wasn't true, but her husband held fast to that notion.

In the end, Cecily considered that first session a success. Dr. Alexander's calm words and caring eyes as she sipped her tea made it successful. As her husband aptly put it, round one: Dr. Alexander. Cecily believed Larimore would like Naomi off-the-bat (Kyle, too)—especially "prudencesphere" (Naomi's metonymy for common sense).

Dr. Alexander held off prescribing drugs for her, and that furniture cast a glow of sunshine toward the icicles outside her office window. Cecily clung to those two unrelated thoughts and images circling her mind as she and Oscar sat in Dr. Halim's office.

Dr. Halim *would be* prescribing drugs, and his furniture was as dark as the news he'd given them.

Hours later, she stared at her plate, thinking no circumstance of a lunch date could provide cheer after that discussion with Dr. Halim. They were quiet in the car, Oscar's anger (and fear) a pall along the miles as he drove, leaving it figuratively as cold inside the car as it was outside. But he still wanted to have lunch.

She wasn't that hungry, but her not eating would only irritate him—adding to his irritation over Dr. Halim's news. Besides, he was already annoyed with how she ate her food; his occasionally flaring nostrils said so.

Since she was a little girl, she'd always had a thing about holding fried chicken. She liked fried chicken, even added an occasional splash of hot sauce sometimes, but holding a piece of the cooked dead animal in her fingers didn't sit well. She ate chicken wings, legs, or thighs with a knife and fork—as any self-respecting person would. It had nothing to do with being prissy and everything to do with the gross-out factor. Cecily ate her fried chicken with a knife and fork; she wasn't the only one in the world to do it. When they first started dating, Oscar thought it was cute. He wasn't of that opinion anymore.

She should've ordered something else.

He stopped eating his meal and watched her use utensils on her fried bird wings.

Cecily stopped cutting the meat on her plate. "Sorry." She lowered her knife and reached for her Fanta orange soda, pretending to need a refresher. If she was going to eat that chicken, she'd have to pick it up. She'd done it before when eating fried chicken with him (only to end up vomiting in the ladies' room soon after); she could do it again. Instead of picking up her chicken, she used her fork on her mashed potatoes and green beans—both seasoned well and flavorful.

Oscar went back to his steak and baked potato. Steak wasn't the best choice, given the news they'd just received, but anything else wouldn't have been *cheerful*.

Although it sat at the table with them, taking samples of their food and enforcing silence, Cecily didn't want to think too much about Oscar's PAH diagnosis ("severe," Dr. Halim had said). "Do you not want to go to Janyce and Hank's party now?" She cringed internally while picking up the drumstick part of her wing and taking a bite. Her stomach lurched as she placed the food back on her plate, practically dropping it.

Oscar smirked as he swallowed. "Why? Because of Halim?" He scoffed with a headshake, his friendly-muttonchops facial hair making him look like someone from the 1800s. The look didn't suit him, but he was always trying new things with his hair, and Cecily didn't knock that. He took a swallow of his Pepsi. "You'd like that, wouldn't you? That would be right up your alley. Try to deny me some fun just because some quack interpreted some numbers and knows a bunch of gobbledygook words." His iron-brown eyes were full of challenge, but Cecily saw the fear in them, too. Still, he was in one of his moods, and she'd just have to deal (as always). "Maybe I'll get a second opinion."

Cecily took a bite of potatoes. Dr. Halim was the second opinion.

"Or a third, or whatever the fuck number. Maybe I'll do that."

"I'm not trying to d-deny you fun, Oscar. I j-just thought—"

"You just thought it'd be the perfect excuse for me to wallow and be pitiful. Well, I want us to go. It'll be the best fun I've had all year."

She guessed being with her (and her episodes) wasn't much fun. Cecily didn't blame him. "Well, let's p-pick up the stuff for the p-punch on the way h-home." She didn't want to go to the party. Since Christmas two years ago, crowds bothered her. Not as much as before, but...

Her husband rolled his eyes and sat back with a grumbling sigh. "You never listen to me. Guess I need a degree for you to hear the shit I say."

She didn't know what he was talking about. Say what, when?

Her expression must have shown her confusion, because Oscar mocked her cruelly. "Duh. You may have those degrees, but you can be so— Anyway, I told you this morning I'd gotten the stuff for the punch and put it in the freezer in the garage."

Cecily didn't remember that conversation. She'd been in the freezer this morning; no punch-making ingredients were freezing there. Were there? Cecily sighed; she hated being unsure of things (something happening more regularly). She scrunched her shoulders to her neck for an instant. "I'm s-sorry. Must've missed that."

"Like I said: you don't listen. No wonder your children stay away from you." He went back to his steak covered with sautéed onions and mushrooms. The baked potato rested half-eaten on his plate, slathered in butter and sour cream. The meal was supposed to cheer him up, but while he ate heartily, the "cheering" didn't transfer to his current disposition.

Cecily swallowed that insult with a green bean. She guessed she'd be ornery, too; if she'd received news her heart and lungs would fail her within the next several years—guaranteed. "I l-listen to you, Oscar. So, you're d-doing Tornadoes this time?" She didn't address his comment about Marcus and Chelsea.

Oscar nodded and grinned. "Yeah, the Mabrys love it, 'specially that Hank." He chuckled.

Cecily chuckled, too: that was true. Hank enjoyed the tornado punch so much, he had Oscar make some specifically for bottling and consumption later. Hank tried to make them on his own once. When they didn't meet his expectations, Hank insisted Oscar had left something out of the recipe. Oscar hadn't, and Hank believed he hadn't, but Hank was a good-natured man who enjoyed maintaining that tease running between the Brooks and Mabry couples. She liked Hank.

Oscar forked some broccoli (the only thing yet uneaten on his plate). "Got a few wings left, Cecil. At least finish that one you started." He chuckled again.

That brief discussion about punch for the Mabrys' upcoming party may have cheered him, but referring to her as "Cecil" instead of as "Cecily" was a cruel joke he insisted was all in fun. There was nothing cheery about that "joke" as far as Cecily was concerned. She'd asked him more than once not to call her that, told him it hurt her feelings, but he replied she didn't *get* him. That, if he said it was all in fun, she shouldn't be so sensitive. But the reason he called her that wasn't funny at all: that to him, she was more masculine than feminine. It was why (he said) she needed to keep her hair styled and out, why he needed to approve her clothing sometimes, why she needed the contacts. She lived with it. He didn't call her that name often, and it was better than that *other* term not-of-endearment he sometimes used.

Fighting nausea, she picked up the flat portion of the wing she'd started on and took a bite. She nodded and smiled through the queasiness as she looked at her husband and tried to think of anything other than knowing she held a piece of a dead animal in her hand. She didn't know why cutting the chicken versus holding it (dead was dead) mattered, but it did. The taste didn't bother her; it was the *touching*. She put the chicken down in a similar rush as she had before.

Oscar grinned back. "See? It's not so bad. You don't have to do that prissy eating."

The irony of him sometimes calling her "Cecil" because he said she was more masculine, then deterring her from doing something prissy (and thus feminine) occurred to her. Still, she held in a retch and nodded, timing her need to go to the ladies' room.

Oscar glanced at the hand that dropped the chicken and reached for a napkin. "That is some freakish shit."

Cecily chewed and finished wiping her fingers. He was in a mood for sure. Her ability to use either hand indiscriminately, be ambidextrous, pissed him off for reasons Cecily had yet to decipher over seven years of trying. "I know. Sorry." She usually concentrated on using her right hand when with him, but he'd noticed her switching off, as he liked to call it, "willy-nilly."

Oh boy.

He scoffed, his gaze at her hands almost a glare, and then he went back to his food. "Freaky."

She wasn't a freak, but she didn't dispute him. "Little girls' room..." She left the table, needing relief from the disgust swirling in her belly.

She returned (her stomach empty and mouth refreshed) to their cleared table, her leftovers tucked away in a white plastic bag emblazoned with the restaurant's blue and green logo. Oscar had cleaned his plate, leaving no leftovers, so he now enjoyed a bottle of Corona.

Cecily approached the table, thinking of stopping for some fresh flowers before going home. Besides lifting her spirits, they would commemorate a successful first session. Hopefully, these flowers would last more than a few measly days (she often wondered why she ended up with bad bunches of flowers so regularly).

Oscar turned his head as he took a swallow of his beer. He gestured for her to sit.

As she moved closer, she recognized the crease in his brow showing irritation (again). She smiled, holding in an internal sigh of dread. What was the problem now?

Cecily sat, seeing he'd ordered a cup of tea for her; her favorite, too: Earl Grey. With the temperatures they would walk into again soon, Cecily appreciated it. The tea would also soothe and counter her experience picking up that chicken, but she was sure Oscar didn't go that deep with it. "Thank you."

He nodded as he set his bottle on the table. The crease only furrowed one eyebrow now as he held the Corona in one hand and stared at it with displeasure. "This thing costs almost twice as much as it did the last time we came here. And, I'm telling you, the damn bottle is smaller."

This again. Cecily stirred her tea to speed the cooling as it steeped.

"Shit's annoying." Even in the short-sleeved shirt, perspiration dotted his upper lip, neck, and temples.

"Cost of making and marketing the product rises; price of the product rises accordingly." Cecily shrugged. He'd complained about this to exhaustion, but there was nothing to do—except stop purchasing.

Oscar gave her his one-eyed squint. "So, I guess you're just Miss Wall Street now, huh? They don't have to make the bottles smaller. They can still give you the quantity you're used to and have been paying for all this time. I'm saying, we're paying more but getting less. That won't make sense—ever; I don't care how many degrees you have to try and explain it to me."

Sometimes she could get away with ignoring him. Cecily tried that now. She took a sip of her Earl Grey, adding nothing to it.

Oscar frowned, that crease deepening as he watched her.

This frown, however, wasn't from anger as it shifted into a soft grin of confusion. "No sugar? Yecch! I don't see how you do it."

Cecily chuckled and set her cup down, the contact lens in her right eye giving her trouble. "You should try it."

Oscar's iron-brown eyes turned inquiring.

Cecily nodded and pushed her cup toward him, offering him the opportunity to try something *she liked* for a change.

Her husband finished guiding the cup toward him. He kept semi-mistrustful eyes on her as he lifted the cup to his lips. He sipped once, twice, and then put the cup down, staring into the tea. "Interesting." Oscar looked up at her with this odd expression that would've been cute if Cecily weren't wary about what it could mean. "What's that I taste in it? It's black tea, but..."

"Bergamot."

"What?"

Cecily gave a low titter. "Bergamot. It's from the rind of fruit, like oranges."

Oscar nodded thoughtfully. "Oh..." He took another sip.

Cecily raised an inquiring eyebrow at him, finding the tea discussion a highlight of her day, second to her session with Dr. Alexander.

Oscar nodded, giving a *not-bad* bend to his lips. He pushed the tea back her way, not unkindly.

"Need sugar?"

"Nah, I guess not." He used the cloth napkin with a circular swipe over his face to clear the dampness.

Cecily held the cup to her lips before taking another sip. "See?" She sipped gingerly; the tea was good but still hot.

"Yeah, but that other tea needs sugar. I don't care what you say." He chuckled and reached for his beer. "Come on." He finished the Corona in three short swallows, then set the bottle down with a sigh transitioning into a soft belch. "If you're not pressed to see the bottom of the cup, we can go. I'ma hit the head."

She wanted to stay and finish it, but she nodded. "That's fine. We n-need to pick up your p-prescriptions, anyway, and I want to s-stop and get some f-fresh flowers on the w-way home." She also needed to attend to her eye. If she had to choose, she much preferred the dry feeling from her contacts, as if her lids were held open before a blowing fan, as opposed to that *other* dryness that sometimes left her panicky. That dryness was akin to the rough and painful irritation of a sandstorm blowing in her eyes. Rubbing and blinking helped with that fan-blowing feeling—no dice when the sandstorm raged behind the lenses. This was more fan-blowy: her eye watered some but was less irritated; it could wait.

Oscar's eyes shone something unkind before he pulled his lips back from his teeth. "No problem. Need to get cigarettes, too, so..." The challenge in his eyes begged her to say something about it.

Cecily, seven years in, knew better. "Okay. I'll meet you up f-front."

As Oscar headed for the men's room, Cecily picked up the check and her bag of leftovers and headed for the front to pay the bill, her thoughts returning to images of a mustard-yellow seating group.

He'd indirectly challenged her to say something about him getting some cigarettes, but Oscar left the carton in the store. She waited patiently behind him as he stood in front of the display case, mumbling a curse-filled debate with himself before he mumbled some excuse about not getting them. Cecily didn't care the reason; he'd made the right choice. The downside: he was more agitated by his desire for a cigarette and not having one. Needing (wanting) a cigarette, on top of supporting the "rip-off" that was doctors' prescriptions with his copay (which he didn't pay, she did), Oscar was in a foul mood by the time they reached home. He didn't take it out on her during the ride, though; there was that.

Oscar pulled into their garage, pulling mighty close to her Devin, and Cecily had the feeling he threatened to hit her car by accident on purpose. He didn't take anything out on her during the ride home, but they were home now. He turned the car off and swiveled his head and shoulders her way. "Think I might be able to take the Deville out for a spin? Now that I'm dying and shit?"

Cecily looked at him.

His words were mean, spiteful, full of more challenge, but his eyes held the fear that last question carved in his soul.

Cecily clutched her bouquet of Narcissus, Pepperberry, Phlox, cyclamen, star of Bethlehem, and Queen Ann's Lace tighter. She regarded her husband, really looking at him in the seconds it took her answer to leave her lips. His light complexion looked lighter, pale even; the ever-present perspiration seemed wetter somehow; his breathing, more noticeably labored these past few months, carried a low-level rattle in the car's quiet; something sour in his breath traveled over the mint in his mouth, and Cecily saddened although she fought not to show it. Her husband was dying.

Again.

Her husband was dying (again). That was the heart of the matter. Cecily pushed down the self-pity and mustered a smile. "Wanna take it now?"

His eyelids fluttered with surprise at her words. Devin was the one thing considered hers; it surprised her he didn't take it over (yet). Oscar shook his head with a grin; the agitation pushed aside (if only temporarily). "Maybe later." And then the grin flattened into a straight line of anger, his brow creasing in tandem. "I hate..." He looked away, staring past her through the car window, out at the wall with the garden tools.

Cecily resisted reaching out and touching him for fear of him pushing her hand away and hurting her feelings. "You hate...? What do you hate?"

He shifted his gaze back to her and bared his off-white teeth, the brown in his irises dead and stiff like the leaves on the cold ground; no warmth to be found. "I hate...this!"

He was talking about what was happening to him; Cecily empathized. "I know." She opened the glove compartment. Inside, tucked under the owner's manual to their Infinity Q70, was a pack of Newport cigarettes with two lone sticks remaining. Cecily pulled the pack out, listening to Oscar's soft gasp as she pulled one out and handed it to him. They knew he shouldn't have the cigarette, but desperate times called for desperate measures.

Oscar accepted the cigarette while taking her flowers from her, his expression hard to read. "I'll water these for you. Come on." He turned away and exited the vehicle without another word, entering their kitchen through the access door.

It was something he never did, and so Cecily never expected it. Still, every once in a while, she wished Oscar would hold a door open for her, or maybe pull a chair out for her (not out *from under her*: Oscar's weird sense of humor sure made that a possibility), or perhaps any of the various ways a man showed appreciation for the woman he was with. She missed her husband; Roland was one door-opening, chair-pulling-out son of a gun.

Sighing with the memory of a man long gone, Cecily left the car for the house, ready to get out of her clothes and jot down the stuff she remembered in Dr. Alexander's office.

View of the freezer stopped her. Cecily paused and stared at it, trying to remember Oscar telling her he'd purchased the ingredients for the punch for the Mabrys' upcoming holiday party and stored them there. Holding her bag of leftovers in one hand, she gripped the freezer door handle with the other, reluctant to open it.

If the stuff was in there, she was crazy. Okay, been there, still doing that. If it wasn't in there, it meant Oscar was crazy—not exactly the better option.

Cecily snatched the freezer door open as if to catch the frozen foods doing something they shouldn't. Chuckling at herself, she stared inside. The frozen foods weren't doing anything untoward—not even sharing their space with the ingredients for Oscar's tornado punch: no orange juice, pineapple juice, or flavored rums to finish chilling in the kitchen fridge. Nothing in there but cartons of butter pecan ice cream, some of her Greek yogurts, some frozen dinners, and packages of various types of meat already seasoned and marinated for later use. So she was right, and Oscar was wrong.

But why didn't that make her feel better?

Cecily closed the freezer door and went inside.

Lounging on her bed in sweatpants and a Delta State T-shirt, her notes about what she might have remembered tucked away in a small notepad stuffed in a pair of her socks (she had no idea why the secrecy), Cecily enjoyed a glass of Shiraz and listened to music by Nina Simone through her wireless headphones. Eyes closed, head back to her pillow, she grooved to "Do What You Gotta Do," singing along in a quiet voice and feeling jazzy-bluesy from the vocal talents of Miss Eunice Waymon.

She loved her Nina.

Sensing a presence as "Trouble in Mind" floated through her ears and brain, Cecily cracked an eye open. She startled at seeing her husband standing at the foot of their bed. His expression always sent a spear of something bleak and cold into her abdomen, just about the spot where that knife went in.

Part grin, part sneer—she never knew what to make of it because she never knew what she'd get from it; that look didn't always mean a hurt. No foolproof way of gauging this expression created unsettledness in her. What else was new?

Cecily smiled tentatively, responding more to the grin than the sneer part of his expression. "You scared me."

Oscar didn't smile back, but that meant nothing. With Oscar, you just never knew what was coming. "Say that again."

Cecily frowned, knowing what that meant. She hesitated, thinking about how it meant something altogether different when a certain someone else wanted her to repeat words and phrases. Speaking of which, tomorrow was spa day at JAH Tech.

The sneer part of her husband's expression pushed through more. "Y-You scared me."

Now the grin part advanced through his features, but the grin wasn't that much better than the sneer. "You know, you even put that hick twang in your singing?" He then mocked the way she pronounced "scared" (adding this exaggerated drawl on the "A") before leering at her with a headshake and chuckle. "I can't believe you still talk like that."

The Shiraz and Nina had mellowed her some, so Cecily eyed him calmly. She'd lost some drawl since moving up here years ago. Her brothers reminded her of that often. Oscar making fun of her Mississippi accent was old hat now, habit; a part of the give-and-take in their marriage. But it sometimes led to more than gibes and teases, putting Cecily on edge despite Mr. Shiraz. "Sorry."

Her husband scoffed. "Anyway, I came up here to ask about the punch bowls. I want to finish setting up, make sure I have everything. They're not in the cabinet under the island or on the bottom shelf of the pantry."

"Check the cabinet in the dining room breakfront?"

His expression brightened. "That's right, damn." He turned to leave. "Oscar...?"

He paused by her dresser and put a hand to it. He'd climbed the stairs long enough ago to listen to her singing her Nina, so his breathing should have settled, but no. He turned to her. He'd changed clothes, too: to one of his standard sweatsuits—a faded cyan one Cecily still wondered where he got it (and why he insisted on wearing it). "What?"

"There isn't any stuff for the punch in the freezer."

Oscar made a face. "Yeah, I know that."

"You said you already had it stored in the freezer in the garage."

Oscar peered at her, his brows furrowing more with curiosity. "Are you getting worse? That's not what I said."

Uncertainty (all too familiar lately) coiled her insides, spiraling into her chest. She removed her headphones. "Yes. At lunch. I'd asked if—"

"I said I *needed* to get the stuff for the party to put in the freezer, not that I already had it."

"No, that's not... I said, let's pick up the..." She was sure he said he'd already gotten the stuff and stored it in the freezer. But nothing for tornado punch was in the freezer, so maybe she did misunderstand.

"See? You don't listen. Guess what I say isn't important enough. You keep yourself in a state of confusion when you don't listen, Cecil."

That pet name rankled, but Cecily focused on trying hard to remember their lunch date and what they said about the punch for the Mabrys' holiday party.

"Let it go. You've been doing that so much: hearing and seeing shit that wasn't; it's almost a part of you. You're seeing a psychiatrist for a reason. Give it time...and maybe leave the wine alone."

She rarely drank but wanted something to decompress with after today's full plate of events. However, she was nowhere near intoxicated. A rare-occasion drinker, she hadn't even finished the glass, but maybe Oscar was right. She sighed. "Right. Thank you."

"It's what I'm here for." A mint clacked against his teeth.

"I love you."

Oscar turned to leave. "Back at you."

"You put my flowers in water?"

"Oh yeah, I watered them. They're on the kitchen table as we speak, spreading their flowery joy." He sounded a low snort-laugh.

Cecily didn't know what was funny, but Oscar had an odd sense of humor. "Oscar?"

He sighed (hint of impatience) but turned back to her. "Yes, Cecily?"

"We... We don't kiss or touch like we used to..." She sounded meek and pleading. She wasn't trying to, but she couldn't help it, either.

Oscar sighed again, his impatience clearer. "Not this again."

"I'm just saying."

"We had sex the other night."

That wasn't the same thing, and Cecily knew Oscar knew it; she was talking about affection, not sex (although one didn't negate the other). "But..." *But with the news we received, we should take time to be closer and bond.* She, however, didn't want to remind him of Dr. Halim's diagnosis...and prognosis.

"But...?" He used his handkerchief across his perspiring brow.

Cecily discharged a resigned breath. "But nothing. Never mind." She stared at the unopened magazine resting by her thigh on the bed. A picture of hyenas on the hunt graced the front of her National Geographic (NG), bordered by its renowned yellow frame. Oscar said NG was an uppity, White man's periodical, but Cecily didn't care. She had an NG cover framed and sitting on her desk at work—one with two male giraffes in combat. She loved giraffes; they were such majestic creatures.

"Fine." Stuffing his hankie back in his pocket, he came over to her.

Cecily looked up at him. He wore a tentative smile, but that still didn't mean anything. With him, you just never knew.

He bent down, placing his lips on hers. When she put a hand on his shoulder, he pushed his tongue into her mouth with the usual poky stiffness. She was used to his kiss.

They kissed for some seconds, Oscar's mint helping to make the kiss more pleasant than it would've been had he not had it. Perhaps his treatments for the PAH will help with that, too. Hoping for the opposite but knowing what to expect, Cecily parted her eyelids to slits. Oscar's eyes were wide open, looking at her as they kissed; a habit weird and creepy to her. She shut her lids (the darkness much better than Oscar's stare).

When she drew her hand from his shoulder, Oscar pulled back. "How was that?"

Weird and creepy. Stiff and poky.

But she couldn't say any of those things to him. Not ever.

Cecily smiled. "Just fine."

Chapter Six

Home Skillet

S hopping? Done. Wrapping? Done. Holiday plans? Only a few, but made and in the works.

Naomi sat at her desk, staring at the brace on her wrist. Accidental bumps against the brace didn't cause the excruciating pain it had days before, so there was some improvement, some healing.

With a sigh, she removed the brace. Hesitant but powering on, she worked her left hand and wrist, clenching and unclenching her fist, turning and bending her wrist. Minimal pain—until she tried twirling with her wrist, sending a sharp reminder up her arm to her elbow. Naomi winced, bit her lip, and let out a breath. She wasn't out of carpal-tunnel jail yet, but with the brace on, she could write some; not at length, but a few notes during a session would be manageable. She put her brace back on, listening on low volume to J.S. Bach's Prelude No. 1 in C major from *The Well-Tempered Clavier*.

It wasn't "Jingle Bells," but to each their own.

Mr. and Mrs. Brooks were due for their appointment in about fifteen minutes. They were her only appointment for the day, the last scheduled before the holiday break. If her patients struggled, however (and the holiday season lent itself to increases in depression and mental stress often), they had a special phone number to contact her for urgent help or counseling—the "DNA hotline."

After her session with Mr. and Mrs. Brooks (she allowed for longer than an hour if the couple needed), Naomi made plans to begin her holiday by visiting Mr. and Mrs. Phillips this afternoon. Viv sent several texts with emoji of excited happiness and words of thanks, but they hadn't spoken; Naomi looked forward to hearing more about Rick being home—and not just for the holidays.

But that was later. In keeping with the holiday spirit, she even wore jeans with an ugly Christmas sweater instead of business attire for her only appointment today.

Naomi gazed out her window, the icicles now nubs and no longer threatening, having melted with the round-forty degrees outside. The fangs were more like baby teeth. What difference four days makes. But December still looked cold and unforgiving out there. Her poinsettias, positioned in vases along the picture-window's interior sill, helped brighten the bleakness.

Her thoughts shifted to her incoming patient.

Part of her approach with Cecily would be through cognitive restructuring: continuously challenge the poor woman's thoughts and beliefs regarding her capabilities and value. Although they didn't use to be, Cecily's current notions of her role as wife were implicit but false, and Naomi wanted to work with calculated discretion for her to see that.

As it was, Oscar had a grip of control over Cecily, over their marriage. Naomi needed Cecily to see that submission, which had its valid role in a marriage for *both* parties, didn't mean giving total control to someone. Cecily's surrender to Oscar's manipulations rendered her ineffectual in establishing her confidence, independence, and value as a person, let alone as a woman.

The approach would be to challenge Cecily's thoughts of hopelessness and denounce the degrading, belittling, disparaging internal sermons Cecily lived with. It would be delicate work, but Naomi could do delicate and in-your-face; most times, she preferred the latter.

She couldn't do critical incident debriefing; Cecily presented as too fragile for that one-stop-shop approach. But using imaginal exposure to guide her through what happened two Christmases ago may have to be coupled with some in vivo exposure and helping Cecily face the trauma that is her relationship with Oscar. She needed to help Cecily become habituated to asserting her true self in therapy so that she could do so at home and elsewhere, instead of avoiding the stimuli created by being under such a closed and oppressive situation.

Responses to traumatic events (experiences involving a threat of death or serious injury that evoke fear, helplessness, or horror) could be

categorized but were never typical. And treatment for it varied. Naomi
wasn't a big fan of doctors using critical incident stress debriefing; it
rated a colossal waste of time to her, because she had yet to see solid
proof of its effectiveness. Cognitive behavioral therapy, or CBT, showed
promise, but the newer experimental drugs raised thorny questions.

With PTSD, traumatic events resulting from intentional actions, such
as the home invasion, presented a higher risk for severe PTSD manifestation than those resulting from impersonal disasters. In her view,
medicine had its role, but most people could cope with traumatic experiences if left to their own devices.

Because Cecily suffered through the crime of home invasion, the CBT
approach was ideal.

So, where to begin? That was never a simple question with treating
people. The beginning sometimes meant somewhere in the middle or
even the end. Cecily had acute stress early-stage PTSD, so the going
could be tough, but it was doable. She'd already determined Cecily's situation wasn't a one-stop-shop situation requiring the simple approach
of critical incident stress debriefing. Psychotherapy had its place with
Naomi, always. She, however, figured combining cognitive restructuring
with bits of imaginal exposure thrown in (given recent success with its
application), could work. She could use some in vivo exposure, too, but
a "real-life" situation lent itself to having Oscar's participation—but he
was the heart of the problem.

In Cecily's case, imagining or reimagining the trauma outweighed
reliving it outright, but she'd have to see. She might implement some
stress inoculation training toward the last remaining sessions; meditation and relaxation methods to reduce anxiety worked wonders even
for the un-afflicted. Ultimately, her purpose was to redirect Cecily's
conditioned responses: to the home invasion, but foremost, to Oscar's
narcissistic dominance.

At the core of any psychiatric counseling, however, was *talking*.
Talking founded everything else. No treatment or approach, cognitive,
medicinal, or otherwise, would happen if no one talked. All psychiatrists
or therapists did the *talking thing*. There were multiple treatment approaches, but every single person with a medical license in the mental
health profession (and some without said license) effected talking with
a patient to treat their mental stresses. Couldn't get around that in

any form or fashion. You talked, and they talked, and you asked more questions to get them talking more.

Very little happens, very little progress made without the talking.

But with cognitive behavioral therapy, the talking took on different looks, different purposes. Therapies to treat PTSD patients could be targeted on the PTSD symptoms alone to help a patient, or they could go an indirect route with focus on other areas of life impacting a patient's mental well-being, such as their familial relationships or job stresses.

From Dr. Lewis's notes, Naomi surmised his focus was on the stress inoculation training part of therapy more so than the exposure or restructuring areas of CBT. She wanted to combine and refine these parts with Cecily, starting with some cognitive restructuring and then the exposure with elements of stress inoculation weaved throughout (to reduce her PTSD symptoms). Before Naomi could lead her into intense mental imagery related to events two Decembers ago, Cecily needed to make sense of the memories from that night.

Naomi turned to her credenza and prepared her session beverage of warm, orange-spiced tea with a hint of lemon—adding a splash of Hennessy X.O. (a surprising flavor enhancer). Letting her tea steep and cool to a tolerable temperature for session consumption, Naomi turned back to her desk. She picked up a Friday newspaper (today's selections: the *Washington Post*, the *New York Times*, the *Wall Street Journal*, and *USA Today*) for her weekly perusal, absorption, and analysis of the nation's psychological state. She didn't have time to get deep into the articles, but that was fine; it would do to fill the time. She was ready for Cecily and Oscar; ready to begin work.

A knock on her door interrupted her review of the Arts and Entertainment section of the *Washington Post*.

She looked up to find her resident, Dr. Veronica Stewart, grinning at her. "That sweater is too much."

Naomi smiled back. "Ugly?"

Her resident snickered. She was 27 and very bright, with dark, burnished-maple skin and long, ropey dreads of a contrasting shade of crimson she styled many ways, and which always left wafts of coconut in their wake. Veronica was taller than average but still overweight for her five-eight height, although not grossly. "Oh my God, yes! The colors and

the bulbs, with the tinsel, the snowflakes, plus the way the reindeer—
Oh yes." She chuckled, shaking her head while holding the doorknob.
"Mister and Missus Brooks are here. Mister Brooks is in the men's
room."

"Okay. I'm ready. Send them in when he's done. And uh, I suggested
Khalid get you something similar for Christmas."

Veronica's eyes widened. She then smirked disbelief before looking
unsure. "You did not. ...Did you?"

Naomi shrugged and picked up a section of *USA Today*, pretending
to get back to Friday's reads. Khalid was Veronica's fiancée, and no,
she didn't suggest an ugly Christmas sweater for a gift idea, but the
uncertainty kept Veronica guessing (an element of fun for Naomi).

"I'll send them in." Chuckling, Veronica closed the door.

Naomi folded her paper and set it aside. She adjusted her eyeglasses
on the bridge of her nose, picked up her Cambridge mug full of tea, then
sat in her counsel chair, session timer ready.

Cecily walked in with a sincere smile, her hazel contacts twinkling with fakery. "He's still in the men's room, but Doctor Stewart
said it was okay to come in." She dressed more casually in a pair of
Brunswick-green slacks and a white blouse—looking Christmassy (although Naomi didn't think it was her intent).

Naomi stood and smiled. "Sure is." She gestured to her seating group.
"Have a seat."

Cecily eyed her ugly Christmas sweater and chuckled as she hung up
her coat. "Cool sweater."

"You think?"

"Oh, most definitely." Cecily walked back, her laughter heartier as she
gazed at the sweater again. Naomi now interacted with someone closer
to the real Cecily Edana *Jamison Cooper* (she wasn't so sure about the
"Brooks"). The rosacea had cleared considerably.

The women sat (Cecily choosing the loveseat this time).

Naomi started the recorder and reached for her mug. "So, ready for
the holidays? Any big plans other than visiting Larimore and going to
Odessa's?"

Cecily nodded pure enthusiasm. "Going out to dinner with Marcus
and Chelsea and my grandson. Party at the Mabrys'."

Naomi suspected Oscar wasn't included in that first outing. "'Party'?"

Cecily nodded, looking less than excited. "New Year's."

"Testing that triumph over the ochlophobia, huh?"

Cecily hunched her shoulders. "Something like that. I'm looking forward to it."

Naomi saw that wasn't true but said nothing, believing Cecily's ochlophobia could've been a derivative of an avoidance symptom of her PTSD, as well as an extension of Cecily remaining unsure of people's motives. "So, which restaurant for Christmas dinner?"

"Haven't decided yet. Someplace child-friendly but nice, you know?"

"I do know. They grow up fast, don't they? They're infants and then starting first grade in the spate of what seems like months instead of years."

"I know! Little Roland just started walking, *I thought*, and now he's trying sentences!"

"I bet he's a joy."

Cecily's expression conveyed sadness before she nodded and smiled more brightly with new grandma pride. "He is—a blessed joy. I don't get to see as much of him as I'd like, but..."

"And why is that?" Her question didn't mask the meaning behind it.

Cecily braced her gaze on her. "You just dive right in, huh?"

"Most times, yes."

Bringing those hands together (as she did in session days ago), Cecily went quiet.

Since they were into it, Naomi took things further while Oscar had yet to join them. "Let me ask this, then: Do you believe people have a *true* self, and a '*what everyone else sees*,' a 'public' self? Are they always separate, always the same?"

"...Depends on...on whom the interaction is with." She looked pained.

"Fair enough. ...Do you feel *safe*, Cecily?" Her random question, wasn't.

Cecily frowned, but it wasn't with confusion, but more with wondering how Naomi determined it was even a viable question. Her stomach growled. "Excuse me."

Naomi nodded her pardon, waiting.

Cecily began wringing her hands. Her saturnine disposition reclaimed itself with her gaze at the books on the bookcase along the wall behind the sofa.

"We may not answer those questions in here today, but they do need exploration and an answer, Cecily."

Cecily turned that perfect hair and those fake irises toward her. "'Safe' has many meanings, Doctor Alexander."

She noticed Cecily hadn't stuttered once. "Oh, I agree. But the answer should be 'yes' to all of them, regardless."

"I know, but—"

The door opened, and Oscar whisked in, in a flurry of burgundy and gold. The NFL season hadn't ended officially for Washington, but technically it had (several games ago), yet Oscar wore the colors as if that mattered not: vintage Redskins cap, gold hoodie, and these dark-burgundy fleece sweatpants formed the team-rooting ensemble. His eyes narrowed on her and Cecily, dispatching an apprehensive suspicion before he smiled. "Whassup, Home Skillet?"

Everyone was in a casual mood today. And, "Home Skillet" wasn't going to work, either. But it was Christmas.

He chuckled as he approached the loveseat. "Ridiculous sweater..."

Eyes on Oscar, in her peripheral vision, Naomi noticed Cecily tense. Oscar's eyes widened with hilarity. "It's perfect!"

"Thank you." The three laughed a few seconds, but Naomi recognized Cecily's guffaw held relief.

Oscar removed his hat and sat beside Cecily, and Naomi was taken aback at that show of indoor manners.

She, however, almost coughed at the profuse and semi-offensive stench of Oscar's fragrance. Cecily's nose wrinkled, too; Naomi wasn't alone. "What're we wearing this morning, Oscar?" She touched her nose to show what she referred to.

He displayed a satisfied smile, a piece of mint candy moving on his tongue. "Number one classic: Aramis. You like?"

Once upon a time, she did like it—on Tyson, back in the day. *Way* back in the day. And "classic" Aramis may be, but not this much of it—ever. "It's nice."

Cecily swallowed. It wasn't obvious, but Naomi noticed it: Cecily picked up on her sarcasm.

Oscar leaned back, sending an arm along the back of the loveseat and behind Cecily. "So, what're we talking about today?"

"Oh, a little bit of this, a whole lot of that." Naomi sipped her tea.

Oscar shook his head. "Here we go."

Chuckling, Naomi set her mug down.

He gestured at her brace. "See you're exercising it, working it. Trying to get it back in good shape, huh?"

"Something like that. Now, I'd like to talk some about Cecily's life *before* the attack, as well as give some attention to the events on a night two years ago."

Cecily frowned. "All of that today?"

Naomi shook her head. "Yes, and no. But we're just touching on them today. We'll delve more once we return from the holiday break."

Cecily nodded (rather nervously).

Crossing an ankle over his knee, Oscar looked doubtful himself. "I...I remember little about the attack. Sorta blocked all that out." He tapped Cecily's shoulder using the hand resting behind her.

Cecily nodded her agreement. "M-Me, too."

"Don't prod or prompt her, Oscar. Please."

"I didn't." He didn't attempt an innocent look; his words held challenge.

He didn't intimidate her. "Yes, you did." And if he became too aggressive in here, well...Naomi hoped he didn't.

"Please, don't," Cecily pleaded. She looked at her. "He didn't p-prod me, N- Naomi. But..."

The damn stutter was back. "Yes...?"

Cecily shrugged. "But if you w-want to t-touch on it, think it'll help. I...I g-guess that would b-be okay."

He prodded her, but Naomi left it alone. Cecily addressed her by her first name, though, so Cecily felt a level of comfort with her—good. "Okay. We're just focusing some on what you *do* remember, as we did a couple days ago."

Cecily gave a quasi-yes tilt of her head.

Oscar looked less convinced, but he wasn't Naomi's focus, so who gave a hey-nonny-nonny?

"Okay, so, Cecily, before we start on that, I want to ask about your tinted contacts..." Naomi paused, observing their reactions to the mention. Surely, they didn't think she believed they were her real irises.

Oscar smirked.

Cecily pulled her upper lip in for an instant. "What about them?"

"Are they prescription?"

Cecily's eyes darted in her husband's direction. She looked down at her hands. When she looked up at Naomi, she gazed as if again nonplussed at how she dove right in. "No, just p-personality."

Naomi started to reply, *take them out then*—because they weren't part of her personality; not the inner, truer Cecily. At least Cecily didn't venture to fibnation by telling her they were medicinal. "Oh, okay. Now, your pre-therapy questionnaire said you collect comics."

Grinning, Cecily bobbed her head.

Oscar rolled his eyes while Naomi grinned back. The question intended to reinforce those things about Cecily—*pre*-Oscar. "Marvel or Detective?"

"Oh! Marvel all the way. Although, I do like a few DC characters."

"How long have you collected them?" Just a little more...

Cecily tilted her head back with a reflective smile. "Larimore and I started reading Daddy's in junior high. I was high on Daredevil, while he followed the X-Men. Between the two of us, there's a good sample of other key ones: Iron-Man, Spider-Man..." Eyes brightening with the discussion, Cecily's body posture became less inward, more open. She didn't stutter.

Naomi hadn't heard the Marvel heroes' names—tweaked with Mississippi flare—quite that way before.

Oscar scoffed.

Naomi ignored him. "I don't follow them to great detail, but I like Doctor Strange, Nightcrawler. From DC comics, I'm a fan of the Flash. Also, Archie Comics was a favorite as a teen."

Cecily cheesed and nodded; tickled Naomi related.

Oscar stared at the center table as if contemplating either reaching for the water to pour, or a magazine to leaf through (although he could reach for the one he had last session—he hadn't read it).

"I don't read them as much as I used to."

"Understandable. You sell 'em?"

Cecily shook her head, her expression so pure with caution, she looked offended. "Oh no. I won't. Saving them for my grandson. Now, if *he* wants to sell them, that's fine, but not me. Several collections are over forty years old and worth a good penny."

Oscar wore the oddest expression: something secretive, unfriendly.

Naomi continued. "I understand you're a financial consultant and manager. That's right up your alley; what you went to school for."

Cecily nodded. "I like numbers,...and I don't."

Naomi chuckled. "Understand completely. But you've held other jobs. Done things besides the 'numbers'?"

Oscar frowned. "What's with all the—?"

Naomi gestured to shush him, and Oscar's eyes narrowed before he turned to Cecily. Naomi shifted attention back to Cecily, too.

Cecily's eyes held concerned curiosity. "I... I've been a waitress and a bank teller—but I guess that's back to the 'numbers.'"

"As it were, yes. Did you like waitressing?"

Cecily's nod was full of truth. "I did, yeah. Meeting all kinds of people, giving them excellent service—perhaps brightening their day..."

Oscar shook his head and scoffed. "She can get Pollyanna on you quick. Even at her age."

"Nothing wrong with that. We all need to sometimes." Eyes on Cecily, Naomi noticed her reply relieved her. "How long did you wait tables?"

"Only about a year or so. Roland did a stint as a cashier at the Kroger. We were getting married soon, and we worked extra hours to ensure we had a cushion."

"Settlement money held in trust?"

"Yeah. They didn't finalize things yet, and I looked at it as nothing being guaranteed. But either way, Roland and I *wanted* to work."

"Considering you two were still pursuing degrees, mighty industrious of you."

Cecily's shy grin carried pride. "It was...a fun time."

"Something like that could put a strain on things, on a relationship, but I suppose it brought you closer?"

Eyes darting toward her husband, Cecily hesitated before giving a minimal nod.

Oscar stared at the magazines on the table.

Naomi let the silence meander, wanting Cecily's thoughts on the *before*—and maybe have Oscar's thoughts in that direction, too.

"Okay. Now, tell me about your middle name. Irish, isn't it?"

"Edana." Cecily rolled her eyes upward. "Yeah. I don't know what my parents were thinking."

"Means 'fire,' right?"

"Yes. My mother said it fit me. Said I was a fireball in her belly and came flaming out at birth." She chuckled, her expression strange, as if fond memories of her mother battled not-so-fond memories of her. "My dad would say it fit me later, too." Cecily shook her head with a kind smirk, memories of her dad unmistakable as fond ones. And the stutter disappeared. It was the damnedest thing.

Oscar pushed out a breath. "What's with this memory-lane crap?"

Disregarding him, Naomi raised eyebrows in question to Cecily. "And does it? Fit you now, that is?"

Cecily wore that validity-of-a-viable-question expression again. She turned to the window and went silent.

Oscar (having poured water) sat back with his cup of refresher and sighed. "She's not fiery, Doctor Alexander. Never has been. Cecily's one of the sweetest pushovers you'll ever meet. So, all this talk is mute." His words were smoothly critical of Cecily while sounding complimentary.

Cringing inside, Naomi left the mute-moot correction alone. "'*Never*'? You've only known her about seven years." She kept her challenge mild but with enough emphasis for her patient's benefit. Surely, Cecily picked up on Oscar calling her a pushover—regardless of how *sweet* a one she was.

Cecily frowned at something outside the window, and Naomi hoped she had her thinking—if only a little.

"That's long enough. If you've been fiery all your life, it would've been evident whenever I met her. Cecily's not like that. Maybe her parents wanted the name to come to fruition for her or something."

Oscar had a point, Naomi guessed, but Cecily's deepening frown toward the window suggested not (answers on her pre-therapy questionnaire said "not," too). Oscar wasn't considering having met Cecily soon after losing Roland. Naomi, however, was keeping Roland's death out of the discussion for now, wanting Cecily to focus on who she was before that sad event—and who she still is. And, he knew the word *fruition*, but not the difference between moot and mute? Go figure.

Oscar shrugged and drank his water, and Naomi wondered how his doctor's appointment went.

The silence that followed, Naomi hoped, allowed Cecily time to ruminate about comic books, and waitressing, and her name, and all the other teeny, tiny things that made her up.

Oscar, however, couldn't take it. He reached inside his hoodie pocket, pulling out a pack of Newport cigarettes.

"This is a non-smoking building, Oscar. Sorry."

His eyes widened with annoyance before he smiled with a dismissive shrug; those teeth needing a strip or something to improve their appearance. "Whatever you say."

It wasn't what she said; rather, the CDC and the state of Maryland got together on that one. But his passive-aggressive response provided Naomi additional insight into how the man worked.

He put his cigarettes back, shaking his head. His friendly-mutton-chops beard needed taming, but the look was growing on her.

"It...It also means 'zealous.'" Cecily now focused on Naomi's desk.

"True." Naomi checked the timer.

Cecily chuckled; her eyes signaled it was at something specific.

Naomi turned to her desk. "What?"

"There's no breeze or anything, but...Einstein's nodding at me."

Naomi checked her deskmate: her Einstein bobblehead. He did seem to agree with whatever conclusions Cecily had drawn in her head; the delicate bobble (more up-and-down than swirling) said so. She turned back to the couple. "Yeah, he does that—but only when he agrees with your thoughts." She let the joke linger, but Cecily goggled her as if she'd spoken some mystical truth.

Oscar, true to form, scoffed with a headshake, placing his empty cup on the table.

"But there's no breeze. No one bumped the desk or anything." The confusion in Cecily's eyes also rated mildly curious.

Naomi noticed Cecily hadn't stuttered once during the whole memory-lane exchange. She rechecked her deskmate: no movement now. Weird, but strange shit happened every day all over the world. Shit like flashes of truth and aura-flickers, for example. She turned back to them with a shrug. "Now—"

"I'm sorry." Cecily's hands began a partial wring and then stopped.

She understood its root causes, but Naomi was determined (before it was all over) to work on that habitual response, too. "Nothing to apologize for, Cecily. Not in here. Now, I want to dabble discussion on the two of you before moving on to the invasion."

Oscar obliterated his mint and swallowed. "*Us?* What for?"

Naomi maintained her matter-of-fact gaze.

Oscar turned to Cecily, suspicion furrowing his brow and making his upper lip quiver. "What does she want to talk about us for?"

Cecily looked at him, eyes wide and fearful, but she spoke in her usual, modulated tone. "I d-don't know, honey."

"I'm just touching on the basics before getting into the nitty-gritty."

It took a second or two for the couple to break their gaze before Oscar sighed and sat back. "Oh. Is that all?"

"I don't know yet. But that's all...for now. So, how did you meet?"

Mollified, Oscar sent his arm behind his wife again. "Shopping at Walmart. Married seven months later."

Cecily nodded (her eyes not yet returned to normal size).

Well, seven didn't prove lucky for Cecily in this case. Naomi turned to her. "And how did things go from there?"

Oscar parted his lips in reply, but Naomi's expression paused him.

Cecily sat forward some, her smile almost genuine. "Oh, I was hooked: the quiet talks, going on city tours, renting movies and chilling on the sofa. You know, the usual." The glimmer in those fake irises suggested the "usual" had been nice—but was now *unusual.*

"And you don't do those things anymore?"

Oscar issued his standard scoff-headshake, then turned to his wife.

Cecily startled. It was slight, but there. "Sure. Y-Yes, of course." She sat back.

"And is the sex satisfying, Cecily? Does Oscar bring you to orgasm?"

Oscar drew his arm from behind Cecily and sat forward, confused anger making his face redden some. "What?! You go from how we met to, is she climaxing during sex?!"

Again, Naomi gazed back plainly.

Eyes back to normal size, a tiny smile of embarrassment curved the corners of Cecily's lips.

Oscar blew his cheeks out, working the bill of his cap with intermittent squeezes. "Seems to me, you went from basics to 'nitty-gritty' mighty quick." He scoffed, giving his cap another squeeze. "Man, this is driving me crazy."

Naomi pulled her mug to her lips, murmuring, "That's a short trip."

Oscar frowned. "Huh?"

"Nothing. Now..." Naomi quasi-leaned toward Cecily.

"Why aren't you asking me if I climax?"

"You aren't the patient." Besides, who was he kidding? "Cecily...?"

"I...I do, y-yes. Every t-time."

Now see, adding *every time* messed her up. Naomi held in her own scoff. Even she didn't climax *every time* she and Kevin were intimate. Not that it was solely about that—not for a woman. Still, Naomi mentally converted that "every time" to "rarely" and kept it moving, thinking about one woman who no doubt climaxed whenever intimate with her husband (if not multiple times). Naomi smiled and nodded. "Good." She checked the session timer. This session revealed a wealth of information for her to ponder over the next two weeks, but she still wanted to delve deeper. "Do you love Oscar?"

Instead of her eyes softening with warm emotion or looking confused by the question, Cecily looked fearful again. "Y-Yes."

At least 80 percent fibnation. *At least.* "Tell him."

Now, Cecily looked confused (and still fearful).

Oscar scoffed. "I don't know what any of this has to do with her episodes." But he sat back in expectation, ready to hear the majority-lie all three in that room knew existed.

Cecily turned to her husband, her eyes wide, anxious. "I love you, Oscar." She didn't stutter, but the words sounded wistful—as if she wanted the words to be true.

"Love you, too." Oscar's words weren't sad but came out in a rush, sounding more like "luvatoo"—as if he wanted the words to be over with. Adding this dismissive glance Cecily's way, he neither looked Cecily in the eye nor said the words with any genuine feeling. He sat forward again and looked at Naomi. "Now, there. Can we move on, please?"

"This is my session, Oscar—with Cecily. You're here to help, but..." Naomi shook her head, telling him in but so many words, he wasn't directing this therapy, so he needed to slow his roll. She understood if the couple was uncomfortable professing their love in front of her. Many people (herself included) were uncomfortable with outward displays of love and affection, especially verbal expressions. But Naomi didn't get that vibe from them at all. Seemed it had nothing to do with discomfort and more with...pretense.

Oscar's glare at her revealed his propensity for violence against women, so Naomi decided her Glock-17 would rest at the small of her back for all future sessions with the couple. She didn't notice any telltale signs of violence against Cecily—nothing she could *see*, but Naomi didn't assume there wasn't any. She doubted Oscar would try anything, but a person only needed to be wrong once.

Maybe she should name her gun.

"I l-like your p-poinsettias, Naomi."

"Thank you. I don't do a tree here in the office, but..." Naomi shrugged.

"Yeah, those flowers always tell you what season it is, huh, Home Skillet? And you have yours in vozzes instead of planters. Nice."

Really? *Vozzes*? Boyfriend was from right here—not Europe. "I like the organic experience of seeing the stems in water. Using vases of differing shapes creates a bit of fancy, too."

It went quiet, Naomi's eyes on her patient.

Cecily stared at the poinsettias. She whispered, "Merry Christmas,"—and then went to the floor in a fetal curl, screaming incoherently at the top of her lungs.

Ignoring Oscar's sigh and eye-rolling, Naomi went into action. She dropped to the floor, positioning in front of Cecily. She didn't touch her. "It is *now*, Cecily. Daylight. Naomi's office. Morning." She repeated those words with calm seriousness, not trying to talk over Cecily's screams and wails.

Tears leaking, eyes tight, Cecily trembled, going on about bad smells and blood and gingerbread and black boots and being cold. There was concern about Marcus and a call to Chelsea. She apologized for wetting herself (in the *then*; she hadn't wet herself presently).

Naomi repeated her words to bring Cecily back.

Oscar dropped to his knees. He reached to touch Cecily, but Naomi, using a vehement headshake, deterred him.

Genuine concern filled his eyes before he (incredibly) looked annoyed again. "It'll be okay, Cecily. No one's there." The words were hollow; he sounded almost...bored. His bromide, disguised as benevolence, was wanton—particularly in this dire situation.

Naomi continued her grounding litany to Cecily.

After three minutes, Cecily jolted and reached outward, clutching Naomi's upper arm in a viselike grip. She opened her eyes, heaving, but the incoherent screams ceased. Trembling, Cecily stared at her.

Naomi held her gaze, working a slow-paced nod. "It is *now*, Cecily. Daylight. Naomi's office. *Morning.*"

Cecily's head movement mimicked hers. Her stomach growled.

"Say it with me."

Cecily's gaze fell to Naomi's mouth as Naomi restarted the litany. Soon, she was saying the words with Naomi, until Cecily closed her eyes, exhaling a long, heavy breath. When her eyes fell on Naomi again, her focus was much better. "I'm sorry." She still gripped Naomi's arm.

"It's okay." Oscar rose from his knees and sat on the loveseat.

Naomi clenched her teeth to keep from speaking to him. He didn't know any better, but his *It's okay* suggested Cecily did something wrong, and it pissed her off. She peered into Cecily's eyes. "It is now, Cecily. *My* office. You did nothing wrong. I don't want you apologizing in here." She said, "in here," but she hoped that soon translated and extended to everywhere else, too. "Were...Were there poinsettias then, Cecily?" The two remained on the floor. Naomi would stay on that floor with Cecily for as long as she needed.

Cecily shook her head, still gripping Naomi's arm. "No. Not...Not where I was. Kyle sent them earlier that week, and they were in our bedroom, but—" Her grip tightened.

"There doesn't have to be direct connection, Cecily. Breathe..."

Cecily took a few deep breaths and paused. Eyes locked on Naomi's, she mouthed: "*Please help me.*"

Naomi inclined her head in assertion. She'd do that (and more). She kept her eyes on Cecily's, listening to her breathe and get it together.

Cecily's grip on her arm loosened until she released her.

Naomi propped on her elbow, a hand supporting her head. "Ready?"

Cecily giggled and nodded as she started rising.

Oscar assisted helping his wife up. "This is what I'm talking about, Doctor Alexander. She needs something on the more-intense side."

Naomi rose and sat, grabbing her Cambridge mug for the refresher she needed herself. She sipped slowly, breathed evenly as she watched the couple settle in their seats again.

Cecily poured herself some water. She drank and then held that cup in her lap as if it were a lifeline to the present, her eyes on the poinsettias again.

Oscar stared at his running shoes.

Naomi allowed the silence to linger. She was in no hurry to wrap up, given what just happened. Before sending them on their way, she needed to be comfortable Cecily was okay. And she still wanted to touch on events from that night. "It was dinnertime that night, correct?"

Cecily shook her head, then nodded, her response vague. "Little Roland's first Christmas was so sweet. Of course, he had no idea what all the fuss was about." She offered a frowning-smile at the poinsettias.

"She's asking about *that* night, Cecily." Oscar lifted his eyes from his shoes. "Yeah, Doctor Alexander: dinnertime."

Naomi nodded. Cecily's shift in topic was an example of avoidance: a defense mechanism to offer escape from the anxiety created by her question. Since they were early in the sessions, Naomi allowed the redirect, noting the avoidance response. She went about touching on events from that night another way. "Who's the detective working your case, Cecily?"

Hand rubbing her side, Cecily winced. "A um...Detective Saunders. Reginald Saunders."

Naomi startled inside. The name was too familiar, but it shouldn't have been. Unless he transferred. Detective Reginald Saunders: the same detective who worked the investigation involving Jonathan Rast. Middle initial: "Q." The likelihood of two detectives with the same name working cases within such proximity: farfetched. He must have transferred. Must have. Such a small world.

She watched Cecily distractedly soothe her side: the area where they stabbed her. Although Cecily winced, Naomi doubted it was from actual physical pain. First avoidance, and now this...conversion display in response to discussion about the invasion (another defense mechanism); Cecily was a walking textbook of symptoms, which was odd. "...How much do you obsess over it not being solved, Cecily?"

Eyes on the flowers, Cecily hefted one shoulder. "I wouldn't say 'obsess,' but it baffles me."

Naomi nodded her understanding. "The DNA?"

"Yeah. I mean," Cecily turned to her, "with all the hype over DNA capabilities..." she shook her head and turned back to the flowers.

Oscar crossed an ankle over his knee, hoisting it closer with a sigh. "True. My job as a security guard gave me exceptional experience to be a detective, so I have what it takes, but up against stumpers like this..."

Naomi didn't know what police force would hire him based on his unarmed protection of the Family Dollar, but okay. "Well, don't give up hope, Cecily. DNA could also stand for Do Not Attempt. As in, your DNA will eventually bring you down, so don't attempt crimes."

Her patient guffawed. Just threw her head back and belly-laughed at that. The sound was light and silly sounding, but hearty, too.

Naomi sat taller, a lightness in her limbs. Round two: Cecily.

Oscar watched his wife laugh, his mouth semi-smiling with this mix of wariness and puzzlement.

Cecily eased her laughter, pointing over at Naomi. "That... Oh, that was good."

Naomi returned a slanted grin. "So, I see."

"Yeah, that was pretty good," Oscar agreed.

Cecily straightened her posture. "So, no, I don't obsess. But with the DNA and all the info I supplied—" Her eyes widened. She glanced in Oscar's direction and went still.

Oscar startled and positioned as if to help with another PTSD occurrence, but Naomi didn't move. This wasn't that; Cecily's expression reflected recognition and remembrance.

Naomi set her mug down and scooted forward. "And we'll pause here, lady and gentleman."

Oscar's mouth fell open. "*Now?* She looks like she's—"

"Cecily's fine." Naomi looked at her patient. "Whatever that is. Let it marinate."

Cecily nodded and closed her eyes. Whatever the memory was, it was painful and unsettling; her breathing increased as if fighting tears. She then opened her eyes, sending Naomi a pained, watery gaze. "But I don't know if it—"

Naomi nodded, knowing what Cecily was trying to say: she didn't know if it was an actual memory, or her mind playing with her. "That's why it should marinate."

Cecily breathed easier. "Okay."

"What? What needs to 'marinate'?" Oscar sat forward, too, and snapped his gaze to his wife. "Tell me, Cecily."

"No, Cecily."

Mr. and Mrs. Brooks each sent gazes her way: Cecily with surprise, Oscar with dislike.

"Let it marinate first. Then share when we resume. Okay?"

Cecily bowed her head in affirmation.

Naomi eyed Oscar. "Don't pressure her about it later, either. *You* let it marinate, too—inside Cecily. Some of this she must do without us."

He didn't look too comfortable with that idea, not at all. "Yeah, okay. Fine. Whatever. Are you that paranoid, you think I'd—?" He shook his head. "I wish you thought enough of me to include me in whatever's going on here." He resumed focus on his shoes.

Cecily turned toward him, her lips parted to appease.

Naomi waved her off. Her eyes stern, she mouthed "No" to her. Oscar's passive-aggressive stance fazed Naomi not. She'd seen all kinds in her office—*all* kinds. She realized this passive-aggressiveness was likely more menacingly manipulative at home. "You'll be included, Oscar—when the time is right."

Oscar, eyes on his shoes, scoffed.

Cecily stared, openmouthed, with shock (or something close to it) at being stopped from doing what she's been doing since meeting him.

Naomi stood. "And on that note... You all have a delightful holiday. Cecily: twice a week?"

"Yes. I'll be here." She studied the floor.

"Head up, Cecily. You have my special number if you need me sooner. Consider it the 'DNA hotline.'"

Oscar tilted his head, looking more annoyed than curious. "Huh?"

Cecily's mouth curved upward with mild amusement. "D-N-A: Dr. Naomi Alexander."

Naomi grinned back with a nod and shrug.

"Cute. But what about me?"

Cecily gawked at him.

Naomi frowned at him (refraining from saying, *What about you?*). What did he want her crisis number for? He wasn't her patient—not in the actual sense. Oh, he needed psychiatric help—but that was a different matter. "Cecily's the focus, Oscar."

"Right. It's only about me sometimes."

Naomi didn't respond. She smiled at Cecily. "After New Year's."

She beamed back. "Okay. Have a Merry Christmas and prosperous New Year."

Naomi smirked at her.

Chuckling, Oscar settled his cap back on his head. "You sound like a greeting card, Cecil." He retrieved a small Altoid mint container from his pocket, depositing a white pellet on his tongue.

Naomi noted the intentional mispronunciation but didn't react.

Cecily's smile faltered, something like pain rippling through her countenance. "Sorry, I know." She looked at her husband, a weak warning in her eyes as she shook her head.

Oscar's chuckle grew into light laughter. "I'm just teasing. Stop being so sensitive." He sent his gaze toward Naomi with a bright smile of dim beige. "It's just a nickname, but she gets so uptight."

It wasn't a kind nickname from what Naomi could tell, despite Oscar's joviality over it, but some things Cecily had to do herself. And it would come, but later.

Cecily chuckled, the sound uncomfortable to Naomi's ears. "I'm n-not uptight. Oscar has such a w-weird sense of h-humor, that's all."

That wasn't all, but the session timer would sound any minute, and Naomi was moving into a mental space where her analytical neutrality was fading fast. She could be in-your-face, but she did it tactfully and with good timing; she was slowly losing that position with this couple—she had to keep Cecily's health at the forefront. Denying her sensitivity and offense to the nickname under the excuse of Oscar's weird sense of humor was nothing but a defense mechanism. *"Cecil."* Naomi scoffed inward. *Nickname my ass.* She extended her hand to Oscar, sending her eyes upward to look in his. "Be well."

Oscar's hand claimed hers, his palm sweaty-moist. "A'ight, Home Skillet. Happy Holidays."

Naomi pulled her hand back. If he calls her that next session, it will be the very next thing on the agenda. "Thanks." She turned to Cecily. "And I have a token for you..." Naomi walked over to her credenza and opened the side panel: a tiny gift bag sat shelved inside. She retrieved it and came back to Cecily, gift bag extended.

An odd light filled Cecily's eyes, suggesting gifts were a rarity. "Thank you. Can you give gifts?"

No. "It isn't a gift like that; it's in line with therapy. You can wait to open it at home."

Cecily glanced in Oscar's direction, and Naomi envisioned him badgering her about it (and not kindly) as soon as they were out of earshot.

Oscar leaned closer, peering toward the bag, his posture almost threatening, but Naomi remained quiet.

Cecily reached inside the bag, an anticipatory smile bending her lips. Naomi didn't know whether to be touched or saddened by Cecily's excitement upon revealing the contents. "Oh, cool! Relaxation CDs." There were three; she turned the top one over, reviewing it.

"So now everyone knows. Convert them to whichever digital listening format you prefer, but put them to use between sessions."

Cecily nodded, still excited over receiving the CDs.

"Have a pleasant holiday. Spoil that grandson."

Cecily wore a hesitant smile (the true hurt from that nickname still in her eyes). "Of course. You have grandchildren?"

Naomi thought of Leslie. "Not just yet."

Oscar scoffed. He smirked as he studied the floor, shaking his head, and Naomi knew what that was about: the idea of her having sex and making children didn't reconcile inside him.

Cecily's eyes flitted as if she, too, got the same meaning.

Both women ignored him as Cecily extended her hand.

Naomi shook firmly.

"Is... Is your arm okay?"

"Just fine. Don't apologize."

Cecily's mouth transitioned from uttering the automatic apology into a smile. "Okay." She pulled her hand back and headed for the door (giving her gift bag a tiny shake).

Oscar saluted with his Redskins cap and followed his wife.

It was silent as Naomi watched the couple leave her office and close the door. She heard Oscar wishing Veronica holiday greetings, calling her "Home Skillet" as they departed.

Already packed for an extended time away from her professional office, Naomi picked up her mug and finished what remained of her tea. She turned to the door as it opened, and Veronica popped her head in, wearing this smirk of annoyed incredulity.

Naomi let out a muted laugh. "I know. I'll speak to him about it when they return after the holidays. I don't like it, either."

Veronica's smirk changed to an appreciative grin. "Good. That it?"

"Pretty much: session summary and next session framework. I'll handle it. Enjoy your holiday. Be safe, Doctor Stewart."

Veronica's smile brightened. "Thanks, Doctor Alexander. You, too." She closed the door.

Naomi entered her private bathroom to rinse her mug, ready to visit her family.

The afternoon sun warmed some of the chill off the forty-three-degree temperature outside, but as she rang the doorbell, Naomi believed she experienced some residual indirect internal coolness from that session with the Brooks couple. She heard multiple footsteps before the door pulled wide, Rick Phillips smiling brightly as he held his son. "Sup, Sis!? Ha! Love the sweater!"

Lord have mercy. "Thank you. Hi." Grinning, Naomi stepped inside, giving RJ a tickle causing him to giggle and squirm in his father's arm.

Rick gestured at her sweater with his free hand. "So, you go'n be ready for Christmas Day, then?" The plan was for everyone to wear either ugly Christmas sweaters or football jerseys from their favorite teams. The vote went for the ugly sweaters.

"Oh, I'm covered. There's more where this came from." Smiling, she leaned up and Rick leaned down for a kiss in greeting, their cheeks brushing with respective pecks. He smelled of some deliciously wonderful— "Well, my goodness!" Naomi swept her gaze around their foyer, across the living and dining rooms, into where she could see parts of the kitchen and family room: Christmas every damn where!

Naomi laughed. She lowered her packages to the floor and hollered.

Viv came in laughing, shooing and shushing her while swiping at her in fun. "I know! Stop laughing!" She hugged her.

Naomi was so busy cracking up, she could only return a partial hug.

Rick chuckled. "Just give her a minute..."

Amused to her core and holding her belly, Naomi backed toward the chair in the foyer and sat, the Phillipses gazing at her with happy eyes. Rick and RJ wore jeans and T-shirts, socks but no shoes, while Viv wore gray capris, a black tank top, and slides (her toes polished neon-green). "Okay. Okay. Wooo! ...Okay. Just..." Naomi surveyed the house again: the pine garland wrapping the banister—with tiny white

Christmas bulbs woven inside blinking merrily—sent her into bales of laughter again.

She soon had Rick and RJ laughing.

Viv, her lustrous chestnut hair tousled with bangs, held out for as long as she could—and broke down, too.

The four laughed (RJ following his parents' lead) until Naomi could finally pull it together. "Wh-Where's Alna?" A new arrangement of family portraits adorned the wall behind Rick.

Rick put RJ down. "She's downstairs with Zenobia."

RJ headed into the kitchen-family-sunroom area and disappeared, calling his sister's name—or something close to her name.

Viv reached down for Naomi's packages. "Yeah. Zen's been here, or Al's been at her house since the school break started. They're getting their science project out of the way. I'll put these under the tree. Come on here."

"Yeah, before we wake my dad." Rick extended a hand to Naomi.

Naomi playfully smacked it away. "Please." She stood, hoping to see Rick's father, Eugene.

Her brother backed away with a grin. "A'ight, a'ight. No need for violence."

Chuckling, everyone headed in the direction RJ disappeared.

Naomi settled on her customary barstool as Viv went over to this big-ass Christmas tree in the corner of their family room. Naomi just shook her head. She noticed Mrs. Phillips had quite the pep in her step as she moved about. "So, how'd you like the cookies?"

Grinning broadly, Rick thumbed toward the fridge. "Stopped and bought another box before we came home."

"Guess you liked them fine."

His expression suggested *Damn skippy*, but he didn't say it.

She missed hearing that from him.

A chessboard with pieces situated mid-game sat over by the fireplace. Naomi gestured in its direction. "Whose move?" She heard RJ downstairs with his sister and her friend.

"Rick's."

Naomi stared at the positions. "Hmm... Good game. How long?"

"Two days. Get you something?" At the fridge, Rick's gaze turned inquiring. "We have olives."

Touched, Naomi grinned but shook her head. "Not now. I'll get it when I'm ready."

Rick raised a mischievous eyebrow. "There's something, like sweet buttermilk, in there, too."

Naomi returned a knowing smirk. "I don't doubt it."

Rick winked.

Naomi enjoyed that wink and eyed the entry wall, taking pleasure in viewing the big spoon (three and a half feet long). With its ornate artistry along the handle and inside the bowl, the wooden spoon hung vertically, awaiting Viv completing the fork to fill the space next to it. Viv finished the spoon a couple months ago, and the fork had been her newest distraction effort. But Rick was home; the specific need for distraction was over. Naomi wondered when the fork would find its way to its walled companion, figuring that spoon may be lonely for a time (and who knew when she'd start on the knife).

The television was on: *Merry Christmas, Charlie Brown* frozen mid-play. Viv reached for the remote. "He's not watching this now..."

No sooner had the screen gone blank, when young Master Phillips bounded into the kitchen from the basement and then into the family room. RJ (having turned two last month) possessed energy Naomi didn't remember seeing before. He considered the dark television screen and then looked up at his mother.

Rick laughed low. "You can watch it later, little man. Time to eat first; take your nap. Come on."

His mother's disrespectful treatment of his television viewing forgotten, RJ grinned and grabbed his miniature dump truck from the center table and returned to the kitchen—and his father.

The interaction was notable to watch, RJ's behavior quite understandable. He was only two, but he was still a person; with fears and concerns—even those he couldn't express clearly. RJ responded to Rick's entrance into his life quickly, fully. Perhaps Viv's careful reinforcement of who Rick was over RJ's beginning years helped solidify the transition and acceptance. Or maybe the boy just looked at the man, noticed the uncanny resemblance—and subconsciously understood the man's importance in his young life. Who knows?

Naomi only now noticed R&B and Soul Christmas music playing low from the entertainment center. "Winter Wonderland" by the Miracles was on. Christmas every damn where. A storage bin marked "Kwanzaa" sat near the entrance to the sunroom. Rick and Viv had a beautiful home: cozy, despite the grand interior.

Rick started unhooking the table portion of RJ's highchair.

"No. Sit *down*." RJ pulled a chair from the kitchen table and maneuvered his little self into it. He began rolling the dump truck tabletop while he waited. Naomi noticed he used his left hand more and more, but it was still too early to know his handedness.

Viv chuckled as Rick re-latched the tray to the rejected highchair.

Naomi chuckled, too. "Well, somebody's asserting more independence."

Rick grinned and moved toward the stove, stopping RJ's truck-roll on the table. He rubbed his son's head as he passed him. "Play with it on the floor, RJ, not the table." He headed to the stove, where Naomi could see (and smell) he'd already prepared something for his son's lunch. Viv cooked, but she often said Rick enjoyed it more than she did.

RJ left his seat at the table, pulling his dump truck to the stone-tile flooring to play with it there.

"Yeah. Since Rick's been home, that little boy doesn't want to do anything he doesn't see his father doing. Rick doesn't sit in a highchair, so now, this. Come on in here, Naomi. Let the menfolk occupy the kitchen."

Naomi left her barstool and stepped down into the family room, taking her usual spot in the leather lounger. She noticed something akin to a story portrait gallery on the wall across from the entertainment center: pictures (some new, others not so much) designated members of Alna and RJ's family tree. The framed pictures surrounded a vintage "Waiting Room for Colored Only" sign; the additional, more subtle meaning didn't escape Naomi. She'd check the wall out later. It was a beautiful display; Viv must have been excited while putting it together.

Viv sat on the sofa, patting the area beside her. "No. Sit *down*."

Naomi changed her seating, both women laughing at Viv's sweet mimic of her son. With Rick several yards away in the kitchen, their discussion was still private. Nat King Cole's "The Christmas Song" played on low. She sat back. "So, catch me up."

Viv shifted closer and sat forward, turning her body more toward her. "Well, first—"

"And don't thank me again."

Viv focused those coal-like irises on her with a wry grin. "Oh. Okay, fine. Well, the Smithson and the Spirit of Baltimore were nice, as always. There were walks along the harbor. We took body-shots off each oth—"

"Viv, you didn't start that last load, did you?"

Viv looked over at her husband, shaking her head. "No. Why?"

"Go'n put our shirts in."

"That's fine. RJ's pajamas from last night are still upstairs, so..." Viv returned her attention to Naomi and lowered her voice. "Now, where—?"

"Body-shots." Naomi grinned, lowering hers, too.

Wearing a sweet yet secretive smirk, Viv lifted and curled a foot under her and leaned closer, smelling of sandalwood and camellia. "Yes. And well, we took care of pressing necessities."

"I'm sure."

Viv sighed with a blush. "Girl, he stuck the needle on this record and played a beautiful symphony...for hours, working that Rock of Gibraltar in his pants like..." She lowered her head and shook it.

Naomi chuckled.

"We prayed together first, though. And then it was on, that man reminding me of positions I'd forgotten about." Viv lowered her head with another shake. "My husband's marketing career has some amazing side benefits from his creativity. We did some things in that suite..." She paused and shivered with erotic memory before lifting her head with another sigh. "Naomi, I wanted it everywhere." She raised an eyebrow. "He put it *everywhere*." Viv shifted her attention to Rick (busy in the kitchen with RJ) for several seconds before turning back to Naomi. "And God bless America."

Naomi almost hollered but, wanting to keep their discussion low-key, laughed low instead.

Viv laughed with her before growing more serious. "Hearing Rick's soft moans, his low, masculine grunts and nasty words of arousal, the change in his breathing with his excitement, Naomi: music to my ears. I'm more aurally-focused regarding sex; I like to 'hear' it: words, emoting sounds, noises from physical contact. So, finally being able to hear Rick once again being a man with me was just..."

She knew these things about Viv already. "Heaven. I get it, Viv: a near-thousand-day wait."

Mrs. Phillips sighed her relief at that being over. "One of the main things we did, something we'd both been sorely missing, yearning to do: wash each other's hair—so arousingly personal. But there were also periods of lying in the dark with Rick and talking, the music low..."

"Sounds cozy."

Viv wore this women-only expression confirming the summation. "Oh yes. And Rick's taken up smoking a pipe on occasion: like his dad."

Naomi nodded, knowing what that meant for her friend. It was also favorable info: men smoking a pipe seemed a lost indulgence of cool. Cigars were the rage now, but a man smoking a pipe... "You already enjoy kissing him when he's had his bourbon, but now, with the added flavor of pipe tobacco mixed with the bourbon on his tongue..."

Viv grinned. "I can't stand cigarettes, and Rick can't, either, so that works out. It's not a regular thing with his pipe; mindful tobacco is tobacco. But, girl, when it happens..."

"It's a treat," Naomi concluded.

"Fuck the dumb stuff." She rolled her eyes with teasing but excited exasperation. "But now, I'm learning all these tobacco-pipe terms: Billiards, Apples, and Canadians; stems, shanks, chambers, and bits. Getting shotgun kisses from him..." Viv's eyes had that sparkle from Manje—but intensified. "Just as nice as weed to me: the flavors in the smoke, on his tongue." Viv blushed. "We, uh, we did it on the balcony, with the view of the harbor. Thankfully, it was a mild night. Being on the balcony, both of us naked under Ricky's coat, him making my body feel like the Fourth of July." She glanced toward the kitchen. "Naomi, Ricky is very... He's very... Put it this way: Rick is quite intuitive and attentive regarding the female anatomy. He doesn't just 'call it in' if you know what I'm saying."

Naomi nodded. Listening to this was just plain-old fun.

"Women have differing needs, but Rick's basic shit has universal female appeal. He doesn't do the courtesy kiss and squeeze, then be ready to get his. Rick's never been like that. He gets it's not just his dick I want; I want his hands, his mouth, his whatever, giving me pleasure."

"Right."

Viv made this odd expression, part-secretive, part-arousal, then closed her eyes before looking at her. "Although his erection alone is enough to get me there."

Naomi chuckled, having little doubt about that. *Nine inches...*

"Out on that balcony, Rick stood behind me, his fingertips at my waist, and kissed down, from my nape to the small of my back. Gently nipping all over me while his hands—" Viv closed her eyes with a shiver. "His soft lips and the brush of his facial hair as he moved his mouth over me..." Viv looked at her. "I learned his philosophical approach to sex our first time, and it's a wonderful philosophy, Naomi."

"I'm guessing you've put those toys away."

Viv hoisted her shoulders. "They no longer serve as a substitute for him, but..."

"As an addition to the fun."

"You got it. And we have toys for him, too, so..." Viv giggled like a schoolgirl (an endearing sound).

Naomi shook her head with amusement. "You two are not playing."

"Nope. We're picking up where we were in our marriage before shit went south, but remembering shit did go south. If that makes sense."

"It does."

Viv nodded, looking over at her husband. "Have you ever kissed for a half-hour, straight?" She turned to her.

"Maybe a full minute, but a half-hour?" Naomi shook her head.

"Twenty-seven minutes. Until we could finally fall asleep. It wasn't all heated tongue-action. But we took time, with our mouths, to 'talk' to each other without speaking. That man's mouth..." Viv shook her head. "Twenty-seven minutes, girl. In the dark? With slow jams playing softly?" She winked. "Try it. It doesn't have to be R-and-B slow jams." Viv grinned. "Try it with your Bach or Boulogne or Brahms or Chopin or whoever. Price, Vivaldi."

"Well, if I did, it wouldn't be soon."

Viv searched her eyes. "It's time to call him, Naomi. I doubt Kevin has moved on; he's really into you."

"That's what I'm cautious about, Viv."

Viv scoffed. "Sounds more like fear than 'caution,' but okay. It's time to call him."

"Listen to you! Anyway, I've been thinking about it."

"No more thinking. ...Seems maybe you haven't moved on, either."

Spotting several blanket throws on the sofa, Naomi grinned, noting two throws in particular: one for Howard University (Viv's) and one from

George Mason University (Rick's). Each had graduate degrees from the University of Maryland, but she didn't see a representative throw from that institution. "You two have been true couch potatoes."

Viv grinned. "Mainly to binge-watch several shows down here, catching up on the ones we watch together, yeah." Her expression sobered. "Don't change the subject."

Silence between the women followed. Naomi stared at the Phillipses' coffee table, suddenly immensely interested in RJ's book on beginning dictionary words.

"Do you love him, Naomi?" Viv spoke with concerned friendship.

Viv was her friend. She was (the list wasn't long to begin with). But Naomi considered mental and emotional explorations something that originated with *her* and flowed outward to others—not the other way around. The seconds grew full and ripe with wait for Naomi's answer. Running through the last couple years of her life in a matter of seconds, she had the answer; it just wouldn't travel over her tongue—not readily.

Her friend waited patiently, while in the kitchen, Rick and RJ engaged in a quiet but lengthy discussion about animal sounds. She scanned the family room. The only picture of Rick Naomi remembered being on display was the wedding photo in their dining room, but Viv was on a mission to return the house to normal: a childhood picture of Rick now rested on the console table. It was a school photo of him in his uniform (navy tie and white shirt). He looked 12 or 13, beginnings of facial hair, big smile with braces shining, the red eyes suggesting the photographer snapped too closely to the lens—but he didn't. A childhood picture of Viv and Patrice rested beside it. Viv enjoyed woodwork; she made the console table—a lovely piece of furniture.

"...Yes." Naomi expected her answer to emerge soft and hesitant from her lips, but it didn't. Once upon a time (while on a date at Six Flags America), she'd prematurely told Kevin she loved him. But that was then.

Viv reached over and popped her leg. "Phase one complete."

Naomi shrugged; that much was true, she guessed. She sensed Viv's eyes on her as she focused on the airplane and kangaroo on the cover of RJ's dictionary. A few Louis L'Amour books were stacked: western novels from Rick's youth. Maybe he was getting back into them. Several Donald Goines novels were also present, two from the Kenyatta series.

"The Good House" by Tananarive Due was opened but turned pages down on the table (a horror reread for Viv).

"I hope... I hope I'm not overstepping when I say Tyson would approve, Naomi. As you once said: it takes nothing away from what you had with him."

Naomi stared at the violin on the cover of RJ's book, reflecting on that conversation she'd had with Viv some years ago while dining in DeTante's restaurant. She indeed said something similar to Viv regarding Viv's situation with Rick and Jonathan Rast. Given the circumstances of what happened to him, Jonathan's family chose not to sue, so (thankfully) Rick and Viv didn't have the added ordeal of a civil suit, too.

In the kitchen, RJ made his points on the beauty of dog barks, while his father countered with his views on the sounds cows and horses made.

Naomi shook her head. "You're not overstepping, Viv."

"You know, I still relive that moment Mark shifted, and my husband, the absolute love of my life, was sitting behind him. So, phase two: call Kevin, Naomi. Get it back. Get it on. *Live*, Naomi."

Naomi glimpsed the room, scanning randomly.

"What?"

"With all this philosophical illumination, just looking for the meditation mats, the Buddha, and the incense."

They laughed at that, and then Viv turned serious again. "I'm not saying everything is all lollipops and unicorns. We've already had a few tiffs since he's been home. Two of them were on me, and the one on him was because of me, but we'll leave some credit on his side just the same." Viv winked. "We're not over here in some romantic fantasy world, but for us now, the imperfections enhance, not detract. I know that sounds hokey, but that still sums it: because I also remember running up the stairs to find my husband..." Her lips turned downward before she startled from that sad memory. "So, call him, Naomi. Call Kevin."

She would. She didn't know when, but she would. And just maybe, she knew what she was going to say.

Viv looked over at Rick. She turned back to Naomi, holding her gaze. "What is it, Viv?"

"The first time Rick cheated, and...well, maybe even the other two..."

"Uh-huh...?"

"It wasn't dispassionate. Wasn't just a dick-thing."

"I see. Blaming yourself a little for those, are you?"

Viv scoffed with a headshake. "You've got to quit with that shit, girl."

Naomi smirked at her.

"I guess. There's no excuse for it bottom-line, but I... I get it."

"You believe you gave him reason to feel justified."

Viv dipped her chin in concession.

"You chea—?"

Viv shook her head. "When it all started, no. But there was an occasion, involving my ex, where I did something giving Rick every reason to believe I cheated. And then, that second time, it was after Halsey—"

"You can stop right there, Viv."

"And just like that, you've filled in the blanks."

Naomi shrugged. "I've spent half my life exposed to all kinds of human behavior and relationship scenarios, Viv. Comes with the territory."

"Yeah, but still."

"So, in therapy, when you asked why..."

Viv shrugged with a sigh. "When he thought I cheated, he cheated. Although it wasn't the case then, it was a tit-for-tat deal for him. It was early in our marriage. We were adults but young, not mature in that respect, so okay, I can understand it some. But then, when I struggled and wanted nothing to do with him for over a year after Halsey: he cheated. That last time, we were having problems, big fights over having another baby. Believe it or not, I was ready; Rick wasn't. It created a wedge between us, I guess; so, he cheated. I wanted to know why, whenever we were having major issues, why that was always the fucking route for him to take, you know?"

Naomi nodded her understanding, remembering their cryptic uses of *go-to* and *resorting*, and Rick's *not really* when they were in therapy with her. They never circled back to explore it further—and here it was.

"And then that motherfucker said, 'because he could.'"

"Viv..."

"I'm good. It still pisses me off sometimes, but not drastically. Just... Argh! Men! You know?"

Naomi chuckled with a nod. She steadied her gaze on her friend. "So, what would you have wanted his course of action, his response to whatever was happening, to be? To wait it out? Talk it through?"

"Both. I mean, shit, marriages have crises sometimes. It's not a free pass to— Anyway, I'm saying, let's get to the other side of it, talk it out. We always talked through the other shit we went through, so—" Viv shook her head. "No. Therapy is over. *That's* over—all of it. We didn't delve extensively years ago, but we covered the gist. We've gone over it, and we get where we went wrong. Moving on. The end."

Naomi laughed. "Okay. Gotcha, sweetie. You're right."

Viv looked over at Rick. "Girl, I was so horny for my husband while he was away. Of course, I was. Those quickies were good, they helped, but they didn't allow for how we like to roll. But I don't know what to call what I'm feeling for Ricky now that he's home. It's hotter than just wanting sex with him. Sometimes I want him so badly, I think I might hurt him. My head fills with all kinds of X-rated stuff I think might put the fire out." Viv turned to her. "And I'm talking *triple-X*, my psychiatrist friend."

Naomi grinned.

"It's a constant, sensual *ache* for him. It's too bad God didn't make them like us, with the ability to engage back-to-back-to-back without pause. Rick can repeat, but not like what I'm talking about. Because, with what I'm feeling for my husband, his dick would be out his pants every five minutes."

Naomi hollered; Viv was something else. She also knew Rick's ability to repeat was part natural, part...something else.

"What's so funny over there?"

Viv winked at her man. "Girl-talk. Mind your business."

"Yeah, a'ight, Lady Blue."

Naomi knew Viv would share some of their discussion with him later. "How'd Louise do?"

"...When we arrived at Tim and Lou's to pick up the kids, she held on to my husband, Naomi, for a long time."

"What?"

Viv's nod was sad. "Even Tim looked at *me* funny. I didn't comment, but I don't know how things will play out now that Ricky's home. I've implied knowing the real, but have said nothing to Lou 'officially.' I mean, how do you tactfully broach that conversation? *'Hey Lou, we're supposed to be tight, like sisters, but check this: I know you're in love with my husband and once caught him off-guard with a kiss'...*" She shook her head with a shrug. "We're still friends, sort of, but we don't hang like we used to; things're different now."

Hearing the way Viv said "Ricky," Naomi knew Viv didn't limit using that affectionate moniker to general conversation regarding her husband. She also sighed it, whispered it, moaned it—in the heat of passion with him.

"You know she visited him biweekly?"

Naomi just looked at her. Biweekly certainly wasn't necessary.

"I know. Would've been more often, but, well, he has the nerve to be married to me and seeing me at least weekly."

"She didn't mention the visits to you?"

"A time or two, but overall, no. Rick told me."

"So...?"

"Rick was ready to hurt her feelings, reject her visits. But I told him, no, just tell her it'd be better if she brought Tim with her."

"Big of you. And did she?"

"Eventually." Viv released a hissing breath. "She's been calling, texting: wanting to set up time to get together and hang. But it's tainted, Naomi. When Rick was locked up, she didn't make this much effort for the two of us to get together, repair what's left of our friendship. *Now,* all this interest? It's just efforts for her to be around Rick."

"Sorry, sweetie."

Viv shrugged. She shook her head with a frown of anger morphing into an expression of regretful indecision. "Part of me wants to cuss her ass out, Naomi. I do. Just lay into her ass, punch her dead in her face, and be done. But I'm trying to be bigger than that. Trying to be less 'straight-no-chaser' and take that high road of tolerance and understanding. Trying *so* hard."

They shared a brief laugh, and Viv looked toward the kitchen for quiet seconds, watching Rick with their son.

Naomi went quiet, watching her friend.

A soft smile brightened Viv's face.

"What, Viv?"

Viv looked at her, eyes shining. "His side of the bed isn't empty anymore."

Naomi nodded with a warm smile of her own. "No, it isn't." She sat forward. "What're you guys doing at the end of January?"

Viv rolled a shoulder. "Al has her violin recital that week; other than that, nothing. Still wrapping our heads around the flurry of this past week."

"Great. I have tickets to this annual charity formal—"

"The Wonderland of Giving Ball?" Viv's eyes widened.

Naomi smiled. "You know it?"

"Yes! We haven't been since the year before Rick was— Anyway, those tix sell out by October."

"True. A select few of us get plenty freebies to invite our doctor associates. I write a check, but don't go every year. I try to go every few years. Interested?"

"Of course." She shifted to rise. "Let me get the checkbook..."

Naomi settled her back down. "Key word: *freebie*."

Viv shook her head. "Key word: *giving*. We'll check online for the sponsored charities this year and pick one." A cheerful grin swept her face. "I'm excited! Thank you." She leaned and hugged her, filling Naomi's nostrils with the oils of sandalwood and camellia.

"You're more than welcome. Stop by and get your tickets. I'll have four for you."

"Bet. How's tomorrow?"

"That's fine."

"Inviting Kevin?"

Naomi laughed. "You don't quit, do you?"

Viv's eyes changed again, more solemn than before. "Black love must thrive, Naomi. No, I don't."

Naomi considered Viv's words. "You're right. But I'm still not sure about everything yet."

Viv shrugged. "Get sure."

"Viv, come here a minute. You, too, Sis. Look at this..."

Naomi rose with Viv and entered the kitchen; Carla Thomas's "Gee Whiz, It's Christmas" floated around them.

With lunch over, Rick had given RJ a brief pass to play with his truck (and food) tabletop. RJ Phillips used his left hand to transfer peas from his plate to the dump bed of his truck, his little face stern with concentration. The peas were a perfect size for the small truck. He took one from the bed and ate it. Remnants of gravy, mashed potatoes, and bits of roasted chicken dotted his plate. The milk in his cup was half-gone. RJ backed the truck to his plate and dumped the peas onto it with a toddler laugh. A bright and solid tangerine color suddenly surrounded the toddler (visible to no one but her), and Naomi's heart warmed from the figurative 'sun' of joy surrounding Rick and Viv's son.

The adults chuckled as Rick reached for his wife, guiding her under his arm. He kissed her temple as she leaned on him.

Alna and Zenobia came up from the basement, giggling about something 12-year-old girls found funny. Alna sighed. "There. Finished and ready for Miss Norton's class. Hi, Doctor Alexander." Smiling (her face an echo of her mother's), Alna approached and hugged her tight.

Naomi hugged back. "Hi, Alna. Got that science project done and out of the way, huh? Rest of the holiday free?"

Alna gazed at Naomi's sweater with a chuckle and a kind headshake. "Too much." She nodded. "Yeah. Daddy made me. But I'm glad."

Zenobia moved to the refrigerator. "I'm glad, too, Doctor Alexander." She retrieved a bottle of apple juice. "If I'd had another partner for this project, I know we'd be rushing to come up with something the weekend before returning to school. Thanks, Mister Phillips." Zenobia felt right at home as she went to the cabinet for a small plate and then helped herself to some mashed potatoes and gravy (although she'd be better off with some yogurt or a salad; she was cute, but on the chunky side).

"You're welcome, Zen." Rick looked over at Naomi, gesturing toward the stove.

Potato peelings in the sink (for the garbage disposal, she imagined): the mashed potatoes were from scratch. The peas: frozen, not canned. Rick also prepared spinach. The food looked and smelled good, but Naomi shook her head. "Maybe later."

"Your son almost ruined a week's work when he came downstairs." Alna rolled her eyes tongue-in-cheek.

Rick sat at the table with his son, wearing this tiny grin. "Almost, but he didn't. Focus on the upside."

Alna set eyes on her father, a mischievous grin bending her lips. "Share your peas with Daddy, RJ." She snickered.

Rick's gaze at his daughter combined warning and humor. His relationship with her was cute already.

"Yeah, sweetie," Viv said, chiming in on her daughter's semi-prank on Rick, "give Daddy some peas, too."

RJ lit up with a big grin. "Peas!" He reached for one from his truck, holding it outward for his father to eat.

Rick glanced at Viv. "I'm go'n get you for this."

"Mm... I sure hope so."

Naomi chuckled as Rick allowed his son to put a pea in his mouth.

Rick chewed the pea with a pained, smiling expression, trying to appear as if he considered peas a good thing.

Alna giggled. "Peas are *good*. Aren't they, Daddy?"

Still holding that frozen expression of false enjoyment, Rick nodded and chewed.

RJ clapped, not old enough to detect his father's lack of sincerity.

"That's right: watch Daddy eat his veggies, too, RJ," Viv chirped.

RJ giggled, "Peas!" and put another in his father's mouth.

Rick spoke through that fake (albeit still gorgeous) smile while chewing. "Viv..."

"I know; you're getting me later. I can't wait." The loving heat between the couple was palpable.

Zenobia blushed to high heaven.

"You have several more to go, Daddy." Alna snickered, and everyone except Rick chuckled.

When RJ reached for another pea, Rick pulled back and stood. "A'ight. Good job, man. All finished!"

The ladies laughed while RJ started trying to get down.

Rick stopped him. "Daddy's go'n wipe your face and hands first, man."

RJ waited patiently, and Naomi was impressed.

Rick went to the sink and rinsed his mouth. Viv chuckled as he retrieved the pitcher of sweet tea from the refrigerator, poured some, and gargled with it.

Naomi couldn't believe it. "Is it that bad, Rick?"

Rick finished his gargle and set the glass down. "Yes." At the sink, he dampened a paper towel.

"You don't like *any* vegetables, Mister Phillips?"

Viv turned to Zenobia. "He likes fries, some potato salad. Tomato sauces are okay for like spaghetti or pizza. He'll sometimes do onions, lettuce, and tomato on a burger or sandwich, maybe black olives or green peppers on our particular pizza. Other than that, no, sweetie: he's not a fan of anything else, anything *real*."

Naomi added an addendum. "Maybe if covered in peanut butter."

Rick and Viv chuckled at that, while Alna bobbed her head.

Rick wiped his son's face with care. "I like corn."

Viv shook her head. "You *tolerate* corn, baby." She shifted attention back to Zenobia. "But now he'll be downing them like they're delicious treats—just like he did for Al: carrots, broccoli, peas, squash..."

Rick tolled a quiet, unhappy groan. Finished wiping RJ's face and hands, Rick helped him down. "Nap in a minute, RJ." He took RJ's soiled shirt off and tossed it in the laundry room off the kitchen.

Viv moved to the table for his plate and cup. "You can play for a little while, sweetie."

RJ jetted to the corner of the family room where his toys were.

Naomi looked at his parents. "His room must be a toy store: there's never been much down here."

Viv shook her head. "Not much in his room, either."

"The 'toy store' is tucked away in the basement bedroom closet." Rick finished his tea.

"We decided, when he was in utero, to rotate those suckers on him," Viv relayed as she rinsed RJ's dishes, "instead of putting everything out at once."

Rick handed her his empty glass. "Oh yeah. Basic math. Except his Duplo Blocks: he enjoys those."

Zenobia dropped her fork to her plate. "Oooh! Do the song! Do that song!"

Alna went to the refrigerator while the other eyes fell on Zenobia.

Naomi looked around. "Song?"

Viv shook her head with a tiny smirk; Rick lowered his with the same.

Alna grabbed a spoon for the yogurt she retrieved. "Yeah. Mommy and Daddy act out the duet to 'Baby, It's Cold Outside.' It is kinda cool."

Viv smiled at her daughter. "Well, thank you, Al."

Alna shrugged with a grin and sat opposite Naomi at the island counter.

"So, do it. Please?" Zenobia scooped the last of her gravied-mashed.

Rick sent his gaze to his wife.

"I'd like to see it. Go ahead." Naomi smiled her encouragement.

Mr. and Mrs. Phillips exchanged a look as Rick went to the entertainment center.

Viv pulled a juice glass from the cabinet for her drink prop. Moments later, Vanessa Williams and Bobby Caldwell began their duet of "Baby It's Cold Outside," and Viv started her tuneful regretful rejection as Rick returned to the kitchen with his melodic plea in reply.

Zenobia struck the countertop with merriment.

It was "kinda cool" watching Rick and Viv act out the lyrics to the song, Rick moving close to cajole his woman into spending the night instead of heading out into the ice and snow. Viv flirted her waffling rejection, showing how much she wanted to stay despite propriety. The couple sounded good together (no surprise).

By song's end, Rick had a hand to Viv's waist, nuzzling her neck. He pointed the remote at the entertainment center and paused the music.

Naomi clapped with the girls, Zenobia cheering, "I love when they do that song!"

Viv blushed some as her husband's nuzzling intensified.

"Song's over, Daddy." Alna's half-grin contradicted her dry comment as she smirked sweetly at them. Watching her parents' pure affection and love for each other was healthy for her—especially because it wasn't new; she'd witnessed their affection since she was little. But seeing her parents' love survive such hardship carried lasting benefit.

Rick cleared his throat and pulled back with a peck to Viv's cheek. "Right." He stepped back into the family room and made a move on the chessboard while looking back at his wife, his Jimi Hendrix T-shirt and relaxed-fit jeans showing his toned physique.

Viv's scoff was lighthearted. "Yeah, okay."

Zenobia giggled. She made this googly-eyed expression at Alna, mouthing, *He is so fine*, and likely believing her interaction (regarding being smitten with her friend's dad) went unnoticed.

Naomi chuckled to herself as Alna returned an upward eye-rolling scoff with headshake. "Anyway. Can I go over to Zen's for a little while?"

"Well, I see we have a full house." Eugene Phillips stood in the areaway leading into the kitchen. Tall and lean, the elder Phillips personified Viv's description, reminding you of what a near-70 Sam Cooke would have looked like; he was pretty handsome—gray and all.

"Hi, Pa-Pa." Alna, positively enamored of her grandfather, moved over to him. She hugged him around his waist and put her head on his shoulder. "Did we wake you?"

Eugene voiced a warm, rumbling chortle. "No, Birdie." He kissed the top of Alna's head, then looked around at the others.

The interaction between Alna and Eugene reminded Naomi of Leslie with Boppa, Tyson's father. Boppa passed away last year; Leslie still showed signs of mourning his loss.

Viv turned to Naomi. "You know Naomi, Dad."

"I do. Naomi: the other 'daughter' I never had." He smiled at her. "Good seeing you. And I thank you for all you've done for my boy."

Naomi went to him, shaking the hand not wrapped around Alna. He smelled good, too: like wintry spices and hints of pipe tobacco. Her smile at him was full of care. "We're past the thank-yous. And yes, it is good meeting again."

Not a man of many words, Eugene returned a single nod.

Alna appeared thoroughly content to lean on her grandfather as Naomi returned to her barstool.

Zenobia finished her juice. "Hi, Papa Phillips. Ready, Al?"

Alna nodded and kissed her grandfather's cheek. She inquired of her mother: "Can I?"

Viv shook her head. "Not until Zen washes those dishes. And did you finish vacuuming upstairs?"

"Uh-huh. Before Pa-Pa laid down."

Naomi was again impressed. If Zenobia felt that much at home (helping herself to food and dirtying dishes), the Phillipses gave her the same responsibilities as if she were a part of their household.

Zenobia gathered the few dirty dishes and proceeded with the task.

"Hungry, Pa-Pa?" Alna looked up at him. When he shook his head, she pecked his jaw and went to finish putting the food on the stove away.

Eugene, however, wanted something: he moved to the fridge.

Rick stood by the entertainment center. "Viv, c'mere."

RJ was content for the time being, moving between the sunroom and his toys in the family room.

Knowing what Rick wanted, Viv kicked off her slides. "Excuse me..."

"White Christmas" by Otis Redding came on. Naomi looked over to see Rick drawing Viv close. The couple danced.

Everyone else went about their whatever, as if everything was regular, paying Rick and Viv little mind (although Naomi noticed Zenobia sneaking peeks over at them).

Papaya juice in hand, Eugene stepped down into the family room, sitting in the leather lounger. He watched his son and daughter-in-law, a gentle smile on his face.

Head lowered and eyes closed, Rick held Viv close, subtle mouth movement suggesting he spoke or sang low to his wife while Viv caressed his head.

His little hands holding toys Naomi didn't recognize, RJ came over to his grandfather and climbed into his lap: a sweet scene if ever there was.

No one spoke; only noises from the kitchen reorganization, the song, and RJ's "conversation" with his toys surrounded them.

When the song closed, Viv kissed Rick's cheek. "Me and You."

"You and Me, Viv. All the way." Rick held her gaze for a beat and then smiled as he pulled back, giving his father some dap before he stepped into the kitchen. Still smiling (the man was plain happy), he winked at Naomi.

Lord have mercy.

Naomi smiled back.

Rick sat at the table. "Make sure the basement is straight, too, Al."

"I will. Come on, Zen."

The girls hurried downstairs, Zenobia sending Rick a glance of adoration he didn't see.

Viv stood by the chessboard, studying it.

Eugene held his bottle of juice up and level for his grandson's consumption. "He's getting sleepy."

With a final slurp, RJ climbed down from Eugene's lap and returned to his toy corner before taking something into the sunroom.

Deciding Eugene's papaya juice looked mighty good, Naomi rose and headed for the fridge. She took the long route, wanting to satisfy her curiosity over something. Using her Big Sis status, as she passed Rick, Naomi sent a hand to his hair and semi-ruffled it: thick, full, the curls rough and dry. His roots weren't tightly-coiled nor silky-straight, giving the sensation to her fingers and palm of something crinkly-soft yet gently spiky—nice. She resisted grabbing into it. "Viv tells me you're smoking a pipe?" She moved to get her juice: the entire second shelf stocked with a variety of them.

"Check." Pulling her hand from the chessboard (she maneuvered the white pieces), Viv looked at Rick with this intriguing smirk.

Rick smirked back, grinning at his wife before responding to Naomi. "Yeah: few months now."

Naomi returned to her fave spot in their kitchen. "Like father, like son?" She opened her bottle and swigged thirstily.

Eugene chuckled as Viv joined them, slipping back into her slides. He hand-checked his shirt pockets with an acknowledging grin. "Speaking of which..." Soon after, a warm, cherry-woody scent wafted into the kitchen as Eugene Phillips puffed on this rather sizable pipe with a shape unlike ones she'd seen before.

Naomi didn't know, so she'd better ask somebody. "What type of pipe is that, Mister Phillips?"

Eugene turned his turtle-brown eyes on her. "'Eugene' is fine. Or 'Papa Phillips,' 'Pa-Pa,' or heck, even 'Dad.'"

Naomi sent him a warm-hearted smile. "I'll bounce between one or two of them."

Rick's father smiled back, and Naomi wondered why some female senior citizen hadn't snatched him right up. "I smoke my trusty Pot or Half-bent Billiard," he pointed to his pipe, "but I whip out, 'Maverick,' my big boy Oom-Paul here—especially during the holidays." Alabama cadence weaved through his speech.

Naomi decided she'd read up on tobacco pipes, gather some knowledge. She wouldn't have personal, private tutoring (as Viv received from Rick), but if the subject came up again, she could hold her own in a conversation.

Alna and Zenobia returned from the basement. "I moved it. It's set up at the back of the storage room: RJ's afraid to go in there."

Viv stood by Rick, her hand moving over her husband's hair, the fingers playing nimbly. "Good thinking. Okay, you can go. Back by five, Al; we're all going out."

"I know: dinner and the light show." Alna kissed her mother's cheek. She entered the family room and kissed her grandfather, who smiled up at her. "Bye, Pa-Pa." After a parting rub to her brother's head, she returned to the kitchen, her eyes on her father conveying a touching little-girl happiness and love for him. Her hug to Naomi was just as tight as her hello hug. "See ya later, Doctor Alexander."

"Bye, sweetie. Bye, Zenobia."

"You can call me 'Zen.'"

Naomi nodded, but she'd call the child what her parents named her.

Alna went to her dad and kissed his lips. "Back by five, Daddy."

"Okay. We'll practice some moves tomorrow."

Alna's eyes brightened. "For real?"

"Sure. It's something we've always enjoyed. The end."

She kissed his temple. "Okay. Bye."

"Be a lady." Rick's fatherly parting advice to his daughter moved through his caring gaze at her.

"Always, Daddy." Alna plucked her small purse from the chair seat next to Rick. "Come on, Zen."

Zenobia hugged Viv. "Okay. Bye, everybody!"

Everyone sent assorted parting words to her.

However, as Zenobia entered the laundry room to exit the house, she turned back. "See ya later, Mister Phillips!" She passed Viv and smashed a lengthy peck against Rick's cheek before dashing away.

Rick startled, looking dumbfounded as his wife hollered.

The girls were gone.

Naomi laughed, too.

Rick shook his head, leaving it alone, while Viv stepped inside the butler's pantry.

RJ began fussing with his toys, upset about something not happening his way.

"Told you he was getting sleepy." Eugene rose from his chair and picked up his grandson. "All right, little fella. You, the blocks, and that payloader need a break."

Head on Eugene's shoulder, RJ's lower lip poked in sad irritation.

"Yeah. It's time for his nap." Rick stood.

"'See ya later, *Mister Phillips*,'" Viv teased with a high-pitched, flirty voice, placing fresh napkins on the counter as she moved toward him.

Rick cleared his throat, blushing hard as Viv edged closer, and it was interesting to see. He exhibited continuous disquiet with compliments or interest regarding his physical aesthetics—even those from his wife. Naomi remembered seeing some of that during therapy with them years ago. However, Rick's blush vanished and changed to something more interesting when Viv reached him. "I got your 'Mister Phillips' right here, woman." He pulled his wife close and kissed her, his tongue moving with hers for a quiet moment as Viv cupped his cheek.

"Get 'er, Rick." Naomi chuckled and polished off her papaya juice, turning the bottle to check the label for the brand details; she'd have to get this brand in the future.

When they parted, Viv pushed Rick's forehead with a forefinger, shaking her head at him with a sweet smirk before turning to Naomi. "I told him Zen had a little crush on him already; he didn't believe me."

Shaking his head, Rick looked away, appearing uncomfortable again. Not quite blushing, but...uncomfortable and...sad. He wasn't a patient anymore, but Naomi wanted to explore the roots of this behavior: compliments bothered Rick—beyond self-deprecating embarrassment. Viv's empathetic expression as she looked at him and caressed his head, told Naomi Viv knew the root cause; she seemed sad, too.

Rick instantly welcomed the distraction of Eugene entering the kitchen, holding a sleepy-looking RJ.

Eugene set his pipe in this small porcelain bowl (containing Rick's yo-yo) on the counter. "I'll take him upstairs." He looked at his son. "Trip to the boneyard later? Round or two of Matador or All Fives before turning in."

"Sounds good," Rick said, with a grin showing how much he missed his father (playing dominoes or whatever).

RJ lifted his head and reached out for his daddy.

"Wait a minute, RJ." Rick grinned at his son, his paternal pride coming through. "Well, that's my cue. A'ight, Sis..." He came over to her, that smile of his creating some internal havoc.

Lord have mercy.

Naomi stood for the hug Rick wanted to give her.

He moved close, lowering his stance. Fingertips to her waist, he kissed her cheek; his way of greeting women he considered himself close to. "If you aren't here when I return, see you Christmas?"

"Christmas." He smelled deliciously of ambergris, violet leaves, and semi-woody verbena. The moment passed, but even without second-hand knowledge from Viv, the gentle pressure at her waist and the tender brush of his lips and mustache told her, au fond: Rick Phillips possessed extraordinary sexual prowess (she felt the same thing at Manje Trankil but ignored it). A knot of something quite inappropriate coiled between her legs. Naomi pulled back. "Excuse me, would you?"

Rick frowned. "You okay?"

Naomi grinned. "Just fine." She hurried to the powder room. Door closed, she paused before the mirror. "You know there're hordes of psychiatric terms to explain how and why you felt that way, don't you?"

Naomi stared at herself. Yeah, she knew plenty of terms, but none of them mattered. The only word that did? "...*Wrong*." She looked upward, gazing at the ceiling light fixture. "Where's the mercy I keep asking for?" Her faculties gathered, Naomi washed her hands and left the powder room with a chuckle: apparently, She wasn't dispensing any mercy right now—Naomi would just have to "suffer."

When Naomi emerged, Viv was the only one still downstairs; she sat on a barstool at the island counter, browsing a store catalog. Christmas music still played on low. Naomi paused next to the door leading to the basement and the adjacent wall, gazing upon a framed collage of pictures of RJ (also new since her last visit).

Viv joined her in front of the collage. "Rick and RJ."

Naomi gaped at her.

Viv nodded (she'd freshened her lip-gloss). "Yep: *both*. I restored some of Rick's childhood pictures from when he was the same age, then made it a point to eliminate as much background as possible. I've been working on it for months. You can't tell which is which, can you?"

Naomi moved her eyes over the pictures, doing her best to identify those of Rick.

Viv chuckled. "It's taking some time, I see." She viewed the collage, too. "Rick's 'mini-me.' I like saying: it's like they're twins, only thirty-eight years apart."

Naomi nodded, giving a faint titter. "You could say that, yeah."

"There's a difference. But I'll leave it to you to figure it out." Viv grinned with one brow arched.

"I'll try my best."

"Since he's been home, often when I look at Rick with RJ, I feel this crazy desire for him. It's weird; something about having given birth to his *son* turns me on in a way that's hard to explain."

"I think I understand, Viv." And she did. She remembered having similar feelings toward Tyson soon after Jassiel was born. But that...was a time long ago.

Viv stared at the collage. "His *second* son. Our rainbow baby. And that little face, looking like his daddy; he's such a sweet little boy, Naomi."

That was true.

"They should be asleep by now. Wanna go up?"

Naomi looked at her friend. "Rick, too? Already?"

Viv nodded. "When he sat at the table before the girls left, I knew he was sleepy. He's been up since yesterday. Rick has crazy energy, but even superheroes take naps."

Naomi chuckled, thinking about her newest patient's penchant for comic books.

Viv headed toward the foyer. "Come on. Let's peek in on 'em."

Naomi followed.

They paused outside the closed door of RJ's bedroom, and Viv kicked her slides off. She opened the door, and they entered a world of cars and construction vehicles.

Daylight filtering through only had the option of curving around room-darkening drapes—except for one window where the opened drapes allowed light.

Shirtless, sockless, Senior and Junior were on Junior's bed, RJ lying prone atop his father, his face in Rick's neck, Rick's right arm curled around him. Both were knocked out: RJ's breathing sounded mildly congested, Rick's low and even but deep. Gazing down at them, Viv spoke at a quasi-whisper: "Since Rick didn't get to be with RJ regularly as an infant, one way he bonds with him has been skin-to-skin naps."

Naomi watched the sleeping males, feeling maternal.

"RJ is very attached to his daddy, hardly wanting me."

Naomi spoke low. "Rick doesn't snore?"

Viv shook her head. "No. If he's, like, dead tired, maybe a little."

"I see we've retired *Sesame Street*." Wheel loaders, backhoes, dozers, and racecars had replaced the Big Bird and Elmo decorations, but the number of books multiplied, too. Still, his room wasn't a toy store.

Viv grinned and nodded, pointing at her husband. "He's been busy—and it's only been a week."

Naomi grinned as Viv turned away and started straightening RJ's books, puzzles, and cars in the corner. She used long seconds to run her eyes over Rick, moving from toe to head.

Given he practiced martial arts (something he still practiced and even taught while incarcerated), she expected gnarled, cracked toes and feet. But Rick's size-thirteens (she knew his shoe-size from events leading to his arrest years ago) were unblemished, the toes long and finely shaped. Light patches of fine hair brushed the midfoot. She moved her eyes upward, over the denim covering his legs and the swell representing a part of him for Viv's eyes only. Naomi continued her upward gaze, taking in the cinnamon-brown muscles sculpting his torso. *Lord, have mercy, I said.* Some 20-year-old men didn't look this good, let alone 40. His fraternity brand etched his right shoulder. The hit-master did excellent work: the scarring intricate but discernible and neat. RJ rested more on the right side of Rick's body: she noticed a tattoo over Rick's heart.

"This little boy..." Viv sighed as she straightened.

Naomi released a soft quasi-laugh.

Rick's tattoo was compelling: a bridge over roiling water. "*Vivian E.W. Phillips Lives Here*" displayed across the bridge decking. The wording below the image was harder to make out, but Naomi read: *My BOTW. TNP. Epic love.* The "BOTW" was clear: Bridge Over Troubled Water. But Naomi wasn't sure what "TNP" meant. An alluring line of fine hair trailed the middle of his abdomen, leading to what Naomi now titled his "Naughty-Nine" (that name was *porn-worthy*, wasn't it?). Suddenly flush, she joined Viv at RJ's play corner and helped her finish shelving the remaining books.

Done, they returned to stand closer to the sleeping males. Viv gazed down at them. "You know, the other day I peeped in on them, and this image turned me on so, I woke Rick up."

Naomi contained her chuckle. She looked around. "No binky, or blankie?"

Viv shook her head. "RJ doesn't have one, but this week, his 'binky-blankie' has been his father."

The chuckle surfacing this time was harder to keep down.

Viv grinned. "Yeah, seeing Rick and RJ do their father-son stuff is special. Rick took RJ to get a haircut and to the grocery store with him: a sweet moment. Girl,...I still remember the afternoon we likely made RJ...or even that sex a couple days later." She reached for Rick's hair and played lightly, making Rick sigh deeper into sleep. It went quiet as Viv gazed at her husband. "He... He gives me a contact-high."

That, for sure, went both ways. "What's 'T-N-P'?" Naomi whispered.

Viv turned away, using a thumb to lower the waistband of her capris at the back. Centered on her lower back at the base of her spine: a tattoo like Rick's with the bridge over roiling water, *"Rick A. S. Phillips Sr."* written on the bridge surface. Beneath the water-bridge image: *My BOTW Forever. TNP. Epic love.*

Viv turned back. "T-N-P: Take No Prisoners. I got mine a few months ago, after seeing his. That boy did *not* want me to add that 'S' in there."

Naomi didn't think Viv the type. She grinned. "You've both been busy. Never figured you to get a tramp stamp."

Viv returned a quick shoulder jostle. "It's about more than that. Much more. But whatever. This is a permanent-type deal I'm involved in here—till the death. I'm Rick's 'tramp'; as it should be."

Rick stirred.

Blushing, Viv resumed whispering. "He says he enjoys reading that when he's getting it from behind."

"I'm happy for you, sweetie."

"Thank you. I know I'm prattling, giving a little TMI, but I'm just so—"

"Don't explain; it's perfectly understandable, Viv. You and I: we say what it is. It's fine."

There was a long pause as Viv watched Rick and RJ. "...If this is a dream, Naomi, wake me up. Please. ...Because it means he isn't really here. And that's... Well, that's more of a nightmare, not a pleasant dream."

"Rick's home, Viv. No dream."

With a somber nod, Viv placed a soft peck on Rick's forehead and one to RJ's temple (making him snuggle deeper into his father). She lifted RJ's burgundy comforter partially over her husband and son, plucked RJ's pajamas from the foot of the bed, and tipped toward the door. "Come on. We did well to last this long without waking one."

They left Senior and Junior to their nap and peeked in on Eugene in the guest bedroom, who wasn't sleeping, but reading the newspaper and smoking his pipe, a talk-radio station playing on low from the alarm clock on the nightstand. He looked up and smiled at them.

Viv blew him a kiss and closed the door. "I love that man. Rick is a lot like him." She headed back downstairs. "Rick wanted to go down for him right after we picked up the kids."

"I'm sure Eugene was overjoyed."

Viv glanced her way upon reaching the foyer. "Brought me to tears."

Naomi didn't doubt it.

"So, we packed him up and brought him home for a few weeks—longer, if he wants. But if I know my father-in-law, two weeks will be enough before he hints about wanting to go home." Holding the clothing from RJ's bedroom, Viv headed for the laundry room.

Naomi paused before the family portraits. Yes, Viv had been busy, too. New professional photographs were taken, processed, and returned to Viv for framing—all in short order. There was a picture of Rick Naomi found captivating. Rick looked down and away to his left, in partial right profile; Viv's left hand rested against Rick's right cheek, her wedding set visible. Rick held Viv's left wrist, his wedding ring visible. Rick's expression in the portrait reflected contemplative melancholy: particularly appealing.

Viv returned. "Yeah, that's my favorite."

Naomi viewed the other pictures. Viv's photograph was similar: she looked to her right, in partial left profile, but looking more upward and smiling. Rick's left hand rested on her shoulder, his fingers touching her neck, his wedding band visible (hands well-groomed). Viv's left hand rested on her husband's (her wedding rings visible). The specific lighting on these two portraits accentuated Rick's and Viv's faces, the contact of their left hands. The eleven-by-fourteen-inch framed pictures were situated, not side-by-side, but such that they complemented—as if the couple gazed at each other: Rick down at Viv and Viv up at him.

There were also smaller-sized shots of Rick with RJ and with Alna, of Viv with RJ and with Alna, of the four of them together, of the couple alone, of the kids alone; the various shots representing both comical and calm elements.

Looking at Alna and RJ, both children amassed appealing features from each parent (sometimes the opposite happened). Although Naomi wasn't yet sure what RJ picked up from Viv. But it had to be something (Rick's sperm couldn't do the whole deal).

Viv tugged her arm. "Let's have some cider."

Christmas songs playing, Naomi helped herself to some lunch. Not a fan of peas, she had the spinach. Rick could burn; the man didn't like vegetables but knew how to cook and season them. After her meal, she sat on the sofa with Viv, sipping warm apple-cider garnished with cinnamon sticks, and chatting (Viv interspersing the conversation with subtle but sweet pleas regarding Kevin's case for a relationship renewal).

Naomi didn't let it show, but she received the messages kindly.

Viv was discussing a letter from one of Rick's dalliances, when "White Christmas" by the Drifters came on.

Naomi froze. This song was important on a level derived from the flash of truth moving through her.

Viv leaned close, her voice conveying concern. "Naomi, you all right?"

Naomi stared at Viv, listening to the Drifters, her mind racing with jumbled, unclear images from a night and place where she wasn't present.

Viv shook her. "Naomi!"

She needed to play this song during Cecily's therapy. "I'm okay, Viv. Sorry. Had a thought about treatment for a patient."

Viv sighed her relief. "Oh. Okay."

Naomi stood. "I want to hear more about that letter, but I'm gonna scoot. You'll be through tomorrow?"

Viv nodded as she rose. "Rick and I will, yeah."

"Cool. Rick's never been to my spot."

Viv shook her head, a teasing smile playing around her lips. "Nope."

"After eleven."

"Okay. And you're coming over for Christmas?"

"Yes. Les and I will be here around three. We'll see you the day after at my house for brunch and Kwanzaa-Umoja."

Viv smiled at that, but then looked suspicious. "And Mark's thing?"

Naomi returned a hedging smirk. She hadn't decided on attending Mark Dilworth's combination New-Year's-Eve-slash-Welcome-Home-Rick party.

"Well, try to make it. Bring the New Year in right," Viv smilingly encouraged.

Nodding, Naomi hugged her friend. They said their goodbyes.

Naomi was home twenty-three minutes later.

After a refreshing (and odd) solid five hours of sleep, Naomi did her yoga first thing, showered, and then worked on the Brooks case in her home office. Leslie was home, piddling between the top floor and the basement, adding extra touches to the holiday decorations around the house, focusing most on the kente cloths, muhindi, drums, and other Kwanzaa celebration items in the great room on the main level. When the doorbell rang for a second time at one-thirteen p.m., Naomi knew Leslie was deep in decorating mode.

"I'll get it!" Naomi left her office for the front door. "Hey, there!" She stepped back.

Viv and Rick entered her foyer with big smiles as they removed their coats. Dressed casually (Rick in sunglasses), they tended (subconsciously) to coordinate colors. Today, it was unintended derivatives of blue in the shirts they wore with their jeans. After hugs, Naomi led them to her living room, where everyone settled into light chatter.

"Leslie, Viv's here!"

"Oh! Cool! There in a sec!"

Naomi shook her head. "That girl..."

Rick and Viv chuckled as they listened to Leslie's approach.

She entered, sounding breathless. "Just wanted to get that— Oh. Um... Hi...?"

The three of them stood as Leslie moved closer.

"Les, this is my husband: Rick. Rick, this is my art partner, Naomi's daughter: Leslie."

Rick extended his hand. "Hi, Leslie."

"Hi, Mister Phillips." Leslie shook his hand but didn't sound like herself, and Naomi knew why.

Rick drew back, a quizzical frown on his face. "'Mister Phillips.' Is it like that?" His smile faltered.

Leslie shook her head as she released his hand and gazed up at him. "No. I, uh... Well, no..."

Naomi reclaimed her seat. "Visit awhile, Les. Park it and chat."

Leslie startled as Rick and Viv reclaimed their seats. "Okay, but I wanna show Viv my latest. Be right back."

Rick watched her departure. "She okay?"

Her husband was clueless, but Viv wore this knowing smirk; she had to be used to it.

"She's fine. Been bouncin' around here all morning, getting things ready."

Leslie returned, struggling to carry her latest sculpture.

Rick jumped up and took it from her. "Where're you putting it?"

Leslie, words failing her as she gawked at him, pointed to the floor in the general area near Viv, and Rick set it down as directed.

Viv leaned closer, inspecting, her brow furrowing with what Naomi knew were photography ideas.

Leslie sat in a chair near Naomi, awaiting Viv's comments.

Rick sat close to Viv on the sofa, reviewing the art with her.

Viv turned to him. "You can't really appreciate with those on."

Smirking, Rick removed his shades and continued his examination.

Leslie did a subtle double take with a whispered "Oh," making this tiny choking-cough-gasp sound. She turned toward her mother, mouthing, *"Oh my God!"*

Naomi uttered a faint titter.

Viv chuckled, too, wearing that perceptive smirk again. "This is good, Leslie. I like the shaping here..." She moved her fingers along the mid-to-lower portion of Leslie's piece.

"Thanks," Leslie responded distractedly, mouth parted, her gaze roaming Viv's husband as he inspected her sculpture.

Eyes still on the sculpture, Rick's slow nod conveyed favor. "Yeah. Nice, Leslie. I'm a fan of abstractionism. The use of energy you show here..." He trailed a hand over a portion toward the bottom of Les's sculpture and smiled at her.

Leslie startled again with his words (and likely that smile), looking as if caught with her hand in the cookie jar. "Thank you."

Naomi and Viv chuckled this time.

Rick took Viv's hand as he sat back. "What?"

"Oh! Excuse me a minute." Leslie rose. As she passed Naomi, she looked heavenward, giving God a surreptitious thumbs-up while whispering, "He's a *masterpiece*."

Rick leaned forward. "Beg pardon?"

Leslie turned back. "Oh, uh... I said, 'two *at least*'—as in sticks of butter: for the cake I'm baking."

"Oh." Rick shifted his attention back to Leslie's sculpture.

Naomi smiled to herself.

Leslie turned to her. "Ma, can I see you for a sec? Want some clarification on this recipe."

"Sure." Naomi headed after her daughter but turned back.

Viv put a hand up. "I'm home. Go 'head."

Naomi looked at Rick: "And if she's home, so are you."

Rick nodded his appreciation. "Thank you."

"I'll give him a quick tour, Naomi. Go see about that 'recipe.'" She still wore that knowing smirk.

Realizing Viv knew what was up, Naomi headed for the swinging door of her kitchen. She may go open-concept one day, but she liked her swinging doors; they were a home interior throwback to the styles of 1950s and 1960s (albeit periods societally unstylish for her people).

She didn't get through the door before Leslie was all over her. "You didn't say a *thing*!" she whispered.

"About?"

Leslie stared at her, shaking her head with wonder and gesturing toward the closed kitchen door. "Ma, he is... Oh, my God!"

Naomi grinned. "Yes, he's very."

Leslie firmed her gaze, still whispering. "No, Ma. I know some fine men. But he's like... I mean, he is just..."

"Yeah. All of that you *didn't* say."

"Viv didn't have his pictures up, and I didn't pry, but Lord!"

"That was likely to help her cope." Naomi guessed Leslie didn't venture into the Phillipses' formal dining room (where there was a photo of Rick); if you've seen one set of table and chairs with china cabinet and sideboard, you've seen them all.

"Such dramatic *symmetry* in his features... Unh." She scoffed. "He's created some whole new category of handsome."

Naomi chuckled her agreement, valuing her daughter's artistic take.

"What the hell does he have on? He smells like something mysterious and sultry, but still refreshing and light."

"I'll ask Viv. Want it for Trevor?"

Leslie shook her head, staring into the double bowls of the farmhouse sink. "Wouldn't smell the same."

Naomi shrugged. Different body chemistries likely made that true; didn't mean it wouldn't smell nice.

"That smile, and his voice, the bowed legs. Tall, body's cut, and..." Leslie shifted focus from the empty sink to look at her.

Naomi smirked at her daughter's rundown, surprised Leslie took such swift inventory of him. "And his *eyes*. Yes, Les, I know."

Leslie shook her head in awe. "Those lashes. And the color's so... It's like some weird special effect going on in them. People consider hazel eyes pretty, but Rick's eye-color..."

Naomi agreed, thinking about Cecily's artificial lenses. "And he's a nice man, too. *Good* people."

"RJ does look like him, but I thought, you know, he's a baby, toddler, whatever; they're small and cute anyway. But Rick is..." Leslie gaped at her for emphasis. "Ma."

"I know, Les. Can I go back in there now? Do you have clarification on the recipe for this cake you aren't baking?" Naomi scoffed in jest. "'Two *at least*—as in sticks of butter.'"

"I had to think fast, think of something rhyming with 'masterpiece.'"

"So I gathered." Naomi raised an eyebrow. "Done?"

Leslie gave a shuddery exhale. "Yeah. I'll be out in a sec." She fanned herself. "I just need a minute here... Whew, Lord!"

Chuckling, Naomi left the kitchen to rejoin the Phillipses.

She returned to find Viv grooving to "By My Side" from Godspell, singing along as she stood by the kinara on the mantel, while Rick worked his yo-yo as he reviewed her music collection of CDs and LPs.

He turned to her. "You ever just pull the albums for the liner notes, like back in the day, listening to the album as you read?"

"Many times."

Rick nodded his appreciation, gesturing toward her home's general interior and her music collection, then warmly assailed her with his radiant smile. "Impressive."

Naomi smiled back. "Thank you. Consider it home. Wanna play Uno?" She was more in the mood for Scrabble, but Rick and Viv were only there for a quick visit. Viv enjoyed Scrabble, too (no surprise there).

They didn't play Uno (Viv said Rick sometimes gets too competitive, and so declined), but to Naomi's surprise and delight, Rick demonstrated his technique with a yo-yo. They hung around talking, and Naomi gave Rick the extended tour. He loved her kitchen but commented her game room looked unused—which it did because it was. During that time, Naomi gave the couple their tickets to the ball in January.

The couple stayed for another half-hour before she and Leslie saw them to the door. Rick had been pressed to see the Wizards play live, so he and Viv were going to a game downtown later that evening.

In awe, Leslie watched them leave. "Viv didn't talk about Rick much when he was away, but I understand why she held on to him. I would've waited for his fine ass, too."

Rick's looks had little to do with it for Viv, but Naomi chuckled.

Leslie laughed, too, but grew serious. "I know it was only an hour, but I don't think I've ever seen love between two people like that before. And, I'm sorry, Ma, but not even between you and Daddy. Don't get me wrong: I know you and Daddy loved each other. Very much. But today, watching Viv and Rick together, for even that short time... You see the authenticity of their love and friendship. It's not just 'they're married,' so they love each other. Watching them, you...*see* a ride-or-die that has history and isn't flavor-of-the-month, you know?"

Naomi considered her daughter's words.

Psychiatrists were rarely off duty. Her visit with Rick and Viv yesterday (and today) embodied a sense of warmth and...*home* (having little to do with Rick's release), giving her perspective on relationships she'd ignored for some time because she hadn't had good opportunity to witness it. "You might have something there, Les." She nodded thoughtfully as she headed to her office. "Yep. You just might." She closed her office door, thinking more about Leslie's observation, reflecting on her last therapy session before the holiday break.

'Safe' has many meanings, Doctor Alexander, Cecily had said.

Naomi stared at her desk. "Viv is safe with Rick, Rick safe with her. Conclusively. *All* the meanings. You... You see it, feel it,...*know* it." Once upon a time, she worried about Viv's safety with Rick, but the circumstances then were unique.

But...*safety*: physical, mental, emotional, sexual. That's what the essence of this is with Cecily: the benevolent umbrella of safety in a relationship, not broken by overt violence or the hidden, non-physical violence of deceit and treachery. That concept would also form the essence of her therapeutic approach with her newest patient, arming her against such broken benevolence. Treating Cecily for the PTSD stemming from the home invasion was important. But in her gut, Naomi knew: Cecily's home-invasion PTSD was...secondary to another violation, unaddressed but vital.

The coming sessions may require more structure than Naomi's usual exploration through sometimes random dialogue. The structure involved with cognitive behavioral therapy allowed for better focus on the reasons for Cecily's negative thinking. Within the frame of the CBT approach, Naomi had specific opportunity to make Cecily aware of more effective ways to respond to problematic situations.

Drugs, too, could soothe traumatic stress throughout various symptomatic stages, but she didn't want to prescribe medicines without finding out more about what was going on with Cecily; Naomi was not one to straightaway whip out the prescription pad. Most of the antidepressants introduced over the last decade were about as equally effective, but she'll review the side effects and use that as her starting point. The pre-therapy questionnaire revealed Cecily's sound sleeping sessions were sporadic but occurred. To help her sleep better (look who's talking), she could begin work with some benzodiazepines, see how Cecily does on those. Although Cecily experienced that recollection in session, Naomi didn't believe antipsychotics were necessary. SSRIs could come into play later, but she could make progress without them.

Review of the side effects would dictate, so she had to pick her poison. Cecily needed regular sleep patterns; bupropion's insomnia and headache side effects could interfere with that. Venlafaxine sometimes resulted in dizziness and nausea, and even mirtazapine and sertraline caused sexual problems. Naomi realized Cecily experienced problems enjoying sex (with Oscar) currently, so any medications exacerbating that was a double-edged sword, because that arena was another topic requiring some analysis.

It was all a bit of trial-and-error: all the drugs could produce a side effect or two, but not necessarily the same ones (even though the treatment purpose was the same). Cost wasn't an issue for Cecily, so after some trial-and-error, it may be a matter of Cecily's preference: what side effects she could live with and still get better.

Antipsychotics were out (Cecily didn't have schizophrenia). So: a combination of benzodiazepines for relaxation and sleep with antidepressants for tension and sadness? Maybe. The benzos, though, could interfere with Cecily's memory. So, maybe not. Then again, there was always—nothing. No prescription. Naomi wasn't one to be pigeonholed in her therapy approach; she didn't like being limited to the norm.

Psychotherapy could replace meds, but meds helped ease the *reach* of therapy, treating symptoms impinging a therapeutic approach.

A future session could be a class on trauma and triggers, with teachings on what trauma is (it's not as straightforward as people think) and the effects of such frightening events. Maybe expound some on relaxation and anger control, and show the different emotional identifiers tied to trauma reaction. She could also throw in tips on sleeping, diet, and exercise—it all helped contribute to overall well-being.

Drugs could soothe traumatic stress symptoms: benzodiazepines for anxiety, not sleeping; antipsychotics for intense anger and outbursts. Eventually, SSRIs could help with symptoms. But in the end, nothing helped *prevent* PTSD from developing.

Like December, PTSD could be fickle. It could manifest without warning, then "disappear" for months before deciding to return in increments (rather than all-at-once) for round two or ten. Triggers could be blatant, or subtler and seemingly unrelated. Sufferers went through the trials of PTSD differently, but all experienced the core symptoms related to the illness: intrusive and upsetting recollections, avoidance pursuits, or displays of increased anxiety (sleeping problems, extreme outbursts of emotion). Cecily lapsed into an episode at seeing the poinsettias—a trigger or reminder both blatant and subtle, sending her into a bout of reliving combined with hyper-arousal.

A saving grace: Cecily hadn't turned to substance abuse or developed suicidal tendencies—both of which sometimes happened with trauma victims; it was a coping strategy best avoided. Still, drugs weren't an automatic cure-all for treating people with PTSD.

Being the victim of a crime was the figurative cherry on top, but Cecily's mental struggles had several root causes needing attention. For one, she didn't manage her emotions well; the first two sessions illustrated that. Not showing or expressing emotion or responding to different situations with the same emotion was just as bad as over-emoting. For another, Cecily had a substantive amount of relationship conflict with Oscar stemming from what Naomi determined was emotional trauma (even unbeknownst) attributable to his relationship abuse. If she had to guess, any trauma bonding with this couple was one-sided, or at least lopsided. Naomi, however, felt those other factors would dissolve with steady swiftness with Oscar out of the picture.

Naomi sat in the chair before her framed Elizabeth Catlett lithograph from Tyson, listening to Coleridge-Taylor's Symphony in A minor, Op.

8. The moody violins in the piece fit her viewing of the art as she focused on the etchings more in the center and pondered a most pressing case.

Medical theories and pharmaceutical concoctions aside, Naomi didn't ignore the common-sense element: Cecily's marriage to Oscar was toxic, unhealthy. In some instances, there appeared something close to a bit of Pavlovian conditioning was in place. With certain of Oscar's tone or expression, Cecily responded as if one of Pavlov's dogs, with either fear or attempt to appease him—something going beyond the normal human interaction responses to emotion cues.

Oscar showed classic "egosaurus" traits. As Leslie mentioned (regarding Rick and Viv), Naomi didn't readily see a ride-or-die vibe between the Brooks couple; quite the contrary—especially on Oscar's part. But Cecily seemed none the wiser, the idea of Oscar wishing her harm as foreign as the Slavic languages. This wasn't unusual. Good people rarely embraced suspicion: they struggled to imagine people doing the type of stuff they weren't capable of. It's why a narcissist could go undetected for years, if at all.

"'White Christmas' by the Drifters," Naomi said, remnants of her flash (while sitting with Viv yesterday) dancing out of reach. She could never right-off "replay" the darn things. "Never mind that. The *song*, Naomi. It's important."

In session, she asked Cecily about a person's true-self versus a public-self, and Cecily went middle-of-the-road with "it depends." But Naomi believed the internal often battled the external. It was why part of the session delved into aspects of Cecily's life having nothing to do with Oscar—aspects in place *pre*-Oscar. Without getting too bogged down in Freud's id-ego-superego concept, in Cecily's case, Naomi believed Cecily's issues stemmed from her external behavior being in direct conflict with her true or inner self. Naomi herself theorized, when it needs (all else being equal), the mind attacks itself to protect itself from being compromised and attempts to set things right again. And this righting manifested in many ways.

But compounded with the fundamental matter of Cecily's event trauma suffered during the home invasion, things became, not a danse macabre, but a delicate dance—with a bit of the macabre.

"Get ready, 'Home Skillet.' I'm on to you."

Now, what should she name her gun...?

Chapter Seven

Her Refuge

C ecily hung up the phone, feeling so much better. The air in the room seemed lighter.

She held off for as long as she could, tried listening to the relaxation tracks, but Dr. Alexander provided the number to the "Bat-phone" for this very reason.

Something unfriendly flitted around the edges of her mind, but she didn't want to know what it was. Something unfriendly, threatening to bring on one of those...episodes.

She was at work—and *that* couldn't happen.

So, she called Naomi.

She didn't know what she expected from the phone call, but it still wasn't what she got. Naomi spoke with calm assurance to her. Not patronizing, but calm, asking her (weirdly) a lot about her life in Mississippi. She'd done it in therapy the other day, too. Cecily didn't know why that was so important, but ten minutes later, she breathed easier and felt...

Stronger? Cecily shook her head. Maybe *stronger* wasn't the right word, but she felt better, less "episodey," and that was the point.

She never used the pen and pad in either session, although it was right there. ...She's...left-handed!

Realizing that about her doctor had nothing to do with anything, but that was how her mind sometimes worked—always putting tiny observations together here and there to form the various categories of trivia filling her head.

Except observations about that *night. Try putting those together.*

She thought about the fun time at Christmas dinner instead, about the thankfully uneventful time spent with her children. Rather than dining at a restaurant as planned, Cecily, Marcus, and Chelsea cooked dinner at Marcus's (little Roland happily underfoot). It worked out that way because Oscar began hinting about joining them. Switching to dinner at Marcus's sent a subtle message Cecily didn't have to voice aloud—and contributed to the uneventful aspect of things.

Cecily gazed through her office window at the barren trees sending their bleak and bare branches heavenward in search of the sun's warmth. "What happened?"

She'd asked that question so often during the last seven, eight years of her life, it became a rhetorical joke. But very little was funny—because Cecily knew the answers to that question (and there were several answers), meant facing and accepting or changing and rejecting many truths easier (and safer) to ignore.

Besides, she knew what happened.

Spotting a last holdout of leaves high on a branch of a tree in front of the leather goods store across the street, Cecily grinned with memory. Both of them put their best foot forward those first months. She was more withdrawn then. After losing Roland, she'd moved to DC for a fresh start, but Marcus and Chelsea made a better go of it than she had by a long shot. A part of her thrived vicariously through them, but there wasn't much personal success in the moving-on department on her behalf. Dating was so far on the back burner; it teetered falling off the stove. And then she went shopping for laundry detergent at Walmart.

Oscar showered her with gifts, attention. The gifts weren't extravagant—which was fine. Cecily giggled, thinking about the tokens and trinkets he presented, most strange and unrelated to her likes or interests. It was the thought that counted. Then.

Oscar's whirlwind of charm and energy, the flirting and general excitement he spread, provided ideal distraction, helped her move on. Marcus and Chelsea were happy for her then, but they were teens—amid their own share of activities and distractions. Oscar seemed happy with her, interested in her and being with her, and Cecily enjoyed every moment. Their sex left much to be desired, but Oscar more than made up for it in other areas of their relationship: she was a sucker for long talks, nature walks, and classic movies.

When the fun extended past month three, Cecily figured she'd found a keeper. Oscar was enthusiastic, intense and drunk on life, and there was never a dull moment (except when intimate with him), and Cecily drank from his well. And although she began paying for everything at some point, that didn't matter; their bond was strong. Or, so she thought, until about month four or five after they were married, and she began secretly calling him "Mr. Hyde" sometimes.

It began with complaints about meals she'd prepared, about her choice of attire. Worsened with insults about her person, her looks (hence the contacts and her forever-coifed hair), her competence, and then the hurtful nicknames and random pinches and punches started. By then, Marcus and Chelsea were long over their teenage activities and distractions, long over Oscar.

Swallowing a sigh, Cecily headed back to the front. She sat at her computer and continued working on reviewing the financials for the last quarter. She didn't need the money, but working at JAH Technologies, Inc. offered something money couldn't buy: peace (of mind, of...spirit). Cecily enjoyed working at JAH Tech. The environment wasn't rushed; even in this fast-paced world, they were more concerned with quality than speed.

She'd worked at JAH Tech over four years now, managing the company's finances and portfolio, and although they had an admin person, she helped with some of the administrative functions, too.

Speaking of their admin person, Cecily glanced over at Rhonda Peterson: on the phone, as usual. Cecily sighed. She could go back to her office and leave Rhonda to the front (Terrence was on vacation), but she enjoyed being out front, too: interacting with the interesting people coming in for business. She didn't work in her back office much; when she did, it was for quiet concentration during the final stages of analysis and reporting—a time approaching come mid-January. But now, maybe, she'd go there for private episode-avoidance calls to the Bat-phone.

Laughing, Rhonda hung up. "She is so crazy." She headed for the coffee-klatsch table topped with a box of pastries, the cinnamon and sweet dough aromas still wafting through the shop. Rhonda grabbed a cup and sent a frown toward the back, where the other offices and computer workrooms were. "When're they coming out of that meeting?" She turned to Cecily, still frowning. "Weren't you supposed to be in there?"

She was, but she couldn't join the meeting feeling so uneasy as she did before calling Naomi. "Something else came up."

Rhonda nodded with this curious smirk. "He'll update you." Average height, with long black hair (Cecily heard her saying something about a "lace front" before), she wore her usual tight blouse and short skirt, leaving little to the imagination. Her shoes were perilous five-inch heels. She'd been with JAH Tech for eight months, but that, so far, seemed to be Rhonda's uniform.

Somewhere inside, Cecily was a little jealous (she wasn't 23 anymore), but when you've got it, flaunt it (and all that), right? She looked at Rhonda, wondering what her curious smirk was about (and semi-knowing what it was about). "I guess he will: a side meeting of sorts."

Rhonda turned back to the klatsch and filled her cup, adding splashes (not dashes) of hazelnut cream. She shook her head, stirring in her sugar. "He'll update you, using all those obscure dictionary words like he likes to do—and I don't mean computer-talk." Cecily couldn't see her face, but she imagined Rhonda smirking again, but with a warm smile.

"He's an educated man, Rhonda. He likes to express himself using more than the common vernacular."

Rhonda turned to her (black hair swishing) and paused. She stared with kind eyes, the smiling-smirk no longer Cecily's imagination. "I see you've picked up the habit."

Cecily resisted blushing. But she didn't pick up anything; she was an educated woman. It was a shame how younger generations assumed you were doing something special and maybe even snooty by choosing to use a variety of words uncommon but applicable. And neither of them beat anybody over the head with exotic word usage.

Rhonda scoffed. "Shoot, if I had a company based on my name, I'd be breaking people down with my...'vernacular.'"

Both women chuckled.

Rhonda stared at the pastries before plucking a napkin and selecting a doughnut with chocolate sprinkles, using nails curving from their length (How did she type with those?). "He's a sweetie, though. *Really cute*, too. You know what the 'A' is for?"

Cecily frowned, confused by the question.

Rhonda rolled her eyes upward with a sigh and sat at her desk. "In JAH Technologies, Inc. His name is Joshua Hall, so I got the 'J' and 'H.'"

She sipped her coffee. "Maybe it's for Anthony, or Andre, or Antwon: something like that." She peered at Cecily for confirmation.

Cecily held in a chuckle. Rhonda joined the staff eight months ago, but every day since, she somehow centered at least one conversation around the owner of the company they worked for. "The 'A' is for Ambrose: Joshua Ambrose Hall." She experienced a tiny thrill at saying his full name aloud but cleared her throat to counter it.

Rhonda stared dumbfounded for a second before her nose turned up, not with disgust, but with a crinkle of surprised confusion and curiosity. "'Ambrose'? That's... That's..."

"Different?" Cecily offered, wanting to help her find a word.

"Yeah; not what I was expecting at all."

Cecily chuckled as she turned back to her monitor and the fourth-quarter numbers: they looked good. JAH Tech was doing well.

Rhonda sipped her coffee, repeatedly whispering Josh's full name for long seconds. "Sounds like it should be on a building or something."

"Guess that's why it is—*this* building, anyway." Cecily rose with her coffee mug and headed for the klatsch table, feeling self-conscious about her simple belted sheath dress and two-inch almond-toe heels (she wasn't 23 anymore). There were mortifying times she teetered in five-inchers herself, but that subject was best suppressed.

Rhonda giggled. "You're funny." She scoffed. "I can't stand my middle name. 'Heather.' What kind of mess is that?" She rolled her eyes, another scoff stressing the comment.

"It's nice."

Rhonda issued scoff three. "It's a White girl's name."

Cecily smirked, then smiled at the three arrangements of amaryllis she bought for the shop; they looked vibrant in the window, brightening the shop atmosphere.

"You like flowers, huh?"

Cecily smiled. "I do. Fresh ones in a room offer a bit of fragrance, a bit of happiness from nature."

Rhonda wiped her mouth. "That why you bring them in?"

"You could say that."

"I might bring some in."

"That's fine. I don't own the idea of liking fresh flowers." Cecily reached for a packet of English Breakfast tea and began its preparation.

Laughter traveled from the back. Male laughter: Joshua and his sons formed the meeting group. Cecily checked the wall clock. Seems things were going well as the meeting wound down. Josh didn't have to update her; they'd already gone over the highlights of the meeting beforehand. But he'd set time aside to give her a summary. Her name wasn't on anything, but he often treated her like it was, sometimes even said...they were partners. Tea prepared with three packets of sugar substitute and a dash of milk, Cecily walked back to her desk, sipping gingerly.

"You don't like coffee? You never get any."

Cecily shrugged as she moved the mouse on its pad to open a new screen. She had the financial-management and portfolio-management applications opened together. "I like the taste, but I'm not a regular drinker." She smiled inside: Naomi was a tea-drinker, too.

More laughter came from the meeting room.

Rhonda scooted closer to her desk as if preparing to look busy. "Listen to them... Guess it's all good."

Cecily didn't respond.

"Think Malcolm's cute?"

Cecily paused her review of the current month's expenses. "Huh?"

"Well, he's my age,...and he's looked at me with interest sometimes. Just wondering what you thought about him."

If I were male and 22 and often worked with a 23-year-old female wearing asset-advertising clothing, I'd be "interested," too. "All three Hall men are attractive."

Rhonda nodded emphatically with her shining grin. "Facts. ...How old is Mister Hall? Thirty-eight or so? I think he may have been a teenager when he had Malcolm. Those specks of gray in his twists..." She paused as if fighting the words that pushed forth. "I'd...I'd do him, too. Unh."

Josh was 45, turning 46 in less than two weeks, but Cecily shrugged, moderately shocked at Rhonda's last sentence. She seemed obsessed with those in the meeting room. Rhonda knew Josh liked yo-yos and James Brown, but Cecily rather enjoyed knowing personal details about him that Rhonda didn't (like his Ohio upbringing and love for the Negro Leagues; how he likes chicken salad and spaghetti, but kiwi and pineapple, not so much; how the slight bump in his nose came from it being broken his sophomore year in college). She'd told her his middle name; that would have to do for the sharing portion of the day.

"I like the way Mister Hall dresses: the jeans-and-sports-coat look?" Rhonda nodded with a wink. "Kinda hot." She started typing. "Have plans for New Year's?"

"A party, I guess." Cecily focused on the portfolio software.

"You 'guess'?"

The meeting room door opened, and Cecily was glad; she didn't want to discuss the Mabrys' party. She wondered if Naomi would—

"Are we ordering in? Or do you all have plans?" Josh's warm but nasal voice preceded the men's entrance into the main area. He had allergies that lessened in the winter but never left him.

"I'm meeting Janyce today, so I'm out."

His eyes of molasses (much like his skin) registered disappointment before he grinned. "So, we're ordering your favorite, then?"

She had to admit she enjoyed seeing his trace disappointment over her not joining them. "No."

"Sure? I'll have them add extra deli pickles."

She hated deli pickles, and Josh knew it. "In that case, I'm most sure. Since I won't be there, knock yourself out."

Joshua chuckled. "Where you from?"

Cecily came right back. "Where *you* from?"

Joshua watched her, waiting the necessary beat before they both said, "Cleveland!" and shared a light laugh. He added a checked vest with his ensemble today; something he did from time to time. The tattersall pattern of yellows and navy-blue popped against his brown blazer and pale-blue button-down. Josh wasn't exceedingly tall at five-eleven, but he had an athletic build: the low-rise, straight-leg jeans fit him well.

Malcolm and Bradford Hall laughed with them.

Rhonda frowned. "What does that even mean?"

Brad headed for the pastries, his white #92 Reggie White, Philadelphia Eagles jersey bright and fresh-looking. His longer, shaped fade glistened with healthy moisture in the office lighting. "Just a joke between Dad and Missus Brooks. We taking the tree down today?" He didn't elaborate on the private joke (his father was from Cleveland, Ohio, while she was from Cleveland, Mississippi). Maybe Brad wasn't as interested in Rhonda as his brother (if Malcolm was all that interested).

The idea of taking the tree down saddened Cecily, but she focused on the numbers on the screen as Josh headed her way.

Malcolm grabbed his backpack from behind the counter and headed to the rear again. His shadow-fade haircut looked fresh for the holidays. "Fine with me. I'm starting the networking config for Mister Nolan. Come on, Brad." Cecily checked for any looks of "interest" originating from Malcolm toward Rhonda: so far...nothing. But maybe she was too old to know what to look for anymore.

Brad spoke around the cruller in his mouth. "We're ordering lunch." He bit down, chewing with this mischievous grin (and looking very much like his father). He was tall and lean, molasses-brown like his dad, looking like he needed some lunch, but at 19 and active in college sports at Lincoln University, he burned everything up quickly.

Shorter than his father and brother, and more wood-brown (like his mother) than molasses, Malcolm scoffed as he moved out of view. "You *are* lunch: a meathead. I'm down for whatever. Order for me." The sound of a door opening and closing followed; he was in Workroom Four (containing the setup for Mr. Nolan).

His chuckle blending with Rhonda's, Josh stood behind Cecily, a hand to her chair. His Polo-Blue wafted delightful hints of melon, geranium, and moss. "Should hear about the government contract soon."

He sounded hopeful. Although the contract was small, it went a great deal toward expansion for JAH Technologies, Inc. Cecily was just as hopeful. "That would make a great Christmas gift." She moved her mouse on its pad to open a new window.

"It would, Cecily. Belated or not, landing that DOD gig would be..." He trailed off, but he didn't need to finish.

Cecily loved the way he said her name. He practically whispered the last syllables—as if it were the sweetest, most precious word he'd ever heard (that was her private take). She reached for her mug and studied the screen (also glimpsing everything in her desk mirror).

Brad licked his thumb. "Four left. Wrapping these for Hadji?"

Hadji was an orphaned "homeless" boy who frequented the back of the business park; homeless in the sense he shuffled between foster families who were always "between places." Eight years old, he was as streetwise as they come, but humble and respectful whenever he approached JAH Tech for a handout. He enjoyed school, and several teachers in his school extended themselves to give the boy food and shelter. Joshua made numerous attempts with authorities to get a proper situation for the little boy, but either those same authorities allowed bureaucracy to let Hadji fall through the cracks, or Hadji was quick on his feet enough to resist getting "snagged" (as he liked to say).

Hadji, though, cute as a button, always visited JAH Tech at least two or three times a week, and he and Josh would always steal away for fifteen, twenty minutes of one-on-one. Cecily suspected Josh wanted to care for the little boy full-on, but she wasn't sure what stopped him. They hadn't seen Hadji in a day or so; his visit loomed.

"Yeah, wrap those up. We're overdue for that little man coming by and rattling his psittacisms with glee. I'm sure he has plenty of holiday tale."

Cecily chuckled her agreement, while Rhonda rolled her eyes upward in kind exasperation at Josh's word choice. Cecily chuckled at that, too.

"It's dead, Dad. Closing early?" Brad closed the box of pastries.

"It's still early, but we can, Smeek. I have a teleconference sched—"

The door to the shop opened, and a short, stocky, middle-aged Black man barreled in, trying to balance several laptops in one arm. He looked over the faces before settling on Josh's. "You, Josh?"

"I'm *Joshua*, yes. How can we help you?"

The man looked surprised at the correction. "Oh, sorry, man. Yeah: you guys service computers?" His walnut-brown, clean-shaven face was sweaty despite the cold, reminding Cecily a lot of Oscar. And he had a weak nose: not small of itself, but weak—his other features took over, making his nose negligible (again reminding her of her husband). Cecily considered strong noses an important masculine feature.

Brad wiped his hands and went over to the man, assisting him with his technical load, and the man looked pleased to get the help.

Rhonda met Brad at the counter as he set the laptops down. She glanced at the gentleman. "They do a bunch of everything."

Joshua shifted around Cecily, moving closer to the man as he closed the shop door. "Well, we focus on networking and database services for small businesses, but we can troubleshoot most hardware and software issues for the average user, too." He extended his hand to the potential client. "Joshua Hall: JAH Technologies Incorporated."

Cecily locked her screen and joined Josh as the man gripped his hand, pumping with a smile. "Benny Sparks. Oh, good. Thanks, man. Can you do a rush?" He ran his gaze over Cecily as she stepped up. "Your wife, I take it?" Still smiling, Benny extended his hand to her.

Heat moved in a diagonal zigzag through her face to her extremities. She shook her head, her hand moving into Benny's. "No. I—"

"This is Missus Brooks: CFO. Can't say if we can do a 'rush.' All depends on the problem and what you mean by 'rush.'" Josh led the man toward the reception counter and the stack of laptops.

Cecily followed, wondering when it was he assigned her the lofty title of CFO.

His wife...

Thirty-nine minutes later, Benny Sparks headed out of the shop, a broad grin brimming, several of Josh's business cards and brochures (pulled from the reception table by the Christmas tree) in one hand, two sturdy bags holding the repaired laptops in the other. There were five laptops altogether, but between Josh, Malcolm, and Bradford, the repair was quick. It wasn't a virus, but Cecily gathered it was some other technical issue with registries or something. The Hall men were well equipped to deal with computer maladies, both simple and complex.

Joshua earned his BS and MS in Computer Science from UMD-College Park, specializing in software development, but he preferred the hardware side. He held many certifications from CISCO, Microsoft, CompTIA, and others, including his CISSP, CISM, and CSSLP. Malcolm had CCNA, MCSD, and Network+ certifications, while Brad had his CCNA and worked toward getting his Network+. Both Hall boys were computer-science majors (Malcolm earned his BS from Wilberforce University last spring). Cecily only had a broad understanding of those certifications, but didn't need an in-depth grasp to be proud of those accomplishments.

Rhonda and Brad were on the lunch run, and Malcolm was in the back; only the three of them were in the front area.

Benny waved the hand holding JAH promo material. "Josh, man. Thank you."

Josh smiled, but it wasn't a full one; the mustache in his Cavalier goatee twitched with annoyance. "It's *Joshua*, and you're welcome. Have a safe New Year."

Benny knocked his forehead with the heel of the hand holding the cards and brochures. "Right. Thank you, *Joshua*. Sorry, man. I keep— Anyway, I'll refer this place to others." For emphasis, he raised the hand holding the cards. "You're a lifesaver!"

Josh chuckled. "I don't know about all that, but I appreciate the kind words and support, Mister Sparks. Looking forward to meeting with your team next month to outline the client contract agreement and network setup potentiality."

"'Benny' is fine, man, and next month: you bet." He was gone.

Cecily returned to her desk, feeling Josh's eyes on her. She unlocked her laptop, displaying forecast numbers for the upcoming first quarter.

"Sure ya gonna pass on lunch? It's a working one: exploring marketing options for the spring."

Something soft and sweet swirled within his question, making it absolute necessity she meet with Janyce and not hang at JAH Tech for lunch ("working one" or not). Looking at him, Cecily nodded. "It's best."

He arched his brows at her. "'Best'?"

Cecily shrugged, feeling cornered over her Freudian slip. "I'm— I'm sorry. You know what I mean."

"Well, no, I don't, actually. Why is it 'best'?" He frowned curiosity at her, his mustache twitching again, but not with annoyance—something quite the opposite. A tiny vertical break in the hair over his lip marked a scar there since he was 12.

Cecily closed the program and reached for her phone, thinking of a good redirect. She spoke to Josh as she texted her lunch date. "Give you a chance to come up with another knee-slapper." She looked at him. Since he discovered her fondness for a good joke or pun (knock-knocks and riddles were faves, too), Josh fired one at her at least weekly. She looked forward to them.

Josh sent her a sweet smirk (making it even more necessary she lunch with Janyce). "You're on." He smiled, showing that tiny gap between his upper far left incisor and left cuspid, which Cecily considered darling.

Her phone chimed. She texted Janyce back, then headed to her private office. "Well, you have time."

"Your court jester shall have your *blague* ready upon your return, my queen." His use of French sounding authentic, he added a bow and hand-flourish in what was only part humor.

Knowing his eyes again followed her movement, Cecily fell in character as she entered the hallway. "Be warned: I must smile, Fool, or it's...*off* with your head!" She cackled as she disappeared into her office, listening to Josh's chuckle behind her.

"You eat like a bird." Janyce shook her head as she eyeballed Cecily's plate, her eyes conveying the criticism not camouflaged by her words of general observation. "That how you keep your figure?"

Figure? No, she wasn't overweight, but she wasn't 23 anymore; she wouldn't use having a *figure* as something to describe herself, either. Cecily shrugged. "Not as hungry now, I guess."

Janyce scoffed. "You always say that."

Cecily didn't think she did but kept quiet; Janyce was in a mood. She didn't have as many packages stacked in the vacant chair beside her this time—perhaps the reason for such sourness.

Janyce pulled her scarf tighter around her neck. She dined with it on; dabs of marinara sauce dotted the front. "I hate winter. So damn cold! That global-warming stuff must be a crock."

The environmental threat wasn't a crock, but Cecily wanted to avoid the snide remark she'd get if she tried to explain what the concept meant. She shrugged instead. "March'll be here in another eight weeks. Warmer weather's coming. Hold tight, Jan."

"More like April, which is another twelve weeks. March isn't all that warm. Keep that hanky you keep in your pocket ready."

Definitely in a mood.

Janyce reminded her of Oscar sometimes (reminded her more of her mother, too). Her phone chirped. Cecily checked it.

Speak of the devil (literally?); it was Oscar: *What're you doing?*

Cecily texted back, "Lunch," hoping she could get away with a short answer this time. Sometimes she could.

Oscar came right back: *Ur desk? U go out?*

Cecily sighed (he wanted details today) and texted where she was and with whom. She finished her Fanta. Nothing back from her husband (Mr. Hyde was satisfied).

"That Oscar checking on you again?"

Cecily nodded, wanting to vanish before her eyes. "Sorry."

"You tell the truth?"

Cecily frowned at her friend; of course, she told the truth. "I did."

Janyce shrugged, swirling her finger in the leftover sauce on her plate, licking the finger clean. "Good. You can be so sensitive, Cecily. It's just a sign of love. I have software on Hank's phone telling me where his phone is."

Cecily wondered if Hank knew of such dealings, wondered if Oscar had done something similar to her phone and was testing her. She changed the subject. "I could use another spa day."

"I'm sure. That company you work for must be making buckets. Only those Fortune-Five-Hundreds do that ritzy shit for their employees." She reached for her apple martini and finished it.

JAH Tech was doing well, but the spa days had more to do with personnel being less than ten (thus, the splurge was affordable)—and with the owner being into such holistic health and healing measures. The serenity, the aromas, and speaking as much or as little as she wanted all contributed to one hour each week, sometimes carrying over an additional day or two of good feeling, which she treasured. "I don't know about all that, but it's a cool benefit."

Janyce stared at her before she grinned. Her very-black dreads were pulled back from her face with a thin headband. Those blackest locks stood in harsh contrast to her burlywood complexion.

"What?"

"Just...the way you talk sometimes."

Cecily swallowed. Janyce was on about her accent—again. Cecily didn't understand why that remained such fascination for her and Oscar. Still, doubt and embarrassment locked in her chest. She was caught between embracing where she was from and rejecting it. Their jibes about her being from Mississippi sometimes made her feel ugly, feel...*less*.

"Your brother's at Lorton. He still talks like that, too?"

Her head felt extra heavy with the nod she gave Janyce. "Sorry." She wasn't sure why she apologized, but it usually kept the peace (and all that). "It's not as bad as it used to be." That was just an extension of her apology and leaned more toward rejecting where she was from rather than embracing it, but appeasing was just easier. *You've become such a wuss.* Cecily gave Janyce a wan smile and, having finished her soda, reached for her cup of cooling Earl Grey.

"How long was he sentenced for again?"

"Eleven years."

"And how long has it been?" Janyce frowned with attitude, but Cecily didn't know why. Out of martini and only faint streaks of sauce left on her plate, Janyce opted for the piece of breadstick left in the basket (and used it to sop those last streaks).

Too long. But Cecily preferred keeping discussions about Larimore close to nil. Time for another topic detour. "So, ready for tomorrow?"

Janyce smiled, the petulance lifting away from her features. For a woman, she had a large nose (and hairy sideburns), but her smile lessened its dominance. "Oh yes. Hank can't wait." She tapped a shopping bag in the chair next to her. "Got a new outfit."

Janyce bought a new outfit every week, but Cecily held her tongue. "I'm looking forward to it, too." That wasn't entirely true (pretty untrue, actually), but, speaking the words aloud, maybe they would manifest into truth. "We could use some fun." Now, *that* was entirely true.

Janyce's expression in response was curious and piercing, but Cecily also saw a glint of irritation. "You have to allow the fun, Cecily. Our party last year was a blast, folk talking about it for months afterward, but not you; oh, no." The curiosity in her gaze pushed through more. "Isn't part of healing after a tragedy, forgetting about it? It was two years ago. You're healthy; your kids came out of it okay. Just...I don't know...try to forget what happened and move on. Defeat the sadness by standing up to it and spitting in its face."

Cecily started to ask for some water to go with that forget-being-raped-beaten-and-stabbed pill, but she chided herself; Janyce was only trying to help.

"You think about it every day, don't you?" Her large brown eyes held this weird, subtle glee.

Cecily nodded the slightest, thinking, for someone who encouraged her to *forget about it*, Janyce found ample opportunities to bring the subject up whenever they were together. She also perceived her friend took perverted interest in mentioning the invasion to stir unease within her, so she could feel superior and feed her own ego (that gleam of glee in her eyes seemed to say so). Cecily didn't think that about Janyce often, but sometimes she did. "It's with me every day, in some form or another, so I can't help it."

"I understand. But like I said, you're alive; Chelsea and Marcus are over it. If it wasn't for that call from the Exxon station..."

"That is a blessing, yes."

"Would've been a better blessing if they hadn't—" Janyce sucked her teeth with a soft scoff, her brow furrowing with what looked like memory. "Anyway, still no word on the diamond teacup brooch?"

Shaking her head, Cecily drew her upper lip in and shivered against the nonexistent cold of the restaurant, doing her best to curtail the slithery rise of another episode. She wondered (speaking of blessings) if the anonymous caller called after she prayed to God, or if God was already on it—and answered her prayers before she prayed.

Swirling despair began in her middle.

Please, not now, Cecily. Don't do this now.

Too late. "Sorry, Janyce. Would you excuse me?"

"Sure. Wh—"

Purse in hand, Cecily already had several steps toward the ladies' room before Janyce could say anything more. It wasn't bad smells or music this time, but voices and images burgeoning the nausea filling her belly as she closed the stall door, thankful for the privacy of bathrooms in this restaurant separated by entire walls (rather than the standard coated steels or heavy plastics of typical bathroom panels).

Call Naomi.

Cecily shook her head against the wall, her fists balled and tightening in resistance to the flow of unsettling emotions. She couldn't call Naomi for every little thing. She didn't want to overuse the number, didn't want to piss the doctor off.

Nausea created the need to vomit, but as Janyce pointed out, she hadn't eaten much; the dry retching over the toilet irritated her throat.

Cecily sat perilously on the edge of the toilet seat, covering her ears while shutting her eyes tight. Her covered ears did nothing to silence the voices; her clamped eyelids did nothing for the images rebounding behind them. "Please..." The episode she avoided earlier by calling Naomi, listened not and forged ahead...

She was 15 and then 42, 42 and then 17, back to 42: alternating sounds and scenes from her youth and from two Decembers ago melding and separating at warp speed. She heard her mother's backhanded insults, saw her mother's intimate tantrums of disappointment with Cecily during private audience. Cecily saw and heard those men degrading her, watched black boots and keychains march past her line of sight as she lay bleeding and dying again. Chelsea's moans and calls from that night reverberated. Marcus's silence echoed louder. Her mother, those men, Chelsea, Oscar: all of them crammed into the stall with her, making her miserable (and making themselves at home). "Please..."

No one listened,...and the voices and images continued.

"Hello? Ma'am?! Do you need help?"

Curled into a teetering ball on the toilet seat, face wet with tears, Cecily responded to the unfamiliar voice crashing through the disturbing drone of those others. "Yes?! I mean, *no*! I'm— I'm okay. Just nauseated."

Silence from the other side. Cecily saw the shadowy reflection of someone standing outside her stall door. The scant view underneath showed portions of blue patent-leather pumps. "...Ma'am?" Whoever it was, wasn't convinced.

Cecily uncurled herself and reached for the toilet paper, the voices and images dissipating. "Really, I'm fine. Sorry. I tried one of the new drinks on the menu." Cecily focused her attention under the door to her stall as she wiped her face and blew her nose, wondering if she'd revealed the real aloud while curled on the toilet.

"Oh. That'll do it. Have to be so careful when going random on a menu. You sure?"

"Y-Yes. Just needed a minute."

Those patent-leather pumps stepped away. "Sounded like it. Okay." A door to another stall opened; Ms. Patent Leather handled her business.

Cecily hurried from her stall. After a quick hand-wash and face swipe part two, she said, "Thank you," to the lady and stepped into the hallway on the woman's "No problem." She paused with her back to the wall, composing herself before rejoining Janyce.

"That's better!" Cecily placed her purse on the table and sat with a fake sigh of relief.

"You should've told me your stomach was upset. We could've postponed—"

Cecily shook her head. "Nothing that deep, Janyce. I think the little I ate didn't agree with me." She didn't like lying, but the situation called.

"Think I want dessert..." *And if you're gonna lie, make it look good.* She could take whatever she selected home to Oscar.

Janyce smiled. "Oh, good. Me, too."

Ten minutes later, Cecily reviewed the dessert options for what felt like the tenth time, sensing Janyce's stare through the laminated trifold rectangle. She didn't want to pick wrong, that's all—because she wasn't picking for herself. Choosing wrong could go so bad.

"*Really*, Cecily? I hate when you do this." Janyce long ago selected key-lime pie and now waited no-longer-patiently for Cecily to pick something. "You sounded like you already knew what you wanted."

"I know, but..."

"It's a *dessert*, Cecily." Janyce huffed more exasperation. "Why do you get into these modes where you overanalyze *everything*?"

Chocolate cake? Cheesecake? Parfait? She could text Oscar and ask him, but she wanted it to be a surprise (and she didn't want to open the door for him to add something else). Cecily then ordered something for his dinner, anyway. She avoided insults about her cooking if she went the takeout route—although, sometimes...she didn't avoid them, and Oscar got shots in, anyway. Cecily viewed the menu, deciding on an entrée and dessert now. It would be a surprise, but if she didn't choose correctly... And then it hit her. Since Janyce reminded her so much of Oscar today... "I'll have the key-lime, too."

Janyce scoffed (much like Oscar). "Finally!"

Oscar's key-lime (and dinner) in hand, Cecily left the restaurant with mixed feelings, her mind and body trying to de-episode itself while preparing to shift back into JAH-Tech mode as she hopped back on the red line (toward Grosvenor) and headed back to work.

Perhaps I am too sensitive, overanalyze everything...

She'd had this conversation with herself many times. The control Oscar wielded, his meanness, wasn't as bad as she made it out to be. She just needed to learn more about how his mind worked, that's all. They were only seven years in; their relationship was still in infancy by some measures. With time, the unsettledness would settle.

Oscar texted: *Back at the office yet?* Cecily texted back: *Almost*, as she ascended on the subway escalator, wondering how long things would take to...settle. Wishing for a hat and scarf, Cecily used her pocket-handkerchief on her tearing-from-the-cold eyes as she walked the few freezing blocks back to JAH Tech, her mind awhirl about many things: Oscar, her episode in the bathroom, little Roland, key-lime pie...

Her thoughts circled Janyce's comments about that anonymous caller. She doubted ever mentioning the stones and shape of her missing brooch to her, but those considerations vanished once she opened the shop door.

She inhaled the joy even before she saw the tiny white bag on her desk or the bucket of goodness on the reception table: snickerdoodles from the Great Cookie at Iverson Mall. Temple Hills was a trek from JAH Tech, but always worth the prize.

Rhoda's flirty cackle came from somewhere in the back; the responding low chortle coming from at least one of the Hall sons. Sadly, the Christmas tree was down; tinsel remnants dotted the floor. Bags and containers from a local sandwich shop filled a small tied-off trash bag near the front door. The radio was on. Station WMMJ (Josh's favorite) played on low (amid an ad run).

Josh was on the phone. He smiled upon seeing her enter the shop, but it faded with his attention back to the phone call. "I prefer 'Joshua,' please. Yes. ...No problem." His smile resumed its brightness. "...January fifth at nine. Sure. ...You're welcome. Happy New Year to you, too. Goodbye." He hung up. "How was your lunch date?"

"Nice, thank you very much. How was your sandwich?"

His shoulders jerked ambivalence. "They added mayo, but I ate it."

"Hungry?" She liked talking to him.

He shrugged again, this time with a nod. "I was, yeah."

Cecily picked up the tiny white bag from her desk. She hadn't ordered dessert for herself during lunch but now had a sweet tooth; the cookies would be perfect. "And these?"

Josh's eyes twinkled as he approached her. "A bit of celebration..."

She watched him, seeing that line in his mustache twitch with the smiling-smirk emerging from his lips. "You got it?"

He nodded at a slow pace. "They called a half-hour ago. *We* got it; a late Christmas present for sure."

"Or early birthday." Getting that government contract was such good news for him.

"Yeah."

"Congratulations, Josh!" Nothing but happy for him; Cecily hugged him. He pecked her cheek in their embrace, his Polo-Blue sending wafts of delicious tangerine and basil around them. Their congratulatory hug lasted seconds.

"Thank you, but it's your win, too, Cecily."

The way he said her name... Cecily gripped her bag of snickerdoodles tighter. "Thanks."

"I mean that." His brown eyes twinkled interestingly again with whatever they had twinkled with moments ago.

"I know you do."

Josh leaned against the desk. "I'll be getting the official award letter and documents soon; we scheduled the meeting for next Thursday."

"Cool."

"You'll be there?" His question was both request and confirmation.

"Of course," Cecily assured with a smile.

Josh gestured at her bag. "So, eat a cookie and make it official."

She began opening her bag. "Did you have one?"

He stood erect, shaking his head with a grin. "I haven't. Had Smeek make the run around the beltway for them. The kids took handfuls from the bucket to the back, but I didn't partake yet."

"Well, then..." Cecily reached in for a cookie and offered her opened bag to him. Peabo Bryson's "Reaching for the Sky" played overhead.

"Thanks." He held his cookie up between them. "To government contracts and...reaching for the sky."

Cecily touched her cookie to his in a toast. "To reaching for the sky." They bit and chewed, listening to Peabo for quiet seconds. Peabo's lyrics, however, had nothing to do with business expansion and everything to do with—

Cecily shifted her gaze and closed the bag, putting it in her purse. "So, what's happening on the fifth?" Her need to change subjects was rampant today.

"Meeting on preliminaries for opening the second shop." Josh finished his cookie with a bite.

"I see." Cecily finished hers.

"Need to think prepensely about using more-intensive marketing; take this word-of-mouth success to the next level."

"I agree." She possessed limited marketing knowledge, but they did need to increase focus on such an essential part of business growth. She'd have to focus more on the marketing budget for sure.

"Can you lead that piece for me?" He sounded hopeful again.

She didn't want to disappoint him, but she knew little about marketing. "Oh, I don't know, Josh..." Her stomach knotted with nerves, the stress over his request growing. "Research it maybe—"

"That's all I'm asking, Cecily." He smiled. "I... I trust your judgment. You have good instincts."

She didn't believe she did. *Don't waffle, Cecily. Not this time. Have some balls (like you used to).* "I'll give it a try, sure."

"Good, because I consider you JAH factotum." He looked out the shop window. "The trees have little foliage, still somewhat niveous after last night's dusting, but the birds...have chosen to nidificate just the same."

She peered through the large window and the trees-in-winter lining the street, finding Josh's observation on point: tiny nests dotted some of the upper snow-lined branches.

Joshua turned to her, solemn. "There's some other news..."

Cecily gazed up at him, curious. His twists looked healthy and moist (he wasn't balding yet), but he'd get them tightened and trimmed soon.

"You had a phone call while you were out."

Cecily's thoughts went to her husband. "Okay. Is there a message?"

"...From Larimore."

Cecily went cold. Josh knew about Larimore, but... "You... You accepted the call?"

"Well, *I* didn't, but once Brad said yes, he handed the phone to me. We didn't mean any harm. I just thought..." He looked so uncomfortable, but Cecily resisted cupping his cheek to reassure him. "Just thought you'd want to know if anything was wrong with your brother."

She loved Larimore, but she didn't want him calling outside their agreed schedule—especially if nothing was wrong—and especially not at her *job*. It just made things easier on her end. "He's... He's all right?"

"He sounded fine. Wanted me to make sure you understood that. Appreciated me taking the call but said he'd try you in the morning—your scheduled day."

She checked her cellphone: no missed call from her brother. There was, however, another status-request text from Oscar. She let her husband know she was back at JAH, then sent her eyes back to Josh. "But why was Larimore early calling me? Why not my cell?" Her embarrassment regarding her jailed brother speaking with Josh took a backseat to the confusion and alarm over Larimore calling outside their routine. She wondered if something was wrong, and he wanted to discuss it.

Josh shrugged. "Can't say, Cecily."

"I know. I'm sorry."

"Don't apologize." He placed a hand on her shoulder. "You okay?"

"Yes. I ju—"

"There you are! 'Bout time." Rhonda placed a paper pack on the copier and traipsed over to the Great Cookie bucket for a 'doodle.

Josh didn't turn to Rhonda. He focused on her.

Cecily now held his molasses gaze. She nodded. "I'm okay."

Josh gazed into her eyes seconds longer, confirming, before lowering his hand. He stepped away just as Malcolm and Brad emerged.

Malcolm set his backpack onto his shoulder. "A'ight, Dad. I'm out."

"Get Up Offa That Thing" by James Brown was on; Joshua's eyes were closed as he head-bobbed to the beat. "Okay."

Brad smiled at his father, shaking his head at him. "That's the ticket for your birthday: lock you in a room with nothin' but the Godfather of Soul playing." He went for another 'doodle.

Josh eyed his sons with an approving grin. "Happy birthday to me."

Chuckling, Cecily sat at her desk, doing her own head-bob—and fighting images and thoughts of spending his birthday with him. She had a unique present for him and hoped he liked it.

Rhonda loaded the copier, her body bouncing to Mr. Brown's beat as she did.

The song ended, and, lunch officially over, Josh switched the stereo broadcast back to muzak. "Getting my new skis will be gift enough."

With the brothers' glance at her, Cecily changed the subject for them. They went all-out in purchasing a new special edition Negro Leagues jacket for their father, not skis—and they didn't want to blow the surprise by talking about it. "Did Hadji come by?" She started internet research on marketing terms and concepts: give herself some background (on topics her business degree didn't cover).

Josh's smile answered the question before he spoke. "Yeah. Little man is something else. Told him to see if he could come through before closing—bought him a sandwich."

Cecily smirked. "He'll be through." But she worried about that little boy alone on the streets—no matter his streetwise savvy.

Rhonda sat at her desk. "For sure."

Malcolm popped his brother's back. "Come on, man."

Brad grabbed his bag. "See you tonight, Dad." Both Hall sons went over to their father, giving him parting power-handshake embraces.

Malcolm headed to the back and the exit there. "Bye, Missus Brooks. Later, Rhonda."

Rhonda blushed. "Bye."

Brad "Smeek" Hall came over to Cecily. He leaned down and kissed her temple, smelling a little like sandwiches, cologne,...and computer circuits. "Bye, Missus Brooks. Coming in tomorrow?" His bay-brown irises twinkling, Brad's inquiring smile was much like his dad's.

"For a little while, yes."

He whispered, "Thanks for the redirect" to her and headed after his brother. "Bye, Rhonda."

"Okay." Rhonda blushed again, giving Cecily the idea Rhonda's druthers went with either Hall son (and she'd "do" their father, too).

"It's quiet, Rhonda. I've decided against closing early, but traffic's light: Missus Brooks and I can handle whoever comes in."

Cecily clicked to download a list of standard marketing terms. "Like Hadji—and giving him his sandwich."

Josh let out a warm, playful chuckle. "Yeah, like that." He reached inside his leather bag for his yo-yo.

Rhonda grinned and began shutting her desk down. "Thank you, Mister Hall. I still get tomorrow off?"

Josh worked a basic yo-yo throw. "Yep. With pay. See you Tuesday."

Listening to the muzak, Cecily and Joshua watched Rhonda's closing-shop ritual. It took less than two minutes. Rhonda went over to Josh with a happy sigh and hugged him with her parting thanks and New Year's wishes. Completing her winter-weather prep by donning hat and scarf, she waved to Cecily with a smile and was gone.

Cecily opened the financial-management software to log the payroll. "I've downloaded a few documents with some marketing terms and concepts. I'm a complete novice, but a cursory review shouldn't prove too hard."

"Say that again.?"

Cecily did her best not to blush. Whenever Josh asked her to repeat certain words or phrases, it had an altogether different overtone than whenever Oscar or Janyce asked her to repeat herself. Josh enjoyed hearing her accent, allowing Cecily to embrace where she was from rather than rejecting it (as she'd done earlier). "I said..." She repeated the last part of her previous sentence for him—the part she knew he wanted to hear again—and feeling far from worthless...or ugly.

He grinned, nodding with appreciation. "Printing those for me, too?"

Cecily sent the documents to the printer. "As we speak."

Joshua headed for the copier, wearing a slanted grin. "Thanks." The doorbell at the back rang as he handed Cecily her set. He checked his watch. "Hadji might be early." He collected his laptop, carrying it and the papers from the printer. "I'll work in the back. You got the front?"

She could've opted to leave early, too, but it was unspoken understanding she liked (*preferred*) the time at JAH Tech. "I do."

His eyes did that thing again with her response. "Want me to bring you a bottled water, juice? Anything?"

"I'm good." She reached for the bagged meal and key-lime pie and handed it to him. "If you'd put this in the fridge for me?"

"Sure." He headed for his back office.

Cecily changed the stereo back to radio station WMMJ. At her desk, she finished the payroll, then scanned the marketing pages she'd printed. Her talents were in finance; she had minimal confidence in herself on this aspect of the business (not to the extent Joshua had in her), but she could comprehend beyond college level, which only helped.

"Smile" by Lyfe Jennings came on, and although this was maybe her fourth time hearing the song (it got little airplay), she always paid close attention to the lyrics, finding the song inspiring.

She worked quietly; the oldies offering calm yet encouraging background noise. She smiled as she listened to Josh and Hadji's exchange in the back; hearing the two make each other laugh (and all that).

Only two people came in and scheduled appointments for network setups, but that was good (given the slow day). They lost themselves in states of productivity at their respective stations.

Dusk approached when Josh emerged from the back.

He handed her some papers. "I made notes on what I've read so far."

Cecily added them to her note-ridden papers. "Okay. We'll compare and combine next week?"

Josh nodded. "Well, we still have an hour until closing, but we can knock off now; I'm sure you and Oscar have New Year's preparations to get a head start on—with the party and all."

"I guess. But I'm not going anywhere."

Josh wrinkled his brow, his lips bending into an almost-smile. "What?"

"Entertain me, Fool! My joke!" She sometimes surprised herself with how relaxed she allowed herself to be here. This place was her refuge. Cecily squinted in mock warning. "The Executioner awaits..."

Joshua Ambrose Hall tossed his head back and roared, his Adam's apple bobbing in sincere glee. Once his laughter died, he smiled at her, that sliver of space between his upper far left incisor and left cuspid just as inviting as it wasn't supposed to be. "Okay, Cecily. I didn't forget."

Cecily began the (sad) task of closing her desk down for the night. "I'm listening, Court Jester."

He turned the stereo off and came back to her. "Okay. Here goes. I know you've heard this one, but it can still stir a classic laugh: What do you call cheese that doesn't belong to you?"

Cecily frowned curiously, her analytical mind trying to solve the riddle. He believed she'd heard it before. She liked a good joke; didn't mean she heard them often. Not wanting to overanalyze (per Janyce), Cecily gave up. "I don't know. What?"

Now Joshua frowned. "Seriously?"

Cecily did her best not to be embarrassed, giving a hesitant nod as she shut her computer down, feeling a tad embarrassed anyway.

Joshua grinned, giving his punchline pregnant pause. "Nacho cheese."

Cecily cracked up. Threw her head back this go-round and laughed. The laughter conjured memories of Roland, but that was okay. She spotted Joshua trying to determine whether she was humoring him, but his smile soon showed he was pleased to find she wasn't. "Oh! Okay. That was good. Your life is spared."

Josh wiped his brow in mock relief. "Whew! Thank you, Your Majesty." He scanned her desk and then looked at her. "Ready?"

She wasn't, but she nodded with a sigh. "Yeah. You?"

"Not yet. I'll walk you to your car, but I need to close shop: trash out, registers closed, workrooms straight. You know: the usual."

"I can help."

"I know. I appreciate that. But get your holiday started with Oscar."

"I'm back in here tomorrow, Josh."

He shook his head as he grabbed her coat. "No, you're not. I appreciate your *anti*-presenteeism for this place, Cecily; I do. You show up regardless, and your productivity rocks. But JAH is closed tomorrow. I just decided." He held her coat open, and Cecily slipped inside it. "It's cold out there, Cecily. Where's a hat, scarf, something?"

She tried not to have hurt feelings behind him telling her not to come in tomorrow, tried not to be disappointed over him closing the shop; she knew he meant well. And why she didn't wear a hat or scarf wasn't up for discussion, ever. "It's a short walk to my car; I don't need them." She had complete access to the shop and could come in if she wanted, but Joshua was sending a kind message of sorts; she'd take the day. Cecily grabbed her bag. "Oh. My package..."

"I got it." Josh stepped in the back and returned in short order with her (Oscar's) package. "Here you go. Come on."

Seven minutes later, she was guiding her Infinity Q70 toward home. Glad she drove (instead of taking public transportation), Cecily rode with the music off, ruminating her day, but inevitably, her thoughts shifted to either Oscar or Larimore.

Although Larimore wanted Josh to ensure she understood he was okay, Cecily remained uneasy. She couldn't remember Larimore ever calling her outside their established touch-base-and-catch-up calls: him calling her at her job and outside of their routine was cause for concern. "No use stressing over it, Cecily. You'll talk tomorrow." At a traffic light, she said a small prayer for her brother, and continued driving home, her heart sinking with each mile falling away the closer she got.

"Cheer up. If he likes what you've brought him..." Cecily grinned over that scenario, imagining and expecting a smile and hug from her husband upon receiving the bag of goodies—Mr. Hyde nowhere to be found (for the time being, at least). She anticipated Oscar's being pleased translating into an evening of watching television together maybe, or,...anything not involving the cold indifference most times filling her evenings. *You've got the party tomorrow. Oscar's looking forward to that. Between the food tonight and the party tomorrow, you should be good for a bit.*

Maybe. Maybe not. With Oscar, you just never knew.

Cecily sighed into the car's interior. "Am I being too sensitive? Too stressed about everything and overanalyzing?" She shrugged and changed lanes, giving the notion targeted thought. If she considered some of the other marital situations she could find herself in, she had to admit she was better off compared to what others endured. Oscar never blacked her eye or broke a bone—so there was that. And being with her was no picnic, either: her episodes and overall feebleness surely drove the average person up the wall.

Feebleness since when, Cecily?

She turned onto the roadway leading to her development, unwilling to answer: the feebleness began before the invasion, began after shopping for laundry detergent at Walmart. Passing the Exxon station, Cecily focused on it before returning her eyes to the road. She revisited Janyce's words at lunch earlier about the gas station and her brooch.

An anxious breath snagged in Cecily's throat before it stuttered out of her.

Larimore, episodes, Janyce, Mr. Hyde: it was all just too much. "Think about marketing for JAH." That was another source of stress but different; she shifted thoughts to the few terms and concepts she read about and kept her thoughts there for the remaining minutes before arriving at her home on Hemingway Lane.

She pulled into her garage and took the few minutes she needed before entering her home. Marcus sent a text: a picture of little Roland wearing the outfit she bought him for Christmas. That picture did the trick. She grabbed her belongings with a smile, thinking about Joshua's joke.

"'Nacho cheese'..." she scoffed with a chuckle and went into the house, not knowing little would be funny for the next few days.

Chapter Eight

Much Ado (about nothing)

H e had a taste for chocolate, but she brought home...key-lime pie.

He saw in her eyes how much she wanted him to be pleased, and that was always her mistake: she let him see the hope. The food was tasty, though, as good as Cecily could've done. And although annoyed she didn't bring home something chocolaty, he gave her what she want-ed (needed). He laughed and kissed her cheek in thanks.

Appearances were everything.

When she came in, he could tell she was feeling pretty good about her day. He often tried to offset those good vibes she got from being at work, but he planned to stop by JH Computer Company unannounced—to throw Cecily off and see what the big draw was—so he allowed the good vibes from her day to linger. He'd bring her back down. He always did. Bringing her down led to her trying harder next time—and that's what it was all about. Cecily was in this thing where she wanted "affection" from him; he'd use that to his advantage (the medication had his dick sending good signals again).

Oscar snickered. His wife was a wonderful source of entertainment. Maybe he'd leave her alone. But...

He spat in his spittoon and took another swallow of Corona, rubbing his chest to soothe the stupid flip-flop thing his heart insisted on doing sometimes (at least the heartburn went away). He loved Corona. Halim wanted him to stop drinking, too, and he would—after the Mabrys' party (maybe). He stared at his bottle, wanting it to be bigger for what he (Cecily) paid for it.

Guess I should tell her that asshole son and snooty daughter of hers called.

He scoffed at the commercial for car insurance during a rerun of an old *Adam-12* episode, thinking they likely called Cecily's cellphone. That was the one thing he couldn't fully control: her cellphone activity. As much as it irritated him, controlling her cellphone use or controlling her even having a cellphone could be a deal-breaker. Cecily was a pushover and all, but even rats fight back if forced into a corner. Janyce told him about some spy shit he could put on her phone, but he was doing well with the texting check-ins—maybe he'd look into that *Mission Impossible* shit later.

He sensed Marcus's distaste for him through the phone; the boy had no home training from what he could see, showed little respect. Dude didn't like him. Okay. Still, this was his house, and he was fucking the punk's mother; some respect should come with that. The daughter was a little better, he guessed, but she was quieter, like she became autistic or some shit whenever she had to interact with him.

He had to admit he'd wanted to spend the holiday with Cecily, have dinner with them at that restaurant they'd planned to go to. He never said as much, but Cecily was pretty, nice to look at and talk to, and sometimes that Pollyanna shit of hers had its place—like Christmastime; so yeah, he enjoyed spending time with her now and then.

But then Cecily started talking about moving the celebration to Marcus's place, and well, fuck that. Marcus showed no respect for him in Oscar's own home; Oscar could only imagine how he'd be treated sitting up in Marcus's townhouse (with that punk-name brat running around, too). So, he ended up spending time at his sister's house instead. Cecily dropped by and all—but it wasn't the same.

He didn't give her shit about her children much, either—he could see that being a major deal-breaker if he pushed it to the point he wanted to. Bottom line: he had the insurance coverage, the attorney-thing, and Plan B in operation. He'd have the last laugh.

If you live long enough...

Oscar sucked his teeth, using the remote to switch to the NBA channel. He was working on that, dammit. Speaking of which, he reached for his prescriptions on the end table and downed his pills with two swallows of Corona, finishing the bottle. He tossed the bottle into the recycle-bin with a sigh. Plan B needed to move along quicker—or Plan C may involve a rerun of Plan A. Controlling and influencing Cecily's perception of things was easier. He knew she sometimes realized something wasn't quite right anymore, but the doubt and fear she lived with now (that he helped her live with) kept her under his wing.

But that Dr. Alexander wasn't going for any of this. He could feel it. And he wasn't sure what to do about it. Which was why Plan C...

Bored with the basketball game, he swiped his sweaty brow with the hand towel he kept nearby and headed upstairs.

He wasn't winded when he reached the main level, but the extra breaths he needed as he paused in their kitchen told him he needed to move around more. Halim didn't want him doing anything (including fucking) for the next few, but this wouldn't work, either. Seemed like the fatigue was getting worse. Irritated, Oscar stared at the vase of flowers on the kitchen table.

Her and those flowers: always thinking they were a pick-me-up.

He went to the sink and opened the cabinet underneath, reaching in the back for his jar of special-made watering mixture: water, vinegar, ammonia, and his piss. He never poured much in the water, but enough to give it a tinge of oldness and mildew. The solution hurried the withering, because they hung around for longer when he didn't add it. Today, however, because he was more irritable, he added a few extra drops: fuck being cheerful. Fresh daisies wouldn't help his punk-ass-heart problems. Flowers watered, Oscar headed for Cecily's office.

He paused in the doorway, seeing if she'd been in her office since last he was.

Yep. A few folders were stacked neatly on her desk, along with some paper-clipped sheets. She kept separate holders for pens and pencils on each side of her desk blotter. She had everything on the desk aligned, in its place. He stared at the pairs of scissors in separate holders: one for left-handed use, the other for right-handed use.

That antidextorious shit of hers was weird; he didn't like it. It was like she had one-upped him somehow. His wife was an organized person, liked structure. She didn't freak out if things weren't organized, but Oscar could always tell when it bothered her. With a smirk bordering evil (to anyone looking at him), Oscar went over to Cecily's desk. He switched the scissors, placing the right-handed scissors in the holder on the left side, and vice versa for the left-handed scissors. Smiling to himself, he mixed pens and pencils in both containers (he didn't do the pen-pencil mix often—but enough to keep her confused). She would ask him, as she always did, if he'd been in her office, messed with anything, and he would tell her, as he always did, that he had his office setup in the basement and didn't need any of her high-sadity shit, so no, he hadn't been in her office.

Sometimes, though, she didn't ask him anything after he'd moved stuff around—and he wondered uncomfortably about those times. Oscar flipped through those papers and folders (something to do with marketing) before shifting them around. Satisfied, he headed upstairs, listening to the shower running.

As expected, Cecily was in their bathroom when he reached their bedroom. The water hadn't been running long: he had time.

Her Chanel handbag was on the floor next to her nightstand. He reached for it and sat on her side of the bed, turning on her lamp to see better. He fingered through Cecily's purse, checking for nothing and everything. She went to the Great Cookie for snickerdoodles. She hadn't mentioned that during his text check-ins. Okay. Oscar took a cookie and closed the bag. Holding the cookie between his lips, he reached for her wallet and helped himself to fifty of the one-hundred-eighty dollars in the bill slot. She wouldn't miss it. Even with those two degrees, Cecily didn't pay attention like that. When you're a millionaire, who's counting?

Oscar scoffed as he stuffed the money in his pocket. Valentine's Day was coming; he'd need the extra cash—especially with his seasonal shit abandoned.

He picked up her cellphone: locked. He'd tried several combinations of numbers (her brats' birthdays, birthdays of those brothers), but so far, no luck. She didn't have the passcode for his phone, either, but then, he didn't use one: he wasn't at all worried about Cecily checking his phone—she knew better. Oscar returned her phone, thinking of a way to make her give him the passcode. He could use guilt (usually successful), but he needed a reason for bringing up her having the passcode and his needing to know it. He trusted her, but he needed to *see* everything, be...*sure*. The cellphone could be a deal-breaker; he had to go about this right. It was important to make her feel she had privacy—without giving her any. He stared at the bathroom door, pondering busting in, and changed his mind. He'd long ago gotten rid of the idea of locked doors around here; she hated when he walked in on her in the bathroom—regardless of what she was doing.

Oscar checked his watch: almost time for hour blocks of *Good Times* and *The Jeffersons* on BET. Hopefully, the reruns were from the earlier seasons, the ones with James Evans and the first (and true) Lionel.

Chuckling, Oscar put his wife's belongings back in place and turned out her light. At the bathroom door, he turned the knob: unlocked. Good. Just checking.

He bit his cookie as he left their bedroom and headed for his man-cave, looking forward to drinking another Corona while laughing at James Evans and George Jefferson.

Sitting in a quiet corner of Applebee's, Oscar did his best to control his laughter. Odessa often said he had a sensitivity chip missing, but whatever, the shit was funny. Cecily laughed with him as she cleaned the spilled Fanta as best she could until the waitress returned, but he could see she didn't find it funny: orange soda stains splotched her jeans and tan sweater. There was light attendance in the restaurant, understandable for New Year's Eve, but those few heads turned their way, expressions hesitant on whether it was okay to laugh, too.

"You c-could help m-me, Oscar." Cecily mopped and blotted with the too-wet napkins in her hand.

He could, but the soda was rolling her way; she could get it better. "You're doing fine." Finally calming his laughter, he tossed his napkin her way as the waitress stepped up to get the job done. "Here you go."

Cecily stood as Jackie lowered her wet rag to their table. "I'll be b-back." She hurried to the ladies' room with her purse.

Jackie watched her departure. "It's not too bad, is it?" She was short and brown with big titties, her hair cornrowed into prison braids reaching her back.

He pulled his eyes from Jackie's ass just as she looked at him for an answer. He shook his head, finding her nose-piercing a turnoff; she'd have been one he fucked for the tittie-fun, then left alone. "Nah."

Jackie went about the task, drying and clearing and replacing. He guessed small talk wasn't a part of her training.

Oscar wasn't good at small talk, either, so that was fine. He watched her titties bounce and sway in her Applebee's uniform, watched her ass move with her twists and turns to reset their table. He spotted a gentleman several tables over, giving Jackie the same eye-roam. They exchanged looks, nodding silent agreement about the waitress (and fucking her for the tittie-fun), before the lady sitting with the gentleman popped his arm and he returned his attention to her with a guilty chuckle.

Table cleaned and reset, Jackie started away. "I'll bring her another soda. Your order will be ready soon."

"Great. Oh!"

Jackie turned back. "Yes?"

"Can you add extra deli pickle to my wife's order? She loves 'em."

Jackie frowned. "But she said *not* to add pickles to her burger order."

Oscar shook his head. "You misunderstood."

Jackie shrugged. "Okay, will do."

He watched her ass move away. Once it was out of view, he people-watched, waiting for his wife's return. She was probably in there working like crazy to get those stains out of her sweater; he believed it was one of her favorites. He imagined her expression when her order arrived with pickles: a combination of hurt, confusion, disgust, and surprise. She may suspect him of adding the pickles to her order, but she wouldn't say anything, likely blaming Jackie instead. Cecily's habit of denying or downplaying shit worked to his benefit.

Oscar picked up his glass of ice water, shaking his head. Cecily liked fresh cucumbers, but not pickles. What the fuck? That didn't even make sense. She said it was both the taste and texture of pickles that bothered her. That "texture" thing sounded snobby, and he was determined to put some sense in her head about it. Not that he was all that fond of pickles himself, but her reasoning was a problem for him. Oscar scoffed, "Texture." Crunching on ice, he turned toward the restrooms. She was taking a mighty long time.

He'd popped a mint in his mouth when she finally returned to their table. Just like he thought: she'd worked hard to get those stains out of that sweater. There was a tiny orange streak about the hem of her sweater, and her jeans were damp in spots, but she looked good as new. Sexy. "That's better."

Oscar chuckled. "Now, back to our date—after that brief interruption." He didn't mind saying mushy shit like that. Well, most times he did, but not today.

She smiled at him, and his dick jumped. Halim prescribed that medicine with instructions for him not to fuck, but that medication made him want to do nothing but. He wasn't hitting it like he used to, but things were looking up. He'd take it easy, but sex was on the agenda—and soon.

Jackie had already returned with a fresh Fanta, which Cecily sipped. "So, the meatballs are r-ready for t-tonight. You've g-got the Tornado p-punch barrel already over there. Only thing left is p-picking up the cake for Janyce. It's r-ready, so we can pick it up on the way h-home."

Oscar nodded; he looked forward to the party. Maybe the new year had something different in store for him. "That's cool."

"I p-pressed your slacks and p-picked up your shirt from the c-cleaners. Did you like the n-new cologne?"

"Oh, yeah. It's fine for tonight." He wasn't wearing it, though. He'd wear his Lagerfeld; it was a classic. She'll be disappointed, but oh well.

"Good. Still trying to d-decide if I'm w-wearing the pantsuit or the d-dress..." Her eyes held inquiry, as if waiting for him to decide for her.

She came correct with that, but Oscar shrugged. "Either of them looks nice on you, so..." The white pantsuit would be better in line with the party theme, but he said nothing.

"Thank you. And if I wear my hair p-pinned up, it'll be m-more carefree for s-socializing..." She looked at him again.

Without speaking, Oscar let her know that wasn't the right decision. He stared at her for meaningful seconds before checking his phone.

"Well, I could do a nice b-bun at the b-back instead..."

Oscar said nothing, keeping his eyes on his contact list.

"Oscar, it'll likely be h-hot in there."

That was true, but she knew the rules. He heard the plea in her voice, but he never fell for that weak shit. He closed the contacts app and opened his text messages.

Cecily sighed and sat back, turning her gaze outside.

Matter solved.

They were quiet until Jackie arrived with their dishes. "Enjoy. Let me know if you need anything." She turned away.

Oscar reached for the pepper to add to his surf-and-turf, watching the confusion, hurt, surprise, and disgust cross Cecily's face as she examined her plate. He held in a grin while seasoning his food.

With a glance at him holding a shade of suspicion, she looked toward Jackie as if to call her back, but sighed instead.

Oscar dug in. "What's the problem?"

"Sh-She added p-pickles."

"Oh. Just put 'em to the side. Are they on the burger, too?"

She lifted the bun, another unhappy expression crossing her face. Those little red splotches had virtually disappeared. "Yes. Ugh." She delicately, almost distastefully, removed the pickles, placing them on her appetizer dish. "I'll still t-taste them." She added the two quarter-slices of deli pickle to the round-cut ones on the plate. Pickles everywhere.

Oscar munched a shrimp. "I seriously doubt that. Don't start."

She crossed her arms and mumbled, "I'm n-not starting anything. I d-don't like p-pickles," looking like a schoolkid as she pouted at her plate. "And j-juice is t-touching the bun. I can't eat this." She shifted the plate toward the table's edge and looked around for Jackie.

Oscar sliced his steak. "You're telling me, you're going to waste that food and the chef's time because some juice is on the bread? You're overreacting...as usual." He forked his meat.

"Sorry." Cecily stared at the rejected order. When she folded her upper lip in, he knew she was going to attempt to eat it. With another sigh, she guided the plate back in front of her.

"Is the bread soaked with it, Cecily?"

She looked more closely at the burger and shook her head.

"Well, there you go. At least try the damn sandwich. This is a lunch date: you need to eat something" He made that last statement sound more caring and concerned than necessary, for appearance's sake.

How he phrased that last sentence made her wan smile brighten. "I guess. And you're r-right." She ate a french fry.

When she reached to pick up her burger for a (tentative) bite, Oscar stopped her with a hand to hers. "Use your knife and fork, maybe. Like you do with fried chicken. Don't wanna touch wet bread if you don't have to." He hated when she ate her chicken that way, but he was trying to get some pussy later. He wasn't a rapist, so he had to play the game.

She smiled even brighter, her eyes showing a different surprise at his suggestion. "I can d-do that." She then cut her burger into moderate pie-slice-like wedges and forked one. "H-Here goes…"

He paused consumption of his fries to watch what developed (pretty much already having a good idea).

Cecily put the food in her mouth and chewed maybe twice before she frowned and grabbed a napkin to spit the forkful in. "Nope, can't do it. Blech!" She shook her head, covering her mouth (and the retch behind it) with a new napkin.

Oscar snickered and bit a fry. "Unreal. Maybe that was a bad section. Try again."

Her eyes told him she didn't want to, but he told her with his eyes, she'd better. He pressed his foot onto hers for good measure.

She winced and tried again, this time chewing and swallowing. She sipped some Fanta and rose from the table. "Scuse me, Oscar."

Although he wanted to, he didn't laugh or say anything else. He called Jackie to the table and asked her to remove the offending order. Keeping his later goal in mind, he also asked her to bring back some new fries and a couple of dressed-up sliders for Cecily—no pickles. Told her his wife was vomiting this very moment from all those pickles. Jackie gave him a look of annoyed confusion but fuck her. He returned to his plate, having a good time with his grilled shrimp.

As Cecily returned, he watched the hesitancy and dread in her eyes shift into warm surprise upon spotting her plate gone. "She took it away?"

Oscar nodded. "Yeah. Told her to. She's bringing you a fresh round of fries and some sliders."

She kissed his cheek (and his dick jumped again). "Thank you."

With a shrug, he reached for his drink. "No problem. Next year, though, pickles: your New Year's resolution."

She sat with a sigh of relief, not answering him, but she didn't have to: it wasn't a request. She reached for one of his fries and bit a portion, chewing as her eyes roamed the restaurant. He liked when she did shit like that. "Might need a n-nap before the p-party."

He chuckled sincerely at that, making his wife grin. "Yeah, maybe. Think I need a haircut?"

Cecily scanned his hair and face. He was balding now and tried compensating with fuller facial hair. He'd started tiring of the muttonchops look but wasn't sure what to try next. She shook her head. "You g-got it cut last week. A few wh-whiskers trimmed m-maybe."

"You'll take care of it for me? Before the party?"

Cecily nodded, finishing the french fry. "Okay."

Jackie returned with new food for Cecily. "Sorry about the mix-up. It's on us."

Seeing Cecily about to part her mouth with an apology of her own to tell them it was okay, that she'd pay for the order (such a pushover), Oscar spoke. "Good. That'll work."

Jackie sent him another annoyed look he didn't care about and stepped away.

Cecily dug in, lifting a tiny burger and biting it in half.

He laughed at that, finding his wife cute when she let go (sometimes). "Slow down."

Laughing at herself, she put her burger down and nibbled another fry. "I know, right? Didn't r-realize I was so h-hungry."

"Because you hardly eat, Cecily." He wiped his brow and back of his neck with a napkin.

She stared at him, as if determining whether this was getting ready to be a thing, but it wasn't. He was actually in a fairly good mood right now. Seeing all was well, she reached for her Fanta.

"No gray earls with the burgundy monts?"

She chuckled and shook her head. "Earl Grey with bergamot. And not today."

He hated if she corrected him, but that fairly good mood was doing its thing (mostly). "Oh. And, you're sure you don't want to blow the party, go to that Night Watch service? I'm not going, but if you wanted to..."

"It's okay. I'd p-prefer we do whatever it is, t-together."

"Cool. ...Why aren't you working? You love it so much."

"Shop's closed. N-Not opened for b-business until next w-week."

He heard trace sadness in her reply. "Wow. That would be great for me. Sure wish I had a job like that: willy-nilly hours and shit, hanging around computers that do the work for you..."

Cecily opened her mouth with a response and then folded her lips together instead, and he didn't like that at all (good mood or not). He saw the change in approach alter her expression. "I can see about—"

"Computers aren't my thing." He didn't know what her initial response was, but she cleaned it up well. Her efforts to please and appease him never failed. He had her trained well—like one of Packluv's dogs.

He'd done his share of data entry (so he could work computers), but he only said what he said to make her think he cared about his limited employment situation. Working nine-to-five 365 days a year wasn't his thing, either. Those who worked for some personal fulfillment bull-shit (like his wife) were only making excuses for getting caught in the rut-wheel of life. It was much wiser having time to enjoy the world—and if you can manage it on someone else's dime while still having the finer things in life, more power to you.

She opened her mouth again, folded her lips again, changing her initial reply again, and it irked the shit out of him. She kept biting her tongue on some smart-ass answer or something. Where the fuck was this coming from? The fairly good mood grew shaky.

Cecily finished that first slider and ate a fry. She sipped some Fanta. "Well, let's n-not worry about that right n-now. We'll investigate f-find-ing something you're m-more interested in once w-we get into the new year." Her smile was hopeful, a tad pleading.

She'd cleaned up her response again, but he remained pissed over her needing to clean it up at all. "I'm not worried. You forget: I've been a security guard. I know my way around a crime scene, know a thing or two about police procedure. Got contacts on both sides of the line, so I could make detective if I put my mind to it."

She nodded agreeably, but he could've sworn a tiny smirk was in it.

He needed to rein her ass in. "Plus, there's that other thing I told you about..."

The fear shooting through her hazel eyes satisfied him. She nodded again (no sign of any smirk).

Better.

Years ago, before he locked shit down legally, he'd hinted he'd killed someone—and only trusted her to keep his secret. It was some shit he tried on a humble, but it worked; she believed it, and it was his trump card ever since. Guilt-ridden or fear-induced sex was better than no sex;

he wasn't a rapist. "So, I'm not worried. The right job will come along; maybe in law enforcement, maybe not."

Cecily pushed her plate aside: she'd eaten a good portion, considering. "I'll wait on d-dessert till the p-party. Want anything else?"

Oscar gazed at his plate: empty except for the broccoli he always ordered but rarely finished. She preferred eating out to avoid him saying something about her cooking, but Cecily could cook—it was his job to make sure she didn't get her head too big about shit. "Nah, I'm good."

Cecily called for the check. She looked longingly at the lady a few tables over (who also prepared to leave), putting on an entire ensemble of winter-wear: coat, scarf, gloves, hat...

He made Cecily keep her hair always styled and in place to please him, telling her it helped keep her looks up, told her she was stronger for being able to withstand the cold—unlike the other soft females needing cover. Hats and shit messed her hair up. Even if the wind blew, she'd have to restyle her hair if she wore a hat, so why bother? She finally got the message with his punch to her upper back after coming in with a hat and scarf on. And although he bundled up sometimes, her ability to tolerate the shit he pulled was a weakness, making it his job to take advantage. She put up with it, accepted it—that was on her; it wasn't his fault.

Jackie returned with the check, ensured everything was fine, and walked away as Cecily reached for her credit card.

Oscar stood and grabbed his coat from the back of his chair. Cecily stood, wearing that stupid look of hoping he'd help with her coat, but he ignored her as usual. It was stupid because she still hoped after all these years when she knew he didn't do that lame-ass shit. "I'ma hit the head first. Meet you outside." He walked away on her soft sigh, doing his best not to be irritated by it.

It was shy of three in the morning before he finally got what he came for, although it looked like he wouldn't.

The party turned out chill—almost. The tornadoes were a hit, and while Cecily moaned and dreaded reaction to them, everyone loved her sweet-and-sour meatballs. Hank had a mix of music jumping, so Oscar got in a few good-foot grooves with some lady guests (ignoring the painful yet familiar heartburn that should've burned off hours ago).

Some men there were nothing but assholes: opinionated, self-absorbed punks who came off a little lazy to him when they weren't interested in joining his downline. But he wasn't there to win friends, just party and bring the new year in right. And he would have...if Cecily hadn't left early.

He messed up by not telling her they switched the décor and attire to a black-and-white party theme. Janyce passed the news on to him, telling him she'd called everyone else and let them know and for him to tell Cecily. Okay. His bad. He guessed he could've said something when she chose the red dress to wear instead of the white pantsuit, but okay, fuck it, he didn't. They got there, and Cecily went through the whole embarrassment phase over being the only one not in black or white, but as the party rolled on, he thought she'd come around and gotten over it. She sat at the end of the sofa, smiling politely while exchanging small talk, so he thought she was good.

But then, as he watched her, he saw her doing that deep-thinking shit. Saw her looking around at everyone and then glancing down at herself, saw her go to the powder room a few times. Even so, again, he thought she was good. She came back to the sofa and chilled, but she wasn't all there, doing more of her deep-thinking shit that annoyed him to no end—because it made her look slow or something, retarded. What did she have to think so long and hard about?

He came over to her a few times to be sure she was cool, and she said she was—until she wasn't and had blown the joint. Janyce told him she'd left, and he used powers he didn't know he had to remain calm and unaffected, acting as if her leaving early was a part of things all along. She ended up going to church after all: that Night Watch service she'd said she preferred they both went to.

When the countdown came, he was in the powder room himself (listening to the whoops, hollers, kisses, and well wishes for a happy new year), staring in the mirror and wondering how to address the situation. He returned to the party and jammed with a few female guests for another half-hour before saying his goodbyes. He was horny as hell when he got home (a long-missed feeling), but his wife was still out watching the night, and he mentally battled how he wanted to handle things when she got in, versus how he *needed* to handle things (to meet a pressing, horny objective).

Having gotten the heartburn to settle (and craving a cigarette), he'd made it a point to be in their bedroom when she came home (instead of brooding down in his man-cave), expecting her to have an attitude and show some of that kick she used to have (before the breaking). However, when she entered their bedroom around two-thirty, humming "Auld Lang Syne," it seemed the church service did her some good. Or so he thought.

The argument (if you want to call it that) lasted maybe fifteen minutes: her stutteringly whining and bitching about him not telling her about the attire change; disappointed he didn't wear the new cologne she got him; some nagging shit about him flirting with the female guests—making much ado about nothing. He'd told her as much, and at last got her down off her sadity high horse in much the opposite way he usually went about things with her.

When he spotted the moment in her eyes greenlighting getting some pussy, he took full advantage, playing to her silly need for affection. He rubbed her arm or shoulder (couldn't remember which), held her for a quick second, and then kissed her, pushing his tongue into her mouth to move shit along.

Whenever they French-kissed, he watched Cecily, liked being sure her eyes were closed. Women closing their eyes during a tongue-kiss showed their weakness, vulnerability, and desire to be owned. Her eyes fluttered open every blue moon to find him looking dead at her as they kissed. It didn't bother him in the least. Nah, he wasn't one of those mushy dudes, closing his eyes and shit—he liked to see what was going down on *her* end, liked seeing she was totally under his spell.

Oscar heard her soft pleas for him to slow down, to be "softer" with her or whatever, but she always said that shit, and he rarely paid any attention to it, and he still got the pussy. He could've paid more attention this time, he guessed, but he was still pissed about her leaving him at the party, so her needs weren't on the list this time.

He grabbed Cecily's breasts and thrust into her from behind, giving her some talk, and doing his best to make it last as long as possible (he didn't know when his dick would be firing right again). They didn't do it face-to-face often; doggy-style was the usual order of the day because he didn't like kissing while fucking, didn't need her caressing him and shit while he was getting some—it was too distracting. All of that was best left to romance novels. He sometimes gave it to her that way on their anniversary (or her birthday or something) because he knew she liked it, but he mainly needed her to shut up and bend over.

His nuts began singing their wonderful song. "Oh, shit!" He pushed in hard and shot inside, giving her what she came for. The sex they had the other week was fine, but these meds had shit back on point! Cecily fell to the bed as he pulled out, and he smacked her ass in appreciation. He checked out his dick: swollen like a motherfucker! He was already working with something serious, but Halim's pills put him on super or some shit. Halim also mentioned needing to monitor his liver function because of the medication, but Oscar wasn't worried.

His wife stood and pulled that dress back down over her nice butt. Cecily was slender but had meat where she needed: her ass and tits.

He kissed her cheek. "That was good."

She gathered her stockings and stuff from the floor with a half-smile. "Thanks. I love you."

"Back at you. Happy New Year." He stretched, feeling 40 again (or hell, even 48 again). "Want me to finish unzipping?"

"H-Happy New Year. N-No, I'll d-do it." She turned for their bathroom.

He unfastened his pants, adjusting his boxer-briefs to re-tuck his softening penis. "A little TV?"

"Okay." She closed the door. The shower started soon after that.

Oscar sat on his side of the bed, working to control his anger again. Well, not *anger*.

It never failed: after sex with him, she showered. He never said anything, determined not to give her any idea her always showering afterward bothered him, but it did. Had she showered after in the beginning? He believed she did. He scoffed. His breath wasn't the best these days, but the mints helped, and yes, he sweat a lot (and she knew why), but he was never funky by any means. So, what was her problem? "Man, fuck her. Long as I get some." He whispered it (not really feeling that way about it at all). Sighing, he grabbed some lounge pants and a t-shirt from his chest of drawers to change into for bed.

Cecily took forever to emerge, so he opened the bathroom door: combing her hair. She startled upon his entry, with this expression both sad and...annoyed. She wore a t-shirt nightgown as established. Although his dick was less and less cooperative over the last, she could only wear pajama bottoms during *that time*. Nightgowns made for easy access if he wanted some during the night; he didn't want to fumble with lowering pants over her butt, preferring to lift her gown and stick it in when the need called.

She smelled nice and fresh from her shower.

He sniffed the air. "Might want to take another, Cesspool. That one didn't take." He laughed and closed the door on that hesitant and hurt expression of hers. She never appreciated his sense of humor. Sometimes she did, but most times she didn't.

Oscar climbed into bed and turned on the television, a mix of emotions making him uncomfortable; he wanted to enjoy having busted a nut, but something about Cecily was changing, and he didn't like not being able to put a finger on what was different. Did Dr. Alexander show her that fucking secret door already? He scoffed and changed the channel. He'll get shit back on track—and soon. "Come on, Cecily!"

She exited their bathroom and joined him, climbing under the covers on her side. "Wh-What're we w-watching?"

"Not sleepy yet, so the news should help me in that direction."

She chuckled softly (she got his humor sometimes). "That's fine."

Damn straight. Cecily enjoyed watching the news, but it bored the shit out of him. The world was fucked up; that was the gist—no need to tune in every day to see that shit. He put a hand to her thigh as they watched, and her faint sigh told him that was a good move on his part. He knew what to do—when he felt like doing it.

Some political news story came on about some local politician "making a difference." He nudged his wife and pointed at the White lady bullshitting about changing the situation in a neighboring county. "You've done pretty well having those two degrees, but *she's* doing something with her education, huh...?"

"I...I guess."

He looked at her, gripping her thigh tighter. "What?"

Cecily pulled the covers up around her while slinking lower into them. "Y-Yes. She's done something with her education."

"Unlike you."

"Un... Unlike m-me."

He nodded and kissed her cheek. "You haven't done *bad*, though, so it's all good."

Nodding, she focused on the television.

Oscar watched the news, getting sleepy. He cut some quiet cheese and settled into the mattress to call it a night. Pretending to be looking for the remote, he shifted the covers to open the oven and send the smell her way. "Want to set the timer— Oh, here it is..." He grabbed the remote and set the television timer for auto shut-off after thirty minutes.

Wanting to see just how much had changed with her, Oscar watched his wife out of the corner of his eye. If she acted like she detected nothing, they were still in a good spot. If she reacted negatively, some realignments and adjustments would be necessary.

His eyes didn't water from the smell, but it wasn't one of his mild ones, either. But Cecily never so much as twitched her nose in response.

Yeah, they were good.

She usually meditated during her morning run, focusing on nothing but the sensation and sound of her breathing, but she couldn't manage it. So, instead, she sat in a corner of the coffee-shop in the mini-mall three miles away from home (the distance of her halfway point during her run). Cecily gazed out the window at the busy activity, sipping her tea, watching others prepare to leave another year behind. She checked her watch: she'd head back in another five, ten minutes.

Maybe the late start had her out of sorts. She would've finished her run hours ago by now, but she couldn't do anything this morning until she heard from her brother. Turns out he had good news—*very* good—so all her worrying was for nothing.

And Larimore's good news should have freed her mind to allow for good meditation during her run (when she finally got around to it), but that wasn't in the cards; she was too preoccupied with the Mabrys' party tonight. She shillyshallied between looking forward to the party and dreading it, mostly wanting the day (and that party) to be behind her.

Cecily sipped and watched the mini-mall activity. She liked peo-ple-watching. The lemongrass tea was soothing and flavorful, but her snickerdoodles would have topped things off. She only had four left (she'd spent a good five minutes this morning ruminating the belief there were five left in the bag, before deciding she'd miscounted—or not), and bringing them on her run would've been awkward and uncalled for, so she'd planned to enjoy her snickerdoodles with some lemongrass tea during one of her many quiet (and lonesome) moments sure to arise over the coming days.

Nina Simone's "I Think It's Gonna Rain Today" floated on low through her earphones as she people-watched, the song on repeat. Thoughts about the party stirred the anxiety she maintained a close friendship with, so Cecily allowed her mind to wander to places of daydreams, where she could disconnect with the here-and-now. It was always better in the daydreams: the atmosphere was welcoming, there was tea aplenty, and the people were always so...*friendly*...

"...Missus Brooks? A refill?" The voice traveled over and through her Nina.

Cecily startled and looked up, removing her earphones. She was a semi-regular here; a few personnel knew her by name.

Kara smiled politely, holding a fresh pot of hot water. "Tea refill?"

Cecily looked in her cup: empty except for the wet tea bag resting at the bottom. She didn't remember finishing it. "Oh! Well, no..." She checked her watch: those five, ten minutes had come and gone—thir-teen minutes ago. Where had the time (and the tea) gone? Cecily re-turned her gaze to Kara and smiled. "No, thank you. Need to head back, and on the quick." She stood, placing her earphones in her ears. "Tell Portia 'Hello' from me, and you all have a Happy New Year, okay?"

Kara backed up with a nod and smile as Cecily stepped past. "I will, and you, too! See you next year!"

Chuckling, Cecily stepped into the cold of New Year's Eve and stretched some, thinking it would be best to wear the white pantsuit to the party instead of the red dress. She wanted to wear the red, though, so she'd have to see. She began her run with a jog, getting her blood pumping to counter the winter temps. "Wear the red, Cecily. Face those fears, girl." Grinning to herself, she headed home, surprised she could get in some meditation this time.

Several hours later, Cecily checked her sweet-and-sour meatballs for the hundredth time, believing she could still taste those pickles from her lunch date with Oscar. She'd brushed and gargled since, but pickle juice haunted her nose and throat passages. The pickle-fiasco at Applebee's still had her irritable and on edge, but she was determined not to let it influence the rest of the evening—and the party. The idea was to end one year and begin the next, jamming to the beat. Sounded good. Sounded...like a plan.

Even with Oscar's silent treatments about her hair and his job situation, his practically flying off the handle over the pickles, Cecily had to admit their date (Oscar's words, not hers this time) went far better than usual. It gave her hope, and she held on to it, because hope was a good thing. She turned the heat down on the meatballs to keep them warm instead of overcooking and smiled to herself, recalling their discussion about her working (at JAH Technologies) and Oscar not so much.

"Where was that coming from, Cecily?" She checked for her husband's whereabouts, sighing her relief he wasn't near. She shrugged internally. The sarcastic replies to Oscar's comments about working (replies remaining on her tongue and behind her lips), were new only because they usually stayed in her head and never, ever, traveled so far as to pause on her tongue, making her think on her feet and utter more suitable replies to his complaints about his (non)-employment status.

She had plenty money and didn't mind sharing it with him. But she wasn't a fan of laziness, for laziness' sake. If he didn't work a job, she would be fine with him volunteering his time. Her husband, however, seemed far from that type, yet he bitched and moaned about not working—when Cecily surmised (down in that part of her she only visited rarely) he was fine not being employed. She could never say those things to him (she knew better), so the strong desire to voice her views (even sarcastically) was...shocking. Good thing smarter heads prevailed—or she would've been a (painful) no-show for the party. Oscar never broke bones or blacked eyes, but he did enough; he didn't have to break or blacken.

Uplifted over Larimore's good news, Cecily headed upstairs to trim Oscar's hair and get a nap before getting ready for the party.

The lady or woman in red may have had its positive connotations, but Cecily didn't feel any of them applied as she sat on the sofa at Janyce and Hank's house, music blaring and people dancing or socializing: people in varying combinations of black and white (a guest or two in silver). Of the fifty-plus people there, she was the only one in red—and all the more miserable for it.

She'd been leaning toward the red and so went with it because she wanted to make a personal statement. Red was the color of blood, so she avoided wearing it since the attack; she had enough non-direct reminders of what happened to her, including the scar on her abdomen: direct reminders of blood weren't necessary. So, for the party, she was taking a page from Janyce's book by wearing red and facing her fears. Oscar watched and sighed his impatience as she dithered wearing the white pantsuit or the red dress, and uttered not one word about the attire theme change. That hurt her feelings, because Cecily knew Janyce passed the update on to him; she'd said so upon seeing Cecily in red.

One positive Cecily grabbed at was facing her ochlophobia. Her fear of crowds was improving by lessening, such that she considered herself better in that arena. With the charity ball coming up in late January (and the increased number of people attending), the Mabrys' party was an excellent precursor.

Cecily smiled and laughed at the innocent jokes at her expense over her odd-man-out attire, engaged in small talk with some of Janyce's friends, and watched as Oscar engaged in more than small talk with some of Janyce's friends. Oscar's nose wasn't the strongest, but he looked stylish in his white shirt and black slacks, the trimming she applied to his hair adding something extra. She was okay with some flirting, but wasn't so okay when he didn't even flirt with her.

Just leave.

That imperative gave her the warm-and-fuzzies, but Cecily stayed put awhile longer, occasionally stepping into the powder room and convincing herself to soldier through. She danced with Hank (since her husband hadn't approached her for a dance) and laughed and talked more with Janyce's friends (accepting compliments about her meatballs), until the cliquishness began permeating the party atmosphere, and she found herself mostly sitting on the sofa and smiling politely. The dancing, laughing, and socializing of fifty-plus people also raised the temperature inside the Mabry home—and Cecily wished she'd been allowed to wear her hair up.

She sat on that sofa, the woman in red, eminently the non-life of the party, with the music blasting and the guests jamming, but the silence of looming loneliness echoed deep inside her. People often emphasized distinctions between being alone and being lonely when discussing their social status, but Cecily didn't feel any clarifications were necessary for her: she was both. Oscar checked on her (halfheartedly), but he wasn't a source of comfort, so Cecily didn't bother him with the details. However, she rose and circulated through the house to not irritate him over her being a wallflower.

One half-hour rolled into the next, the current year yielding to the incoming one. But something changed for her as ten o'clock moved toward eleven o'clock—and it wasn't a change for the better. She couldn't put her finger on it, but something about being at Hank and Janyce's made her unwell, reminded her, for some ungodly reason, of the attack two years ago. Why?

Cecily got some punch, deciding to stand and people-watch to suppress whatever was brewing instead of sitting and dwelling on it, but that only helped a little. Something about being there stimulated tinges of having an episode. Something (Furniture? Decorations? Refreshments? Music?) reminded her of being raped and stabbed and beaten.

Leave, Cecily.

With Oscar nowhere to be found, Cecily did just that, giving Janyce a good parting excuse. Ignoring the cold icily coursing under her heavy coat and going for her nylon-covered legs, she hurried to the car, figuring (hoping) Oscar would be okay walking less than a block to their home after the party. She just had to get away. Going home, however, wasn't an option, either; she'd do nothing but think and obsess about why the Mabry home became a trigger, and she feared she'd break down into a worse episode if she did that.

Such a winter of discontent.

Wrong outfit. Oscar's flirting. The Mabry home suddenly giving her the creeps. Lonely among many. Bad omens were out tonight, determined to thwart any of her attempts to face what happened to her with positivity and resolve. Why was she such a magnet for bad juju?

She started the car and turned the heat to full blast, wishing she had a hat or scarf to curl around her head and ears while she waited for the interior to warm; she'd tried sneaking wearing a hat before—with unfriendly results. Cecily clutched her pocket-handkerchief, watching the cold, stiff night through her windshield, trying to understand why her life was so different now, why *she* was so different now.

That line of thinking, however, almost always put twisty knots in her belly, creating its own version of episode-like feeling. And now, a memory from that night wanted to push through again. It swirled and teased just out of reach again, an annoying occurrence. Weeks ago, she'd tried hard to allow it to surface, ready to have the memory free her from the despair—but that was weeks ago.

Cecily pulled off, knowing where her escape awaited, determined to keep the memory buried for now.

It was two-nineteen a.m. when she pulled into their driveway. She parked and waited, listening to the radio with a mellow weightlessness in her chest and limbs. The Watch Night service (Oscar called it *Night Watch*, but she dared not correct him) was uplifting, informative, and she thoroughly enjoyed it. She hadn't been to one since the year before...the incident.

She pulled her phone from her purse, accessing her text messages: three weird ones from Oscar (not threatening, but oddly, concerned?), texts from Janyce, Kyle, Marcus, Chelsea, and one from Joshua.

Josh's text came right at midnight, wishing her a Happy New Year and including some words of inspiration with spiritual overtones. It wasn't a group text, either, just from him to her. Josh only texted her regarding business matters or for something like holiday greetings, so seeing his text was a pleasant surprise, primarily because the message was a little unlike him. Josh wasn't atheist (he was borderline agnostic, if anything), so seeing his inspirational text dotted with spiritual references was...interesting. Maybe she was rubbing off on him. She reread his text, his words reaching into her, steadying her pulse.

Cecily listened to a replay broadcast of the countdown of what was now "last year's" hits. She guessed she was giving herself some time, preparing for Oscar's response to her leaving the party early. But she could never brace herself or prepare for what Oscar would or wouldn't do because, with him, she just never knew. That unpredictability of his (well, she knew what to expect from him in certain circumstances) kept her wary, unsettled. But it was a new year doggonit: the Watch Night service inspired her...differently. Maybe it was time to let him know how he failed *her* for a change—especially tonight. Cecily turned the car off and entered the house, humming the chorus to "Auld Lang Syne."

She climbed the stairs with a bit of attitude despite her anxiety, her mood darkening more with breathing in the aldehydes, sandalwood, and Tonka beans of Oscar's Lagerfeld. She'd bought him a bottle of Giorgio Armani Code as a surprise and to change things up. It was, she thought, a nice way of telling him she was tired of smelling only either Aramis or Lagerfeld on him. Those odors kept her in the past (with the Gingerbread Man).

Only she understood why (maybe Naomi would), but she believed a change that small could go a long way. She could never express it quite like that to him, so she bought the new fragrance and tied it to the Mabrys' party, hoping for the best. However, that hope was dashed when he got in the car reeking of Lagerfeld. She didn't comment, just went to the party with him—to find she wasn't dressed right...

After a deep breath, she entered their bedroom.

Oscar sat on his side of the bed, bent over, a glass containing a mixture of baking soda and water on his nightstand. He looked at her, this weird mix of threat and concern in his eyes.

"It's better if you stand or sit up. Staying bent over like that can prolong it." She entered her closet and kicked off her heels, leaving her purse and coat there, too. She returned to find him standing as he finished the glass of heartburn relief.

He set the glass down. "Hello."

"H-Hello."

"How was church?"

Although the service was great, she shrugged to assuage him. "Okay. And the p-party...?" Here it was.

He faced her. "Well, that's just it. You would know if you had stayed. But I can see you've got your nose out of joint about something, so let's have it."

Cecily swallowed as he stepped in her direction. He rarely cared if she was upset about something, but his posture suggested he did care, so she didn't know what to think. "I...I was the on-only one in r-red, Oscar. Why d-didn't you t-tell me about the attire ch-change?"

He made that face as if to mimic her, but shook his head with this strange smirk. "I thought you knew."

"But the white p-pantsuit was *right there*. You s-said n-nothing."

He shrugged and went to his chest of drawers, removing his watch. "I thought you knew."

She went silent. She guessed it was reasonable for him to assume Janyce told her, but Janyce had said she'd told him to tell her about the change. Cecily sighed, a part of her still believing he didn't tell her on purpose.

"That it?"

He was prompting her to get things off her chest, and when had he ever done that? "Well..."

"I'm listening. For the moment, anyhow. Go 'head. You wore the red and stood out from the crowd. Most people would love an opportunity like that, but not you. What else?"

Now she felt stupid. He had a point (although that wasn't the point). "Why didn't you w-wear the Armani f-for me? You didn't t-tell me about that, e-either."

He dropped a low chuckle, shaking his head again. "I didn't know I had to say anything to you."

Cecily looked at him, again finding his nose unflattering and forgetful. "Well, I th-thought you said y-you were w-wearing it—when we were at l-lunch earlier."

"I wore what I like, what works. Stop trying to change me."

"I'm n-not."

"Oh no? Getting me new cologne without seeing how it would smell on me, wanting me to check with you if I wear it or not—!"

"That's not what I—" She went quiet.

"Why don't you like what I wear?"

"It's not that I don't like it..." Her shoulders grew stiff.

"So, what is it, then?" Challenge pulsed through his question.

"It's a n-new year: I thought you'd w-want to t-try s-something new."

"Because you don't like *old* Aramis or Lagerfeld."

Cecily shook her head. "No, Oscar. It's n-not that."

He scoffed. "Anyway, is there anything else, Your Majesty?" His words simmered with restrained anger, his snide address to her sounding nothing like that address coming from someone else.

It was no surprise she wasn't getting anywhere with him by expressing her feelings, but she forged ahead, getting it off her chest for her own sake (there'd been no pinching or punching—so there was that). "The...The f-flirting."

"The what?" He sounded angrily confused.

"The way you w-were standing with those w-women at the p-party: the laughing, t-touching their arms, those l-looks you were g-giving them, leaning on th-them. ...You...You d-didn't do any of that with m-me."

Silence swelled for some seconds, and then he laughed softly, shaking his head.

She didn't think anything was funny (but that was Oscar). "What?"

"*You*, that's what." He edged toward her. "You were jealous."

"May— Maybe a little. But that's not the p-point."

He stood before her, his Lagerfeld stronger than it needed to be. "Oh, but that's the whole point, because I wasn't flirting. Socializing, being polite, yes. But not flirting. You've got that part wrong."

She frowned. "H-How do I h-have that wrong?"

"Because men and women consider different things 'flirting.' I wasn't flirting. It was all in your head, if you ask me." He rubbed her upper arm, much like he did a few women at that party, but the gesture was so unexpected, she went mute. "Just your imagination, Cecily. I wasn't flirting. If I was, you'd be more than a little jealous."

That was true, she guessed. She sighed. "You're r-right. I'm s-sorry."

He lowered his hand from her arm, and Cecily had to admit she liked it being there. "No problem. But you know how you are, Cecily, how you can get. Think first before you start bitching and accusing."

She nodded her agreement; she could do that.

"Anything else?" He stepped away and popped a mint before coming back to her.

She could hear in his question he didn't want there to be anything else, but... "I th-think...I think things w-would be b-better if...if we showed m-more affection..."

Her husband sighed and rolled his eyes. "This again? What is it with you and this mushy shit lately?" His eyes hardened with a hint of cruelty before softening again, his expression growing into that unkind smirk. "You won't be happy unless I'm curled, all snug and warm, up your butthole."

She blinked at him, finding the way he twisted things so unfair.

"Won't you?"

Her spirit deflating, Cecily shook her head. "That's n-not what I'm s-saying."

He made that expression as if to mimic her mockingly again but changed course. What was up with *him* tonight? *That* was the question. "We show affection, Cecily. It may not be all lovey-dovey twenty-four-seven, but it works for us. Leave it alone."

She started to say, *Works for you*, started to remind him the affection was greater in the beginning, but she knew better.

He rubbed her arm again, giving it a kind squeeze. "We done?"

The threat in his words (they'd better be done) contradicted the strange warmth in his touch. Cecily nodded, deciding to take what she could get.

"Good." He gripped her arm, guided her close, and hugged her briefly before shoving his tongue into her mouth.

She supposed they were making up, but it all felt very one-sided, because while he was well past eight, moving on to a hard nine, she struggled to get up to four.

He pulled her closer, pressing that definitive hint of bulge against her thigh.

Cecily pulled back from his stiff, poky kiss with a brief gasp of, "Wait," before he pushed his tongue back into her mouth and began unzipping her dress at the back.

He'd curtailed his smoking, but the minty sourness of his mouth still made extended kissing difficult. But she wanted to get closer to his number nine level of arousal, so she continued their kiss. She didn't need to part her lids to check if his eyes were open; she could feel him watching her kiss him—and that was creepier than seeing it for herself. Still, she needed more of a gentle approach. "Slow down, sweetie. Let's just—"

He released her with a growl of annoyance. "A'ight. Damn!" He stepped back and released his erection through his zipper. "This is what you came for...right here..." He reached for her arm again, guiding her lower.

Yes, it was all very one-sided. Accepting her new seven-year normal, she lowered to her knees and got on with their usual.

He exhaled. "Yeah. That's it. Get at that Big Bopper. Don't be shy..."

Cecily mouthed his erection. His penis was harder than it had been the last few times they had sex; maybe that was a side effect of his new medication. Harder was undoubtedly good (or could be under different circumstances), but her husband was in no way...bigger. Oscar may have had a "bopper," but there wasn't anything big about it. If memory served her correctly, her current husband didn't have the length and girth of her first.

Rest in peace, Roland.

Oscar grunted and guided her to stand. "Turn around. Bend over..."

She turned and faced away from him, lifting her dress over her rear before lowering her nylons and underwear to her ankles.

He reached inside her dress (opened at the back) and sent his hands around her body to lift her bra over her breasts and take them in his hands, and she couldn't tell if his low grunt of "Soft tits..." was compliment or complaint. He used his hold to her breasts to guide her into a bend forward, pushing his erection inside with a grunt of sexual pleasure.

Cecily closed her eyes, supplying the standard responses to his sex-talk as he thrust into her, going to that mental place where things were less humiliating and much more tolerable. Little was required of her during these times; she didn't have to move or grind with him to give some sensation back. He only wanted her doing that sometimes, and he usually let her know when. She recollected telling Dr. Alexander she climaxed every time she and Oscar had sex. She felt bad about fibbing to her doctor, but she also believed Naomi knew the real.

"Oh, shit!" He pushed in deeper with his climax. That was long for him; maybe the medication affected his stamina, too. Yet these side effects, too, had one-sided benefits—she benefited not. It was all much ado about nothing.

She semi-fell to the bed as he pulled out, glad it was over. She needed to shower. When he smacked her butt with this grunt of satisfaction, she experienced a degree of womanly pride for having pleased him, still determined to take what she could get. She stood and pulled her dress back down. She'd already stepped out of her nylons and panties while Oscar did his thing.

Oscar kissed her cheek. "That was good."

She proffered a wan smile, battling a mix of feelings, and picked up her clothing. "Thanks. I love you."

"Back at you. Happy New Year." He stretched, wearing this silly grin on his face. "Want me to finish unzipping?"

"H-Happy New Year. N-No, I'll d-do it." She turned for their bathroom, making sure she didn't hurry.

The sound of him opening his pants and enclosing his penis followed her. "A little TV?"

"Okay." She closed the door. Fighting tears as she approached the shower stall, she now hurried—to wash away the last ten minutes.

The new year was almost six hours old, and Oscar snored beside her as she lay in bed, staring at the unmoving blades of their ceiling fan, clad in a nightgown standard (if it wasn't her time of the month). He'd done little lifting her nightshirt from the back during the middle of the night and pushing her face into the pillow for nearly a year now, but rules were rules. He, however, made plenty use of the "no locked doors" rule: walking in on her in the bathroom, whether she was combing her hair, changing a pad,...or having a bowel movement.

She sometimes still felt his punch to her stomach upon her initial protest, telling her she didn't have anything anyone was trying to look at, so she needed to get over herself. And while the deed was in both their names, she paid the mortgage—but she didn't lock any doors.

Cecily released a trembly sigh and covered her mouth, swallowing an urge to weep, and doing her best to send away many things (*this year*) associated with the man lying next to her: the sound of him calling her that awful nickname (there was nothing endearing about a cesspool); the shame from him making her feel her academic accomplishments were subpar; the mortification of enduring his flatulence without remedy, escape, or comment (not even jokingly). ...Doing her best to push away vestiges of the nightmare that had awaken her. She didn't have many nightmares about what happened to her (she was more "episodey" than "nightmarey"), but when she did, they were hard to shake off.

If my two degrees bother him so, why doesn't he finish and get his?

Just another of the litany of repeated questions and observations she'd ruminated over her years with him, the answers still a mystery.

She lay there, wanting nightmare-free sleep, watching daylight overtake the dark spaces in her bedroom, and listening to the sounds of her husband sleeping. Roland snored, so she was used to sleeping with the sound, but Roland's snoring didn't sound so alarming. She sometimes worried about Oscar's hard snoring but kept her worries to herself; he'd just turn it into something unfriendly if she mentioned it.

Cecily reached for her headphones; she'd listen to Nina.

No. With the way you're feeling, you need to call Naomi.

It was New Year's Day, and early at that; she couldn't call her. Besides, she'd called her the other day.

In the end, with despair and heartache and irritation and anger and confusion and dejection threatening to swallow her whole, the need for solace and understanding won out. Cecily left their bedroom in search of a quiet corner in another part of the house, the number to the Bat-phone clutched in her hand.

It was two o'clock when she got around to preparing the Hoppin' John for dinner. Cecily stood by the sink, picking the greens, listening to "Just Ask the Lonely" by the Four Tops (set to repeat).

Dr. Alexander had picked up on the second ring, sounding nowhere near the sleepiness Cecily expected. The doctor could've been just getting in from partying, or answered while out partying, but Naomi didn't strike her as that type. The half-hour on the phone with her comprised mostly silence; Cecily sometimes breathing into the phone for long minutes before finding her next words. But Dr. Alexander didn't rush her or signal-sigh or anything. When she mentioned her nightmare, Naomi stopped her from recounting it, instead telling her to write it down, and that's when Cecily confessed about her sock with the notes. Her doctor said it was a good idea—and didn't ask to know anything about what she'd written.

Their conversation ended with Naomi overviewing the meaning of Watch Night (expounding on some of what Cecily heard during the service earlier), adding some brief anecdotes on mental and spiritual renewal and restoration. Her doctor didn't talk long (maybe five of the thirty minutes), but with those few short (comforting) sentences from Dr. Alexander, Cecily began feeling better. Not good, but *better*—which was all she was trying to do. She returned to bed (and Oscar), able to lay her head down for some sleep. When she awoke, Oscar had already returned to his man-cave.

She hummed along with Levi Stubbs and finished prepping her collard greens, the blackeye peas soaking.

Marcus, Roland, and Chelsea were coming over. It had been a while, so it was a great way to start the new year; Cecily looked forward to it. They loved her, but wanted no parts of her husband, so the holidays were the only time they indulged the family thing, and it was strictly for her benefit. Cecily knew she'd only see her children on their turf as the year drew on.

As with Oscar, she'd take what she could get (and all that).

Her children failed to understand, Oscar's controlling behavior was his way of showing he cared about her—that's how she preferred to look at it, anyway. She sometimes lost track of things she did (like moving those marketing files around in her office), sometimes got confused or upset unnecessarily. The episodes only compounded everything. Although he wasn't a mushy type of guy (anymore), that was okay; not all men were. There were aspects of a relationship more important than emotional security, affection, and good sex. She could do worse.

She paused her music and removed her earphones.

Do you feel safe, Cecily?

Cecily startled at the thought, Naomi's question rebounding in her brain with unavoidable significance now that no music traveled through it. To avoid its significance, however, she went to the pantry for the rice, deciding to let the grains soak, too. She shifted thoughts to marketing terms and concepts, running over those she had a pretty good grasp of as she moved about the kitchen.

She filled a pot with water, thinking about Josh's text coming in at midnight. The other holiday-sentiment texts she received came in after twelve-thirty a.m., closer to one a.m. It occurred to her: she was on Joshua's mind when the hour struck (thus, likely *before* it struck). There may have been little to no importance to that on Josh's end, but in that secret part of herself, Cecily let it be important, let it be special (she took what she could get).

The pot over-filled with water, bringing Cecily out of her reverie with another startle (she startled so easily nowadays).

Rice situated and sitting on the stove, she turned her attention to seasonings. She enjoyed bacon on occasional weekends (until two Decembers ago). Otherwise, she didn't do pork other than the holidays when seasoning vegetables and other holiday dishes called for that Southern touch. She seasoned foods during the year with turkey meat.

But with Oscar's health issues, she stared in the refrigerator at her seasoning options, unsure of how to prepare the greens and blackeye peas. She could go with the turkey necks and either hear Oscar's appreciation over considering his health or hear his anger over her coddling him. The neckbones and ham-hocks could go either way, too, with him saying either she was trying to kill him, knowing he had health issues, or thanking her for not treating him like a health case.

The refrigerator motor started, telling her she'd pondered the options too long.

You know you don't do this at work, right?

Maybe so, but she wasn't at work. Picking wrong could go so—

"What time is everything?"

Cecily startled and turned to him. "You sc-scared me."

Oscar smirked. "What else is new? What time?"

"They should b-be here around s-seven. You h-hungry?"

He shook his head. "Nah. Got the greens and peas started?"

"Not yet. I wan—"

"I'll do it. Let me handle it." His expression was hard to read. He cooked every blue moon. He didn't do cakes and desserts, but his main dishes were pretty good.

Still, his offer threw her. "What? W-Why?"

"Because you've been a basket case. Who knows what we might end up eating after you're done? They stay away from you as it is; you don't need to alienate them any more than you already have."

"Oscar, I'm f-fine. I'm not d-doing anything st-strange to the food."

He shrugged with this doubtful look in his eyes. "Maybe, maybe not. Just let me do it, Cecily. Sit down, relax, let that mind of yours de-stress, so you don't stress us out by getting all... Well, you know."

She did know. But she wouldn't do anything to harm her children or grandchild. "Oscar..."

"Your husband is offering to cook for you, but you gotta make it a thing." His upper lip suggested wanting to sneer at her.

Cecily closed the refrigerator. "You're right. S-Sorry." She gestured at the stove where mixed greens, blackeye peas, and rice awaited final prep and heat. "It's all yours."

He scoffed and headed toward the stove. "And do something about those flowers. I don't know what color your thumb is, but it isn't green."

Cecily frowned at her flowers. They did seem to be fading fast. The water had a tinge, but...

She shrugged and grabbed the vase, emptying the water down the drain. The faint odor suggested maybe a fungus was present with this batch. Sometimes her flowers thrived; other times...she got a bad bunch. Wouldn't stop her from getting more; she liked fresh flowers and the resulting spirit-lifting—even if they wilted sooner than expected.

After discarding the flowers, Cecily went to the refrigerator for a yogurt, thinking maybe they could prepare the meal together. "Using the turkey necks, or...?"

He stood at the sink, pouring the water off the rice. "I don't know, Cecily. Let me do this my way. I don't need you supervising while I cook. Believe it or not, no degree is required for this."

Embracing the melancholy so familiar to her, Cecily headed on upstairs. She'd keep out of his hair and stay in the room reading, maybe get a nap and de-stress, as he suggested. The kids would be an excellent distraction...

But the kids weren't a distraction. Little Roland was sick, so Marcus didn't want to bring him out. Without Marcus and Roland as additional buffers, Chelsea instead asked Cecily to come to her for dinner. Cecily considered it for about an hour before calling her daughter to say she'd just stay in. Oscar didn't pretend to be disappointed the dinner plans were canceled, having fixed himself a plate and taken it to the basement.

She ate alone at the kitchen table, reviewing the financials for JAH. The food was appetizing, but she would have enjoyed it more while dining with others. Cecily raised her glass of lemonade and clinked it against the vase (now devoid of fresh flowers). "Happy New Year."

And that solitary toast planted the tiniest seed for change.

Chapter Nine

Me-Phi-Me

O scar stared at the treadmill display panel, both annoyed and disappointed as he willed the counter to say he'd gone farther, that he had fewer minutes left. Sweat poured off him, dampening the multiple surfaces around him, but the sad part was, he perspired so profusely anyhow, there wasn't much difference.

"Fuck." He huffed and slowed his semi-jog to a walk, already knowing he'd pushed himself too far too fast. But it was a new year; he was taking a page from his wife's book. Cecily liked plugging her ears with music or even one of those auto-dial books and running in the mornings. She listened to that bass-sounding, sometimes hard-to-understand, moody Nina Simone more than anything else, whether she was running or just sitting around the house. Maybe he'd give the auto-tune books a try; listening to a book might be better than reading it (he bored easily). But he needed to slow his roll on the treadmill before—

Oscar grasped a handrail and pushed the button on the panel for the machine to stop. He paused after the walking belt stopped, feeling his legs tingle along with a weird motion sensation even though he was still. "How does she do this shit?" It was barely eight o'clock, but his wife had been up, exercised, showered, and was gone. She practically ran out of the house this morning, off to that computer company in the brutal January cold. From the basement, he sensed a different excitement and energy coming off her through the floorboards and down through the ceiling as he listened to her movement.

He reached for his damp towel and dampened it more with a swipe over his face before he stepped down. He inspected himself in the mirror, seeing if his Corona belly was any smaller. Not that it was all that big, and he knew eighteen minutes on the treadmill likely wouldn't show any change (but it might).

He gripped his bottle of Gatorade and gulped, keeping his eyes on his sweaty form in the mirror. His hair, thinning by the hour, lay matted in damp, wavy strands against his scalp. He probably should have some sort of healthy shake or power breakfast to go along with this new exercise regimen, but he hated most of that stuff. He couldn't stand apples. People found that strange, but that was the deal: no raw apples, cooked apples, apple pies, apple strudels, or any of that mess. He didn't like nuts, either, and his lactose was very tolerant because he couldn't stand milk. He liked a banana now and then, and he'd deal with a fruit smoothie—if Cecily made it. He liked eggs, so he could have a scrambled-on-toast, but the health-nut assholes whined about the yolk, claiming egg-whites were better. That was the thing about all these health fads: there was always a catch. He'll just have the rest of the onion rings from dinner last night (he loved onion rings), a glass of orange juice (something healthy), and a cigarette (giving life the finger).

There was always tomorrow: he had another 360-something days to get it right.

His belly as soft as it was eighteen minutes ago, Oscar surveyed the workout room, looking forward to all of it, the workout room and the five-bedroom colonial housing it, belonging to him soon. He closed his eyes with a sigh. People pretended they didn't, but he kept it real: he valued money, having expensive things. He could see his sister and baby brother sitting around the family room drinking one of those fancy bottled waters they liked (not Deer Park or Aquafina, but the top-line shit like Fiji or Pellegrino), grinning and talking, giving him props and finally extending the respect he should've been getting all along. That alone would be worth everything else. He'd have to catch up on his world events; Odessa and Otis (like Cecily) watched the news and kept up with news, activities, and events in the community.

Running a hand over his belly, he scoffed. He wasn't troubled about the world because all that extra shit wasn't his problem. His only concern was his world, because he could do something about that: he was founder and charter member of the OJB chapter of Me-Phi-Me. But he could watch a news program now and again (maybe tune in to that snobby *Jeopardy!*); make himself able to give feedback to his sister and brother for appearance's sake.

Oscar stared in the mirror at the wisps of hair plastered to his pate, contemplating going to one of those hair clubs. Why God gave him the good shit (from his mother) when He had every intention of it falling out, Oscar didn't know (God had a sense of humor, all right). He was determined to do something about it, though, because he wasn't going with either of the usual hair-loss solutions: White men liked that comb-over shit, while Black dudes wore a cap every-fucking-where. Men who shaved it all off went about it right; maybe that could be his new look—once his plans gelled. Cecily often mentioned he should shave his head, said she thought he'd look nice bald, but he wasn't ready yet; some adjustment was necessary before making such a drastic move.

"A'ight. Enough on my makeover..." With an annoyed glance at the now-empty Gatorade bottle (smaller size but higher price), he tossed the bottle in the recycle-bin (Cecily had the damn bins placed every-where). He yawned and recoiled at the offensive odor of his breath, both puzzled and irritated. He hadn't brushed yet, okay, but the sports drink should've camouflaged it. At his next visit, he would ask Dr. Halim about it again. Although he shouldn't be doing Halim's job. Halim should've already been on top of it. Doctors, man: bunch of—

With the whole day ahead of him (the entire month or quarter, for that matter, until he got his next gig), Oscar left the exercise room for the kitchen, his mouth watering for the onion rings from last night.

Showered, dressed in his favorite gray Redskins fleece sweatsuit, and stomach full, Oscar stood in the sunroom smoking a cigarette, watching the squirrels and birds scamper and hop across the backyard lawns. He was having what he liked to call, one of his Cecily moments (except for smoking the cigarette): she liked trees, animals, nature, and all that shit. *The $10,000 Pyramid* would be on soon, but he wanted to get his hands on those legal papers before settling down and enjoying the show. He needed the life insurance policy, powerful attorney, and even those papers he'd signed but never looked at. They weren't in the locked drawer of the desk in their bedroom, in Cecily's closet or nightstand, so he put himself in Cecily-mode to give himself an idea of what she might have done with them. The safe deposit box was a possibility, but she often said that wasn't a good place for those documents in an emergency. So, where the fuck were they?

He passed gas while watching two deer cross their neighbor's yard, and smiled to himself, thinking about his wife. Women were the weaker sex and all, but they couldn't be allowed to let their dainty ways ignore having their share of stinky moments. Women (and some punk-ass men) tried being more discreet and shit, but fuck that; belching and farting were natural bodily functions. He rid Cecily of all prissy notions about him passing gas early in the relationship. He'd trained her to accept and not respond to any odor changes, and although he wouldn't have cared if she let go around him, she never did. Speaking of which... Pulling out his phone, he texted his wife: *What're you doing?*

He expected her reply in three, maybe five minutes at the latest.

Oscar finished his cigarette and opened a sunroom window, allowing the second-hand to flow out and be dissipated by the fresh air flowing in. He sprayed some air deodorizer, too. He did his best to keep his smoking limited to the basement, but whenever he lit up in another part of the house, he did what he could to lessen the evidence because his wife didn't smoke, and he cared about Cecily's feelings—on some things.

But caring about some of her feelings wasn't enough to keep him interested in keeping things going. There were only so many ways he could use guilt and insults to keep her where he needed. She'd had her tubes tied and was past the baby-wanting stage, but he insulted her mothering skills because it made him feel better about his absentee-dad status. He didn't want the kid (well, *adult*, now), but he wasn't letting Cecily think she was any better at parenting than he was.

Still, none of it provided the satisfaction it used to. They'd reached a lull or something. He'd gone as far as he could with Cecily; it was time for a fresh start—with her money. Cecily's money wouldn't only put him in good with his family, he'd have an even better hold over his next female; he'd hold all the cards.

It wouldn't be enough to divorce Cecily. He watched the woodland creatures, not realizing he clenched his teeth. Cecily was attractive, intelligent, wealthy. He couldn't just divorce her because she could easily move on. That whole idea pissed him off to no end. He owned her, had her primed—for only him.

Oscar headed upstairs to search her drawers for the papers before the game show started. Her office was next.

Twenty minutes later, Oscar sat in his chair in the basement, television off—and no legal documents. He was irritated but not worried. He didn't need them right this minute; Cecily likely tucked them in one of her unique places for safekeeping. Going into Cecily-mode didn't work, but that was okay; he'd ask her about them, get around to getting his hands on them in the next few. He contributed to his spittoon and tilted his head back onto the chair cushion with a sigh.

Yeah, he'd gone as far as he could with this. He bored easily and could only thrive off her hurt feelings for so long. He had many chances and ways to keep Cecily under his thumb (physically, verbally, mentally: he knew the game), but she was already securely there. And, as long as Cecily kept wanting or needing affection from him, he had her on lock.

But with that weird energy coming through the ceiling this morning, something told him that lock was loosening—and that was a problem. Oscar entertained ideas for Plan C. Plan B was good but would take too long. This time next year, he wanted to be months under a different marital status—and a different financial one.

He shook his head and glared at the ceiling, barely in touch with the rising anger filling him. "There're times when I hate you. There are. But there's no leaving this, so..." *You have to go*. He didn't say that last out loud as he turned on the television, simply savoring the certainty of it.

It was long past the expected five minutes and Cecily hadn't texted back, but Oscar's mind was on other things.

Chapter Ten

Boogie Shoes

One week to go. That summed her mood as she worked on the marketing budget (or rather, stared at a possible one).

She had another week to go before resuming her appointments with Dr. Alexander. Although she'd spoken with Naomi over the holiday break, Cecily needed, *wanted* the face-to-face time with her. She didn't feel episodey, but the new year hadn't gotten off to the best of starts.

She sat at her desk, fighting an urge to weep with pity for herself. It was her first day back at JAH Tech, and she'd rushed to get here, but her mood remained glum. And while that may have had something to do with Joshua not being on site yet, Cecily avoided thinking about it that way.

Cecily balled the paper towel containing remnants of her lox, bagel, and cream cheese breakfast and tossed it in the trash. The meal was tasty but did little to lift her spirits. That wasn't unusual, but that was part of the problem: the everyday normality of her being in low spirits was growing burdensome, tiring—and only added to the melancholic joylessness of things.

"How do you eat that stuff? Isn't that White-people's food?" Rhonda burped against the back of her hand. Her three-quarters-gone bacon-egg-cheese biscuit and half-empty bottle of Coke sat on her desk.

"It may be a Jewish mainstay, but it isn't 'White-people's' food, and I eat it by biting, chewing, and swallowing—because I like the taste." Cecily heard the annoyance beneath her biting reply. "Sorry, Rhonda."

Rhonda's wide-eyed expression reflected surprise, not hurt feelings. She frowned with concern. "You okay?"

Cecily cringed with that question, holding in another harsh response (*No, dammit!*). There were only two people she didn't mind asking her that question, and they weren't Oscar, Janyce,...or her children. But Rhonda meant no harm. Her concern was sweet. Cecily forced a smile. "A little tired from the weekend, I guess. I'm okay. Thanks."

Rhonda nodded and returned to her breakfast, skimming a newspaper section as she ate. Her reading the paper wasn't new, but Cecily was always pleased to see it.

Cecily stared at her monitor, looking at the screen but not seeing it, going over the humiliation, sadness, loneliness, and confusion (the ever-present confusion) of the last few days.

Stop feeling sorry for yourself and fix it.

That was the idea, so she was eager to resume her sessions with Naomi. She needed to make some progress with her own issues and get better, so she'd be better able to help Oscar. If she got better, and they got Oscar feeling better, he'd be less... Well, be less everything, and that could only help their relationship. Everyone was extra mean when they were sick. They didn't know how long he'd been living with his diagnosis—it could've been there all along, making him so...

If she were better, she'd also be able to help bridge the gap between Oscar and his siblings. She saw warm qualities in Odessa and Otis; she believed she could get them more receptive toward their brother. Oscar complained about her relationship with Kyle and Larimore, but Cecily believed he wanted the same thing for himself. Oscar was sick and didn't really have family (other than her), which made him mean and angry; she felt sorry for her husband.

She glanced in her small desk mirror and sighed at the prickly red splotches across her nose and cheeks: her rosacea flared up despite the medication—another thing she had to improve.

The radio was on low, but Lyfe's "Smile" sounded through the overhead speakers. Surprised (and pleased) to hear it again, she closed her eyes with imaginings related to the lyrics.

The sound of keys and the alarm being reset at the rear entrance startled her. "Joshua here. Hey, all."

Rhonda folded her newspaper closed and called back, "Hi, Mister Hall." She began clearing her desk to start the day. "Need to review the inventory for the workrooms."

"Okay."

"So, you and your husband had a wild-party weekend, huh?"

Cecily looked at her.

"Your being tired? From the weekend...? New Year's stuff?"

"Oh, yeah. Party and stuff."

Rhonda snickered. "I didn't get in until noon on the first."

"You should be tired, too, then, huh?"

Her coworker responded with a middling wave of her hand, suggesting she was a little tired. "Does Oscar party hard?"

"No more than anyone else, I suppose."

"The Hall men probably partied hard. I can see Mister Hall jamming with some woman."

Cecily stood. "Excuse me, Rhonda." She locked her computer and headed to her back office. She needed a moment—and wasn't in the mood for Rhonda's gossip session. Listening to her semi-obsession with Joshua could get uncomfortable—and she could see Josh "jamming with some woman," too.

"Oh, okay."

Hearing faint strains of "Bewildered" by James Brown, Cecily welcomed the smile curling her lips. She wanted to pop her head in and say hello officially before retreating to her office.

His door was ajar. Instead of busting in, Cecily paused outside it.

Josh stood by his desk, lip-synching to his favorite artist and unbuttoning his shirt from its hanger on a wall-hook. He was shirtless, his undershirt at the ready on his desk. He preferred to commute in a clean T-shirt or polo and put his dress shirt and blazer (and sometimes tie) on once he arrived at JAH, but this was her first time witnessing the ritual—and she couldn't tear her eyes away.

She stared at the contoured molasses that was Joshua's torso as it contracted and relaxed with his movement. A centaur with a yellow rose in its mouth formed the tattoo on his upper back on the right, just below his trapezius muscle. The tattoo represented his fraternity affiliation: Iota Phi Theta. Since her feet weren't working, Cecily watched her boss dress for the day, thinking about how he came from the projects of Ohio, how poor his family had been. When Joshua was eleven, his mother walked out on the family, leaving his father to support him and his sister. Joshua maintained minimal contact with his mother, but had been very close to his father. After his father's death, the insurance payout paid for his college tuition loans. He and his sister, Dimitra, remain close even though she still lives in Ohio.

Her focus on his six-pack abs (noticeable even from the side), Cecily watched Josh's muscles and tattoo disappear beneath cover of his undershirt as he slipped it over his head. Now bopping his head to James ("Popcorn" came through his player), he reached for his gray dress shirt, looking good in only a white T-shirt.

Embarrassed (and admittedly aroused), she stepped back and hurried to her office.

She spent five minutes berating herself for the arousal she experienced watching Josh. And although, personally, she and God were in a tenuous status, what with her still not understanding why God abandoned her, why He allowed several men to beat and rape her, why She allowed her son to be shot and her daughter to be raped, Cecily spent another ten minutes in prayer asking forgiveness for it.

Acknowledging and embracing her mood being improved because Josh was there (she'd take what she could get—spurts of happiness included), she headed back to the front. She spotted Joshua's prized possession hanging on the coat rack as she passed his vacant office: his Negro Leagues jacket. That jacket was produced in recent years, but the one his boys were presenting for his birthday was going to knock Josh's socks off: an original leather jacket worn during the era. Cecily wished she was there to see his face when he opened it.

"...—eeting about the contract award from DOD this Tuesday..." Rhonda read from her computer screen.

"Right. And add that bit about the MOU." Josh spoke as he stared at his laptop, sitting at the portable computer station he liked to use whenever he worked in the front for a change of scenery. When she entered, Josh smiled at her, gesturing at her desk. "Good morning. That matutinal routine of yours has you crunching numbers early, I see." He reached for his tumbler (filled with some herbal concoction he'd prepared at home). He wore black slim-fit jeans with his light-gray dress shirt and a Glenurquhart-plaid jacket blending blacks and grays. His stone-gray Chelsea suede boots matched the stone-gray day outside.

Cecily glanced at Rhonda (shaking her head with a kind smirk at Josh's word-use), then smiled at Josh, and it dawned on her how little she'd smiled lately. "Good morning. A few draft reports to get an idea of what we're getting into."

His twists shook with his chuckle; twists freshened and trimmed, his shape-up flattering his hairline. "And what're we getting into?"

Cecily sat at her desk. "Jury's still out."

Josh nodded, resuming focus on his laptop.

Cecily frowned. Her right-handed scissors were missing, and the left-handed ones were in the wrong slot. Someone tossed an orange highlighter atop her calendar booklet. "Someone been at my desk...?" She viewed the others in the room, her body trembly with the disruption to her space.

Josh and Rhonda exchanged a look, and then each raised a hand.

Rhonda lowered her hand first. "Sorry, Missus Brooks. I grabbed the wrong scissors. Malcolm borrowed mine, and they're still in the back." She approached her, returning the right-handed scissors.

"And I'm guilty of not putting the highlighter back in the holder." His eyes conveyed his apology.

Cecily accepted the scissors from Rhonda with a heavy sigh. "You know, it may seem weird to you, but I like certain things a certain way. All I ask—"

"We get it, Cecily."

She focused her attention on him. "Do you, Josh? 'Get it'? I'm not so sure." She believed he did *get her*, and she didn't know why she suddenly felt so...angry, but here it was. And she didn't want to send her anger toward him, *least* of all him, but someone needed to hear her.

Rhonda headed toward the rear of the shop. "I'll...I'll be in Workroom One. Sorry, Missus Brooks."

Cecily kept her eyes on Josh. When Rhonda was gone, she continued. "You know, I understand those workrooms stay in constant disarray by the nature of the business: computers and parts everywhere. But I'm the one who organizes them, only to be frustrated when they get messy again. And now, the same with my desk."

His gaze hardened with the tightening in his jaw, but his expression was neutral when he stood. He smoothed his mustache using his thumb and index finger, though: still upset. "I've apologized for misplacing the highlighter. Rhonda, too, for the scissors. No one is out to 'frustrate' you, Cecily. We can only apologize and be mindful if there's a next time.

But as far as the workrooms...?" He sounded less-nasal now—especially with the sincerity lacing his words.

Cecily nodded, her anger mixing with something else as she put the scissors down. "Yes?"

"No one has ever asked you to straighten them. You do that on your own, so feel free to stop anytime. It's greatly appreciated, so thank you, but..." He slowly shook his head, reconveying she could stop organizing the workrooms whenever.

And, just as filled as she was with the displaced rage, it just as quickly dissipated. "I...I enjoy straightening the workrooms."

"That's what I thought. Kinda had the feeling doing it was therapeutic for you."

She tensed when he said "therapeutic" but nodded. "It is. Sort of."

His gaze on her softened with this curious frown. "So, why're you blasting me about the workrooms?"

Cecily detected the humor, but new anxiety over their minor spat blocked her from receiving it fully, intensifying her urge to weep. "I know. I'm being too sensitive, overreacting as usual. I'm sorry, Josh—" She nibbled her upper lip to stem the stream of emotions crashing into each other. The last thing she wanted was to lose it in front of Josh.

"Whoa! Hold up, Cecily!" He was beside her before he finished speaking, placing a hand on her shoulder. "Maybe we're both overreacting, huh?"

Cecily didn't move, didn't speak. She couldn't just yet.

Josh lowered his hand. He didn't speak, just standing with her and waiting.

She pulled it together, staring around the shop, listening to the muzak, hearing sounds of Rhonda piddling around in Workroom One. This turned into much more than it should have. Finally, she bobbed her head. "I guess we both were, yeah." A part of her wanted him to put his hand on her shoulder again—if for nothing than the reassurance it provided.

He didn't put his hand to her shoulder, but Cecily sensed him wanting to—which was just as good. "What can I do? Anything? Aside from never borrowing your highlighter again."

The laughter pushing forth was raw and rather loud, but Cecily didn't care; it felt good to laugh.

Josh laughed with her, bringing Rhonda out from hiding. "What? What's so funny?"

Their laughter died, and Josh's eyes turned inquiringly serious. "We good?"

Cecily nodded (glad the whole thing didn't go far left). "Yes. Sor—"

He placed a finger over his lips, stopping her from apologizing, then turned to Rhonda. "Nothing. Just an icebreaker." He sent Cecily a conspiratorial wink before returning to his workstation.

Rhonda sighed as she returned to her desk. "Oh. Thought you hit her with one of your jokes again."

Cecily approached the coffee klatsch for some much-needed tea. "No, not yet, Rhonda. The year's just starting..."

"Oh, but I'm ready. I'll hit you with it when you least expect it." He wore a mischievous grin.

Rhonda scoffed. "Oh boy. What'd you do for New Year's, Mister Hall?"

Cecily's ears prickled; she wasn't sure she wanted to hear this. She focused on the teas, staring hard at the tea packet options. *You can't pick wrong with this, Cecily. Dag! No dangerous outcome here.* Still, she didn't move.

"Go with whichever gives you that a-place-for-everything feeling."

Smiling at hearing the smile in his voice, Cecily selected the pomegranate tea.

Josh answered Rhonda. "Oh, I took things light this year, Rhonda. Waited for the hour to turn, sent a text, and called it a night."

"No parties?"

Cecily added sugar, not wanting to be pleased by his response.

"I had a few I could have attended, but nah. Like I said: took things light."

"And you only sent *one* text?" Rhonda's question implied her disbelief.

Cecily looked Josh's way as she finished prepping her tea. She recognized him making it a point not to look at her—very telling.

"Yeah. Just the one...to only one."

Rhonda scoffed. "Uh-huh. And what was *her* name?" Her question was teasing; she didn't (rightly) expect a response.

Cecily walked to her desk, sipping gingerly while watching Josh pay extra-close attention to his laptop. She opened the marketing budget again.

Rhonda stood. "Sorry, Mister Hall. Is it okay if I run to the pharmacy for my mom's prescription? I'd like to get it while it's on my mind."

Josh didn't lift his head or eyes. "Twenty minutes long enough?"

"Yes."

Josh nodded his approval (but she'd better be back in those twenty minutes).

"Thank you!" Rhonda grabbed her coat, scarf, purse, and was gone.

Cecily changed some figures for a different budget preview while Josh focused on whatever he was working on, and the muzak played on.

The Matter of the Text He'd Sent Her stood, hands on its hips and foot tapping, waiting for one of them to say something. "...Thank you for my text, Josh. It was very apropos."

Josh eased his eyes her way. "I'm glad. When you didn't reply, I thought I'd overstep—"

"Oh, no. Not at all. I'm sorry: it was very sweet."

The relief in his eyes was also sweet. "Cool."

"Sweet...and unlike you?"

Josh grinned. "Believes but doesn't know, isn't the same as doesn't believe and doesn't know."

She was aware of levels of theism. She'd been struggling with her own levels since Roland died. "You're right."

"So, cut me some slack. I allowed my spiritual self to surface."

"Good for you." Cecily sipped. The tea was yummy.

Joshua sipped from his tumbler and sat back. "See, the problem I run into most is not getting past that air of exclusivity religious folk project. The churches I've walked into in search of...whatever, I've gotten looks of suspicion, rejection. Now, *I'm* fine," he shook his head, "but that's not what God intended."

"Well, that's the human element disappointing you, Josh, not the Godly one." Sounded good anyway.

Josh appeared introspective. "And so, I am where I am with it all."

She smiled at him. Where he "was" was fine. He believed—and that was most important (although it shouldn't have mattered or been any of her business). "You're a work in progress. We all are."

He smirked and stood, switching the background noise from muzak to the radio. "Just until street traffic increases."

"Fine with me."

A rap song was on. Cecily didn't know the name of the record, but she'd heard it many times before—and the voice was unmistakable: Tupac Shakur. She went back to her figures, singing along in her head.

"You know, God made rap and hip-hop, too. Made all that."

"True."

He focused on whatever he was doing on his laptop as he spoke. "We may get carried away with using it, but that's God, too—even non-gospel rap. Don't get it twisted. God's blessings of and through the talents He gives us, regardless of expression: singing, writing, computing, analyzing? It's all God, for real."

"Thought you were agnostic."

"Agnostic theist, not atheist. *That's* the key." He sipped his herbal-protein smoothie concoction with a grin.

Cecily chuckled, already understanding. She so enjoyed talking with him. She envisioned God doing a little rap about Her creations.

Joshua's grin turned curious. He lowered the volume on the stereo using the remote. "What?"

"Just seeing God doing His rapping." Cecily stood and adopted a rapper's pose. "You know, I made the world in just seven days."

Laughing, Josh adopted a similar stance in his seat. "Created people: they got some *crazy* ways."

They giggled together, then resumed their respective tasks; that disagreement (or whatever it was) over and behind them. She didn't have to worry about a sneak attack regarding the topic later, no painful grips to her upper arm from out-of-the-blue to reinforce some previous message. Here, she was free to agree...or disagree...without penalty for her views.

"Working on budget options for our upcoming marketing pursuits?"

"Among other things. You want to get someone knowledgeable about this, though, Josh. I'm not—"

"There you go: selling yourself short. We want rough numbers for implementing a marketing strategy, not the strategy itself. The numbers: that *is* you."

She nodded at him. "Okay. In that case, based on what I've read so far, I have four potential budgets."

"Which likely is based on viable marketing strategies..." He smirked at his laptop, not looking her way.

Although he didn't see her, Cecily smirked back; he had her on that one. "Yes. Okay."

"Can I look at what you have so far, or...?"

She waved him over. "No, it's fine. As you said, they're rough numbers, so..."

Josh made a few additional keystrokes and came over to her.

He reviewed a scenario or two with her, but discussion detoured into a joking but informative and serious discussion regarding the portfolio management and accounting software applications she used. Because his forte was computers, his knowledge of QuickBooks Enterprise, FreshBooks, and Intacct impressed her. Then again, she shouldn't have been. It was his money and his business: he should have been knowledgeable about what was used to manage it. He interspersed requests to have her repeat certain words or phrases to hear her accent. While discussing his power-of-attorney and executor-of-estate, there was also an aside regarding his investment accounts, including his 401(k)s, IRAs, brokerage and savings accounts. Her end of the conversation flowed with ease; she was in her element with this finance stuff.

Discussion over, Josh checked his watch as he headed back to his desk. Rhonda wasn't back yet.

"Give her a few more minutes. You're a bit of a scofflaw, Josh; you know how it is." Traces of his cologne wafted around her. It was new, but she knew it was in the Ralph Lauren family. Smelled nice.

Josh released a breezy laugh. "That is not the same thing, and you know it."

It wasn't the same, but Cecily liked teasing him about his habitual resistance to paying tickets. "Still..."

He sighed and sat. "Fine."

"So, what're your plans for your birthday?" She wasn't sure she wanted to know.

"Well, now that I'm not going skiing, not sure. The boys are taking me out, but that's about it."

"Still taking things 'light,' I see."

He shrugged. "My New Year's resolution."

"No Kristin?" Saying the woman's name created low-level turmoil in the pit of her stomach. She hadn't heard mention of her in months, but that didn't mean anything.

Josh made an odd expression but kept focus on his laptop. "Nope."

"So, what're you gonna open?" She sounded distressed. She heard it. "You have the boys' gift, but what else?"

He turned to her, brow furrowed. "Huh?"

She went mute, her words having revealed more than she intended.

He smiled softly. "I'm turning forty-six, not six. My gift from Malcolm and Smeek is fine. And even though we're divorced, it's amicable; Angela always acknowledges my day with something."

"And me."

"So that's three. More than plenty. Why?" His fingers hovered his keyboard.

Mute again, Cecily shrugged and adjusted the sleeve of her dress.

"Big fan of opening lots of gifts?"

That wasn't it. Not exactly. She couldn't recall opening a genuine present showing some thought and originality from Oscar; not since before they married. His go-to gift now was a card with money, and, when examined truthfully, considering his infrequent employment status, she realized he (in essence) was returning her own money. She pretty much paid for everything—including her birthday, anniversary, Mother's Day, Valentine's Day, and Christmas gifts "from him."

"Cecily...?"

"I don't get gifts."

He stared at her as if knowing she blurted her response. "At all? I mean, well, except for those from me."

"Not those from you, no, but..." Josh's tokens of remembrance, of Christmas and her birthday, were small but big in thoughtfulness: gourmet teas; herbal bath tea kits; tea bag holder; running vest; framed poster with infographics on tea trivia (currently hanging in her back office); her runner's alarm (which she carried on every run without fail); tea tins in the shape of novels (on display on her kitchen counter). She even had a tea lab from him she had yet to use (but looked forward to going "mad" with one day). Cecily shrugged again, her mind racing for a change of subject. How did she keep getting into these corners with him? "Cards with money or gift cards."

He smoothed his mustache (annoyed and dissatisfied with her answer) but kept quiet for a bit. "Well, that's okay once or twice; sometimes you're stuck for an idea but want to give *something*."

Cecily nodded her agreement, wondering how one can get stuck for an idea so...regularly. Her cellphone chimed a text notification. It was Oscar: *What're you doing?* She returned her phone to her purse with more determination than hesitation.

"Still, a gift should be something you put even a little thought into."

She agreed, but a change of subject popped into her head. "Brad pledging Iota yet?"

Josh's warm smile reflected how much he loved his "Smeek." "This year's spring line, yeah."

"Proud Papa?" At one point (her sophomore year at Delta State), she entertained pledging a sorority: a toss-up between S-G-Rho and AKA. She'd since developed a leaning toward the ladies of pink-and-green, but, alas, never pursued anything.

Josh nodded. Malcolm was already his fraternity brother. "Little bit. I'll be legacy: times two." He rechecked his watch, and this time Cecily said nothing: Rhonda needed to get back (and on the quick). He looked at her. "I hope she's okay—"

"But she's pushing it. I agree."

"Mind if I take another look at those last two marketing budgets?"

She pulled up the information and situated them side-by-side on her monitor. "Here you go."

He leaned on her desk and stared at the numbers, subtle hints of mint and ginger wafting around her.

Cecily remained quiet, giving him time to review without interruption, when "Beautiful" by Joe came on. She watched Josh, noticing his attention to the information on the screen splintered because his head moved with the music. "This your jam?"

"I like the song, yeah." He turned to her. "You should, too."

"Me? Why? I've never done those things he talks about."

He shook his head at her with a trace of pity, making her uncomfortable. "Yes, you have. With Roland, Oscar—and me."

Her mouth went dry.

"The song is about the woman's beauty *as a person*, Cecily. And you've done those things for me. Not necessarily in a romantic sense, but you've breathed for me without you even being aware of it—especially this last year or so with JAH Tech. ...And that's beautiful, too, Cecily. You're beautiful."

That going-mute thing happening to her again, Cecily stared into his gaze of molasses, the words *not necessarily,* rebounding in her head. She then went warm as his gaze fell to her lips, and warmer still with her gaze lowering to his lips: plump but not fat, and...they looked soft.

The song ended. Ads rolled.

He walked away. "Shit." He sounded angry.

She worried he was angry with her. "What is it?"

"Nothing. It's all good." He stared out the window, his back to her. Seeing the pedestrian traffic outside was heavier, he tuned back to the muzak with a chuckle. "She'd better get back here." Seemed he needed to change subjects.

"Any minute now..."

She wasn't far off. It was another three minutes, but Rhonda returned with prescription in hand and what was a good excuse: she'd had a minor fender-bender from someone rear-ending her.

They got on with the business of the day. She checked her phone periodically. Oscar didn't text again, and Cecily left well enough alone.

Days later, with the success of the government contract meeting behind them, the JAH Tech, Inc. team sat around the front of the shop, chatting and enjoying the typical after-the-holiday lull. They had a special guest with them, sitting at the desk Terrence vacated with his return to college: Hadji. His elementary school was closed because of heating problems, so Hadji made his way to JAH Tech, and now sat, working on his homework, his tongue sticking out of the corner of his mouth in concentration. She'd been working at JAH for over four years, and Hadji had been a regular for going on two.

They'd just finished a working lunch, continuing discussion of plans for opening the second shop, about Malcolm being ready to manage it (he had several certifications now and a BS degree). He was green, so he wouldn't truly be flying solo (Josh would guide), but Malcolm looked excited and sounded ready. They again touched on needing alternative marketing approaches for JAH Tech, and Malcolm offered ideas, but Joshua wanted her to continue research and reconnaissance.

Rhonda and Malcolm circulated, gathering everyone's lunch refuse.

The recent spa day still with her (how she loved those!), Cecily balled her sandwich wrappings and napkins. She finished her fruit-smoothie with a slurp, appreciating Josh ensuring the sandwich shop kept any semblance of a cucumber fermented in spices away from her selection. She'd stepped out when they placed the order, and her sandwich came with pickles ordinarily—but Josh was thoughtful to remember.

"Finished, little man?" Josh partially sat on his desk, working his yo-yo, his eyes on the 8-year-old. He wore a suit to the meeting earlier; his tie was loosened at the neck.

Hadji nodded and closed his book with a snap. He wore one of the three shirts she usually saw him in, his jeans needing a run through a wash cycle. Hadji, however, never smelled dirty. "Yes. I like spelling homework: it's easy."

Cecily smiled at him and extended her hand, thinking of little Roland being in school one day. "Let me check it."

Hayden Joshua Leeds (the serendipity of his middle name, that his birthday was days after Josh's, didn't escape her) hopped down from his seat, papers in hand, and approached her with a grin. "It's right." His hair needed combing, but somehow that made him cuter.

Brad raised an eyebrow at Hadji. "Confident little—"

"A'ight, Smeek."

Smeek smirked at his father. "Third grader." He headed toward the back. "Workroom Four: deliverable for Servitch and Walls."

Malcolm paused his lunch-straighten with Rhonda, holding Cecily's vase of fresh flowers. "Need me?"

Brad scoffed as he disappeared into the back. "Have I ever?"

The response elicited a low laugh from Joshua, who put his yo-yo down before sitting at his workstation and opening his laptop.

Cecily reviewed Hadji's work: so far, everything looked in order.

"Still keeping who gave you the yellow rose a secret, Mister Hall?" Rhonda sent him this hesitant, inquiring smile, gripping the garbage bag mid-pull from the receptacle.

Josh focused on his screen. "I am."

Cecily tensed as she resumed reviewing Hadji's spelling. She bought the rose on impulse when getting fresh flowers for the shop (strangely, these always lasted much longer than those at home). It was part thank-you for his inspirational text since she felt bad about not replying, and part nod to his Iota affiliation. She'd put it on his desk in his office, but instead of leaving it there, he grabbed a vase from under the sink in the breakroom and placed his rose on his workstation up front. Rhonda had been bugging him about it ever since.

Malcolm chuckled and headed to the back. "Give it up, Rhonda. He'll die with that information."

Finished with clearing after lunch, Rhonda followed Malcolm (no surprise there) to Workroom Four.

Cecily handed Hadji his homework and rubbed his head. "You were right: no mistakes."

The little boy turned wide, expectant eyes to Josh. "Mister Joshua..."

Josh chuckled. "I heard." He reached in his drawer and tossed Hadji a neon-green yo-yo. "Good job."

"Yay!" Hadji darted toward the rear section.

"Hey!"

Hadji came back. "Huh?"

Josh pointed. "Hat and coat, man." He frowned as he stretched and rubbed the back of his neck.

Hadji hurried to snatch his winter-wear from his chair.

Watching Joshua, she wanted to massage his neck and shoulders (however briefly) to ease the tension; he had a lot going on. "Hadji, come here. Let me zip you up."

Hat crooked, coat halfway on, but yo-yo held tight, he came over to her, and Cecily cozied him up properly to go outside.

She pecked his forehead. "And must you yo-yo outside?"

Hadji nodded, grinning broadly. "So I don't hit nuffin'."

Cecily winked at him. "Good thinking. Stay right behind JAH, okay? By the windows so Brad or Malcolm can see you."

"I will!" He pulled away and dashed for the rear exit.

Josh called after him, still rubbing his neck. "Ten minutes, Hadji! Gotta get you back."

"Okay!"

Both she and Josh shook their heads with chuckles.

Josh used the intercom to advise those in Workroom Four to keep an eye on Hadji. "...You're good with him."

Cecily shrugged and shook her head; she didn't know about all that.

"No, you are. How you speak to him with such sincerity. It's like you make his minor triumphs your own." Josh removed his tie. "But not just with Hadji. The recent meetings are examples; you're all in, Cecily. You express true happiness at anyone else's good news. ...It's a cool quality."

Her husband sometimes considered her a simpering wuss for empathizing with others, but she didn't want to think about Oscar. The last few days had been exceptionally quiet in their home.

Oscar was in what she liked to call one of his "freeze-outs" where he said little to her, but the silence wasn't the break it should have been, instead swelling with an intangible doom. Sometimes he came out of the freeze-outs with little to show for it, but other times...

Well, she called him Mr. Hyde for a reason.

The door opened before she could thank Josh for the compliment. Their regular courier, Mackenzie, came in smiling brightly, carrying two packages. "Hey, folks! Happy New Year!"

Cecily raised a hand in greeting. "Hey, Mack. Same to you."

Josh stood, extending his hands for the parcels. "Whassup, Mack?" Even sans tie, he looked good and sexy in his navy suit, and there was no use denying it. She was married, not dead (and all that).

Mackenzie (late 30s) walked over to him, her uniform clean and fitting, her makeup highlighting her features. She was attractive (reminding Cecily a lot of the singer, Sadé), and she always had this specific look at Josh whenever she interacted with him. Cecily didn't think she was up on what flirting looked like with the younger generation, but Mackenzie wasn't much younger than she was; Cecily recognized the signs. She grew uneasy and self-conscious whenever she had to witness the two of them. "'Whassup' is wanting to know why you can call me 'Mack,' but I have to stick with 'Joshua.'"

Josh accepted the packages and put them down. "It's my name."

Mackenzie handed him the digital clipboard to sign. "No kidding. But I've been delivering here almost a year. 'Josh' is more personal. You know: 'Mack-n-Josh,' 'Josh-n-Mack'..."

Cecily adjusted the collar of her dress and stood, trying to think of an exit phrase. She gathered Hadji's homework papers instead.

Josh chuckled as he signed. "How was your holiday?"

Mackenzie laughed. "Don't change the subject." She touched his arm, adding a caress. "No dice, huh?"

Josh smiled and shook his head, returning the tablet. "Sorry, I prefer 'Joshua.' But don't go away angry."

Mackenzie sent him one of those looks again. "Couldn't if I wanted to." She caressed his arm again (Josh lowered his head with a shake) before heading for the door. "Y'all be good!"

Josh smiled, and Cecily wondered if he closed his eyes while kissing. "A'ight, Mack. Or is it 'Mackenzie' now?"

Mackenzie paused in the opened doorway, letting the stiff January day in. Her eyes moved over Joshua slowly, meaningfully, before she looked in his face. "Oh, for *you?* 'Mack' is just fine." She gave him this wink that took forever to finish, waved at Cecily, and was gone.

"There goes your birthday date."

Josh scoffed and walked toward the rear, studying the packages he held. His Polo Classic drifted her way: pine, juniper, carnations, and leather commingling with aromatic bliss. "Pshaw. Not hardly."

That surprised her. "No?"

Josh shook his head. "No." He paused in the archway and passed her an exploratory look. "You know, we're all pitching in to help get the second site into shape in the coming months: cleaning, painting..."

"Yeah. What about it?"

He stared at her, his eyes twinkling with that unnamed thing again before he smiled with glimpses at her dress, her hair. "That's more of a baseball-cap-and-ponytail type exercise: old jeans, faded T-shirt...? Think about dispensing with being 'runway' ready." He grinned.

She swallowed hard and handed him Hadji's bookbag.

Joshua's grin faded. "I say something wrong?"

She shook her head.

"I'm just saying, you're always so polished. I look forward to seeing you with your hair down—or rather, *up*, as the case may be. And Oscar's free to help, too: the more, the merrier, the sooner we're finished." He winked and headed to the back. "Taking Hadji home. Back soon."

Fifteen minutes later, she had the shop to herself, finishing a three-way teleconference with Kyle and Larimore. Laughing, she hung up softly on her brothers teasing each other. Her contact lenses rested in their case on her desk; she wanted a break from wearing them while alone in the shop. She turned the player on and switched from muzak to the radio for the company and distraction. Tension and unease (and dread) increased with her day at JAH ending—and her time to go home drawing nearer. She worked quietly, enjoying the solitude.

The well-known horn opening for "Boogie Shoes" started, and she jumped up, getting her frolicsome groove on with K.C. and the Sunshine Band. She was alone and contemplated taking her stress-relief to her back office, but Cecily danced freely in the front, not caring who saw.

It was a rare but good moment for her, so she embraced it, indulging in a combination hip-swirl and spin that was so 1975, it wasn't funny. Disco was in the house and Cecily invited one of its imaginary guests to dance along with her. She laughed and partied with K.C., her mind's eye seeing the shimmery ball above her, its glimmer of reflective light on the floor. She was just a kid when this song was popular, but she wasn't a kid now. Cecily laughed...and danced.

Winded but still chuckling, she went to the radio and turned it off for a second, wishing for a replay.

She startled at seeing Josh in the archway separating the shop zones. Her chuckles died with the hand she brought to her chest. "Oh!"

He leaned against the abutment, his smile suggesting he'd been there for most of her stress-relief session. "Don't mind me." He pulled out his cellphone. "As a matter of fact..." Seconds later, those "Boogie Shoes" horns blasted into the shop.

Cecily held his gaze, afraid to move at first (he twitched his shoulders to the beat), but she loved this song, so practicality surrendered to its total disregard. She threw her head back and boogied, that imaginary disco ball spinning and glittering above her and bringing 1975 back front-and-center. She sensed Josh's closer proximity. He danced with her while maintaining his distance, his footwork revealing his own level of enjoyment. His short twists bounced as he grooved, the flecks of gray in his hair pleasing the eye. After doing samples of the Robot and the Disco Finger, they soon adopted a matching shoulder-move to the chorus, having fun with K.C. and his Sunshine Band.

"Boogie Shoes" ended, and Cecily (winded again) saddened just a little. "That was fun!"

Josh closed the app and put his phone down with a chuckle. "Oh, yeah." He glanced toward the windows. "And we have an audience..."

Cecily turned to see five people peering in, clapping and smiling. The gentleman wearing a heavy light-brown parka opened the door. "Nice! What were you dancing to?"

She finger-combed her hair, straightened her dress. "'Boogie Shoes.'"

Chuckling and nodding, the man re-closed the door. They watched him talk to the others, likely conveying the song's name. The people smiled, offering either a wave or thumbs-up before moving on.

They breathed together in the ensuing silence, getting their middle-aged winds back. Josh considered her long and hard. "No contacts."

Cecily shook her head, feeling awkward and wishing she'd kept them in, believing he likely preferred her with them.

Josh's eyes stayed on hers. "So,...*hickory*, not hazel."

"No, not hazel." No one had ever described her eye-color before, had ever isolated the particular brown her irises were.

He slowly nodded his approval, and again, his gaze trailed to her lips.

The moment was there, swelling between them with a warm sweetness that was honest and...going on four years old.

Josh stepped back. "Shit." He studied the floor.

"A bit of déjà vu happening here." Strangely, she felt calm, experiencing a personality déjà vu having nothing to do with today—and everything to do with twenty, fifteen, even ten years ago.

He nodded, grinning at the floor tiles. "I know, right?" Josh lifted his head, his gaze both piercing and pleading with something not matching his next words. "Forgot Hadji's homework."

Still calm, she simply looked at him. Calm wasn't new (but it was). "Okay." The folder with Hadji's papers was on her desk. She handed it to him. "Dropping it off on the way home?"

Josh accepted the folder with a deep breath, clearly uncomfortable. "Yeah. So, what made you drive Devin to work today?" He was good at this. The swollen moment still existed between them, but there was nothing to be done about it; a change in subject was warranted.

It was true she preferred public transportation, but her Deville looked sad as she headed for the bus stop this morning, so she'd turned back, keys in hand. Cecily shrugged and sat at her desk. "He can't just sit. It's not good for him, so..."

"Makes sense." He went to his workstation and started his laptop with a sigh. "Need to work on this script for Vosage Unlimited."

Cecily resumed her duties, too, working on projections for the year.

They worked in silence for all of eleven minutes when Josh stood and headed for the player.

"Silence killing you?"

"Something like that." The remote was on the reception counter. He aimed it, turning the radio back on.

Peabo Bryson's "Reaching for the Sky" came through the speakers.

Josh Hall put his hands on the counter and dropped his head with this sighing chuckle. He looked over at her. "Guess it's part of the current rotation." He spoke with a bit of apology.

"Seems like it. Just let it play, Josh."

He nodded and went back to his workstation. But he didn't work, and she didn't either as the song played, both just listening (and glancing at each other) until the song ended—only to roll into Roberta Flack and Donny Hathaway singing "The Closer I Get to You."

Cecily swallowed, her body tingling with a serendipitous rush as she watched Josh's eyes widen before he cleared his throat, looking awkwardly around the room. Again, they didn't work, both listening to lyrics seeming louder and smoothly message laden.

Their glances at each other grew more frequent, and Josh had cleared his throat five times before the song ended and rolled into something more obscure. With nervous chuckles, they returned to their respective tasks.

They worked in peace (Roberta and Donny still echoing in her mind), the numbers on her screen telling her a story, when an icicle of fear eased into the pit of her stomach, near where that knife went in. She hadn't been thinking about anything fearful, merely working the numbers, so the randomness of it was more unsettling than if she had been dwelling on something terrible. She was used to it, but she hated it.

"Cecily?" Josh stood.

No, not at work!

Panic, familiar and unrelenting, began its job with her, doing away with this "resurgent" Cecily of the last day or two at JAH Tech and bringing her back to Earth, preparing her for the return home—and whatever waited if there was an end to the freeze-out once she got there. How dare she think (for even a minute) that she was okay? "Scuse me, Josh...!"

Time must have skipped, because she was shivering under her desk in her back office, weeping with whisking images from a frosty night two Decembers ago, while Joshua called for her from the other side of the door. His call wasn't panicky or forceful, but calm, compassionate, reassuring. "Cecily..." That was all he said intermittently for the next few minutes, and Cecily focused on her name coming from his lips, much like she did in Naomi's office when Naomi was speaking to her as she lay on the floor trembling, and everything was...wrong.

Her sessions with Dr. Alexander couldn't come fast enough.

The moment less intense but not over, Cecily carefully got to her feet. The door wasn't locked, but he chose not to violate her space, didn't enter and try to force her to get it together, and that touched her. She opened the door and looked up at him, ashamed and wary. "I'm s—"

He shook his head and guided her into his embrace. "Shh..."

Cecily held on to him, taking comfort from his hug that was friendly and nothing but (although that secret part of her acknowledged it would've been fine if it was more than friendly). She closed her eyes and breathed in his Polo Classic, purposely reliving those images torturing her while she cowered under her desk.

Calmer, but still on edge, she finally pulled back.

Holding Josh's caring, conferring gaze, she nodded confirmation she was okay—or at least less episodey. He smiled softly and turned away with a gentle squeeze to her shoulder before he disappeared into his office, once again giving Cecily her space.

Except for parting words, they said nothing more, but before she left JAH Technologies, Inc. for the day, she had more to write in that notebook in her sock.

Oscar continued freezing her out, so her evening at home was uneventful. However, she sensed something different and darker behind this freeze-out. She sensed it, but she was also too sensitive at times, too analytical—it may have all been a case of her overreacting (again) and reading too much into things.

Cecily slept alone, slept peacefully.

She dreamed about a moment swelling with a warm sweetness that was honest...and ended as it was supposed to.

Chapter Eleven

Simpatico

N aomi completed dictation regarding her psych-maintenance session with Willette Hargrove (whom she'd just finished counseling), saving the voice file to the file folder "WH47318" on her laptop with a sigh. Willette had lost weight over the years, but there was little progression regarding the woman's antipathy toward her sister, so Naomi doubted her professional treatment made any headway. She could say she kept Willette from outright killing her sister—that would have to be the silver lining (a rather dubious distinction).

She tolerated the maintenance or drive-thru cases; they were part of the job. But she remained most excited about the early and middle sessions with a patient, where the exploration and discovery could be intense and cathartic. Documenting healing and positive progression for a patient was a rush—much like surgeons getting off on using the scalpel.

Naomi smiled at the now-defunct file folders titled "RVP35719" and "JMTW18921" and logged off, preparing for the Brooks couple, who would arrive soon (file folder "CEJ51279").

The holiday break didn't pull her away from work entirely, but it was a change of pace from previous years. There was more socializing, and...she and Kevin were back on, having just returned from a two-day medical conference together (make-up sex had its own brand of *rush*).

She'd called him as Viv advised, her reconciliation speech rehearsed and ready. Kevin answered the phone; she said, "Hello," he greeted with, "My Sankofa Bird," and his next words were to invite her to come with him to the conference.

When he arrived to pick her up, his new tight-boxed beard made an instant impression. She invited him in, and they briefly discussed what happened between them, touched on their differences (non-deal-breakers). During the getaway, they enjoyed each other's company, moving forward instead of dwelling backward.

For a psychiatrist, on a personal tip, Naomi wasn't for much talking—on her end, anyway—and Kevin understood that. He understood and accepted much about her that, upon reflection, she was thankful for. Naomi checked her watch: Kevin was in the air, in-flight nonstop on his way to Ghana. She wouldn't be hearing from him for another eight hours at least. She wasn't a worrier, but she needed to keep occupied.

Naomi turned on her stereo and listened to more of her playlist featuring the Swan Silvertones, an old-school, traditional gospel group based out of Knoxville, Tennessee. "Love Lifted Me" instantly worked its magic. Today's gospel music was okay (she enjoyed a song or five), but it didn't move her the way old-school gospel did. Listening to the likes of the Swan Silvertones, the Soul Stirrers, Mahalia, Albertina, James, the Davis Sisters, or the Five Blind Boys evoked a warm, spiritual fullness in her chest that stirred and comforted her.

Naomi reached for the Brooks file. Twenty-five minutes before Cecily and Oscar arrived: she had solid prep time. She'd acquired the police report and the CSI documents (courtesy of her renewed relationship with Kevin) and started with review of those. Looking at the details of the crime, Naomi shook her head: the Brooks home-invasion date *will live in infamy* for Cecily, too—for an undividedly different but just as devastating reason.

Finished reviewing crime documents for the time being, Naomi turned to her credenza: Viv's wood sculpture of the Rod of Asclepius occupied the center. Naomi placed it on her desk. The couple presented the sculpture as zawadi celebrating Kwanzaa-Kuumba, and Naomi treasured it. Viv put remarkable detail and artistry into making it. Maybe she should keep it at home instead of at the office. But it was here now, so Naomi used it as a focal point while pondering the upcoming session.

She had every intention of including Cecily in some decisions regarding her treatment: any meds, the approach going forward. Having a stake in her mental well-being would more likely lead to full recovery and deter a relapse.

Her psychoanalytical-cocktail would now introduce some Solution-Focused Therapy (SFT). She'd ask Cecily (and maybe Oscar) an exception question or two and see what she gets. Hopefully, the questions will stimulate realizations of positive coping experiences Cecily can use when she's stressed, but Naomi would have to see. She'd later introduce a scaling question or two before finally hitting her with a miracle question before it was all over. The Miracle Question: that would be the kicker. For now, though: CBT with a touch of SFT was the order of the day.

She was shifting focus, interjecting more cognitive restructuring with some challenging questions about that night...and about her relationship. She may provoke a bit of fear and maybe some anger, but that was the point; Naomi needed to test some of Cecily's automatic thoughts for her to see them, reinterpret them, and maybe gain a new (or perhaps not-so-new) viewpoint on the matter.

Cecily maintained a positive outlook regarding others, but that outlook no longer turned inward with how she viewed herself and her life. She moved between bouts of emotional numbness to hyper-alert for danger (yet easily startled or frightened) to periods of overwhelming shame and guilt. Her memory, too, may be problematic—but Naomi wasn't sure if that problem was chronic or intentional or maybe even a subconscious desire to avoid specific memories.

She'd use a derivative of reality testing by playing several versions of "White Christmas" for Cecily while in therapy with her and observe her reactions (if any), because she wanted to bring internal feelings about the song out into the external world in which it played (her office). Whichever session she introduced the music, Naomi expected reaction to the version by the Drifters. She'd take it from there. Purposely triggering patients was ill-advised—but what happened in a doctor's office usually stayed in a doctor's office, only coming to light under special (and rare) circumstances.

Maslow wrapped it all in a nutshell (with a neat little psycho-analytical bow on top), so Naomi used it when analyzing a case or two. Concerning Mr. and Mrs. Brooks, Naomi believed Cecily had her physiological needs met—she took care of that herself. But now, Safety and Security? Loving, Belonging? Recognition and Esteem? Those were interfered with severely (if not inhibited altogether).

Before Roland's death, sure, Cecily may have approached a point of self-actualization. But Roland died, and although not dependent on him, he was Cecily's partner and lover. That crisis left her vulnerable to the Oscars of the world.

Naomi knew the game well, able to see it from Oscar's perspective: woo Cecily in with a false love of life (the first few sessions with him told Naomi he did *not* have a love of life); make Cecily cling to his false goals of wanting a committed relationship; present a false drive for pursuing personal empowerment; and foster euphoria in their relationship...until Cecily was hooked, line and sinker. It blueprinted the narcissist's way since the time of man. She'd seen it all before, having helped many men and women overcome their emotional addiction to something that no longer exists—because it didn't exist in the first place.

Informal greetings over, Naomi sat before Oscar and Cecily, tea in hand.

In their initial session, the couple sat on the sofa together, Cecily taking Oscar's hand in solidarity. The second session had them together on the loveseat—until Cecily found it necessary to lie on the floor. This time, Cecily hung up their coats, and when she rejoined them, she elected to sit on the sofa—instead of next to Oscar on the loveseat. Her decision could've been based on memories from last sitting on the loveseat, but Naomi didn't think so. She couldn't read too much into it, but there was a takeaway to be gleaned (she sensed it).

"So, how was your holiday?" Naomi set her Cambridge mug down.

"Warm-up?" Oscar lifted an eyebrow while popping an Altoid mint. He dressed more businesslike with a shirt and tie, but his turquoise tie didn't knot fully at the top, showing the top button of his dress shirt—a pet peeve of Naomi's (if he'd unbutton that top button, too, she'd be okay with it).

During Cecily's DNA-hotline calls to her, she'd stopped Cecily from revealing Oscar's recent health issues (she was Cecily's doctor, not Oscar's), so she didn't know any new specifics regarding his health, but he looked better in the face: perspiration was still present, but his light complexion didn't look as washed-out.

"Something like that. But it's also to find out about your holiday." Naomi turned to Cecily. "Did you have Christmas dinner with Marcus and Chelsea as planned?" Having spoken with Cecily over the holiday break, she knew the answers already, but Oscar needn't be aware of that.

The glint in Cecily's not-really-hazel eyes as she nodded indicated she appreciated the ruse. "We had Ch-Christmas dinner at Marcus's, and then I j-joined Oscar over at O-Odessa's. It was f-fun."

Something in Oscar's eyes told her he didn't agree. "If you say so."

Cecily glanced in her husband's direction but shrugged Naomi's way. "It w-was quiet but st-still celebratory."

Oscar scoffed.

"You don't agree, Oscar?" Naomi nodded her encouragement at him. "Speak freely in here."

"Christmas was fine. Cecily spent it with her family. I spent it with mine." His expression hardened with challenge. "But since Odessa and Otis can't ever find a solid fifteen minutes to visit our house," he scoffed again, "I didn't stay long at Odie's, and I spent the same fifty dollars on their gifts that they always spend on mine."

His tit-for-tat thinking regarding his siblings reflected the classic passive-aggressive criticism a narcissist uses, so she resisted offering the adage it was the thought (not the gift) that counted. And any mention of the reason for the season could end with the two of them coming to blows. "I see. So, how was New Year's...?" Again, she knew about Cecily's miserable transition into the new year from Cecily's call New Year's morning. The question was Oscars.

Cecily placed her elbow on the sofa arm but said nothing, her discomfort with the question obvious (given her focus on everything other than Naomi or Oscar).

Oscar chuckled and nodded (but sent a warning glance toward his wife). "It was good. The party at Hank and Janyce's turned out better than I expected; we partied hard."

Naomi reached for her tea and let the lie stand. "Did you now?" She sipped and watched the couple. They were the same, but something was different. Only more talking could reveal what that difference was and dictate whether she could exploit it positively for Cecily or avoid (to sidestep something negative from Oscar).

"Before we get into her crap, can we...?" Oscar tugged on his tie.

Naomi wished he'd leave his tie alone; it only drew her attention to it not being snug at the neck. "Yes? Can we...?" She left his "crap" reference alone for the time being. Although Oscar hedged with unusual hesitancy, Naomi knew better: something inimical brewed behind his gaze at her. She hadn't named her gun yet, but she had it—tucked at her lower back.

"I'd like to talk some more about that spiritual-compass stuff."

"Okay."

Cecily's attention was now on her husband.

"Well," Oscar cleared his throat, "I just have some questions..."

Naomi waited. She could only answer his questions from her perspective; she was only the authority on her approach to spirituality, no one else's. "Go 'head. Just know, I can only speak for me."

"Oh, I know." Oscar smirked unkindly, and Naomi wanted to call her brother to come kick his ass.

Instead, she extended a hand in gesture for Oscar to proceed.

Cecily seemed frozen in place.

"Do you think God cares about a person listening to certain music or using drugs or alcohol? Are they wrong or evil for doing it? I mean, Jesus turned water into wine..." He had an attitude, but Naomi sensed it wasn't with her.

Naomi sipped her un-spiked tea. How interesting his question arose on a day she hadn't yet indulged. And the whole wedding-at-Cana analogy was so overused it was ineffectual. "People get carried away with their views and instructions on being 'godly,' sure. But for me, as far as substance abuse is concerned, God already designed the human body to address that. She's made these plants with their effects, bestowed humans the brains to cultivate them for certain purposes. But now, He also gave us physical reaction to misuse. The body gives you the 'good stuff' if used properly, in moderation, or whatever—but the body isn't designed for abuse; the physical effects are violent, damaging,...fatal." Naomi twitched a shoulder. "Seems flawed to believe She condemns one for it."

"You don't believe the devil made that stuff to pull us from God?"

"Well, if I believe God is the beginning, end, and Creator of everything."

Oscar jerked his chin in accord. "Gotcha."

Cecily nodded, too, her attention on Naomi now. She wore a re-flective smile. "And music reflects God blessing individuals with talents. She gave us the brains to be selective about what pleases our ears—selective, but not judgmental. Hip-hop and Rap music have their virtues—aside from the gospel versions." She wore that reflective smile of some memory again—and she didn't stutter.

Naomi nodded with a grin. "Okay."

"Sorry. N-No one was t-talking to m-me."

Oscar scoffed his agreement.

Naomi ignored him and shook her head at her patient. "No, no need for that, Cecily. I agree." She turned to Oscar. "Anything else?"

"What about free will?" The challenge and attitude were gone, his question carrying more genuine curiosity.

"You tell me." Naomi put her mug down and jotted a note to herself.

Oscar glanced at her notepad with suspicion, then shrugged. "Free will—maybe it's exactly that; God created us and gave us this planet to do as we wished: free will." He frowned with irritation. "On the flip side, coming from the interpretations of those other religious fanatics about free will: what's 'free' about it? Supposably, God gave us free will, right? Suggesting without fear of retribution. But so many teach free will with the implied threat of hell and damnation if we choose 'bad' things." He lowered his head with a slow shake before lifting his gaze to her. "God's will be done. Well, what is free will? Isn't that God's will?"

She usually cringed when people used "supposably," but Oscar's pontification showed his post-high-school education. "I like to think so."

He looked surprised. "So, you agree?"

It pained her to nod, but she did.

Oscar nodded back, pleased as he sucked his mint.

"They say God is a s-selfish God, a j-jealous God, but then p-preach selfishness and jealousy are wr-wrong." Cecily's soft words carried a trace of annoyed disappointment.

This time, Oscar's scoff was in solidarity with his wife as he nodded his agreement at her. "Yeah." He fiddled with his tie.

They looked at Naomi.

Naomi observed the couple, ready to begin therapy. This was therapy of a sort, but the focus was Cecily, not Oscar. And, watching them, she saw genuine interest from Cecily over the discussion, but something quite different from her husband. Naomi suspected all this spiritual-compass talk centered around something specific for Oscar—as if contemplating something.

If she could use a flash of truth, now would be great; the foreboding feeling wasn't enough.

Oscar crossed an ankle over a knee. "What? You disagree? Cecily's done all right for someone with her education level, and I'm an extremely logical person, so..." The unvoiced conclusion behind his trail-off was that Naomi should be in steadfast agreement with them. His oblique passive-aggressive dig regarding Cecily's education, within the backhanded compliment that was really criticism, revealed his resentment over Cecily's academic achievement.

Naomi exchanged a glance with Cecily, pleased with the knowing look in her eyes; if he were so "logical," he'd realize spiritual matters had little to do with book smarts. It would also be logical for him to contribute more to the household—but that was another matter. "Cecily made a valid point."

Oscar hoisted his ankle closer with a smile of pride, those teeth making him look more like the Grinch than the proud husband.

This couple wasn't in love, but they shared a minimal bond over their ponderings about spiritual and religious things. Interesting. Naomi reclaimed her mug, eyeing Cecily as she sipped her rose tea. "You said you prayed during the attack."

Cecily nodded, her perfectly styled hair bouncing subtly.

"But in the aftermath, in the *now*, did things turn you away or draw you closer to God?"

Cecily tugged the hem of her tan skirt and crossed one black pump over the other. "I fluctuate."

Naomi sipped, appreciating that most-honest answer. "Cool." She leaned forward, speaking to Cecily. "Turning to religion or God after a traumatic event is fine and dandy, but also understand, one must also use their *common sense* to help resolve issues. God gave us that, too."

They exchanged another look of understanding, but Cecily only said, "The 'prudencesphere.' Sure."

Oscar, however, sat forward, as if to remind Cecily of his presence. Cecily's eyes widened.

Naomi sat back. "Okay. We'll touch on this again as we move through other topics, but what I'd like you to do, Cecily, before we get into meatier things," she noted Cecily's fearful expression, "is have you give me a brief biography of your life through age seventeen."

Oscar scoffed. "Again, with the—? What has this got—?"

Naomi put a finger over her lip to quiet him (which he didn't like at all). "The focus is Cecily now, Oscar. You're here for support." She turned to Cecily. "It doesn't have to be in detail. I want to get a better feel for your pre-adult life." Cecily had already shared plenty, but this angle of therapy held unique application.

"See if something about her brought this on, huh?"

"No, Oscar. You can't 'bring on' a random attack."

Oscar reached for a magazine. "Right." He flipped through pages. "Go 'head, Cecily."

He was good, but Naomi was better: reaching for the magazine was a tell. She gestured for Cecily to begin.

Cecily Jamison finished in the spate of thirteen minutes (a minute for every year since actual memories formed), and many of those minutes deliberated, not on Kyle or Larimore or her father, Bennett, but on her mother, Yolanda. Listening to Cecily's narration, Naomi discerned a hint of narcissistic flavor to that mother-daughter relationship. Cecily loved her mother, but she was not Cecily's treasured member of her family—that title was a tossup between her father and Larimore. She didn't talk long about her childhood, but she shared enough to relay she was fairly happy as a kid. As Naomi requested, Cecily stopped at a period shortly after her high-school graduation. Cecily turned 18 the following October; months later, her parents were dead.

Eyes on either Naomi or the Einstein bobblehead as she spoke, Cecily stuttered sparingly.

Naomi paid little attention to the magazine-skimming Oscar. "Very good, Cecily." She chose not to explore the mother-daughter dynamic, hoping to get into it when session attendance was lower. "Now, pick it up from that chance meeting at a local Walmart to buy laundry items."

Oscar chuckled, giving his wife a sideways glance. "Guess she wants you to skip the period with that punk-ass ex."

Naomi shot him a look, her patience with him wearing thin. His fleer regarding Roland was uncalled for (and Roland wasn't Cecily's ex). She would have Cecily recount her years with Roland, but that was for a future session.

Oscar's sneer was fleeting, but he responded to her expression by returning his attention to the magazine.

Cecily stared out the window, appearing frightened but...annoyed again. The recurring annoyance was a good thing. She sighed, then began recounting her beginning years with Oscar.

Naomi listened. Oscar flipped pages.

Her years with Oscar were fewer, so Cecily's narration was shorter, but it went as Naomi envisioned—almost verbatim. She, however, recognized when Cecily approached discussion of changes in their relationship, because her sentences trailed off into new, unrelated ones or faded altogether. Cecily frowned with angry confusion as she spoke (or avoided speaking), signaling a hurt over much she didn't understand about the current state of her marriage. She said nothing of physical or mental abuse, glossed over their arguments, making it all sound fairytale normal. But Naomi was excellent at reading between the lines of every unfinished sentence (and Cecily's calls to her during the holiday break also conveyed something different). This recited version was for Oscar's benefit; reaffirming the notion Oscar's participation in these sessions was a hindrance. She'd garnered all she needed from him; solid work with Cecily needed to continue without him.

Cecily shrugged. "...So, it's fine. We h-have our ups, r-right, Oscar?" She turned to him.

Oscar flipped to the next page.

"Oscar?" Cecily frowned, not curiously, but nervously.

He took his time looking up. "Oh, I can speak now? Didn't know I had to say anything, didn't realize I was a part of the discussion." He focused on his wife with a slow nod. "But yeah, we have our ups." He lowered his eyes to not read again.

Cecily's acknowledging chuckle wavered with wariness. "Yes. And I g-get through the d-downside of the cycles okay. I'm n-not always w-walking around on eg—" Cecily swallowed.

Oscar swallowed, too.

That would be "eggshells," ladies and gentlemen. As in: being overly careful dealing with a person or situation because they get angry or offended easily—and the consequences that entailed. Cecily's cryptic use of "downside of the cycles" said more about their relationship than she intended. Naomi mentally noted and filed. She sipped her roses and put her mug down. "Okay. Fair enough. Now..."

"Uh-oh." Cecily pulled the multicolored accent pillow from the sofa and onto her lap.

"Yes, but no," Naomi hinted.

Cecily frowned. "No?"

Oscar lifted his eyes to her and paused his page-flipping. "No?"

"We're getting there, to discussion about that night, but not yet—"

Cecily sighed with relief. "Oh! Because..."

Naomi raised an eyebrow. "Because...?"

Cecily's posture stiffened. She didn't respond.

Naomi allowed her time to gather her thoughts while Oscar set the magazine next to him on the loveseat cushion.

The seconds rolled, approaching a minute, when Cecily gripped the pillow and whispered: "It's j-just, I don't kn-know... Everything is..." She looked bewildered, uttering, "I don't know what happened."

She wasn't talking about the night of the invasion. Laypersons often used the term *gaslighting*, but Narcissistic Abuse Syndrome or NAS had stages for the unsuspecting victim. Naomi didn't consider the stages independent and finite, but fluid. Cecily used the term *cycle*, which suggested she moved through the honeymoon-disbelief-defense-depression stages in a pattern of sorts, even likely experiencing multiple stages simultaneously. Right now, disbelief weighed Cecily down. Naomi sat back and crossed her legs. "Take your time."

Oscar stared at Cecily with a wary contempt which slid into concern upon catching Naomi looking at him.

Naomi resisted smirking. "We'll talk about it when you're ready, Cecily. No worries."

Her patient's fingers tightened on the pillow she held while her eyes beseeched Naomi. "But it *is* a worry, Doctor Alexander. I'm a m-mess. You want me t— when I can't d-do anything right lately. I d-don't trust m-my own mi—"

"Cecily, stop." Naomi remained legs crossed, arms on the armrest.

Cecily took a hiccuping-gasp and pulled her upper lip in, apology in her eyes (traces of shame, too). "I'm sorry."

Oscar remained oddly quiet.

The present stressful moment appeared derived from discussing the night of the invasion. However, Naomi still detected something different about the couple, still detected a takeaway at hand: very little of what's been happening in today's session had anything to do with what happened two Decembers ago—and everything to do with the last seven years of Cecily's life.

Having withheld information about what's been going on in her marriage, having covered up how Oscar's treated her (for years), something has Cecily *tired* now, tired of going along with the program. She wasn't at a point of revolt and confrontation yet. That required twofold therapy: for the NAS existing with her husband and the PTSD resulting from the attack—therapy sessions conducted without Oscar.

Naomi had plenty work to do, and time was of the essence because Cecily and Oscar both approached some figurative precipice, with Cecily's hopefully leading to empowerment and self-fulfillment, and Oscar's leading to... Well, Naomi didn't get the same positive vibe about Oscar's "precipice."

"We can take a break, Cecily, or end the session altogether." Naomi wasn't ready to end the session, but Cecily's needs were the priority. "What do you need?"

Cecily's expression changed to one of confused wonderment as she pointed to herself.

Naomi nodded.

"I...I want to get on the other side of this." Her words were soft but not weak.

Oscar nodded with his standard scoff. "Amen." He narrowed his eyes at Naomi. "Enough with these trips down memory lane, Naomi. Do something."

Oh, I will. Naomi reached for her tea.

Cecily hugged the pillow to her body, speaking to them with a murmur. "I...I w-want to get on the other side...," she glanced toward her husband, "no r-repercussions."

She wasn't talking about her PTSD. She wasn't. Not solely. *No repercussions* was critical, but Naomi couldn't get into that last part; she'd have to circle back.

Oscar turned to Cecily with an expression Naomi couldn't read, but somehow suggested he also knew she wasn't talking about the home invasion. He looked down at the magazine, and back at his wife, then back again. He nodded, appearing to struggle with something. "You'll get through, Cecily. You know, because I love you." Those last three words came out in a mumble so fast and low, Naomi's brain delayed determining what he said.

Sometimes people expressed something sincere with discomfort, but that's not what this was: he was forcing the phrase because he believed it was a suitable spot to stick it.

Oscar lifted the magazine and put it down again. He looked at Naomi. "Cecily may not need a break, but I could use one. Mind if I smoke?"

And that was the thing about him. His request was basic passive-aggressive challenge, because he'd interpreted her "sorry" in answer weeks ago regarding his request to smoke as a weakness in her character he wanted to take advantage of.

He wasn't the first narcissist in her office, wouldn't be the last.

Naomi replied with her own element of challenge. "I do mind, OJ. There's no smoking in this building." She held his gaze. She may blink first, but she wouldn't be breaking eye contact first; that would be Oscar. He wouldn't like it, but it would be him. Her name wasn't Cecily.

Cecily brought a hand to her mouth upon hearing the "violation."

Oscar's eyes flared stonily before he brandished his not-pearly-whites. "Right. Just messing around." He reached for the water and poured himself some. He sipped, his stony leer scanning her office. In the pre-therapy questionnaire, he revealed he disliked being called "OJ" anymore—not since the O.J. Simpson trials. Cecily told her the nickname left a nasty taste in his mouth.

And since his attitude left a nasty taste in Naomi's...

It wasn't the most professional, mature response—but it felt good.

Cecily lowered her hand and reclaimed the pillow. "So..."

Naomi uncrossed her legs. "Sure you don't want a break?"

Her patient shook her head. "But I agree with Oscar. How much more of this memory-lane stuff do we have to do? I don't see how it's doing any good with my PTSD."

Oscar flipped a page with a scoff of agreement. "Tell me about it. This isn't getting us anywhere from what I can see."

He was in a hurry for resolution. Cecily seemed in a hurry, too. But both needed to understand: recovering from PTSD wasn't a one-off event. It was a gradual, ongoing process still with a few bumps (especially being compounded by NAS). Memories of a traumatic event didn't disappear. Still, Cecily's handling of the emotions tied to the memories could lead to recovery—something that didn't happen in a session or two...or six. Working with Cecily to help her increase the number of *safe* memories relating to what happened (and replace her fear-based ones) would be instrumental in Cecily overcoming PTSD stresses. But Naomi wanted to start with safe memories unrelated to the home invasion.

Naomi smiled at Cecily. "Well, in this case, what you *don't* see, is what you'll get."

Cecily smirked kindly.

"Ready?" Naomi sat forward.

Cecily glanced in Oscar's direction. "No, but..."

Naomi laughed softly. "I'll accept that. I'll be gentle."

Cecily chuckled, something other than jocularity wanting to push through those fake contact lenses. "If you say so."

Naomi addressed Oscar. "There may be moments where she needs your help with—"

"I'd be happy to." His patronizing wink-and-smile sickened her.

She jotted more notes with only the faintest twinge; the carpal tunnel was behind her. She sat up. "Okay, Cecily. Let's start with that morning after your run. Did you work? Go Christmas shopping?"

Fingers tracing the pillow's shape, Cecily stared out the window at the sunny January day. Sunny, but freezing. "You like ice cream in winter?"

Oscar looked up with a raised eyebrow. "Cecily..."

Naomi shook her head at him and replied to her patient. "I enjoy it year-round. You?"

"Peach sorbet in the spring." Cecily kept her attention turned away.

Naomi came right back. "Pineapple sherbet in the fall for me."

Oscar expressed his perplexity with a headshake.

"Did you have ice cream that day, Cecily?"

Cecily, focusing outside, shook her head.

Oscar sat forward. "She obviously doesn't want to talk about it. All this mess about ice cream."

It wasn't "mess," but Naomi probed differently, anyhow. "Let's talk about the dishes prepared that night. Did you all cook as a family or bring dishes separately?"

Cecily went stiff as she gazed out the window, and Naomi remembered bacon was a prominent factor from that night. Cecily shook her head and nodded in one motion. "I've been researching marketing for my job. It's not my strong suit, but I enjoy learning new things."

Oscar gazed at his wife, his brow furrowed with confusion and irritation, but he kept quiet. His aura flared around him, a ringed image of a muddled charcoal-gray and dark-red (as she'd envisioned for him weeks ago), but with it was this dark-green, creating an overall brownish hue to his aura.

Sensing his ill-health, Naomi believed it rooted the darkness of things, but there was also lots of negative energy in that commingling of dark-red and dark-green. She liked the color brown, and natural brown auras indicated earthy, rustic gravitations. But years of auric sightings left her with less enthusiastic notions regarding murky brown auras from blends. And, between Cecily's gray-themed aura (which Naomi believed remained static since seeing it last) and Oscar's red-green, brown one: gray-brown or brown-gray—it was not a good mix in the relationship arena.

Cecily's change in subject was simple defense mechanism. Naomi's questions about the home invasion weren't targeted (not yet), but Cecily was uncomfortable discussing that night—or day. The questions, however, still created anxious thoughts in Cecily's mind; she didn't want to think about associated memories or feelings, avoided recollection because of what any relived details might reveal—thus, she suppressed them by coming up with another subject or anything unrelated to the home invasion as distraction. Naomi let her. "Nothing wrong with that; marketing's crucial in business."

With the ensuing silence, Oscar replaced the magazine next to him with one from the center table.

Naomi watched her patient, watched more tension stiffen her body with the passing seconds.

"...Those months right afterward... Nothing but chronic anxiety, lows...only going lower. My days were fragmented. I...I would grow panicky—sitting still. I could have a low that wasn't so low—and that was a 'good' day, but then...those super-low days were waiting." Cecily rocked from side-to-side. "...Didn't want food, nothing substantial, anyway... If anything, I subsisted on junk back then: candy bars, cakes.

I don't even like a lot of that stuff. Lying awake for hours... If panic or anxiety wasn't taking over, sometimes I was just...unable to...*move* for fear of...*everything*. I'd be numb to my surroundings, detached, and then...respond to the littlest thing." Cecily turned to her, her false-hazel eyes almost glaring. She still rocked. "It's exhausting."

Naomi noted the use of present tense. She hadn't prompted Cecily to recount her mental or emotional state in the months following the event, but despite Cecily's attempts to suppress discussion of the actual night of the crime, there appeared to be subconscious need to reflect on what happened after. Cecily still experienced bouts of those PTSD symptoms, but they were less concentrated, as time offered a form of healing (however minor).

Cecily stopped rocking, and her gaze remained fixed on Naomi. "And I didn't tell her the shape. I know I didn't."

"Good." Naomi had no idea whom Cecily didn't tell the shape of what, but it was important. Her patient's demeanor said so. Naomi jotted a few notes and checked the session timer. She'd already factored in extra time for each session of the Brooks case; she was good on time.

The intensity of Cecily's gaze softened with surprise at Naomi's response, but Oscar's sigh drew Cecily's attention.

Naomi didn't want her focusing on Oscar. "Can I ask why you stayed in your home, Cecily? Why didn't you move?"

Cecily's attention was back with her, eyes wide and mouth parted with curious surprise. "I...I don't know."

"Okay. Now, instead of a minute-by-minute retelling, I'd like you to simply name key words regarding your experiences from that night."

Cecily frowned. "No blow-by-blow?" She sounded relieved.

Naomi shook her head. "Words. It can be as many as you want, but must be more than three."

Oscar scoffed and shook his head. "Pointless."

Naomi turned to him. "I want you to do the same."

He almost smiled at that, but then nodded and assumed the grave expression applicable. "It'll be hard, but okay."

Naomi swallowed the smidge of bile rising from his response. "You first, then. Sometimes the hard things are easier if we plunge ahead."

Oscar closed the magazine and sat straighter. "Well,...well-orchestrated,...cold,..." He frowned as if on cue. "...Horrific."

She didn't know why, but Naomi thought he sounded proud when he said, "well-orchestrated." "And...?"

He looked confused. "You said three— Oh, '*more* than three.'" He reached for his tie, tugging on it. "And...I guess,...unsuccessful."

Naomi watched him. That last came out with his trademark scoff, showing what could only be irritation. It didn't fit (or maybe it did).

Cecily stared at Oscar, her fingers working the decorative buttons on the throw pillow. "Unsuccessful?" She sounded hurt.

"Yeah. Because whatever they really came for, they didn't get: just some trinkets. And we all made it through."

And while that reasoning made sense, he still sounded pissed-off about it.

Lips turned upward in understanding, Cecily nodded. "Right."

Oscar looked at Naomi. "How was that?"

Scary. Revealing. Puzzling. Eerie. "It was fine. There are no good or bad answers here."

Oscar nodded and went back to his magazine.

Naomi turned to Cecily.

Her patient exhaled.

"Just words, Cecily. No elaboration—unless you feel the need."

Cecily turned to the window, hugging the pillow while working a button with her fingers.

"Take your time."

"At least three..."

"Four."

Staring out at the sunny bleakness of early January, Cecily's features relaxed more with recall of that night.

Maybe a minute passed, and then Cecily spoke to the window. "...Pain, gingerbread, closet, tape. ...Twinkling lights, screams, silence, pain, burned bacon. ...They wore dark-blue. ...Crescent moon. ...It was in the closet. ...Gunshots, urine, icy. ...Music wouldn't stop. ...Rumbling, click-beam-buzz-whir, Chelsea. ...Couldn't breathe. ...No Marcus..." Tears trailed her cheeks as she continued, speaking in soft, modulated tones that, despite the subject at hand, reflected key inference of Cecily's inner self, her inner strength. "Pine, slippery rust, scuffed boot. ...Pain. ...Pinky-ring too big. ...Blood. The door burst open,...and I...I..." She went still and quiet.

Normal response to trauma was flight, fight, or freeze. She wasn't there, but Naomi believed Cecily's response during the invasion was *freeze*, because she'd already suffered the semi-trauma of losing her husband and relocating to start a new life. In that moment, when the door busted open, another trauma was happening again: the fight in her was gone; fleeing didn't work the last time, so she...froze—much like she did now.

"See? She's got it all mixed up, Doctor Alexander."

"Her words can't be taken as chronological, Oscar. Have you heard these things from Cecily before?"

"No, and that's just it: she didn't even mention me. I was there. And they wore *black*, not blue. What 'closet'? And a loose Mason birthstone pinky-ring fit with black tape would've fallen off. We would have it. She's conf—"

Naomi sat forward. "Unh-uh! Don't use that word in here."

He tossed the magazine on the table. "Hold up. You don't tell me—"

"Oh, I do. *In here*, I tell you." She was in the wrong arena with him now, but he wasn't her patient.

"Please don't."

They turned to Cecily, who gazed out the window.

Naomi sighed, reflecting on details in the CSI report. *Blue* fibers were analyzed. There was also mention of those fibers coming from...the hall closet. Either Oscar didn't know this information, or he knew and wanted to guide Cecily's memories. Naomi couldn't tell which (but knew which way *she* listed). There was, however, nothing about a pinky-ring in any of the reports. Oscar went more specific with *Mason*, *birthstone*, and *fit with black tape*, but he may have also seen the ring in his repressed memories. But the perpetrators wore gloves, didn't they? "You're right, Cecily. I apologize—to both of you."

Cecily nodded absentmindedly. "Thank you."

Oscar fiddled with his tie. "Yeah, thank you. Accepted."

"But I meant what I said, Oscar."

His glare dissolved into a dismissive shrug. "Whatever you say."

Over him and all that he represented, Naomi turned to Cecily. "...Whether it's 'men in black' or 'men in dark-blue,' why do they always follow the cliché with the dark and intimidating? The crime is intimidating enough. So, why not wear, say, shamrock-green?"

Naomi watched Cecily, watched the corners of her mouth turn upward, watched her lips (shaded a dusty rose) part and show her teeth. Cecily's teeth parted next, and then her head went back, the laughter sounding urgent and fresh. "I know!"

Oscar chuckled. Naomi did, too.

When her laughter faded, Cecily focused on Naomi. "I like it just being the words, and not..." Her face was tear-stained.

"Okay." Naomi reached for the box of tissues on the table and handed them to her.

"Thanks." Cecily pulled a few tissues and blotted her face.

"Sure." Naomi sat back. "What I'd like to do before we close shop is bring a little more focus to that falcate shape. Can we do that?" She wanted to see if this was the shape Cecily referred to earlier—the one she didn't tell a mysterious *her* about.

Oscar sat forward. "To the what?"

Naomi kept eyes on Cecily. "The keychain."

"Oh. Coulda been a banana; she didn't see it all that well."

Cecily's expression and posture suggested entertaining that, but Naomi shook her head at her. "Could've been, Oscar. But it's the shape I want to focus on, regardless."

"You mean, *irregardless.*"

Naomi started to respond, but Cecily's subtle smirking headshake stopped her, and it surprised and pleased Naomi to see it: because this wasn't a warning based on fear over correcting her husband, but a conspiratorial suggestion as if to say, *let him be wrong.* Naomi changed course. "My bad. So, Cecily, using just words..."

Cecily nodded and turned back to the window. She didn't need a full minute to begin this time. "...Maroon, shiny, capital W? ...H? ...Tip broken, different key attached..." She frowned but said nothing more.

The only things Cecily mentioned, not in the reports, were the tip being broken and her reference to letters ("W" and "H?"). Cecily sounded unsure about the second letter; may as well have been "R" or "B." Were they related to the trinket maker or manufacturer? A person's initials? Naomi jotted more notes. There were severe limitations on what Naomi could share regarding session discussions, but Cecily had full reign on this—she should let Detective Saunders know about the new things she remembered.

"It was *brown*, Cecily, not 'maroon,'" Oscar offered with a flip of a page. He sounded sullen and bored.

This time, Naomi held in a chuckle. The dude couldn't help himself. It was classic; he couldn't even allow Cecily her own memories without putting his influence on them, making them fit his needs. In certain lighting, brown and maroon likely looked the same, but Naomi perceived Oscar wanted to imprint *brown* in his wife's head. Because confusion between brown and maroon was possible, Naomi couldn't say *brown* was an outright lie on Oscar's part, but she didn't put it past him: he had sizable Bushwa City acreage in the land of Fibnation. It was the narcissist's way. She expected Cecily to amend her statement and change the color from maroon to brown, but Cecily continued frowning toward the window without responding.

"You need to focus more on that *night*, Doctor Alexander. This route won't get us anywhere." Oscar scoffed, "Shapes..." and shook his head.

Naomi ignored him; she wasn't giving him any more opportunities to guide Cecily's memor— A flash hit her: a glittery teacup sticking out of a jewelry pouch and resting on a wooden surface. The reverie faded. No rhyme, no reason. She didn't know if it tied to this patient or some other or neither (yet). But: teacup jewelry. Okay. Filed.

Cecily briefly folded her upper lip in with a sigh. Her frown disappeared when she released it. "Spring is coming."

"Peach sorbet, here you come." *Teacups...*

Her patient grinned at that with a gentle nod.

"Is there anything you'd like to discuss, Cecily, before we wrap up?"

Oscar closed the magazine and placed it on the table, and Naomi almost heard *Thank God!* in the gesture.

Cecily shook her head. She turned to Naomi with a hint of a smile. "I did well in here this time, didn't I? It wasn't a waste?"

Most of the connotations of being "in therapy" were negative, but attending therapy sessions and getting better didn't mean someone was suffering a mental collapse. Sometimes a good therapy session or two was just enough to help a person resolve marital conflict or anxiety related to a job, sexual issues, sleeping problems: the list of source-stresses was endless—as were possible treatments. Naomi reached for her tea. "Well, since there is no true *good* or *bad* for the patient during therapy, I'd have to say yes to the former and no to the latter." She sipped her roses. "I haven't prescribed anything for you, Cecily. But we can experiment with low-dosage Lexapro or Luvox for your anxiety; see how that does you. It's up to you."

The hint of smile faded. "I...I don't know."

Naomi smiled brighter to reassure. "Good answer. Let me know when you do. Now, a minor shift in gears before you leave..." She was going into a modicum of Solution-Focus, beginning with some Exception Questions.

Cecily looked fearful before her expression changed to curiosity; Naomi recognized Cecily's trust in her solidifying. Good. "Okay." She now held the pillow on her lap casually.

"A few questions. As always, take the time you need to answer."

Cecily nodded.

Oscar opted to get more water. Seemed hard for him to sit still.

"Question one: Can you identify any times you don't have your...'episodes'?" She still didn't like that word, but it was a point of reference for Cecily (and Oscar).

Cecily's gaze focused behind Naomi—in the general area of Einstein; he was a point of mental refuge. Naomi watched closely as her eyes lit up, softened, and then those things faded as Cecily turned to her. She shook her head and jerked her shoulders.

"Okay. A shrug suggests there may be a time; you're just uncertain. Question two: Can you identify whatever is different about that time, such that you don't experience PTSD symptoms?"

Attention on Einstein, Cecily whispered, "The environment."

Naomi let the not-so-cryptic statement ride. "Fine. Here's question three: When are you most chill?" She started to replace *chill* with *yourself,* but she'd save that for later questioning.

Finished his water and fiddling with the cup, Oscar sucked his teeth. "When she's jogging her head off at five a.m., or listening to that man-woman, bass-sounding, Nina Simone."

Although she sensed Oscar's contempt, that didn't mean he was wrong: her morning jog or being plugged into Nina were possibilities. "Cecily...?"

Her patient drew her upper lip in again and held it there, hugging the pillow tight as she stared at Einstein. "I do like running, listening to Nina, spa days at work..." But she didn't sound very "chill" right now.

"Okay. We'll stop here, Cecily." Hearing about the spa days was good news; they offered a level of stress inoculation training.

"I know. They're simple questions, but I can't even—" She wasn't worked up, but Naomi recognized Cecily getting there. "I'm sorry. I must be nervous, getting all stressed-out and conf—" She'd internalized much of what she likely heard Oscar or others say about her, to where she accepted the words as truth: a form of introjection.

"No, Cecily." She hoped her tone settled the matter.

Cecily looked at her.

Naomi shook her head. "That word isn't allowed in here for now." She was referring to the word *confused*, but the word *sorry* also applied. Cecily's habitual apologizing pushed beyond good manners, being polite. It served as a strategy to *stay safe*—primarily from the ever-present threat of Oscar's craziness. However, she's now transferred that safety-net expression to cover all bases and keep herself safe...from everyone—to keep all anger and disdain away if she can.

Cecily pulled her lip in again and nodded before turning back to Einstein.

"What is this: a classroom? Don't say this, don't say that..." He crumpled the cup and tossed it in the wastebasket.

"There are things to learn in here, so we can go with that." Naomi offered him a smile she didn't feel. She turned back to Cecily, who still contemplated her Einstein bobblehead. Naomi turned to look at him, too, and then back at Cecily. "You know, he contributed a classic definition of insanity."

Oscar headed for their coats. "Oh yeah? What's that?"

Naomi watched Cecily. Cecily knew the answer; Naomi felt it. She waited because she wanted Cecily to recite it.

Oscar paused. "Well?"

Cecily locked eyes with her. "Doing the same thing repeatedly and expecting a different result."

Naomi nodded subtly. Round three: Cecily.

In her peripheral vision, Naomi noticed Oscar shrug. "I don't get it." He sighed and grabbed his coat. "A'ight, Cesspool—"

Naomi turned to him and stood. "That's word number two for you. Don't call her that. Not in my presence." There was only so much of this she could take—and not lose her license to practice.

Instead of anger, Oscar expressed curious confusion. "I don't mean it like that. It's just a nickname, all in fun." He likely believed he sounded convincing, but seeing Naomi wasn't to be persuaded, he scoffed and turned for the door. "Fine. Sorry. Whatever. Guess I'm not meant to win a round. I'm going to the men's room. Meet you outside, Cecily. Later, Doctor Alexander."

Yeah: much.

Naomi sat as the door closed (hearing him call Veronica, "Home Skillet"). She jotted notes, letting the silence linger, allowing Cecily a much-needed moment.

"...I'm sorry. We're creating all this turmoil in your office. But don't think badly of him, Naomi. Oscar means well. His sense of humor is a little off, and he's not the best communicator, but not everyone is. All marriages have their rough spots, and I'm no piece of cake: he just wants me to get better."

Naomi jotted her notes, classifying Cecily's response as rationalization and a typical defense mechanism. Cecily likely told herself varied versions of the same at least once a day now, continually attempting to reason-away her marital situation in rational terms to avoid accepting the reality of it. Naomi glanced her way. "I hear you." Thinking about the potential sex-related side effects of Cecily taking an SSRI (and reflecting on a recent discussion with Viv), Naomi posed a question: "Do you respond more to aural or visual stimuli as far as sex and arousal?"

"Huh?"

"Sounds left field, I know. But it isn't."

Cecily stared at her before lowering her gaze to her shoes. There was a pause before she answered. "I...I don't know, or rather, I don't...remember anymore." When she lifted her gaze, she looked ashamed.

"No embarrassment in here. No good or bad answers, remember?"

"So,...the Lexapro or Luvox: you think I need to be taking something."

"No."

Cecily's brows knitted with bafflement. "But..."

"You need to get well. Whether that journey entails help from pharmaceuticals at this stage? I'm leaving that up to you for now."

"I see."

"But as these sessions progress, a prescription may be in order, Cecily, because the questions will get harder, probe deeper. That means talking about the rape and other traumatic things from that night. Discussing it aids having it lose its power."

"Janyce said, 'a part of the healing after a tragedy was forgetting about it, moving on from it'..."

"Well, you'll never forget it, Cecily, but there's some validity with the 'moving on' portion of what she said; you don't want what happened to handicap you to the extreme."

"I understand. And that's 'Janyce': with a 'Y,' not an 'I.'"

Naomi chuckled, not getting Cecily's need to clarify. "Okay."

"I know. It's habit."

"...Your fondness for Nina Simone..."

A tiny smile creased her lips; the fondness was deep. "What about it?"

Naomi held her gaze. "Beyond the music, her personal story..."

The tiny smile faltered. "I know it, and it's a part of it, yes."

Naomi nodded. Made perfect sense.

"They loved each other...in the beginning."

"Maybe. Could've been something else."

Her patient's eyes, those fake lenses, gleamed with curiosity...and knowing. It was a nod without her moving her head.

Naomi shrugged. "For human beings, love has relative meaning."

"I guess." Cecily stared at her hands. "'Love is patient, love is kind. It does not envy, it does not boast, it is not proud.'"

"Well, yes: we often reference chapter thirteen of Paul's First Epistle to the Corinthians in the New Testament as a definition of love. But I believe he's referencing Divine Love, not romantic love. This Divine Love, if you will, is for all people to extend to whomever; it's not restricted to husband and wife. Romantic love is a strange animal because it embodies more of the human element." Naomi discharged a summarizing sigh. "Thus, everything in that arena—"

"Becomes relative." Cecily lifted her head, her eyes searching Naomi's. "And so, *that* love...we must define for ourselves."

Naomi winked. "Yes. But let us hope there's still some Godly to it."

Cecily nodded and lowered her gaze back to her lap.

Silence followed, Naomi jotting more notes. Cecily broke it with a whisper of "Lickety-split."

Naomi paused her note-jotting to lift her eyes Cecily's way. "From that night?"

Cecily slowly nodded.

"Let it marinate. You like nature? Trees and parks, trails...?"

"I do, yes."

"Thought so."

"Why?"

"Because I want you to spend as much time outdoors as possible."

Cecily looked perplexed.

Naomi grinned. "I know, sounds weird, but trust me. Take extended walks aside from your usual, okay? Take new routes, see different parts of the great outdoors. Maybe even during a light rain..."

Cecily gazed at her, a curious yet hopeful happiness in her not-hazel eyes. "How will that help?"

"It's something you like doing, anyway, so do more. The seclusion, the peace and relaxation from nature's sounds... Trust me. You like nature, the outdoors; be outside as much as possible. Bundle up: but enjoy nature." Naomi sent her a deliberate gaze. "Meditate, listen to Nina or the relaxation music I gave you."

"I already do. I like the tracks featuring babbling brooks."

"I'm glad. But other than hanging out with Mother Nature, try doing something *outside* your comfort zone."

Cecily looked unsure about that one, but that was okay.

"...And find a *confidant*, Cecily. Someone that'll listen and not judge. I don't care who it is—because it may not be the people it's supposed to be. You feel me?"

Cecily tilted her chin in concession.

"If not a friend, join a PTSD support group: they already get where you're coming from."

Cecily nodded again; this time, her eyes held more determination. "I will, Doctor Alexander. And...there is someone I can talk to."

"Good. Like I said: I don't care who it is."

"It's not Janyce." Cecily's mouth then worked as if wanting to reveal who it was.

But Naomi meant what she said. She shook her head, telling Cecily it'll keep.

Naomi stopped the recorder, noting Cecily's lack of stutter during that private exchange. Minutes later, alone in her office, she remained in her counsel chair, scanning her notes from the Brooks sessions.

Cecily exhibited a variety of disorders in her inability to cope with the trauma of the home invasion and the resulting PTSD—all of this exacerbated by the pre-existence of NAS. Cecily didn't exhibit any issues with sleeping, and she needed to explore more of Cecily's eating habits, but so far, she detected key problems with anxiety and personality. A few rounds of CBT could change those for the better.

And after this session, Naomi realized her therapy with Cecily may have edged into being threefold instead of twofold: 1) treatment for her PTSD derived from the home invasion; 2) treatment to release her from the grip of NAS derived from meeting Oscar; and 3) treatment to help Cecily solve a vicious crime committed against her, derived...from meeting Oscar.

Naomi sat in her great room, nibbling a York Peppermint Pattie while reviewing yearbooks she pulled from the basement, listening to a playlist of Celtic music. Tracey Hewat's "(The) Firelands" circulated.

Leslie and Trevor were in the last stages of Christmas-Kwanzaa dismantlement, returning her four-level home to normal. She still thought of Leslie's previous boyfriend, Scott (with the pleasant voice and conversation), but alas, Leslie relegated Scott to the friend-zone some time ago, dashing Naomi's hopes for a Scott comeback. Leslie and Scott kept in touch, but as friends—Trevor was her romantic focus for the last couple years. In that time, he'd grown on her. He only had Leslie by an inch or two; if the two were going down Nuptials Road, Leslie should probably wear flats. But knowing her daughter, Leslie could give a frig about that stuff; she'd wear five-inch heels if the mood so inspired.

Rick and Viv were due to arrive soon, and she wished Kevin was stateside to join them, but he wouldn't be home from Ghana for another two days. Kevin enjoyed the time spent with his family, but her phone discussion with him thirty minutes ago let her know he was also ready to come home, ready for them to resume being back together.

Naomi flipped a page in the high-school yearbook from her junior year. She missed him, too. It was a new arena for her: at 47, she hadn't finished "cooking" yet, still had some learning about herself.

Naomi reviewed the pages, seeing faces she knew but people she didn't know, gazing into the eyes of former classmates and doing a bit of psychological profile. There was innocence there, yes, but Naomi also saw in those eyes, hints of what many of those futures held. She saw suicide wishes, restrained rage, political cunning, burgeoning alcoholics, and purposeful philanthropy, but mostly, marrieds-with-children-and-day-jobs. She searched the faces for anyone who rose to a particular prominence: nope. That wasn't surprising, but she expected different from her college yearbooks, expected to see a classmate or five who'd had media coverage on some scale. She'd still see hints of future mental breakdowns, broken relationships, and drug addictions—but that was a given. The images reflected the truth that is life. "*Veritas vos liberabit,*" she whispered with a gentle smirk, finding the motto of her alma mater, Johns Hopkins University, apropos on multiple levels—especially in therapy.

With the Phillipses arriving any minute, Naomi wanted to study that collage of Rick and RJ. Viv said there was a difference, and Naomi was determined to find it, so she'd taken a picture of the collage for private viewing at her leisure. She'd been studying that cotton-picking collage for weeks, still with no idea who was who; their resemblance was eerie (a nice eerie). She looked forward to Rick and Viv visiting; hanging with them elevated her spirits.

Smiling, she tucked the RJ-Rick collage photo inside one of her coffee-table books, thinking about the couple on New Year's. She went to Mark's shindig and had a good time. When the hour drew near, she watched Rick and Viv's tradition of engaging in a deep kiss seconds before the new year turned and continuing that kiss for seconds afterward, desiring to close one year and bring in the new one the same way. The couple hadn't been able to bring in the new year that way for the last two Januarys; their kiss translated hotter than she'd seen between them. She toasted but didn't hug strangers as the new year rolled in. Later, she'd been home for all of ten minutes when Cecily Brooks called.

The doorbell rang.

From two flights up, Naomi heard Trevor say, "Cool! They're here!" As the two headed down the stairs, she wondered if her daughter was aware of Trevor's infatuation with Viv, wondered if Trevor was aware of Leslie's blossoming infatuation with Viv's husband.

She listened to them open the door and greet Mr. and Mrs. Phillips and their son, listened to conversation as coats were removed and hung up—and detected something was off.

"Ma!? They brought snickerdoodles! I'm addicted to these things!"

She was. Naomi aimed the remote at the player and paused the Celtic music set. She stood as Leslie, Trevor, Rick, Viv, and RJ entered her great room (RJ in Viv's arms). "Hi."

The couple wore smiles part-genuine.

Rick set the Great Cookie bucket and a silver gift bag on the coffee table. "Yeah. 'Addicted' is a good word. I believe they've included an addictive as their secret ingredient." He placed his gray GMU cap back on his head and approached her, greeting with a hug and peck to her lips. His irises appeared redder, and his smile (as beautiful as it was) seemed forced; he was upset.

Rick stepped away, and Naomi approached Viv.

Viv wore jeans and a long-sleeved green-camouflage tee ("Must Love Robots" emblazoned in yellow across the front). Her hair, straight and parted on the left, framed full-bodied around her face and over her shoulders.

Viv smiled with her customary "Hey, lady" and leaned close for a hug, but she appeared more upset than Rick despite the warmth of her greeting. Her body oil blended orchids and cinnamon. Naomi hugged RJ before Viv set him down with a rub to her son's head. "Excuse me, would you?" She hurried into the kitchen.

RJ headed for his father, who stood by the fireplace. He didn't ask to be picked up, content with hugging his father's leg.

Rick's hand came down, stroking his son's head, but his jaw was tight as he focused on the far wall and her painting by Archibald Motley. He and his son were dressed similarly in sweats by Adidas.

The silence wasn't uncomfortable, but it wasn't comfortable, either.

Leslie shot her a look, and Naomi nodded.

Leslie nodded back, but Trevor picked up the baton. He retrieved RJ's bag and pulled a book out. "Hey, RJ. Want me to read you a story?" The low afro-fade and strategically cut sideburns gave him a rapper's look (at 25, he had the age), but Trevor earned his bachelor's degree in history and substitute-taught third graders at an elementary school in Bladensburg (while working on his graduate degree). Not that he couldn't parlay the look into a rap career; rap artists these days started with much less.

RJ turned to Trevor with a nod, and Leslie approached RJ with an encouraging smile as she took his hand. "Come on, RJ..."

RJ knew his surroundings and liked Leslie; he didn't protest.

Rick palmed his son's head before letting him follow Leslie. "Not that one, though, Trevor. Read Keats' *A Snowy Day*. That's his joint—if you read it right." He smiled, but again, it didn't have its familiar brightness. "Don't just say the words, man."

Trevor nodded as Leslie headed past him with RJ in tow. "I got it, Mister Phillips: read it with feeling."

Rick adjusted the bill of his cap and pointed at Trevor in a gesture of confirmation before Trevor followed Leslie and RJ out of the room. He returned his attention to the painting.

"...Don't let this linger, boy. Get in there."

He issued his signature curt-nod and turned for her kitchen, pushing through the swinging door.

Naomi paused in the silence, hearing a chair pull. She allowed the couple some respectable minutes and then went to the swinging door on the other side of her kitchen, glad she hadn't gone the open-concept route yet. Some might consider her being nosy, but this was her house, and she was wildly curious; all bets were off.

She cracked the door open: Viv stood by the stove, Rick sat at the table, gritting his teeth. Viv held her lowered head in her hand, shaking it. Naomi eased back, allowing the swinging door to close. She listened.

"...It just slipped, Rick."

"Yeah, I know. That's the problem." Oh, he was hot.

"I didn't mean it the way it sounded, baby. I swear." Viv's tone was hard to place: pleading and sorrowful, yet still remnants of anger.

Rick sighed. "I know that, too." He sounded hurt, pissed, but understanding. "...Don't call him 'Jon,' Vivian. I am *not* well-handled. I pray the need for his name to come up is nil, but whatever the case, *don't call him 'Jon.'*"

Rick spoke low, but each syllable pierced the quiet with utmost sincerity. Cruelly loving Viv aside, Viv had better heed his words. If the need to speak of Jonathan Rast arose, she'd best not reference Jonathan using her onetime nickname for him. Although nowhere near the levels of three years ago, Rick still suffered intermittent violent surges. He wouldn't direct violence against Viv (that's the one thing he would never do), but it was best Viv didn't rile his anger over that "Jon" point.

Naomi didn't blame him, shit. She suspected he always would percolate with bits of rage underneath it all; a subconscious part of his personality now surfaced and morphing with his conscious personality (couldn't put *that* genie back in the bottle). The bonus? Rick used sex to help tame the restless surges associated with Intermittent Explosive Disorder—and his wife's sex drive matched his needs stroke for stroke. Those two: hot for each other since day one. Only now, it was heightened in the aftermath of events three years ago. She wasn't so sure Viv wanted therapy to help with *that* side effect of his IED.

Rick sighed again, and then Naomi heard the chair scrape.

Viv sniffed.

"Anything I can do, baby?"

"...I can't stop replaying the words from Lynelle's letter in my head. And I know it's counterproductive to our thing, Ricky. I *know* that."

Naomi shook her head with a trace of sadness. Viv and Rick were in such a good place, so in love, but Viv just couldn't let things be. Her flash of truth about Cecily weeks ago interrupted Viv's talk about that letter from Lynelle—the dalliance who ended up catching feelings for Rick. She and Viv hadn't talked about it since, and, listening to the couple now, Naomi wished they had.

"...C'mere, Viv."

Sensing Viv move closer to Rick, Naomi listened.

"Look at me." His words were low but loving. There was a pause, and Naomi envisioned Viv looking up at her husband. "Enough of this."

Naomi sensed other movement and cracked the door enough to see them beside the fridge, Rick guiding Viv, backing her to the wall. He placed one hand next to but above Viv's head, gazing in her eyes. Viv looked up at him, her eyes angry yet vulnerable. After a lengthy pause, Rick spoke: "I love you."

Viv replied, "I know," and Naomi reclosed the door.

"I want only you, Lady Blue. You're all I've *ever* wanted."

"...I know that, too. Same here, Ricky."

"Then we gotta get past this, baby. I don't wanna keep coming back to this,...when we have so much to look forward to."

"You're right."

"I thought we forgave each other?"

"I have."

"Not if you keep dwelling on the negative, giving me attitude about the past and taking it out on me in the present when I didn't do anything." Traces of anger laced his response, and again, Naomi didn't blame him. Viv told her the first few arguments she and Rick had since his return were Viv's fault; this issue filled the same bill.

Viv sniffed and exhaled a rippling breath.

"Do you love me?" That mellow baritone of his dripped with such unintentional magnetism, Naomi nodded trancelike in answer for Viv.

"You know I do. More than words could express."

"So, decide, Viv. I did my shit. You did yours. That's dead and done. *Over.* It's you and me. We've learned a hard lesson about dealing with crucial conflict between us; to work through the hard shit *differently.*"

"We have. Tough lessons."

"So, decide. Leave the past where it is and not let it interfere anymore. Choose *us.* Okay?"

"I have chosen us, Rick."

"Not if you keep going back to our old shit, Viv. You haven't." He sounded frustrated. "You're the one told me all of that was over. At the Smithson. Remember?"

"You don't think about it? About me being with Jonathan?"

Naomi envisioned Rick's jaw tightening. "Every once in a while, yeah. I'm not go'n lie. But it's *rare*, Viv. And I don't let it interfere with what I want to have with you past the day I die."

"Right. I'm sorry, sweetie," Viv sighed. "Can't say I won't think about it anymore, but I'll take a page from your book and not let it interfere, not dwell. ...And not take it out on you when I do think about it."

"Thank you."

Smiling to herself, Naomi stepped away, giving the couple some privacy; they were on the right track. She, however, could only stay away for so long. Naomi returned to the rear kitchen door and peeked in.

The couple was in the same place she'd left them, but now Rick had the fingertips of one hand to Viv's waist. Rick lowered his head and kissed her, his tongue moving with Viv's. When he pulled back, he gazed at her with a soft smile but some fierce love. "All the way, Vivian."

Viv grinned up at him. "All the way, baby. I love you. I'm sorry. Okay?"

Rick nodded, and Viv drew her arms around his neck, kissing him again.

Naomi backed away and returned to her great room, leaving Mr. and Mrs. Phillips to it. She sat on the sofa and picked up the yearbook from her first year at JHU.

It was several minutes more before the couple emerged from her kitchen, Viv leading Rick with a finger link. "Sorry about that, Naomi." She bore a sincere smile, Rick's cap now on her head, her hair tucked behind her ears. The green and yellow in the GMU logo complemented her camouflage tee.

Naomi closed her yearbook and stood. "You're home. Don't apologize. You know better." Her heart warmed seeing this older couple showing good, sexy, fun love wasn't limited to couples in their 20s or 30s, nor did it fade with age—and that it still had its bumps along the way. "I'm just glad you addressed it, didn't allow it to spoil your visit."

Rick shook his head with a chuckle and released his wife's hand. "Basic math. So, what're we doing? Anything specific, or just hanging?"

"Let's just play it by ear—*after* Naomi opens her gift."

Naomi grinned and reached for the silver gift bag. Telling them they didn't have to get her anything was pointless—especially since she did the same thing with them. "Where's Alna?"

"Recital rehearsal with Li'l Tim. She's coming; Lou's dropping her off." An odd but fleeting expression crossed Viv's face with that last, but Naomi didn't think she was aware of it. Viv went for a cookie.

"Kevin has something for you, too, Rick." Naomi pointed to a gift-wrapped box on the window-seat. "He's texted twice, asking if you'd opened it yet, so I'm guessing he's not pressed to be here."

Rick raised an eyebrow and cleared his throat. After years of interacting with him, Naomi determined his throat-clearing was selective and not a motor tic disorder. Seemed he had different throat-clearings with different meanings. As expected, only Viv knew the difference (irritated, blushing, uncomfortable, aroused, actually clearing his throat, or a combination); her smirk suggested she knew what this throat-clearing meant. Naomi surmised he was uncomfortable. He smiled, though, as he walked to the window-seat. "A'ight. Ours isn't a gift like that, just a neighborly token, but let's open together."

Naomi grinned. "Sounds good."

Minutes later, she popped a tasty Cerignola olive from the jar into her mouth (her gift from them, along with a jar of select Dalmatia black olive tapenade) while she and Viv watched Rick explore his gift from Kevin: a Venere rusticated half-bent Canadian by Savinelli with related accessories including a tin of Dunhill Durbar pipe tobacco. Naomi mentioned Rick's new indulgence to Kevin once, and he purchased it while they were at the medical conference.

They watched Rick marvel over his present: a little boy with a new toy. He had his tobacco-pipe leather carrying case out (a gift from Viv), transferring and organizing the items from Kevin. Rick spoke Italian. Viv had his case engraved, *È tutto basato sull'amore*: translated, means, "It's All About Love"—one of his favorite songs by Earth, Wind & Fire.

Viv leaned down, whispering in her ear. "*Thank you.*"

Naomi grinned; she knew Viv well. Kevin's gift translated to Rick later giving Viv shotguns after drawing from his pipe, allowing her a taste of pipe tobacco smoke; quite arousing, according to Viv—so the pipe and accessories were Viv's gift, too. "Gotcha, Viv."

Viv stared Rick's way, running a musing gaze over him. "Yep."

Rick looked over at them. "Beg pardon?"

Viv shook her head. "Nothing, baby. Do your thing."

"But don't get too absorbed. You have something else over there...from me." Naomi smiled at her brother, smiled at that curious and surprised expression; adorable without him trying. She realized the gift-giving bordered excessive, but this couple had been through a lot, partly deserved but mostly not. She extended the goodwill to them because, reason number one: it lifted her spirits.

Rick smiled with a questioning, "Seriously?"

And his smile and expression were reasons two through infinity.

Lord have mercy.

"Yes. So get on with it."

Rick turned to the black gift bag, lifting out the card. "Mister Richard Alden...Stannis Phillips Senior." His upper lip did this little thing, signaling he wasn't a fan of "Stannis," but he eyed her with a kind smiling-smirk saying he was cool with her using it. But with that little thing he did with his lip, Naomi decided to follow his wife's lead and stick to "Richard *A.* Phillips" going forward.

"Read the card later. Just get to the good stuff." Naomi winked.

Nodding, Rick reached in, peeking past the tissue paper. "Woo-hoo! C'mere, Viv! Check this out" He brandished a broad grin and pulled the tissue paper out in a rush as his wife came over to see. He sounded a joyful laugh upon the gift's full reveal: a rare copy of Christmas music by EWF from their early years. The LP was signed. Rick couldn't take his eyes off the album, so Viv reached in for what remained in the bag: packages of Reese's cups and a bottle of Four Roses bourbon. Smiling, she nudged her husband's arm with the bottle of Four Roses, and his mouth fell open more at seeing it. He gawped at her. "Naomi..."

Viv's expression matched her husband's. "Thank you so much. But what's going on?"

"Yes. Thank you, *largely*. But Viv's right: this is... Wow..."

Naomi snacked another olive in answer.

Rick looked at Viv. "The end." Viv nodded, and Rick returned to the EWF album while Viv organized the other gifts, putting everything in one bag (except for a Reese's cup Rick wanted). From upstairs, Leslie's and Trevor's laughter blended with the giggles of a two-year-old.

Naomi accessed her phone, texting Kevin about Rick's reaction to his gift. She could've recorded it and sent that, but oh well, TLTB.

Soon after, Naomi and Viv were alone in Naomi's library on the fourth level, sitting in leather club chairs and gazing out at rooftops and the DMV horizon through the huge picture-window. As expected, they talked some about Rick. Viv attended Rick's initial session with Dr. Newble. Rick's sessions would resume in March, with Viv scheduled to attend once a month. The couple liked Dr. Newble, so they were off to a good start. Dr. Newble would reevaluate Rick at year-end to determine whether continued counseling was necessary as part of his probation.

One thing not part of his probation was court-ordered community service. However, Naomi learned from Viv that, also beginning in March, Rick imposed his own version of community service by signing up one Saturday a month to mentor convicted juveniles on transitioning back into school and family life and getting employment.

Naomi considered that alone worth more than a rare, signed EWF Christmas album.

Since psychiatrists weren't ever officially off duty, thinking about Cecily Brooks, Naomi broached exploring the Phillipses' relationship more. She turned to Viv. "Do you feel safe, Viv?"

Viv gazed out at the view. "With Rick? Absolutely." Her words didn't waver, and she didn't clarify or modify, Naomi guessed, because she meant it in whatever way (and all the ways) Naomi did. "He has all aspects of my well-being in his care. I assure you." Viv turned to her. "Why? Because of when he choked me?"

That wasn't why exactly, but she couldn't reveal her hidden reason for the question, so Naomi simply shrugged.

"Well, I feel completely safe with Rick, even encouraging him, as my form of therapy, to be rougher sometimes during sex—because I believe he needs a little sexual intensity to curtail the surges for violence he sometimes has."

"Okay."

Viv turned back to the view outside. "Professional therapy will do its thing, too, but I'm moving about the prudencesphere, using a dash of your philosophy about applying common sense."

Naomi chuckled with appreciation, thinking, Viv's sex drive likely needed some of that sexual intensity, too.

"...Rick would never hurt me, Naomi. I *know* that, not just believe it. It's not a hunch or intuition, but a gut realization that I am the exception to receiving any displays of his propensity for violence. I'd...I'd say there're only six people in that category: me, Al, RJ, Papa Phillips, Mark,...and you. That would be the main list. There's a secondary list, sure, but circumstances would dictate. And strangers? Well..."

Naomi knew, years ago, she was *not* on that main list. "I agree, Viv." She decided she'd continue asking Cecily variations of the same question throughout future sessions to see if anything, *anything* about her answer changes; it would be a relationship-safety barometer of sorts.

"He wouldn't do anything to separate us again, but he has to be careful."

"So, you and Rick are inseparable, huh?"

"In terms of our love and commitment to each other: definitely. But now, we're not joined at the hip. We'll be 'breaking' from each other."

"You will?"

Viv grinned and then shook her head. "Not right now. Oh, hell no. Got too many dates at Takoma Station Tavern to get out of our system."

Naomi shook her head in fun. The couple visited the DC pub several times since Rick's return. The tavern, with its cozy atmosphere of live music, food, and drink, was a favorite haunt of theirs; they indulged in reacquainting themselves with the place.

A wonky smile curved Viv's lips. "Yeah. But we've outlined a plan to implement weekend breaks."

"Interesting."

"Weekday evenings are family time until the kids go to bed. The weeknights are for us to talk or, uh, ahem, *bond*."

Naomi grinned.

"We'll be alternating having Saturdays to ourselves to indulge in our divergent interests; I do my thing while Rick takes the kids. Alternate Saturdays, Rick does his thing while I take the kids. Al's old enough to make her own plans sometimes. It isn't off the table, but we won't spend nights away or anything like that, but we can take the entire day on into night if it calls. And, of course, it's perfectly cool if one of us doesn't want to take our day. Regardless, Sundays are for the four of us in some form of family-time groove."

Rick already established how he'd use one of his Saturdays. "I see you're working on keeping complacency at bay."

Viv returned a long, contemplative nod. "That's dangerous for a marriage, Naomi. Routine is one thing; a working-eating-sleeping part of life can be routine. And that's okay."

"But complacency ended up being a wake-up call of sorts."

Viv didn't respond for some seconds. "Yeah: complacency..."

"Sort of led you down your particular path with Jonathan."

Viv nodded, lips bent downward. "Which set off the rest..."

Both women went quiet, reflecting on events years ago.

Viv took a loud breath, startling Naomi.

Naomi grinned.

"So yeah, Rick and I will take our healthy breaks. And soon, one weekend bi-monthly will be just for Rick and me alone—no kids. It'll be Friday night through Sunday evening."

Naomi chuckled.

"Don't laugh. We may recruit you or Leslie to babysit some of those weekends."

Naomi loved Viv. She did. "I'd be happy to."

Viv smiled and turned back to the window, her beauty breathtaking in the natural light (baseball cap and all).

"And, as much as Leslie fawns over RJ, I'm sure she'd be happy to."

"She fawns over my husband, too, but that's another story."

Naomi didn't know what to say.

Viv looked at her with twisted lips. "Naomi, please. I don't care about that. Rick is good-looking, sweet, and charming. Leslie's an adult, but she's young. I remember being a young twenty-one-year-old lost in love with a mature nineteen-year-old. That nineteen-year-old is now forty and carrying some serious, grown-ass, effortless, masculine appeal, so I get Leslie's perspective. It's self-explanatory and innocent enough. Unlike Louise's feelings..."

The withheld anger ringing clear whenever Viv spoke about Louise required the couple address that unresolved issue—and soon. "Right."

"Leslie's crush on Rick? It's sweet."

"Because Rick is oblivious."

Viv grinned, nodding. "He just doesn't get it, Naomi. Has no clue. Now, if a woman overtly compliments him or violates his personal space with explicit meaning, he'll pick up on that. He's uncomfortable with it, but he recognizes that much more readily than picking up on the subtler cues coming his way. He's unaffected by or about his looks or the effect his looks and personality may have on others. And although I know why..." a tiny frown of anger creased Viv's brow fleetingly as the reason resonated within her, but she recovered, "it still fascinates me."

She'd already determined a root-cause existed for Rick's behavior, but given Viv's fleeting frown in anger, Naomi wondered what rooted Rick's disregard for his looks, but she let it go; Rick's humility heightened his attractiveness. "Yeah, me, too—and I do this mental shit for a living."

The ladies tittered.

Viv stood, affixing Rick's cap more securely. "Come on; I want a cookie. Let's see what the rest of the crew is up to. RJ needs a nap." She picked up the Edgar Allan Poe compilation she selected from Naomi's shelves and headed for the stairs.

"Don't forget: I want to see that home video."

"Already started working on a copy; I didn't forget. I got you."

Before they headed down, Naomi double-checked she'd secured her Glock-17 (still no name) in the safe in her closet.

They came downstairs to more of RJ's giggles (having himself a good time) and paused at the entrance to the great room, watching Rick delight his son with yo-yo tricks. The electric-blue orb spun, twirled, and sparkled through the room, making RJ bounce on Leslie's lap with glee, hollering, "Again!"

Viv bit her bottom lip (suppressed desire for her husband).

Les and Trevor prepared a light snack for everyone, and Viv put RJ down for a nap afterward. They watched some of *Good Will Hunting*, Naomi and Rick bonding over the part where Will ridiculed the ivy-league grad student in the bar (a shared favorite scene). Naomi spotted her daughter slyly staring at Rick during the movie—something gone unnoticed by unsuspecting Trevor.

Rick and Viv got in a game of pool (ensuring they made *use* of her game room); Leslie and Trevor paying close attention. Naomi got a kick from seeing the younger couple shadowing the older one, trying (in vain, Naomi thought) to capture whatever intangible elements Rick and Viv possessed.

Game over (Viv won), they sat around the table, a game of Tonk closing with Rick's win.

"You're some sort of cardshark, huh, Mister Phillips?" Leslie beamed at him with excitement. Her cherry-tinted wash-n-go afro looked full of life, suiting her daughter's artist lifestyle.

Rick shook his head but smiled. "Not at all. And technically, it's *cardsharp*, Leslie, not 'cardshark.' A '*P*,' not a 'K.'"

Her daughter paused and looked around at everyone, seeing Viv's agreeing nod. "Uh! I've been saying it wrong for years!" She laughed at herself, making everyone chuckle with her.

"Not necessarily. It's a regional thing. But I like acknowledging the distinction." Rick shuffled the cards. "Can I ask you a question, though?"

Leslie nodded, curious yet wary (though still a tad moony over him).

"Why is it you call my wife 'Viv,' but I'm 'Mister Phillips'?"

Leslie looked perplexed. The blazer she wore with her t-shirt and jeans had been her father's (which she had altered to fit her).

"Hey, I get the respect-your-elders thing, but uh…" He glanced at Viv, then regarded Leslie, thumbing toward Viv. "She's older than me, so…?"

Viv bit her bottom lip with a smile, her lower body movement suggesting she playfully kicked him under the table.

Rick laughed, reaching across the table for Viv's hand. He fastened his eyes on Leslie. "Call me 'Rick.' Okay?"

Leslie nodded, gazing at Rick with this awed, google-eyed expression rendering her infatuation with him transparent, but she recovered, trying not to blush. "Uh, okay."

Rick nodded curtly and resumed shuffling, oblivious to the whys of Leslie's response. He shot Trevor a look. "You, too. Enough with the 'Mister Phillips' jazz."

Naomi looked at Viv, who shook her head and looked upward with a knowing grin and sigh. "Another one bites the dust." She rose and went over to her husband.

Rick looked up at Viv. "Huh?"

Viv pecked his lips. "Nothing. Let's get some music on."

In all the exchanges during their visit, Naomi anticipated hearing Rick say, "Damn skippy," but it hadn't happened yet. And she didn't know why, but not hearing him say it bothered her.

Rick watched Viv head away from the table, those eyes roaming Viv's lower body, focusing on how her camouflage tee fit her waist and rounded over her derriere. He bit his bottom lip in obvious meaning, and Naomi withheld a chuckle, thinking about Viv biting her bottom lip when watching Rick.

Trevor, too, ogled Viv longingly (his camel-brown skin looking rather flushed with tacit desire), and it was good Rick's attention was elsewhere: Naomi didn't think Trevor was on any of the free-from-harm lists—not yet. Rick rose, heading for the player. "A'ight, Lady Blue, I have something in mind. Just need to see if Sis has it…" He went over to her digital jukebox.

Turns out, she did have it, and now the couple hand-danced in the middle of her great room to "When We Get By" by D'Angelo. They danced so well, with such familiarity, it equated seeing what their lovemaking was like. They weren't grinding on each other or anything, but the way they brought their bodies close and then parted in the groove and bounce of the music, this erotic give-and-take existed between them almost subliminal. There was no mistaking how good their sex was. The intimacy conveyed with their body movements made it pleasantly uncomfortable, such that you wanted to avert your eyes but couldn't take your eyes off them.

Naomi saw the same sentiment echoing in Leslie's and Trevor's viewing of the dancing. Although Rick led most of the dance, like lovemaking, they switched lead without a misstep. There were moments when they traded glances, speaking love with their eyes, and other moments when their smiles at each other told a tale of sensual, deep friendship. Naomi experienced intense pride seeing it; she couldn't wait to see them all dressed up and dancing at the upcoming charity ball.

Unfamiliar with hand-dancing, Trevor tried to emulate Rick as he danced with Leslie, and partway through the song, Rick and Viv gave Trevor and Leslie some beginning hand-dance moves. Rick danced with Leslie (over-the-moon), while Viv danced with Trevor (looking just as smitten). The younger couple had some ways to go, but Naomi suspected that had more to do with being hormonally distracted by their dance partners.

Naomi splintered her attention between watching the kids dancing and her text conversation with Kevin when Rick seized her hand, bringing her to the middle of the room to hand-dance with him. Holding her phone, she jumped right in, surprising herself and everybody else as she followed his lead; she hadn't hand-danced in ages—not even with Kevin—that was a Tyson thing. Viv added to the fun (to Leslie's and Trevor's cheerful calls) as she positioned behind Naomi, dancing with Rick, too. Reading Naomi's dance cues, Viv stepped when Naomi stepped, and Leslie kept hollering, "That's so cool!"

Rick danced with her, but his eyes often fell on the woman dancing behind her, and Naomi saw up close the depth of feeling coming through Rick's gaze at his wife.

With Leslie and Trevor attempting to hand-dance again as the song closed, Naomi smiled and stepped from between Rick and Viv to allow them to finish. "When We Get By" ended, followed by Aaron Neville's rendition of "Stand By Me." Rick's smile at Viv showed he'd programmed the song to follow D'Angelo's.

Rick guided Viv closer, and they danced with a mix of hand-dancing and slow-grooving (Trevor and Leslie again, watching closely). This dance displayed more intimacy; the lyrics held special meaning for the couple (given the last three years). But it had a sweetness, whereas the faster-paced hand-dancing showed something more primal.

"Stand by Me" rolled into New Birth's "It's Been a Long Time (You for Me, Me for You)," and Naomi smiled with an understanding nod. Rick held longtime affinity for the older stuff, the songs he grew up on, and this song carried an even deeper meaningful association for the couple. The sweetness transitioned into something more intense as they danced, their movement more emotional (and sexual).

Rick held Viv close after the song ended, and Naomi recognized carryover emotion moving through both as their mouths locked, tongues twirling. Viv eased fingers into Rick's hair.

The room went quiet (except for Trevor's low but audible grunt).

Kiss ended, and holding Viv at her waist, Rick dipped his head and pecked Viv's collarbone. "Go'n check on our li'l man..." He left the great room for the stairs, heading for one of the spare bedrooms on the second level, and Viv watched his departure.

They settled around the great room, Naomi making her point about the 1997 deaths of Princess Di and Mother Teresa. It stuck in her craw that those two women died within days of each other, yet the media covered Princess Di non-stop, while Mother Teresa received a mere footnote. Leslie groaned for her not to get started on that again as Rick returned from checking on his son.

"He's still sleeping, listening to Brahms's 'Violin Concerto in D major, Opus seventy-seven' somewhere in his dreams: that's what was playing."

Naomi stared at Rick. The music playing for RJ was from a CD she burned but didn't label, so it surprised her Rick recognized the music.

Her surprise obviously showed. Rick raised an eyebrow at her as he reached for a snickerdoodle. "What? You think you're the only one on the classical music tip? I know a little sump'n-sump'n."

Her real brother was dead (thirty years now), but she couldn't ask for a better stand-in than Rick Phillips. "Apparently." Naomi wondered if RJ liked clarinet concertos; she enjoyed them immensely.

Rick laughed and sat next to Viv, and everyone socialized awhile longer, talking, joking, and passing Naomi's yearbooks around. Rick asked Naomi to call Kevin, and he thanked him with a live voice instead of through Naomi's text. Kevin laughed his surprise, which reflected being touched by the call. She then put Kevin on speaker for the gang to say their hellos. They ended the call and resumed hanging out, Naomi looking forward to speaking privately with Kevin later.

Viv soon headed for the stairs. "I don't want him sleeping too long..." She reentered soon after with RJ in her arms. As soon as RJ saw Rick, however, he wanted out of Viv's arms. Viv put RJ down, her eyes holding low-key aroused interest as RJ ran to Rick.

RJ headed toward his father's lap at full toddler speed and a leap, and Rick used his hands to slow RJ's forward motion and keep his son's airborne parts from landing into his privates. "Whoa! Careful, little man. Go'n send Daddy curled to the floor, jumping into me like that."

Trevor chuckled his male understanding.

Viv and Leslie chuckled, too, but Naomi swallowed with the tingling sweeping across her face over the mere idea of Rick's genitals.

Rick settled RJ on his lap. RJ leaned back on his father, sucking his lower lip, just chilling as his eyes moved over everyone. His resemblance to Rick blared.

Naomi shook her head. "Rick, you spit that little boy out." She turned to Viv. "Just the vessel, huh?"

"Isn't it a shame? All that work: sickness, fatigue, weight-gain..." Viv scoffed with a headshake. "RJ's eye-color is darker than Rick's, but other than th—"

"*That's* what it is!" Mystery solved.

Viv nodded, wearing this acknowledging smile. "The collage: yes—that's the difference."

"That's probably you, Lady Blue. Maybe he'll have your drastically dark color...and hopefully, with no issues." The couple exchanged a private but understanding look.

Naomi was curious about possible issues with RJ's eyes but didn't pry.

Viv sent Rick this cutely dismissive glance. "Anyway, he has my ears, but that's about it. Everything else is Rick's: face, body type, fingers and toes, the same rough but soft-yet-dry curls in his hair texture. Oh, but RJ has my adenoids, apparently..." Viv had her adenoids removed as a toddler; RJ's surgery was next week (Naomi sensed Viv's nervousness about it). Viv shook her head.

"Hey now, my daughter is the spitting image of her mother. Making me nothing more than the donor."

Viv smirked at him. "I see some of you in her. Al has your nose, complexion—"

"And I see you in RJ."

Naomi put a hand up. "So, you guys are gonna fight about it?"

Viv winked at Rick, getting a wink back in response. "Yeah."

Leslie giggled. "Yeah: so they can 'make up' later."

Exchanging smirks, the couple began that silent-conversation thing.

RJ tilted his head backward, speaking upside-down to his father. "Peenbu'er."

Leslie's mouth fell open while Viv just shook her head. She looked at Naomi. "Spit him right out. Rick's clone. I'm telling you."

Trevor laughed and headed for the powder room.

Rick chuckled as he gathered his son to him and stood. "What? He likes peanut butter. Has nothing to do with me."

Viv hollered. Just let loose with laughter. "Yeah, okay, boy."

Rick smiled back, then turned to Naomi, eyebrow raised in inquiry.

Lord have mercy.

"We have JIF brand: your preferred."

His warm smile in response reflected the good things about life. Rick kissed the top of his son's head. "Coming right up, buddy. Come on..." Carrying his giggling son over one shoulder, Rick smirked at Viv before kissing her cheek as they passed her, taking their son into the kitchen for some peanut butter.

Viv popping her husband's rear as he passed didn't faze Naomi, but Leslie looked almost beside herself. "You don't worry about peanut allergies?"

Viv shook her head with a shrug. "He's over two now, so..."

The fellas returned, the littlest fellow content with his small serving of skinless apple slices with smears of peanut butter. Naomi asked Rick if he was ready to return to work, and Leslie, former marketing major, got into discussing various theories in marketing strategy with him.

Leslie swore by the Innovation Theory (developed by someone named Jacobson). She pointed her cookie at Rick for emphasis, adding a headshake. "You can't tell me that creative destruction, born out of an inherently uncertain and disequilibrium business sector, doesn't lead to long-term profitability."

Rick believed competition faltered without adopting a bit of something called "Zagare's Game Theory" (whatever that was). "Leslie, there is a level of uncertainty to be expected, yes, but when you're able to figuratively 'walk' in your competitors' shoes and gain analytical perspective for the success of your own firm, using an understanding of probable outcomes? That strategy wins hands down."

The two parlayed different points Naomi had no clue about, but Viv put the brakes on it. "Why don't you two agree to disagree, and let's move on."

Rick nodded and smiled at Leslie. "Your knowledge regarding strategy formulation processes and strategy implementation concepts surprises me. You were an art major?"

"BA in Sculpting, yeah. But *after* three years studying international marketing." Leslie glanced at her with a smirk.

Naomi smirked back; it all turned out fine. She now worked toward her master's in art.

"Three years makes you legit—especially since you're G-Mason alum, too!" Rick laughed, giving Leslie a high-five, and then they both smiled, yelling: "Patriots, brave and bold!"

Naomi shook her head (along with Viv and Trevor shaking theirs).

Rick cleared his throat. "So, look, Les, since we both agree with the Narver and Slater cultural perspective on market orientation, we'll agree to disagree on Institutional Theory." He smiled at her.

Leslie nodded with a grin, and Naomi resisted stepping close to keep her daughter from swooning to the floor, thinking Leslie might be somewhat pissed at having changed her major (for no other reason than having even more in common with Rick).

Rick issued his brusque nod. "Done."

"Now that class is over, anybody feel like playing Quirkle? Scrabble?" Trevor sent his gaze around to everyone.

RJ finished his last apple-peanut-butter slice. "More?"

"No more, RJ." Viv grabbed a wet-wipe and cleaned her son's hands, getting the few tiny smears from the hardwood floor. "Here, sweetie." She handed him his sippy cup filled with water, then spoke to Trevor:

"You already know Naomi's and my vote, but we'll be leaving once Lou drops Al off, so make it a low score to win if it's Scrabble."

Music playing in the background, they ended up playing both. Naomi had long ago combined two boxes of the Quirkle game to allow over four to play. Rick and Viv let RJ play their tiles, using the opportunity to teach their son more about colors and shapes. The six enjoyed the music and the tile-laying, the game moving along with ease.

During a quiet moment, as Rick pondered his tile move, Viv watched her husband's hands select and deselect, select and place. She released a whispery grunt, drawing Leslie's attention, and Naomi smiled inside. Viv loved Rick's hands (especially the prominent veins on the back and along his wrists and forearms); that tiny grunt expressed her likely imagining those hands on her in some nice way.

L.T.D.'s "We Both Deserve Each Other's Love" came on. Rick and Viv interlocked hands, and everyone grew quiet. It was the way the couple did it. They moved tiles with their free hands or had RJ do it.

And it was then that their "couple aura" flickered for her (such a rare occurrence). She'd wanted to see a combo-aura for Rick and Viv since they were patients on her couch almost three years ago. Combo auras (with couples) informed her of a deeper compatibility level than individual aura comparisons. Viv's individual aura flickered with the orangish-yellow warmth of amber, while Rick's glimmered with a calm, collected hue leaning toward royal-blue. However, Naomi focused (in the few seconds she had) on that shade of candy-red enclosing them. If this were paint, one would expect the combination of their individual auras to create something near a brown (unfavorable) or some muted blue. But it didn't necessarily work that way with auras. Auras existed as capricious phenomena. That candy-red (brightened by some pink) coming from Mr. and Mrs. Phillips: exciting, enduring, powerful friendship, combined with a loving sexual energy, fiery and passionate. Naomi almost blushed. That their three hues were a composite of the primary colors didn't escape her either.

When the song ended, Rick and Viv pecked the lips.

They paused at seeing everyone looking at them, returning questioning gazes and responding in tandem. "What?"

Good-natured laughter followed, and RJ's excited push of the tiles signaled the switch to Scrabble. Rick displayed his Scrabble acumen, winning with the word *Machiavellian*, and Naomi took professional pause, correlating it to her newest patient.

Oscar's behavior with Cecily filled the bill; he exercised a complex and sinister set of operations within their marriage. The home invasion and the circumstances of their getting together in the first place made it difficult for Cecily to figure things out. In the end, it undermined her mental stability and compounded her attempts to heal, get well.

Cecily didn't realize it, but Oscar's manipulations only reinforced (and actually rewarded) Cecily's exhibits of inadequacy. In upcoming sessions, she needed to elucidate Cecily already had the coping skills necessary for thwarting such a dangerous cause-effect relationship—which likely resulted in Cecily seeking either Oscar's approval or some display of caring about her and her situation.

Louise texted Viv, telling her she'd be dropping Alna off soon. Naomi wondered if any dynamics played out when she arrived.

There was a sweet moment, as Viv stood by the window-seat checking out the EWF album, and Rick came over to her. He placed a hand on the small of her back. "Can I have a chance?"

Viv blushed. "...Yes."

Rick kissed her cheek.

Trevor frowned. "She's already your wife. What're you mackin' for, man? A 'chance' to do what?" He devoured an entire snickerdoodle. His curiosity was genuine; he still had much to learn (some older men, too) about keeping the romance popping after you've "landed" them. Quiet, meaningful (old-school) questions like that were a romantic touch.

Rick pointed something out on the album to Viv and didn't answer Trevor. The message? *Think on it, son.*

Trevor's grinning nod: he'd received the kind men-only message.

Rick kissed Viv's shoulder. "How 'bout a little rice-n-gravy tonight?"

Viv stared at the album, but Naomi read her lips, saying a soft, "Yes." She blushed yet again, and it was the damnedest thing. Naomi saw some of this between them in their therapy sessions—before things detoured. Seeing this side of her friend again was heartwarming. Viv was an empowered Black woman and all, but in this moment, she was simply a woman in love.

"You guys going to have meat with that, or...?" Trevor was being nosy, but Viv's blush told Naomi Rick wasn't talking about food.

Leslie mouthed at Trevor for him to mind his business.

RJ sat on the floor playing with his "laptop." A distinct odor meant his digestive system functioned properly. He got up, pulling at the back of his sweatpants, and went to his father. "Poop...?"

Rick took his hand. "A'ight, buddy. Les, hand me his bag, please." Moments later, he had the task well in hand. "Sis, a buddy of mine, Ellery, has some Wizards tickets Mark wanted, and I told him to drop them off here. He should be here with them shortly."

Naomi nodded her approval.

He looked up at Viv, who stood nearby watching the diaper-change. "Now, this boy just told me, in a word, that he pooped. Still want to wait to start potty—?"

"Yes. And, just so you know how this works: he's supposed to say something *before* he poops."

Rick smirked at her, his golden-auburn eyes twinkling something sexy her way. "Rim shot."

"He's a new two, baby. Two-and-a-half will be better for him. Alna got it earlier and quicker because she's a girl—"

"Let's not start *that* again." Rick rendered mellow amusement.

"Cuz you know it's true; little boys like having that mess on them for as long as they can stand it."

Rick lowered his head, shaking it with a smiling sigh while setting RJ to his feet.

Snickering with Leslie, Naomi joined the fun. "Yeah, Rick: what's that about?"

The ladies laughed (Trevor stepped out of the room minutes ago).

"Uh, I'm go'n find the other testosterone in the house, now. Maybe open my Savinelli pipe from Kevin, smoke some of that Dunhill."

"Good thinking, husband-o-mine."

Rick kissed at Viv with a wink and left the room (dirty diaper in hand).

RJ grabbed the handle of his "computer" and headed after his father.

Leslie watched RJ leave, shaking her head. "Seems RJ's had enough of us women, too."

Nodding, Viv chuckled. "Yeah. He's 'Daddy's little man' these days."

The doorbell rang: either Ellery or Louise. "I'll get it," Rick called.

Ellery Newsome (a graying man in his late-40s and with considerable connections with the DC sports teams) was in and out of her house in under five minutes. He'd no sooner left when Louise arrived to drop Alna off. Mrs. Nguyễn-Collins had enough manners not to let Alna out of the car and pull off—but coming inside for proper hellos wasn't the most comfortable situation for her.

Naomi was proud of Rick and Viv: the couple acted normally, giving smiles and warm greetings as if Louise's betrayal didn't exist. Their congeniality was rooted in having history with Louise and Tim, with their children being good friends. However, in the ten minutes Louise was in her house, she spent nearly seven of those minutes gazing at Rick, such that Leslie kept giving her looks. Naomi subtly warned Leslie off with her own look because Leslie was getting heated.

There was an awkward moment with mention of the charity ball: Viv hadn't used her extra tickets to invite Louise and Tim (she asked her sister, Patrice, and her husband instead). Naomi recognized Louise's hurt feelings, but they glossed over the matter without it becoming a *thing*. The ten minutes (which felt longer) were up, and Louise was gone.

After Louise left, Alna performed a wee section from her upcoming violin recital (to Naomi's pure delight), and the Phillips family prepared to leave. "Can I speak to you two for a second?" Naomi pointed toward her kitchen.

Rick and Viv shrugged and nodded before following her through the swinging doors.

Naomi paused by her island counter.

"Whassup, Sis?"

"I want to say something to you two." The couple's curious-yet-cautious expressions were cute. "Don't stop showing your love in front of others. It's terrific to see. Great to see a mature couple, past their twenties and thirties, showing what good love can look like. Black Love. You're tasteful with it; don't stop showing it to others. And I know you're not 'showing' it, you're just being yourselves, and I'm saying..."

With glances at each other, they responded: "Don't stop."

Naomi shook her head, loving them both. She eyed Viv pointedly. "Especially *you*."

Viv's eyes widened. "What'd I do?"

"You're in unfamiliar territory, but I think you know. And it's not 'do,' it's *doing*."

Rick turned to his wife. "Yeah!"

Viv smiled, pecking Rick's lips with a loving smirk. "Shut up."

Rick's gaze at Viv changed, and Naomi watched him lift his cap from Viv's head and bring their mouths together again for something hotter.

"...Get 'er, Rick."

Her comment made the couple laugh into each other's mouths, giving her glimpses of their tongues gliding together haltingly as they kissed before looking at her with amused, inquisitive expressions. Rick raised an eyebrow with this engaging smile. "W-What is that?" He placed his cap on his head, backward.

"What?"

Grinning, Viv neatened her hair. "'Get 'er, Rick,' 'Get 'im, Viv': *that.*"

Naomi shrugged and headed for the exit. "Don't worry about it. You two, just heed my words." She left the kitchen on the couple's laughter.

Trevor was in the basement as Naomi and Leslie watched the Phillips family walk to the Range Rover. RJ was on Rick's shoulders, Alna and Viv leaning close and giggling at something as they carried purses and bags. Balancing RJ on his shoulders, Rick opened Viv's door for her before settling their son in his car seat. Alna got in beside her brother, still laughing at something with her mother, as Rick settled in the driver's seat. The family, however, didn't drive off right away.

"I know he has faults, Ma. We all do. Viv could probably give a list of not-so-great things about her husband." Leslie sighed. "But it's obvious Rick is a good man—and a magnificent lover."

"Leslie!"

"What? I'm just saying. You know you feel it, too. Viv looks like she is getting UPS deliveries from Rick on the regular, and he looks like she gives it to him good, too. Those dances said everything. The way they move together..."

Her daughter was an adult (almost 23), yes, but hearing such things from Leslie was unsettling.

"Even when they pulled you to the floor—which shocked the mess out of me. Notice the way they looked at each other?"

The Phillipses waved before pulling off, adding a quick blow on the horn. Naomi waved back. "I did."

"They don't just look at each other with lust; there's something much deeper going on. They're best friends, Ma. Will die for the other without hesitation." Leslie turned to her. "And what the hell is up with Louise?"

"I prefer not to get into that."

Her daughter rolled her eyes with a harrumph of attitude still directed at Louise, but nodded her understanding. She returned her gaze to the view through the storm door. "Yep. That's what I want."

"With Trevor?"

"Hopefully. But if not, then with someone."

"I see. Well, Rick and Viv had what you see between them from the beginning. They lost touch with it later in their marriage, but have since reestablished things, coming full circle. Theirs is a natural thing, but sometimes couples must work extra at it." Naomi gazed at her daughter more seriously. "You know a little about what happened. Could you handle what they went through to attain that type of connection?"

"...If it means having something as loving and intense as those two? Then, hell yes."

Laughing, Naomi closed the door, resigned to free Cecily so that she could find something close to what Rick and Viv have—which meant Oscar had to go. They headed for the great room to finish the minor tidying necessary, Leslie trailing behind her. "Feel like fennel-and-sweet-onion pizza with some green olives for dinner? We have Asiago in there, some Castelvetrano olives."

Leslie scoffed. "You and olives."

Naomi chuckled, retrieving a purple Quirkle tile from the floor.

"Haven't had that in a while; that's fine—long as *you* chop the onion. Use that 'impervious-to-onion' gene of yours."

"I see."

"You know what's hot to watch with them?"

They were back to Mr. and Mrs. Phillips. "What?" Naomi returned the Quirkle box to the shelf.

"When they touch hands. They'll interlock or hold hands sometimes, but most times they do this soft, casual interplay with their fingers when they're near one another, even when they're interacting with us and not each other—*hot*."

Naomi nodded; she'd noticed that, too.

"You think Rick is aware of his looks, his...effect?"

"In the sense he's seen himself in a mirror, has likely received plenty feedback regarding his looks from others: yes. Otherwise, no—not the way you mean."

Leslie nodded thoughtfully as she stacked the glasses she and Trevor used. "I can tell. Viv has said she didn't think she was the ugliest person in the room, but I don't think she gets how attractive she is, either."

From the basement, Trevor exclaimed joy over some points scored.

"He always smells so good. Today it was...coriander and tangerine mixed with iris, leather, ginger, some other stuff. I finally had to ask Viv, shit. Sorry, Ma."

Naomi chuckled, wondering if sensitive noses ran in the family. The way her daughter rattled off the scents she'd isolated in Rick's fragrance was surprising. Maybe it derived from her artsy vibe.

"She said it was Artisan Black by—"

"John Varvatos."

"Yeah, that's it."

"Maybe you can get that one for Trevor."

Her daughter shrugged and neatened the yearbooks on the coffee table. "What is 'Lady Blue'? Why does he call her that?"

Naomi believed she had an idea. "Leslie, Viv and Rick are former patients, now extended family. But I don't know everything about their relationship." She requested everyone leave the Scrabble board alone and now stared at Rick's winning word, planning for next week's session.

Leslie opened the bucket of cookies and grabbed one. "You know what I'm going to call them?"

"No idea." Great room tidied, Naomi headed for the kitchen to prep dinner.

"Mister and Missus...Simpatico."

Naomi nodded with a laugh.

Noon the following day found Naomi in her office, enjoying slices of grilled bread with roasted tomato and the Dalmatia olive tapenade from Rick and Viv while reviewing her notes and findings on the Brooks case. The situation there was pressing. She wanted to go through her rehash exercise now because upcoming sessions with Cecily would focus on active recovery—and much less on exposition and supposition. She wasn't sure how she'd extricate Oscar, but she had some days to think about it. Naomi snacked and listened to a playlist combining the best of classical and Celtic music, all while ruminating and extrapolating and contemplating generalities and specifics related to the NAS and PTSD experiences of Cecily Brooks.

Mother Nature didn't discriminate, but she did disseminate.

Humans were born with innate defense mechanisms and adaptive behaviors used to protect the species from extinction. From the early trauma of infant separation anxiety to something as devastating as being a crime victim in middle-age, adaptive behaviors and defense mechanisms (both learned and natural) remained, unconsciously doing their thing throughout one's life by reducing stress, anxiety, and fear. Certain forms of social and emotional bonding were necessary for human survival (people needed people), and its success or failure began with that very first attachment: mom.

While identifying and connecting with mom (or dad) as an initial and primary caregiver was key, Mother Nature inserted new dynamics as a child aged—and mom (or dad) ended up being one's first antagonist as well. And if that love-then-almost-hate dynamic went far left, it could lead to a child relying solely on emotional bonding to...make it through life. Without it, they're lost and unable to...survive.

Cecily's relationship with her mother satisfied and possibly tested that "first antagonist" dynamic. Still, Cecily's relationships with her father and brothers helped her nurture proper bonds with others, which didn't allow Cecily to form unhealthy emotional bonding patterns. And then: Roland died, Cecily met Oscar, and later she was beaten, stabbed, and raped under a Christmas tree.

Most important? Cecily met Oscar.

Honeymoon stages of relationships were a given, but things took on a distinct flavor when dealing with a narcissist. Caught up in the alluring state of euphoria during the honeymoon stage with Oscar, Cecily became hooked by Oscar's attention, combined with his grandiose exploits.

During the initial stages of a relationship, partners sometimes experienced biochemical changes in the brain (and body) created with the release of chemical endorphins, giving people an elated feeling when things are kicking off. Cecily, still mourning Roland when she met Oscar, was susceptible to becoming addicted to the highs of Oscar's (seemingly) over-the-top gestures of romance and attentiveness. Oscar drew Cecily in, such that Cecily soon found herself hooked on him emotionally. Naomi had seen it all before in some form or fashion. And not only with men. Women could be narcissistic abusers, too; a Svengali could have a uterus and bear children. Mother Nature didn't discriminate with penis size, nor did She with the gender of relationship abusers.

Naomi finished her snack, topping it off with a shot of Hennessy X.O. She turned her Baltimore Ravens cap backward before resuming review of the Brooks case, thinking, extrapolating...

What Cecily didn't realize, was Oscar's "perfect match" presentation was just that—a presentation, an...illusion. An illusion designed to draw Cecily in to feed his own narcissistic needs. Naomi was sure Oscar flipped the script soon after they wed. Once Oscar had a convert in Cecily, it was easy to flip the script on her because she was still dealing with losing Roland. Addicted to the relationship in the *before* and now confused by its sudden change, Cecily likely works time and again to get things back to the euphoric state: but Oscar's done with that; his mission accomplished once Cecily was hooked. Without the "drug" of that false happiness at the start of their relationship, Cecily didn't have her drug—and so began withdrawal and more anxiety over the change in things. Cecily likely believed she'd found her second soulmate—and was now bereft at its loss.

The Jekyll-Hyde twists-and-turns Oscar shifts their relationship through, continuously upsets and disrupts Cecily's view of her role in her world and how marital relationships work—especially given the success of her first marriage. Oscar had Cecily hooked, "in love" again, and then, out of nowhere, he turned cold and uncaring toward her. Cecily fell from Oscar's grace: Oscar grew critical. She couldn't do anything right anymore, and everything Cecily tries somehow still ends negatively for her—she's devalued at every turn.

His sudden script-flip left Cecily confused and unbalanced with the unexpected change, making her unhappy and stressed, depressed with her new situation. Her constant apologizing reflected need to keep Oscar's disapproval or anger at bay, an appeasement of sorts to lower herself and build Oscar up to avoid conflict and his (targeted) narcissistic aggression.

The apology held and shifted power on many fronts: Cecily wields it to redirect Oscar and maintain a temporary safe zone, while Oscar accepts it as confirmation of need for the redirection.

Thing was, once a narcissistic abuser reached some figurative peak in the relationship, reasoning with them became...moot. The abuser's peculiar behavior creates confusion for the victim and increases the need to work harder to please the narcissist because they want to get back to that elation from the honeymoon stage. With the narcissistic abuser unwilling to kowtow or surrender their position of power, the target experiences something equivalent to withdrawal, becoming bereft over the loss of the good times, distraught and anxious about the current status, and confused about how they got there. Unconscious defense mechanisms are then used to cope with the sudden rejection, from rationalization and cognitive dissonance to suppression and denial—and victims apply these mechanisms to navigate the NAS existence of their day-to-day.

Naomi shook her head with an annoyed chuckle as she reviewed her notes, reflecting on the last session and Oscar's attempts to guide Cecily's memories. Never mind, the recollections he fed her contradicted the reports. Regularly, methodically withholding facts about a partner's experiences, or switching those facts with lies as placeholders, was part of a narcissist's MO. With NAS, the goal remains using fact withholding and replacement to impact the mental stability of their target negatively, so that they rely on the narcissist, need them to provide the truths about their daily lives. Over time, victims lose their sense of self. Narcissistic abusers get off on the emotional violence of *messing with the mind*—and that's dangerous.

Flipping the script on Cecily entailed gradual, repeated forms of insidious and self-serving psychological manipulations as Oscar picked her mental stability apart for his needs. Into the relationship, the "dance" began, creating a paradoxical vicious cycle (and was likely what Cecily meant when she referenced *cycles* in session).

Naomi could see Oscar's abuses (mental, physical?) becoming more blatant with his perceived increase of importance and power over Cecily. Any hint of Cecily pulling away from him and their relationship, any attempt to reassert her former self, would be interpreted as a threat to his narcissistic needs—making him kick things into a higher gear to regain his foothold by devaluing Cecily even more, using any means necessary: her physical appearance, her intelligence, cheapening her value sexually.

Mr. and Mrs. Brooks were *anti*-simpatico.

She believed Oscar pushed Cecily away with his "disgust" based on his abuses, on how Cecily responded to how he treated her: her displays of powerlessness and inferiority irritate him. Still, he pulls her back to feed his egosaurus needs—which Cecily meets because it's instinctual for her to. Bottom line? Oscar "hates" Cecily—but she'd better not leave him. It was the *better not leave him* part making it necessary for her therapy to accomplish several goals—and leave Cecily alive to see the results.

Cecily's marriage to Oscar reflected a low point, a nadir, in Cecily's life. Thinking about her patient, Naomi recognized the situation as so incapacitating it limited Cecily's ability to be humorous or find the funny—a form of mental fatigue. She laughed, but not often. Cecily carried little emotional baggage, nor did her self-esteem suffer...until meeting him. And while her personality allowed for prompt coping with repeated disappointments coming from being with him, Cecily could be agreeable to a fault; her tendency to always find a silver lining could be detrimental.

Cecily losing Roland not long before encountering Oscar, created an isolated predisposition of susceptibility, which primed her in a way any seasoned narcissist would gravitate to take advantage of. Cecily's personality before Roland's passing, however, was not susceptible. Getting her back to that would leave her resistant to another narcissist trying the same thing with success. If she empowered Cecily to escape from her narcissistic situation with Oscar, to get Cecily to see through Oscar's lethal fog of deceit, she doubted Cecily was at risk of future re-victimization.

It was likely a gradual change, but to Cecily, Oscar became cold and uncaring overnight. Cecily's figurative fall-from-grace in his eyes was hard for her to understand and accept. Naomi saw it all: suddenly, Cecily couldn't do anything right; Oscar's loving words turned critical. Anything Cecily tried in a positive vein with her husband ended up having a negative effect as Oscar's subtle but effective attempts to devalue Cecily included spurts of loving attention to keep her interest—and keep her off-balance. However, on a subconscious level, Cecily realizes what's happening (confusion is but acknowledgment that something has changed), but daily existence in a precarious relationship interferes with her normal and instinctual emotional response. Her continued but often failed attempts to make things right again (walking on eggshells), increased her stress levels, leaving her unhappy and depressed with the situation.

And then, several men broke into her home one December...

Cecily didn't wallow in self-pity about what happened to her two Christmases ago, but the months in the hospital afterward extended the period of loss of control and helplessness often triggering PTSD. After talking and interacting with Cecily, she appears to have a positive outlook on most things other than her personal life, but could not apply those positives effectively in the areas of her life where she needs it most. Naomi noticed her sympathetic ear and calm reassurance making headway, but she now wanted to encourage Cecily to add yoga to her meditation and running, continue the spa treatments her job offered, and maybe add more—activities bringing both the mind and body together toward healing. A calm, soothed body can quiet the mind, reducing various forms of stress.

During the invasion (and soon after), Cecily's mind and body were in shock. Still, she hasn't been able to make sense of what happened or fully process her emotions behind it, thus prolonging her trauma—she's still in a psychological shock. She remembers most of what happened, but her feelings *about* what happened remain disconnected. Naomi needed to do a bit more *in-your-face* to yield revelation and induce the emotion sorely needed to free the additional bonds her toxic marriage has on her.

Aspects of Cecily's personality (unassuming, optimistic) made it easier for her to use her motivational drive as a resource to cope with NAS extremes by rationalizing to assuage conflict, both internal and external. The initial euphoria Oscar manufactured during the honeymoon stage created many false bonds with him, but now a real one existed to the extent they now shared in the home-invasion experience—even if Oscar's experience was likely pretense. Regardless of Oscar's inherent experience, the bond was real and valid to Cecily, and one she clung to. Naomi would help Cecily see these pseudo bonds for what they were.

Cecily accessed many defense mechanisms, but repression was the one doing the most damage. Her repression about the home invasion possibly tied into other mental-protection strategies manifesting, such as denial, rationalization, and conversion. Blocking unwelcomed thoughts and pushing them into the subconscious to avoid related anxieties, instead of contemplating the sources of those anxieties knowingly and purposefully, translated into those unwelcomed thoughts being bottled up—only to emerge in strange behavior patterns. Because Cecily is repressing what she may really know about what is happening to her and what happened to her two Decembers ago (more importantly, repressing knowing who did it), the other defense mechanisms have kicked in to compensate.

Media circles have established: intense stress interferes with eradicating memories. The association of certain events from the home invasion with the correlating emotion lent itself to Cecily's PTSD and to expressing maladaptive and acute stress responses to smaller-scale events. The home invasion and attempted murder sent her natural survival mechanisms into overdrive, thus creating links between her experiences back then to the now. Left untreated, these links could become wound too tightly, becoming permanent and pervasive. Naomi's job required helping Cecily weaken those links through treatment.

Once PTSD is in motion, drugs can only address the symptoms. No prescription can prevent it altogether. But Naomi wondered if the family (Cecily primarily) received doses of propranolol (ideal for blood pressure control and mild anxiety) within hours of the home invasion, if that bolstered her resistance to a later outbreak by suppressing her stress hormones from the outset. Didn't matter now (Naomi was in full swing with treatment), but she wondered.

She'd have to see, but she could also work with drugs interacting differently with the body's reuptake of various neurotransmitters: mirtazapine and duloxetine came to mind. Duloxetine ("Cymbalta" in the commercials) may be a good fit, but mirtazapine, or Remeron, worked a fraction faster than the SSRIs she had in mind. She'd just...have to see.

As far as any side effects causing sexual problems: Cecily seemingly had problems enjoying sex presently; it's not likely a prescription will make a difference—because the fix for that, well... Oscar had to go. *For all intense purposes* (Naomi chuckled to herself, thinking Oscar's misphrase rather fit this time), she needed to turn his gaslight out—at least on her patient.

Naomi paused and poured herself another shot. She changed thinking tactics, moving to her chair near the Catlett lithograph Tyson gave her, finding the etchings soothing and thought-provoking.

Cecily didn't have a histrionic personality, as she directed her need for protection and approval at Oscar (even her sometimes) rather than the world, but she displayed traces of dependent personality with demonstrations of anxiety and some fear that, at times, countered the truer aspects of Cecily's personality manifesting during discussions unrelated to the attack.

Cecily's dependent personality of late wasn't full-blown disorder, but compounded with the PTSD, there was a lot to address. The thing about personality disorders: symptoms overlapped. Someone meeting the diagnostics of one disorder will often satisfy the requirements for another.

Personality disorder had its share of cause-and-effect perspectives; she could use elements from each viewpoint in treating Cecily. She could use some of the psychodynamic theory suggesting dependent personalities were defending themselves against some unconscious hostility, and a bit from the more cognitive arena, suggesting dependency resulted from a person's view of themselves. Naomi still believed Cecily's inner self (nondependent) battled against her outer self (dependent), and that the hostility and anger over suppressing her true self only enhanced the dependent manifestations. To that point, she needed to work with how Cecily viewed herself—to allow her to see the roots of her recent (as in seven years) behavior. Naomi needed to counter Cecily subconsciously telling herself she was powerless, fearful, and weak—when she was quite the opposite.

Oscar's narcissistic personality issues and Cecily's dependent personality issues could be a destructive mix—especially for Cecily. The aggression bubbled just under the surface yet went undetected. But it would present. Eventually. *How*, was the question.

The most interesting aspect was, while Cecily displayed dependent personality, Oscar was the one with the disorder. His need for validation and support from Cecily (not only financial) led to expressions of emotional abuse (physical? Hmm...) and intimidation.

Even more confounding: the notion Oscar wanted to be rid of Cecily despite the dependence. Naomi was sure of it. Weird. People needed people, but people were also nuttier than fruitcakes in June.

Since Cecily's dependent personality stemmed from isolation and emotional abuse from Oscar and not something based on her upbringing, Naomi wanted to continue interspersing therapy with discussion of Cecily's life pre-Oscar. She wanted Cecily always exploring her past life (which fostered very nondependent behavior), so she'd internalize it and get back to life.

Cecily was experiencing PTSD from what happened to her years ago, but the oppressive and abusive circumstances of her marriage to Oscar compounded matters. The trauma event of the invasion was years ago, but Cecily's marriage trauma is ongoing. The two intertwined, and Naomi needed to manage treating both while appearing to be working on only one.

Oscar, because he takes Cecily's symptoms personally, isn't much help. He's aware of her triggers, yet instead of avoiding them, he stimulates them in his twisted view of tough love. Oscar wasn't a sounding board for Cecily's feelings because he had his own wall up (his own agenda). He didn't want to talk about the invasion, yet he was obsessed with rehashing it, guiding the memories. Cecily couldn't depend on his patience with this, either, which further interfered with the healing process—and maybe that was his goal.

The lack of genuine support from Oscar and even, sadly, her children, also contributed to Cecily's PTSD susceptibility. If her coping skills fell short of what she needed to handle better what happened to her, having a sound support system could fill those gaps and make things easier. Chelsea and Marcus underwent trauma as well, but not to the extent their mother did, and recovery for them was quicker—and so, they resumed having the mental resources to help their mother. Their issues with and dislike for Oscar, however, left Cecily alone with her pain and a below-par coping strategy, as she also dealt with the oppressive situation with her husband.

The thing with Cecily was this display of dependent personality disorder Naomi knew, *knew*, was something relatively new—as in seven years new (or whenever it was they met). Her tendency to defer to Oscar, to seek his approval and reassurance for even minor stuff, wasn't intrinsic to Cecily's natural personality. It just wasn't. Naomi knew it. She'd seen signs Cecily was a different person at her job—or anywhere she wasn't with her husband (that "the environment" response to number two of her Solution-Focused questions said it all).

Cecily accepted Oscar's relationship bullying because she was stuck in wanting needs two and three on Maslow's Hierarchy; this needed exploration.

Her therapy approach always considered and adapted to her patients' emotional and educational intelligence; Cecily had high levels of both.

Going forward, she'll check to see if Cecily only talked to her. It was important she share some of what happened in treatment with someone other than her. Not Oscar, but maybe Chelsea or Marcus or her brothers. Cecily's circle was small. This "Janyce" person could be an option (or the confidant that wasn't Janyce), but Naomi wasn't sure. So far, Cecily discussed some of her therapy with Kyle and Chelsea: good. Documentation of her social interactions outside of treatment was also crucial to documenting mental progression or regression.

Regression remained a concern, because Cecily's troubles upended her emotional scale, keeping her on the outskirts of the prudencesphere, kept her suffering from CSD (common sense deficiency), while Oscar...not only avoided visiting the prudencesphere—he couldn't breathe the air there if he did.

And there was that cryptic statement Cecily made regarding she "didn't tell her" the shape of something. Cecily had been adamant about it. Further probing in the session revealed it wasn't the keychain Cecily was talking about. That, too, needed exploration...

A knock on the door interrupted her ruminating and extrapolating. Naomi aimed the remote and paused the music. "Yes, ma'am?"

Leslie poked her head in. "Deep in it?"

"And can use the break. What's up?"

Her daughter entered, hand extended. "Your change from the store."

Naomi accepted the money ($2.37) and peered up at Leslie, stunned.

Leslie nodded her understanding. "Yeah. They've gone up."

"Apparently."

Leslie picked up the piece of abstract woodwork art Viv made (and presented to Naomi for Mother's Day last year). "Talk to them? What're they up to today?"

Naomi held in a chuckle; Leslie thoroughly enjoyed the get-togethers with the Phillips family. It was something Rick and Viv used to do with Tim and Louise. "Talked to Viv this morning: something about Rick wanting to window-shop for a new motorcycle. Other than that, I have no idea."

"Oh." Her daughter nodded as she ran a hand over the wood shapes blending and forming new shapes. Although abstract in formation, this piece, too, showed intricate craftsmanship: Viv was talented. Naomi, however, knew her daughter: something else was on her mind. "You still miss Daddy, don't you? Jazzy?" When Leslie was little, she couldn't pronounce her brother's first name, Jassiel, correctly: the nickname "Jazzy" stuck.

"Every day."

Leslie nodded, keeping her eyes on Viv's piece, but in that nod, she seemed satisfied. She'd recently lost her grandfather (Tyson's father), and now Kevin was back in the picture. Leslie liked Kevin, but after losing her Boppa (a connection to her dad), Kevin's return created trace anxiety over Tyson, somehow losing an abstract level of significance in her mother's life. Leslie wanted to be sure her mother wasn't erasing her father (and brother). She needn't worry.

"Joy and Brendan are coming over. Wanna join?"

Joy and Brendan Giles were Leslie's art mentors and close friends. In their late 30s, they were much older than Leslie, but that didn't matter: Leslie was her own person and liked whom she liked. Naomi shook her head. "Kevin's flight gets in early."

"I don't know why that should matter; you don't sleep, anyway."

"Not for lack of trying, child of mine."

Leslie tittered. "Suit yourself." She leaned and kissed her cheek.

She and Leslie were at some ancillary caring impasse over the last year. Naomi didn't know how they got there, didn't know how long it would last, but a caring impasse was better than an antagonistic coexistence. She examined the whys and wherefores for many people, was paid to do so, but didn't delve too deep with her own stuff (not regularly).

Leslie headed for the door, humming, "When We Get By."

Naomi shook her head. The girl had it bad, and when Naomi thought about it, Trevor and Kevin were drawn to the couple, too, for reasons different and circling the same. Since their recoupling, Kevin more than once hinted his looking forward to seeing them. He hadn't seen Rick in three years (even then, only briefly), but whatever (people needed people).

The door closed.

Grinning, Naomi restarted the player, sending Stravinsky's *Firebird Suite* into her office.

Truly needing a break (her brain was NAS and PTSD "fried" for the moment), she gathered her notes and other materials related to the Brooks case and placed them in her leather satchel, her thoughts on yesterday's fun. It was always a delight watching Rick and Viv do their married thing.

Seeing their combo-aura was special and confirmed much of what was already right before you. Their individual auras, too (consistently ranging yellows and blues, thus far), were very compatible, harmonious. She may never see a combo-aura for them again (likely wouldn't), but she knew that candy-red aura would change to a color darker or muddier, more stressful sometimes (they were married, after all). Yet Naomi also realized the strength of their union wouldn't allow that murkier color to exist for long. She sensed, whatever trials Rick and Viv underwent, that candy-red (brightened by pink) would still dominate.

Viv and Rick weren't so corny they finished each other's sentences (although quite capable of it), and they didn't fawn over each other in some overly mushy way, not at all, but witnessing their interaction, the depth of their friendship resonated and, even with the inanest situations, there remained this current of erotic heat between them. They were enjoyable to watch.

Naomi's soft smile faded with thoughts of Tyson and Jassiel, and her daughter's question. "...I miss them every day, Les." She went to her player, searching for a particular track.

Remote in hand, she sat in the chair near her lithograph and pressed play. "Danny Boy" (as performed by Franc D'Ambrosio) floated around her. She hadn't listened to this in ages.

Naomi relaxed and listened, relaxed and mourned her dead husband: Tyson Daniel Alexander. She called him "Danny Boy" sometimes, when it was quiet, and their version of fun belonged to only them. Tyson was a man unafraid of a flower or a Fuzzy Navel...or tearing during a movie.

Her marriage wasn't perfect, wasn't always happy, but it was good—and that trumped NAS any way you looked at it.

Naomi allowed the music to settle and unsettle her, memories of the son she lost, creating many of the unsettled moments; memories of a little boy who died before she knew him well. Her husband would've turned 48 this month.

The song wasn't long but was long enough. Naomi stopped the player and wiped her eyes, making effort for the active mourning to close until the next time.

She left her office in search of a few snickerdoodles and to watch a couple episodes of *Jeopardy!* on her DVR, considering: maybe the best therapy plan for Cecily...was no plan at all.

Chapter Twelve

Comparisons are Odorous

"Oh! Here it is! Unhh!" He grabbed into her hair with one hand and held his spurting erection in the other, aiming it at her face and sending his release onto the bridge of her nose and her cheek. His heart bounced like a bitch, but he didn't care; those pills had his dick doing good shit again. He took some seconds to watch the evidence of his orgasm run down her face and then released her hair. Cecily gave pretty good head, and sometimes he made her swallow, but this time he wanted the degradation image to further tantalize him. "A'ight. Get up."

She stood, wearing nothing but the whore heels: five-inchers he kept in his closet. Whenever he approached her with the whore heels, Cecily knew what to expect. With his dick on semi-vacation, it'd been a while since he brought out the heels, but he taught her well. He kissed her cheek, then reclined on the bed, still winded. He ran his eyes over her body as she wiped her face. Cecily was slender, but she had a round ass and good-sized tits. That scar (where that motherfucker, Winton, didn't finish the job) gave her an edge or something and turned him on. Her hair was all over the place from him grabbing and pulling on it, but he allowed it to be unkempt during "whore heels."

They were quiet as she took off the shoes and headed into the bathroom for her pain-in-the-ass shower. They didn't have *sex* sex, so why did she still need to shower? He watched her shape leave the room, holding in a chuckle. She'd long gotten over the idea of him going down on her (he helped her get over it)—if she was hot for more, she'd better take care of that while she was in there (since she liked to shower so much). He guessed he shouldn't care if she showered; in a matter of months, it wouldn't matter anyway. In a matter of months, Cecily wouldn't have to worry about showering...or anything else.

He'd gone to that white-noise place inside his head for a few days, saying little to his wife.

He neither liked nor disliked going into the *white-noise*, primarily because he couldn't help it if he tried. He didn't hear voices or none of that stupid shit, but there were thoughts inside the blankness—he just sometimes came out of it, not remembering what those thoughts were. Sometimes, the white-noise left him extra irritable; other times, he was calmer. He was calmer this time, ready to move on—but (since his dick was acting right these days) he intended to get as much sex from Cecily as he could before everything changed.

Penis soft, Oscar sat up and fixed his clothes. That climax was okay. He'd come harder before, but Cecily wasn't all-in this go 'round (again), and his mind kept entertaining the most fucked-up thoughts. His wife's lack of enthusiasm wasn't new, but this time it *felt* different—like that morning she left for work right after New Year's (and every morning since); there was a weird energy about it. Because, even though the head was good enough to bring him off, Cecily didn't even pretend to be into it. Most times he didn't give a fuck about her feelings, but something was changed here...likely because of that doctor bitch. Which brought him to the fucked-up thoughts he'd had while being serviced.

Oscar went to Cecily's side of the bed and retrieved her purse. Valentine's Day was just around the corner.

There he was, thrusting into her mouth, giving her some good talk while grabbing into that thick head of hair, when Dr. Alexander popped into his head. And, while anyone would expect him to lose his hard-on from that shit, he didn't. Their last session, Naomi looked kinda hot in her skirt and blouse; the outfit showed off more of her petite body. She'd styled her hair differently, too: more twisty-curly with a lighter color on the tips in some places. Nice (and proving his point about short hair and pantsuits). Dr. Alexander was on the opposite team as to Cecily; she should've been the last thing on his mind. But there she was, walking around his head, tight little figure in the skirt and heels, bending over that yellow sofa and getting some of his monster dick... He'd also had images of squirting on Naomi's face: all of it, just crazy as hell.

Fifty dollars richer (she'll never miss it), Oscar left their bedroom for the basement to shave his muttonchops. He had plans for tomorrow: hook up with Janyce for some Valentine's Day shopping for their spouses and later meet with Odie and Otis for lunch at Florida Avenue Grill. Shopping with Janyce killed time, gave him something to do. He bought two Valentine's Day cards for Cecily last year, so he'd give her the one left. He needed to pick a gift card to put in it, though; twenty-five dollars should do it. This fresh fifty was going toward covering lunch with his sister and brother.

Oscar checked his watch for the umpteenth time as he stood in Macy's in Pentagon City Mall, watching Janyce check out yet another wrist-watch for Hank. He guessed he should've hooked up with Hank for this shop-for-spouses adventure, but he was closer to Janyce—and Janyce was more the man of the house. Hank wasn't a punk, but he was borderline; that deep voice gave him extra man points.

"I liked the Cartier better." She turned the watch she held over in her hand for the third time. She had beefy hands for a woman. How Hank enjoyed those hams moving over him, Oscar didn't know.

He unloaded an air of aggravation. "I thought Cecily was bad..."

Janyce sent him a nasty look and put the watch down. She picked up the Cartier and handed it to the saleslady. "This one. Thanks." Her jeans and sweater fit too snug, bending and denting into the folds of her fluffy middle. The tight jeans were okay, but damn, no one was trying to look at the rest of that: she needed a larger sweater.

They left Macy's and headed for Sephora. He still didn't know what type of gift card to get Cecily; maybe he could change things up and get one from there, surprise her with something different. She'd be around for a little longer at least, and there was nothing wrong with making them good days, making him look like the adoring husband—appearances were everything. "So, did you make that call? I wanna—"

Janyce shook her head, walking faster. "Yeah, um...about that..."

Oscar kept pace. "Don't chicken out on me."

"Winton's not interested. Said we need to quit while we're ahead. ...I agree. They already feel screwed for moving forward without payment the last time." She smelled like Cecily's flowers in the kitchen; he didn't like it. Compared to his wife's warm scents (which rotated but never reminded him of flowers), Janyce smelled like an old lady.

"Gave you that pricey brooch, didn't I? Couldn't have the paper trail."

"Apparently, Cecily doesn't keep a serious balance in the account you share."

He scoffed. Cecily was loaded, but he didn't bother putting his name on all the bank accounts because she had the children on them, and he figured he had rights to the accounts by marriage. If something happened to her, the kids were minors, and he would logically be executive of real-estate.

But Marcus and Chelsea weren't minors anymore. Fuck. He'd gone about this all wrong. He now knew where Cecily kept the legal papers, but... Irritation set in. "And if they'd done it *right*, everybody would be on easy street." He knew they were going to fuck him over. He had a backup, but didn't have the connections Janyce did. Plan A failed, Plan B would take too long, and now Plan C looked shot; he felt stuck. "Look, I'm an extremely logical person, so, for all intense purposes, that plan was a good one. We almost pulled it off. If it wasn't for whoever called the—"

"We're out. Talk about something else." She checked her phone with this weird look on her face. Her next words were so low, he struggled to hear her: "...And I like Cecily."

Shit. "...I was thinking a carjacking this time."

Janyce sucked her teeth. "Making Cecily the most crime-prone woman in the DMV. They *would* be looking at you, then."

Oscar grabbed her wrist, but Janyce snatched it back. "Okay, wait. I get you're scared—"

"Not scared, not sorry. Find somebody else." She shifted her coat across her arm. "Or do it yourself." Her dreadlocks wound about her head. He hated dreadlocks, but if Hank liked dealing with them, more power to him.

"Are you nuts? Nobody gets paid if she's here, and nobody gets paid if I'm in jail. It can't be me." Sweat poured off him, and his chest began doing that full, flip-floppy thing again. He reached into his pocket for his handkerchief. "Let's find somewhere to sit."

"Sephora's right there. You sit and hold the bags?"

Oscar nodded and pulled a twenty and ten from his pocket. "Get 'er a gift card for me." He handed her the money, needing to sit down.

Janyce shook her head. "Cecily doesn't even really wear makeup. Why're you even perpetrating? You're so fake." Her face crunched inward with annoyance, making her sideburns stand out more. "Just let the marriage die if you're so miserable."

"I didn't say I was miserable. And I'm not being fake. I...I love her." He sat on an unoccupied bench, wiping his face.

She laughed this laugh, making him want to punch her in the face; he hated being laughed at. "Do you even hear yourself?! Try an infusion of feeling next time!" Her laughter faded to a chuckle.

"Don't worry about how I sound." He looked up at her, not liking the angle at all. Janyce was semi-attractive, but certain angles were less flattering. "And Hank still doesn't know anything?"

She shook her head as she lowered her coat and packages to rest beside him. "No. That would be stupid. I graduated 'thank-you-laude,' so I don't have a lot of book smarts, but I have street smarts."

Oscar nodded thoughtfully. "Just checking." He cupped a hand over his mouth for a breath check; it could be worse at certain times.

"Yeah, pop a mint."

He did.

Janyce ran her eyes over his face. "I like that better: the goatee. That other beard style made you look old-fashioned."

"Thanks. Thinking of shaving it all off."

She shrugged and turned on a boot heel, heading for Sephora. Oscar watched her ass as she moved away, his mood darkening with the calming down in his chest. Janyce had him thinking about the money.

He was satisfied using whatever money was in the joint (that balance always hovered around fifteen grand); his expenses were few and Cecily still paid for everything. He took weird joy in selling those stupid comic books and taking a little something from her wallet because he was teaching Cecily a lesson; it wasn't his fault she didn't have street smarts (like him and Janyce). But with Cecily's brats now adults, where did that leave his plans?

He never figured Janyce for a sympathetic person. Now, suddenly, she was "out" and "liked Cecily." She had a point about the carjacking, but it wasn't his fault the idea was lame. It was Winton's and Desmond's and those other two who didn't finish the job, and whoever called the fucking police, that created this nuisance (*"Lickety-split" my ass*). And who the fuck was she to be talking about how and whether he loved Cecily? Love had different shades. Just because he wasn't a punk-ass like Roland and Hank (borderline), and kept his woman under wraps, didn't mean he couldn't love her. He liked Cecily, too, mostly (and sometimes he hated her). Oscar clenched his jaw as he watched the few shoppers. Nobody understood where he was coming from. His cellphone notified he had a text.

It was Odie: *Sorry, Osc. Can't make it. Meeting. Otis sends his regrets, too. Maybe another time. Bring Cecily. TTYL.*

Nobody understood, and nobody cared.

He gripped the phone, feeling another bullshit day brewing. They just didn't want to have lunch with him. He was their flesh and blood, but they liked Cecily better, maybe even loved her over him. He was sure Otis did. Odessa gave him grief about not working, having Cecily work and pay for everything, said he wasn't a man taking care of his household, and he thought Odie was being hypocritical: whatever happened to all that women's lib crap? He texted his sister back, letting her know he was buying. She came back with: *You mean, Cecily's buying, don't you? Can't today. Another time.* Oh, he hated her sometimes! She and Otis thought they were too good, but he'd show them. Real soon.

He scoffed, watching a young man (who should've been in class somewhere) hiking his pants over his ass, leaving 50 percent of his underwear covered instead of the original 20 percent.

So, everyone liked Cecily. Fine. But they failed to realize *he* was the smart one, smarter than they gave him credit for. Cecily had those degrees, but she was also...kind. The kind ones were the suckers in life. Example number one? Cecily and that loser brother of hers, Larimore. A smart woman would've cut ties with his convict-ass long ago, but not his Cecily. She kept the faith, visiting and calling and writing. He could almost hear her talking to that jailbird through the partition, using that calm, soft, modulated, weak-ass voice as she prattled on about her Deville or the weather or snooty Kyle or whatever-the-fuck.

Those bleeding-heart politically correct whiners thought the world thrived on tolerance and compassion, kindness and understanding, and all that give-me-a-break bull. But if you wanted to get anywhere, accomplish anything today, tolerance was weakness—and it was his job to take advantage of Cecily's. Survival of the fittest. Simple. No degree required.

Another nagging realization surfaced: if Dr. Alexander showed her that secret door, Cecily could move on and leave him behind, have her money, a new man, and...everything. *And leave him behind.* It was why he hated her sometimes, why...he couldn't let her go anywhere. He had to keep her pressed under his thumb, squeezing and pressing until...

Man, this ain't right. See someone.

Oscar stretched, sending Whiny-Bitch Voice away. He was fine and didn't need to see anyone—especially not anyone like Dr. Alexander. Leave that therapy-shit to the tolerant and kind. Be damned if he was going to any more of those bullshit sessions, either. Naomi rubbed him the wrong way; so fuck that. One and one was two; he wasn't putting himself through the annoying paces to satisfy some woman's ideal—that's not how this works.

Dr. Alexander ran her sessions like she was fucking Queen-of-Everything: telling him what he could and couldn't say, giving him looks of impatience and disgust, the sarcastic comments. He'd also seen the looks between her and Cecily, doing some secret woman-shit that left him out of the loop without being obvious about it, but he was aware.

Her face popped into his head, making Oscar's middle cramp. She was no Dr. Halim, with her secret doors, double-agent questions, and shit. Like she was Sherlock Holmes or somebody, sleuthing around Cecily's mind (looking for him in there, probably). He didn't like it, didn't need no doctor-detective all up in shit, messing with his plans. Oscar scoffed, his lip curled with unhappy. Quack Halim wasn't doing his job, and Alexander...was doing more than he expected—or needed.

But (and this was the kicker) as long as Cecily kept deferring to him, kept startling whenever he came near, or needing punk-ass affection, it was point: *Oscar.* He watched a bill of money fall from a man's back pocket as he retrieved his wallet, thinking about the many ways he kept his thumb pressed. Cecily's need for feedback and approval from him made her a sucker for the silent treatment (one of his favorites).

Before anyone else spotted the money, Oscar rose and walked toward the bill, tickled at seeing Andrew Jackson's narrow face as he pocketed the money. He spit in a nearby trashcan and returned to the bench, wondering what was taking Janyce so damn long. Her dawdling reminded him of being out with Cecily. He needed a cigarette.

Oscar took out his phone and texted his wife, wanting details on her lunch plans (adding "Cesspool" as a middle finger to Naomi). Lately, she'd been replying more with *brown-bagging it*, and he didn't have a good feeling about that, either, so he added extra instruction for her to pick up some Prilosec before she came home. He didn't need it, he had plenty, but she needed to think about him sometimes while she was out working. That job wasn't everything. She didn't even need to work. Overall, he didn't mind her working, encouraged it, but it also irritated him how industrious she was, how dependable and hardworking, putting all her energy into...accounting or whatever. Seemed like that job came before him a time too many these days. He didn't trust professionals, resented them. From doctors to lawyers to accountants to techno geeks to blah-specialist to blah-analyst, anyone having spent years specializing in how to do something has inevitably found a way to scam people using what they know; it was all a racket to him.

Janyce finally returned from Sephora with a bag of cosmetics and his gift card for Cecily. He gave her the silent treatment, though, letting her know she pissed him off taking so long, but Janyce was more like Delia; she didn't keep trying to get him to talk to her. She went about her business, talking on her phone all nonchalant and shit. He let her off the hook and sparked conversation again, making sure he stayed away from anything related to Plan C. By noon, they considered the outing a shopping success and went their separate ways.

Oscar still went to the Florida Avenue Grill for lunch, giving his brother and sister the finger and treating himself—courtesy of $20.00 from some stranger at Pentagon City mall.

He was home before Cecily and made sure he was in their bedroom when she entered (carrying a small bag containing his Prilosec). Her hesitant smile as she handed it to him said she was still in his grip. He pinched off a smile. "Thanks."

"Sure." She leaned down and pecked his lips, the tiny frown as she pulled away, telling him it was time to pop another mint. "How w-was your d-day?"

"A'ight, I guess." He didn't ask about her day, not interested in hearing about her job successes (or even any failures) and rubbing his nose in him being unemployed.

She nodded and shrugged as she took off her shoes and entered the bathroom.

Five, four, three, two...

She popped her head back into the room, her brow knotted with confusion first and anger second (but the confusion won out). "Oscar, did... d-did you m-move anything a-around in h-here?"

He counted backward from seven before answering. "Really, Cecily? Is that what you think I do all day: walk around the house, looking for shit to 'move around'?"

"No, but—"

"Home not five minutes and already starting."

"That's n-not—"

"No, Cecil. Everything is where it's been. I showered and used my shit like I always do. You're the one straightening and organizing and getting rid of clutter. You do the shit so much; you can't even remember when you've done it." He opened his nightstand drawer for a mint. When he turned back, she was back in the bathroom.

When he got home, he was irritable from Odie, Otis, and Janyce, and then with Cecily at seeing the lotions, soaps, and washcloths neatly stacked in the linen closet. Something about that made it seem like it was *her* house, not theirs. So, he put shit the way he wanted to see it. Yeah, he could've just said that, but what he said was true: she did organize and reorganize a lot. Besides, she focused on that stuff too much: shouldn't be getting all bent out of shape over something being on a different shelf—it was weak and stupid.

When she reentered the bedroom, Oscar couldn't tell what her expression meant. She went to her dresser, removing her jewelry. "Don't forget to give me your tux to put in the cleaners." She viewed him in the mirror.

He still couldn't read her expression. "The charity ball's the end of this month?"

Cecily nodded, placing her bracelet in her jewelry box. "Yeah."

"Okay." He'd never owned a tuxedo before meeting Cecily.

She mumbled: "Hopefully, this party will be more fun."

"That's your problem: you dwell too much on the past. That's over. Just worry about today, about now."

She removed her earrings. "I guess." She sounded funny, different.

"Well, the jacket was already a little big, but I'll need a new shirt:...gained a little weight 'round this middle..." He patted his Corona-belly.

She shrugged. "Balding, gaining weight: it's a part of aging. Some women like a man with maturity, a little meat on his bones..." Still wearing that unreadable expression, she stepped into her closet. "You want pleats on the shirt or plain front?"

That shrug almost seemed to dismiss him. Her expression was unreadable, her tone wasn't soft and hesitant, and she didn't stutter. He couldn't tell if her reply was compliment or complaint. "Pleats." He didn't feel good. Instead of going into her closet and pushing the heel of one of her pumps into her neck, Oscar left their bedroom for the basement; he needed to think.

Hours later, his eyes stared at a rerun of *CSI*, but he wasn't watching. He had a new Plan C.

One he could do...himself.

"I'm shocked you gave up your spa day for this, but this has been fun, so I'm glad, too." Janyce stepped back into the dressing room in a whirl of fuchsia—her decided color for the charity ball.

Cecily didn't think such a sharp pink was ideal for the winter formal, but to each his own (and all that). "This has been fun." She'd taken a break from JAH because she wanted (needed) distraction from thinking about Joshua's birthday and how he may have spent it. She shouldn't have been concerned (and all that), but she was, and there was no escaping that realization. This mini-break helped her deal with not being a part of his birthday celebration, but it also allowed the two of them a breather given what happened at JAH recently: her episode and their "moments" (the number of which seemed to increase lately)—restoring some figurative distance between them. She did text him her good wishes, though, and looked forward to him opening her gift.

You don't need a break from JAH. You need a break from—

Janyce emerged from the dressing room, rejected dresses draping her right arm, selection across her left. "Okay! Just need to get Hank's accessories, and that's it." She tossed the rejected garments onto a bench. "You and Oscar set?"

Cecily nodded and followed her out of the dressing area. "Yes." She tapped the shopping bag in her hand. "Got Oscar's new shirt right here, so we're all set." She welcomed the touch of excitement over the upcoming ball—anything was better than the weight of melancholy and joylessness often clinging to her as if ivy upon a wall. She couldn't breathe for it sometimes, and all she wanted, *all* she wanted, was to make those around her happy so she could...survive another day.

It occurred to her: she didn't feel this way in session. But she couldn't sleep on that yellow sofa (could she?), so she needed to adapt what was happening with Naomi to what was happening everywhere else.

Much easier said than done. "Let's get those studs and cufflinks and then stop at the food court. I—"

"Want a cup of tea." Janyce grinned. "You always want tea. You're also not stuttering today, thank God." Her expression changed, at first probing and then brightening again. "Your eczema looks good."

She had rosacea, not eczema, and Cecily didn't think anyone with eczema would describe it as looking good, but Janyce meant well. "Let's hope it stays cleared for the next forever."

Janyce cracked up as they approached the cashier, making Cecily chuckle, too.

They strolled Arundel Mills on the way to a men's clothing store, in the hunt for studs and cufflinks for Hank. As they walked, they passed the Polo Ralph Lauren Factory Store, and another store was playing James Brown's "Please, Please, Please," as part of their overhead music. Cecily sighed inward: so much for distraction from Joshua. When she saw a little boy struggling with a Spider-Man yo-yo, she burst out laughing at the ridiculousness of it all, startling Janyce.

Having purchased new studs and cufflinks for their men, they sat in the food court (Cecily enjoying a steaming cup of green tea with lemon, Janyce a soft pretzel from Auntie Anne's Pretzels), people-watching and commenting (well, Janyce did the commenting). Oscar didn't need them, but she bought the onyx studs and cufflinks as a potential peace offering. Yes, it was a form of buying his love, and she didn't advocate that ordinarily, but if the token afforded her even a brief respite from his wrath, afforded her an extended period of peace (it worked sometimes), she was all for it.

Seeing a shopper carrying a Kay Jewelers Outlet bag, Cecily turned to Janyce to ask something she'd been curious about since their key-lime pie lunch outing late last year. "Hey. How'd you know the call came from the Exxon station?"

Janyce blinked and swallowed her bite of pretzel. "What? What call? 'Exxon' station?" She sipped her soda.

"Yes. When we were at lunch right before New Year's. You were advising me to get past what happened, saying that things might have turned out worse if it wasn't for the call from the Exxon station." The frequent doubt and confusion threatened to creep in and take over, but Cecily stiffened her body against it, refusing to let it happen; this was important.

But Janyce stared at her for such long seconds, the doubt crept in anyway. "I don't know what you're talking about. You must have misunderstood, Cecily."

Cecily shook her head. "No. Because—"

"If the call was anonymous, how the hell would I know where it came from?" Her gaze turned hard, her steel-brown eyes narrowing and then widening. "Huh?"

Cecily went mute, but not with confusion or doubt this time. In the notebook in her sock, she'd jotted details about the conversation during that lunch with Janyce last year, going over them before coming out with her today. Something wasn't right. But she had enough to worry about with Oscar (and trying to keep distracted from other stuff), so she'd write this down and think on it later.

Maybe it was time to share her notes with Dr. Alexander. Something...wasn't right. Because Janyce revealed some other things during that lunch, Cecily knew Janyce would deny now. Maybe she needed to record her conversations with *certain* people. Cecily shrugged. "I guess. So, what did you say about Exxon...?" Exxon wasn't her imagination; that wouldn't be something she'd just come up with. None of that conversation was her imagination—but she'd focus on one word at a time.

Janyce rolled her eyes in a scoff. "I don't know, Cecily. You know how you do, how you can get. If I said anything about 'Exxon,' it had something to do with lottery tickets, since that's where I get mine. You're so sensitive and paranoid about everything; mentioning a gas station has you all... Well, you know." She used a finger to spread mustard on her pretzel (she was very touchy-feely with her food).

Cecily did know, but that's not what this was. "Okay." She'd write this down and think on it later. "I'm ready. You?"

Janyce nodded, staring at her again. "Sure you're okay?"

She hated being asked that. Cecily put on a bright smile. "I will be. Let's go."

An hour later, she sat parked in her driveway, giving herself her routine regroup time because Oscar was home.

He's always home. You rarely have the house to yourself. You pay for this house, but he gets to enjoy it more than you do.

Reasoning when married people lived together, someone was usually home, Cecily reached for the fresh bouquet resting on the passenger seat. She breathed deeply, taking in the aromas of spray roses, daisy and button spray chrysanthemums, Monte Cassino asters, and limonium, all in shades of white, pink, green, purple, and lavender. She took a healthy whiff to fill her head with memory of the fragrance and counter the other awful smells she'd have to contend with shortly. Cecily offered up a small prayer of thanks for the little things: he'd been mean, but not violent lately; there was that.

She stared at her house, noting the elevation, windows, shutters...

Misery and Loneliness entered the bottom of her Nikes, traveling over her shins, knees, and thighs and picking up Uncertainty and Sadness somewhere around her hips. The foursome laughed together as they continued the road-trip coursing through her, convincing Hope-lessness and Fear to tag along as they passed her chest and neck, traveling upward.

Trembling, Cecily folded her upper lip in and shook her head, not only to contain sobs, but to refuse that carload of unhappiness access across state lines, across the border...to her mind. "Please..."

She was so tired. Tired of doubting events and conversations, her competence. Tired of *episodes* and winters of discontent. Weary of depending on Oscar or Janyce to validate her thoughts and feelings. Not for the first time, she wondered how she ended up...*here*.

"Please..."

Cecily closed her eyes and breathed her fresh flowers, giving them a sample of saltwater. She stayed that way, halfway praying, halfway pursuing happier thoughts—anything to give her the courage to stop crying, open the car door, and go inside. Images of Chelsea, Marcus, or Naomi didn't help; not even thoughts of Little Roland or Joshua eased the turmoil.

It took some minutes, but Cecily finally took a deep breath, turning that unfriendly carload away. She lifted her head and wiped her eyes, blew her nose. She'd been happy once. She'd been happy...*before*. Cecily checked her hair. Holding her purchases and flowers, she opened the car door, thoughts of Roland Michael Cooper easing the pain.

It was late evening when she found herself sitting near Oscar in their family room (him in the big chair, her on the loveseat next to it), feeling none the worse for wear, but entirely uneasy about the occurrence just the same as she divided her attention between the salaries and payroll reports for JAH Technologies Inc. and a rerun of *Law & Order: SVU*.

JAH Tech was a small company; didn't mean you paid small attention to the numbers. Besides, the numbers calmed her, reminded her of God's blessing and purpose for her. There were a few heavy-duty curses God mixed in, too, but she wanted to stay positive.

Detectives Benson and Stabler were on the case, with Oscar (and his backward sense of humor) chuckling at a few dramatic moments.

She was used to being unsettled (marriage to Oscar made that normal by default), but this unease sided funny. Her usual unease centered around some intangible (and impending) doom lurking, possibly, maybe. But not this time, well, not *fully* this time. This unease had its standard gloom component (she was seven years in with him), but also bore some pleasantness about it, leaving her a combo of hopeful and wary and...uneasy—*differently*.

How they ended up watching television together was reasonable and semi-normal and weird, but here they were.

She'd entered the house and called downstairs to let Oscar know she was home (normal). As she reviewed the mail, he emerged from the basement and kissed her cheek (weird), asking if she felt like making salad for dinner (normal). Since she, too, wanted something light for supper (reasonable and normal), she was okay with it, suggesting they add the leftover roasted chicken for more flavor and to be more filling for him. Oscar then offered to boil eggs and chop the tomatoes without one comment about her "inability" to do it properly (weird).

She did her share of washing, tearing, and chopping, a bit nervously, wanting his approval and the respite, but also waiting for that other shoe to drop. It didn't.

Before having dinner, she gave him the new shirt and showed him the new onyx studs and cufflinks for his tux she purchased as a bonus (reasonable). Her husband chuckled and kissed her in thanks, pushing his tongue into her mouth with its ever-present poky sourness (normal, unfortunately, because he was sick—and that was just unfortunate). She peeked to find the expected weird-and-creepy of him looking at her as they kissed, too, but that was okay.

Salads prepared, he took her hand, leading her to the family room with some comment about how they rarely used the TV in there (reasonable but exponentially weird: caution flag). But she so wanted this to be what it looked like, needed to be in a better place with him; she followed along—and hoped for the best. So far, so good.

He didn't even complain about her wanting to review some reports as they watched; maybe he was lonely for her company but didn't know how to say it; perhaps he experienced his own need for more affection between them. And, for the gazillionth time, she wondered if she was being paranoid and a Nervous Nelly and too sensitive about it all.

Stabler and Benson visited the ME's office, getting details about the corpse's condition (she liked the episodes featuring Elliot Stabler).

"Ha. I knew it." He forked a last piece of egg, pointing his fork at the television and nodding. "I told you: I'm an extremely logical person. I knew that shit." He smiled at her or the television or at himself, but it was good to see either way. But then, he looked at her again, and it was yesterday or six days ago or six months ago or six years ago: "Degrees are for those with book smarts—not *street* smarts: where the real-life lessons are taught." His tone and eyes held challenge, but she never bragged about having a double-major, never nagged him about finishing his degree, only encouraged him about it, so she never understood his hostility toward her regarding her academic achievements.

"You're r-right. You n-need good logic for m-most things in life: a l-lot of us d-don't have that." Hating her reply, she returned to her financials, a part of her wishing she was on the ME's table (for real) instead of some actor.

He pointed at her with a click of his tongue. "Good girl."

Benson and Stabler left the ME's office for the perp, getting ready for the climactic courtroom stuff after the commercial break.

"Yeah. Maybe I should go into law enforcement. Being a security guard prepared me in ways you couldn't imagine..." He spat in a cup resting by his foot on the floor. He'd been spitting in it over the last forty minutes—and she cringed with every wet plop. And although a severe pinch to her thigh years ago attempted to convince her "*real* men spit" (that bruise lasted weeks), it was a habit of his she'd never get accustomed to. The thought of that thing he kept in the basement made her stomach turn. He was sweating buckets, and she wondered how he had any water left in him, what with his spitting and sweating. "*Other* experiences prepared me, too. You know what I'm talking about, don't you, Cecily?"

She nodded mutely again at his reference to having committed a crime, feeling the true normalcy of things settle over them, having the usual unease (not much pleasantness about it) solidify and reassert. "Yeah, I r-remember." She looked down at her papers after he nodded and left his chair for the powder room (to rid himself of more water, no doubt). While he was in there, she tried to think of a reason to excuse herself. She could text Chelsea and tell her to call in a few minutes.

Cecily shook her head; something about that didn't sit well. The toilet flushing coincided with the end of the commercial run, and Cecily left it alone. She'd sit and watch the rest of *SVU* with him. It was fine.

Oscar returned and paused next to her. She sensed him looking down at her papers. "Making any headway...?"

She knew he didn't care if she'd made headway, but she appreciated him going through the motions. The sudden change in the aromatic-at-mosphere revealed the release of his silent-but-deadly, and although her eyes watered from the foulness, Cecily smiled right through it. "Some."

"Whew!" He fanned in front of his face as he sat, wincing and rubbing his chest. "Excuse me. Sorry about that one, Cecil. That salad was good, though."

His salad hadn't fully digested yet, so it was likely the result of some earlier meal, but she only shrugged and waved it off with a grin before turning her attention to the television. Cecily felt him staring at her for seconds after, but then he watched Benson and Stabler wrap it up, too.

She was all for accepting her man and all his faults and smells and...functions, but she didn't think there was anything wrong with using discretion sometimes with those functions, being mindful of your partner—and avoiding purposely offending them; she extended Oscar that courtesy for crying out loud. Cecily moved the papers in her lap around some to facilitate odor-dissipation.

She noticed he still rubbed his chest. "Heartburn again?"

"I...I don't know. Feels like it, but..."

Cecily grabbed her phone. She knew CPR, but emergency personnel needed to be en route in the interim.

"No!" He shook his head. "Don't. It's...It's not a nine-one-one type deal, Cecily. Just..." He shook his head again, rubbing his chest.

She stared at her husband, trying to gauge any level of emergency. He was sweating, but his breathing wasn't more labored than usual. Even with his meanness, she didn't want him dying on her. "Oscar..." Her fingers pained from gripping the phone so. He had an appointment with Dr. Halim next week, but maybe he needed something sooner.

He let out a long sigh that was part belch. "There...! It's...It's much better now." He gave her a nod, drawing his handkerchief across his brow before popping a mint.

Cecily stared at him, still trying to gauge, but relaxed her grip on her phone.

Oscar resumed watching the show. "Love you." (Weird.)

"Love you, t-too." Cecily put her phone down and resumed her reports-and-television multitasking. No, she wasn't in love with him, but she cared about him (which was a love of sorts). Oscar changed as she was falling in love, making things change course and killing any progression of those feelings for him. Nevertheless, she meant it in the way they both understood.

The credits rolled as she reviewed the deductions compliance for the staff. Hearing his zipper underneath the sounds from the television, she grew leery.

"I know you're on, so come suck it." His voice was nasally-raspy with arousal. He muted the television.

Once upon a time, when she was married in the *before*, there were soft tongue-kisses and warm touches, gentle nips to her neck with an arousing pinch to her nipple accompanying a romantic cajoling for some fellatio. It wasn't the case *every time* Roland wanted that from her, but it happened often enough, such that it was okay those times he didn't go the extra mile. And that married-in-the-before guy had no problems returning the favor—with joyous results.

But she was married in the *after* now. Things were different. There was no sweet cajoling, no favor-returning (normal).

True, she was on her period (and no, she did not feel like putting his erection in her mouth). She gawked at him, semi-amazed he entertained the extra stimulation to his heart, given the pains he'd just experienced. "Oscar, y-you were j-just—"

He stroked his inches with one hand and waved her over with the other. "I'm fine after that belch. Come on..."

It was his medication; had to be. Seemed he was hard every ten minutes now. And she hadn't climaxed once. Hadn't climaxed since... Well, that wasn't important. To not rile the beast (and to get it over with), she shifted the reports to the side and went to him, kneeling between his legs.

He gripped the back of her head, pushing it suggestively. "There you go. I know you've been waiting. Get on that thing..." He sighed and tilted his head back as she lowered her mouth over him.

She stared at his shirt-covered belly and got on with it, the seconds and minutes feeling like minutes and hours. If there was a positive about any of it, it was the taste and smell of this part of him. As much as he sweat (and given his odoriferous mouth most times), his penis never offended her nose and tongue, only minimally tinged with his natural oils and sweat from the day. This, and only this, was like husband number one. That did not, however, make her want to swallow his release. To hurry things along, make him feel good about himself, and avoid the avoidable, Cecily kicked things into a higher gear.

Oscar released her head, clutching the arms of the chair instead. His entire erection fit in her mouth comfortably. Still, when he was close, she coughed and gagged to suggest she couldn't accommodate his size (interspersing commentary likewise), using her hand on him together with sucks to get him there and timing it such that his semen landed not in her mouth, but in her hand.

She eased her hands from his body, anticipating her shower minutes away, when he lifted his head with a strange grin, looking into her eyes. "That was good. Thanks." He leaned down and pulled her close, pushing his tongue into her mouth—and they were back to weird again.

The stinging pellets soothed and rejuvenated while she showered after sex with him (normal) and ruminated one thing after the other.

Naomi asked if she felt safe. And while the answer wasn't what it should be, Cecily wondered how much of that was her fault. Oscar loved her. He did. It wasn't a mushy love, but a...love. She was "safe" in the sense he limited harming her—he wouldn't kill her or anything; she could say she was safe in that regard. Perhaps her over-sensitivity to everything made her give Oscar less credit than he deserved.

Cecily filled her mouth with water. She spit, moving her thoughts to other areas of safety. She smirked into the showering water, thinking it was likely a good thing her current husband didn't perform cunnilingus on her: the safety level in that regard was low. Not only did she believe he'd be terrible at it—it wasn't a farfetched notion he'd hurt her while doing it—maybe even on purpose (ouch). And there was something wrong with realizing that about him and accepting it as part of his normal behavior, but Cecily only wanted to be soothed and rejuvenated by the stinging pellets and not dwell.

She ruminated more while toweling-off.

Dr. Alexander posed interesting questions, questions giving her pause long after the session timer went off. She liked Naomi. Dr. Lewis made her anxious about his treatment; like she was constantly being tested somehow, but Dr. Alexander spurred a different gut feeling.

Naomi respected her mental space. She didn't make her feel pressured to answer anything or, if she answered, make her feel weird about it. Her doctor seemed to *get* her, seemed to understand without her saying or explaining much of anything. Oscar would continue challenging Naomi and Cecily's decision to stay with her, but Cecily wasn't looking for another therapist—she'd found a keeper.

Their brief not-Ozzie-and-Harriet gathering behind them, they were back in their usual corners of the house. Moisturized and pseudo-thankful her Aunt Flo was visiting (it allowed her to don cozy PJs), Cecily curled in the bed and grabbed her headphones to plug in and tune out now that Oscar had returned to the basement. She missed the things they used to do together. She missed... Well, she missed many things about marriage (and relationships) that didn't exist for her anymore. But specifically, she missed...*that point* when being at peace with losing Roland suddenly changed to heartbreaking anguish having nothing to do with him.

She'd missed it, couldn't pinpoint it for the life of her. What did she do to make him turn on her, make him so...*hateful?* They were happy in the beginning, weren't they? Or was that her imagination, too? Did she latch on to Oscar in some sort of blind hysteria while still mourning Roland, such that she noticed nothing and accepted...everything? All of it, unfortunately, was possible. And the uncertainty was driving her crazy—crazier, it seems, than she already was. She was a numbers girl: facts from figures motivated her, grounded her. This...This constant uncertainty about her personal life laughed in the face of that. Numbers and emotions were unrelated concepts. But she was a numbers girl: doubt and uncertainty unsettled her.

Getting a headache from pondering the same questions she'd been asking for years, Cecily turned her music on for ideal distraction.

Except, it wasn't the distraction she hoped for: "Boogie Shoes" bounced into her ears. Naturally, her mind went to a time she listened to this elsewhere—and then she imagined how Joshua likely spent his birthday (with Kristin?). She considered switching to Nina, and then just let it play. The song lifted her spirits, but there was another reason she let it play. It was pointless to attempt distracting herself from the undeniable. Joshua A. Hall was always in her thoughts somehow or another. And, if she allowed the truth to do its job, she'd admit he wasn't only in her thoughts, her mind; Josh existed elsewhere, too.

"Boogie Shoes" transitioned to "Reaching for the Sky," punctuating that *somewhere else* point. She'd forgotten she'd programmed certain songs to play ("Beautiful" by Joe, and Roberta and Donny's "The Closer I Get to You" were sure to follow). Cecily closed her eyes and listened to Peabo, letting the lyrics speak to her, letting the song...no longer distract her (she would need another day away from JAH Tech). When thoughts of Josh began inching and bending toward what they naturally would while listening to a slow song and thinking about a man (reasonable), she changed to her Nina Simone playlist, both embarrassed and angry with herself.

"Can't Get Out of This Mood" floated into her ears. Cecily listened and prayed. The optics of listening to a playlist with songs reminding her of another man didn't look good, but it wasn't about Josh as much as it was about the snippets of happiness those songs evoked (and she'd take whatever she could get).

Nina sang to her, her songs echoing much of Cecily's alternating emotions. Before long, Cecily grew sleepy. She stopped the music and sent the room into darkness, shifting her thoughts to the upcoming charity ball.

She looked forward to dressing up, Oscar in his tuxedo (dressing up brought out Oscar's better side), hanging out with other people of color sharing in a good cause. The deejay always played excellent sets, the food was tasty, and the decorations were exquisite. There was also an open bar, but that wasn't a source of excitement for her (not that she didn't enjoy a cocktail now and again). Drowsy, she left the misery of her home, daydreaming (or was it evening-dreaming?) about the few hours at the ball, seeing Oscar next to her at their table with their neighbors (she liked the goatee much better on him). She saw them dancing and laughing as she drifted off, the imagined evening progressing in contrast to the Mabrys' New Year's party.

The weekend nearing its end, Cecily sat on the bed sorting clean laundry, listening to the shower running. Oscar rarely showered in their primary (mainly using the basement bath), so they were at weird again. He'd been around more than usual the last couple days, just...hanging around her. She liked it but didn't trust it. Hated it but wanted it.

Oscar told her he wasn't attending any more sessions with her, said she and Naomi needed to try to do it without him. To herself, Cecily claimed *round four: Naomi*, but with Oscar, she said it was up to him. She started to tell him she wanted him there, but Naomi's voice in her head (and maybe some of her own voice) stopped her.

He prepared to go to the Comfort Inn for one of his network marketing meetings.

She could never get into those things and was thankful he didn't make her pursue it with him. Maybe it worked for the chosen few, but to her, the odds against were stacked as soon as you signed up. But Oscar kept at it, one opportunity after another; he tried and...kept trying. She would never say as much to him, but if he'd devoted as much effort into finishing his associate degree—he'd have his bachelor's by now.

Oscar's electric trimmer buzzed as she put his underwear in his chest of drawers. He emerged from their bathroom, towel around his waist. "Man, that felt good!" Her husband's light complexion (more red-bone than yellow) appeared both pale and flush. She usually wasn't attracted to light-skinned men; Roland's skin had been a lovely walnut-brown. Oscar headed for his chest. Sweat beaded even as his skin cooled with the change in room temperature. "It's cold as fuck outside, but wanna go to the movies later?" He dropped his towel, his rear marginally hairy and with the firmness of a nonactive man in his 50s.

Cecily couldn't remember the last time he suggested an actual date. "It... W-Won't it b-be on the l-late side wh-when you finish?"

He tugged his gray boxer briefs on, wearing this thoughtful expression as he nodded. "Yeah. It might. Scratch that, then." He opened another drawer for an undershirt. His hair lay in sparse wavy strands on his head and in moist curly tufts across his chest. His Corona-belly evoked a four-months-pregnant image that would've looked less so if he were taller. Still, he wasn't a bad-looking man at all. He could use a stronger nose, but that was her idiosyncrasy.

She'd take the ask and be happy with that, looking forward to having a few hours in the house by her lonesome. "I h-have n-no idea what's p-playing, anyway."

Oscar scoffed. "Which would've meant an irritating hour or two of you going back and forth with picking a damn movie." He stepped into the bathroom and returned, pausing in the entryway and applying deodorant. "Maybe seeing that therapist will help with that, too. You need something." He scoffed again and returned to the bathroom. He wouldn't brush his teeth until heading out the door; the minty effects of brushing didn't last him long these days—he wanted to be at the meeting before the need for mint-popping began.

Noting he'd relegated Naomi to "that therapist," Cecily said nothing.

"Those children of yours didn't make a New Year's resolution to see you more? They begged off coming to dinner, and we haven't seen hide-nor-hair of 'em since, man. Damn. They avoid your ass like the plague."

His words hurt. Cecily carried her clean pajamas to her dresser. "Year's j-just starting," she called in answer. It was a stupid response, only validating his comment.

He came back, heading for his sock drawer. His slacks and shirt lay across his side of the bed. He sat on the bed and put his socks on.

"Oscar...?"

"Yeah?" He stood with a sigh, reaching for his slacks.

"Let's have f-fun at the charity b-ball."

He frowned, slipping his pants on. "Huh?"

"I mean,...let's h-hang-out, talk, d-dance—"

His frown deepened. "Get it out, Cecily."

She sighed and closed her drawer. "I'm j-just saying, I d-don't want—At the M-Mabrys' party—"

"There you go." He scoffed with a shake of his head. "Every time we're having a chill time, you get to whining and bitching." He looked at her quizzically before his eyes turned stony. "Now you're bringing up past shit again. Your punk-ass dead husband must've got his brain cancer from your nagging. Damn!"

Cecily gasped and swallowed, her face hot and her chest suddenly heavy with sorrow and shock. She couldn't believe what he'd just said to her. She gaped at him, unsure what to do with the rage now twisting and coiling with the shock and sorrow.

"That might've worked with him, but don't try that nagging shit with me—if you know what's good for you."

His threat bounced over and around her with little impact. She remained cloaked by the shock, sorrow, and rage from that cruel proposition about Roland. Cecily couldn't move for it. She needed him to take those words back. Needed the ability to go back in time and fix it so she never heard them in the first place.

He stared at her, his stern gaze softening with seeing her demeanor. He sighed long and hard and came over to her. "Look, I get it: you're still in your feelings about whatever you think I did at that party. But we'll have 'fun' at the charity ball. I'll be by your side, doting on you hand and foot, dancing with only you. I can manage that for a few hours. So, chillax. Stop stressing and getting yourself all worked up again. It's all good." He kissed her cheek and stepped away.

It wasn't all good. It wasn't an apology, either. And there was something insulting about him needing to *manage* being with her *for a few hours*. But he offered her that box filled with black lies and slimy, grimy half-truths, the benevolence behind the words broken and spiked with malice and insincerity, and she accepted it thankfully, almost happily—she didn't get many gifts as it was.

He stood by the bed and looked back at her, and she nodded acceptance of his words. "Good. Now, let me get out of here. I'm going to be late, dealing with this foolishness." He reached for his belt.

Cecily turned to finish putting away the laundry and glimpsed his reflection in the mirror too late.

Pain, clean and sharp, slammed into her lower back. Her ragged inhale cut off her scream from the second blow whacking near where the first one landed, the pain excruciating and isolated. She stopped, dropped, and curled, but it was already over. He'd never been one to go on and on with his torture; there was that. Tears leaking, she lay curled, catching her breath while breathing through the intense throbbing.

Get out of this, Cecily. Leave.

The simple solution that wasn't.

He said nothing, and it wasn't until she heard the familiar clink that she realized the source of her agony: the buckle of his belt. After listening to him put on his shirt, she slowly rose. In the bathroom (leaving the door open), she cleaned her face, fixed her hair, and took two Advil. She'd check her back after he left.

And there was still shock and sorrow and rage from that other thing he said.

Oscar stood at her mirror, leaning close and pushing his insignificant nose back, creating folds in the bridge. "Ugh! Look at this..."

Stomach curdling, lower back aching, she stepped closer to her dresser, breathing in his fresh application of Lagerfeld. His cologne did nothing for her, reminded her of things she'd rather forget. Compared to the fresh and changing scents someone else wore, Oscar just smelled...old. She held in a sigh: such odorous comparisons were...odious.

Cecily watched the white snakes of oil coil from the pores in his nose, holding in a gag. Why he insisted she bear witness, bare her senses to his bodily exercises, she didn't know.

Her husband observed her in the mirror and snorted a laugh. When she covered her mouth with a hand, he looked bothered, wiping the snakes of oil from his nose with a tissue. "That's part of what's wrong with you: no sense of humor."

That wasn't what was wrong—not even close.

Oscar tossed the soiled tissue in the trash. "A'ight, my little Cesspool: brush my teeth, and I'm out."

Ten minutes later, he was. She watched Mr. Hyde leave and then went to the kitchen (so far, her flowers looked fine). She poured a glass of iced mango-peach juice and took it upstairs.

In the bathroom, she took out her contacts. After applying peroxide, Neosporin, and an adhesive bandage to her back (the second blow caused a small cut), she lay down with an icepack on the offended area to ease the pain and bruising, wanting a joint or a drink or...an anything to help camouflage the everything. This wasn't exactly what she had in mind for having the house to herself.

Cecily stared at the ceiling.

Did...Did she make some sort of deal with the devil,...where she somehow ended up marrying him, too?

She reached for her cellphone and set the timer for a half-hour. Whether she slept or only lay there for those thirty minutes, she didn't want to allow stiffness in her lower back to settle in; she'd get moving when the timer went off.

She dozed, coherent thought interspersing with the incoherent stuff, her mind and body trying to work some things out.

He had some nerve talking about her mothering; he was no one's Father of the Year. Keisha wanted no parts of him.

A single word kept flittering close and then out of reach.

She lay there, practicing countless comebacks and versions of standing up to him, but they were all hazily jumbled and more a part of the incoherent stuff. She also heard either Oscar or herself saying, "that's why you need a therapist," in her head, but that was okay because she did need to see one, and she was seeing one: an excellent one who was going to help her get to the other side of...this.

Any time thoughts of the home invasion intruded, Cecily groaned and sent them away; she felt bad enough as it was.

That single word flittered close and then out of reach again.

When the timer sounded thirty minutes later, she'd been asleep for a solid twenty minutes: a nice refresher. The icepack beneath her was now cool, not cold, but the pain was minimal. Cecily sat up wincing, however, from both mild stiffness and the points of impact. She went to the mirror in her closet and checked her lower back, causing additional pain from twisting to see: the bandage centered some bluish-purplish discoloration just above her tailbone and to the right. She only imagined what it would've looked like if she hadn't iced it.

Back in the bedroom, she sat on the bed and sipped her (now watery) juice, idly turning magazine pages.

"...*other than hanging out with Mother Nature, try doing something* outside *your comfort zone.*"

Naomi's suggestion in her ears, Cecily grabbed her glass and headed downstairs, a bit of defiance in her bones.

She paused at the top of the stairs leading to the basement, however, hesitating despite the defiance. This may not have been what Naomi meant, but this was way outside her comfort zone, so maybe it was precisely what she meant. She had little reason to be in the basement. The laundry and workout rooms were on the main floor, and Oscar moved her boxes of comics to a spare bedroom on the uppermost level years ago. There was a storage room down there, but she didn't have much need to stow away keepsakes.

Cecily checked her watch: she still had another two hours before he returned. This was her house (and all that), and she shouldn't have worried about being caught in Oscar's man-cave, but she was worried, hesitant, fearful.

Her feet finally realized what her brain was telling them to do. She turned on the light and headed down the stairs.

Cecily paused at the bottom. She cast her gaze around her basement, wishing she'd gone with the open great room concept than this here: a choppy effect resulting from breaking the basement into multi-purpose rooms. "This house is too big."

She stepped forward, walking gingerly, and passed the leather furniture, his Barcalounger recliner, the 47-inch flat-screen. Cecily opened doors to the other rooms, visiting and looking in: an empty, unused bedroom; the bedroom Oscar sometimes slept in; the storage room appeared orderly. She had no desire to visit the utility room but opened the door just because. Water heater, furnace, sump pump? Check.

She grabbed the remote for the television and turned it on: *Forensic Files* was amid one of its marathon airings. She half expected the channel to be set on a game show, but *Forensic Files* or something from any of the true-crime channels made sense: Oscar seemed too preoccupied with programs of that nature lately. Cecily turned the TV off with a shiver.

She took a wide berth around that spittoon-thing and stopped at his desk. The recycle-bin needed emptying. She set her glass down atop some envelopes and frowned at her framed picture sitting to the side, not so sure it touched her seeing it there.

Cecily smirked at his moderately neat desk, certainty circling her belly: she knew he sometimes changed stuff around on her. She stared at his desk, thinking about moving something around on it, but shook her head. "Next time." She didn't open any drawers or anything; saving that for the next time, too. Glass in hand, Cecily headed back upstairs.

She was midflight on the stairs leading to the top level, reflecting on the last Oscar session with Naomi, when that word, formerly flittering but never fully forming, popped into her head.

She froze, holding the banister and trembling, remembering Oscar's expression while discussing one particular topic.

"Oh, Jesus."

Cecily continued to her bedroom, that word no longer flittering but clamoring: *Unsuccessful.*

Chapter Thirteen

Come Hell or High Water

"**O**h, that shouldn't be a problem, man, sure. Be glad to." Oscar smiled extra hard. He couldn't wait to leave.

"Cool." Joshua pointed to the rear of the shop, toward a hall with several doors. "Hold up a sec; I'll be right back. Help yourself to a doughnut and coffee, man."

"A'ight."

Joshua headed down that hallway, turning left and disappearing, leaving Oscar in the front by his lonesome (Tight-Skirt-and-Heels stepped out minutes ago).

Oscar helped himself to a glazed-twist doughnut and strolled the joint, hearing muffled conversation traveling through the walls. Bougie-ass elevator music played overhead as he walked around checking out the place his wife was always so pressed to get to (except these last few days: what was that about?).

Lots of computer and network gobbledygook decked the walls, a small area had what he guessed were computer parts for sale. He scoffed: computers weren't his thing. Although he would've made a topnotch programmer: he was extremely logical.

Oscar stepped behind the reception and cashier counter without reservation. He scanned the few desks, recognizing Cecily's: neat and organized, finance books, and that antidextorious shit so she could use whichever hand suited her.

With a glance toward the hallway, Oscar went to her desk. He switched the scissors and rearranged some of her decorative knick-knacks, leaving a few papers askew for good measure.

She'd framed the cover of one of those stupid, uppity National Geographic mags—this one with a couple giraffes swirling their necks together. Since when did she start liking those long-necked mother-fuckers? He moved the picture to the other side of her desk and facing the other direction.

Chuckling, he stepped away, moving back to the other side of the counter before GQ-wannabe returned. A vase of fresh flowers rested on the small table with the brochures: Cecily's contribution, no doubt. Oscar curled his upper lip. Too bad he didn't have his special watering solution. He sat in one of the reception chairs and waited, finishing the glazed twisty.

He'd envisioned JH Computer Company as dank and cluttered with computer circuits all over the place. But when he stepped inside, the site was much bigger than he imagined, sleeker. Dude made bank from the looks of the joint. Tight-skirt-and-Heels (Rhoda? Donna?) greeted him, and Oscar lied, saying he was stopping by for Cecily; she was under the weather but feeling better enough to take some work home. Cecily didn't appear sick, but she wanted no parts of this place the last few days: he made the lie fit. Besides, he'd been meaning to check this place out for years.

Josh— Oh, excuse me, *Joshua* came out, extending his hand and correcting him from calling him "Josh." Oscar took it in stride; he didn't give a fuck about the punk's name, wouldn't even be using it after he left the place. Taller than he was, Joshua was good and brown, sorta slim, with short twists in his hair. He could never get with dreads or twists for men: those that had them were trying to perpetrate being extra African or some shit. Joshua had gray in his hair, but maybe he was graying early. He looked...mid-30s, maybe? He wore a blue sports coat and black jeans; his vest had a crisscross pattern from England or some shit, and everything, from shirt to shoes, was coordinated: GQ-wannabe. A nice sweatsuit was coordinated by default; waste of time going through all that extra dressing and shit.

Oscar made small talk with him and Tight-Skirt (Joshua was likely fucking her), and then Donna (Rhoda?) excused herself as she should have, leaving the men to talk. They chatted about nothing, safe stuff, but Joshua used a bunch of words no one heard of to make things interesting, he guessed (showoff: what the fuck was "eggsidyoous"?). Whenever he asked stuff about Cecily, Joshua's answers were kinda vague and noncommittal, and Oscar figured he was too busy banging Tight-Skirt-and-Heels Rhoda-Donna to pay much attention to Cecily. Joshua then mentioned the crew getting together to help get the new site into shape, inviting him to come along. Oscar smiled and lied, telling him it shouldn't be a problem, that he'd be glad to, but he resented him asking. Joshua was big-man, bigshot business owner—hire some motherfuckers to pitch in. Cecily wasn't helping with that shit, either.

Oscar stood as Joshua returned from the back.

Joshua extended a large envelope toward him. "Her voicemail said she'd be back tomorrow, but here's something just in case..."

Oscar accepted the envelope. The envelope was sealed, pissing him off, but he smiled. "Okay, man. I'm sure this'll be fine."

Joshua grabbed a few brochures, extending them his way. "If you know anyone needing what we do..."

Oscar nodded, placing the brochures in the same hand as the envelope. "Of course. Gotta help Black businesses thrive, man."

Joshua smiled. There was a teeny space between two teeth on the left side. "I appreciate that, bruh. Take care." He pumped his hand once.

"Yeah, you, too." Oscar left.

When he got around the corner (a little winded and sweating despite the cold), he tossed everything in the trash before getting in his car.

Appearances were everything. Right now, shit appeared to be going wrong.

Days later, Oscar sat in his recliner, holding the pages from the To Do list from two years ago. "Fuck." He flung the tattered and blood-streaked list onto the leather sofa. He'd messed up with the bank accounts. That nearly $20 million would go to Marcus and Chelsea (and the brat grandson). And although he'd been playing up the niceness, trying to make a move to change shit now would look suspicious—even to Cecily—and he sensed some...some...resistance in her now. It was a quiet, subtle thing, but he detected it. The fuck? She was still herself, still coming correct, but there was something different about it; he just couldn't put his finger on what.

She remembered the closet...

Yeah. Janyce said Cecily had been asking her questions, too. And he'd told Janyce: no worries. Cecily could ask questions all she wanted. Questions were one thing, *answers* were another. As long as she had one without the other, all was chill.

He wondered how the sessions were going. Cecily never wanted to talk about them, and he didn't know what to make of that. Could mean she was frustrated at not getting better (like with Dr. Lewis). Could mean she was making dangerous progress but was afraid to act on it.

Annoyed, he kicked the cashbox. His chest flip-flopped and went heavy. Oscar closed his eyes and took slow breaths, calming shit down. He could still do all right. There was $2.5 million in life insurance payable to him, and he'd have powerful attorney over her investments and shit: he could do just fine. He breathed slowly, looking at it that way. It helped: the fullness was still there, but the flip-flops stopped.

Oscar stared at the blank television screen. The white-noise beckoned, offering another break so soon after the other, but he didn't have the time to sit and veg-out, thinking about weird shit. Besides, sometimes, when the white-noise went away, he was irritable—and he was doing his best not to be.

He spotted the pictures of Cecily from that night and reached for them. Staring at her bound, swollen, and bloodied body (and getting a hard-on), he wondered if they still made film for Polaroid cameras, thinking he might want some pics...for next time—or another video.

You're crazy, man. See somebody.

"See who? Naomi?!" Oscar laughed then, laughed at Whiny-Bitch Voice, and headed upstairs for some pussy. Passing his desk, he noticed a water ring on the top manila folder. He used coasters and shit; must've set a Corona there without thinking about it.

After adding his special watering mixture to her annoying flowers and messing with the books on the shelves in her office (for the hell of it), Oscar plucked a magazine (to cover his still-hard dick) and went upstairs.

He found her on the bed in her usual spot and usual position, doing her usual: resting on her back with eyes closed and headphones on, listening to something—probably that man-woman Nina Simone. Cecily wore a T-shirt and lounge-pants, but she still looked hot. He ran his eyes over her, thinking about how she'd been vulnerable and sad but still had some spunk and edge when he first met her, how the breaking had killed all that women's-lib empowered shit and left her his and his alone, how now, he sensed some spunk and edge coming back.

Sometimes when a broken leg didn't heal right, you had to...re-break it. But he didn't know if he had the energy anymore, didn't think it mattered (given what was coming).

Lightly stroking his erection with his free hand (the one not covering it with a magazine), he watched her lying on the bed. He'll give it to her missionary as a treat. Still shielding himself, he approached her side of the bed, knowing she would startle. She must have sensed his nearness: she opened her eyes and looked at him (tiny startle), pausing her music.

He pinched off a smile. "Hey."

Her gaze turned wary, but not the wariness he was used to. "Hey."

"What's going on in those?" He gestured toward her headphones. "More Nina?"

She shook her head and removed her phones, placing them on the bed. "Just some relaxation stuff." She finger-styled her hair, making it neater for him. The little things mattered. "What's up?" She glanced at the magazine, frowning; he didn't read magazines (or much else).

Oscar sat by her legs on the bed, placing his magazine near her headphones. He hunched his shoulders. Women liked for a man to shrug; made her want to take care of him and shit. His penis throbbed for some action, but he wasn't a rapist; he had to play the game first.

She sat up, concern in her eyes. "You feeling okay?"

He nodded, but when she began reclining and reclaiming her headphones, he grabbed her wrist, making her sit up again. "Think...Think you might get that prescription from Naomi? Is it for pain?"

"For anxiety. And I don't want a prescription, no."

He examined the floor, noticing she didn't stutter (that faded more as the weeks passed, too). "It wouldn't be...for you."

"You're anxious?" She placed her hand on his shoulder, and he knew he had her.

He shrugged again, growing impatient with the game—or his dick was, at least.

"Oscar, I don't know. People sh-shouldn't use their prescrip—"

He scoffed and shook his head, keeping his eyes on the floor.

"You c-could ask Doctor H-Halim for something on y-your own."

He already did. Already had the first one filled. But he needed Cecily to have one, too. Oscar scoffed. "Taking too many things from him already." He sighed. "Never mind."

She patted his back, giving it a quick rub. "No, no. I'll...I'll think about it. Maybe g-get one filled?"

He nodded, knowing he'd convince her to get the other refills, too. "I'm not trying to get hooked on anything. Just...this heart shit makes me so...!" He scoffed more seriously this time because he was sincere: the PAH shit messed with him constantly: physically and mentally.

"Shhh... Okay. I know it's hard."

He nodded again. Getting blue balls with the wait, he guided her hand to his erection and looked at her. "So...So is this."

Her hazel eyes widened with shock, and he almost howled. "What?!"

"I...I was looking at pictures of you, thinking about the past, I guess." He looked away. "We don't have to." He rarely played the shit like this; it was kinda fun.

She probably didn't mean for him to hear her sigh. "No. It's fine."

Magic words. He grunted and slammed his mouth onto hers, shoving his tongue in. He watched her as they kissed, saw the tiny frown. Should've popped a mint before coming to her, but too bad. Pushing her back and moving over her, he raised her T-shirt over her breasts and squeezed on both through her bra. He pulled back from her mouth. "Pull 'em down." He braced above her, working to get his shit out while she pulled her lounge-pants and panties down. She looked everywhere but at him, but so what? He grabbed a tittie and pushed in, finally getting what he came for. Head lowered next to hers, he breathed Cecily's warm, sexy scent from her pillow, images in his head of her and Naomi broken and bloody. As she'd been told and taught, she didn't interfere with his needs by moving with him or caressing him—just took what she had coming.

He thought he'd given her at least two minutes of dick, but he doubted it. He'd been hornier than a motherfucker. It didn't last as long as *he'd* wanted, but he couldn't help it: he'd been hard so long, his nuts couldn't wait (and Cecily had some good stuff). He pulled out and looked down at her. She looked toward the window, but, given her expression, she might as well have had her headphones on. So what? He got his; wasn't his fault she didn't know how to get hers. Should've gotten that shit doggy-style like he started to. Instead of ramming her head into the pillow (like he wanted), he kissed her cheek.

Oscar left the bed, fixing his clothes while she readjusted hers. He knew she'd shower once he left. So what? "Feel like having Chinese?" His nuts felt better, but he remained dissatisfied. Fuck.

"Okay."

He took stock of her. She really was pretty—even without the contacts and shit. "Your usual?"

"Yes, please. Thanks."

"...And you'll get the prescription."

She nodded again, but with less enthusiasm.

"Charity ball's coming up soon." He didn't know why he added that. Oddly, while he wanted to slam her head into the wall,...he also wanted to make her feel a little better or something.

This time her nod carried a small smile. "A little over a week."

"A'ight. I'll place the order." He left her and that magazine on the bed, returning to his man-cave so she could shower in peace.

He returned to his hole-in-the-ground, sitting on the sofa instead of in his recliner. The stuff from that night was still out, but he wasn't worried about it: Cecily knew better than to come down here without permission. The only reason she had to come down before was the comics, for which he now used the smallest bedroom on the top level, moving all the boxes to that room. He visited the comics room, but Cecily had no reason to be in his man-cave. He used to test to see if she ever came down when he wasn't home: she never did. Once he saw he had her trained well, he stopped testing.

Still feeling dissatisfied for reasons he didn't know, he focused on the sex he'd just had...and scoffed.

He was proud of himself, thought he did pretty good. Although he could've just taken the pussy, told her to open her legs and give him some, he went the "sensitive" route. Talking a little, faking an interest. He didn't get mushy, telling her he loved her, and that was for good reason. After a psychology course or two, he knew he was a nature, not nurture, type dude; not into holding, cuddling, supporting emotionally with physical contact, and all that sissy jazz. He was all for nature taking its course in helping somebody get through troubles, letting time and distraction do their thing. And, he wasn't a rapist, but he could've used force, used some hurt to get her cooperation. But that just wasn't his thing—not completely.

Unlike some people, he didn't have a piece of paper to proclaim it to the world (not yet), but he believed he was smarter than most. No, he wasn't book smart, but he had a certain level of intelligence for certain things—like knowing it wasn't necessary or wise to leave serious marks on Cecily.

Although there were times (like earlier) when he wanted to send her head through a wall, he didn't have to abuse Cecily. He kept her right where he wanted her, mostly with his words. The breaking required pain, and he reinforced rules and lessons with a surprise jolt of pain to bring a point home (women were like Packluv's dogs), but he didn't go overboard with it. And you didn't break bones, blacken eyes, or damage the extremities: you kept that shit along the torso (below the neck and above the knees), where it was easiest for them to cover any evidence and protect their pride. Some women didn't let you get away with any of it from the jump (let alone go overboard), but you avoided those wannabe man types (like Delia). Under the right circumstances, with the right woman? Oh, yeah: words were as effective as action in getting a woman off that pedestal and down where you needed her.

Men were stupid when they left major, easily seen marks on the woman's body (definitely the wrong way to go about it). Women were weak and naturally wanted the man's approval, but men have to keep a woman's sense of independence down. Men gotta find that key element inside a woman, that part of her spirit, and break that down first (maybe with a little pain, but see how the words affect her first). Then, for insurance, exercise some power over her, using pain: small pinches or hits, but shit that didn't cause deep marks (yet still brought the message home). His father let his mother run her mouth too much, have too much say. He learned well from his old man: if you don't get control of your woman, they drain you dry using their "mystery" and their pussy—leaving you nothing but an old, hull of a man once they're done.

The key was keeping them off balance with it (the words, the pain) by throwing in some of that "love"—and getting that pussy (always).

He spat in his spittoon.

But he'd played up the sensitive-man part, and she still wasn't happy. Typical. It just proved his theory all along, why he went through no extra pains to get her off. Sex was about the man getting some pleasure while getting the female pregnant. It had nothing to do with the woman getting any pleasure—which was why it was so hard for them to bust a nut, why they had to fake coming. God wouldn't have made it such a hassle if that's what it was about for them, wouldn't have made finding that hoax G-spot such a fruitless treasure hunt. And although Cecily had a fresh vagina, he didn't go down on her because the shit's subservient. He didn't need her getting any ideas of confidence and entitlement—not when he had her right where he wanted. But he'd gone down on a female before.

Oscar sat forward, shaking his head as he reorganized his keepsake lockbox. Going down on them was too complicated. Men's shit? Simple: dick and balls—suck on dick until balls send squirt. But them? Nah. Bunch of folds and openings and shit, some parts too sensitive, other parts needing more stimulation. Complicated. You can lick forever and still nothing. Waste of time—and being between her legs like that made him a submissive punk. Fuck that; that's not how this works.

He hurried and stashed the pictures of Cecily away, stuffing them at the bottom. Sometimes he got hard looking at them, but sometimes they bothered him (like now). Oscar locked the box and put it away in the utility room. With a new plan brewing, he'd get rid of this stuff soon.

She remembered some shit, man.

Oscar shrugged. So. She also wasn't sure if what she remembered was real. He didn't know what was happening in those sessions now, but if Naomi was still doing that memory-lane mumbo jumbo, it'd be a while before they got around to anything important. Oh, the little doctor bitch thought she was slick: calling him "OJ," being an ass about him smoking, giving him looks like he was a child and shit, giving him lip period. She may have been working some secret shit with his wife, but he was time enough for her. He had plans for both of them.

Marcus and Chelsea were a done deal. He needed to let that 20-million-dollar ship sail. He couldn't take a chance trying to wipe out the three of them again (too risky). So, he'd go for his $2.5 million insurance payout at the least. His street smarts could quadruple that $2.5 million easy-peasy.

Plan A ended a failure. Plan B would take too long, was too convoluted, and not guaranteed. But he had Plan C now, which combined the best of the first two with a delightful bonus.

He wanted Cecily to continue the therapy, would encourage it, be supportive. He'd also build a stash of his pain pills and her anxiety meds. Halim didn't give him a big count on the pain pills, so it would take months to build it like he wanted with the limited number of refills he had. But he'd get there, and Cecily would keep going to Naomi. Once he got enough pills, he'd make a smoothie for his wife, claiming it was some new recipe he saw online...

Cecily "committing suicide" while being treated by Dr. Alexander would take Naomi down a few notches, kill her reputation—and he'd kill two birds with one stone: Cecily literally, and Naomi—by destroying her rep (from suing the shit out of her).

Oscar grinned at the blank television, belly rippling and breathing stilted with nervous excitement. He liked this one a lot, and he was doing it by himself.

So, fuck you, Janyce, Winton.

Oscar reached for the phone to order a large kung-pao chicken for himself and a small shrimp-with-black-bean-sauce for his wife. He added a couple egg rolls as partial private celebration.

There'd be no need for any other letters of the alphabet.

He'd see Plan C through...come hell or high water.

Chapter Fourteen

The Charity Ball

(Group Therapy Extreme)

"Ohhh, I am liking this, Naomi..." Antonio finished the last section of finger coils.

Antonio was her barber and now stylist as she got her coif ready for the charity ball this evening. She'd allowed her hair to grow out more for just this purpose.

She and Antonio were a few years in. Antonio was a nice, dark, chocolate-drop of a man who wasn't gay and would've turned her head if he was at least 40—instead of just shy of 30. He still turned her head: cute was cute. He did hair, not gossip, which suited her fine, and he covered her grays well—which served her even better. She was never fond of having someone else do her hair when he wasn't available (the nerve of him).

Naomi continued reading the Connie Briscoe novel in her e-reader. "So glad you approve." They'd gone over several style options over the last few months. He'd given her options for flattened and teased short bobs and pixies, but she didn't want heat—even for the one night. When he showed her a new book with natural hairstyles, she picked the finger coils and suggested the bolder color highlights.

"No, seriously, this is going to be pretty." He finished the last coil and stepped back, checking the look from a different angle. "The caramel highlights weaving throughout, man. It's popping!" He reached over, adding fingering finishing touches, then grabbed the clippers for finishing barber touches. "I want this to set."

She looked at him.

Antonio grinned, shaking his head. "Not hot and not long. I got you. Come on..."

E-reader in hand, she left her chair, following him to the hair dryers.

True to his word, Antonio had her under a cool-warm setting for less than fifteen minutes. Returning to Antonio's station, she paused with joyous surprise at the figure sitting two stations down.

She moved close and waited (much like she did over a year ago). Head down, they were engrossed in their smartphone, thumbing through comments on social media. She smiled at seeing a package of Goldenberg's Peanut Chews candy tucked into the side of the seat cushion (with blue labeling for milk chocolate). "I see I've made a convert..."

Todd Winthrop smiled without looking up. "Yeah." His barber stopped combing, and Todd stood and faced her, still smiling, that chip in his front tooth as adorable as ever. "Hey, Doctor Alex." He hugged her, taller but less lean since last year, his football activities combining with and enhancing what puberty already had well underway.

He pulled back with a full grin, his blue Coppin State hoodie showing its eagle logo in yellow. Coppin State had been his mother, Julia's, alma mater.

She grinned back, resisting ruffling his hair. "Getting a fresh cut for your birthday?" He would be 16 in a week.

"You remembered? Wow. But nah: got a date tonight."

Naomi nodded; she didn't doubt that. "I talked to Jeff over the holidays, but you weren't around. Did you have a pleasant holiday? How's school? Mallory—?"

Todd laughed, the sound heavier with bass than when he was in therapy. "Everybody's fine, Doctor Alex. School's fine. Mallory's applying to colleges. We're..." He nodded with reassurance. "We're *really* good. Ruth's defunct. And Miss Isolynn's..." He grinned again, displaying happiness for his father. "Miss Isolynn's making things better—for all of us. Dad's finally..." He trailed off with a curious frown, giving Naomi no worries.

"Your dad's finally...?"

Todd sat back in his chair and reached for his candy, extending the package to her in offer. His aura flickered a serene sky-blue: (at present) poised and comfortable with life. When she declined, he continued.

"Well, you know how things were for my dad. He was all over the place for so long...just trying to deal with Mommy being gone. He...He once described it as everything running into one another: his days, his emotions, his roles as father, artist, friend, and husband. But now..." The barber resumed combing Todd's hair. "But now he says he has a good handle, no longer navigating such obscure boundaries and floundering."

Jeff Winthrop described his progress to her likewise during their recent touch-base conversation. She didn't keep in touch with many of her former patients, but some...well, some she did. "Good for him."

Several minutes later, small talk with Todd over (she wished him a Super Sixteenth) and Antonio paid and tipped, she left the barber-shop amongst several compliments regarding her caramel-copper finger coils. She wondered if Kevin would be pleased and then didn't give a hey-nonny-nonny; *she* liked them.

The January freeze-over had mellowed big-time, given the fifty-seven degrees it was now. The low for tonight was a tolerable fifty-one: perfect for tonight's festivities.

It was another fifteen minutes before she sat in her newly detailed BMW 540i, watching two ladies with whom she'd just finished speaking. She watched the young Black women approach another unsuspecting business park patron, thinking about her short exchange with them.

Naomi sensed their purpose through nothing more than their smiles as they approached her. Although "tall" to Naomi included almost everyone, the taller, full-figured one with blond braids (soon known as "Tamika") and the shorter, more diminutive one with a school-teacher bun and red lipstick ("Kim") paused her progress, asking her what she would do if a disaster struck.

And because she enjoyed toying with such enthusiasts, Naomi hemmed and hawed, giving vague responses considered standard Christian teaching. She was then told that her prayers wouldn't be enough, that believing wasn't enough, before Tamika juxtaposed the conversation, mentioning something about sacred seals being opened with the end of time approaching and about being prepared for all these disasters happening.

Naomi listened, nodding where appropriate, holding fast to her own spiritual beliefs while allowing them to express theirs, Oscar Brooks flitting through her mind the entire time.

When their discussion turned pushier, a tad threatening through guilt as they handed her pamphlets and informed about an upcoming service, Naomi smiled, asking what her contribution (money) should be. Kim skirted the issue, explaining "giving gestures" only helped to spread the word to others and provided an avenue to the Water of Life.

Naomi now watched the women talking to an older gentleman, her mind still on the "disasters" portion of their conversation. She scoffed, not unkindly.

In her view, humans were bringing on weather disasters by not caring for planet Earth's delicate balance. And God, if nothing else, is receptive to prayer—always. The Bible and most spiritual leaders encouraged it (not that she cared what anyone thought). For them to tell her prayers would not cut it in dire times (prayer being the primary line of communication to God) tickled Naomi. She believed action went along with prayer, but for Naomi, that had more to do with loving others, being charitable in extending yourself to help others.

Still tickled, chuckling to herself, Naomi turned on Richard Smallwood's "T'will Be Sweet" and pulled off.

As she drove home, Kevin texted. She listened via Bluetooth: he would dress at her house instead of his. That was fine; it saved time. She also received two calls on the DNA-hotline: one from Willette Hargrove, the other from Cecily Brooks. Naomi couldn't answer and administer help while driving; she pulled over as soon as opportunity presented.

She called Willette back first, knowing the call would be short. This was all about Willette's sister's upcoming birthday. True enough, it was, and Naomi had Willette calmer after seven minutes of conversation about "Alicia." She treated people of all types, but her Caucasian patients used the hotline much more often; Willette was no exception. With Willette calmed, Naomi called Cecily.

Thirteen minutes after that conversation, Naomi called in a prescription for anti-anxiety medication for Cecily: she needed them to deal with being around many people tonight. Cecily wanted the prescription small and without a refill, so Naomi didn't pry and had no misgivings—she'd get into more about it during their next session. With Oscar having opted out of attending sessions (likely out of some misconstrued protest), conversing with Cecily was easier. She hadn't seen Oscar in weeks, and that looked like it could roll into the foreseeable future; Naomi couldn't have been more pleased.

She pulled back into traffic, resuming the commute home. Cecily's ochlophobia could be a derivative of an avoidance symptom of her PTSD. Given all she's gone through, all that she's going through: at this stage, Cecily remained unsure of most people's motives. Trying to ferret out those with genuine, friendly, or neutral intentions among a multitude of people—when she's having a great deal of difficulty doing it with key one-on-one relationships—would generate the desire to avoid that multitude (or at least request some anti-anxiety meds to manage it).

Naomi drew closer to home, Oscar Brooks on her brain. She hadn't seen him, but he was such an integral part of Cecily's mental distress, Naomi kept mindful of him. This occasion of Cecily being around a group of people had Naomi wondering. With her freedoms limited, Cecily's home was likely its own self-contained police state she tolerated to survive. Many would view such tolerance as accommodating and noble, but Cecily was married to a man who viewed tolerance as weakness—a weakness he nurtured and took full advantage of.

She wondered if Cecily was in store for a Mabrys' New Year's party...part *two*.

The Winter Wonderland of Giving charity ball was an annual event sponsored by multiple African American charities with interests local to the DMV. Rotating annually in various banquet halls or select mansion estates throughout DC, Maryland, and Virginia, this year's event was in Anne Arundel County. From six p.m. to midnight, there would be free-flowing music, food, socializing, and booze—all for a good cause or twelve. The charity balls were about the fun and celebrating philanthropy; there were no long-winded pompous speeches, awards, or presentations—just food, drink, and music. Six hours rated long for these events, but Naomi remembered when it was only four hours long. With increased popularity came increased demand, increased ticket prices, and a more prolonged event duration, but with that also came a significant increase in charity money: six hours it is.

The ball was highly anticipated and well-attended every year. Early-bird tickets were $600.00, and if you snoozed you did lose—to the tune of $950.00. The demographics for the charity ball targeted high-end. A portion of the proceeds from ticket sales went to the charities, of course, but it wasn't called "Wonderland of Giving" for nothing: guests were also expected (although never officially asked) to give a little extra (with a check) as they walked through the door. The varied charity-sponsoring allowed people to select where they lent their support—and guests rarely arrived empty-handed.

Naomi didn't attend regularly but looked forward to going tonight.

NAOMI (6:17 p.m.)

"You have everything?" Kevin checked his inside pockets before looking at her with inquiry. He smelled good, and that midnight-blue peaked double-breasted tux with satin facing looked good on him. His trousers were too long, with a noticeable break, and he wore a Ghana lapel pin (she wasn't a fan of that trend), but all of it still came together well: from his fresh haircut, the mother-of-pearl studs and links, and whole-cut balmorals shined to perfection, to his semi-butterfly bowtie and the fluted white pocket square.

Kevin didn't look his 50 years; thus, 50 looked good on him.

Naomi checked her clutch for her essentials: present and accounted for. "Yes. All set." She turned to find him gazing at her. "What is it?"

He shook his head and leaned close, kissing her cheek. "Nothing. You look beautiful, Naomi; that's all. I like...*everything*." He grinned at her.

Naomi pecked his lips. "Thank you. Everything's looking pretty good over in that driver's seat. Come on." She turned to open her door.

He touched her wrist, pausing her.

She affixed a warm gaze on him. Normally, they wore eyeglasses, but tonight their eyes were unshielded; they fashioned contact lenses for the special occasion. And right now, his saddle-brown eyes cast a curious sparkle.

Kevin tipped his smile to the side. "No working."

"Shouldn't have any patients in there. There won't be a reason to."

Kevin's smirk deepened, but there was humor in it. "An existing reason has little to do with it. It's part of who you are." His Ghanaian accent flitted through, causing her attraction to him to simmer.

Naomi smirked back. "Well, if you know that—"

"No *working*, Naomi." He grinned again, knowing the request was futile (mostly), but wanting her to focus on having fun.

Naomi appreciated it. "I'll do my best. Now, can we go?"

He reached for the glove compartment, unlocked it, and deposited his 9mm Sig Sauer inside. He looked at her, but Naomi shook her head; she didn't bring her Glock (she still pondered a name for her gun). Kevin nodded and locked the glove box. "*Now*, we can go."

Charities supported and coats checked, she and Kevin made way to their Alexander-Oheneba table. Like a classic car refurbished and so pristine and fresh-smelling with new paints, the estate's interior stood out with fancy showroom accoutrements: the halls festive with glittery wintry-like gold and silver tinsel, the main banquet hall simple and tasteful with water bowl centerpieces and candles.

The acoustics of the place were prime. Even with the music playing, people heard it most on the dance floor. The music wasn't as loud at the tables, allowing folk to socialize without screaming at one another. The hall was vast. They also placed tables far enough apart to encourage dancing near the tables.

The lighting, too, was practical yet intentional, providing both visibility and a festive ambiance.

The featured deejay was Curtis "Up-Owl-Nite" Devereaux, a college professor doing his side-gig and loving it. Dressed in a dark tux (maroon? burgundy?), he supplied smooth jazz as background noise during the ball's slow-start cocktail hour with guests still arriving. A digital timer displayed near his station and would change with the next song played. Curtis liked to show the minutes and seconds marking a track, claiming he wanted partiers to see the exact moment a song moved them (an effective touch). She hadn't been to one of these in years, but some things never changed.

Curtis adjusted his mouthpiece and the volume, speaking over the smooth jazz. "All right, y'all. I'll be playing several dedications throughout the night. You all know how it works: just come up and slip me that paper with name and dedication, and I'll take it from there...!" He bobbed his head, pursing his lips to the music, and spoke to the growing crowd again. "Now, because you have gotten yourselves all fancified and dolled-up for a great cause, I'll keep things nice and easy, sticking to the slow to mid-tempo stuff; keep the moisture content low in those fancy clothes. But now, I make no promises as my late-hour finale approaches...!" He brought the smooth jazz back up to medium volume, chuckling along with guests nodding and waving their familiar understanding at him.

Naomi spotted her daughter and Trevor seated at the table. Leslie smiled and stood, waving them over, suggesting they dispense with taking in the hall sights and just come sit down.

Kevin chuckled. "I've missed her."

"I'm sure." She looked at him. "You didn't forget those extra tickets, did you?" She was referring to the tickets for Timothy and Louise Collins. Louise begged for tickets to the ball, having no shame. Naomi continued begging off but finally relented after consulting Viv, and let the couple purchase Kevin's extra tickets (the money donated to Kev's preferred charity).

Kevin took her hand, adopting this odd expression as they drew closer to Leslie and Trevor. "You believe your question came across neutral, but I heard the hope...that I *did* forget." He tapped where his inside breast pocket would be and smirked. "Sorry to disappoint."

Naomi squeezed his fingers with a chuckle.

NAOMI (6:39 p.m.)

Leslie checked her phone for the ninth time and turned to her. "Did—?"

"I haven't heard from them; I don't know when they're coming; and no, I'm not texting her—and don't you bother her, either." Naomi finished her crème fraîche and caviar tartlet in a bite and chewed at leisure, signaling her daughter to stop bugging her about certain guests arriving at the ball.

When Naomi reached for her wine to wash her hors d'oeuvre down, Leslie sat back with a pouting sigh. "Fine."

Kevin and Trevor socialized elsewhere in the banquet hall.

Knowing it would be less than two minutes before her daughter checked her phone for the tenth time, Naomi stood, ready to join Kevin on the other side of the room and check out more of the scene, when she spotted the objects of Leslie's excited angst approaching the entrance.

Naomi sipped and watched the couple, using some of her body language training.

Initially, Rick walked slightly ahead of Viv (as her husband, he was protector first). At the door, they stood together (equal partners). Viv then entered with Rick but moved ahead of him as they walked, Rick's hand touching the small of her back (Rick was her supporter).

Kevin advised her against "working" tonight, but that was like telling a banana not to ripen.

Leslie spotted them, too. "Oh, wow. They...look like Hollywood."

Naomi watched and grinned as men and women took subtle double takes at the couple, sometimes following their progress for a few steps before resuming conversation. Viv finally made eye contact, and Naomi waved them over.

Both smiling at her as they drew nearer, Naomi agreed with Leslie's summation.

Although her black satin shawl still draped her shoulders, it didn't detract from seeing Viv's presentation for the evening. Viv's black high-neck halter sheath dress with silver illusion mesh panels flowed with flattering fit over her form. Those illusion panels glimmered with silvery-metallic beads on the beguiling dress, while the high neck added elegant detailing to the front. Viv accessorized the silvery shimmer with diamond drop earrings and a tennis bracelet. The only rings: that diamond-and-platinum set on her left ring-finger. She'd styled her hair with a chignon twisted high and beaded with sparkling silver stones, leaving sparse delicate tendrils of curl at her nape.

Naomi caught glimpses of three-inch silver T-strap d'orsay peep-toe pumps as she walked, her toes polished a soft iridescent. Viv carried a black peau de soie clutch with a diamond-like fastener; the grosgrain silk matched the facing of her husband's tuxedo.

Naomi swallowed and held her smile, her focus shifting to Viv's date. *Lord have mercy.*

Rick's black tuxedo was single-breasted with a peaked collar and grosgrain facing instead of satin. From the fit, his tuxedo didn't have vents. His shirt was pique with French cuffs and a turndown collar instead of wing (the studs and links looked platinum). Keeping with recent trends, most men in attendance so far wore formal Windsor knots with their tuxes (including Trevor). Kevin and Rick, however, were true formal with bowties (Rick's bowtie knotted into the point-ed-bow formation). Rick's grosgrain waistcoat was the only one she'd seen tonight so far; the other men wore cummerbunds.

His shift to pass behind a chair revealed, not a fabric strip, but a bona fide grosgrain braid covering the side seam of his trousers. Rick's trousers were hemmed to the throat-line of his flat-bow court shoes with virtually no break. His jetted pocket flap didn't have a pocket square, and Naomi recognized this was because he wore a custom-made boutonniere instead (not a blasted lapel pin). She understood the boutonniere's significance: the white gladiolus was Viv's birth-month flower. Men routinely wore carnations as boutonnieres, but the depar-ture was classy. He wore no jewelry except his wedding band, but given those platinum studs and links, Naomi believed a platinum pocket watch lurked somewhere inside that waistcoat.

His facial hair was now a low-key, modified Zappa: clean-shaven ex-cept for his mustache and a fraction of soul patch, losing the chin-por-tion of his former Hipster. It was a throwback to his look years ago. Unobscured by facial hair, the cleft in his chin was prominent now. Limiting the amount of his facial hair was a choice for elegance few other men observed: beards were everywhere tonight. She was used to an inch or three of his rough curls atop his head, but tonight Rick wore the Dark Caesar with a sharp, even lineup: a badass haircut because it was classic and timeless.

And that would be: *Lord have mercy.*

The couple, indeed, looked like Hollywood. Again, Naomi was proud to have helped them overcome a major marital crisis.

Viv hugged her, pure aromal with that intriguing, subtle mix of ros-es and...cloves. The unique body oil carried elements of vanilla and jasmine, too. "Hi! My, this is a stelliferous night, isn't it? The weather finally releasing such a freeze..." Viv typically limited her makeup to shaded lip-gloss, but tonight was exception. Dark, smoky silver and black eyeshadow matched her dress, thinly winged eyeliner accenting her beautiful ebony eyes. She tinted her lips a natural-neutral with a hint of shimmer. She surveyed the banquet hall. "And this winter-themed clinquant is such an exquisite touch. They always go all out."

Leslie leaned forward and kissed Viv's cheek with a smirk. "What kind of night? And what's clinkint?"

"Tis why she's so good at Scrabble, Les." Chuckling, Rick stepped around his wife. "*Buonasera*, Sis."

"Hi, there!"

Rick placed his fingertips to her waist and smiled that devastating smile at her, those strange golden-auburn eyes of his seeing into her, and then kissed her cheek in greeting. His fingertips at her waist again reminded her his masculine power was gentle enough to give her multiple orgasms. He then placed a gentle peck upon her lips, allowing her a brief period of feeling how soft his lips were, of enjoying a graze from the hair above his lip, to breathe, in proximity, the seduction of his cologne which carried sensual touches of vetiver, cedar, and grapefruit to her nostrils: a blend earthy, spicy, and entirely masculine.

Rick's kiss was not sexual (he considered her a sister), but inside that moment, for an instant, Naomi was fully fine with ignoring all rules of society, of morality; her body flooded with carnal desire for the man. The rampant renegade emotion moving through her ruined reason, eradicated etiquette, and destroyed decorum, reducing her to nothing more than a female in heat for him.

As they parted and Rick shifted to greet Leslie, Naomi wanted to reach inside his pants for what was housed there, and use every one of her five senses to explore, taking (and happily accepting) everything he had to offer (all, ahem, nine inches).

She looked at Viv to see if Viv detected the betrayal, but Viv's expression was hard to read as she laughed at something Leslie said. Although fleeting, the feeling didn't pass quickly enough for Naomi, but finally, the traitorous reaction mellowed (yet, unfortunately, didn't leave altogether). "Where're Patrice and Garrett?"

Viv thumbed toward the entrance with a shrug. "Still at the car. Something going on with her dress..."

Leslie guided Viv toward the seating, obviously wanting Viv (and, by default, Rick) sitting near her. "Who's watching Al and RJ?"

"My niece. Reecie and Garrett brought Calais down with them." Viv removed her shawl and sat with a gentle sigh as she looked around with a smile of anticipation and excitement.

For the seating to work effectively, Naomi would be next to Rick at the table, making eating easier because their elbows wouldn't collide. It also meant she and Kevin would occasionally bump elbows, but Kevin had become adept at dining while sitting beside a lefty (much like Viv); it wasn't a big deal. Naomi chided herself for taking selfish pride in having something in common with Rick that Viv didn't: left-handedness.

Over the next few minutes, Patrice, Garrett, Louise, and Tim arrived, completing the party group for Naomi's table. Leslie's mentors, Joy and Brendan, were in attendance, too, at another table. Naomi entertained orchestrating a swap-out of the Collins couple at her table for the Giles couple.

Everyone stood around the table, still in various forms of greeting and small talk, when an aged woman approached. Dressed in a conservative but shiny navy-blue sheath, her gray hair curled and set, she paused in front of Rick, running her eyes over him as any woman of a certain elderly age was entitled to do without comment from anyone even an hour younger. "Well, aren't you *Mister Adonis*? The Lord done used His *good knife* to carve you up, son!" She touched his arm and continued looking him over, nodding her approval. "Yes, *indeed*. Used all your mama and daddy's good genes."

Rick, of course, blushed to high heaven, looking almost pained. He shook his head. "I'm noth—"

Viv linked her arm in Rick's and smiled at the woman, cutting her husband off, her eyes sparking similar sadness and pain underneath the determined brightness. "Thank you very much, ma'am. That's so nice of you to say." Rick's response was habitual and ingrained—but Viv's habit was not allowing him to express the rote response (whatever it was).

The grandam smiled back with a nod, sending her critical gaze among the rest of the group (her eyes paused on Viv with clear approval). Satisfied, she touched Rick's arm again and moved on.

NAOMI (7:03 p.m.)

Curtis "Up-Owl-Nite" Devereaux kept the smooth jazz going while guests greeted and nibbled (before his R&B slow jams and mid-tempo grooves started).

They stood near their table, ladies grouped and talking, their partners nearby doing their men-talk thing, everyone enjoying the atmosphere. Even Louise was on her best behavior.

Naomi sipped her glass of merlot, almost spitting and spraying those around her upon seeing Oscar Brooks approach them. She swallowed her wine, but still almost choked. Her stomach turned with borderline revulsion; she'd been so happy not seeing him. This, apparently, was what Cecily needed anti-anxiety meds for.

I'll be damned.

He looked in her face as he stepped up, but didn't speak, smiling at Viv instead. He complimented Viv's attire, all the ladies looking at him with a curious wariness (mildly amused, if anything). Although turned away from Viv, Rick was within reach and earshot, his shoulder very near Viv's; he undoubtedly picked up on Oscar's flirty interaction.

Ignoring Naomi, Oscar tried naming Viv's hairstyle (chignon) correctly, but kept fumbling the words, pronouncing all kinds of unheard-of variations. Naomi smirked as, meanwhile, Rick inconspicuously extended his hand backward toward Viv, who discreetly linked their fingers down low. Leslie smirked, too (likely because Oscar didn't notice).

Oscar continued making it a point to ignore Naomi, suggesting he didn't care about her, but his actions only served the opposite. He then shifted to commenting on how good the ladies looked (Naomi recognized being excluded, which was fine), soon concentrating his compliments on Viv, saying how good she looked in her dress, now trying to name the style of dress she wore and again failing miserably without warrant (*sheath* wasn't much to fumble over). Naomi deliberated the level of restraint her brother used.

Rick divided his attention for as long as he could before he'd had enough. He turned to them, lifting their linked fingers for Oscar to see. "Whatever style hair or dress it is, it's mine." He was annoyed, not fully angry; even so, it looked good on him; the angles of his tux accentuated the angles of annoyance in his handsome face.

Now, instead of that man apologizing for overstepping with his compliments and full-on flirting with another man's wife, Oscar Brooks grew angry himself. His eyes turned mean as he now gritted on the woman he so tried to impress seconds ago. He glanced at Rick before starting away. "Sloppy seconds, anyway. Uppity cunt."

Patrice gasped. Garrett turned their way. So did Kevin, Trevor, and Tim. Louise's eyes widened with shock. Leslie's mouth hung open with the same.

Naomi lowered her head with a shake: Oscar didn't want to square-up with Rick.

Viv didn't appear as shocked as the others (perhaps she sensed his type), but she leaned on Rick, semi-restraining him. "He was only flirting, Rick. Now his feelings are hurt. Pay him no mind."

Rick gazed at his wife before pecking her lips. He nodded and turned back to the men, resuming conversation.

And Naomi hoped that was the end of it.

However, all hope was lost because, true to form, Oscar couldn't let it go. Several feet away, Oscar continued running his mouth to his cronies, calling Rick "Home Skillet" and adding more offensive comments about Viv, such that others now turned heads his way (including security, who looked akin to secret service agents).

Rick lifted his left hand, using two fingers to beckon Oscar back.

Naomi grew uneasy—for Oscar.

Oscar, wearing an expression of bravado and something else, began making his way back to them.

Viv touched Rick's arm. "No, Rick. I don't want you doing anything that'll send you b—"

"It's okay, Viv. I'm not go'n do anything to separate us ever again. But I've seen his type in prison, baby. I got this."

Oscar Brooks stepped up, sweating and still annoyed. "I'm here. You and what army got something to say?" He was Napoléon Bonaparte in a tired tux.

Kevin, Garrett, Tim, Louise, Patrice, and Leslie stepped back. Trevor, however, focused on Rick, while Naomi stayed close to Viv. Security aimed eyes in their direction.

Rick eased in front of Viv. "I'm an army of one."

Oscar scoffed, puffing air through his lips.

"What's your name, man?" Rick spoke calmly, almost too calmly. Not a good sign.

"'Oscar.' Why?" A white mint gleamed in contrast to his tongue and teeth as it shifted in his mouth.

"Well, you were over there, appearing as if needing to be exorcised. Figured I'd best know your name."

Oscar frowned with, impossibly, more annoyance. "I don't need any exercise. I'm fine."

Rick's eyes remained steady, but a tiny smirk of sarcasm showed the dimple in his cheek. He could have mocked Oscar's misunderstanding of words. Even when angry, the man used diplomacy. He peered at Oscar. "You drunk, Oscar?"

"No."

"Good: there shouldn't be any problem understanding me."

Naomi and Viv were within earshot as Rick leaned toward Oscar's ear. "Oscar, I'm not your 'Home Skillet.' Clear? But hey, come at me all you want, man. I'm right here." He jerked his head toward an exit. "We can go outside, and I can address all your vim and vigor out there under dark cover of night..." Rick then shifted his posture to be more eye-to-eye with Oscar. "...But if you insult my wife again, I will snap your fucking neck in the light of day."

Rick grew quieter with increasing anger instead of louder, so his voice dropped lower as he spoke. Her brother's gaze was steady. He didn't flinch, twitch, or stutter: he meant every syllable (and thus threatening his never-separating-from-Viv-again statement). He didn't rub the scar on his ear, either. Rick resumed his full height, making Oscar look up at him. He stepped back, waiting.

Naomi checked around for Cecily but didn't see her.

Oscar stared, his mouth a line of anger as he battled being prideful versus being sensible.

Eyes on Oscar, Rick shook his head, then leaned close again. "You don't know me, man. And I don't know you."

Oscar huffed an attitude of agreement. "Damn straight."

Rick looked away before bringing his gaze back to Oscar. "But I *do know me*. Fall back, man. Don't put this to the test."

Oscar's eyes registered alarm before he recovered with a look of smarmy contrition. He added a simpering chuckle, and Naomi wanted to vomit. "Hey, I'm sorry, bruh. Seriously. I'm chained down, too." He raised his left hand, showing his wedding band, not realizing that made everything worse. "But I saw her, and she's just— So, I lost my head for a second. Sorry."

Rick didn't readily speak in either acceptance or rejection of Oscar's words, simply keeping those golden-auburn eyes on him (those irises much redder now). "Yeah, okay."

With the situation cooling, security and other eyes turned away.

Oscar nodded and moved to approach Viv and apologize, but Rick shifted, blocking him. "That's unnecessary."

Oscar shrugged, annoyance back on his face. "I was just gonna—"

Rick looked upward, exasperated. "Man, I swear t' God!" He glared at Oscar, speaking low, his irises almost a pure red as anger pushed through more. "...In the light of day."

New alarm filled Oscar's eyes again before the smarmy contrition returned. He put a hand of apology up at Rick and now acknowledged her. "Hey, Doctor Alexander."

"Oscar." She started to reply with, *Mister Brooks*, but that suggested a level of respect for him she didn't have.

Oscar glanced at Viv and headed away.

Viv gently pulled Rick away, having him sit. She rubbed his back and hair as everyone listened to Rick gritting his teeth. Viv did look incredible in that dress. The back of her dress was cut out, exposing even-toned butterscotch-caramel skin and refined, muscular curvature showing the woman worked out.

Rick sighed, surveying those still standing. "Sorry about that. Truly. But dudes like him are such anathema to me." He looked away, shaking his head. "I am *not* well-handled." He wasn't, either: anger still etched his features.

Kevin sat. "He took you there, man. No apologies needed."

Garrett, Trevor, and Tim sat with agreeing scoffs.

Rick sent her a curious but unhappy frown. "You *know* him?"

Naomi returned a subtle headshake. "Let's not."

Rick turned away again.

Viv kissed her husband's temple. "I shouldn't say this, but you look good when angry, baby."

Rick scoffed. "Then I must be drop-dead gorgeous right now."

Naomi joined the others in a chuckle.

Rick, honey, you'd be drop-dead gorgeous...sitting on a rock.

Viv continued caressing Rick's head. "You know 'Oscar' is too short to ride this ride."

Everyone snickered.

Viv then trailed a finger over Rick's facial features. "He's gotta be...this tall, and this complexion, have this cleft, and this scar, and have...these eyes..."

Rick blushed before sending Viv a sideways smirk. "Yeah, but *Larenz Tate* can ride."

Viv pecked his lips, smirking back. "Well, riding privileges *are* up to the discretion of the ride attendant."

"Uh-huh." Rick laughed.

Viv laughed, too, taking Rick's hand. "Come on." She led Rick out of the main ballroom, toward the other rooms of the estate.

NAOMI (7:29 p.m.)

"The recuperative period for our patients is much shorter now with the new procedure, so I believe it's the best way to go..." Althea smiled as she touched Naomi's arm.

"Uh-huh..." Naomi searched for escape. The Oscar fiasco was behind them, but she couldn't stomach Althea's dribble, either. Althea was Dr. Burris's wife. Wife, but not a doctor herself. Dr. Burris was the dermatologist. Althea didn't have patients, didn't administer any "new procedures," so Naomi took offense to her speaking as if she understood patient care with the level a practicing physician did. Dr. Burris may have shared his medical perspective with Althea during pillow-talk—but pillow-talk did not a doctor make.

Searching for Kevin or Leslie, or heck, even Trevor for an escape excuse, Naomi spotted Louise sitting at their table. Tim was at the bar with Garrett. Patrice sat at the table, too, but was deep in her cellphone. Louise focused intently elsewhere, so Naomi followed Louise's line of sight. Louise stared hard at Rick and Viv socializing with others. The couple was having a good time, smiling and conferring with each other while talking and laughing with two other couples (Rick's hand on the small of Viv's back). Louise's forlorn expression ticked Naomi off. She started to go over to Louise and take Kevin's tickets back—or Louise's ticket, mainly; Tim could stay.

Naomi also noticed another woman circling the room. She'd been on Naomi's radar since first spotting her, because this woman also concentrated her energies, not on socializing with others or dancing, but on watching Rick and Viv Phillips.

Althea continued her end of the discussion, Naomi nodding on cue.

Naomi turned attention away from an irritating Louise, seeing the perfect (and expected) escape heading her way.

"Hi, Naomi! Imagine this!" Cecily smiled too hard; she was nervous.

"I can say this has been most unexpected, yes. How are you?"

Cecily glanced at Althea before looking at Naomi. "Can I talk to you? Privately?"

Naomi touched fake-doctor Althea's elbow. "Pardon us." She guided Cecily away sans introductions. Kevin's reminder not to work blared in her mind, but Naomi smiled to herself: she was a banana.

She found a low-traffic spot in an alcove by the billiard room. Wishing she had a glass of...anything, Naomi smiled up at Cecily. "What's up?" She kept her tone upbeat and social, and less, well, work-like.

Her patient stood before her in an embroidered mesh off-the-shoulder A-line gown of deep bronze. Beautiful floral-embroidered mesh skimmed over the A-line silhouette, creating a pleasantly shadowy look. The notched sweetheart neckline added to the overall effect. Usually styled with full curl, Cecily's hair was bone-straight and parted on one side. Her makeup combined gold and champagne highlights to complement the bronze. This departure from her usual look created a sense of sophisticated drama about her appearance, pushing her true beauty forward. She pointed her jewel-toned minaudière in the ballroom's direction, her asymmetric necklace of various brown stones shining in the light. "He's here. Joshua is here!" She displayed flustered and excited and apprehensive and anxious.

Naomi nodded and shook her head in one motion. "Joshua...?" This scenario reminded her of those teen movies and the prom scene where Cecily was the shy, lonely high-schooler, and this "Joshua" person was prom king. "'Joshua' is here. Okay. What do you need?" She didn't know who "Joshua" was, but Cecily's demeanor dictated she care.

Cecily drew back with confused surprise at her response, obviously unused to anyone asking about her needs. "I...I don't know. Nothing, I guess. But he's *here*, and I..." She took a deep breath. "I don't know."

"But it's throwing you off."

Cecily dipped her chin almost shakily.

"Who is he?"

"Joshua Hall: JAH Technologies, Incorporated. We work together, or rather, I work for him."

From the sound, *work together* was more accurate than *work for*. "And you like him." Both knew she didn't mean casually.

She flinched before something close to panic jumped into those artificial lenses. "He's my boss."

Naomi took that as a yes.

Her patient did a great deal of withholding information about Oscar and the abusive goings-on in her marriage (she didn't fully acknowledge it as abuse yet herself). Oscar's spun such an expansive six, seven-year-long web of lies: lies reinforcing the idea Cecily was irrational, imagining things, over-sensitive, or all the above. His lies also carried an underlying message: Cecily had not right nor reason to be bothered by what was happening in the marriage. After six or seven years of it, it's become ingrained in Cecily's thought process, her belief system. Naomi continued probing Cecily about her early years with Oscar, about her life *before* Oscar. Cecily sometimes grew exasperated with the exercise, not understanding there was a method to Naomi's madness.

In the last few sessions, Cecily owned up to knowing the anger Marcus and Chelsea have with her comes from her unwillingness to be real with them, saying she's always giving Oscar a benefit of the doubt he doesn't deserve. They've never liked him, but like him even less because of how their mother protects his image. Withholding information about Oscar and avoiding discussion about him remains a defense mechanism whereby Cecily attempts to prevent family conflict—but the Coopers (Cecily, Marcus, and Chelsea) were only aware of that to the extent they experienced it.

Cecily was doing something similar regarding Joshua, but this withholding defense mechanism centered around avoiding *internal* conflict. Naomi now watched her patient work through that conflict: her eyes darted around, a smile nearly forming before her lips drew downward, and the smile almost forming again.

Finally, Cecily eased out a hitched breath. She looked down, nodding faintly but not hesitantly. "I do, Naomi. I'm sorry." She lifted her head, her eyes teary with distress.

"Well, good for you." She meant that in a way only another psychiatrist would understand, having nothing to do with encouraging infidelity.

Cecily shook her head. "No, it's not. It's wrong."

"It is, and it isn't. But if you're devoting yourself to your husband. You need to begin redirecting your feelings for Joshua."

"That's gonna be..." Eyes wide, Cecily released a breath indicating the apparent impossibility of that task. Her posture straightened. "You're right. I'm not being fair to Oscar. Despite...everything..." She frowned, that internal conflict doing its thing, before she exhaled. "I mean, I know he has my best interests at heart."

"Saying those words and feeling them are two different things, Cecily." It was a gentle reinforcement of the concept of being *safe*: an underlying theme of her treatment.

Cecily's gaze was indecipherable. "We both know Oscar's not the warmest person." She frowned again. "Maybe if I just learn to be more..."

Naomi held her tongue, wondering why Oscar wasn't the one learning to be more of something. Cecily certainly did her fair share.

Cecily's eyes lit with an excited worry. "What am I going to do?"

"Enjoy the ball. Did you take those anti-anxiety meds?" It didn't look like it, but that could be deceiving.

Cecily shook her head and lifted her minaudière, meaning the pills were in there. "Not yet."

"Drinking?"

"So far, a glass of champagne."

Naomi held out her hand. "Seems you've chosen your coping mechanism. I'll take those. You shouldn't do both."

Cecily turned the pills over. "So, just ignore everything?"

"For now. Act normally, go with the flow. You have a few hours left to navigate. You can manage that."

Cecily's eyes narrowed. "Next session."

"Of course. So, be prepared."

Nodding, her patient smiled. "To learn how to 'redirect.'"

"Among other things." She had something more drastic in store but would work the Joshua stuff in if the session allowed.

The drastic measures planned for the upcoming session should give Cecily what she needed to take a critical step toward escape. Her job didn't stop with helping Cecily recover from the PTSD or the NAS but extended to educating Cecily about the traits and effects of narcissistic abuse and how to avoid and counter. Having that newfound understanding and knowledge about the intricacies of gaslighting would only facilitate giving Cecily back her good reality and restore her internal power such that, in the future, she'd be able to recognize signs of narcissism coming her way and be ready to guard against re-victimization. But the explosive element to it all...was the home invasion. And the next session would focus on nothing but.

Cecily smiled, giving Naomi the once-over. "You look nice, Naomi! I like the finger coils with highlights."

Naomi almost chuckled at Cecily's surprise. "Thank you. You look nice, too."

"You don't have to say that."

"I know."

Cecily gave her a look. "Right. You don't work that way. Thank you. So,...ditched the eyeglasses for the gala? Letting us see those brown peepers!" Her excitement was authentic, but still marked with anxiety.

Naomi held in another chuckle. "Something like that. ...Ready?"

"Yes. I know. I'm sorry. I'm taking you away from enjoying the ball, worrying you with my—"

"It's fine, Cecily. Stop it."

"Okay. Thanks, Naomi."

"...You've established power-of-attorney, executor-of-estate?"

Cecily frowned. "Yeah...?"

Unable to discern Oscar's designations (if any) from Cecily's noncommittal response, Naomi nodded.

"Well, here goes..." Her patient turned to head back into the ballroom, but Naomi paused her. "What's the matter?"

Naomi held her gaze, curious about Cecily's reaction to what she was about to say. "Get your own food and drink, monitor it. Accept nothing from Oscar." She doubted Oscar would be so courteous as to bring his wife refreshment, but just in case. She waited.

To Naomi's surprise, Cecily nodded and patted her shoulder, a knowing understanding of the request in her eyes. "I got you." Her eyes then reflected a sad anger before she turned and walked away.

NAOMI (7:53 p.m.)

Up-Owl-Nite was in full swing now, smooth jazz over, dedications rocking, slow and mid-tempo R&B rolling.

Among a myriad of group and selfie photo opportunities, Naomi hugged Kevin around the waist and smiled, taking part in Leslie's round of picture-taking frenzy. Viv returned from the car with her camera and took pictures alongside Leslie, her photographs capturing the entire night—not just the people at their table. Folk used their cellphones for pics, too; lights going off all over the place.

With Viv's attention elsewhere as she captured this shot or that one, Naomi noted Rick often running his eyes over his wife, taking her in from head to toe with a masculine gaze blending love, pride, and arousal. Other times, his gaze at her was softer, and his gentle smiles conveyed genuine interest in her while she was otherwise engaged. Although not meant to be observed, those looks at Viv were sweet.

Naomi understood the frequent requests to get pics of Rick and Viv, to pose with Mr. and Mrs. "Hollywood," but watching Louise, she also had the distinct feeling Louise would later, alone in a quiet spot, review her pics, zooming in and gazing at only one-half of the couple.

She'd also since learned that the woman on her radar all evening was Lynelle Bowden.

Viv identified her after Naomi brought the woman's behavior to her attention. Naomi kept eyes on Lynelle, seeing the woman did little else but keep her eyes on the Phillipses. Lynelle didn't skulk around the ballroom, but her behavior was still creepy and...stalker-like. The woman wasn't unattractive but paled compared to Viv. She wondered if Viv was pleased or annoyed Rick didn't cheat "up." Seeing Lynelle also revealed Rick wasn't about looks (he discounted his own), but in that same vein, he wasn't looking to replace the love of his life.

Naomi sometimes marveled at her ability to have eyes and analysis everywhere. She'd been trained in it, spent medical school specializing in developing the ability to see more than what was before her, to analyze bits of everything in the people around her: body language, facial cues, verbal cues in snippets of conversation. The ability was second nature, but she needed to not cast the net wide at an event like this; there was too much potential for sensory overload—she'd be the one needing a counsel couch before the evening was done.

One would think (if they knew about them) another source of over-stimulation for her would be hundreds of auras flickering, a virtual rainbow of color before her. But Naomi realized long ago: her aura-flickers happened with people relatively still. Too much movement interfered with the transmission or something, which was fine; this was God's ride: she was simply a contented passenger.

Kevin finished his lobster-toast-with-avocado hors d'oeuvre and sipped his vodka tonic to wash it down. "We've only danced once tonight. Is that your plan: one and done?" He smiled, those teeth showing in bright contrast to his carob-brown skin, those saddle-brown eyes sparkling with male interest at her (fetching).

Naomi shook her head, sipping her glass of water flavored with fresh, sweet strawberries. "No. I love Curtis's finale, so there's that..." She formed a sly smile. "But I can fit in a slow dance or two."

He finished his tonic with a look. "Or two. And you're working."

Naomi shrugged. "I'm a banana." She laughed, unable to help it.

Her significant other laughed with her without needing the reason why, and Naomi was glad they'd brought things back; she'd missed him.

CECILY (7:53 p.m.)

She watched her doctor smile and take pictures with the people at her table, watched her sitting and talking with her date, able to reconcile seeing Naomi in a social setting, but still unable to get a read on her; Naomi still wasn't an easy read. Her attire for the evening, however, was on point. Naomi's midnight-blue lace off-the-shoulder gown had a semi-sweetheart neckline, beaded sides, and a high-low hem to complement her petite form (along with three-inch pointed-toe T-straps). Crystal-and-pearl-topped geometric crochet created intriguing detail on the sides. Her sapphire jewelry provided the perfect offsetting touch. Naomi in heels and a skirt wasn't new; she wore suits and such in session, but this was an altogether different setup.

With a mild grin, Cecily sipped her glass of zinfandel and shifted her attention to the rest of the gala activity. This was her third drink, but who was counting? Cecily giggled to herself and sipped. Apparently, she was: she was a numbers girl, after all.

She dabbled in critiquing fashions as she sat alone at her table, taking in those dancing, talking, eating, flirting, and laughing. Only a few men wore bowties with their tuxes (including Josh); the majority wore formal Windsor knots (to her, a rather tired, less formal trend). And, men opting for the cummerbund, she'd only seen three men with waistcoats tonight (one sat at Naomi's table). Cummerbunds were fine—but only if black or midnight-blue. Wearing colored ties and cummerbunds to match a dress was tacky to her, not formal, but whatever. She wasn't a fan of the monochrome look in formalwear, either: it lacked imagination. Naomi's date and Joshua wore double-breasted tuxedos, negating the need for a stupid cummerbund.

Cecily took a long draw of wine and covered her mouth to contain a tiny belch. Most of the women did a lot of off-the-shoulders, plunging necklines, and mermaids; only a select few were in sheaths or A-lines (like herself). Janyce wore a mermaid dress: a fuchsia off-the-shoulder satin and tulle mermaid gown. Janyce wasn't a drama-queen, but that fuchsia dress carried a bit of drama by its very existence. Those dresses normally flattered a woman's figure—even a full-figured one—but the fit and size had to be right: Janyce's wasn't. Her hair looked stylish, though: the locks knotted and twisted into a flattering upsweep. Those five-inch fuchsia peep-toe ankle-strap platforms weren't flattering and only made Janyce look like a big, bright...pink. Janyce waved her Chanel pouch in pure advertisement, but no one cared; tonight was about the charities.

She'd say none of this to Janyce, of course.

Yeah, people-watching and fashion-critiquing while sipping the good stuff was better than wondering why she sat alone at a table for ten people, better than *knowing* why she sat alone at the table.

Drinking won't solve anything, Cecily.

Cecily took another swallow of zinfandel, glad she picked up two glasses. She wasn't looking for solutions: simple suppression would be enough for the next few hours. And she had a lot to suppress. She needed to avoid thinking too much about what happened to her (then and now), suppress ruminating about why it happened to her and how it could've been prevented. Thinking about those things only led to fretting over who was to blame and who should be punished for it.

And there was the unsettling dilemma of Josh's presence at the ball.

A little champagne or wine would keep all that at bay. Besides, she wasn't a drinker like that—just for tonight—which was why her three drinks (number four on standby) already felt like twice that many.

She spotted her husband near the entrance with other men, laughing his head off. She knew he'd renege on that black box of promises he made the night that belt buckle came down. And maybe she should have been tired of hoping and believing in him by now, but she wasn't yet. Oscar was her husband, and it was nicer once upon a time; it was. She saw no reason they couldn't get back to that. A part of her also believed they were too far along in the nightmare version to go back. But maybe, once his health improved, so would other things.

He seems fine now. Sweating, but fine. Whooping it up.

Janyce seemed fine, too, as she talked with one of their neighbors (and a member of their table party). Cecily remembered seeing her at the New Year's party.

An odd thought about Oscar occurred. Cecily sucked her teeth. Oscar watched her while they kissed but avoided looking at her whenever telling her he loved her (*Back at you.*). How...interesting. All kinds of things popped into your head when you were three glasses in.

Done with fighting the inevitable, Cecily eyed Joshua standing near his table. She watched him engage in talk, trying not to be jealous over the ladies coming up to him, vying for his attention.

Was she just drawn to Josh because of her unhappiness in her marriage? Would any man look better in her eyes compared to Oscar right now? Cecily didn't know the answers, and the wine wouldn't let her ponder it too deeply, but she doubted Joshua would want her—not if he knew...everything.

Just then, the deejay played "Beautiful" by Joe as an anonymous dedication, and she startled with instant memory. She did her best not to look for Josh, but her best wasn't good enough. He smiled at her with a nod toward Up-Owl-Nite, as if suggesting the song was for her. Instead of doing what she wanted to do (rise and join him for a dance or conversation), Cecily smiled, nodded, and turned away with a sip.

He said it was "Unsuccessful"...

That revelation bubbled-up repeatedly lately—and Cecily sent it (and all its implications) away just as repeatedly.

She resumed staring in Oscar's direction, allowing her disappointment and irritation to do their own mix-and-mingle with her inebriation. He looked stylish at the Mabry party, but when not donning a sweatsuit, Oscar sometimes had bamma-fied taste, often shooting for couture extremes and ending up looking tacky. She didn't get to experience the occasional spousal thrill of picking out something for her man to wear for her—not since Roland. Cecily watched Oscar and scoffed.

Although his tie was a bowtie (she'd insisted), it was the only concession he granted. Besides the knot being pre-tied, she hated the bronze color. That bronze cummerbund was upside down (pleats facing downward) and was cold wrong, but her man didn't care. She found a trace of positive about that piece of in-your-face attitude. She bought him a brand-new tuxedo: one peaked instead of shawl, with two side vents instead of that poor-taste single one (although no-vent was topnotch), and the pockets were jetted—and not with flaps (like the one he wore now). But that tuxedo stayed covered and hanging...in *her* closet. Oscar wasn't a sentimental guy, but was attached to the tuxedo he'd purchased.

Cecily took another sip and shook her head. His trousers showed too much break. He wore derbies, refusing to wear the whole-cut balmorals she bought, with his stubborn claim she was trying to change him.

She was the one changed, not him.

Cecily sipped from that third glass, feeling better about it all by the time she got to the bottom.

NAOMI (8:15 p.m.)

With another four hours to go (if they stayed that long), Naomi went over to Cecily and pulled that fourth glass away with a kind warning, almost motherly. If Cecily had taken the anti-anxiety meds, the need for the alcohol, Cecily's need for alcohol to drown her sorrows would've been reduced. Naomi, however, wasn't her mother: if Cecily stayed the remaining hours and didn't heed her warning, she'd be wasted by party's end. But she hadn't gone back to the bar for another.

Keeping one eye cocked on her patient, Naomi stood near the rear entrance chatting about a local news story with Viv, Leslie, Louise, and Patrice. Naomi sensed Louise wanting to reconnect with Viv, but Viv wasn't having it; she was cordial and semi-friendly, but it was nothing Naomi imagined it would be if Louise's inappropriate feelings for Rick hadn't come to light. And although Patrice engaged in discussion, she had a chip on her shoulder. She met Patrice when she came down to help Viv after the birth of RJ. Naomi didn't like her then, and things hadn't improved much.

"—tro buses and the subway. So, I don't know." Leslie bounced a shoulder in indifference.

"If they want to raise fares—" Viv started, but she turned with Rick's touch as he stepped up from behind.

He kissed her cheek. "Sorry to interrupt. Go'n visit the billiard room, play a little pool." He withdrew his money clip from his pocket and handed it toward his wife. "Hold this for me."

Viv grinned. "Think you'll lose it all?"

Rick's lips formed a sloped grin. "I hadn't planned to gamble, but now..." He pulled a twenty from the clip before handing it over.

The couple laughed as Viv slipped Rick's money clip inside her clutch.

Tim, mimicking Rick, plucked a twenty from his wallet before handing it to Louise. Rick, however, had it right: men didn't carry wallets when wearing a tuxedo. "Bringing back double, Lou. Don't worry."

Everyone laughed, and Naomi spotted Kevin and Garrett waiting and chatting outside the billiard room. She'd relieved Kevin of his wallet before they left her house.

Louise nudged her husband. "I think you and Richard Alden nee—"

"Man! Why're you middle-naming me?!" Rick's expression was jovial-smirk, but Naomi also recognized irritation—even with the smile.

Viv's expression was hard to read.

Louise smirked back, and it was so near a flirting expression, Patrice raised an eyebrow. "It's your name."

Naomi kept a straight face as her daughter surreptitiously tugged her dress with unhappy at Louise. Naomi was just glad Louise didn't use "Stannis."

Rick nodded. "That it is."

Patrice leaned forward, speaking to Rick and Viv. "But giving her your money: does it have something to do with your probation?"

"No. But instead of worrying about my probation, worry about paying back that seventy-five hundred you owe us."

Patrice's lip curled with surprised, angry embarrassment. "You mean, that I owe *Viv*. And you didn't have to put that out there."

Viv eyed her sister for long seconds. "No, Rick said it right: that you owe *us*. That money came from our joint account. And you didn't have to bring up his probation."

Rick kissed Viv's cheek, adding a sweet grin. "Anyway. Wanna play?"

Viv sent him a flirtatious smirk but shook her head. "No. Men's business. I'm good. Besides..."

Rick's grin broadened. "We're playing some next weekend."

Viv pecked his lips. "With Ellery and Nedra, yes."

A sad jealousy crossed Louise's face, while something sad and wistful crossed Patrice's.

"A'ight." Rick kissed Viv's cheek again and headed away.

Louise called after them. "*One* game: Tim, Ricky."

Leslie gripped Naomi's arm, Patrice drew back, and Viv bit her bottom lip as Rick returned, his expression saying it all as Tim followed.

Louise's eyes widened with her step back upon seeing Rick's face.

Rick maneuvered past everyone to lean close to Louise. "I'm saying this *once*, Lou: No one, *no one*, calls me 'Ricky' but Vivian. I will not acknowledge nor respond positively to anyone else who does. Are we clear?" He pulled back, maintaining eye contact with Louise.

Louise lowered her head. Her subtle nod in reply held apology, embarrassment, and disappointment.

Tim stepped closer. "Is there a problem?" Louise was out of bounds, and everyone knew it, but Tim still attempted to do his job as her husband.

"No." Rick regarded him, his gaze direct as he reached for Viv's hand.

Tim Collins lowered his gaze with a hand to his wife's shoulder, backing down from that golden-auburn stare that had right to be outraged and protective over something personal between him and his wife.

If anything, Louise's violations were her way of connecting to Rick by one, acknowledging she knew his middle name, and two, using Viv's loving name for him. The "Alden" thing wasn't such a big deal (people often middle-name someone in fun). But calling him "Ricky,"... Naomi was surprised Viv hadn't knocked Louise to the floor before Rick turned back. Her friend was straight-no-chaser, and she'd seen signs of Viv's Delaware roots before, but tonight, Viv was all about the tasteful and peaceful—good for her.

Seeing Kevin frowning from a distance and starting to head back, Naomi waved him off and addressed the others, especially Tim and Rick. "That's enough. You two, go play pool if you're going."

Rick sighed. "You're right, Sis. This isn't fun." He placed his free hand on her waist and kissed her cheek. "Thank you." He then turned to his wife and kissed her lips before giving Tim a nod. "Come on, man." He started away, but Louise's touch to his arm paused him.

Louise glanced Viv's way. "Just Naomi and Viv get kisses?"

Leslie shifted, frowning with lips parted, but Naomi held her back.

Patrice frowned. "Yes, Louise."

Tim decided the chandeliers required scrutiny.

Once again, Viv's expression was hard to read: tasteful and peaceful to the hilt.

Rick shook his head at his sister-in-law to quell her annoyance. "It's fine, Pat." He then acquiesced to keep the peace, giving Louise, Leslie, and Patrice kisses on their cheek (it was such an awkward gesture). Rick kissed Viv again, his lips on hers for extended seconds.

"Why'd you kiss Viv again, Rick?" Leslie snickered and smirked as if knowing the answer.

Rick sent Les a charming grin in response. "My mouth needs to touch Viv last." He winked at Leslie and started away, but now Viv paused him.

Viv guided him closer. "I wasn't finished." Rick's initial blush lessened with Viv's repeated gentle pecks to his lips.

Everyone issued teasing commentary (except Louise, which Naomi understood perfectly).

Rick drew his arms around Viv's waist, and Naomi sensed the couple getting into it. Their pecks exhibited rather hot—leaving you wanting to see more.

Leslie echoed a similar, more direct sentiment. "Kiss! Kiss for real!"

"Leslie..."

The couple didn't use tongues. Instead, Viv caressed Rick's head, and he went to play pool, Tim in tow. They watched the men in silence, Naomi believing all took in Rick's bowed legs and slightly pigeon-toed walk. The man walked with head held high and an assertive swagger, confident and determined but not prideful.

Lynelle came up to him as Rick neared the ballroom exit.

"That bitch!" Patrice stepped in their direction, but Viv put a hand to her sister's middle with a headshake, doing more tasteful-peaceful.

Watching Rick's interaction with Lynelle, Naomi peeped Viv, who caught her eye and smiled. "No worries over here. I'm fine."

She was.

Patrice scowled and scoffed, not getting Viv's tasteful-peaceful.

Rick looked back at Viv and winked, and Viv sighed. "Unh. Case in point." She winked back and kissed at him with a chuckle, blending with Naomi's, Leslie's, and Patrice's. Louise was understandably quiet: no words would do just yet.

Leslie readjusted her jewel-toned earring. "You two are, like, perfect together." Her Aegean-blue asymmetric notched neckline crepe mermaid gown fit her taller-than-average form well, the notches in the unique one-shoulder styling reflecting Leslie's artistic leaning. The entire cherry-colored tint to her hair was gone now, leaving more of her natural dark-brown roots, with an Ombré frohawk style speaking volumes. Tall for a woman, Leslie wore matching kitten heels instead of multi-inchers to remain shorter than Trevor. Naomi guessed those things mattered to her daughter, after all.

Viv sucked her teeth. "Girl, Rick still gets on my nerves. Ask Naomi."

Naomi nodded with a chuckle, seeing Louise roll her eyes upward with a low scoff of jealousy. Of course, Rick wasn't perfect, but the only real complaint she'd ever heard Viv make about her man was Rick's occasional moodiness, that she didn't like whenever he opted to sulk awhile before talking something out with her. Irritating, sure, but small potatoes compared to what some women contended with. Naomi had yet to see this moody sulking, so Rick likely only shared that side of himself with his best friend; he was quite personable around others.

"Dude definitely gets on my nerves sometimes." Viv looked over at Rick: now talking to other guests. He wouldn't get to play pool at this rate. He then smiled at something, and Viv whipped back to them. "But I'ma fuck 'im!"

Everyone laughed but Patrice. "No need to be vulgar, Viv." The chip was back on her shoulder (whatever it was). Three years older than Viv and that same number in inches shorter, Patrice's complexion was lighter, but her features were much less delicate than Viv's. Naomi saw similarity around their eyes and chin areas.

Viv gritted on her sister but didn't respond, looking at Leslie with a gaze reinforcing her original statement.

Leslie grinned with a nod. "If you don't mind me saying, Viv, the thing where he puts his fingers to your waist..." Leslie raised an eyebrow with her unvoiced but obvious question.

Viv scanned their group for several seconds before focusing on Leslie. "UPS, girl. With occasional FedEx when I need it." She tried containing her blush.

Naomi chuckled with her daughter, while Patrice and Louise looked puzzled. Despite their funky attitudes, their outfits were flattering.

Louise ventured outside the dark formal hues with a strapless sand-stone-orange high-low satin dress with side pockets and box pleats carrying a bit of fun with its glamour. She wore her hair in a round bob with a swooping front bang that somehow emphasized her Asian features. She accessorized the sandstone-orange with two-inch cream pointed-toe sling-backs matching her wristlet, and a choker with orange and cream stones.

Patrice dressed more seasonal with a moss-green embellished waist off-the-shoulder satin ball gown with lapel sleeves and a pleated bodice. Her statement collar of green stones offset the V of her neckline and complemented the shimmering embellishment at her middle. Her sling-backs were black two-inch platforms, and she styled her hair in a curly bob. The way she gripped her moss-green envelope clutch signaled how much internal tension she carried about...something.

Patrice's brow bent with snooty attitude. "Why're we talking about couriers and mail? I thought Leslie was hinting at...you know." They knew, but was Patrice such a prude, she couldn't say (at minimum) "sex"?

Naomi cleared the confusion. "It's a euphemism for a man's sexual ability, Patrice—how he 'delivers the package,' so to speak, regardless of how big his 'package' is."

Patrice smirked. "Oh."

Viv explained further: "Yeah. Does he take his time to deliver it right to the front door, ringing the bell and waiting to ensure you receive it? That's a good thing: taking his time, grinding nicely, and holding his climax for as long as possible to continue giving you pleasure."

Leslie chimed in. "Or does he just drop it out of the truck and pull off—the package isn't even on the porch? This is rushed sex, where he comes too fast and leaves his partner unsatisfied."

Louise and Patrice nodded, eyes dancing with the intake of info.

"No orgasm?" Viv shook her head. "Well, he delivered the package, but you weren't home—and the good stuff was stolen."

The ladies laughed low but knowingly.

Naomi summed it up. "A FedEx delivery is more like a very satisfying quickie—delivered right on time. A UPS delivery is a man delivering Undeniable, Unbelievable, Ultimate, or Unique Pussy Satisfaction. ...The 'U' is up to you."

Grinning hard, Leslie winked. "Because FedEx can deliver UPS!"

The ladies hollered and headed back to their table. As they walked, Naomi noted the varied mating games taking place (although most were already married and thus mated): men posturing and posing, women flirting and preening...

OSCAR (8:23 p.m.)

"A'ight, man. Let me get on back in there: do my husband shit." He gave Winton Hollis and Hank each some dap and returned to the table, only to find Cecily not there. Karen and Greg Missenden from two houses down were at the table, but he ignored them. Oscar sent his eyes around the ballroom, pushing his gaze through the glass panels on one wall, which allowed view of the passageway showing the other rooms in this big-ass place. He liked this place better than last time. He finally spotted Cecily standing outside what he called the "piano" room, talking with some woman he didn't know (she wasn't from their table).

Oscar scoffed, "Thank God!" He didn't feel like babysitting tonight; that's for damn sure. He sat (needing a break from Winton and his crew, too) and swiped his brow with a napkin, feeling his insides settle and calm with his relaxed posture. He'd played it off, but he couldn't stand and joke for extended periods; plus, those mushroom-parmesan thingies must've given him the slight case of heartburn. He didn't like rich-people's food, anyway; should've just kept his distance.

Of all the fucking misfortunes to come down on him at this thing, it was seeing the little doctor bitch in attendance. Shocked the shit out of him, but he played it cool. She looked hot in her fancy dress and heels, and the contact lenses brought out her cute face even more. But his dislike for her messing up his flow with Cecily got in the way of giving it much attention. He still fantasized about fucking her (still crazy-weird to him). Naomi even had a date. He would've expected her to come stag to something like this, but surprise, surprise.

Karen and Greg left the table, offering him one of those fake courtesy smiles and nods. Oscar fake-smiled back, but they could've just left; he barely knew them. Oscar stared at the candlelight centerpiece, enjoying the solitude. He was smarter than most people, extremely logical: this charitable shit was nothing but a scam. Yeah, Cecily's big-ass check was for something called "Monument Academy." Everyone who submitted checks had them made payable to one charity or another, but that was probably the other end of the scam. The people who owned this building donated its use, but who paid for the food and booze? Kind people were just suckers, falling for some soft spot in their hearts that was nothing but guilt about something else. Him? He came for the atmosphere and the show, liked putting on a tux and mingling with these other deep-pocket assholes. But there was only so much talk about politics and business he wanted to do. The music was good; he liked that, too—especially the deejay's finale.

Oscar watched his wife smile and talk with another lady who came up. He'd told her she'd do fine at the ball, but she never listened to him (what he had to say wasn't important enough). One minute, she's sitting alone, sulking like a kid (and drinking?!); the next, she's got plenty conversation for some uppity bitches. He didn't like it, but he didn't feel like being bothered, either, so he'd give her a break. He thought he saw that Joshua dude here, too, but Cecily hadn't noticed; they obviously traveled in different circles—Joshua didn't have time for Cecily's moping ass, either.

Cecily sure looked nice; he'd give her that.

Another woman was here, though, that... Damn!

Oscar sent his gaze toward Naomi's table, but the woman in that sleeveless black-and-silver dress wasn't over there. He already knew she'd be in his head tonight as he went at Cecily. He didn't know when she'd get out of his head. She was tall and fucking gorgeous. Her dress showed only her back but told him: nothing but sexy-ass curves moved underneath it. That dress wasn't tight and didn't have to be, shit. His whole body went warm when he saw her, his dick twitching like crazy. Bunch of men were eye-fucking her, too. What did her husband expect, letting her out like that?

Oscar nodded to himself. He was the only one to approach her. He wasn't a punk-ass like the rest; he let the woman know. Yeah, okay, he may have overstepped, but that wouldn't stop her from being in his thoughts tonight—husband couldn't do shit about that.

He watched the people, readying to get another drink, when he saw Janyce coming out of the ladies' room, and he went hot for a whole nother reason. Oscar got to his feet and headed her way, stepping around people and excusing himself across the ballroom. He saw her fuchsia ass approaching the rotunda foyer and caught up in time to grab her arm and pull her into one of the empty rooms.

She jerked her arm, but he had a good grip. "What is wrong with you?! Get off me!"

He released her. "What're you doing?!" He was so mad, his head hurt.

Janyce looked him up and down. "What?"

Oscar reached for her little purse, but she would let him take it. "Why did you bring that here?" Oh, he wanted to drop her ass!

"It's mine. No point in having it if I can't wear it. But I know I can't wear it yet, but I just wanted to have it with me."

"You stupid bitch."

She got in his face with a huff, smelling (again) like Cecily's dead flowers. "Call me that again, and your balls will become your tonsils." She stood straight with a deep breath, smoothing her dress.

"Keep that brooch in your bag. You're threatening everything having it here."

Janyce gritted on him. "Just stay out of my way."

He walked away to keep from losing it completely and beating the shit out of her.

NAOMI (8:41 p.m.)

"Thanks, Charles." Naomi accepted her fluted glass of sparkling water and fresh peaches from the bartender, still chuckling over his joke about sobriety. She strolled the ballroom, listening and watching, watching and listening, getting a kick out of it all.

She took particular interest in seeing Rick and Viv come together to dance to Peabo Bryson's "I'm So Into You." Each was engaged in conversation in different parts of the ballroom, but when that song started, Naomi watched as both abruptly left their discussions to meet on the dancefloor. The couple danced close, not with a grind but a gentle sway, Rick holding Viv's hand to his chest. They talked and laughed between themselves, enjoying the song, the dance, and each other.

Naomi continued her stroll, taking in the party activity, the people...and going into banana-mode.

Humans survived as social creatures. Even the most introverted introvert needed some form of human interaction and exchange—however small. Strong and supple emotional attachments to people and a certain interdependence with them were instrumental in defining certain aspects of mental health. People get angry and disappointed with one another: only natural. But an unhealthy degree of disdain and disappointment when dealing with human interaction is where she came in. Naomi didn't think Cecily faltered in that arena, but her husband was a different story with his demand for Cecily to fulfill his narcissistic needs, and it likely contributed to the one-sidedness in their marriage Cecily struggled with subconsciously.

Kevin smiled, winked, and raised his glass at her from across the room. He pointed toward the dancefloor, implying wanting another dance soon. Naomi smiled back with a nod and raised her glass before continuing her ballroom stroll. She overheard pockets of conversations, noting some people were drunk. But being drunk (and not remembering your words the next day) didn't mean the words weren't true.

She approached Patrice, Garrett, Louise, Tim, and Trevor, standing near a refreshment table. Naomi didn't spot a spark of chemistry between either of those couples, but Patrice's body language broadcast additional unhappiness about something as her mouth moved. Naomi followed Patrice's line of sight as she drew closer to the group: Rick and Viv on the dancefloor.

Oh, boy.

Naomi quietly joined the small faction from Trevor's side.

Patrice sucked her teeth. "I'm telling you: their lovey-dovey won't last. Probably faking all that for the kids' sake: that kind of love is impossible." She cast a baleful glance at the men in the group before scrutinizing her sister and brother-in-law again. "...Men can't love like that. Only at the start—after that, forget it." She focused on the dancefloor, giving a slow head-bob. "Watch. By the time RJ is three, it'll be over." Patrice worked as a corporate mediator, but presently, she stirred nothing but discord, motivated discontent.

Tim didn't see, but Naomi caught Louise's pleased expression at Patrice's summation. Neither woman was in a charitable frame of mind.

Garrett's expression read annoyance, but Naomi sensed it wasn't in agreement with his wife but because of her.

Before this turned any uglier, controlling her anger, Naomi shifted forward, addressing everyone but Trevor. "Show of hands of those who've been incarcerated, or is the spouse of someone who was?"

The Carters and Collinses looked confused and perturbed, but no one raised their hand.

Naomi continued. "Viv and Rick have been through a great deal and have stayed together. It's a testament. And while I realize your relationships are top candidates for Marriage of the Year, leave Rick and

Viv alone. They are on the other side of things now, living their happily ever after. Don't hate. Congratulate. ...And gravitate."

Now everyone looked chastened, including Trevor (and she wasn't even talking to him).

Naomi locked eyes on Patrice. "And saying men can't or don't love like that is selling men short, Patrice. Stop generalizing men with negativity. It's not a victory for either side when you do."

Patrice huffed, and her posture stiffened, but Naomi got all that in the periphery. She froze, experiencing a comforting flash of truth. In it, she saw Rick and Viv, with a teenaged Alna and an older-but-still-young RJ (four, five?), working a puzzle, the scene serene and...loving. The flash was gone as quickly as it descended, but the residual feeling was still warm and comforting (proving Patrice so wrong).

Others flaunted their "seeing" abilities, profited from it. But Naomi was too private a person for such vanity pursuits. Besides, the occurrences were such intensely personal things, making her feel aware of things about people (mostly strangers) that she shouldn't be.

In any event, she'd use the flashes to save lives if and where she could, and the flickers—well, those were only most useful if one was a patient. And neither happened regularly enough for her not to be considered a nut if she went public with it. Kevin would believe her. Leslie. Rick and Viv. But in the end, suffering alone and in silence was best for her mental well-being.

Naomi headed away, sending the two couples a last look of admonishment. She needed to touch base with Cecily.

Speaking of Marriage of the Year, Naomi casually searched for her patient, pleased at seeing married (happily or not) Black folk dressed-up and having a classic good time. From Naomi's observation, only a few couples appeared unmarried.

NAOMI (8:53 p.m.)

She caught up with Cecily outside the gallery. "You haven't blown the joint; that's a good sign."

Cecily offered a smiling headshake. "Not yet, no."

"How long have you been coming to these?"

"We came last year, but not the year before. This is our third." She didn't sound or look drunk; she rode a mild high, at most.

"You like formal dances?"

Cecily squinted. Naomi read emotion in Cecily's fake lenses more easily with each passing session. "You mean, did I attend dances with Roland?"

Naomi held in a chuckle.

"Yeah. I'm on to you." Cecily grinned and nodded, the alcohol giving some clarity, it seems. "Yes, I did, and yes, I do. How's that?"

Naomi left it at that. She didn't want to explore Cecily's experiences with Roland; the mention alone was enough to do Naomi's work for her. Those outings with her first husband carried different associations. "I take it you didn't give Oscar any formal-wear pointers."

Cecily's countenance registered exasperated irritation before it turned wary and fearful. "It's a catch twenty-two for me, Naomi. He hates for me to point things out, but if someone else points that same thing out, he takes his irritation over it out on me for not saying anything." She sent her gaze around her, taking in the festivity.

"How's the Jos—?"

Cecily's eyes widened as she gasped, "Scuse me, Naomi!" and then hurried away.

CECILY (8:55 p.m.)

Cecily hastened toward the fuchsia, her body running hot and cold. She saw the glint only briefly, but the shape and blend of stones couldn't be mistaken: Janyce had her brooch. The one her mother presented her for high school graduation: shaped like a teacup and made of diamonds and genuine opal (her birthstone). A token representing a maternal peace-offering for years of meanness suffered and instilled feelings of inadequacy. The one missing since those men invaded her home.

She ran cold with shock and hot with anger, and then both melded into warm confusion. Why was she carrying it around? Maybe she planned to give it to her as a surprise. But how did she end up with it in the first place?

She knew the shape—and you hadn't mentioned it. You know how.

No. Not Janyce. She just needed to ask her about it. Ask her and get it back.

Janyce stood with Karen Missenden, holding a drink and laughing.

Cecily touched Janyce's arm. "Hey, can we talk a minute?"

Janyce turned to Karen, who smiled and excused herself. Janyce sipped from her glass. "What's up?"

Cecily used her liquor-buzz to plunge ahead. "You have my brooch."

Her friend reared back, face contorted with angry surprise. She scanned the ballroom, then turned to her and leaned close, speaking in an annoyed whisper. "What're you talking about? What 'brooch'?"

She owned one brooch; one holding major significance in her life.

So, there was a telling problem with Janyce asking what brooch she was talking about. Cecily realized that, but that clarity got lost in her buzz, and her wondering if she'd imagined things through a boozy haze. She stared at Janyce, wanting to ask her to open her little Chanel, and afraid of the mental consequences if the reveal showed—nothing but Janyce's personal effects.

"You're drunk, Cecily. Or close to it. Now you're seeing things and trying to include me in your paranoid delusions. I usually go along and try to help, but I'm trying to have fun tonight. Damn, does every day have to be about *that*, Cecily?" She sipped some more, her steel-brown eyes hard.

Yes! Yes, every goddamn day is about what happened to me! Every goddamn day is about avoiding the bad smells and the bad sounds, about moving on to the next hour without cowering or startling or "episoding"! Every day is about what's happening to me...then and now!

"Never mind." Cecily turned away, needing air or Naomi—whichever came first.

NAOMI (8:59 p.m.)

The body and facial cues between Cecily and the woman in the ill-fitting fuchsia mermaid dress were wrong. All wrong. Naomi made her way to Cecily in time to reach her as Cecily stepped past the rear ballroom exit and into the hallway. "Cecily."

Her patient paused. Trembling in her three-inch bronze pointed-toe T-straps, Cecily waved her closer.

The dark rooms on this side of the ballroom were off-limits by implication. Naomi touched Cecily's elbow and guided her toward a darkened room farther down the hallway. "Come on. In here..." They stepped just across the threshold of one room, in minimal violation, using the lighting from the hallway to see each other. "Breathe."

Cecily closed her eyes, taking calming breaths. After a minute or two, her lids blinked open. "That was Janyce."

"With a 'Y,' not an 'I.'"

Trembles gone, Cecily fashioned a droll simper. "Right."

"Okay. I don't want you to get into that. I saw it wasn't good, but let it marinate, okay?"

Cecily nodded with a soft sigh. "That situation just killed my buzz. Is that possible?"

"Sure. Can you do a couple things for me?"

"Yes."

Naomi valued the non-hesitation. "First, remove those fake contacts." Now, Cecily hesitated.

"Make up a reason. Tell him you lost one, whatever."

Cecily bent forward, removing the first lens. "I don't know how I'll get away with this, but..."

Naomi didn't like Cecily feeling she had to "get away" with anything, but it was the state of things—for now. "I have an ophthalmologist connection or two. You'll have a doctor's note next session." She nodded at Cecily, directing her to remove the other one.

Cecily removed the second lens and stood straight, blinking. "Now what?"

Naomi held out a hand. "Give me the 'lost' one."

Cecily handed her one, and Naomi saw the mini relief move through her; she disliked wearing them. "This...This is the 'before' me."

Naomi grinned. "Yes. Let's reclaim some of that, shall we?" She tucked the lens into the inside pocket of her sapphire-beaded clutch.

"Every little bit counts."

"You said it, not me."

Cecily adopted an inquiring smile. "So, what's the second thing? You said, 'a couple.'"

Naomi paused, feeling the certainty behind her next words but unsure of her patient's reaction. "Dance with that 'Joshua' fellow."

The smile faded. Cecily went still, with a panic in her dark-brown eyes not based in fear. "What?"

"I'm not talking about grinding the man into oblivion in the middle of the dancefloor. It doesn't have to be a slow one, but *dance*, Cecily. I've been paying attention. You've been sitting alone, drinking, or making awkward attempts at socializing. We're three hours in, and you and Oscar haven't danced once." Even though she encouraged Cecily to dance with another man, Naomi had no qualms. Dancing wasn't cheating. And Cecily was her priority—not the continuation of that oppressive marriage.

"He likes the fast-paced finale."

Naomi returned a neutral stare. From the looks of things, Oscar had no intention of asking her to dance. "It'll be the most fun you have all night. It's a charitable event; you should be charitable to yourself tonight and allow yourself a few minutes of fun."

"I don't know."

"I do. But if not Joshua, the gentlemen at my table wouldn't mind cutting a rug with you; they're nice guys." Naomi saw Kevin, Trevor, Rick, and even Tim smilingly willing to dance with Cecily. She didn't know Garrett, but he seemed cool, too. She teetered all sorts of doctor-patient boundaries here, but whatever. Sometimes bananas overripened; you still peeled and ate them—or found better culinary uses.

"*Your* table?" Cecily made this odd, blushing expression Naomi wasn't clear on. "That's nice of you, Naomi, but..." She shook her head, then opened and closed her minaudière with a contemplative sigh. "...I'll see."

"That's good enough for me. Now, one more thing, and you can get back to the ball."

Cecily gazed at her curiously.

Naomi was fondly used to the dark color of her irises already. "What's seven times seven?"

Cecily's curious frown deepened. "Forty-nine." Although her expression was curious, Cecily didn't ask her answer; she stated it with bracing bluntness.

Cecily was a numbers girl, and Naomi chose the random math question for that reason. "You sure? Don't get all confused now. You might be too stressed to know what you're talking about."

Music traveling from the ballroom, they stood together in the threshold of some off-limits room, hallway light on one side of their bodies, darkness on the other, Cecily gazing down at her for long seconds. Naomi gazed back. She saw the meaning dawn in Cecily's eyes, and it was such a good feeling. Psychiatrists weren't neutral about *everything*; they just weren't.

"It's *forty-nine*, Naomi. Seven times seven is forty-nine." Cecily's eyes expressed an unvoiced *thank you* as well.

Naomi jerked her head in the ballroom's direction. "Go. Be charitable to yourself."

Cecily smiled and stepped away.

NAOMI (9:19 p.m.)

"Les is talking an after-party." Kevin leaned back in his chair and put a hand to the back of hers, brushing his thumb against her upper back. His touch was lovely.

Naomi chuckled. "I knew that was coming. It's fine." She adjusted his now flattened and askew pocket square.

He kissed her fingers as she did, enjoying the attention. "Come on, let's tour the joint."

An ideal plan. She grabbed her glass of Dom Perignon. "Let's go."

After a partial tour (and brief detour for a lengthy deep kiss), they returned hand-in-hand to Curtis's current dedication. "A'ight, folks. Have another dedication rolling through. Another anonymous one, but it's an eighties goodie. So, to whomever you are, from whomever they are: they can't let go."

"Can't Let Go" by Parris started, and Kevin changed direction, leading her toward the dancefloor instead of their table (where Rick and Viv sat together, chilling and talking). Naomi moved into Kevin's arms, swaying to the classic slow jam. Her man smelled good.

Louise and Tim were on the dancefloor as well. Leslie and Trevor congregated with a youthful gathering in a corner of the ballroom.

Patrice and Garrett stood near the portrait table with minimal inter-action, and Naomi again noted a lack of chemistry between the couple; their body language remained detached all evening. If Naomi had to guess, they weren't having relations—not for a while.

One eye on Cecily (alone at the table yet again, but not drinking), Naomi watched the other couples dancing. Her gaze settled on Louise and Tim. While dancing with Tim, Louise ogled Rick, and Naomi real-ized who the *To* and *From* parties were in this "anonymous" dedication. "Can't Let Go" was from Louise to Rick.

Naomi began guiding her dance with Kevin into Louise's line of sight. She caught Louise's attention, adopting an expression letting her know she knew what was up, and Louise's response did not surprise Naomi: she moved with Tim, guiding him so she could continue focusing on Rick. But when Louise turned her face to Tim's chest with obvious hurt feelings, Naomi turned to see Rick and Viv bopping to the song some before bringing their bodies together to slow-dance for a few beats, then parting again to resume the Bop. An interesting occurrence was the pops of red showing from the bottom of Viv's pumps and Rick's court shoes with their movement—a sexy, allegorical representation of their unity. The rhythmic way the couple moved from one dance into the other and back: entrancing. No wonder Louise's feelings were hurt.

"Can't Let Go" centered on wanting a lover back. The irony of Louise dedicating it: Rick was never Louise's, to begin with.

She realized Louise might end up a patient again—for a reason, having nothing to do with anxiety over a young patient's death. Tim was cute and a quality dude (based on previous history). Nevertheless, Tim often tried emulating the younger Rick. Naomi found it insightful; perhaps Tim was subconsciously aware of Louise's feelings for his friend. Emulating Rick, however, was one thing. *Being* him? Quite another.

The song closed, and Louise rushed out. Naomi pulled back from Kevin to see Rick confirming with Viv to go after her. Was Viv aware of the underlying innuendo as well? And if she was, telling Rick to go after Louise was taking tasteful-peaceful to some philanthropic level, Naomi couldn't believe. Her respect for Viv notched even higher.

"Whoo! Good stuff. Let me hit y'all with another!" Curtis continued the slow jams as some couples left the dancefloor and others joined.

Kevin took her hand, reclaiming her attention. "Get you anything?"

She grinned at him. "I'm not working."

He just gazed back. "Sparkling water with melon this time, perhaps, or a few of the country pâté toasts with pickled grapes? You like those." He was incredibly dear to her. She was working. They both knew it. Kevin merely offered refreshment to keep her stamina up and see it through. She also did the date thing with him this evening, which satisfied him.

"Both, thank you very much."

He kissed her cheek. "Back in a bit." He stepped away.

Naomi watched him, too, for solid seconds, liking what she saw. Seeing Viv alone at their table, Naomi made her way there. She sat as Viv finished looking at her phone. "Hey, lady."

Viv smiled. "Hey, lady." She gestured at her phone resting on the table. "Finally got RJ down."

Naomi nodded, then gestured at the open space by their table. "See you two don't need parquet floors..."

Viv shrugged with a headshake. "Nope. Don't need a dancefloor. If there's room, we can groove wherever."

"Where's Rick?"

"You know where he is. And thanks for trying to run interference."

"Caught that, did you?" It didn't surprise Naomi; she and Viv worked from such similar personality stock: they knew each other well.

"I did." Viv leaned toward her. "And I'm telling you, Lou has only one more time to pull that stunt, Naomi." Her black gaze hardened before she sat back with a sigh, putting her phone in her clutch. "Now, I can't make Lou stop being in love with my husband, and Rick can't stop being himself, so what do you do?"

That was the question.

Viv continued: "And, as good as you are, I'm not sure you can help—because it's an affair of the *heart*, ya know? Not the mind."

"I see what you're saying." But Naomi saw signs of things needing mental-medical intervention; she'd have to see.

"I get that tonight is extra hard on Lou: she hasn't seen him on the regular in so long, and Rick is in a tuxedo. Hell, his being in a tux is hard on *me*!" They laughed together at that, but Viv grew resolute, much of that tasteful-peaceful pushed to the side, if only for this brief venting period. "Lou has only one more time to pull that shit." Her friend looked at her with slight incredulity. "I mean, what *is* that? My husband is off comforting my old friend, who's upset because she can't *be with* him? What the hell?!" Viv turned in her seat, crossing her legs with womanly attitude. "Lou has two times; she's just used one. If there's a second time..." Viv turned those black eyes on her, stern once again (but still beautiful). "*I'll* be the one 'comforting' her." She scoffed, shaking her head. "I've got enough going on with Lynelle being here."

"True. She's only spoken to him that one time, right?"

"Yes."

"Speaking of Lynelle..." They listened to another of Curtis's anonymous dedications: "Misty Blue" by Dorothy Moore. She and Viv searched the ballroom. Naomi spotted Lynelle at her table: eyes closed with this semi-pained expression, her head rocking in tempo with emotion (before sending a furtive glance around the ballroom). Naomi turned back to Viv. "This one isn't so anonymous, either."

"Tell me about it." Viv scoffed with a sigh. "It figures they'd play close together. But I'm good. Let her pine. Men can handle these situations all wrong, but my baby was cool with his shit. I was pleased Rick acknowledged the woman without being rude to her or overly attentive to me—either of those would've pissed me off, not made things better. And he knew no introductions were necessary."

"He's getting it."

"He is. Got it a long time ago, Naomi. But that's because he knows me, too, so..." Viv sipped her wine.

And *knowing* your partner, knowing who they are as people, and understanding their motivations and reactions, was most important to *getting it*, to successfully navigating a relationship.

Naomi spotted Tim near the front. She wanted to speak to him privately if she could manage it. She looked at Viv. "You're good?"

Viv sipped and set her glass down. "I am. Go do your thing."

"I'm *not* working." That meaningless statement had become comical. Naomi grinned.

Viv grinned back with a nod toward the rest of the ballroom. "Go."

NAOMI (9:45 p.m.)

She left the ballroom, intent on catching up with Tim Collins, and ended up having him catch up with her instead.

He touched her shoulder as she stood outside the billiard room. "Having a good time, Doctor Alexander?" He smiled, but there was sadness in it. His A-Phi-A fraternity lapel pin winked at her.

Naomi cut to the chase. "I am, but the question is... Are you?"

Tim grinned wanly, shaking his head. "Same ole Doctor Alexander."

"The one and only." She grinned back.

"True talk." He smiled, his teeth a very flattering feature.

Naomi looked up at him more seriously. "A mini session?"

Tim hesitated but nodded.

Naomi curled her arm inside his and they walked, Naomi guiding him toward the hallway with the off-limits row of dark rooms. Perhaps there was a yellow sofa lurking in one of them. She paused outside the room she and Cecily stood in. "It's relatively private back here..." Unhooking her arm, she smiled up at him. "Let 'er rip."

Tim chuckled but then looked around, not speaking.

Naomi let him warm up without prompt or interruption.

"...I don't talk a lot, Naomi, so everyone probably thinks I'm the dumb one, oblivious to what's going on, but I see how my wife looks at Rick."

And here we are, ladies and gentlemen—a view from the other side.

Tim leaned back against the wall and sighed, studying the floor. "For the longest time, I watched to see if Rick was sending signals or something to Lou, encouraging it." He shook his head, lifting it to look Naomi in the eye. "Rick ain't about nobody but Viv. *Deeply.* Even when he did that other shit, he was still only about Viv."

She nodded, wanting him to continue.

Tim studied the floor again. "I know y'all find that hard to understand, but it's the truth, so..." He shrugged.

Naomi didn't find it hard to understand at all.

"I...I can sometimes tell when Lou is thinking about Rick when we have sex." He swallowed hard.

Maybe he was being respectful, but Tim knew he didn't have to hold back when riffing with her. There was something about him using *have sex* (as opposed to any of the many colloquialisms adopted to mean intercourse) that stayed with her.

"I've..." He swallowed again, his face pained before turning sad and reflective. "I've even woken up to Lou masturbating and whispering Rick's name."

Not surprised, Naomi said nothing.

He looked up at her, and Naomi saw a confession coming. "I fantasize about being with Viv sometimes." He stared at her as if waiting for admonishment or laughter, but when she gave neither, he concentrated on the floor again. "I do. Viv's gorgeous, not even aware of it, just cool and friendly. Lotta men want Viv, Doc; for good reason." He scoffed, his shoulders rising with it. "She's also crazy in love with Rick. Nobody would have a shot, anyway."

"True talk." Like her husband with women, Viv had an intoxicating, enigmatic allure men were drawn to. "Tim, why don't you sit with me, in a more professional setting, and talk about it?"

He peered at her. "With Lou?"

"Well, it would be best. Treating you separately for the same core problem has its drawbacks."

Tim shook his head. "I'm not ready to hear about Lou's feelings for my friend, Naomi. I live with the shit every day. Not ready to hear it out loud."

"I get that, Tim. But you guys can't keep ignoring this. ...Not when it's escalating."

He stared at her for several seconds, then frowned. "'Escalating'?"

Naomi nodded gravely.

Tim gazed around the hallway, taking in the art and décor, seeming to absorb that word before staring at her. "What does he have, Doc? I mean, okay, he's handsome. You don't have to be gay to see that. I'd even say he's got a *Cool Hand Luke* vibe about him. But what the fuck indefinable thing does he have that has my wife 'escalating'?!"

Naomi rattled-off several definable things in her head. Tim already said it: Rick had something *indefinable* about him. His good looks only heightened whatever that ineffable attribute was. Rick was wholly ignorant of his looks and sense of presence, being himself and taking nothing for granted. The *Cool Hand Luke* vibe was full-throttle charisma. Rick carried the unique paradox of being an understated Alpha-male. Combined with his good looks, intelligence, and humility, Rick Phillips was a beast—and Viv Phillips was one of the luckiest women around. Hell, Viv was no slouch, a beast on all fronts herself; Rick was a walking four-leaf-clover himself. Naomi loved them dearly.

"I don't know, Tim." Naomi didn't want to hurt Tim's feelings by listing specifics—the man was feeling bad as it was.

Tim stared at a painting a few feet away. "When Viv surprised us with Rick being home, I was standing next to Viv when Lou came in the room. Well, I should say, surprised *me*. I'm now guessing Lou knew Rick was out; now that I think about it, she was all dolled-up and fidgety that weekend." Tim smiled, still staring at the painting, reflection in his eyes. "It was good seeing him, though. No homo, but I missed him. Love 'im like a brother—and not just because we're frat." His lapel pin seemed to blink in response.

"I see." She noted Tim's repeated offhand assertions that he wasn't homosexual, wondering why men felt the need to emphasize their manliness. These days, people shouldn't give a—

Tim's mouth formed a slight, contemplative grin. "See, Rick's the kind of guy loved, liked, whatever, by both men and women. He's just all around, deep down, *good people*. Just... genuine. So, you love 'im, cuz you feel that coming from him."

"I agree."

"So, I get it from that perspective. It's some other piece I must be missing. I mean, he was gone almost three years, Naomi. *Three years*. In *prison*, mind you. And it changed *nothing* for her. ...The way she held on to him..."

"Well, they say 'absence makes the heart grow fonder'..." *And apparently, sends them into obsessive fixation.* Naomi kept a straight face.

Tim scoffed, shaking his head in understanding (albeit reluctant) agreement. "Tell me about it." He stared in the opposite direction. "Lou keeps..."

"I'm listening, Tim."

"She keeps a picture of Rick and Viv on her nightstand." He turned to Naomi, and Naomi filled in the rest. Lou, under the pretense of Viv and Rick being close like family and so, "reasonably," their picture would be in their room, only had that picture for one-half of that couple. But it wasn't cool having Mr. and Mrs. Phillips up in their bedroom—let alone Louise's nightstand.

"Say something, Tim."

Tim looked away. "I...I imitate Rick a lot, ya know? Trying to figure out his allure. Lou's not just attracted to him, Naomi. I could let it go if that was all it was. People are attractive; people are attracted to attractive people. But she's in love with him. Just all out *in love* with my boy. And I think...I think Viv knows, too."

Seems Mr. Collins was well-rounded on the matter at hand.

His gaze at her firmed. "And 'Can't Let Go' was from Lou to Rick."

Naomi couldn't mask her surprise.

Tim scoffed. "I'm *quiet*, Doc. I'm not stupid." He was one of those few people who could call her "Doc."

"Come by my office. Tuesday, nine-fifteen?" Tuesdays were her counter-sadness days: days she endeavored to distract herself from Tuesday's particularly dark meaning for her. An appointment with Tim to help him deal with Louise's semi-betrayal worked in that vein.

Tim offered a hesitant smile. "I don't know, Naomi."

"Just you, Tim."

"But you just said—"

"Just you for now. I'll counsel you separately for a preliminary session or two, but..."

"But then you want us to come to sessions together."

"Yeah, Tim. I can recommend someone."

Tim shook his head. "If I'm gonna do this, it's gotta be with you."

She had no problem bypassing the rules, but sometimes she bothered to toe the line. "I appreciate that. Rick and Viv are no longer patients, but with them now being like family, I may run into a patient-boundaries slash conflict-of-interest thing, so we'll see. But for Tuesday, just you. Okay?"

"And Lou?"

"Not sure. Shooting for Monday morning." Louise was next.

Tim quasi-smiled again. "Trying to get that stopgap going, huh?"

"Something like that."

"...How 'bout that dance by our table? Pretty slick, wasn't it?"

"It was."

"Yeah. Those two are in deep."

"They are. Very much so."

Tim scoffed. "*I* can see it. *You* see it. *Patrice* sees it—even though she's mad about it for some reason. ...I've heard others commenting; *they* obviously see it." He looked at her, eyes steadfast curious but quite annoyed. "...So, what the fuck's wrong with Lou?"

Naomi had no answer—yet.

He shook his head and headed back to the ballroom. "That's enough 'mini session.' Thanks for your time, Doc. See you Tuesday."

She watched Tim's dejected walk to the ballroom—and his wife.

NAOMI (10:03 p.m.)

Naomi sat at the table with Kevin, Viv, Rick, Trevor, and Garrett, listening to Up-Owl-Nite's grooves (the selections increased in tempo as he approached his finale) and engaging in varied discussion. Leslie, Tim, Louise, and Patrice socialized elsewhere. She hadn't seen Patrice and Garrett together much before or since they stood by the portrait table. Interesting.

Cheryl Lynn's "Got To Be Real" pumped into the room.

Garrett had a plate piled with hors d'oeuvres, munching heartily as he chatted. Cedar-brown and on the stocky side, he had long eyelashes but beady, dark-brown eyes. His full lips were surrounded by hair forming the Winnfield, which reminded Naomi of Oscar's former Friendly Mutton Chops. His black, single-breasted, satin-faced, shawl-collar tuxedo made the mistakes of having only one vent and being accented with a moss-green pocket square, cummerbund, and Windsor tie, but it fit him well. He, too, wore a lapel pin: repping Omega Psi Phi fraternity. His trousers had no break but were hemmed above the topline of his shoes, which, while appropriate, was too high for Naomi's taste. Perhaps she'd been teased about wearing "high-waters" too much as a child, making her extra sensitive. Not a Neanderthal, he covered his mouth with a napkin when speaking (washing his food down with sips of a martini).

Viv reached for her clutch. "If you'll excuse me." She stood, preparing to leave the table. "Wanna check on the kids..."

As he had been all evening whenever Viv left their table or approached it, Rick stood, and Trevor (again) looked up at him with confused curiosity. Kevin didn't rise fully, but his partial rise extended gentlemanly courtesy to Viv. Trevor glimpsed Kevin strangely, too, as Viv walked away (Garrett getting down with his mini snacks).

Kevin sat.

"So, who do you have for tomorrow's game, Rick?" Trevor shifted his plate of uneaten delicacies to the side.

Garrett sipped and swallowed. "I think the Wizards are good for it."

"They haven't lost at home since Christmas," Kevin added.

"Rick...?" Trevor waited.

Still standing, Rick's eyes followed his wife's departure, wearing this cute, moony expression (more attractive than goofy). He touched his top lip with his tongue, hinting where his thoughts were.

Garrett shook his head with a chuckle. "He's gone, man. Save it." It came in like an old television set warming up, but Garrett's aura flickered in for some seconds: tan with red swirls zipping through. Over the years, Naomi found the tan auras to have such interesting variations. If this was Garrett's base composite aura, he was an AT (or abstract tan). On average, ATs were open, friendly, and outgoing (she'd seen much of that from him). However, they could also be forgetful, easily distracted, emotionally withdrawn.

Once Viv was out of view, Rick took slow seconds turning to Trevor, and eyed him with this raised-eyebrow of a smirk holding humor but also mild irritation at being interrupted. "I agree with Kevin. The Wiz have been killer at home these last games. Everybody's healthy, stats are up. They should take it." He glanced Garrett's way before settling his eyes on Trevor again. "I also agree with GC: I'm gone over her."

He sat, and everyone shared a relaxed laugh.

Naomi kissed Kevin's cheek. "Think I'll find Viv. Let the men have the table for a bit." Maybe they could give Trevor pointers on gentlemanly courtesy.

NAOMI (10:09 p.m.)

She didn't have to go far. Naomi bumped into Viv at the rear entrance. "Kids all right?"

"Yeah. RJ was up again when Ricky checked on them, but he's asleep now. He's used to Alna, of course, but not Calais. And now they have him camping out with them in the basement bedroom."

"Fully understand." Naomi reentered the ballroom with Viv, and they stepped into some space off to the side instead of returning to the table. The men had vacated their table and now congregated near the bar, laughing and talking with men not from their table.

Biting her bottom lip, Viv uttered a sighing grunt. "I fuck him."

Naomi snickered. "Uh, yes, you do."

Viv chuckled, too. "I know, that was random, but sometimes I like saying that to myself when my attraction to him surges. And my baby is looking good over there."

"He is, Viv. Expressly. But you didn't say it to yourself."

"Yes, I did. You just happened to be within earshot."

They tee-heed again, looking over at the fellas.

Viv sighed. "I can say this to *you*: something as simple as that boy's mannerisms makes me hot for him, Naomi—especially when watching him do his male thing."

Naomi understood; there was a certain underlying something about how Rick moved his hands or body, the way he laughed or gestured while interacting with others, that drew you.

"...Give me my Rick, Naomi, my...*Romeo*: 'and, when he shall die, take him and cut him out in little stars,...and he will make the face of heaven so fine, that all the world will be in love with night, and pay no worship to the garish sun.'" Viv spoke reverently, still heard beneath Curtis's jam.

Naomi, touched, remained quiet, surprised (or maybe not so surprised) Viv knew Shakespeare.

Soon, a soft smile curled Viv's lips. "Girl, I have been using that man's body as my personal playground. Just...from those rough curls on his head to his long toes,...having an erotic good time with every male inch of him—with dedication...and gusto."

Naomi laughed lightly. "Party on, Viv. For the rest of your life."

"Until it falls off. Motherfucking right. That man can lay some pipe."

They cracked up (causing heads to turn their way); their friendship a comfort to Naomi she acknowledged more easily every day. Laughter subsided, they spied Mr. Phillips. "I'm sure it's reciprocated, Viv."

Viv nodded snaillike. "Yes, Lord. Every inch of me: with dedication and gusto. ...Know what I've been doing lately, though?"

Naomi remained silent; the question was semi-rhetorical.

"Picturing us elderly. Or picturing Rick old and sick, and me, older than him, still trying to care for him. Or seeing the reverse. Envisioning one of us sick with cancer, or imagining him growing bald, or him needing a pill to get his johnson going—"

"Or you, needing a pill to get your libido going."

Viv looked at her with a trace of smirking incredulity. "Anything's possible, but *that* shouldn't be an issue for me—*ever*."

Naomi chuffed a dampened laugh.

Viv chuckled, too, but her eyes turned contemplative again while gazing at her husband. "But, stuff like that, or you know, just..." She jounced both shoulders.

"Sprinkling your fairytale with doses of reality?"

Viv nodded thoughtfully, looking over at Rick. "Something like that. Keeping things in perspective, I guess. And you know what?"

Again, Naomi kept silent.

"It's all good. I want 'im. I'm in, and *that's it*. He's the best thing ever. So,...while I think I've done 'for worse' already... Worse, Poorer, Sickness: bring it on. You feel me?"

"I feel you, Viv."

"It's not always gloom-and-doom I think about. I also think about growing old with him, trying to keep up with any grandbabies."

They chuckled together.

"Rick's trying to get me into martial arts with him, but we'll have to see about that. Me? I'm trying to get him to drink juiced veggies."

"Good luck."

"I know, right?" Her expression sobered. "Rick's love for me... It's..."

"Dangerous now."

Viv turned to Naomi with a hesitant but agreeing nod. "You saw how he was with 'rude dude.'"

Naomi nodded, thinking most about how sexy Rick looked.

"Yeah. It's...dangerous. But Rick isn't psychotic about it."

Naomi kept silent, smirking internally over people not wanting to fully commit (pardon the pun) and go all the way with saying someone may be experiencing some psychosis. Naomi loved Rick. She did. Didn't mean she believed he couldn't be psychotic over Viv.

"I don't believe he'll jeopardize his freedom again, do anything to separate us again, but that dangerous element percolates under the surface for him. His love for me, it's...it's...*entire*. It's scary, but a good scary. I sometimes worry, though,...because Rick still..."

She was talking about Rick's continuing surges of restlessness, his lowering but still-present propensity for violence; an edge he developed after events years ago. You didn't recognize it unless you knew him—and Viv knew him like no other person on Earth.

Viv gazed across the way. "...No one better 'hurt' me, Naomi."

"No, it's best they didn't."

"And it's best no one 'hurt' him."

"All right, now. I hear you, '*Missus* Dangerous.'"

Viv chuckled. They watched their men. "...When Rick was away, I received plenty advice on how to handle it. From friends, family. Except for you, it was negative. Just down on Rick. The basic message? Leave him. Walk away and don't look back. Believe it or not, even from Lou. And in retrospect, I get her angle now. But anyway, just a lot of negativity in my ear. And now that I reflect on it, probably all leading me the wrong way with this; leading me to someplace lonely and unhappy."

"Yeah, probably."

"Being with him is like... Remember when cereal boxes had, like, *real* prizes in them? Solid, hold-in-your-hand, play-and-trade prizes? Not the flimsy tokens they insert now."

"Sure."

Viv nodded reflectively. "That's what this feels like, Naomi. That excitement from seeing the commercial, and then begging your mother to get, hopefully, *two* boxes of the cereal because the prize maybe came in different colors or something, and then reading the back of the cereal box at the kitchen table."

"Right."

"Yeah. Then, digging in the box or pouring the contents into the largest bowl you could find. In reality, those prizes weren't worth much, but that wasn't the point, was it?"

"Not at all."

Viv shook her head in agreement. "Nope. The monetary value meant nothing. Getting the *prize*, Naomi: that meant everything. And you treasured having it—whatever it was."

Naomi nodded with childhood memories Viv's analogy evoked.

"That feeling of seeing the prize plop onto the pile of cereal, Naomi, or gripping it along with cereal crumbs at the bottom of the box. That excited glee mixed with curiosity and anticipation. That...*joy*." Viv went quiet, focusing on her husband. "That's what being with him feels like: Ricky's the prize in the cereal box."

"Nice, Viv."

Viv shrugged as if she were only speaking truth. "It's what being with him has always felt like. Even with that other mess we went through. And I need him." Her eyes on the man she married (who just tossed his head back with laughter at something), Viv bit her bottom lip. "Whenever he touches me, Naomi. Simple, casual moves like a hand to the small of my back or interlocking our fingers: I experience this current of erotic closeness to him, this electric, intimate *happiness*." A soft scoff escaped her lips. "And that boy's kiss..." She eased a slow, musing head-bob. "He's my buddy, my baby. *Our* thing: it's fireworks...at a slow burn."

Naomi fully appreciated that comparison.

"And his eyes, Naomi..."

"Uniquely pretty, yes."

"You'd think I'd be used to them, that they wouldn't faze me after so many years together. But Rick's eyes, those molten-fire irises, do different shit with his *moods*, the reds and dark golds firing strangely sometimes with his disposition."

Naomi had noticed as much—primarily when he's been angered (as with that interaction with 'rude dude' Oscar).

Viv went quiet, watching Rick. "He can be so silly sometimes, which I love, but I also like how he can turn around and discuss something deep and meaningful."

"A good balance. Goofy can be attractive."

"Oh, yes. Rick's smile is to die for. But when my baby laughs, Naomi, there's this crinkle in his nose...just adorable."

"Like ol' Saint Nick?"

Viv smirked with a grin. "Bet you couldn't guess what's been the most unexpected positive about him being home?" Viv turned to her with genial challenge in her eyes.

Naomi came up with nothing. "What?"

Viv stared her husband's way. "... Sleeping through the night."

"Because his side of the bed is filled—with him."

Viv turned those onyx eyes on her, hints of mischief and happiness swirling in them. "Well, yeah."

Naomi smiled but then grew serious. "And the nightmares?"

"...I've startled awake a few times, screaming out my baby's name as the 'monsters' come to take him away, or just scared he's gone again; stuff like that. But he holds and comforts me, reminding me he's right there. It was bad those first few weeks." Viv returned her attention to the men across the way, focusing on one especially. She released a whispery grunt. "...Making love with him, lying on our sides face-to-face, moaning and breathing our arousal, our excitement together,...my hand in his hair, the other roaming his muscles,...all while gazing into the fire of his irises as he moves inside me so *sensually*, Naomi..." Viv smiled a secret smile. "That's been my preferred position lately. But I've also reveled in him roughly snatching my—" She turned to her. "Anyway, you and Kevin have plans for Valentine's Day?"

Naomi adopted a neutral stare. Viv had to know the answer: she didn't do Valentines.

Viv's smirk suggested she did know. "Fine. Since you have nothing major going on, can I ask a favor?"

Naomi continued looking at Viv without speaking but changed her expression to convey the affirmative: of course, Viv could request a favor; she was on a concise list of people who could.

Viv popped a soft grin. "Thank you. I wanted to know if you'd babysit for us that weekend. Not the entire weekend, but overnight from Friday evening to early afternoon Saturday?"

"Getting started on those 'time-alone-no-kids' weekends, huh?"

"Something like that. Ricky doesn't know; it'll be a surprise."

"Good for you, Viv."

"I know," Viv gushed.

"Kevin and I will be glad to. And make it Saturday night instead of early afternoon. Ten, eleven o'clock will be good."

Viv grinned. "Thank you."

"Going out of town?" Naomi grabbed her arm in mock shock. "That won't cause problems with his probation, will it? Can he even stay overnight anywhere other than his home? Will the probation officer arrest him?"

Viv playfully snatched her arm from her grasp. "No, 'Patrice.' Mind your business."

Naomi smirked. "Thought you'd get a kick out of that."

"I did. But no; we'll be local: the Gaylord, National Harbor."

"Nice."

"Yeah. Making sure we have *Love Jones* and *Love and Basketball* to watch in the room."

"Not that you two need a catalyst for sex."

"No. Rick definitely has some blues and funk working my thighs. Hell, he has some calypso and bossa-nova going on in some other places, but that's another story."

They laughed.

"But no, LJ and LB are just classic, romantic Black cinema—and we like to act out some scenes for goofy fun."

Naomi envisioned that goofy fun as something also sweet and romantic for the couple.

"With February being Black History month..." Viv shrugged, looking mischievous.

"Black History is every day, so yeah, right, Viv."

Viv winked, making Naomi chuckle. "If we were leaving town, though, it's just a matter of him letting his PO know. Rick and Irwin are cool. Rick's restricted from drug use; that's about it."

"I know."

"Yes, you do; bless your heart. Then you also know it's a minor adjustment for us."

"Long overdue for one of your... What do you call them?"

"Tree-climbing or Slow-motion getaways."

Naomi smiled. "Yeah, that's it. Quarterly, right?"

"Triannual. And yes: long overdue."

"Hang in there, Viv."

"Oh, we're good. It's not pressing. We've gone this long; a couple more years won't matter. Just miss taking that time with him."

"Something to look forward to."

"Yes. You or Kevin ever...?"

"Kevin doesn't now, and now that I think about it, I don't know about before we met, but I haven't had tea-time since med school."

Viv emitted an exaggerated gasp of shock. "High while studying how to take care of people!"

Naomi returned a smirking-grin. "Along with likely half of all doctors in America."

"Miss it?"

"Sometimes."

"Okay." Viv sighed with a soft smile. "Being able to make plans again, Naomi. Able to plan getaways and trips with him again."

"Special?"

"And exciting."

"I'm sure."

The music volume lowered. "Okay, people. A brief intermission, and I'll be back with it." Curtis stepped away from his deejay setup.

Viv kept her attention on their men. Naomi watched with her.

She'd observed men all evening and noted Oscar's and many other men's frequent crotch adjustments. But Rick made none that Naomi saw, and neither did Kevin nor Timothy. There were also cases where men didn't wear an undershirt: so gross. Thankfully, none of the men in her group committed that major faux pas.

"...You gotta listen to your heart when it speaks to you, Naomi. Not worry about all the advice and recommendations. I'm glad I followed my heart and stuck by him instead of listening to the panel of folks doing more judging than understanding."

Naomi was glad she stuck by him, too. People needed people.

"He's my best friend, and I'm crazy about him."

Naomi and Viv viewed the activity in silence.

"...He's my best friend, Naomi. And I will be in love with him, deeply, *unashamedly* in love with him...for the rest of my life, no matter what."

"I hear you, Viv."

They watched Rick socialize with the fellas, smiling and laughing.

"...Naomi?" Viv gazed in Rick's direction, teary-eyed.

"Yes, sweetie?"

A tear trailed Viv's cheek. "Follow your heart, okay? Pursue something *Epic*. Take No Prisoners. The rest of it, all the bullshit?" she shook her head, "Doesn't matter." Viv wiped away the tear, boring her eyes into Naomi's. "...Fuck 'em if they can't take a joke."

Naomi smiled, noting Viv's radiating beauty. "Fuck 'em."

Viv hadn't noticed, but Leslie, Joy, Patrice, and Louise joined them.

No one said anything for a spell, the ladies' attention directed toward a particular group of men still talking and laughing several feet away. Inevitably, even with adults, there was the natural occurrence of boys socializing together and girls doing the same at these events.

Leslie released a long, airy sigh. "I love men."

Joy Giles pursed her lips, running her gaze over their guys. Big up top and small everywhere else, Joy's exposed almond-brown skin shimmered. Her belted one-shoulder dress drew attention to her middle (not ideal for women with apple body types), but the sangria-red dress was pretty. She had Naomi by an inch or two—even more with the teetering heels she wore. "Mm-hmm! There's just something about a man in a tuxedo, hair lined and tight, smelling all good..." Her hazel eyes widened and then narrowed on the men with appreciation. The tiny stud in her pug nose glistened.

Various murmurs of agreement followed.

Louise swooped her bang from her eyes. "They do look nice over there."

"We can narrow the discussion points to three topics, can't we? Sports, Cars, and..." Leslie turned to them, and they all replied: "Women!"

They laughed, but Naomi knew a select few of those men, depending on the audience, could talk at length about politics, current events, entertainment, or business news, too.

Joy scoffed. "You can tell when they're talking about women. They all do that stupid, laugh-handshake thing."

The ladies nodded, and then everyone but Patrice began imitating it with each other, giving dap or power handshakes and making bass-sounding nonsense commentary, creating more laughter about their men.

As their laughter died, Leslie turned to them. "Yeah. What *is* that?"

"It's disrespectful." Patrice sounded so sour.

Naomi exchanged a look with Viv.

Viv shrugged. "Oh, I don't know. Pertaining women, it's mostly talk. What's the big deal? We talk about men. I like when Rick does his male bonding. Watching the sodality turns me on, sometimes."

Patrice rolled her eyes with a low scoff of unhappy. What was her problem? Naomi thought if she could ever use an aura-flicker...

Leslie frowned at Viv, tongue-in-cheek. "Watching the what?"

Naomi and Joy chuckled as Leslie shook her head, not expecting a reply; she likely inferred the meaning of *sodality* from the context. Viv returned a smiling smirk.

"Not sure if you've noticed, Viv, but Rick isn't paying attention to the women walking past. He only looks if somebody directs his attention. Look, watch..." Leslie touched Viv's forearm, giving a surreptitious nod toward the men.

Some woman walked past, mauve dress hugging.

Rick continued talking.

Garrett (his eyes all over the woman's dress) nudged Rick's arm. Rick turned in the direction Garrett pointed, nodded, and resumed conversation. Garrett gave the stupid, laugh-handshake thing to some neighboring dude they didn't know.

Leslie grinned. "See, Viv? Others might be gawking at the women, but Rick's disinterested. Girl, what you *doin'* to that man?"

"You're young, Leslie. Give it time. He's just into whatever he's talking about. He knows Viv is watching." Patrice rolled her eyes.

Naomi grew irritated with Miss Rain O. Parade. "So, which is it, Patrice? He knows Viv is watching, or he's into his discussion? Because I've seen plenty of men stop talking, eating, drinking, or whatever, to rubberneck a woman passing by. And Rick hasn't once checked for Viv's whereabouts."

Patrice returned a look of perturbance Naomi couldn't have cared less about.

"It's fine, Naomi." Viv turned to Leslie. "Rick's never ogled, not in my presence; he's not an ogling-type dude. But he has a penis, so I know he looks."

Naomi shook her head. "Not tonight, though, Viv. The only shape he's checked out...is yours."

Viv blushed with a quasi-smile. "Well, even when he does, since he doesn't *ogle*, it doesn't bother me. I look at other men sometimes."

Leslie reared back. "Girl, why?! Your husband is fine as sh—" She stopped, looking embarrassed. "Sorry."

Viv returned an understanding grin. "Thank you, Leslie. He is."

Joy sent her eyes upward with a headshake. "*Freakishly.*"

Everyone chuckled except Patrice.

Leslie nudged Viv's arm. "Go over there, Viv. Walk past him."

Viv's mouth fell open. "What?!"

Joy nodded with exuberance. "Yeah, Viv. See what happens."

"Uh, no."

"Please?! Come on." Leslie wavered, her expression pleading.

Viv smirked. "What is this, high school?"

"Maybe. But one of the fun parts of it. Come on," Joy urged.

Viv looked at Naomi.

Naomi grinned, wanting to see it, too.

Viv sighed, shaking her head with a grin. "Oookay..."

"Yes!" Leslie leaned closer to Viv. "Okay, so walk past like the other ladies did. See what Rick does."

Viv gave Leslie a look Naomi couldn't place, but she started away.

The ladies went quiet, watching for what developed.

Viv sauntered toward where their men congregated (Rick talking animatedly). Naomi noticed other men turning heads to Viv. Viv was a head-turner in jeans, but in that dress tonight...

When Viv passed behind Rick, Kevin gave Rick a heads-up nod. Rick turned, seeing Viv walking on. The ladies watched as Rick addressed the fellas, then caught up the few steps Viv had on him. He stopped her with a hand to her lower back. Viv turned to him. There was an exchange between the couple, and then they smiled at each other in that *more-than-friends* way.

Leslie sighed yet again. "Lord. He is just..."

A smile bowed Naomi's lips. "It's good watching them."

"Yeah..." Louise's response was low, but Joy looked at her funny, because it seemed Louise agreed with only one-half of Naomi's summation; that maybe it was good watching *only one* of them.

Joy smiled as she watched them, too. "The way he looks at her. If you can see how he feels about her from here..."

Leslie laughed. "Imagine what it's like receiving it up close and personal like Viv is."

Warm, acknowledging chuckles followed.

"You know,...Rick looks at her like that all the time. When Viv walks into the room, he..." Leslie shook her head with a smile of appreciative reflection.

Also in their view was Garrett Carter, roaming his eyes over Viv. He exchanged the "stupid, laugh-handshake" with the other dude in unmistakable sexual reference to his sister-in-law, the buddy nodding and grinning his total agreement with Garrett. Kevin and Brendan frowned, showing their irritation with Garrett's disrespect. Trevor shook his head with a scoff of annoyance, while Tim watched the couple and then nodded and shook his head in a way that was unclear what it meant.

Naomi glanced at the ladies to see if they spotted it. Various reactions, from mouths hanging open with shock to hands over mouths with embarrassment for Patrice, meant they'd also spotted Garrett's lack of discretion.

Patrice, her face contorted with rage, looked away. Naomi knew people, trained and endeavored in understanding their motivations. So, she didn't need aura-flickers to inform about personality traits. But based on her interactions with Patrice (and discussions with Viv about her), Naomi deemed Patrice to have an aura somewhere in the green family (passionate, down-to-earth, competitive, structured, jealous, harmony-seeker, workaholic). The discord and discontent Patrice brewed regarding Rick and Viv earlier contrasted being a natural harmony-seeker, but people were strange, variable creatures. Patrice's moody displays this evening suggested her green aura (if that was the color) wasn't a bright Kelly-green but currently something muddier and darker, harboring elements of that jealousy and some adverse competitiveness (with Viv?).

Attention back with Rick and Viv; they watched Rick peck Viv's lips and lean close with a hand to her waist, saying something in her ear that made Viv laugh with a bit of flirt.

Joy scoffed kindly. "Unh. These two..."

Agreeing snickers followed, the focus still on Viv and Rick. Eyes locked, there was additional exchange between the couple before they pecked lips again.

"Even their pecks are sensual." Joy sighed.

Leslie did, too.

"That...That is rather sexy." Patrice spoke low, with a trace of painful sadness, and Naomi experienced a pang of sympathy for her.

Viv headed back toward the group, and Rick watched her departure (as he'd done several times throughout the evening).

Joy giggled. "Viv's heading away, and he's *still* lookin'."

Naomi chuckled. *Sittin' on a rock, boy.*

Rick lowered his head and shook it with obvious male meaning, then looked over at his boys.

Kevin smiled in camaraderie and men-only understanding and waved Rick back over, and Naomi's attraction to her man surged some.

Rick turned for another look at his wife. Men were male, but not all males were *masculine*. Some men carried an extra intangible element conveying robust virility intertwined with a captivating persona—Rick Phillips was prime example.

"Damn, look at him!"

Naomi extended kind warning. "Les..."

"You're right. Sorry."

Their men laughed as Rick rejoined them, Garrett grinning in his face as if he hadn't, moments before, coveted Rick's wife. Rick exchanged the well-known laugh-with-a-power-handshake with Kevin, which the ladies welcomed under an understanding, acceptable arena.

Viv stepped up. "Satisfied?"

Leslie nodded her approval. "Nice, Viv. What'd he say in your ear?"

Viv raised an eyebrow at Les, wearing this secretive smirk. "Uh, no."

Joy bounced with excitement, smiling hard. "Ooooh! It was nasty!"

Viv's smirk, while still secretive, also turned knowing: Rick's words were indeed X-rated and only for his wife's ears.

Leslie shook her head, closing her eyes with a sigh. "Just *hot*."

They laughed, but Naomi also noticed the women giving Patrice these side glances in response to what the "experiment" also revealed.

Viv looked around at them. "What's wrong?"

"Nothing, Viv. That was interesting." With her eyes, Naomi let Viv know she'd tell her later, and Viv nodded subtly.

Patrice scoffed.

Louise had gone quiet: both aroused by Rick's display and jealous of Viv being on the receiving end of it.

Leslie sent Viv a happy-shrewd look. "Rick was all into you, Viv; as you saw."

Viv nodded. "Still, we're realistic about acknowledging other people are attractive, too. But it stops there, Les."

"No, it doesn't. Or have you forgotten about his sidepieces?" Patrice's comment was vindictive, but after what just happened, Naomi understood it. Still, her vindictiveness was misdirected.

Naomi turned to her. "Well, more like 'jump-offs' than true sidepieces, Patrice. It makes no difference, but there is a difference."

Viv stared at her sister. "Thank you, Naomi."

Patrice scoffed and turned away.

Leslie frowned with disappointment, her elation over the experiment fading. "Oh."

Viv touched Leslie's arm. "It's okay, Les. Rick did his thing..."

Leslie looked hurt.

"...And I did mine."

Leslie's eyes widened, lips parting with surprise.

Viv nodded, appearing regrettable over that admission, then shook her head. "But all of that is over with now, Leslie."

An obvious question formed behind Leslie's eyes; she wanted to know what happened but knew it wasn't her place to ask.

Viv apparently read that, too. "The reasons are personal, rather complicated. But... Well, that's a whole other conversation, okay?"

Leslie smiled, showing all her teeth. "One I don't need to have."

The ladies resumed watching the fellas as Curtis resumed spinning tracks, starting with Bell-Biv-DeVoe's "Do Me!"

Unable to ignore the lure of the bass, the ladies bounced to the beat, getting back into the dancing swing of things. When the "Smack-it, Flip-it" part came on, the men paused their discussion to sing the lyrics together and then laughed in their men-only way, giving each other dap and looking sexily appealing in those tuxedos as they did.

Some men-only gestures rendered attractive to the female.

Leslie, Joy, and Louise (looking over at the men) sounded simultaneous grunts. Patrice rolled her eyes with a harsh exhale.

Rick caught Viv's eye and winked at her.

Blushing, Viv shook her head at him with a grin as another woman approached the men, walking past in a tight lipstick-red dress. Garrett pointed her out—to Kevin this time. Kevin turned but didn't comment, so Garrett turned to the guy they didn't know (the only one giving Garrett the feedback he needed). New-dude extended Garrett the conspiratorial-laugh-handshake-with-a-knowing-nod gesture.

Naomi exhaled a wispy breath, happy at Kevin's indifference.

Patrice sucked her teeth.

Viv addressed Leslie. "Rick and I are *locked*, okay?"

Leslie nodded, pride and admiration filling her eyes once again.

"We've been through some grievous and unfortunate stuff to reaffirm that. Doesn't mean it's all sunshine and rainbows; we're imperfect people. Perfection is boring. But as far as that loving, *committed*, one-on-one thing... Yeah, we're locked. Fuck the dumb stuff."

Louise mumbled something Naomi recognized as painful acknowledgment of that truth.

Leslie, openly relieved, hugged Viv.

Viv stepped back. "But as I was saying, it stops with looking, Les. Because, as concerns our marriage, Rick is doing what he's supposed to be doing to keep my focus. *If* you get my meaning..."

Leslie issued a knowing head-bob.

Viv winked. "And I'm doing my part to keep Rick's focus. So that, if there's a next time,....his death will be justified."

The others snickered their understanding agreement.

"Oh, it's obvious you two get it in." Leslie winked back.

Viv smiled with a trace of blush but turned to her sister. "And since Garrett is the main one checking out the dresses, Reecie, perhaps you're not." She walked away.

The tension Patrice was causing bothered Naomi—especially during what's supposed to be a celebratory and philanthropic occasion. Naturally, it grew quiet with Viv's departure.

Joy gazed at Patrice with solace. "Sorry you had to see that, Patrice."

Leslie nodded. "Yeah. That is kinda messed up."

Patrice whipped around, glaring at Joy and Leslie before her expression changed to exaggerated confusion. "See what? I don't know what you're talking about." She left them, her walk heavy with patent fury.

Naomi watched Viv access her phone. She appeared to be texting.

Moments later, Naomi noticed Rick check his phone. He read for a few seconds and then looked up, scanning the ballroom, stopping when he spotted his wife. The couple exchanged a look across the room, Rick gesturing at Viv with inquiry, asking if she wanted him to come to her. When Viv shook her head, Rick winked and returned his attention to the fellas. Viv left the ballroom.

OSCAR (10:09 p.m.)

Oscar watched Naomi and that major dime standing and talking at the rear of the ballroom. He kept his distance (he wasn't trying to be around Naomi, anyway), but he couldn't keep from seeking that other one out in the ballroom, looking her over, imagining...

He'd been checking out Black-and-Silver-Dress (and her husband) a lot. The husband did the right thing by stepping to him, he guessed; it was an all-man move he respected. He wondered if he was from Mississippi like Cecily, though; sure sounded like it.

And while husband was too attentive to Black-and-Silver for Oscar's tastes, he figured he must have a handle on that fine-ass bitch, must know how to control all that beauty without hitting it and leaving marks—like *he* did. He knew she had a banging body. Not solely because of the dress, but because that dress didn't hug her skintight to show it. Sometimes women wore their dresses too damn tight. Prime example: Janyce. She was on the heavier side—and that bright-pink-ass dress only brought more attention to that because of how it fit her. Big women could be sexy as shit—they just needed to go about it right. Women believed men think, "the tighter the dress, the better," but nah. For a little bedroom entertainment, maybe, but at something like this? Nah.

Yeah, Black-and-Silver was pretty as shit, had a hot little figure. Oscar scoffed and shook his head as he watched her and sipped his drink. *Probably a prude in bed; the mega-fine ones usually are—all that beauty and those curves going to waste.*

Cecily was fine, too. Oh yeah. But he had her handled; won't allow her to *know* she's fine: can't keep a handle on 'em if they know they have options other than you. Cecily probably believed he fucked some others since they've been together—but he wasn't a cheater. He let her think it, though: point, Oscar.

Irritated about Naomi being there, Oscar checked out their table. Cecily and Karen were talking, Cecily smiling at something Karen said. She seemed to be coming around, having a good time. If she wasn't, too fucking bad; wasn't his fault she didn't have the personality for this shit.

Janyce and Hank were on the dancefloor. Although not parties at their table, Winton and his wife also danced. He hadn't danced with Cecily; saving his energy for the jamming finale. Yeah, he made some jive promise about spending the evening up her ass, but she knew the deal: he couldn't exaserrate himself—needed to save all that for the finale...and fucking her later. He could at least dance a slow one with her, but she looked like she was okay. If she wasn't, he'd let her complain about it either before or after he got the pussy.

Oscar turned his attention to the dancefloor. So far, Janyce left the fucking brooch where it was, thank God. If Cecily had seen that shit...

Winton spun his wife and smiled. Oscar could take or leave him, but Winton was a Mason—and he was doing his damnedest to get Winton to sponsor and get him in. He hadn't been paid for it yet, but Winton also raped and beat his wife two years ago,...and Oscar worked up to one day asking him...what that was like.

NAOMI (10:33 p.m.)

She didn't do line-dances, but Naomi stood beside her table, enjoying watching the others do one. She didn't know if this line-dance was the Baltimore one, or the Chicago one, or the Atlanta one, or just what (she knew the Wobble, Cha-Cha, and Electric ones: this wasn't any of those), but seeing those shades of brown (including Trevor, Leslie, Rick, Joy, Kevin, and Brendan) in fancy, formal clothing being quite unfancied and informal at the moment, was a treat.

Although several people and rows away from Rick (a respectable distance), the Lynelle-woman seemed to be getting her own secret treat going as she often focused on Rick's body movements (the distinct red bottoms of Rick's court shoes flourishing with his steps). Viv sat this one out and was elsewhere, but Lynelle best maintain that respectable distance.

Cecily watched from her table, her cued shoulder movements showing she "line-danced," too—from her chair.

Spotting Oscar across the way, Naomi began profiling him...

He valued money, material things, and had a backward sense of loyalty. Signs of weakness were wrong to him and thus something he exploited; he thrived off others' hurt feelings (particularly Cecily's). He resented professionals (like herself) and had little respect for public servants (like his sister). Naomi observed him, speculating some positives, some good qualities. Everyone had them, so they were there—underneath the mountainous rest of it.

She'd come up with a few, when Viv stepped up beside her, a glass of sparkling water with fresh peaches in hand.

"Almost over. Having a good time?"

Viv grinned and sipped. "I am, Naomi. This has been very..." she trailed off, her eyes roaming the activity.

"I'm glad. ...What fragrance is your husband wearing tonight?"

Eyes on the activity, Viv spoke without looking at her. "Smells good as shit on 'im, doesn't it?"

Naomi let the truth set her free. "Yes, it does."

In profile, Viv's expression fused a sweet, knowing smirk. "He's wearing Hermès Terre d'Hermès." She sighed, still taking in the gala. "...So, what was the deal after the whole 'see what Rick will do' experiment? My sister."

"We all watched Garrett looking you over with hungry, I-don't-care-if-she-is-my-sister-in-law eyes, then give the guy next to him the knowing-laugh-handshake with clear implication of— Well..."

Viv turned to her, lips parted with shock. Anger moved through her dark eyes before filling with sympathy. "I'm sorry."

"You did nothing wrong, Viv, but I get it."

Viv went quiet.

"He's likely been attracted to you since way back, Viv. He's been respectful, I take it; seeing you had no clue about his desires until now."

Viv's onyx eyes held confusion and worry. "I'm sorry."

Naomi now realized Viv's apology was for the situation's impact on her sister, not for any guilt over it.

"For Patrice."

"Yes. That she witnessed that. Men being men is one thing..."

"Gonna tell Rick?"

"In all honesty, Naomi, Rick probably already knows."

Naomi nodded. That was true. Rick didn't have "flashes of truth" like she did (that she knew of), but since knowing him, she'd gathered he was highly intuitive about many things.

"I can find out if he's already aware, though. I'll see."

"Okay. Let me know if I can do anything."

Viv shook her head with a scoffing-chuckle.

"What?"

"I knew I should've given those extra tickets to Mark and Barbara instead. Mark can dance, shoot."

Naomi and Viv had a good laugh at that.

CECILY (10:39 p.m.)

The night waned, and she had yet to dance, but that was okay; she had fun chair-dancing, she guessed. Naomi advised her to throw caution to the wind, but Naomi also knew better (at least Cecily did).

Out of nowhere, her husband sat next to her. "Hey."

Cecily blinked at him; she'd barely seen him tonight. "Having fun?" She didn't know Oscar's answer—because her body flushed with a rush of different things: Josh approached their table.

Josh smiled and extended his hand to Oscar. "Just wanted to say hello before the night was gone."

Oscar smiled and pumped Josh's hand. "Hey, man. Yeah, what's up? Thought I recognized you."

Recognized him? Cecily let the thought go as she accepted Josh's warm hand. She nodded instead of speaking, not trusting her words or how she'd sound.

Josh stood behind a chair, holding the back of it. He wasn't quite six feet tall, but he sure looked it in that black double-breasted tuxedo with the satin facing and shawl collar. Instead of no vents, he went the still-appropriate double-vent route (single vents were just a no-no). His jetted pocket held a puffed pocket square of pebble-gray complementing his mother-of-pearl studs and cufflinks. He'd taken his twists out for tonight and now wore this short, unkempt 'fro with a clean line-up shaped to perfection. He'd trimmed his Cavalier facial grooming to the Hollywoodian, giving him a refined look.

Josh wore no jewelry other than his Iota lapel pin. He accented his pleated French-cuff turndown with a pebble-gray bowtie knotted into the butterfly. Cecily preferred turndown-collars to winged ones. She'd already noticed (those times she looked without looking) he wore trousers with satin braiding and hemmed with a mild break over black pinched-bow pumps. With her once-over, she knew: he wore button-suspenders, not clip-on; that he carried a money clip, not a wallet. Her Joshua (sometimes she liked saying that to herself) looked dapper.

He gestured at her and looked at Oscar with a nod toward the dance-floor. "If it's all right with you, I'd like to dance with Cecily. See how my coworker grooves to the beat..."

Her husband waved a dismissive hand. "I don't care, man. Take her. But unless you want a fat ugly pumpkin on your hands, I suggest you bring her back by midnight!" He howled at his joke as he pulled out his phone, and Cecily wished her fairy godmother would make him (or her) disappear.

She knew Josh well. Josh returned a wan smile (being polite), but he smoothed his mustache using his thumb and index finger: Oscar's response bothered him. "If you say so." He turned eyes to her, extending his hand in invitation. "Cecily?"

Lord, the way he said her name!

Cecily stared at Joshua (feeling Oscar's eyes on her). He already knew how she grooved to the beat; they'd danced together recently. And she appreciated Joshua coming correct, respecting Oscar (and all that), but she hesitated, fearing Oscar's wrath later.

Cecily, if you don't dance with that man, be charitable to yourself for just a few minutes...

Giving in to her human desire to have fun and enjoy herself, Cecily accepted his hand and tried to speak as casually as she could (given her insides were melting). She shrugged as she stood, playing things off even more. "Sure. No harm in it."

Cecily understood when Josh released her hand before they headed to the dancefloor (guiding her by the hand was too loving, too romantic), but she still hated feeling his fingers leaving hers.

"Outstanding" by Gap Band wound down as they reached the dance-floor, and Cecily expected another faster-paced jam to start, but "I Wanna Know" by Joe came through the speakers instead.

Josh conferred with her visually, those eyes of molasses asking if she still wanted to dance—even to something slower.

Determined not to overthink it, Cecily inclined her head in a yes.

Josh took her hand, guiding her closer, but not against him. His hand was warm, strong. He held one hand and sent the other to her waist, keeping a certain distance between them any nun-chaperone with a ruler would approve of.

Cecily placed her free hand on his shoulder and danced with him. He smelled of something new (still likely Polo), and Cecily had a hard time concentrating for the delicious scents surrounding her.

NAOMI (10:39 p.m.)

When he approached their table, Naomi knew who he was. She hadn't been introduced, he hadn't been pointed out, and all she had was a name, but she needed nothing else. The man approaching Oscar and Cecily was Joshua Hall.

If Rick Phillips was an eleven (no, not ten, and no, she shouldn't use Rick as a barometer for handsomeness, but as her daughter said, that man was in a category of handsome downright new and thus warranting a barometer for the others), she'd say Cecily's Joshua (again, not a good idea, but whatever) edged a solid eight (ten still being the highest number possible for those not named Richard A. Phillips Senior).

Watching that man approach the table and shake hands, the way he stood firmly behind the chair and spoke, the way he rubbed his mustache (at something seeming to annoy him), and then extended his hand to Cecily, Naomi almost went over there, figurative bullhorn in hand, with message to the three of them: *Yes, Joshua, my patient will dance with you and leave this place with you and leave that narcissistic abusive asshole of a husband behind, because she has feelings for you and I believe you're good for her!*

But alas, she stood with Viv and watched the scene play out, doing nothing but rooting for Cecily to dance with him.

When Cecily accepted his hand and stood, Naomi responded with a fist pump. "Yes!"

Viv looked at her. "What?"

Naomi spotted Rick near the portrait table, trying to get Viv's attention. "Nothing." She gestured in Rick's direction. "Rick wants you."

When Viv turned to him, Rick smiled and beckoned her. Viv's quick laugh was dainty and full of blush. "If you'll excuse me…"

"But of course." Naomi returned attention to Cecily and Joshua making their way to the dancefloor, and Naomi looked forward to seeing Cecily boogie down. However, as they reached the dancefloor and the tempo changed, Naomi worried Cecily would balk. When she didn't, Naomi sighed her relief.

Naomi divided her attention between Cecily and Joshua, Viv and Rick, doing her best to remain neutral on all fronts (although she could see Joshua liked Cecily more than casually, too). Joshua and Cecily talked and danced, their bodies a distance approved by society-at-large, while Rick had his wife backed to the wall, a hand to her waist, singing portions of Joe's "I Wanna Know" to her, the couple smiling and talking when he wasn't singing. Assured in his masculinity, Rick clearly didn't care what other men would think of his attentiveness to his woman. During moments things turned meaningful, Viv cupped Rick's cheek. The distance between Cecily and Joshua was greater than that between Viv and Rick, but each man beheld the object of his affection with equal intensity.

When the song ended, Joshua held Cecily's gaze for several seconds before nodding and escorting her back to her table.

Naomi issued another (albeit private) fist pump.

Kevin kissed her cheek, startling her. "What're you so happy about?"

Her fist pump wasn't so private, after all. "Numerous things."

Kevin pulled her chair, and Naomi sat with him, telling a little of what she could about recent developments.

CECILY (10:41 p.m.)

"So, what do you have to say for yourself, Missus Brooks?" Josh's smile held a hint of mischief as Joe sang his ballad. He smelled tantalizingly of roasted coffee mixed with mango, berries, and nutmeg.

"Huh?"

"Well, first: *Hello*, Cecily." He bowed his head.

"Oh. I'm sorry. Hi, Josh. You didn't say you were coming to this."

"You didn't, either. But, the way you've been avoiding me tonight, this last week, I'm guessing that was on purpose."

"I'm not avoiding you, Josh."

"I beg to differ. You've laughed and talked with a few people tonight, but you shifted away every time it even looked like I might head in your direction. Not that you need to—" He shook his head. "Anyway, this is my first time at this event. You?"

"Third time." Her three-inch heels provided additional height, but she still looked up at him. "It's a wonderful cause; they feed you well..."

"That's true. They've gone all out with the hors d'oeuvres. Except the kiwi. Yech!" He frowned accordingly.

She rolled her eyes in fun and popped his shoulder. "They cut the skin off, Josh. Geez!"

Josh smiled while scrunching his nose. "Still." He added a shiver of disgust for effect. "A bit too crinose for me. Sorry."

They shared a hushed laugh, and these were the best three minutes she'd had all day. "Coconuts have hair..." She smirked at him.

He smirked back and nodded, but there was something sad about it as his half-smile evaporated. He looked at her. "Why didn't you want to say 'hi' to me?"

Oh, they needed to be alone somewhere!

The look in his eyes, the hurt in his voice; they just needed to be alone (and she not married) so she could wipe the pain away.

Having no excuse, she shrugged.

The hand at her waist tightened. "...You haven't danced tonight."

"You haven't, either." So, yes, they were both well aware of the other without having spoken. Cecily held his gaze, both allowing that fact (of neither having danced until now) to sit between them.

"True." He glanced away before looking into her eyes. "...If you don't mind me asking, what're you wearing? Your fragrance...?" Those molasses irises appeared hesitant but curious...and subtly turned-on, so her scent didn't bother him (not negatively, anyway).

"I don't mind. It's Samsara by Guerlain." She wanted to ask what the heck that was *he* had on. "I...I don't wear it often."

His slow nod told her how much he liked her fragrance.

With her eyes, she signaled his new haircut. "I like the 'fro."

Josh semi-smirked, his scent enhancing his new look.

"What?"

"How does the moon give the sun a haircut?"

She felt her own blushing smile with her shrug. "How?"

The playful tease in his molasses irises danced. "...Eclipse it."

Her body jolted with contradiction: wanting to give Josh a laughing hug yet needing to be mindful of Oscar. She laughed mildly as he chuckled with her, hoping her eyes and smile conveyed how good she thought his joke was. "You get a pass for the coming week, Jester."

"Thanks." His chuckles soon died with his focus on her. "So,...no contacts again." Absolute approval moved through his gaze at her.

Cecily resisted smiling at seeing his pleasure. "No contacts."

Josh grinned. His gaze then lowered to her lips.

She focused on his eyes, because if she lowered her gaze to his lips, gazed at that line in his mustache, she didn't want to be held responsible for whatever followed.

Cecily fully expected and so wasn't surprised when he looked away, mumbling "Shit," as he had times before. She noted his profile as he looked everywhere but at her, wanting, quite frankly, to push fingers into his gray-speckled kinky 'fro...and her tongue into his ear.

His lowering lids suggested similar issues on his end.

Never mind a ruler: a yardstick between them would do nothing to curtail the underlying heat of attraction moving between them.

Finally, he turned to her. "Listen with me, okay? Just dance and listen, and I'll take you back to Oscar."

Cecily nodded. "I can do that."

They finished dancing to "I Wanna Know" in silence, Cecily knowing Josh meant many of the lyrics for her. And she wanted to tell him: what turned her on, what made her cry—that he already was the one who made her smile.

The song ended and his hands to her body tightened, telling her not to move just yet. She waited, holding his molasses gaze until, seconds later, he nodded and released her.

Peabo Bryson's "Let the Feeling Flow" started as they walked back, and Cecily wondered if Josh experienced the same tremor of *a something* as she did (oh, how she wanted to let her feelings flow—and reach for the sky). The way he turned to her suggested maybe he had.

Josh escorted her back to her table (Oscar having vacated it again).

"And this, is where I leave you. Thank you for the dance, Cecily." He lifted her hand and kissed it. "Enjoy the rest of your evening."

"You, too, Josh." She sat and took out her phone (to avoid watching him walk away).

CECILY (10:51 p.m.)

It was a table for ten, but it would seem only she was aware of that; other than Karen, no one sat at the table except her. Many other tables were also vacant, guests preoccupied with dancing, talking, and socializing in a more vertical-type situation. Janyce hadn't been at the table in a long time (since the brooch incident?), but she could have; she'd already dismissed the whole thing. Had to be those glasses of wine making her see things; Janyce wouldn't do that to her.

What is seven times seven?

She saw Oscar standing alone by the hors d'oeuvre table and started to wave him over to come sit with her, but changed her mind for fear of being embarrassed by his rejection. She was generally over him reneging on his promise for them to hang together tonight, but she didn't expect to be this far into the ball without having danced with him once. Yes, he needed to conserve his energy (and all that), but she wasn't asking him to breakdance for her. He hadn't been mean or rude to her tonight (except for equating her to a "fat ugly pumpkin"), but Oscar was giving her the silent treatment for a reason she didn't know.

She sure could use an earful of Nina Simone right about now. An earful to lose connection with a world that had Oscar in it. She watched the guests partying, daydreaming about what that would be like—under different circumstances.

Maybe she should take Naomi up on her offer and get a dance in with a gentleman from her table. Or even dance with Naomi's group of ladies together—that could be fun, too.

When Naomi suggested she dance with any of the men from her table, Cecily couldn't help blushing: the gentleman in the waistcoat was incredibly handsome. She could see herself stumbling and misstepping: embarrassing herself for gawking at him and not paying attention to what she was doing. She chuckled to herself with images of that scenario. All the gentlemen appeared friendly, but Cecily liked the one in the waistcoat because he was so attentive to his wife. Watching him, he was right out of the 1930s, with the respectful standing and chair-pulling and hand-touching and refreshment serving and... Well, she enjoyed watching him and his wife. She was in the ladies' room when Oscar had that run-in with them earlier. Thankfully, things didn't go far left.

Naomi's date was handsome and carried an old-school vibe like the guy wearing the waistcoat, but she didn't focus on him as much, she guessed, because he was her doctor's date (and on some level, any focus on him seemed weirder). She wondered if Naomi's date knew the secret to being able to read her and get a fix on what was going on inside Naomi's head; Cecily was sure stumped.

Her thoughts shifted to her dance with Joshua.

Josh holding her but not closely (being respectful), swaying on the dancefloor together, shouldn't have been, but was the highlight of her night. Alone at the table, she imagined the dance sans respect for Oscar, their bodies touching while they talked and laughed privately as the music serenaded them.

Cecily nibbled her upper lip, trying to push Josh out of her mind. Naomi said she needed to redirect her energies to Oscar if she was devoting herself to him. Cecily shook her head and scoffed. Naomi probably had some tricks up her sleeve to help with that, which was good, because Cecily didn't think she'd be able to achieve redirection without help. Her connection to Josh wasn't just physical, wasn't just because she was unhappy in her marriage. She and Josh were on a path of genuine friendship. She didn't want to redirect from that.

Still thinking about that dance with Josh, Cecily chuckled to herself again, this time with a trace of self-pity. She hadn't had good sex in years, but during that dance with Josh, her hormones worked on all cylinders, giving her those pleasant trembly, anticipatory feelings in certain places, the good female places. Readying for something...futile.

She'd already picked up on a few single women (and a couple of married ones) flirting with Joshua. Her chest burned and her stomach stiffened with a dropping sensation. She didn't want to be jealous but couldn't help it. Watching Josh smile and talk (but not dance), she wondered what he did for sex, wondered if he was still with Kristin. She hadn't seen or heard him mention another woman in long months.

Pornographic images of Josh in the act popped into her head, and she startled, sending the offending (but arousing) thoughts away.

Cecily concentrated on other ball activity, needing a drink or an hors d'oeuvre or those anti-anxiety meds. She heeded Naomi's warning and drank nothing else alcoholic; maybe she could get the meds back.

James Brown's "Bewildered" came on, and multiple folk cheered their appreciation for the selection.

Smiling to herself with the thoughts any James Brown song evoked, Cecily turned to find Josh looking over at her. His grinning nod, referencing the music, made her laugh.

A hand touched her shoulder.

Cecily looked up into the eyes of a man who had possibly stolen her contacts. He was tortilla-brown with a headful of brown wavy hair, thin lips, and ears that stuck out. His nose was prominent, bordering wide yet pointy. Big, wide, and pointy weren't negative to Cecily, but his nose just wasn't strong to her. Strong noses were a very nuanced thing. His hazel eyes glimmered as he extended his hand. "Care to dance?"

It was clear he expected her to swoon with a sighing "yes," and accept his hand. He wasn't a throw-back as far as looks go, but he wasn't the most handsome man in the room, either—as he apparently so believed. She'd noticed a few tonight that "out-handsomed" him by a long shot (her Joshua included). He smelled of some citrusy-cedar scent. Mr. Suave's subtle smirk already had them dancing and her giving up the goodies in a back room—if *he* was so inclined.

It pissed her off. Naomi wasn't an easy read, but this dude was so full of himself, he was ugly with it.

She took deliberate seconds to look him over before shaking her head and smiling. "Not interested, but thank you." She could've simply said, *No, thank you*, but she wanted to send him a message.

Mr. Suave nodded and walked away, shock and anger in his eyes. His trousers were too long, too, and he wore a red carnation boutonniere with a silver pocket square. She scoffed. Stylists didn't recommend it, but a man could get away with wearing a boutonniere and pocket square together under one condition: both must be *white*. She didn't take a class on formal attire etiquette, but she knew stuff.

Karen and Adele returned, and Cecily chatted with them; they seemed friendlier tonight and not as cliquish as at the New Year's party.

She didn't wave Oscar over, but he had come closer to their table, talking with that "Winton" dude and Hank again.

Janyce still stayed away.

OSCAR (10:51 p.m.)

Her contacts were out. He'd get the fine points on that later.

When Joshua asked to dance with Cecily, he jumped at the offer for her to dance with someone else, so she couldn't say shit when he did. He needed to conserve energy for the finale, but if he wanted to dance with someone, now he was free to without Cecily being able to moan and bitch about him flirting.

Oscar watched them dancing, holding in a laugh. Poor man must've felt sorry for her. He stood so far apart from her. That may have been out of respect for him, but Oscar didn't care about that petty shit; he had Cecily on lock. Besides, there was also a point where Joshua couldn't even look at Cecily as they danced. Ha! He felt sorry enough to ask for the dance but could hardly stand to hold or look at her once they got going. Joshua couldn't have been 40 yet, but gave the middle-aged woman some "play" to be nice, but then, he could barely follow through with it. Guess, being charitable to Cecily, Joshua ended up with the short end of the stick. Oscar held in another laugh.

Nah, he had no worries about Mr. GQ-wannabe. He didn't bring a date. Probably came stag to have his choice of young hunnies. Oscar nodded; he could appreciate that.

Husband of that serious piece-of-ass in the black-and-silver dress was all in her pretty face, singing and talking to her up against the wall and shit; working hard to get some later. Oscar scoffed; he never had to play it up like that to get between Cecily's legs. He did enough to appeal to her soft side sometimes, making her feel her *woman* thing, but that was it. Black-and-Silver must be an ice-queen in bed for all he was doing, damn! Some men learned the hard way, romancing women and shit forever instead of locking them in before changing shit up, teaching they didn't need all that lovey-dovey crap: it drove a man away.

When the song was over, Joshua walked Cecily back to their table, adding the punk-ass move of kissing her hand. Cecily took out her phone as soon as she sat—unimpressed with Mr. GQ-wannabe (and she was a sucker for that punk shit). He'd trained her well.

With a grin, he people-watched. Some random dude approached their table and said something to Cecily. He watched her shake her head, saying words, and dude walked away. Joshua's charitable effort must be catching: all the punks were approaching the wallflower. But she'd done the right thing by turning dude down: she'd only had permission for that one dance.

He watched Cecily sitting at the table. Karen and Adele returned and sat, all three women chatting about something. He couldn't be sure, but he thought Cecily looked...happier.

Oscar finished his beer and set the bottle on the table with a belch. He'd dance a slow dance with her. He was the husband, after all. Need to show Mr. Husband of Black-and-Silver and Mr. GQ-wannabe he owned some quality goods; they couldn't show him up.

Seeing the menfolk back near the table, he sauntered over.

CECILY (10:55 p.m.)

Cecily talked with Karen and Adele, but her attention wavered. She made out snippets of Oscar's conversation with Hank and Winton, and something about their discussion bothered her. Cecily didn't know what bothered her or why, but listening to them talk was both familiar and...revolting.

She tried focusing on Karen talking like a dog behind Janyce's back about her fuchsia dress, and on Adele's laughing co-sign with Karen, but the conversation and laughter to her left pulled at her.

When it hit her what bothered her and why, why the discussion sounded both familiar and revolting, Cecily was stunned.

She reached in Karen's direction, patting the cloth-covered tabletop. "Excuse me." Cecily collected her purse and stepped away. She headed toward the ladies' room but changed direction upon seeing Naomi enter the ladies' room with two other women from her table.

NAOMI (11:03 p.m.)

Having taken care of their lady business, Naomi stood with Les and Viv in the vestibule, watching those two freshen their girly. Usually heavier than the men's room, traffic in the ladies' room was light.

Leslie applied lipstick, eyeing Viv in the mirror. "Y'all dance a lot?"

Viv added dabs of body oil to her wrists and rubbed them together. "No more than anybody else, I guess. We get up if we're sitting at home listening to music and something good, slow or fast, comes on. Why?"

"I don't know." Leslie shrugged with a smiling-blush. "I like the way you and Rick move together. Like you've been doing it so long, you anticipate what the other will do."

Viv propped against the side of a colossal wingback chair. "Well, isn't that what most longtime couples do?"

Leslie shook her head. "You're not getting what I'm saying. It's beyond looking like you've been dancing together a long time. It's much more sensual than that. I first saw it weeks ago when you and Rick danced to 'When We Get By.' When you dance together, it's like your bodies are talking to each other."

"Uh, okay. I see." Viv hunched one shoulder. "Well, our bodies are 'conversing.' There's an undercurrent of desire there, sure. That desire translates into how we move together, the rhythm of the desire, I guess. We've always bonded over music. Maybe that's what you're seeing."

Leslie's second headshake included a mischievous grin. "All I know is, you two were dancing, but those watching were getting worked up."

Viv laughed. "Okay. That's the first I've heard *that* before."

"Yeah. Like the 'Can't Let Go' dance. With the back-and-forth between slow hand-dancing or 'bopping' as my mother calls it, and then embracing to dance close. The way Rick holds you..." Leslie made an odd expression before continuing. "You two were talking while you danced. Something you said made Rick laugh, but you two didn't miss a step. Girl, it was hot."

"I'm sure plenty other couples looked the same way, Les." Viv gazed at Leslie with wary curiosity.

Leslie looked at Viv. "I thought so, too, so I watched some other couples. Some had a little chemistry, yeah. But it was nothing compared to what was happening at our table."

"You should see them hand-dancing, and Viv has her eyes closed."

Leslie gazed openmouthed at Viv, pure admiration filling her eyes.

Viv turned to her with mild surprise, and Naomi recognized Viv trying to recall an opportunity for her to witness that. "How'd—? When'd—?" Viv shook her head with a tiny smile when the memory popped in and nodded. "We dance that way sometimes, yes."

Leslie hadn't yet closed her mouth. "Wow."

"No, 'wow.' I just feel the rhythm of Rick's body, pick up the signals in his hand as we groove together."

Leslie grunted. "*So* hot."

Naomi lowered her head, shaking it with a faint chuckle. That was Les's apparent go-to adjective for Rick and Viv.

Viv stared at Leslie, appearing uncomfortable with Leslie's open adoration. "Plenty of couples do that, Leslie."

Leslie shrugged, "Okay," her patronizing response sweet.

"We were just *dancing*, Les. Sure you aren't biased?"

"Maybe. I love you guys. But again, *strangers* looked impressed and turned-on as they watched you two. Nuff said."

All three laughed as they exited.

Naomi searched for Cecily as they returned to their table. Although she wanted to explore Cecily's reaction to dancing with Joshua, Naomi left well enough alone; she'd speak with Cecily before she left.

She'd pursued reinforcing who Cecily was before she met Oscar, challenged some of the current traits Cecily displayed. Treating Cecily for her PTSD and the NAS involved correcting the subsequent personality disorder manifesting. Strangely, a person's personality offered a degree of immunity to developing certain psychiatric illnesses. Personality, by itself, reflected a commingling of heredity, temperament, learned disposition during upbringing, and behavioral responses to one's environment, all or most of it formed during youth. However, when a person's personality comprised mostly weak traits, it allowed problems related to dependent personality disorder to manifest and exhibit as social anxiety or depression or somatoform issues. A personality dominated by weak traits made resisting certain psychiatric problems more difficult. Cecily's adoption of dependent personality during her years with Oscar could be derived from many psychodynamics at play.

Naomi sat and talked with her group for maybe two minutes when she spotted Joshua Hall alone at the portrait table.

A banana cream pie was now in order (or banana pudding or banana flambé or...).

NAOMI (11:09 p.m.)

"Most people try to find pictures with their faces and move on, but not you." Naomi stood next to him, checking out the professional pictures. The portrait table was just that: a collage of memories, photos taken at events from previous years.

Joshua smiled, and Naomi liked him; his response could've been different. "Well, this is my first one, so..." He shrugged.

"O-ho! A newbie!" Naomi extended her hand. "Welcome, and thanks for donating. I'm Naomi."

Joshua chortled, his handshake warm and firm. "That's me: newbie Joshua Hall. And thank you." He sounded as if he had allergies. He was even cuter up close, making Naomi push that edging-eight to a solid nine. His brown eyes were gentle and caring, with a hint of mischief. His skin tone was a rich molasses. "I take it you're a seasoned veteran." He smiled, showing this tiny space between his upper far left incisor and left cuspid in his otherwise straight, white teeth. His mustache had a thin line of scar tissue, and his nose had been broken once upon a time, but neither detracted from his cutie-pie.

Naomi nodded. "I'm hit-or-miss, mostly miss, with these events, Joshua, but I've been a supporter every year for the last eight years, yes."

Joshua resumed checking out the photos. "So, what's your trade?"

"Medical. You?"

"Technology." He scanned the ballroom. "You're 'hit-or-miss'? This seems pretty nice."

She liked him, period. "And they're all like this. But 'parties' aren't my thing."

He tilted his head back with a short laugh, and Naomi knew Oscar had to go. "They're not my thing, either."

"But you're all for the cause."

He nodded with assurance. "Of course. I don't care about the money—as long as it goes somewhere *good*, ya know?"

"I do."

He surveyed the ballroom again, and Naomi could have sworn he searched for someone in particular. "It's like, yeah, we have deep pockets, but this isn't about the 'brag.' We're doing something good with it and celebrating that philanthropy." He hunched a shoulder. "Nothing wrong with that. It's once a year..." He looked at her, his brown eyes pushing that mischief forth more. "That's *doable*." His words held part challenge to her over parties not being their thing; telling her in a good-natured way, she didn't have to be hit-or-miss, that *they* could handle one party a year.

Oscar had to go.

Naomi formed a slow, somewhat crooked smile. "Message received, Joshua. Guess I'll see you next year." She prepared to part, but he frowned at her. "What's wrong?"

He shook his head with this curious grin. "Oh, nothing. I often have to correct people from calling me 'Josh'; I prefer 'Joshua.' But I haven't had to say anything to you."

"So, I messed up your rhythm? Had your correction all set and didn't get to use it, huh? Throwing you off?"

He laughed again. Laughed hard. The gray at his temples and in his lined, unkempt 'fro made him look extra distinguished despite the silly moment. And he was working that double-breasted tuxedo (except for that Iota lapel pin, but pish-posh).

Oscar who?

As he continued laughing, Naomi touched his arm and started away. "It was nice meeting you, *Joshua*. Enjoy."

He kept chuckling. "Nice meeting you, Naomi. You, too."

NAOMI (11:13 p.m.)

When she returned to her table, Kevin was on the dancefloor with Viv, dancing to "Freedom" by Grand Master Flash. At the table, Rick, Garrett, and Tim adopted the rapping roles of the Furious Five, performing the lyrics and laughing together.

When Viv and Kevin returned, Viv danced with Garrett while Rick danced with his sister-in-law. Rick and Viv also danced with Leslie and Trevor, respectively.

Naomi noticed, however: Tim didn't ask Viv to dance. She suspected Tim didn't want to give Louise excuse to dance with Rick.

Louise, however, seemed determined to push the boundaries.

Naomi sat close to Kevin (his arm on the back of her chair), listening to his summary findings regarding a forensics case he had, when Louise cackled, evidently having had one too many. There was something about her being so happy Rick was home...and then she began lowering her bottom toward Rick's lap.

Viv turned away, her fist balling around a napkin. She may have been used to the idea of Louise having feelings for Rick, used to women flirting with him—didn't mean she enjoyed seeing it. With Louise, she exercised the patience of Job.

Patrice stood, and Garrett put a hand on her wrist to keep her from doing whatever that was in her eyes she planned to do. Naomi, however, still detected distance between those two.

Kevin pulled his arm from behind her, frowning at the development.

Naomi was glad Tim was in the men's room and Leslie was at Joy's table (she no-doubt would've co-signed with whatever Patrice's plan was). She believed Trevor still lurked around the big-screen TV in the sports lounge.

And Rick's athleticism, his martial-arts training, afforded him the reflexes to instinctively avoid Louise settling on his lap. He cleared his throat and shifted away with ease, giving Louise an annoyed smile with a mumbled, "Thanks," and reached for a seething Viv's hand. "Come on, Lady Blue."

The couple headed to the dancefloor and "Happy" by Rick James and Teena Marie.

Garrett guided Patrice to sit. "I think you've pushed it as far as you can, Lou. Maybe you should sit and chill for a sec."

Louise stared toward the dancefloor (her bob less round). "But all I was say— Everything's so *different*." She pouted drunkenly and sat just as Tim returned.

Naomi held in a smirk. *Well, yes, Louise. It can alter things when it's discovered your dear friend has fallen for your husband and tried to kiss him.* And Naomi didn't believe it was ever okay for Louise to park her rear on Rick's lap—not even back in the glory days of their friendship. *That's still very much the same, Mrs. Nguyễn-Collins.*

Tim sat next to Louise and leaned back, putting his arm on the back of her chair. "Rick and Viv decided to get another dance in, huh? So, what's the discussion...?"

Patrice scoffed and turned to watch her sister. She had major internal beef about something since arriving at the ball, but she also had a protective streak over Viv—something Louise needed to watch out for.

Garrett sighed. "Nothing, man. Sports, tonight's fashions, you name it. Kevin's got some side conversation going on with Naomi about cadavers or some shit."

Everyone but Louise and Patrice hollered.

Tim turned to his wife, who alternated focus between her glass and the dancefloor. "You good, Lou?"

Louise offered a sighing-smile and pecked her husband's lips (to Patrice's soft scoff). "Yes. Be right back." After a fearful glance Patrice's way, Louise made her break for it, Patrice staring hard after her.

Kevin leaned close. "Time to be—"

"A banana. I know." Naomi cupped his cheek and kissed his lips. She checked the DNA-hotline first for any emergent emergencies. Seeing none, she left in search of Louise.

NAOMI (11:29 p.m.)

She soon found Louise alone in the music room, but in the interim, she had to calm her anger with Louise several times. Louise stood at the far end, where it was darker and more secluded, gazing out a window.

Naomi approached Louise, her sympathy bordering nil. "What the hell are you doing, Louise?!"

Louise gazed out the window. Naomi noticed her glass on the piano. She placed it on the discard tray outside the door and returned. "Rick and Viv are into each other; they aren't thinking about you."

"I know."

Naomi crossed her arms, seeds of annoyance sprouting. "You're pushing it, Louise: calling him 'Ricky,' the flirty looks at him, that not-so-anonymous song dedication, and just now, that bull with trying to sit on his l—"

Louise snapped around, teary-eyed. "I *know*, Naomi!" She turned back to the window.

Naomi waited, settling her own nerves. That wasn't the best approach, but Louise wasn't her patient.

"I've...I've tried to get a handle on this. I have. But trying to stop loving him is like..." She scoffed, shaking her head with apparent hopelessness. Silence echoed before she sniffed and continued. "This shit is bad, Naomi. Whenever he comes near me,...it means *everything*."

Naomi already expected her subsequent admission.

"When I'm doing Tim, I can't help fantasizing I'm with Rick."

"You need to turn all that toward Tim, Louise. *Your* husband...instead of Viv's."

"The way he kisses... He is so sexy, and he's funny, smart..." Louise turned to her, and Naomi then listened to her rattle off a litany of Rick's personality traits and physical attributes she adored.

After nearly a minute, Naomi had heard enough. "You know what else he is, Louise? He's *Viv's*." She was glad she warned Viv years ago against further discussing with Louise what she and Rick did sexually.

Louise turned back to the window, speaking above a whisper. "I don't care."

"So, you're just going to risk your friendship for something that will not happen?"

Louise uttered a chuckling-scoff. "Viv and I aren't as close anymore. Not since she realized—" Her gaze fell on Naomi, curious and suspicious. "How'd Viv know? I never confessed anything."

Naomi didn't respond.

Louise turned back to the window. "Anyway, I get it, so I don't blame her. But *you two* are closer than ever, so..."

"Viv has room for more than one close friend, Louise."

Louise cackled, then mimicked her in a mocking, singsong tone: "'Viv has room for more than one close friend, Louise.'"

Naomi counted backward from ten.

Louise blew a thin breath, puffing her cheeks. "I'm sorry. You're just trying to help, I know. I love Viv, Doctor Alexander. And even though this has strained things, Viv's my girl for life. But what I feel for Rick is..." She turned to her. "I'm *lost*, Doctor Alexander. When it comes to him, I'm— I'm just...lost."

"They're *happy*, Louise. Rick and Viv are in love...and enraptured."

She turned back to the window with a suck of her teeth. "It's like they're *too* happy. Like Patrice said: it's almost too good between them to be real."

"Look at me, Louise."

Louise turned to her.

"You've known this couple for so long, since before they married. Claim to know them so well. You tell *me*."

Louise looked away. She stared at something inconsequential for long seconds and exhaled before looking into Naomi's eyes. "It's real. It's...mad legit. It's back to like it was when they were dating, to how it's been for most of their marriage." She looked away again. "They had that brief funkiness leading up to the Jonathan-thing, and then they started seeing you. ...Rick went away, but it's even more intense between them now that he's home."

"So, leave them alone. Be happy for them. Be their friend."

Louise's eyes changed to something raw, sober, and borderline psychotic. "I've already told you. With him,....I'm...I'm in a different *place*." She chuckled then, and it was the strangest sound. "You know,...Rick:...he...he has pretty feet for a man."

Naomi didn't respond to that (everyone had their thing). "Why don't you come by my office Monday?"

Louise made that strange-sounding chuckle again. "Want me back on that burgundy sofa again, huh?"

"It's yellow now."

"Oh. ...That picture of him in their foyer... *Lord*." She stared out the window for quiet seconds before turning to her. "Monday."

NAOMI (11:35 p.m.)

Tim had "disappeared," and Louise hadn't returned; Kevin and Garrett were in the billiard room watching a game in play. Naomi stood near the rear of the ballroom with Leslie, Trevor, Joy, Brendan, Patrice, and Viv. She spotted Rick returning from where Curtis was set up.

"—class or something." Joy pointed at Viv and Rick as he stepped up, referring to their varied dance moves (a rehashed discussion courtesy of Leslie's burgeoning infatuation with Mr. and Mrs. Phillips).

"It's not something you *teach*, is it? I mean, basic moves, yeah. But the rest of it?" Viv shook her head (and Naomi agreed).

Joy adjusted the belt of her dress. "I guess. But the 'Can't Let Go' dance with the bopping and then switching to slow-dancing and then back again—"

Miss Rain O. Parade scoffed. "All that wasn't even necessary. One song, one type of dance. Just showing off, if you ask me."

Viv's expression changed, and Naomi knew she'd had it. Naomi winced prematurely at the venom she saw about to spew, when Rick leaned and placed his lips on Viv's with a lengthy peck to keep her from spewing it.

Patrice rolled her eyes. "Whatever."

Leslie, Joy, Brendan, and Trevor looked on with snickers or smirks.

Rick pulled back, gazing into Viv's eyes for solid seconds with an unspoken exchange. A breezy mirth saturated his expression, and he gave Viv this sloped smile that was just—

Viv smiled back with a subtle nod and left it alone as Rick interlocked his hand with hers.

Rick cleared his throat, looking around at everyone. "I believe a change of subject is in order?"

Joy and Brendan did the honors, discussing the charity they supported: Young Playwrights' Theater. Brendan talked excitedly about a few plays drafted by youth who were active participants. Rust-brown and muscular but with wide hips, a couple more inches in height would've topped him closer to five feet eleven—and lengthened him such that his pleated shirt and Windsor tie didn't protrude so much through his tuxedo jacket. Brendan's perpetually-deep dimples, however, made you smile—even if he wasn't smiling.

"All right, ladies and gentlemen. Have another dedication rolling through. This one to a 'Lady Blue'..." Curtis haphazardly sent the spotlight around the ballroom, searching for "Lady Blue" to everyone's low chuckles as they waited for someone to step forward.

Viv lowered her head with a blush as her husband headed away with a grin.

Those in their circle stared kindly at Viv as Curtis continued his spotlight search.

"Okay, I've got one-half of this here, and he is no 'Lady.' Don't be shy, now. I'm not starting the cut until 'Lady Blue' gets here. ...Don't let me have to check the ladies' room."

Many in the crowd giggled, heads still turning in their search.

"Go on, Viv." Naomi nodded encouragement at her friend; Viv still navigated new emotional territory, explored novel aspects of her personality with Rick being home again.

"Yeah, Viv. Don't leave Rick hanging," Leslie said.

That got Viv moving. She turned to meet her husband on the dancefloor, to the low claps of those finally relieved of the mystery.

Naomi and crew followed, moving closer to the dancefloor.

Rick put a hand up to Curtis, telling him to wait. He removed his tuxedo jacket and headed their way with it, but, seeing Louise close by, he handed her his jacket and returned to Viv, nodding at Curtis to continue as he took Viv's hand. In only his waistcoat now, Rick's cut physique displayed more prominently. Naomi smirked as several women exchanged looks with women-only meaning.

Sittin' on a rock, boy.

"All right. Now, we're cooking. We'll let them start the dance, and then, everyone, feel free to join..."

Moments later, "Lady Blue" by George Benson started, and Viv lowered her head with emotion. The couple danced, doing more of those combo bopping-alternating-with-slow-dancing moves Leslie and Joy were so impressed with. As Mr. Benson sang and the couple danced, Leslie turned to her with wide eyes, beaming with the lightbulb coming on regarding Rick's affectionate nickname for Viv.

The song played, but no one joined Rick and Viv yet; people mainly standing around and watching, singing along. Trevor and Kevin voiced loud and enthusiastic commentary from the sidelines, and Naomi had no idea when her man joined the fun. Their commentary, however, now had people looking their way with smiles and chuckles.

Watching the couple dance, observing others watching the couple dance, the entire scene proved more special, because it illustrated Rick and Viv's chemistry, not while dancing slow but more so during their hand-dancing moments, which translated a deeper level of intimacy and connection, such that Naomi was sure Louise and Lynelle were (painfully, woefully) fit to be tied. Those pops of red from the bottoms of their shoes only emphasized that intimacy-and-connection point.

Naomi took in cues from those around her: wholly enthralled. And if Viv chose this moment to close her eyes while hand-dancing with her husband, the place would erupt.

She surmised Rick dedicated the song to Viv to reassure his wife and send a message to others (male, but particularly female). Naomi scoped the crowd, searching for two women *she* meant the song for at least: Louise and Lynelle.

Lynelle was on the other side of the dancefloor, farther in the back, but she watched the couple dance; it was too dark on that side for Naomi to read her expression. And Louise? Naomi watched as Viv's longtime friend held Rick's jacket, sniffing it on the sly.

Being sure not to make a scene but wasting no time, Naomi moved to where Louise stood and eased his jacket from her arms. She returned to Kevin and her original spot (Tim and Garrett were now smiling onlookers). Trevor and Leslie watched the couple dance. They became a rooting pair, with Trevor sometimes calling out, "Hold her tight, Rick!"

or Leslie voicing, "Yeah! Hold 'im, Viv!" creating waves of sporadic chuckles at Trevor and Leslie's excess enthusiasm.

George Benson finished his jazzy-bluesy serenade, and Rick drew Viv close, pecking her lips as people clapped. With others looking on, the couple chatted while in each other's arms.

Curtis turned the lights up on Viv leading Rick by the hand toward the ballroom exit. "Uh-oh, it's time for some grown folks' business!"

Guests laughed, clapped, and whistled.

Naomi watched Louise cover her mouth and excuse herself.

A guy standing next to Garrett murmured, "I wouldn't mind being a fly on the wall of *their* bedroom tonight. Damn!" and several men-only chuckles followed.

Naomi watched the couple exit. Viv led Rick toward the cloakroom. Shortly after, they headed outside to the garden mezzanine, Rick carrying his coat.

Up-Owl-Nite got things going again with "Pop Life" by Prince. The night waned; Curtis seemed pumped and ready to roll past midnight if the people wanted. With the number of people crowding the dancefloor and jamming: the people wanted.

So, too, were people stopping by the window to see what Rick and Viv were up to. They were being nice-nosy, and Naomi was no exception. She paused by the window to check on her fam: the couple stood under a tree, Viv leaning onto Rick, both cloaked inside Rick's charcoal-gray wool dress overcoat, talking and laughing, sometimes kissing. Between the Patrice, Louise, and Lynelle messes, they deserved this mini break from all that for some quiet bonding. She didn't need that candy-red to flicker for her; it was there. She saw it without seeing it. They weren't alone on the mezzanine, but they might as well have been with their position away from the other few people out there. Naomi was sure they'd return in time for Curtis's finale.

She spotted Cecily several feet away and farther down, also gazing out at Rick and Viv. Naomi waved.

Cecily sent a semi-smile and wave back.

CECILY (11:47 p.m.)

Midnight was minutes away, and Curtis showed no signs of stopping. Worked for her; she wasn't in any hurry to go home.

Cecily waved at Naomi and resumed viewing the couple in the garden mezzanine.

She found herself (for the third time) at the window, watching the "Lady Blue" couple from Naomi's table. Watching them made her both happy and sad. Glad to see good Black love, not on a movie screen but happening right in front of her. Yet she was sad God had taken her good love away from her, replaced it with whatever this was she had now, that didn't even hint at love (not really), and then topped it off with a nice, juicy home invasion as a Christmas present.

Yeah, she was a bit wistful at that.

Besides, out here, looking out at them, she didn't have to be near—

"Okay, folks. My jamming finale's in about an hour. You heard right: they've given us the run of the joint. Their mistake, not ours! Let me know your thoughts. Are we rocking this for another hour or what...?!"

The yells and whoops in response answered that. Chuckling to herself, Cecily viewed the garden mezzanine as Curtis started another track. She breathed the whiff of cardamom, coffee, mango, and pepper before the hand touched her shoulder: Joshua.

"Staying to the end?"

Cecily turned to him with a nod, believing she wore the most idiotic grin. "I think so, yes." Oscar could end their evening in a heartbeat, but she didn't want to think about that. She gestured toward one of the many clocks placed throughout the estate. "If I don't turn into a 'fat ugly pumpkin,' that is." She was trying to make light of Oscar's joke, doing her best not to let show how much it hurt her.

Josh scoffed a puff of air. "I paid him no mind, Cecily." He ran his gaze over her. "There isn't an ounce of 'fat' on you. ...And you're quite far from 'ugly.'"

Not uncomfortable with his gaze but needing to turn away from it, Cecily resumed watching the Lady Blue couple. Joshua moved closer, sending that new fragrance her way as he stood right behind her, and she sensed Joshua looking her over again, the warmth of his breath skimming her shoulder. This whispery but emphatic grunt from Josh confirmed her unspoken appeal to him, and it was so nice to hear; creating an additional source of self-pity.

Cecily focused on the view outside. "Look at that. They make each other laugh."

Joshua now watched the couple, too. "Yeah. Looks like it."

When they began kissing (rather hotly now, with "Lady Blue" caressing her husband's hair—along with other movement inside that coat), Cecily sighed. "I can barely remember what that's like."

"What what's like?"

Cecily went quiet; she could talk about this with him, but she couldn't talk about this with him.

"What's wrong, Cecily?"

"...Did you catch them dancing to 'Can't Let Go' by their table?"

He chuckled. "Yeah, I did. Enjoyable to watch." Cecily sensed his gaze roaming her again. "...You can have those things, too."

Cecily held in a scoff; that ship sailed long ago. "You...You smell nice, Josh. I haven't smelled that on you before. Still Polo?" She didn't care for people standing so close behind her (not for two years now), but that wasn't the case at all right now; she so liked the position of his proximity.

"Thank you, Cecily. Still Polo, yeah. I save Polo Double Black for special occasions."

She turned to him. "It's very nice, Josh." She couldn't stress that enough; he smelled divine.

"I like what you're wearing, too: the Samsara. ...Where're your contacts exactly?"

She didn't want to use Naomi's lie; Josh didn't deserve that. She told him the truth. "I...I don't like wearing them. So, I took them out." She didn't mean to reveal she didn't like her contacts; that was more truth than she wanted to share.

He frowned. "Well, so why—?" Josh shook his head. "Never mind. You have your reasons—and they're none of my business. Pardon me, Cecily."

"It's okay." It wasn't his business,...but she wanted it to be.

Gazing into her eyes, he shifted some. "I want to say, your hickory irises...have a dark but fiery wildness about them I like...very much. My unsolicited opinion: your natural eyes are prettier." He hadn't said, *I love you*, but those words were a derivative equivalent—and his eyes never left hers as he spoke.

She turned back to the window and the couple under the tree.

From the ballroom, "The Closer I Get to You" sounded, and Cecily closed her eyes with another sigh, wondering what was going on with the song selections playing in her life these last weeks. Sensing Joshua's closeness, smelling him as Roberta and Donny broke it down (yet again), Cecily stiffened and fought tears, refusing to open her eyes and see the Lady Blue couple, too. It would be too much.

"...Josh?"

"Yes?"

"If I ask you to walk away now, will you understand?"

"Sure, Cecily." She sensed him staring at her again. Josh started away, but purposely brushed his hand against hers.

Cecily winced with the pleasurable torture of his fleeting touch.

He was gone.

NAOMI (11:47 p.m.)

Uninterested in taking her eyes off them, Naomi watched her "brother" and Viv do their loving thing (was Viv now her "sister-in-law" then?).

Knowing how much Rick loved music and dancing (especially regarding Viv), she had an idea to go along with other plans for a tentative clinical study for which she only had preliminary formulations. She was twelve steps ahead in knowing how she wanted the study to go. Rick would do the favor she wanted; she was his little big sis, after all.

"So far, you're looking at twelve for Leslie's after-party: our table, plus Joy and Brendan. She's on a roll." Kevin stood behind her, hugging her as she saw Joshua approaching Cecily.

"Okay. I need to tell that girl: that's it, no more invites."

Kevin chuckled. "Better hurry. Might be a party of twenty by the time you get to her."

"Better not be. But I have no problem uninviting."

"Don't I know it." He hugged her tighter.

"Kev?"

His lips brushed her temple. "Yes?"

"Ever tried anything stronger than whiskey?"

"Cocaine. Weed. I was a young man then."

Eyes on Mr. and Mrs. Phillips, Naomi gave a considering nod, surprised to hear *cocaine*. "And how do you feel about those now?"

Kevin nibbled the side of her neck. "Not interested in doing coke. But having a little ganja here and again might be nice." He pecked her earlobe, his hold to her body tightening with other interest. "Why?"

Naomi shrugged, enjoying his hold and the subtle whiffs of gardenia, lemon, lotus, and incense in his Black Orchid cologne. "Learning more about you."

"Mm..." He paused his nuzzles, watching Rick and Viv with her. "An after-party might be fun, but I was looking forward to being alone with you. So, Les is... How is it—?"

"Cock-blocking." He'd lived in the US of A for decades, but the correct way to use some colloquialisms and phrases still escaped him. Once they were alone, she wanted to explore more of his past; she didn't realize how little she knew about his youth—not that he knew about hers in any great detail.

He kissed her cheek. "Yes. You going to be much longer?"

Naomi shook her head.

"...They are fun to watch, aren't they?"

Naomi nodded.

He squeezed her waist secretly, suggestively, and stepped away.

Rick and Viv took their time returning, and Naomi soon stood among several women also taking a long gander at the couple.

Whatever Viv said to Rick made him wink at her with a smile.

One of the women sucked her teeth with a tsk. "Okay now, this is a damn shame. Who *is* this dude?"

Another woman chimed in. "That smile. ...There must be a law somewhere against a man looking *that* good. I mean, seriously. ...A law...*somewhere.*"

Naomi smirked, holding in a chuckle while the other women chuckled aloud.

A woman standing to Naomi's right sighed. "There're several pieces of vacuum-sealed eye-candy here, but *this* one..."

Naomi grinned at the woman's reference to being married as "vacuum-sealed" while the other ladies sighed in concurrence. They shifted forward some, gathering closer for discussion.

A third woman pulled a tissue from her frame bag. "I already gave him my panties when he walked in the door, shoot. I don't have any more."

Woman Number One scoffed. "He can have mine, then, shit. He is giving off some serious BDE."

The ladies giggled on the hush, and Naomi couldn't help joining them; this was fun. She also smirked inside, considering BDE another 'indefinable thing' about Rick Tim couldn't identify. Naomi eyed Joshua walking away from Cecily, but there was a good vibe about it.

"They killed it with that dance. Sweet but intense: very sexy." Woman Number Two lifted eyebrows at her. "Aren't they sitting with you?"

Naomi nodded, feeling the proud Sister-Mama.

Woman Number Three (needing the tissue) looked around at the others. "Have any of you seen him at these before? Ever seen him and his wife during the deejay's close?"

Naomi turned for answers; the women shook their heads. Two women wore red, one in dark burgundy, the other in gray.

Woman Number Three (tissue, wearing burgundy) smiled this shrewd smile. "I advise you to do your best to be near them for Curtis's finale."

The women returned questioning looks.

The woman kept the smile but shook her head and waved that tissue. "That's all I'm going to say. You won't be sorry."

Naomi figured she and the Phillipses attended the charity balls in different years—missing each other. Now, she was curious, too.

Woman Number One (in red) sipped from the glass in her hand. "I wonder how long they've been married?"

The ladies turned to her for an answer. "Eighteen years."

Woman Number Four (in gray) nodded. "Yeah. I've been sorta checking them out all evening—especially him."

The ladies returned perceptive chuckles.

The woman in gray continued. "No, but he's been such a gentleman to her tonight. Standing whenever she approached or left their table. The soft kisses on her cheek or the touches to her hand while his attention was elsewhere. Not ogling other women—even when she wasn't around. Just a *gentleman*. Attentive to her, but not clingy and possessive, you know? Nice. Especially if they're eighteen years in."

Woman Number Three raised an eyebrow. "My! You have been paying attention."

Woman Number Four blushed, shaking her head. "I know. I just heard it. Hopefully, my husband wasn't paying attention to me paying so much attention to him— Uh, I mean, *them*."

Chuckling again, the ladies dispersed.

Feeling five feet six without heels, Naomi walked her proud Sister-Mama self back to her table. Leslie invited no one else, so the after-party attendance topped-off at twelve. While talking to Kevin, she noticed writing on a napkin before Leslie's seat and picked it up.

Leslie wrote the names of the people in their table party, placing them in hearts according to their assigned pairs. She added other decorative drawings on the napkin, creating a miniature piece of artwork.

Smiling in response to Kevin's smirk at her, Naomi pocketed the napkin in her purse as a memento—feeling unusually sentimental.

NAOMI (11:57 p.m.)

She stood by the portrait table again, this time viewing the photos more closely, spotting several familiar people—personal and professional. Naomi also replayed the few minutes spent with Joshua Hall and turned to see Cecily selecting a few hors d'oeuvres from the refreshment table. The sponsors always served an assortment of kickshaws (both vegetarian and hearty) to meet a variety of dining needs. They kept the food and drink flowing until late—and from what Naomi observed, Cecily accepted no food or drink from Oscar (and she saw Oscar bring Cecily a drink—which Cecily smiled her thanks for but pushed to the side). Cecily also hadn't consumed any more alcohol, so she'd return the anxiety meds when they next spoke (she'd hold on to the contact lens).

During the earlier part of the ball, Cecily spent much time alone, looking lonely but also checking for Oscar's whereabouts often, as if wanting his company (and disappointed at not getting it). But in this latter part of the evening, Cecily appeared content to flow solo.

She spotted Viv doing more of her photographer-thing, snapping pictures capturing the entire night.

Naomi turned back to the photos.

The thing with Cecily was this display of dependent personality disorder Naomi knew, *knew*, was something relatively new—as in seven years new (or whenever it was they met). Her tendency to defer to Oscar, to seek his approval and reassurance for even minor stuff, wasn't intrinsic to Cecily's natural personality. It just wasn't. Naomi knew it. She'd seen signs Cecily was a different person at her job—or anywhere she wasn't with her husband. Cecily allowed Oscar's intimidation and acquiesced to unpleasant requests because she craved needs two and three on Maslow's Hierarchy. But Naomi was determined to get Cecily to see the Cecily who *didn't* tolerate verbal, physical, or emotional abuse. Cecily lacked the motivation and drive to assert herself, avoided justified anger. It wasn't an easy fix, but doable.

Seeing the gang back at her table, Naomi returned to complete the group.

NAOMI (12:01 a.m.)

Everyone at her table hung around, laughing and talking (Rick, Patrice, and Garrett standing), waiting for Curtis's finale, when, inevitably, the subject of sex came up (as it tended to do around a group of grown-ass people socializing).

Rick looked around at them. "Hey, I've got a question: How many licks does it take to—?"

"As many as it takes, boy." Viv shook her head at him with a smirk. "Sit down and stop playing."

Rick shrugged back with a grin.

They all chuckled, except (again) Patrice, who rolled her eyes. "Sex jokes aren't funny."

Rick looked at Garrett. He made a subtle fist-thrust gesture, referencing intercourse, and thumbed in Patrice's direction, asking Garrett if he and Patrice were having sex.

Garrett shook his head and sat. "It's been a while."

So, that was her problem (or part of it). As suspected.

Patrice frowned at her husband, just sour. "What's 'been a while'?"

When Rick and Garrett didn't respond, Patrice correctly inferred what the guys were referencing. She scoffed, "Sex is overrated," then sucked her teeth with a huff and looked away.

Rick turned to Naomi, surprising her. "Is sex overrated?"

Naomi returned a smiling-smirk. "No."

Her brother nodded and turned to Louise. "What about you? You think sex is overrated?"

Louise's eyes softened for Rick inappropriately before she changed her expression with a dismissive scoff. "Course not."

Especially not if it were with you, little brother.

Rick addressed Leslie. "I know you're on the younger side, but…"

Leslie replied with a simper, flirty but not offensive. "And I'm giving you a 'younger side,' *no*."

Rick grinned.

Patrice's attention was back with them. "Unh-unh. Poll the men, too."

Viv rolled her eyes upward with annoyed exasperation as Rick looked around at Kevin, Trevor, Garrett, and Tim. "A'ight, fellas: how do you feel about trips to the Bermuda Triangle?"

Naomi chuckled; Rick was too much.

The men returned variations of the renowned playa bark, semi-appealing in this instance.

Rick turned to Patrice, who folded her arms in a mini-pout. "You didn't ask your wife."

Without even glancing at Viv, Rick raised an eyebrow at his sister-in-law in such a knowing way, no words were necessary.

Patrice's expression remained static.

Rick cleared his throat. "Okay. Well, I'm very comfortable, and I'm sure I'm speaking for both of us when I say, it's *FIRE*: Frequent. Imaginative. Riveting. Exceptional."

Viv looked Rick over in an exaggeratedly appraising way. "Ohh, yes. A-*men*!"

Leslie and Trevor giggled.

Louise lowered her head with a cough while Naomi chuckled with Kevin and Tim. Garrett had grown quiet.

Rick caught Viv trailing her gaze over him and paused. His initial blush in response changed to a look of desire. "You and me."

Viv held his gaze, giving it right back to him. "Me and You, boy."

Rick turned back to Patrice. "Definitely *not* overrated."

Patrice turned away. "I stand by what I said."

Rick stared at Patrice before taking his seat next to Viv. He frowned at his sister-in-law with confusion as he took his wife's hand.

Louise glanced at Rick's and Viv's interlocked fingers, a hurt expression crossing her face before adopting something less damning.

Rick continued looking confused. "Well, maybe you ain't doin' it right. Missin' a step. Sump'n."

Naomi held in her laughter, but Trevor wasn't as successful.

Garrett scoffed. "Well, first, you gotta be *'doin' it'* to begin with."

Everyone went quiet.

Patrice glared at her man. "No, you didn't..."

Unlike the harmonious compatibility of blue and yellow auras (as with Rick and Viv), if Patrice's aura were indeed green, it would be only moderately compatible with Garrett's abstract tan. But they've held fast with twenty years of marriage—so many things worked between them—but something wasn't working right now.

Having noted the lack of intimate chemistry between Garrett and Patrice all night, Naomi now theorized Garrett's manly expression earlier about Viv was tied, not only to Viv's beauty, but to Viv's openness regarding intimacy with her husband, combined with his own wife's blatant disinterest as of late. In that light, Naomi had better perspective and a more tolerant view of Garrett's earlier behavior.

Ever the impromptu host, Rick broke the tension. "Well, ladies and gentlemen: that concludes the *survey portion* of our evening."

Everyone laughed—even Patrice cracked a smile.

Rick exchanged a look with Garrett (who nodded), then returned his curt nod. "We'll be back." He shifted to face Viv and leaned toward her, looking in her eyes. Viv smiled and caressed his cheek while nodding at something unvoiced between them. There was more unspoken exchange between them until Rick kissed Viv's lips with a lengthy peck before heading to the bar with Garrett for what Naomi assumed was some man-talk about the bedroom issues with Patrice.

With the uncomfortable silence, the other men soon left the table, too, Kevin giving her thigh a gentle parting squeeze.

Viv swung a sympathetic gaze toward her sister. "You okay?"

Patrice's eyes were stern, but she showered them with a plastic smile. "I'm fine. I'm not thinking about Garrett...or your husband's comments."

Maybe that's the problem.

Viv echoed something similar. "That's too bad."

Patrice's mouth fell open.

Viv stood. "I'll be back."

Watching her sister walk away, Patrice's full lips curled and flattened as she sent her chin high and turned away, but the way Patrice's right hand clutched her upper left arm informed Naomi she was not only angry but embarrassed.

Leslie covered her mouth with what Naomi recognized as withholding laughter. "Excuse me." She left the table and caught up with Viv.

Louise was head-down, looking sullen.

Not one to be hanging around people she didn't care for, Naomi went to speak with a few colleagues at a neighboring table.

Heads cooled, everyone gathered at their table again short minutes later, now joined by Joy and Brendan. The conversation was light, very generic, making a dogged point to steer clear of anything sex-related.

Brendan bobbed his head, grooving to "Brick House" by the Commodores. He looked at Trevor and Leslie. "I know you two want Curtis to play the current stuff more."

Trevor shrugged. "Can't do current dances to this stuff."

"You can't even do older dances, man." Rick's eyes were playful, in line with his teasing smirk.

Leslie giggled, kissing Trevor's cheek. "Yes, he can!"

Trevor twisted his lips at Rick (his respect for him still quite plain). "Thanks a lot, Rick."

"No problem. I'm here for you, bruh."

Varied chuckles in fun followed.

Trevor shrugged, bobbing his head. "But it's still good music."

Rick nodded, and his expression made Naomi tense, anticipating *Damn skippy* falling from his lips. "You better know it."

Viv stood. "Oh, I don't know. You can still get your groove on doing current moves to the classic stuff." She swirled her hips and then tugged the hip portion of her dress, doing a quick but subtle twerk toward Rick, looking over her shoulder at him. "Right, Rick?"

Rick watched Viv's moving rear in those quick seconds (using what had to be superhuman restraint not to touch it) and then sent Kevin, Tim, Garrett, Brendan, and Trevor a look entirely men-only. His boys responded with men-only looks, smirks, or subtle nods.

"Right, Lady Blue." He retrieved his pocket watch from his waistcoat (yep: platinum) as if checking how long they had before the ball ended.

"Viv, please. Tone it down."

She'd long stopped moving, so there was nothing to tone down, and Viv scowled at her sister accordingly. Rick guided her into her seat next to him. Kissing her cheek, he interlocked their fingers.

Now, Tim frowned at Patrice. "She's flirting with her *husband*, Patrice. What's the problem?"

Joy nodded, also looking at Patrice with mild irritation. "It is a party, after all."

"Yeah. They're married and around family, Pat. Married people have sex. Well, *most* married people." Garrett looked away, shaking his head.

Another awkward hush followed, and then Rick frowned with humor, sending his gaze around at everyone. "Didn't...? Didn't we cover this already?"

Everyone chuckled, including Viv, who still appeared perturbed by her sister's...perturbance.

Rick focused on Patrice, his eyes offering compassion in line with gentle admonishment. The angles in his face seemed sharper, his irises a touch redder.

Patrice bowed her head to him in apology.

Rick responded with his signature curt nod.

Patrice looked at her sister.

Viv sighed with her own forgiving nod, her fingers curling tighter with Rick's.

NAOMI (12:13 a.m.)

Having had enough of Patrice and Louise to last her a good while, and considering some uninvites to drop that twelve down to ten for Leslie's after-party (Tim and Garrett were still welcome), Naomi found a relatively private spot near the rear of the ballroom for some decompression and people-watching.

She watched the guests, observing signs of attraction moving through the crowd as men and women passed one another, interacted. It was a natural phenomenon of biology, having little (directly) to do with any immediate desire to be unfaithful (if already married or attached) and everything to do with male and female hormones and the physiological intricacies of human mating in its most basic form.

Women's eyes softened when gazing at an attractive male, or they pushed their bosoms forward in subconscious invitation and to appear more desirable. Naomi noted smiles brightening and women's voices registering a tad higher when speaking to said male. For the men, the subtle indicators were similar when looking at or interacting with a female deemed attractive: voices lowered while postures straightened to appear taller to the female of the species (and thus more appealing).

Parties weren't her thing; didn't mean there weren't good takeaways and tidbits to enjoy about them.

She spotted Viv socializing across the way. She wondered where Viv's husband was, when he stepped up beside Naomi.

He gazed at Viv with a tiny, reflective grin and sighed.

"Something wrong, Rick?"

"Nope. Quite the opposite."

"Just checking."

Rick continued focusing on Viv. "Naomi...?"

"Yes, Rick?"

"Just wanna say, I love you, Sis."

Naomi swallowed. "I love you, too—and don't thank me again."

"Okay. Long as it's understood."

"It is."

Rick rocked on his feet once. "Can I talk to you? Plain English?"

"Prefer it no other way."

He nodded in Viv's direction. "She's something, huh?"

"She is."

"Look at her, Naomi. ...And she's mine."

"I'm glad the love between you and Viv is still—"

"It's more than 'still.' It's... I don't even know what to call what this is between us now, Naomi."

"I hear you."

"You probably think it's because I'm newly home—"

"No. That has nothing to do with it. Because I also saw a lot of this between you still—when things were rough. I know you and Viv were an incredible match from the beginning. That your marriage flourished and then suffered from all-too-common weaknesses of one, contentment and complacency, and two, improper conflict resolution: resulting in infidelity on both sides. That now, everything's as it was and should be. The stars are realigned. As you and Viv like to say: 'The End.'"

Rick nodded, bending his lips with appreciation at her synopsis. "Sounds about right." He shook his head. "Doesn't matter. This isn't a love stint because I'm out. We've been together a long time, through some serious shit. We're in this, Sis. This is an eonian-type deal."

"I know, sweetie."

"Our thing: it's natural, unpretentious. A man needs that. I have that with Viv."

Viv also considered their thing *fireworks at a slow burn*. "I know that, too. Good for you."

"...And her body is my sanctuary."

Neither could resist chuckling.

"I know. But it is, Sis. My wife still has me jacked up."

Naomi smirked, shaking her head at him.

"Yeah, but besides her body, which is uh... Well, look at her."

"Don't have to. She's snapped it back and then some. Some of that weight-loss was from depression."

"Because of me."

"Yes, sweetie. But, despite that period of depression, Viv looks good, healthy. Everything is—"

"Soft and silky, tight and right: nothing but sinuous curves. I have me some Hollywood-fine—right here in suburban Maryland."

Naomi suppressed an all-out howl. "Okay, Rick."

Rick winked at her with a smile and resumed watching Viv.

Sittin' on a rock, boy.

"Never mind that body. My wife has always had the best attitude regarding our sex. It's the *attitude* about it, Naomi. Even when our bodies age and start to 'go,' if Viv still has the same attitude about it? Aging won't matter as much."

Naomi cleared her throat. "Well, just so you know, Viv still feels sprung, too."

Rick looked at her, wearing this self-deprecating smile. "She said that?"

He was adorable. He was.

"I mean, I know how she felt about our sex *before* I left, but you know," he shrugged, "now that I'm home..."

Naomi nodded her understanding, giving him a knowing look. "*Sprung.* No change, even more intense for her now. You've got skills, my brother. It's hot and good to her, Rick."

"Naomi!"

"How do I roll?"

He smiled. "I know, but still."

Smiling, she shook her head at him. "'Plain English.'"

"No shit."

"Yeah shit. You're telling me, since you've been home, you don't know how your wife feels about the sex you're having?"

Rick blushed, then shrugged. "I do. But hearing she spoke it into the universe, telling you I have her 'sprung': *that's* different."

They snickered.

Rick continued monitoring his wife. "Can I rattle off about that woman over there? Will you give me a few minutes just to lay it all out?"

"That's what big sisters are for."

He glanced at her with a grin and curt nod before focusing on the woman he married, who was several yards away speaking with a tuxe-do-clad elderly gentleman using a cane. "Naomi, she's... Fine. Smart. Viv has the best sense of humor, cracking me up sometimes, man. She's caring, an exceptional mother. A lady most times, but can be 'street' when she needs, letting her Delaware roots show."

"I've seen a bit of that. Oh, yeah."

"Notice how all that love for language arts and grammar falls by the wayside when she's pissed?"

Naomi laughed, leaning on Rick's arm with it. "Yes!"

Rick nodded with this knowing grin before the grin softened. "She makes me feel like I'm the center of her world, yet lets me know her world doesn't revolve around me. That's important."

Naomi agreed.

"And she's... She's *female*, Naomi."

Naomi looked up at Rick, perplexed. "Well, yeah...?"

With a smiling-smirk, he shook his head. "I don't mean she has a vagina, so she's female. I mean, she's... Viv's...a woman in the best ways, Sis. She's strong but still feminine. She can hang with the fellas but still be a girl about it, you know?"

His meaning clearer, Naomi nodded.

"Viv's got that woman's know-how and intuition going on, but she's smart as shit, too. I don't know if you've seen it, but Viv has a secret geek in her relating to technology, data systems..."

Naomi laughed. "Yeah, I've noticed."

"But she's not obtrusive with it, Sis. You're not constantly reminded she has a brain in her head."

"That's true. I know her profession because we're friends, but it wasn't until we were talking with one of Leslie's college buddies majoring in computer science that I got to see and hear Viv in her element."

Rick raised an eyebrow. "Saw her 'Super Geek' shirt underneath her clothes, didn't you?"

Nodding, Naomi chuckled, "I did."

Rick chuckled with her. They watched Viv.

He turned to her with a conspiratorial smile. "She's also—" Rick cleared his throat.

"A freak in the bed. I think I got that message moments ago."

Rick laughed, and it was a wonderful sound. "...You know how some men step out to experience shit their wife won't do?"

"Of course."

"Well, that wasn't my issue. Other shit influenced it, but overall, I was just a dumbass."

"I'll accept that."

Rick smirked and then looked over at Viv with this calm, loving expression. "Yeah, when it comes to sex, Viv's an Almond Joy, straight-up. She'll try shit—even if only once. Hell, she comes up with shit herself. Unlike her sister: such a Mounds, man."

Naomi stared up at him, curious about this description new to her. "I'm waiting..."

Rick grinned. "Almond Joy: feels like a nut, as in she enjoys making a man bust a nut, busting her female nut. Scuse my—"

"Plain English, sweetie."

"Right. And, uh, Mounds..."

"I think I got it, little brother: doesn't feel like a nut, and so, isn't interested in any kind of, um...'nutting'..." Rick smirked sweetly at her, and she grinned, "whatsoever."

Rick smiled, just as sexy as the day was long. "There you go."

"Cute. Is this description something men commonly use to denote a woman's sex drive?"

Rick hefted his shoulders. "In my small circle, yeah."

"You came up with it?"

He shrugged, and Naomi saw the truth as *yes*.

"Uh-huh. And how do you know Patrice is a 'Mounds'?"

"Garrett."

"Of course. So, your wife's an...'Almond Joy.'"

"Yeah. Viv doesn't let her tech-geek brain interfere with a good boning. Sometimes she'll let me use her female without making a bunch of intellectual interplay necessary. Sometimes, I just wanna fuck 'er, Naomi. No drawn-out foreplay, no extensive philosophical discussion, or deep, emotional diatribe. Just slide my hard shit into her desirable body and do the damn thing. Just bust a nut. Viv gets that. Believe it or not, sometimes Viv just wants the straight-up, too. Except for some deep tonguing, there're times when she's not interested in any long foreplay sessions or a lot of verbiage, either. Just wants me hard-and-ready to get her off, rough and raunchy, so that she can, as she calls it, 'empty her purse.'"

"Oh, I like. Very apropos."

"Yeah, she's something." He watched Viv, his expression turning contemplative. "But if I am needing sex with her, coming from emotion and love, Viv lets me feel what I feel without making me out to be a punk for showing it. And lately, I've been needing it and wanting it with her in that way, wanting to *make love with her* more and more." Rick spied Viv. "The way she breaks me off, Naomi..." He shivered again and turned to her. "No woman, before her or..." Rick winced, expressing the pain he still carried regarding his infidelity, "...since her, has ever broken me off like Vivian. No woman. Whatever the fuck stupid-ass mistake I made, trust and believe that fact right there, Sis. Viv gives me the total experience—not just an orgasm. Our sex...it's often mind-blowing. I'm talking, making my toes curl and shit."

"I'm guessing that's part of that 'FIRE' you mentioned earlier."

"Damn skippy."

"There it is!" Her chest softened and lightened with a cool rush; the elation (over finally hearing that expression from him) was pure.

Rick returned an acknowledging smile, unintentionally but cruelly appealing. "Yeah, Naomi, Viv's got some serious birthday cake."

Naomi chuckled, more to herself than anything. She was used to the objectifying references to women as pigeons, dimes, chickens, thots, and the like, yet Rick's references to his wife using multiple comparisons to sweet treats were far from demeaning. "'Birthday cake'?"

"Yup."

"No 'muffin'?"

He bent his lip in sardonic humor.

"I take that to mean she has the whole delicious package: physical features with a nasty mindset and female skills with her body which renders sex with her... I believe 'mind-blowing' was used."

"Yes. Viv's all-around assets make a man wanna celebrate being born...male."

Naomi laughed. "Birthday cake."

"Yes. My baby knows what to do with a dick. The end. Knows what to do and all kinds of ways to do it. Viv does shit personal to my likes and needs, of course, but the woman also has skills with universal appeal. I'm telling you, Naomi, Viv can take that golden-brown hourglass of hers and have every motherfucker in here weak with sexual pleasure in that under-a-voodoo-spell way. *Capisci?* Our sex..." Her brother shivered and trailed off with a lowering shake of his head before he pinned her with a look. "I still have the occasional wet dream about her, shit."

Naomi chuckled.

"Viv's got it all, man. She's—" He dropped his head and shook it for emphasis again, but this time with emotion, unable or unsure how to finish, but Naomi got it. She also experienced a few flutters of arousal with Rick's masculine talk. "That's enough 'Plain English' on that. Suffice it: Viv gives it to me, *right.* ...It would be ungentlemanly of me to elaborate further."

Naomi smiled to herself; he was a gentleman, too.

After another quiet moment, Rick exhaled. His eyelashes cast tiny fluttery streaks of shadow on his face. "To be able to *sleep*, Sis. Just be in her arms, have her in my arms, or simply lie next to her and sleep like a log. No words for it. I hadn't been able to just *sleep* in so long."

"Makes sense, sweetie. I'm sorry."

Rick shook his head, indicating no apology was necessary. "I...I have nightmares sometimes."

"Understandable."

"What I remember most about that place? ...The constant sound of doors and cells opening, closing,...locks engaging..." Rick shook his head as if to erase memory, and cleared his throat. "Now, when I wake in the middle of the night, angry and scared, and I reach out for her... She's *there*, Sis. Viv's right there."

Empathizing, Naomi nodded her understanding and patted his shoulder. He and Viv suffered nightmares. The shared experience, as each comforted the other through their version of night disturbance, likely intensified their bond. "I get it, sure."

"Being with my wife, my closest friend again, Naomi: fucking wonderful. ...I can cry with her or for her, Sis. Pray with her. Talk about everything and nothing. Viv's just cool, Naomi. Her face and that body are hella-nice. She's gorgeous. But Viv's not all 'I know I'm fine. Here, bow down and kiss my ass,' with it. Viv will take that lovely face and that shapely body of hers, put on one of her favorite tanks topping a pair of her sexy tanga panties, then lay me down and get her female mojo going on..." He went still (likely reflecting on his wife in her tank-and-tangas, "mojo-ing" him), before clearing his throat and continuing: "...Reminding me, ever so nicely, that *she* holds the power: in my heart, between her legs, in those black eyes of hers."

"I see."

"Her *eyes*, Sis..."

"Yes, I know."

"I used to consider them dark-brown; no one has *black* irises, right? But Viv's irises, they're...black as all get out. Just big and round and...*black*. They can level me with one look. I often lose myself gazing into them: those dark, mysterious, onyx pools of liquid night."

Naomi laughed with love. "Talk it, little brother!"

Rick blushed. "Her kiss,...the way she moves her tongue with mine... It's enough to make me stop and ponder life."

"Preach."

He offered a self-deprecating grin. "All that chestnut hair, so full and healthy, shimmers of auburn when the light hits it. It's pinned-up now, but when it's out and wild, and I'm pushing my fingers deep into it..."

Naomi heard the love, pure and deep, coming through his voice.

"And when she smiles at me, especially this certain smile she has..." His gaze at Naomi possessed an interesting mix of smirk and happiness. "It slows the world's rotation just a little."

Naomi grinned, noting the parallels between her one-on-one conversations with these spouses; Viv also mentioned Rick's eyes, his smile, mentioned sleeping soundly, and touched on special components of their friendship.

Rick watched his wife. "Yeah. She still flirts with me, too. Still makes me feel a little chase is necessary; turns me on like shit. Viv still keeps a bit of mystery about herself to intrigue me, but not in that frustrating-irritating way women can throw on a man sometimes."

"Okay..."

A feathery grunt escaped him. "And that thing she does? When she caresses my head?"

"Uh-huh?"

He shook his head with an approving scoff. "Viv doesn't know it, she's just being my wife, but that move is one of the smoothest pieces o' shit in her arsenal, Naomi. The way she moves her fingers over my hair with these fleeting soft scratches to my scalp... Or if my hair's longer, the way she caresses my head, grips my hair, and gently scratches my scalp all in one swift motion. It's comforting, but...she's also making some shit *stir*, if you get my meaning." Rick closed his eyes and shook his head again, lowering it with feeling. "Unh! Lord, have mercy." He looked into her eyes with distinct meaning.

Naomi laughed.

Rick chuckled but grew serious again. "Oh yeah. But besides all that, Sis, Viv's...compassionate, forgiving." He watched his wife. "I almost fucked it up. Going after shit I could've done without—because I chose pettiness and spite over my heart."

Naomi silently agreed.

He nodded inchmeal. "Yeah, I hear you. That bullshit almost cost me the best thing that ever happened to me. Almost cost me my wife, my...life. They're the same."

They watched Viv mingle and smile.

"Did you remove your wedding ring when you—?"

"No, I didn't. Not ever."

"Okay."

"They knew I was married, Naomi. I didn't hide that. That first time was only me getting back at Viv because I believed Viv and her ex—"

"I know."

"She told y—?"

"Only in so many words: I filled in the blanks myself."

Rick wore an understanding but shrewd smirk.

"But that's the first time. The second? The *third*?" Naomi caught herself, pulling back the anger she felt for Viv.

"I hear it, Sis. Okay. The second time...?" It went quiet between them. "I'm surprised Viv didn't tell you—"

"She touched on it, but..." Naomi waited, wanting to hear his side.

Although Rick and Viv were former patients, none of this came out in therapy. That wasn't unusual; patients didn't always *let it all hang out* in session (and sometimes, the half-truths and non-truths outnumbered the truths). The couple discussed their infidelity, but Viv's questioning and Rick's reason for it were cut-and-dried. Subsequent events cut therapy short and so didn't allow for further exploration. The little she knew came from talking with Viv as their friendship blossomed during Rick's imprisonment.

"So, you know we've lost babies." His tone was mildly detached, as if speaking from memories.

"I do." Viv miscarried a girl midterm before having Alna. And then the couple became pregnant again. "Viv carried to full term with—"

"Halsey. Our son. Named after his uncle,...and stillborn." He scanned the ballroom.

She put a hand to her little brother's back, suppressing the warm feeling the sensation of his muscles under her palm created. "I know. I'm sorry."

Rick subtly nodded acceptance of her sympathy. He sniffed, swallowed. "And so, after losing him, Viv was going through her shit, I was going through mine. Both of us believing we were mourning together, but we weren't. For a long while there, she wanted nothing to do with me. Just...*nothing*. For over a year. My baby wanted nothing to do with me for what felt like forever. And I thought she— Thought we..."

He believed Viv was leaving him, thought they were over. While still mourning the son he'd lost, Viv appeared another loss.

Naomi lowered her hand, her heart just sad for the couple's situation. "No need to continue, Rick. I... I've filled in that blank, too."

He scoffed with a pitiful headshake, and Naomi let some silence offer its version of comfort.

"So, when you and Viv were in the therapy, and you said you cheated 'because you could,' that was for the third time?"

Rick looked at her, his strange-but-beautiful golden-auburn eyes hard to read. He shook his head. "That's a logical conclusion, but no; it applies to the whole fucked-up thing. But that third time... More of that 'improper conflict resolution.'"

Naomi resisted grinning. "I see." From talking to Viv, that conflict also stemmed from matters related to having another baby.

"'Because I could' applied because there was no excuse, Sis. I didn't have to choose to cheat, but because I could, I did. Ultimately, it's the choice, the decision, Naomi, not the justifications. You feel me?"

"Yes. But 'because you could' didn't mean 'just because.'"

Rick gazed at her for a long moment, the reds and dark golds in his irises shifting as Viv described, and Naomi ignored the goosebumps prickling her arms. "Exactly."

Naomi nodded back.

Rick returned his attention to the ball activity. "Anyway, no, I didn't remove my ring. Not wearing my ring didn't mean I wasn't married."

"Very good."

"It...It was strictly a physical release for me, Sis. I swear. When we were...'broken,' and Viv wasn't—" He exhaled, shaking his head. "Never mind. A fuck-up's a fuck-up. But I wasn't in it for any emotional shit, no relationship bonding. My ring and my words let them know I was bonded with someone else—*utterly*. They needn't get all close and attached; *not* that kind of party. After Halsey, a part of me always hoped Viv would come around—although it didn't look like she ever would."

"I see."

"That first one was cool with it; that lasted a couple weeks, I think. Just getting back at Viv—for something it turns out she didn't do. I didn't tap that last one but what, once, maybe twice, and I was done going that route, so..."

"Well, you mentioned your trysts being short-lived."

"Yeah. After Viv and I talked through the episodes more during her visits, she nailed down the specifics. Women are particularly good at pinpointing dates and shit in a relationship."

"Yes, they are. It's that larger hippocampus at work. Unfortunately, women have reason to."

He nodded solemnly.

"Talking about them also helped you two realize *when* you cheated: helped you both see the 'why' for it, so to speak."

"True. It was a retaliatory move, Sis. When we were in those shaky situations, I retaliated by cheating, believing...it was the only 'weapon' I had. Our talks helped make that clearer."

"Good thing it was only three to talk through—although, that *isn't* a 'good' thing."

"Right," Rick sighed. The two went quiet, Naomi watching the ball activity, Rick now watching Viv again. "So yeah, they were cool with a lay-don't-stay situation. Well, except Lynelle, of course."

"Of course. She's here at the ball, isn't she?"

"Yeah." He looked upset; his jaw clenched tight.

"Don't let that interfere, Rick. Viv's fine."

"I know she is. Viv's badass. Still..." Gazing at Viv, Rick's expression softened, then turned painful again.

"I'm doubting you gave those others your all."

Rick shook his head. "No, I didn't. Most shit belonged only with Viv. I remember, in therapy, you said something about how it didn't sound very appealing because I used condoms and still pulled out." He scoffed. "Guess that says something right there." He looked at her, shaking his head. "I didn't go the whole nine with them, Naomi. I didn't. With them, it was the basics: got my rocks off, helped them break off a piece or two. But it wasn't anything close to how Viv and I—"

"I know, sweetie. I get what you're saying." What she didn't say was, helping the women break off a piece *or two* without "going the whole nine," said more about his sexual skills than he realized.

"Their..."

"Plain English, sweetie."

"Their climaxes were secondary to me, Naomi, while Viv's are..."

"Primary. Your entire focus."

Rick nodded, his attention across the way and running all over his wife. "Yes. Working Viv's body, making her come: the point, the whole point, and nothing but. I get mine, too, of course, from my indulgences—a superb bonus."

Naomi grinned.

Rick winked at her. "Ensuring her pleasure leads to her wanting repeat performances, so..."

Naomi laughed, realizing she'd just heard some of that philosophy Viv spoke about last month.

Her brother laughed with her only briefly. "Yeah. But despite the walls I put in front of Lynelle, she...she still wanted more. Still wanted...*me*. Even after it was over."

Naomi smiled inside with the recurring notion therapy sometimes continued—long after official sessions ended. "Over for *you*."

Rick frowned. "Beg pardon?"

"Come on, Rick; she fell in love with you."

He shrugged. "I guess."

"No guessing. You slept with her for the longest period; am I right?"

Rick's hesitant nod conveyed his discomfort over the current topic. "Three, four months, yeah. And I hate myself for it. For all of it."

"Wonderful."

Rick looked at her.

"Plain English."

"Right."

"You're a sweet, spirited, charming, intelligent, caring man, Rick, with exceeding sex appeal. You talk about Viv, but you're exceptionally handsome and apparently have exceptional bedroom-skills to go with those looks—even without going the 'whole nine.' Lynelle fell in love with you. And from what I've observed tonight, she still is, Rick—terribly."

Rick went silent. He cleared his throat a few times, evincing his embarrassment and unrelenting reluctance to accept compliments about his person or physical attributes.

However, Naomi suspected compliments about his career work or athletic performance were another matter; he likely accepted those more easily and with humble pride. She also suspected the reason he didn't respond well to comments about his looks required a session or three in her office to explore it further. Because it wasn't just normal blushing Rick did when mention of his looks arose. When one complimented his looks, he displayed high levels of discomfort, mild distress, and some worry (hurt?).

Interesting.

"Uh, thanks, Sis."

Naomi hoisted a shoulder. "Ice is cold. The sun is hot."

"But just from sex? I know people sometimes like to distinguish, saying something wasn't 'an affair' to mean it was something more, something deeper. Well, I'm making no such distinction. If 'affair' has some lesser meaning, then that's what I had with Lynelle. And that was so long ago. I mean, I know women develop attachments differently than we do. But Lynelle and I didn't 'date,' Naomi. No romance—not from my perspective. She only had my office phone number, and while I had her other numbers, I only contacted her from work, contacted her for some sex. I'm sorry for how that sounds, but it's the truth.

"There were no lunches or dinners or movies or whatevers. No sexting. No long talks over the phone. There were no strolls in the park.

None of that. With any of them. For a few months, Lynelle and I spent around an hour together once, maybe twice a week. I guess some of that time was talking, but bottom line, it was...me trying in vain to fill a singular void—and using Lynelle's body to do it."

Naomi heard Rick's frustration and annoyance, his dissatisfaction with and disappointment in himself, and, no longer needing to be neutral with the Phillipses, she appreciated hearing it. Few of her male patients expressed any of those things regarding their instances of infidelity; most were more defensive.

"So, Lynelle wasn't—" He scoffed with disdain. "I fucked her, Naomi. Got her naked and fucked her. The end. Again: sorry if the straight-up sounds heartless." He shook his head. "I...I avoided tonguing her. Tonguing is an intimate act evoked by a certain level of desire or passion, by an ultra-sense of connection, and I had none—for any of them. I honestly don't believe I even held her hand. Sure, she tried acting like it was more than it was, but my wall was up, I assure you." He then winced with a sigh of seriousness. "Despite those slip-ups, I love being monogamous, prefer it—it's a turn-on for me. ...I wanted *my wife*, Sis, I swear. I wanted *Vivian.* Basic math. Hell, I...I even called out Viv's name sometimes, shit. But Viv... She didn't want me—or so I thought." He scanned the ballroom, confusion and annoyance moving across his chiseled features.

Naomi's heart tugged. Rick and Viv weren't patients anymore; she didn't have to be impartial—her heart tugged, listening to him. "How'd you end it? Redirect fade to black? Cold turkey cut-off? Phone call...? Text...?"

He looked in her eyes. "I met with her and told her I was done."

Naomi nodded her approval over that admirable approach: he was a man about it. "As you said, women develop attachments differently. I've already covered the type of man you are. Those qualities for sure came through during those 'talking' periods, so...Lynelle fell in love with you." Speak of the devil, Naomi spotted Lynelle staring in their direction. She stood near one of the many huge plants adorning the ballroom, appearing forlorn (even from a distance).

Rick stared at the floor, giving it a musing nod before he shrugged and lifted his head with a weighty sigh.

"But Rick, not just Lynelle. So...So is Louise."

He dropped his head again and shook it, a heavy, drawn-out sigh of "Fuck" crossing his lips.

"Yeah, I know, sweetie."

He lifted his eyes to her. Those golden-auburn peepers told her he was oblivious before he discovered it, that he did nothing (that he knew of) to bring it on, that he hadn't the faintest idea on how to address it.

"She's a family friend, like family, for decades. I get it. You and Viv are handling it well."

"I guess. It's just all so..."

"It sure is. I may be able to help, though."

Rick still appeared uncomfortable, annoyed even. "I'm not perfect, Sis. I have my shit, too."

"Oh, Viv can attest to that."

His eyes registered humor before they grew confused and concerned. "So, what—? I mean, why—?" He shook his head, unable to express his confused concern, but Naomi read him: he wanted to know what was so special about him. Wanted to know why women, other than Viv (he very much wanted Viv's interest), fell for him.

This man had no clue about his appeal. None. Rick was an understated Alpha-male, his charisma and intelligence both subtle and potent during casual interaction with him, but the vulnerable aspects of his personality and his humility (and there was a definitive root cause for it) made him attractive as hell.

Naomi placed a hand on his arm. "Let it go, Rick." She stopped herself from calling him "Richie." Not for any romantic reasons, but for maternal ones—because she sensed this distress had something to do with Rick's childhood (and he was "Richie" until age 18).

Rick nodded, scanning the room. "You'd be surprised how many women don't care about the guy being married."

"Actually, I wouldn't."

Rick gave a scoffing-chuckle. "Right. Forgot whom I was talking to."

They watched Viv.

His erection is nine inches!

The thought burst in, causing all kinds of internal havoc and mayhem with its rudeness (and arousing inappropriateness).

Naomi coughed, trying to shoo the thought away.

"You good, Sis?"

She looked up at him with a reassuring smile, tight and false.

Nine inches!

Size doesn't matter.

That's the doctor talking…not the woman. You heard that woman at the window: 'some serious BDE.' Nine-thick (and porn-worthy). Unh!

Shut up. Go away.

Naomi silenced the internal discussion, giving Rick a reassuring wink to sell the smile. She touched her throat, cleared it. "Just a tickle."

Nodding, Rick returned his attention to his wife, his gaze a mixture of longing and apology. "…She could have walked away, Naomi."

"But she didn't, Rick. She stayed and suffered through it with you. Her love never wavered, sweetie."

Rick's nod was slow, thoughtful. "Yeah, and that's God right there. Nothing but God blessing me, and I'm so grateful."

"I know you are."

He released a low scoff. "'Ride-or-die.' People use that expression to describe their devotion, but when it's time to 'die'…"

"That is where those words are tested, yes." And in the end, most backed-off that declaration—something easily said—during the good times. Viv, however, did her fair share of "dying" with Rick over the last three years.

Rick kept eyes on Viv. "…Viv tell you we were blood siblings?"

"No," Naomi marveled, "You two did the whole pin-prick-and-blend thing?"

"More like *knife-nick*-and-blend, but the night I proposed: yeah."

"Seriously?"

"Kinda corny, but we did, yeah. There was a moment that night…" He trailed off, and Naomi knew the moment inspiring the juvenile ritual was far from corny.

"A moment still holding powerful meaning for you now."

Rick didn't answer. "…I've only known, only *loved* like this, once in my life. …I belong with her: *that woman right there*. My partner and best friend. My connection with Viv goes way beyond the sexual, Sis. Way beyond." A soft, reflective smile curled the mustache over his kissable lips, then faded. "I need my baby. And if she'll have me, for as long as she'll have me, and frankly, now, even if she *won't* have me:…I'm hers. Forever."

"I can see that."

"Should life throw us any more curve balls? I don't give a fuck." Eyes on Naomi, he gestured toward his wife. "*Hers*. Forever."

Naomi nodded her understanding, thinking about the trials having tested their marriage: infidelity, losing two children, an imposed separation due to a prison sentence. "You two have already had a few curve balls, sweetie. I want to think the worst is behind you."

"I believe it is. We're good, solid,...*in love*, Naomi. I'm not saying everything's perfect."

"You two sure seem like it." But she remembered their apparent falling out at her house a few weeks ago—lovingly resolved in her kitchen.

Rick shook his head, his eyes serious. "You're not with us twenty-four-seven; it's not perfect at all. We still have shit to work through. Viv and I have never been big on heated arguments, but we argue—just not often. We get irritated with each other, just like any other couple, but overall, it's as close to perfect as I'll ever need. And my wife has a certain viewpoint about 'perfection' that says it all."

Naomi nodded. Like she said: they were an incredible match from the beginning...and the stars were again aligned.

Rick nodded back. "She makes every struggle worth it. I couldn't love another after having this with Viv. The woman keeps me at ease."

Viv headed in their direction, pausing to speak with guests and looking quite the lady as she smiled and socialized.

Rick grunted low (expressing arousal and attraction). "That walk of hers, Sis. Damn. That sass-with-class combo in her feminine stride. Just does something to me. And her voice? All throaty, but soft and shit."

"You are gone, boy."

"Damn skippy."

Naomi smiled. "Uh-huh." He smelled delicious: heart notes of gunflint, pink peppercorn, and geranium leaves teased her nostrils.

"That mole on her collarbone... Viv is wearing that dress, too; making matters a test of wills." He shook his head with male approval and grinned. "Forty-two: firm, stacked, and fully packed!"

They shared a "sibling" laugh.

"Taking my baby out for Valentine's Day. Got tickets to 'Butterflies at Night': that African dance theatrical production playing downtown. Those are the tickets Ellery dropped off; they're for that Friday."

"Thought those were tickets to a game for Mark?"

"I know you did, and let Viv keep thinking that."

"Gotcha. Viv'll love that."

"She will. I know I will, too."

Naomi waited.

"Hey, I've read a review or two, heard some underground talk: a lot of sexual undertones, themes, and suggestive dance going on. All while sitting next to my off-the-chain wife? Oh yeah. I can already feel Viv's hand gripping my knee in excitement."

Naomi laughed (fighting intruding thoughts of Rick's likely erection with Viv's hand on his knee).

"Yup. Got it all planned. Mark and Barb got the kids that evening."

Naomi realized Viv's Valentine's surprise for Rick might cause a logistics issue. "Let Kevin and me do it."

Rick looked at her. "I said, 'Valentine's Day.'"

Naomi smirked. "My hearing's fine."

"Mark and Barb have plans for late Feb, so they're cool, but even if you don't have plans, Kevin might have plans for you."

Naomi firmed her gaze. "Kevin knows better."

"You're not even go'n be together?"

"Yes. To watch Alna and RJ."

Rick's mouth curved with this gentle smirking grin.

Naomi gazed back, praying she was used to his looks one day soon. She waited patiently for the Lord to (finally) have that mercy she'd been asking for; just sprinkle a little mercy-dust to make her impervious to his sculpted features and stop the occasional tiny internal tremors whenever she laid eyes on the man.

Rick's smirk changed to a smile.

As a matter of fact: *Lord, have mercy!*

"A'ight, Sis. You and Kevin got 'em. Thanks. Six-nineteen good?"

"Make it five o'clock. Or, in your case, shall I say, five-o-*three*. That way, weather permitting, you two can get there early, stroll nearby, have a drink or light dinner..."

Rick arched an eyebrow at her. "For someone who doesn't do Valentine's Day..."

"That has nothing to do with knowing romance. And it just sounds like you and Viv."

He nodded. "If it's not too cold, yeah. We sometimes like to walk and talk, flirt some. Okay. Cool."

Naomi grinned. "My pleasure."

Rick grinned back, but the grin dissolved with the question behind his pretty eyes.

"What?"

"Would you really have shot me? Years ago, when I came to your off—"

"I know what you're referring to."

Rick gazed down at her, waiting.

Naomi's thoughts shifted with memory to that day Rick came to her office, his propensity for violence high. "Yes. I love you, but yes."

He issued a faint nod. "Okay."

"Would you have snapped my neck...or whatever it was you had a mind to do?"

Rick's gaze turned neutral, and Naomi could see him mentally reliving that day, too. "I don't know."

Naomi returned a subtle nod. "Okay."

Rick smirked at her and returned attention to his wife, who now laughed at something Kevin said as he passed her. "I know her, Sis. Viv knows me. We...We *know* each other; you get me?"

"I do."

"Every idiosyncrasy, every...peccadillo. Our love, the friendship: it's— *we're* entrenched. Viv has all of me, Sis. My love for her is...fervid."

Naomi nodded, knowing Viv felt the same for him.

They watched Viv interact with the guests.

"A man can be head-over-heels, Naomi. We can. Head-over-heels in love. And not just when shit is new, when the pussy is new. We can be years, decades in, and still be head-over-heels. But it's...it's gotta be *four-corners right*, is all. I know it goes both ways. I know that. But a woman's not go'n get what she's looking for from us, if we're working with less than four corners. That doesn't mean she has to be perfect because that's all relative. Men aren't as one-dimensional as you all—"

"Excuse me?"

Rick smiled. "Sorry. As *many* of you think."

"Better."

Rick smirked with a nod. "We have different needs as for a mate, too. Have our own definitions of the 'perfect' woman. All that stuff I said about Viv: that's *my* perfect—what turns me on about a woman. Not every man would find what I said about her attractive or in line with *their* perfect."

"I guess."

Rick frowned with a sarcastic nod of disbelief. "I know. Weird, right? What's *wrong* with them?"

Naomi chuckled, so enjoying this discussion.

Rick's smirk shifted to something gently musing. "So, they don't have to be perfect—but they gotta be our particular perfect for them to see that...that *thing* they wanna see from us. And we may not show it in the overt ways you'd expect. But if you really know us, know who we are inside: you'll know when we're feeling and expressing that *thing* to you. Even if nobody else gets it or understands it, as long as *you know* we're showing our love, you'll be straight."

"I get that, sure."

He shook his head. "Doesn't mean it's go'n be candy and flowers, or dinner and a movie. It may be buying an unrequested package of Skittles for you. But if you know him, know who he is as a man, then you'll know that package of Skittles is him telling you, you are 'the shit' to him, hands down." He shrugged. "Women get caught up in what's 'supposed' to be expressions of love, but men are different. We can do the 'supposed to' things: a lot of men out here buying flowers for women who can't stand flowers, hell, maybe even allergic to 'em, just because it's standard practice."

Naomi chuckled.

"Yeah, we can do the 'supposed to' things. But if it isn't genuine or only a means to an end of either shutting you up or getting some slit, who cares?"

"True."

"And that 'spend quality time with me' shit?"

Naomi grinned. "Uh-huh?"

"Goes both ways, too. You want us walking around a museum for some culture? Then dammit, next time, come with us to those smash-up, drag-out, explosions-with-little-dialogue action movies you hate."

"You like museums."

Rick shook his head with twisted lips. "Come on, Sis. You know what I'm saying. I'm not talking about *me,* per se."

"I know. Just messing with you. Lighten up, boy."

He offered her a playful grin before continuing: "Thing about Viv is, except for the occasional impromptu flower bouquet, she doesn't care about that overt, over-the-top, lovey-dovey shit. But guys have it, Naomi. Just like the women. We just need all four corners. We'll work with less than four, but you're not go'n see that *thing*."

"I hear you. Now, tell the truth: the Skittles...?"

Rick grinned. "Yeah, that was us."

Naomi grinned back. "I knew it."

They watched as Viv (closer to them now) tossed her head back in laughter at something the woman talking to her said.

Rick grunted low again. "Damn, she is just..." He spoke with such emotion, Naomi could finish Rick's sentence with all kinds of loving, sexy things about Viv she imagined him expressing. "That smoking-hot body...birthed our children, delivered my *sons*, my little man." His words, while still heavy with arousal, also carried pride and respect, a strong affection for his wife. And Naomi knew Rick loved and cherished Alna, that she occupied a special place in his heart, but RJ was his *son*, and well, it was as ancient as the tribes of Africa—sons carried a deeper level of importance for men.

They watched Viv.

Rick tilted his head with a tiny grunt. "My, she's most pulchritudinous, isn't she?"

"Viv rubbing off on you?"

Rick grinned. "Oh, yeah." His response carried several meanings.

Finished one conversation, Viv continued heading their way, pausing at tables with a smile and brief chat.

Rick ran a hand over his hair, uttering this low, grunting-sigh of, "Viv. Shit...," riddled with arousal.

Naomi swallowed hard.

Rick turned to her. "What time is this thing over?"

Naomi howled, and it helped redirect her focus more appropriately. After her laughter settled, they watched Viv. "And Viv? All four corners, huh?"

"Sis, she's filling up corners I didn't even know I had. She owns me, Naomi. Viv's my first thought in the morning and my last as I fall asleep at night. The woman gives me a contact-high." His expression changed to something Naomi couldn't place. "Viv's just cool, man. My favorite person. I like her!" He shook his head. "There's no me without her. Sometimes I feel like I love her so much, I might hurt myself."

Naomi laughed.

"You laugh, but I'm dead serious. That's my brown sugar right there. My shawty. My *lighthouse*, Sis. Yes, Lord. There's only Viv. I'm...I'm so deep into her, Naomi. So deep. ...Locked on her like a missile."

Naomi grinned her understanding, appreciating another parallel of discussion with Viv, and their being *locked*.

Viv stepped up, smiling curiously. "Now, why is my husband over here looking so seri—?"

Rick pulled her close, looking into her eyes. "You are...a most remarkable woman, Vivian. Damn."

Naomi noted Rick used "Vivian" whenever his level of sincerity deepened.

Rick held Viv, planting soft kisses on her face.

Viv appeared taken aback. "Uh, thank you...? I find you pretty extraordinary, too."

Rick nuzzled her neck. "Mm... You always smell so good."

With surprised, confused, and inquiring eyes, Viv asked her what the deal was.

Naomi returned a *girl, go with it* gesture, and Viv held her husband, caressing his back.

They pecked lips with extra tenderness, Viv now caressing Rick's head. And that was all very tasteful and sweet and respectful, but Naomi just wished to the heavens they'd use a little less tact and use some tongue, for crying out loud.

The way they held and kissed each other, however, was still a very personal thing to be near. Naomi started back toward their table (seeing Lynelle shift her attention elsewhere, too).

Too busy watching Lynelle, Naomi bumped into a taller man, making him drop his keys. "Oh! I'm sorry." Closer to the ground than he was by default, she lowered to pick them up for him—and went cold.

The keychain was a maroon crescent shape—the tip broken.

Doing her best to keep her icy veins warm in order to, well, keep her cool, Naomi turned the keys over in the tiny seconds she had before she stood and handed them back, trying to capture as much as she could visually. She'd trained to mind the details: seven keys, a date, one key fob (Mercedes), Freemason keyring...

Standing erect, she handed the keys back (he wore a pinky-ring secured with black tape), offering some fake compliment she didn't remember about the uniqueness of the trinket. The man (six feet, clean-shaven, coconut-brown, earring left ear, bulbous nose, pointy chin, brown eyes, large gums) smiled his "Thanks," saying he needed to get back to his wife "Lickety-split," and walked away (high butt, slue-footed).

Her blood back to normal body temperature, Naomi returned to her table, mindful of another detail about that set of keys: the name "Winton Hollis" engraved on the back of that broken-tipped crescent moon.

NAOMI (12:43 a.m.)

Conversation circulated at her table, but Naomi couldn't devote her full attention to it with thoughts of the keychain and Cecily in her head; she was a banana-split. She'd already planned something more heavy-duty for Cecily during an upcoming session, but now she had to weigh tonight's recent developments.

Under Oscar's tyranny, the mental (and likely physical) torture Cecily's endured for the past six, seven years triggered a personality change. Cecily's constant states of confusion or fear, the loneliness and general unhappiness and melancholy, render her such that she expects her husband's extremes of hostility. She didn't believe Cecily's true personality would allow it, but Naomi, herself, had every intention of not allowing Cecily to carry the effects of those constant states of fear and confusion into the future (whether or not that included Joshua).

The Oscar-less sessions with Cecily provided opportunity to document various manifestations of defense mechanisms. Cecily often made offhanded comments about how fortunate her life was compared to others who were "really" abused, or suffering some serious illness, or compared to a multitude of worse scenarios a person could find themselves in. This social comparison, comparing her situation to others' potentially worse ones, reflected Cecily's acceptance of Oscar's treatment; Naomi needed to help Cecily see that faulty reasoning for what it was.

Idealization was a common defense mechanism for those suffering under the dynamics of NAS, but Cecily didn't use it extensively. Although Cecily often stressed Oscar's positive traits (ambitious, confident, decisive, for example), she didn't go so far as idealizing Oscar in lieu of (reluctantly) acknowledging his more dominant not-so-good (abrasive, cruel, apathetic, devious—among others). And although the good aspects of Roland's personality exceeded the not-so-good ones, she didn't idealize him, either.

They made significant progress in the Oscar-less sessions, but Naomi realized she could only do so much to influence what happened once Cecily left her office. She needed those close to Cecily to offer emotional support, provide patience, and even encourage her. Cecily's circle was small (as was hers), so this support had to come from other than her husband: from her children, from close friends. The "Janyce" person seemed a friend, but given that earlier exchange, Naomi wasn't sure about how good a friend she was. Janyce showed traits more in line with...Oscar. And so, Cecily continuously bumped against a pseudo wall of broken benevolence. Because, between the two, Naomi believed their seeming benevolence was nothing save tiny shards of malevolence wrapped in the feigned guise of warm compassion.

Deciding to include him for appearance's sake, if he ever returned to the sessions, Naomi would guide Oscar on his role as supporter, but she doubted its success. This was the frustrating part—only being able to help but so much.

Cecily "feeding" Oscar by doing his dance with him (allowing the treatment, going along, trying to be better for him) was another unconscious defense mechanism she used to keep safe, but in so doing, she lost touch with her genuine personality from these exercises of pacifying, conforming, and appeasing.

Some aspects of Cecily's personality, her ability to empathize, be compassionate, were attractive to those with narcissistic tendencies like Oscar. Cecily wasn't a weak person, but the kind and gentler traits of her personality gave her a certain tolerance for putting up with a lot of Oscar's bullshit—if for no other reason than to make him feel good about himself.

Oscar adopted different personas as he guided their relationship through different NAS phases: the Idealization stage of false euphoria and happiness, into the Devaluation stage, where the curtain was pulled on all that glory in the Idealization stage, and finally, the self-explanatory Discard stage. Naomi didn't believe Cecily and Oscar had reached the Discard phase, but they approached it. The problem? Naomi believed Oscar's discarding carried deadly implications for Cecily.

And where did Joshua Hall fit in all this? Recent sessions revealed Cecily often teased and sometimes made jokes at work, without realizing it was part of her inner nature coming through because Cecily often worried about where it came from—despite memories of when she and Roland used to laugh. Naomi didn't know until tonight that Cecily shared that lighter side of herself with Joshua, but great: it fit.

When Cecily started with Oscar, it was all exciting, romantic. Even if it wasn't real (on Oscar's part), it was to Cecily, and the honeymoon stage did its thing to capture her into the snares of NAS. Oddly, Naomi believed Cecily was experiencing a similar euphoric stage with Joshua on a different, more subtle scale. Still, it had an originality and genuineness stemming from Cecily's inner self, her *true* self—and not the wounded, in-mourning, detached self she was when she met Oscar.

Knowing she'd get another opportunity to speak with Cecily before she left, Naomi went to Curtis with a slip of paper.

NAOMI (12:45 a.m.)

"Okay, fancy people. I've got the last slow one coming up. Phil Perry's 'Call Me' will be it for the slow songs before my jamming close, so if you want to get close before you leave for the night... Given the first two minutes of 'Call Me': if you're dancing to this and you're not already in love, you will be. And if you're already in love during the first two minutes? This is a charity event, ladies and gentlemen: keep it clean."

Varied laughter followed.

"Going once, going twice... I'll give you a second to decide."

Naomi sent her gaze around her table: no one seemed interested in dancing. She wasn't having that; Phil Perry's "Call Me" was one of her favorites, and she was feeling oddly festive. She agreed with Curtis: the first two minutes of "Call Me" were enough to make anybody want to get between the sheets. "Everybody: up."

Kevin and Trevor were the first to rise, each reaching for her hand and Leslie's, respectively. When Rick stood and took Viv's hand, Garrett and Tim followed suit with Patrice and Louise. They headed to the dancefloor for one last slow dance.

Naomi held Kevin, feeling his body movement through his tuxedo and breathing in the goodness of his scent. She watched the others dance, noting the effortless glide of Trevor's and Leslie's bodies, Tim's and Louise's near-robotic movement, and Patrice's stiff, resistant movement with Garrett.

Naomi saw Cecily and Oscar slow-dancing, disgust trumping her initial surprise. Through multiple moving bodies, she spotted Joshua off to the side, looking at his phone and not dancing, and she had to admit being happy about that. She didn't wish him not to have fun and enjoy himself, but she had a different idea for him to have fun and enjoy himself—beyond tonight. She was no matchmaker, had no interest in it, but once Cecily got on the way to well again, she presumed the matchmaking between those two would take on a natural life of its own.

Rick and Viv danced, holding each other with eyes closed. This time, the couple did a tasteful slow drag (instead of a slow side-to-side sway), already in love but "keeping it clean" per Curtis's instruction—and still looking hot despite all the tastefulness (the countless looks of interest coming their way, said so). While they were in the garden mezzanine, Viv had loosened Rick's bowtie and unbuttoned the top button of his shirt. That look on him, with the neck and leaf of his bowtie hanging down... Well, Naomi understood Viv's particular fondness for it.

Having watched them dance throughout the evening and over the last few weeks, images of their lovemaking flashed in her mind, and Naomi saw the synced but X-rated rhythm of his masculine cinnamon and her feminine butterscotch brown bodies blending and moving together in loving ecstasy, each using their entire body to please the other.

Her mind's eye saw Viv under Rick and on top of him, saw Rick behind Viv and in front of her. She saw them vertical and horizontal and positions combining both. Rick's thing about sex only in bed was far behind them, and so Naomi saw them, tongues thrashing, not only with a bed as backdrop, but with trees and closets and car seats and rooftops and public restrooms and grassy fields, the flashes of the raw and utter intimacy between them whizzing by with the varied possibilities and positions she knew they explored.

Watching the couple move together (and after her talk with Rick), reminded Naomi, not only were Rick's sexual skills exceptional, Viv gave as good as she got: Rick Phillips was happily whipped.

Naomi sent her observations to the others in her party. Louise held Tim but stared longingly at Rick again, much like she did earlier. Leslie stared at Rick and Viv, too, but with special admiration. Viv's commentary regarding some of what happened in their marriage likely helped solidify them as relationship heroes in Leslie's eyes. Patrice and Garrett danced, but looked like they didn't want to be. Lynelle danced with a gentleman, but, like Louise, her focus was Viv's husband.

CECILY (12:45 a.m.)

She'd comfortably resigned herself to not dancing with Oscar tonight, but Curtis announced the last slow dance, and Oscar turned to her. He sat beside her for the last forty minutes, practically ignoring her, and then suddenly wanted to dance. He didn't mention her not wearing the contacts, but it would be a hot topic later. Cecily didn't care. She'd deal with it like always; she'd had two bright spots tonight and held on to them, not caring *why* they were bright spots.

Arms around Oscar's shoulders (she was taller than him now with her heels on), she swayed with him to Phil Perry's unique singing voice, trying to breathe as little of Oscar's Aramis as she could. Cecily stared through the people, getting glimpses of the Lady Blue couple from Naomi's table; they looked in their own world as they grinded gently. Watching them, she couldn't help where her thoughts flowed next.

She searched for him, her heart fluttering upon seeing his handsome form and then leaping at seeing he wasn't dancing with anyone. He probably had a few numbers of potential future dates, but that was fine; tonight, he was in her presence, and she didn't want to look at it—hearing snippets about other women in his life was much better than seeing it (although her imagination could be torture sometimes, too).

Oscar's hand to her back lowered, brushing against near where he struck her with the buckle. The abrasion had healed and the soreness all but gone, but the area was still sensitive; Cecily tensed. Yes, it pleased her seeing Joshua not dancing with anyone, but she didn't want to be slow-dancing with Oscar, either.

NAOMI (12:49 a.m.)

"Call Me" ended, and Curtis's voice traveled to them in the fadeaway. "Okay. That one was for the ladies. Now, this one...is for the fellas..."

Silk's "Freak Me" flowed to them, and Naomi shook her head on Kevin's chest as she listened to low rumbles of bass in the ensuing male chuckles (and dog barks).

She noted changes in how the men held and moved with their dance partners, in how Kevin now moved with her. And even with Rick's hands lowering ever-so tastefully down Viv's body, they kept it clean with the change in their grind, but the way the couple held each other signified the song's effect on them, too.

"Freak Me" faded, and Naomi saw signs of people recognizing the jamming finale loomed. People finished drinks or hors d'oeuvres and secured loose valuables, preparing to shake their booties. Joshua tucked his phone in an inside pocket, casually moving (in her opinion) to a spot nearer Cecily. Naomi chuckled, noting a few women from the window-watch trying to stand with their husbands near Rick and Viv (per Woman Number Three's cagy suggestion). By the time the last seconds of the ballad rolled past, the dancefloor population had ballooned.

The horns blared with K.C. and the Sunshine Band's "Boogie Shoes," and Curtis "Up-Owl-Nite" Devereaux's jamming finale was upon them. Couples pulled apart, now dancing with their mate in a new, faster-paced way, the crowd giving various calls of dancing excitement. Naomi danced with Kevin (like Mark Dilworth, she could do her thang), keeping her eyes on everything around her.

She saw Oscar entering the men's room, but Naomi had every reason to believe he'd be back: supposedly, this was his favorite part of the ball. Cecily danced on, with an abandon and light in her eyes showing how much she liked the song. Joshua was near her but not, yet there was constant eye contact between the two, both smiling and dancing together but not, until Joshua moved closer to her. They made a choreographed move to the chorus with their shoulders and hands, and Naomi realized they'd danced to the song before. Cecily looked at ease—and happy.

CECILY (12:53 a.m.)

"A'ight, he's about to start the finale. Need to hit the head first..." He pulled back with a kiss to her cheek as people began joining the dancefloor (including Josh).

"Okay." She watched him walk toward their table, and Curtis shifted from ballad to boogie to the crowd's cheery calls and yells.

Cecily embraced stress-relief mode as she had weeks ago and danced to "Boogie Shoes." Knowing Josh danced near her, she smiled every time their eyes locked as they partied...and then he was shifting closer. Cecily didn't care; they'd danced to this before—and dancing was safe ground (especially with a dancefloor full of people around). They danced together, falling into doing their little move to the chorus, and Cecily also embraced the idea of him being her partner in ways beyond this dance (if for only the duration of the song). She was so tired of being unhappy and episodey. She would accept it and endure it, but right now, a little stress relief was in order.

Light on her feet, lungs fluttery and light, too, Cecily danced with him.

K.C. talked about boogieing, doing it till the sun came up, until he couldn't get enough, and Cecily blushed—because, looking at Joshua, she applied the more suggestive meaning toward him in her head. Tiny flutters of desire did its proper job with her, too, and Cecily banished those as efficaciously as she could. She enjoyed dancing with Joshua but wanted Oscar to hurry on back. They didn't do it often, but she enjoyed dancing with Oscar, too; he could dance—and she needed to begin that "redirection" Naomi talked about.

NAOMI (12:55 a.m.)

Curtis's finale fully underway, after K.C., they partied to Maze ("Before I Let Go"); Chubb Rock ("Treat 'Em Right"); Chuck Brown ("Run Joe" and "Bustin' Loose"); Marvin Gaye ("Got to Give it Up"); Funkadelic ("One Nation Under a Groove"); Doug E Fresh ("The Show"); Montell Jordan ("This is How We Do It!"); Usher ("Yeah!"); and Rob Base ("It Takes Two"), among others, as Curtis played his dance club-mix full blast, giving a taste and solid sample of each song before blending it into the next cut.

The last few tracks were a full run of EWF, and Naomi gleefully anticipated her brother losing his E-W-Effing mind.

Naomi, however, was amid understanding Woman Number Three's cryptic advice.

Rick and Viv sometimes broke from dancing with each other and now included dancing with members of the opposite sex near them and with each other. They danced with friends and strangers, enjoying the music and the event. The women from the window-watch exchanged nods, looks, laughs, and Woman Number Three raised her hand to them saying, *I told you so*, and *You're welcome*.

Some women turned around, proffering their rears for Rick to dance up against, but he had none of that—even backing up to avoid it if necessary. The only (natural) exception was Viv. Times Viv faced away from him while dancing, Rick sometimes held Viv's hips, moving his pelvis against her rear as they danced (doing that male side-lean to watch his body on hers).

When dancing with other men, Viv, too, managed deft and delicate dancing navigation and maneuvers in making sure her male dance partners stayed respectful (and some tested the boundaries).

Oscar had returned, and Naomi was surprised seeing how well he danced; the man had moves. He may have been an asshole, but he was a dancing-his-butt-off asshole (pardon the pun). Naomi chuckled to herself and grooved with Kevin (and Rick and Trevor).

While dancing, Rick signaled the men near him to loosen their ties, using a gesture where he tapped his neck and then performed a throat-cut motion with two fingers. Men smiled and obliged, but most men removed instead of loosening; many wore pre-tied ties and so tucked them into their pockets. It was much sexier fun watching the few men who wore actual bowties do a nice little pull to release the bow and leave the ribbon draping their necks.

Seeing Kevin's bowtie draping his neck, Naomi appreciated Viv's penchant.

EWF's "Let's Groove" started, and Rick Phillips roared his pleasure, kissing his wife's lips with a laugh before going into his zone. Watching him move was an exercise in—

"Let's Groove" rolled into "September," and Naomi and Kevin gave Rick a run for his dancing money as both danced harder and pumped their fists in common during a song with their birth month as title.

"September" flowed into "In the Stone," and Rick centered himself before his wife, dancing with only her now. Partying hard, he sang every lyric, every nuance of an ad-lib, giving head movements and facial expressions showing his absolute Earth, Wind & Fire joy. The couple also performed a few choreographed moves to the beat, showing how much both liked the song and enjoyed dancing to it together (a cadent display of their marital history).

Cool blasts of air flowing from above kept the philanthropic attendees cool during their music-based exertion from Curtis's finale, but Curtis had one more song to play after the EWF run.

NAOMI (1:05 a.m.)

The EWF run ended (to the whoops and claps of everyone).

"I appreciate that. Thank you. But looka here: get some water, catch your breath. There's one final dedication for the night, and then it's a wrap until we meet again next year."

People looked around; murmurs of curious confusion echoed as they dispersed to their tables for beverages and breath-catching.

But Curtis didn't give them long at all. "Okay. Here we go, folks. This next one's for everybody—and it's not about dancing this go-'round. The doc says: don't save it for Sunday morning: spread some love now."

The Staple Singers' "Touch a Hand, Make a Friend" floated at moderate volume into the ballroom.

People grinned at each other (Kevin nudged her and kissed her cheek), and Rick smiled and nodded his approval. He pointed at her, confirming she was the "doc" Curtis referred to. Naomi nodded subtly, and her brother smiled and nodded more emphatically, giving her a thumbs-up. He pecked Viv's lips before getting on with the program, mingling and shaking hands, wishing others Godspeed. Naomi smiled inside at watching Rick bob to the music as he shook people's hands, encouraging the elderly ladies to do a tiny groove with him before he released their hand, enjoying the music, message, and moment; he was something else.

Shaking hands and extending well wishes to others (she and Rick long ago learned to resist instinct and shake with their right hands), Naomi noticed Oscar making his way to shake Rick's hand, who accepted, long over the mild dust-up earlier. Tim also shook Rick's hand, which Rick appeared to find strange, but, having talked with Tim, Naomi understood what it was about.

Complete strangers, Cecily and Viv shook hands.

Naomi also monitored Lynelle, noticing her cautious approach to shake Viv's hand. When Viv saw her, Naomi observed Viv's immediate response; her body posture indicated outrage and protection, and Naomi moved closer.

To Naomi's surprise, by the time she moved within inches, Viv accepted Lynelle's hand and engaged in light conversation with a confidence Naomi found commendable.

However, as Lynelle tried to step away, Viv didn't release Lynelle's hand, stopping her. She had some parting words—and the masquerade was over.

Viv leaned in, still holding the woman's hand. "What? You taking this opportunity to see me up close? I know who you are. So, for the sake of this event, Lynelle, I'm shaking your hand, being cordial. But let me provide some clarity." Viv gripped tighter, making Lynelle wince. Viv smiled brightly, guiding Lynelle even closer. "I know all about your letters to Rick and your attempts to see him. When he finally called you weeks ago, I was with him, listening and guiding."

Lynelle peered at Viv, her heavily false-lashed eyes trying to widen in surprise despite her apparent need to still wince from Viv's grip (Viv was stronger than she looked).

Naomi stayed close, biting her bottom lip for several reasons while still shaking hands with others.

"Oh yeah. Calling you? That was *my* request," Viv revealed. "Wanted you to have some closure—have him answer those questions in your letter. But I was right there, listening to you asking to see him, to you wanting a meeting for lunch: 'It's just a harmless meal, Rick.'"

Lynelle stared and swallowed, floored by Viv's direct quote.

"Went to Atlanta for Christmas? Saw your aunt, who turned...ninety-five, is it?"

Lynelle's mouth fell open, and those fake eyelashes batted with shock. Because, even in relaying the conversation to Viv, Rick would've stuck to detached generalities. He wouldn't have revealed all that to Viv—she must have heard it firsthand.

Viv scoffed and gritted on her. "It's so tacky of you to use this moment, of the song and sincere glad-handing, the charitable meaning for it, to approach me. So, although we're here for a charitable cause, I'm not feeling very charitable right now." Taller than Lynelle, Viv adjusted her stance just enough to be eye-to-eye (à la Rick). "I know my husband's heart. Know why he ended up with you. Rick isn't interested, Lynelle. So give it up, let it go, move on. Your world will have to be 'Misty Blue.' Because, if you *ever* approach my husband for something inappropriate again, you and I will be 'Breaking News.'" Viv released Lynelle's hand with a toss.

Even with that hand-toss, Naomi admired how much of a lady Viv's been about the whole thing (because she could also see "Delaware-Viv" taking her earrings off and smearing on Vaseline petroleum jelly).

Patrice glowered their way and now moved in their direction.

Lynelle batted those fake eyelashes before looking Viv up and down. Her expression tried for a haughty bravado contradicting what Naomi read in her eyes: simple fear. "Let...Let him tell me that to my face."

The heat in her trace Cuban ancestry surfacing and shoving all the tasteful-peaceful to the side, Viv bit her bottom lip and drew her fist back (demonstrating those Delaware roots, too), but Naomi grabbed her before she could bring the punch forward.

Lynelle flinched and backed away as others turned attention their way (thankfully, Rick wasn't near).

Naomi pulled Viv away.

"I'm okay. But she *tried it*, Naomi. The fuck?!"

"I know, Viv. Opposite direction. Come on, sit down."

Body postures showing they'd witnessed some of the exchange (and seeing Viv upset), Leslie, Patrice, and Louise approached their table, ready to beat some ass. Trevor, Tim, Garrett, and Kevin stood together, looking but not approaching.

Viv sat. "I'm sorry. I didn't want to end the evening with *that* negativity." She put her forehead to her hand with a slow headshake.

Leslie, Patrice, and Louise offered varied versions of reassurance no apology was necessary, and Naomi agreed, but her pulse quickened and her breath hitched watching Viv's husband making his way to them.

"What happened?" Jaw set, he spoke calmly. He hadn't witnessed the exchange with Lynelle, but seeing his wife's demeanor from across the room was all he needed.

Naomi listened as Leslie, Patrice, and Louise recapped their version of what happened, doing their best to mitigate the situation by telling Rick Viv was okay, etc. Naomi filled in the story gaps for him. Joy Giles joined the group, concern on her face.

Viv maintained her head-in-hand position, her eyes shielded.

Done listening to the continued recapping and mitigating, Rick raised a hand, quieting them. He went to Viv.

"I've been meaning to say this to you about her, Midnight: you could've at least cheated *up*." Patrice scoffed.

Rick fastened a steady gaze on his sister-in-law. "It wasn't about that, Patrice. But, if you must know: cheating 'up' from Viv?" He shook his head. "...Not possible."

Patrice nodded her approval as Joy murmured, "Aww..."

Viv didn't look up or acknowledge Rick's words.

Rick turned to Viv, eyebrow raised. "Vivian, look at me." His command carried loving authority.

Viv lifted her head, locking eyes with her husband.

It took a millisecond. "Aw, hell no. I don't care if she *is* female."

He started away, but Viv grabbed his wrist and stood. "No, Ricky. I'm fine. She got the message, baby. Let it go, please."

Rick turned his wrist to take Viv's hand in his. "I'm so sorry."

"No, Rick. Your part ended years ago. That's *over*. Don't apologize."

"I can break it down for her again: 'to her face.'"

"I'm sure," Viv sighed. "But no: we've given this too much attention as it is." She went into his arms.

Naomi nodded as she waved their men on over. "Amen."

Patrice kept her gaze locked in Lynelle's direction. "She'd best take her ass home and *heed* the message."

"Yeah." Leslie placed hands on hips.

Rick and Viv said nothing, hugging it out.

The fellas stepped up, getting updates from their partners.

As she updated Kevin, Naomi watched Cecily enter the ladies' room. Wanting to speak with Cecily before she left, she pecked Kevin's lips. "Back in a bit."

NAOMI (1:21 a.m.)

She found Cecily emerging from the ladies' room, and they now stood in the threshold of that dark room again, along the corridor at the rear of the ballroom. Cecily appeared calm, but Naomi detected anxiety and trace fear increasing. It would be time to go home soon—and all the hundreds of buffers from the ball would be gone.

"...You haven't stuttered tonight."

An expression, curious and knowing, and part-smirk moved across her face. "No."

Naomi didn't know what that look meant, but she liked it. "You haven't stuttered in recent sessions, either."

"I know." She maintained that bizarre expression.

Naomi left it alone, knowing there was something to explore there later. "Have you ever seen the movie *G*—?"

"*Gaslight*. Yes, I've seen it. Kyle gave me a copy." She shook her head. "That's not what this is." That stubborn determination was more defense mechanism.

"So, what is it, then?" Her question rang with more challenge than she intended.

To that, Cecily had no response.

Naomi reached inside her clutch. She pulled out a slip of paper, handing it to Cecily. "Something for your secret note stash."

Cecily frowned. "For my sock?"

Naomi withheld a grin. "If that's still the holding spot, yes. Wait to open it. Resist looking at it until after our next session."

"What is it?"

"That's defeating the whole purpose of the 'wait.'"

She smirked and nodded (albeit fearfully). Her natural eye color suited her so much better. She looked down, taking slow breaths. Finally, she looked at her. "I really could do without the cloak-and-dagger, Naomi. I have enough going on."

Naomi was proud of her and let that show through her smile at Cecily. "So, open it."

Cecily opened the slip of paper and read, a soft smirk bending her lips. She nodded, wearing that bizarre expression. "I'll add it to one of my playlists; put it on repeat."

"Sounds good. Just listen to it a time or five. Keeping in mind—"

"The definition of insanity. I know. I'm paying attention, Naomi. Even though it doesn't seem like it sometimes, I am."

Naomi now stood before someone closer to the true Cecily Edana Jamison. "I believe that."

"Thank...Thank you for being here, Naomi."

"Well, I'm here for Thrive DC."

Cecily smiled at the small joke. "Right. On behalf of Thrive DC..."

The two chuckled. "Cecily, can you tell me more about that 'environment,' where you least experience PTSD symptoms?"

She rolled both shoulders. "Not much to tell. It's when I'm at work. I mean, I have epis— I experience symptoms there, too. But it's so rare. ...Sorry, I was about to say 'episodes.'"

She was, and Naomi was glad she corrected it, but that habitual apologizing would take more and longer—because it was both defense and survival mechanism. "I noticed." She didn't have to ask if Joshua had anything to do with it. It went without saying: he calmed her (without trying). She could parallel how Viv's presence and personality calmed Rick. "So, it's safe to say, being at home..."

Cecily sighed and looked away. "I don't know, Doctor Alexander. It's like, every time I think we're settling in, things going well, getting...to the other side of this, Oscar,...he's unhappy again, *angry*." Eyes sad, she shook her head with reflection. "The hurtful words start again, the putdowns,...the pun— Just...mean and unhappy. I can never figure why I upset him so." She looked near tears, the NAS-Cecily taking over again. "I can't say anything, so, most of the time, I let things go, because I know if I call him on any of it, he'll blame me somehow. He'll tell me I'm too sensitive or that I criticize everything." She turned to her. "I'm far from critical, Doctor Alexander—in the way Oscar means."

"I know."

Cecily's gaze intensified. "Well then, you also know I can't leave. Oscar's meanness, his unhappy,...can get pretty ugly." Naomi saw reflection of the abuse she suffered at his hands move through her eyes before she turned away. That was the closest she'd come to admitting his abuse wasn't just mental and emotional. "I'm stuck, Naomi. Just help me with the episodes. Please."

"No."

When Cecily turned back to her, tears streaming, her mouth hung open with hurt feelings.

Naomi shook her head. "I will not 'just' help with your PTSD. It's all wrapped up in there together, Cecily. But I'll get you to the other side. Whatever that means for you, Cecily, I'll get you there. Okay?"

She dabbed her eyes. "Yes. Thank you."

Naomi nodded, understanding Cecily's fear of Oscar taking revenge if she left him. She also appreciated the high likelihood of such a response by him. Losing Cecily, her leaving, would mean Oscar losing what he most valued: money, possessions, and the flaunting and bragging and pontification rights tied to having both, which fed his egosaurus by getting him the attention his narcissistic personality needed. "Cecily...?"

Cecily sniffed and stood taller, her eyes clear. "Yes."

"You're far from nasty-critical, but you wear your heart on your sleeve; you're more transparent and open with your emotions."

She frowned. "Okay...?"

"Going forward, except for our sessions,...be less transparent. Can you do that?"

"I think so. But, with *everybody*?" Her eyes widened with distress; she wanted to remain completely transparent under specific (Iota lapel pin) circumstances.

"...*Almost* everybody." They both knew who was excluded.

Cecily's soft sigh of relief confirmed it.

"Did you two say 'goodbye'?"

"No. Not necessary. It's back to the grind on Monday, so..." Sounded like she wanted to say goodbye, though.

They weren't in session, but Naomi wanted to take advantage of this time with her. Some Solution-Focused Scaling was necessary to gauge how Cecily perceived her situation. By having Cecily scale or grade answers to her questions, it allowed Cecily to think first, using her brain, rather than speak directly from emotion. Cecily, after all, was a numbers girl. "I have a question."

Cecily quasi-nodded. "Okay."

"More than one, really."

"Here we go."

They shared a chuckle.

"Ready?"

"Sure."

"Give me a number."

"Forty-nine."

Naomi held in a smile, not surprised. "Okay. Now, 'forty-nine' will represent 'perfection,' the best, goodest."

Cecily smirked but nodded. "*Premiere*. Got it."

"Close your eyes."

Cecily did.

"Okay. Let's imagine you're in a building with forty-nine floors. Floor forty-nine being—"

Eyes closed, Cecily bent the edges of her mouth upward, showing some teeth. "The Penthouse. Got it. This is fun."

"So, I see. Now, each floor is swankier the higher you go. Cecily, you walk on the elevator..."

Cecily nodded, lifting her hand as if to push an elevator button.

"Very good. Now, I want you to push the button of the floor representing how well you're coping with what's happened to you."

The smile faded.

"Breathe and think about it before you push."

Naomi watched Cecily calm herself, watching her facial expression change with her consideration until she pushed the imaginary floor. "Nineteen."

The number was low (just over a third of the way), but it was honest, which was most important. "Okay. Get off on your floor and open your eyes."

Cecily opened her eyes. Naomi recognized her getting ready to ask if her answer was good, but she stopped herself. "Now what?"

"Floor Nineteen: lumpy twin bed with threadbare coverings and a thirteen-inch fat-back black-and-white television. Tell me: what would it take, say, to get you to the twenty-ninth floor...with a nicer bed and a bigger screen TV? We're talking full-size instead of twin, nineteen-inch color TV—still fat-back: flat panels start after floor forty."

It went quiet for about a minute. Cecily looked at her. "I have an idea. Do you want to do this now?" She sounded ready, and that was all Naomi needed.

Naomi shook her head. "We don't have the time. But..."

"Next session." Cecily grinned.

"Of course. The idea, always, is to have you regain your power of 'No,' which you've lost along the way. But I want to ask something I asked in one of the early sessions..." Naomi looked into her eyes. "Do you feel *safe*, Cecily?"

She stiffened and gazed back, her eyes pleading and wary, before shaking her head.

Naomi nodded her understanding. "That's okay. You will be."

Cecily took a breath but looked puzzled, disbelieving. "With Oscar?" She shook her head at the improbability of that.

"I didn't say that."

Cecily stared at her in fraught silence, and Naomi saw the combo idealization-intellectualization mechanism to defend Oscar leap into her eyes. "My marriage to Roland wasn't perfect, Naomi."

"Point taken. But with him,...you were *safe*." She didn't give Cecily chance to respond. "Now, let's get back before they send a search party."

They ambled to the ballroom. "Want your meds back?"

Cecily shook her head. "You know anyone who knows marketing?"

"A connection or two. Why?"

"For JAH Tech. Things are happening, business growing—"

"But marketing's not your bailiwick. Or Joshua's."

Cecily emitted a sighing-chuckle. "Correct."

She was mixing worlds, knee-deep in shades of gray here, but it was decided. "Let me think on it."

"Thanks."

As they approached the rear entrance, Naomi had one more nugget. "Have you thought any more about those initials you remembered: the 'W' and...'H,' I think it was?"

Cecily startled with a hiccup in her step. "Nope. And you're right: we have little time to do that now. Be safe getting home, Naomi." She hurried away, that lie floating in her wake.

NAOMI (1:37 a.m.)

House lights up, Curtis packed up, the bar closed, and refreshments gone; only a few hangers-on were milling around the ballroom. Naomi's crew awaited her return, and when she stepped up, Leslie talked plans for the after-party.

"So, I'm thinking coffee and desserts, people. More music..." Leslie looked at her for confirmation.

Naomi shrugged as Kevin took her hand. "That's fine. But by 'desserts,' you mean...?"

"We have those mini cheesecakes in the freezer, the tiny éclairs, the mini-Bavarian cream puffs..."

Garrett pointed at Leslie. "You had me at 'éclairs.'"

Rick returned from the men's room, moving close to Viv and holding her from behind with his arms around her waist. Chin to Viv's cheek, he looked around at everyone. "What's the discussion?" He kissed on Viv while awaiting an answer.

"We're...We're all h-heading to Naomi's after this...f-for coffee and satisfying...any sweet-tooths..." Viv's raven eyes softened with arousal as she spoke with stutter and pause.

"Mm..." Rick shifted back some, one hand to Viv's shoulder, his other hand with fingertips to her waist. He glanced at Viv's rear, at his body's nearness to it, surely imagining intimacy with her. His testosterone made him look, and he didn't stare, but he was glancing at his wife (not some other woman), so it was all good. Split-second of distraction over, Rick held Viv from behind again and kissed her cheek. "We're go'n go home first, right?"

Garrett snickered with an amiable-yet-knowing nod.

"Unnecessary. I packed a change of clothes for us, just in case; so we don't have to."

"Oh. Well, how proactive of you. So thoughtful and resourceful... We're going home first, right?"

Viv turned her head to him. "Why?"

"Got something to show you."

Viv glanced at Rick sideways. "Boy." Naomi, however, discerned her wanting him, too.

"Come on. I'll show you mine. You show me yours..."

After a night of flirting, emotion, innuendo, and dancing, it was no wonder Rick was ready for private time with his wife. Ready to show her the many things he wanted her to *see*.

"You'd rather waste gas and time by going home, when we can head over there from here?" Viv smirked at him with this loving look denoting she already knew the answer—because his desire to go home had nothing to do with practicality.

Rick just looked at her.

Viv gazed back, her smirk bordering a soft, knowing smile full of flirt with him.

"Yes. Like I said: got something to show you."

Patrice folded her arms. "Uh, you have houseguests, Midnight."

"Don't remind me."

Naomi pondered the origins of that nickname.

Viv nudged Rick, giving him a look over her shoulder; the two doing that silent-conversation thing. Viv soon curled her hand behind Rick's head for a kiss.

Leslie shook her head. "Hot."

Louise sighed, "Anyway!" while Patrice rolled her eyes, adding: "Yeah. Kiss him, Viv. Don't swallow him."

Naomi bit her bottom lip to keep from speaking.

Please let this happy couple be happy. They've been to hell and back and stayed together. Relish their triumph and shoot for the same thing. Damn!

Viv broke her kiss with her husband. Hand still to the back of Rick's head, she turned to Louise and Patrice.

Having known Viv a few years, Naomi recognized Viv was pissed; she now had every intention of trying to swallow her husband. Rick's anticipatory smirk indicated knowing as much, too.

Viv handed Leslie her clutch. "Hold this for me, please." Giving Lou and Patrice a pointed look, Viv turned in Rick's arms, kissing him properly.

Naomi was glad to see them do some real kissing, instead of all that polite pecking. "Finally!"

Leslie chuckled, "I know. *Thank you!*" while Trevor whistled.

Rick and Viv engaged in lip nibbling and soft tongue touches, with moments of more heated tongue action, but they didn't try to slob each other down (likely saving that for the privacy of their bedroom).

"That's right, Viv: kiss your baby daddy." Leslie grinned.

Mild laughter ensued, and Rick wore this subtle smirk (seemingly in response to Leslie's reference to him) as he broke from Viv's mouth to kiss her neck. Viv closed her eyes with a deep sigh while caressing his head. If the couple had a homemade sex-tape, Naomi presumed those watching them now would pay to see it.

Someone across the room cat-whistled, validating her presumption.

Still kissing Viv's neck, Rick spoke breathlessly: "We're... Unh shit... We're going home first, right?" He sent a hand toward Viv's rear but stopped at the rise, his fingers resting with full implication.

Viv spoke with a similar, worked-up breathlessness. "Oh, hell yes."

Sporadic chuckles followed.

Naomi smiled. "'Kisses don't lie,' Viv?"

Viv raked her nails across the top of Rick's head. "They sure as hell don't, shit." With that, Viv grabbed Rick's head, pushing her tongue into his mouth and making her husband moan with it.

The move was outside Viv's norm; she was in unfamiliar territory. Perhaps recent events (and people hating) caused Viv to step outside her normally reserved self and expressly show her love for her husband. Whatever the reason, it was good to see and healthy for Viv, even if she didn't realize it.

Leslie and Trevor laughed with soft claps.

Garrett's eyes bugged, while Patrice looked away.

Kevin chuckled, but his arousal burgeoned because his grip to her hand tightened.

Eyes closed, the couple indulged in each other's mouths, their tongues dancing with heated tenderness, Viv's hands to Rick's hair and face, Rick's hands roaming his wife's waist and back.

The two unwittingly served as aphrodisiac to those around them; Naomi, too, wanted some private time with Kevin. With the passing seconds, Leslie now turned away with a blush (and likely arousal) while the guys fidgeted from a similar root cause.

Louise and Tim looked on with interest. Louise watched hungrily, lips parted, her tongue subtly mimicking as if she were kissing Rick. The girl had it worse than bad for him.

Naomi also observed Lynelle hanging back and watching from off to the side. Her body posture suggested longing (for Rick) and apprehension (over Viv and Rick).

Look on, honey. And take Viv's advice and move on. Rick isn't just her husband: he's her man—lying in bed with Viv every night. You never had a bed with him. You,...were never in the running.

The couple finally parted, a delicate line of spittle connecting their lips before falling away. However, they stayed hugged up, and Naomi suspected (given that intense kiss) they likely waited for Rick's erection to subside.

Viv whispered in Rick's ear, and he shook his head, whispering something back—and Naomi knew she was right: virtually nine inches of hardness pressed between the couple.

Rick rested his forehead on Viv's for quiet seconds.

With a tender kiss to Rick's cheek, Viv eased his tuxedo jacket off his shoulders. She slid the jacket between them from the side facing everyone and handed it to Rick, so he could conceal himself where he needed.

Rick stepped back, casually holding his jacket in front of him.

Naomi noted Louise's concentration in the area of Rick's obscured crotch and wished she wore her brace again—if only for the few seconds it would take to bonk Louise on the head with it.

Rick turned to Garrett. "A'ight, man, look: before we head to Sis's..." He smiled at her, and Naomi blushed inside with pride. Rick had a way of making you feel special, as if, for that moment, you were the only person in the room.

This man upset her balances, making it difficult to maintain her standard neutral objectivity and cool on the inside, but on the outside, Naomi showed little emotion as she nodded back.

Rick turned to Garrett. "We're going home first and..."

Viv used a thumb to wipe a smear of her lipstick from his face with affection, and Naomi spotted Louise frowning displeasure at the loving display; she looked outraged.

Rick interlocked his hand with Viv's, gazing at her.

Viv gazed back curiously but with heat.

"...I live you, Vivian."

"I live you."

Rick leaned close, placing a soft, sensual peck on Viv's lips, their mouths slightly parted.

Leslie grunted her approval. "Black love, people."

Nodding, Trevor placed an arm around Leslie's shoulder. "For real."

Rick pulled back with a grunt of his own. The couple gazed at each other, the intensity between them pulsating around those close and watching, until Viv sent him a flirty smirk. "Finish your thought, baby."

"Right. Where was I...?" Words all low and distracted sounding, seemed Rick couldn't look away from Viv's "liquid night."

Trevor chimed in. "Going home first."

"Oh, yeah. And then I'm..." Rick dragged his eyes from Viv's to look at Leslie. "I'ma take care of some things with my 'baby mama.'" He winked at Leslie (making her blush) before turning to Garrett. "I suggest you take care of some things, too, man."

Garrett nodded while Patrice harrumphed her displeasure, looking indignant (but also excited).

One hand still interlocked with Rick's, Viv held her free hand out to Leslie for her clutch. "So, we'll be there anon; just going home first."

Rick grunted low again, biting his bottom lip while trailing his gaze over his wife. "Oh, yes."

Viv cut her eyes his way. "Down, boy."

Rick echoed this deep-barreled chuckle in reply.

Viv turned back to Leslie. She released Rick's hand, running her freed hand over Rick's hair (his eyelids fluttered with the move). "Suffice it: we'll be late." Viv winked.

Kevin released Naomi's hand to hug her waist. "Time to get that 'FIRE' started, Rick?"

"You know it. Had an *intimately close* friend of mine testifying ever since she put that dress on, man." He wore a cunning smile as he extended Kevin a power handshake, and the males snickered with nods; the men-only reference to Rick's "intimately close friend" made them give these smirks hardly veiled with meaning. Rick then trailed his gaze over his wife with explicit implication, before he scoffed low with a headshake, his eyes still roaming Viv. "Hell, we may not even *make it* home."

The other men roared their jovial understanding, exchanging hand-shakes and giving daps, while Louise looked ready to kill—or burst into tears.

Viv blushed profusely as Rick interlocked their hands again (still looking her over). She turned to Leslie. "So, Les..."

"Uh, no problem. Sure." Leslie giggled.

THE AFTER-PARTY

Daybreak was only hours away.

Naomi gazed upon her framed picture of the Phillips family, hold-ing an almost-empty coupe glass of Henney Brandy Alexander (Kevin added a perfect extra dash of nutmeg), unable to stop grinning. When they arrived, the couple presented it to her, and she placed it on the mantel in the great room. She had a (barely used) game room and substantial spaces on the upper and lower levels, but her great room on the main floor was where everything happened for entertaining guests. Naomi did little of that herself, but her daughter hosted plenty.

Also on the mantel, next to the framed portrait, another gift; this one from Kevin: a Sankofa bird figurine made of pigmented ebony wood. He brought it back from his trip to Ghana weeks ago but only presented it to her before leaving for the charity ball. His sometime nickname for her was "Sankofa Bird," and he believed her profession rooted elements of Sankofa anent treating her patients. The egg on its back shone a muted golden sheen. Naomi didn't know if the mantel would be its ultimate resting place, but its perch there seemed ideal for now. And as much as she appreciated such a thoughtful gift, something about receiving it bothered her (and her grin faded some).

Trevor now served as deejay, programming songs in her digital juke-box. He stood near her built-in, consulting with Rick on selections.

Joy and Brendan were on their way.

Hostess Leslie had stopped bouncing around with setting out refreshments and decks of cards but was now upstairs doing God knows what.

Naomi had to resist chuckling every time she took a gander at Patrice and Garrett over on the huge sectional, Garret sitting back with an arm behind his wife, Patrice talking animatedly to him—no trace of sourness. What a difference a quick detour home makes.

While Patrice and Garrett attempted to recapture something missing between them, the vibe between Louise and Tim carried more distance than at the ball. Perhaps there was an argument during the drive over. Since they came from the ball, they were the only two still wearing their charity ball attire (although Tim had dispensed with his tuxedo accessories, wearing only the shirt and trousers). Tim sat at the table, talking to Kevin (who looked cool and fit in his jeans and sweater). Louise sat alone at the end of the sectional, reading a magazine. Naomi, however, read dissatisfaction flitting through both faces.

Naomi experienced a level of dissatisfaction herself. At the ball, Cecily reminded her much of high school when she'd come to her, telling her Joshua was there. Now, as she spotted Louise's frequent secretive moony glances at Rick, noted the soft breaths Louise took whenever he came near, Naomi considered it so eleventh grade, but it shouldn't have been—Louise wasn't 16 but over 40; it was irritating. And yes, she deemed Cecily's situation something different.

She resumed focus on the Phillips family portrait to redirect her moody-blue, and the edges of her mouth turned upward once again.

"This picture isn't going anywhere." Viv stepped up next to her, grinning. She wore a white high-collar button-down shirt, slim-fit blue jeans, and tawny-brown lady-Timberlands. Her shirt was untucked; it curved over her jeans, showing her shape. Her hair was out now, flowing over her shoulders. And although Viv's shirt was high-collar, Naomi caught glimpses of the hickey Rick put on her—the one she didn't have at the ball.

Naomi couldn't resist. "Things got pretty hot-and-heavy at the Phillips household." She used her eyes to mean the mark on Viv's neck.

Viv blushed. She'd changed her body oil: something carrying elements of honeyed wood. "I told him people could still see it. It's not that obvious, is it?"

"Not really. There's a peek of it when you turn your head or your shirt opens. Having your hair out helps obscure it. But it's fine, Viv."

Viv shook her head with feeling. "Girl, I haven't had a passion-mark in years. But Rick was..."

Naomi grinned. "Yes...?"

"Well,...he put it there as we were..."

Naomi smirked: male-dominant missionary. But vertical, horizontal? "Uh-huh, and...?"

Viv smirked back. "Put it this way: my husband was in a moment where he uh..."

Naomi leaned closer, leering with humor. "You don't have to finish this, but 'he was in a moment'... Uh-huh...?"

Viv smiled. Her beauty exuded a comforting, radiating quality: like a cozy warm fire during a snowstorm. "Rick was doing something, making it difficult for him *not* to put it there. How's that?"

"I bet!" Laughing with Viv, Naomi spotted Louise sending an unhappy look their way.

Viv gave her a deliberate look as their chuckles died, then closed her eyes, lowering her head for emphasis before returning her gaze. "Our sex, Naomi... The touch of Rick's tongue... What that man does with his mouth and hands, his...penis. Multitasking like a— He tears down my walls, girl, making them shimmy and shake!"

Naomi snickered in fun.

"Oh, he's nasty." Viv exhaled a grunting-sigh. "But a good, *loving* nasty. He makes me moan, Naomi. Moan long...and deep."

"With 'dedication...and gusto'?"

Viv smirked with a nodding look of confirmation. "But that's the growling he makes me do, not the moaning."

Naomi laughed, just having a good time with Viv Phillips. Based on Rick's earlier comments about Viv's freak-in-the-bed status, the couple regularly got down-n-dirty with each other.

Viv chuckled, giving Naomi a conspiratorial glance. "We almost didn't make it to this little soiree."

"And your sister?"

"Yeah. Garrett helped her empty her purse. Can't you tell?"

"I can, yes."

Viv gazed around the room, and Naomi could tell whenever she focused on Rick.

Naomi leaned closer, using her eyes to mean Viv's neck. "So, is that your 'yes' spot?"

"Oh, definitely. When I'm hating him? And thus, the answer to everything is the *opposite* of what Rick wants the answer to be?"

"Right...?"

"If the offense is minor, and Rick starts mackin' his apology, pulling me close and kissing or nibbling my neck while talking his persuasive male shit in that voice men only use for such occasions?"

"Uh-huh."

"Girl, every answer becomes quite agreeable." She jostled one shoulder. "I'm a sucker for that, as most women are."

"I see."

"I think Rick knows, but he doesn't exploit it."

"How'd he like the yo-yo?" Viv ordered a unique yo-yo for Rick but had it delivered to her house. She'd been excited about it. The plan was to make more of a presentation to him, but with the mixed company and underlying issues, Viv used the library on Naomi's fourth level to present it privately.

Viv's secret smile said it all. "...He liked it very much."

"Nose crinkling?"

Her friend's smile changed. "Yes!"

Naomi nodded, imagining the delight between the couple. For Viv's smile told her: Rick's joy was hers.

"I see you have something new on the mantel—one I didn't carve." Viv gestured at the Sankofa figurine. "Very nice. That from Kevin?"

"It is. Presented it before we left for the ball."

Viv lifted a side of her mouth in humor. "Your nose crinkling?"

Naomi lifted the opposite side of her mouth in humor. "Not quite."
They shared a brief titter, Naomi glad she didn't have to explain herself
to someone working from such similar personality stock. She finished
the last of her HBA. "Can I ask you something?"

"Of course."

Naomi considered Viv for some seconds.

Viv returned a curious expression of her own. "What?"

"You and Rick have this thing where you 'talk' to each other without
parting your lips. I mean, like, *conversations*."

"Okay, 'Dwight.'"

Naomi grinned.

Viv's eyes grew intense before softening with emotion. She nodded
reflectively. "It developed over our years together but has intensified
since... Well, you know."

Naomi did know.

Viv shrugged. "I can't explain *how* we do it, though."

"Oh, because that was my question." The phenomenon was unknown
to Naomi—she had nothing medical to explain it, either (although she
had a personal theory or two). But then, she had nothing medical to
explain her flashes of truth or aura-flickers, either (and the personal
theories there left much to be desired). "Well, it's interesting to watch."

"You mean, weird."

"I don't mean that at all, Viv. Honestly."

Viv smirked before grinning acceptance of her words, but then made
an odd expression. "You know, I...I was somewhat turned-on by Lynelle
being there tonight."

"...Because she's in love with him, still wants him. Rick busted her
open: emotionally, sexually. It's indirect confirmation of his virility—and he's yours."

Viv watched her husband (much like she did at the ball) as answer.

"And Louise?"

Viv's expression changed, conveying anger and hurt before turning
neutral. "No. *Not* the same thing. Nowhere near turned-on by that one."

It wasn't the same thing—not at all. "I must say, Viv: you've handled
the 'messes' from the ball with...aplomb."

"As opposed to how you know I *could've* handled it."

Naomi grinned. "Correct."

Viv scoffed. "And they were testing my limits, Naomi. I'm telling you. Especially Lynelle."

"Like I said: aplomb."

She sighed, shaking her head. "Thanks. I guess."

"...He wasn't all-in with those others, Viv. Rick didn't 'invest' his heart and mind, just his...penis. He's only been all-in...with *you*."

"I know, Naomi. I believe that. I wasn't all-in with Jonathan."

"True. That type of compartmentalizing: not impossible for women, but much easier for men."

Viv nodded inchmeal, looking over at Rick. "You know 'Midnight Train to Georgia,' right?"

"Of course."

Viv gazed forward, reflective.

Naomi understood. The crux meaning of those lyrics was how Viv felt about Rick and their marriage: that she'd rather follow him to be in his world (and whatever that entailed) than not have him in her own.

"And he'd rather follow you, Viv."

Viv, her eyes on the after-party activity, nodded inchmeal again. "I guess it all works out then, huh? Because he's good, Naomi. Good to me, good for me, good with me. Just a *good* man. And I believe, all the painful rest of it, in the before, only reinforced what we mean to each other, who we are...together."

Naomi bobbed her head in slow consideration.

Viv turned to her. "So, what's your 'yes' spot?"

"...Inside of my left wrist."

Viv grinned. "A'ight, a'ight. Sexy. Kevin know?"

Naomi hesitated before nodding (thinking on his kisses there before guests arrived). This girl-sharing thing wasn't new between her and Viv, but she still hesitated (some old habits didn't die at all). "So, no qualms with people knowing you and Rick went home for some horizontal refreshment before coming here? Or was it vertical?"

Viv offered a slanted smile. "Both. And there was a bit of diagonal amorous congress going on sometimes, too."

Naomi snickered.

"But, no. No qualms." She sucked her teeth. "Please. We're married. Like Garrett said, 'married people have sex.' Besides, if we hadn't..."

Naomi leaned closer. "Yes...?"

Viv raised an eyebrow with her smirk. "If we hadn't gone home first, Rick would've been social and cordial, but not the charming, jovial, fun Rick you know and love. Your sweet 'little brother' would've been a little less *sweet*."

Naomi hollered, drawing others' attention (and noticing more of Louise's displeasure).

"Yeah. If the situation won't allow, Rick's pretty good about getting it later. Tonight, however: not up for debate."

Remembering Rick's state toward the close of the ball, and as he talked to her about Viv, Naomi understood. "Okay, Viv. Gotcha. A woman can only hold out for so long. You did it for us, then."

Viv offered an agreeing shrug with a headshake. "That's all I'm saying. I was looking out for my peops, so I took one for the team."

They laughed.

More like, took nine *for the team, but who's quibbling?*
Thought I told you to go away?

Later, Naomi, Viv, Patrice, Louise, and Joy socialized in the kitchen, music traveling to them from the great room.

Patrice was talking about her daughter's first semester at Hampton, how she'd been bugging her aunt Viv for details on pledging AKA, when Rick entered, heading for the fridge. He wore a blue, gray, and brown striped buttoned-down shirt, jeans, and gray Timberlands, and Naomi wondered what Rick *didn't* look good in. From suits to sweats to the charity-ball tuxedo to the after-party jeans and Timberlands, the man dressed up or down with consistently pleasing results.

"Scuse me, ladies..." Rick retrieved a Corona Extra and looked at her (three-eleven a.m. shadow dotting his face). "Think you need to get in there, Sis. Kevin wants to get a card game going, looking for Spades partners..."

Naomi groaned in fun and hefted her brows at Rick and Viv. "You in?"

With mutual glances, they each shook their heads. Viv touched her upper arm. "We're opting out this go-round. Sorry, sweetie."

"Tim and I will play," Louise volunteered.

Rick chuckled, giving a playful scoff. "Yeah, take 'em up, Naomi: that's an easy win. Lou's pretty good, but Tim sucks."

Everyone laughed as Rick pecked Viv's cheek. He turned to leave the kitchen when Louise jumped on his back. "No, you didn't! Tim's not that bad!" She laughed, lightly punching Rick's shoulder. "Take it back! Insulting Tim's card skills...!" She laughed and "defended" Tim's honor while riding Rick's back and hitting on him. "Take it back! He *can* play!" She laughed.

And everyone laughed, too.

At first.

But then, Louise's playful strikes became these rubs on Rick's body in her playful fighting with him about "insulting" Tim.

Louise's obvious sexual excitement from her interaction with Rick pissed Naomi off.

Joy frowned, mumbling, "Well, wait a minute now..." with confused yet concerned disapproval.

Rick's fleeting expressions of anger conveyed being uncomfortable now, but he was trying not to make a scene.

Viv's smile faded, her following words grave yet calm: "Louise, that's enough. Get off my husband."

Everyone quieted.

Patrice's lip curled with attitude. "Yeah, Lou. What're you doing? You've been borderline all night, and now your 'play fighting' seems like you're trying to get you a sly freak-on." Given Patrice's behavior at the ball, Naomi and Viv looked surprised at her support. Was it because Garrett *emptied Patrice's purse?* "Did you hear my sister?! Get off him like that, Louise. You drunk?"

Louise looked around, embarrassed, but instead of jumping down and off Rick, she slid down his body, running her hands over him as she descended.

Rick's irises flamed redder, and Naomi recognized him resisting throwing her off him.

Joy's disapproval deepened the lines in her brow. "What the...?"

Viv surged toward Louise, but Naomi grabbed Viv's wrist (keeping her from losing her cool again).

Viv paused, but Patrice picked up the baton. "Oh, hell no, bitch!" Now, Viv gripped Patrice's arm, stopping her.

Louise's eyes widened with shock at Patrice's protective hostility, but she finally placed her feet on the hardwood floor and sent her gaze there, too. "Sorry 'bout that. Guess I am sorta tipsy."

Naomi, however, knew better. She loosened her hold on Viv's wrist, and Viv released Patrice.

Rick adjusted his posture with this grunt of aggravation, then headed toward the door.

"Unh-unh."

Rick turned to his wife. After a bit of that silent-conversation thing, he came over to her.

Viv cupped his jaw. "Where're you going?" She pecked his lips and looked up at him, running a thumb over the stubble on his cheek. "Huh?"

With a heavy sigh, Rick shook his head. He bent his forehead to touch Viv's, and Viv caressed his head, pecked his lips again.

Naomi watched the tension leave Rick's body.

Joy nodded her approval. "Grown folks' business. Sweet."

Viv pulled back, looking into Rick's eyes.

Rick nodded. He pecked Viv's lips and headed out but turned back. He stared at Louise for several seconds, his expression alternating between annoyance and sympathy, and then turned to Viv, extending his beer bottle toward her. "Want some?"

Viv eased a nod, her eyes brimming with understanding.

Grinning, Rick moved close to his wife. He swigged from the bottle and placed his mouth on Viv's, delicately transferring beer droplets into her mouth before kissing her deeply.

Tickled, Naomi popped her brother's shoulder. "Get 'er, Rick."

As they had weeks before, Rick and Viv paused kissing and turned to her. Rick handed her his bottle of Corona and winked. "Watch me work." He turned back to Viv with a kiss, slow and teasing. His right hand rested at her waist as he pushed his left into her hair, kissing Viv harder and pressing his body to hers. A faint moan came from Viv.

Joy chuckled. "Watching them never gets old."

The couple's kiss deepened, both issuing whispery moaning-gasps into the other's mouth, when Rick pulled back with a grunting-sigh, his lips a breath from Viv's. "Shit, girl. Can't get enough of you." He reclaimed her mouth, his grips to her body showing intensity before their kiss began deceleration.

The couple parted with a closing peck, and in their gaze at each other, Naomi recognized *"Kisses don't lie"* passing between them. Viv then smiled at Rick, shaking her head (at something else going unsaid between them; the part Naomi couldn't decipher).

Rick's eyes roamed Viv's face. "If the mild weather holds, wanna hang at Lake Artemesia this weekend?" He spoke low with his inquiry for a date.

Viv nodded, her eyes roaming Rick's face with blushing interest. "Sounds good. We can bring Zenobia along as company for Al."

Blindly accepting the bottle from Naomi, Rick pecked Viv's lips once more before heading toward the exit, toasting them with his beer. "Ladies."

Patrice teased her brother-in-law with humor. "Bye, *'Tiger.'*"

The ladies (except Louise) giggled.

Joy grunted. "Yeah. That was the truck driving up to initiate a special UPS delivery, girl."

Rick looked perplexed. "A what?"

Female giggles followed, and Rick settled his gaze on Viv. "Tell me later?"

Viv held Rick's gaze with a gentle nod while sending heat across the room to him. "Or, I'll show you."

Patrice and Joy murmured in teasing jest.

The couple exchanged a private look before Viv joined the ladies in laughter.

"You guys looked like pros with that beer." Joy turned to Viv. "Looked kinda hot, but never tried it myself. It's not weird drinking from his mouth like that?"

Viv gazed into her husband's eyes while answering Joy. "I've swallowed that, much more personal from this man; what's a little beer?"

Naomi smiled as Patrice and Joy indulged in giving various teasing calls of approval. Patrice licked her index finger and pressed it toward her sister, making a sizzling-hiss noise.

Joy high-fived Patrice. "You ain't never lied! Call the FD!" She laughed. "Go 'head, Viv!"

Ignoring Louise's pain-filled grimace at Viv's response, Naomi chuckled, remembering Patrice's behavior at the ball earlier, her admonishments to Viv about being "vulgar." Patrice wasn't of that opinion now, more amenable to a little dirty innuendo. Maybe the bedroom session with her husband released some tension.

Viv continued looking at Rick, wearing a women-only smirk.

Blushing hard, Rick pointed his beer behind him toward the front exit. "I'm going that way now."

Viv held his gaze, something else low and sweet but unsaid passing between them. "Okay."

With a parting wink at Viv, Rick left.

Naomi watched him go, shaking her head with a smile.

Forget People Magazine's choice; he is the sexiest man alive.

As soon as the laughter faded with Rick's departure, Patrice shifted attention to Louise, her expression hard and unforgiving. Joy levied a glare at Louise with similar contempt. Viv looked at Louise, not, her eyes on Edna Lewis's *The Taste of Country Cooking* resting countertop.

Patrice's upper lip curled with her grit on Louise. "You best read the room."

"I'm sorry, Viv. I don't know what got into me."

Viv didn't respond.

Joy scoffed. "Well, with the way you were rubbing all on him and sliding down his body, we all know what you *wanted* to get into you." She sucked her teeth, shaking her head with a derisive sigh. "Not cool." Joy placed a hand of amity on Viv's shoulder and left the kitchen.

It went quiet, and Patrice went to the fridge. "Oh, goodie..." She retrieved the carton of buttermilk (leftover from making biscuits last weekend) and poured herself a glass, and Naomi recalled a therapy session with Rick and Viv years ago. Carton away and milk in hand, Patrice returned to them, her eyes angry and hard on Louise. "So, the ball wasn't enough. You bring that foul mess to this thing, too?"

Louise gazed upon Viv with open sorrow. "I'm so sorry, Viv. Please."

Viv stared down at the glass of ice water she held atop the counter, turning it by degrees. "...You can't have my husband, Lou. Not while I breathe. But you can have what's left of our friendship." Viv shot Louise a narrow look. "Or, you can't have my husband, Lou...and we can be *done* with this friendship. That was your last 'I'm sorry.' My patience and understanding with this can only go so far."

Patrice swallowed with an almost-choke. "'Patience'? Did they—?"

Naomi, Viv, and Louise spoke simultaneously: "*No!*"

Viv focused on Louise as she spoke. "No, Reecie, they didn't. It's um..." She shook her head and sipped her water.

Naomi finished for her. "It's all one-sided."

Patrice sighed her relief, but then scoffed. "Well, if you ask me, if *that's* what's going on, your friendship should already be dead."

Louise mumbled, "But nobody asked you."

Naomi expected things to be on ten (or even twenty), but Patrice surprised her when she turned eyes to her. "This is your home."

Patrice's statement implied: out of respect, had it not been the host's home, Patrice would have cleaned Louise's clock. Naomi nodded and quirked her lips. "It is."

Louise's hand-to-mouth: she received the message.

Patrice winked with camaraderie and turned to her sister. She rubbed Viv's shoulder and kissed her cheek, sending Louise a scathing look as she left the kitchen with her buttermilk.

It remained quiet for a spell. Viv sipped her water. Louise continued pleading to Viv with her eyes, but Viv wasn't looking at her.

"Louise has agreed to see one of my colleagues about it, Viv. After an initial consultation with me, of course."

Viv still wouldn't look at Louise, taking in Naomi's kitchen instead. She sipped her water with a straight face. The seconds passed. "Good."

Naomi spoke with quiet tact, knowing her following words would bother Viv more. "Tim...Tim, too."

Viv shifted her eyes to Naomi, those black irises filled with shock and embarrassment. "Tim...?"

Naomi nodded, and Viv scoffed with a headshake. "This is so..." She shot Louise a stern look. "Poor *Tim*."

Louise began her whine, "Viv, I'm sor—"

Viv's expression cut her off; she was tired of hearing it.

Louise sighed. "So, what now, Viv?"

Viv sipped her water, looking pensive. "...*You*? See Naomi's colleague. Rick and I will continue our married life together. And...Naomi? Well, Naomi does whatever necessary to keep me from going to jail. Hopefully, Tim is okay after all this; I like Tim." Now, Viv sighed. "But for now, let's just go on in there so Kevin can play cards."

With an appreciative pat to Naomi's shoulder, Viv left the kitchen.

Louise stared after her. "I don't want to lose her."

"Yeah, well, that's on you, Louise."

Louise dropped her head and heaved a sigh of, "I know," before looking at Naomi. "Time?"

"Time...and you climbing over the Mount-Everest issue of loving and wanting her husband," Naomi confirmed. "Finding Rick attractive is one thing. Okay. There's...really no getting around that one. But you've crossed a sacred line, Louise. Loving Rick—*in that way*—is major friendship violation. You know that."

Louise dropped her head again. She closed her eyes. "God, he's amazing."

Naomi didn't respond.

"It's not fair."

Naomi waited.

"Viv... She...She gets to *be* with him: in the evenings, the middle of the day, the wee hours... Gets to snuggle with him,...kiss him... Viv gets to see and touch and feel and play with his—" Louise took a hiccup of breath.

"And you get to do the same with Tim—and Viv doesn't."

Louise wore this almost-pout, saying there was no comparison.

"Viv's his *wife*, Louise. Comes with the territory: all that seeing and touching and feeling and...ahem...'playing' she gets to do."

Louise looked hurt. "The way they look at each other, even when it's a laughing moment."

Naomi nodded her agreement.

"Viv... She's...She's been pregnant by him, carried his babies." Louise winced. "Viv...gets to *know* him."

Naomi believed Louise's focus was Viv knowing Rick biblically (especially given what appeared painful points over Viv being pregnant by Rick), but she probably meant the other, too.

Louise's brown eyes doubled in size. "Did you see the way she wiped her lipstick from his face?"

Naomi saw it, but she better remembered Louise's expression at seeing it. Whatever it was about that loving but inconsequential gesture of affection between Viv and Rick resonated within Louise.

"He told her he loved her, well, *lived* her—in front of *all of us*."

Naomi frowned her confusion before getting the point Louise wanted to make. "True."

Louise nodded, then paused with a considering look. "I'm guessing 'live' means something deeper than love for them..." Her gaze solidified. "But he looked Viv in her eyes and told her. With emotion. *In front of everybody.*"

Naomi just looked at her.

"And it wasn't some special occasion, either. Men don't do that shit, Naomi. I don't care how in love they are: men don't make casual, sincere public declarations like that."

Naomi disagreed with the validity of that statement. These generalizations about men were bothersome to her sometimes. Patrice was guilty of something similar at the ball.

Louise looked pained again. "Viv doesn't even like a lot of PDA."

Once upon a time, that was true. Viv wasn't usually one for excessive displays of affection in front of others, but she was in new emotional territory. "Come on, Louise. Let's rejoin—"

"Did you see that passion mark on Viv's neck?"

Naomi leaned back against the island counter and nodded, holding in a smirk regarding her hickey discussion with Viv earlier. "I did."

"Of course you did. You notice all kinds of shit no one else is paying attention to. You're like this mystic ballast who's aware of everything—the unobserved observer."

Naomi held her tongue.

Louise looked toward the stove, her gaze unfocused. "That's a little out of character for Viv to let that be there, let it show—even though she's tried to conceal it. ...Must've been so good, neither of them could stop while he put it there. ...I know he did it while in missionary with her as he thrust inside, grinding his—"

Naomi cleared her throat.

Louise's eyes found hers dazedly as if startled from a daydream. "I know he did. Rick can fuck like—"

"Louise, let's go."

Louise nodded, maintaining that faraway look in her eyes.

Naomi started for the kitchen exit, but Louise didn't move. Unwilling to leave a semi-unstable Louise alone in her kitchen with the knives, Naomi returned to her spot. "Louise..."

"...And Rick's...a praying man, Doctor Alexander."

Naomi didn't have a reply for that accurate but left-field observation.

"He always smells so fuckin' good. And...Viv gets to just *be* with him. She gets to touch him anywhere...everywhere...whenever she feels like it." Louise appeared stricken. "They love just hanging together. And they laugh together, Naomi." Her gaze turned piercing. "After all that's gone down, they still *laugh* together."

"Well, yes. They're friends, Louise."

Louise looked away. "...He calls her. She calls him, listening to that voice of his over the phone. Viv gets... She gets to know things about him no one else does." She shifted her gaze to the overhead plaque, which read: *Blessed meals with Blessed people. Let the Food and Fun begin.* Louise stared at it for quiet seconds and then blushed. "Have you seen Rick's feet? He...He has some pretty feet."

What in the world?! Louise commented on Rick's feet at the ball. The woman fixated on many, if not all things Rick Phillips. *Oh boy.* She'd research whether something tied to Vietnamese culture rooted Louise's preoccupation with Rick's feet. "Okay." There was nothing else to say to that, either.

"Rick's voice, Naomi. When he speaks, how he says 'go'n' with that Southern lilt, or 'weren't' sometimes sounding like 'won't.' That way he says 'here' and 'water.' When he sings..." Louise was freestyling now, just running the list of her Rick-Phillips obsessions.

Naomi let her; Louise had some things to get off her chest. With this expressed now, Monday can be a session of solid work.

"How he moves his body..." Louise echoed a feathery sigh of arousal. She looked at Naomi, a question burning in her eyes. "He doesn't turn you on? Interacting with him, being *near* him... It doesn't make your whole body stir for him, Naomi? Just take your clothes off for him and let him do whatever the hell he wants with you—because you *know* it's gonna be all good?!"

Naomi didn't respond, determining (and hoping) all of that was rhetorical. She held in a chuckle, thinking, Louise perhaps had an idea about Rick's "package" from girl-talk with Viv, but Naomi knew, while Viv and Louise were tight once upon a time, Viv didn't provide personal specifics in terms of Rick's actual dimensions to Louise; that wasn't a part of Viv's personality (she didn't really share it with Naomi—it was a slip of the tongue as she spoke from emotion). If Louise knew Rick's erection size, she'd be slobbering and ready for a straitjacket.

Not that a man's erection size had all to do with his ability to please a female sexually; an enormous erection could hinder pleasant sex, but misconceptions abounded.

That's the doctor *talking.*
What are you still doing here?!
Helping you keep it real.
Shut up.

A woman's vaginal passage (from entrance to cervix) was only so long but, like penises, some vaginas were deeper than others, and uteruses tilted differently. Rick's size apparently didn't interfere with hot relations with his wife; he likely modified how he (ahem) used it. Most women were satisfied with a solid six, and girth with rigidity meant more than length (long, narrow, and semi-hard fell well below the desirable line). But, Naomi supposed, it was better to have well-nigh nine inches and only use six, than to only have five—and the woman need six.

Louise sniffed. She whispered now, her eyes on the African figurine on the counter. "Those two sure love kissing. Pecks, deep ones. Rick can kiss like shit. And Viv... She gets to *kiss* him."

Naomi remained unaffected. But she'd mentioned the kissing before, too. Feet and lips: okay. "Women have different kissing needs, Louise. You don't know you'd like the way Rick kisses."

Louise wore a smirk of incredulity. The look said: *Yeah, right.*

"Rick isn't perfect, Louise. With all that's happened in recent years, you must know that."

Louise smirked again, this time with a reflective look in her eyes. "Yeah, he said that same thing to me at the ball: he wasn't perfect. I know he isn't. It's not about 'perfection.'" She pointed toward the kitchen exit. "It's about him, just standing or sitting in your great room, Doctor Alexander. Rick cheated because he believed Viv cheated, then because Viv treated him like shit for so long after they lost the baby, and he thought Viv was done. He didn't just—" She shook her head, empathetic frustration denting her brow.

Naomi heard Louise's support for Rick, understanding he only cheated in response to major crises with Viv (employing a targeted improper conflict resolution).

Louise sighed. "Look, I know his breath stinks upon waking, that he has gas and bowel movements like everyone else. I get that. It's about who he is as a man—*period*. It's about knowing him twenty years and finding him one of the finest men, if not *the* finest, I've ever known. And I'm not talking about his looks, Naomi. That crazy-handsome face. His smile and those goddamn eyes. That diced body. Rick's looks only make the rest of him as a human being that much more special." Louise gaped at her as if trying to explain a basic tenet, and Naomi wasn't getting it. Louise shook an index finger toward the exit for emphasis. "It's about him just being on this *planet*." She lowered her hand, staring at Naomi as if waiting for her point to hit home.

Naomi swallowed. This was going to be a bitch to work through with her: Louise dined heartily—from an empty plate.

A part of Naomi was glad it would be someone else's case (read: headache), but she fleetingly worried for Rick and Viv's safety.

Louise shook her head with an unkind smirk and scoffed. Asians were often characterized as having facial features that made determining emotion from their countenance difficult. Naomi had no such problems reading emotion from Louise. Louise's feelings regarding Viv, regarding losing her friendship with Viv, vacillated between wanting to keep Viv as a close friend and restore their now-dead bond, and anger with Viv for having the man she desperately wanted for her own. "She wouldn't have even dated him if it wasn't for *me*. She was all hung up on him being two years younger, about them attending different colleges. *I'm the one* convinced her to go out with him for the fun of it—as a short-term distraction from that asshole, Isaiah."

Naomi knew as much already. But what did Louise want, a cookie? "Well, good for you, Louise: helping a friend find true love." She hoped she didn't sound flippant (she was out of cookies).

Louise didn't acknowledge Naomi's words; she looked away, frowning. "Tasting his tongue..." She murmured: "They say all good things come to an end."

Naomi clenched and released her fist in a count of five under her breath. She and Louise were comparable in stature: she could take her on if need be (or call Patrice back in to handle the dirty work).

"I take it that's what you're hoping for, Louise. And, if it is, that's awful; you're not Viv's friend. Hell, you're not even Tim's. But I'll tell you this..." Naomi pointed toward the kitchen exit as Louise had done moments ago. "*That* good thing will end only with the death of one. Trust me. And if it's Viv first, I'd bet the farm, should he decide or feel able to carry on for his children whom *he made* with her,..." (Naomi added that last on purpose—and Louise's responding wince indicated the desired impact), "he won't pursue anything serious with anyone else...and certainly not with *you*. Viv is *it* for him. He *lives* her. So, I suggest you digest and put it to rest because it's for the best."

Louise studied the floor. "It's...It's not fair." When she spoke again, it was barely above a whisper. "Damn... He felt so good. I...I get wet whenever he comes near me."

"Okay, that's it. My patience and understanding can only go so far, too, Louise. So, let me give you a piece of my mind, for my peace of mind. Rick and Viv are my very *dear* friends. Like *family* to me. You know that. I've allowed you time to release some inner thought, but enough's enough. I *am* Viv's friend. Rick's, too. Maybe even *Tim's* at this moment. If you cannot control yourself, Louise, I'll see you to the door."

Louise lifted her head as if to speak, but then dropped her head again. "You can call me 'Lou.'"

Naomi sighed, thinking she may take Cecily's anti-anxiety pills (still in her clutch) herself—especially if another hour or two remained of hanging around Louise. "Come on. Let's join the others. We can explore this more on Monday."

Upon leaving the kitchen, they had Louise's misfortune of entering the great room in time to see Rick and Viv ending a deep kiss.

Louise made an odd sighing-scoff noise and excused herself, making a hasty exit with a beeline for the powder room (nothing dangerous in there).

Patrice (still annoyed with Viv's friend) watched Louise's retreat to safety. "Yeah, well, that's not *all* they do, honey! Married and in love, dammit! Get your mind right!"

Leslie, Trevor, Brendan, and Garrett looked confused, while Joy nodded with this acknowledging simper.

As the powder room door closed, Viv and Rick looked around at the others to see what Patrice was talking about. They then focused on Patrice, both with smirks of admonishment.

Patrice shook her head with a scoff. "Now that I know what I know, I'm not pussyfooting around with her—unlike *the rest of you*."

Something about that made Naomi like Patrice a little more.

Tim frowned with concern and irritation but kept his head down, focusing on the cards.

Naomi, too, felt concerned irritation over what transpired in her kitchen.

With a parting touch to Rick's arm, Viv came over to her. "What's wrong? You okay?"

Naomi didn't care about her next words; Viv came first. She'd often walked a fine line between her personal and professional lives. "Be wary of Louise, Viv. She wants your husband—and she's *fixated*. You're 'friends.' Okay. So maybe it's complicated. But be careful, sweetie."

Viv nodded, her onyx eyes concerned, accepting, and knowing all at once. "It's not all that complicated. Not anymore. Got it. Okay. Come on; we're supposed to be enjoying ourselves."

"She still the family dentist?"

Viv looked at her for seconds, the concern gone, but the accepting and knowing remaining.

"For the nonce."

Naomi nodded, appreciating Viv's penchant for the English language. "Good."

Viv nodded back. "Now, come on."

Naomi chuckled as she followed Viv to rejoin the after-party.

Dawn approached as music played, and everyone socialized in smaller groups, having a good time. Kevin, Tim, Louise, and Joy were at the table chatting (Kevin and Joy enjoying cups of coffee). Louise was all over Tim, giving him this extra attention, overt but insincere. But if that was what Louise needed to do to keep coming correct? Naomi wanted her to go for it (Tim was none the worse for wear from it). Patrice sometimes rolled her eyes whenever she spotted Louise's excessive kisses and rubs on Tim. Naomi shared looks with Viv about it.

Viv, Trevor, and Patrice stood by the built-in bookcase laughing at something on Trevor's tablet (Trevor constantly glancing at Viv with infatuated interest). Naomi talked with Leslie, Garrett, Brendan, and Rick by the roaring fireplace about the virtues of Looney Tunes versus

Merrie Melodies cartoons. Leslie and Brendan did more listening than talking, but they were familiar enough to contribute an opinion or two. Rick worked his new yo-yo as he spoke; a big kid in the moment.

The desserts needed to be put away. Although Garrett helped himself to most of the éclairs, everyone was content chilling with a beverage of choice, likely having their fill of hearty hors d'oeuvres at the ball.

Although socializing separately, Rick and Viv sometimes checked each other out when the other wasn't looking. If Patrice couldn't see these two devoted long past RJ's third birthday, Naomi sure could (her flash of truth aside). With Garrett having administered a level of sex therapy for his wife, given Patrice's subsequent improved disposition, maybe she had a more positive outlook for her sister. All Patrice's earlier funkiness may have stemmed from her need for an explicit intimate connection with Garrett. Rick suggesting Garrett *take care of some things* worked out—even benefiting those not in their bedroom.

Sex wasn't the absolute equivalent of intimacy and connection, but one or both partners wanting but not getting it or doing it (for whatever reason)... That lent itself to a new (but related) set of relationship problems. Positive sexual experiences mattered; if anything, they kept men in the *sweet* zone (just ask Viv). And maybe not having *that* was the root of all evil.

At one point, Rick put his yo-yo down and went over to Leslie. He whispered in her ear. Leslie grinned and nodded. She went over to the music player, pushed a few buttons, and then "Ebony Eyes" by Stevie Wonder came on. Rick had everyone up and singing along, grooving and laughing. But soon, everyone (except Louise, conveniently preoccupied with her phone) was singing mostly to Viv because it was clear Rick meant the song for her. When the song closed, everyone expressed appreciation for Mr. Wonder's talents. Leslie paused the music.

"Thanks, Les. I wanted to request it at the ball, but this here is better." Rick winked at his wife.

Viv's slight smile held a blushing appreciation. "Thank you."

Kevin returned to his seat. "Yeah, man, thanks: that's one of my favorites." Naomi resumed wearing her eyeglasses, but Kevin still wore his contacts. His new facial hair and those saddle-brown eyes spoke warm pleasantries to Naomi's secret self. They'd had a quickie in the shower after returning from the ball. The night was still young.

Rick nodded at Kevin and pulled Viv close. "I see your gorgeous black irises in my dreams, woman."

Viv appeared unable to hold Rick's gaze: she lowered her head.

"Your eyes *are* pretty, Viv." Trevor's voice cracked with his soft but-rushed admission, and then he hurried into the kitchen, to Kevin and Garrett's low chuckles and Joy's soft giggle.

Seemed hasty exits were in fashion tonight.

Viv looked up, replying, "Thank you," but Trevor was gone.

Leslie shook her head with a teasing smirk, and Naomi was proud of her response.

Games of Boggle and Sorry! were in force at different ends of the table. Viv, Tim, Joy, and Kevin played Sorry!, while Brendan, Garrett, Leslie, Trevor, and Louise played Boggle. Naomi enjoyed checking out both games instead of playing (as did Rick and Patrice).

The after-party music, still infused with good stuff pre-1999, had much more of a Leslie-Trevor (post-1999) influence.

After game time (Joy and Garrett won their respective games), everyone sat around the table, engaged in flowing discussion with changing topics. The sun crept higher, but no one cared: it was Saturday.

"Neighbors Know My Name" by Trey Songz came on, and Patrice pulled her husband up to dance. Leslie and Trevor danced, and Naomi struggled to avoid thoughts about the lyrics as they may have applied to her daughter.

Rick and Viv didn't dance, but sent glances the other's way as it played. The couple then shared a long look until Rick raised an eyebrow at Viv, directly referencing the lyrics. Viv flushed in response, touching the hickey area on her neck.

Louise, seeing the exchange, left the table unhappy, almost angrily. She hadn't rubbed and kissed on Tim enough to repel her Viv-Rick jealousy yet.

Joy, however, wore a secret smile at seeing their exchange.

Naomi chuckled to herself. Her eyes being everywhere: sometimes gets to be exhausting.

Kevin wanted to play cards again. The rest watched as Kevin, Tim, Louise, and Leslie got in a few hands of Spades. Viv approached Rick as he sat at the table watching the card game. She leaned her hip against his shoulder and watched, commenting on the card plays while lightly caressing Rick about his head and shoulders.

Rick affixed his gaze on Naomi, and she nearly hollered. His pointed, expressive look was strictly *Naomi-only* in direct reference to their charity-ball conversation: Viv's casual caresses were turning him on.

Naomi nodded her understanding, and they both chuckled.

Kevin turned to her, grinning. "What?"

Naomi glanced at Rick and Viv (Rick winked) before focusing on the game. "Nothing. Private joke. Your play."

Rick tilted his head back to Viv for a deep kiss.

Soon after the card game, the Collins and Giles couples left.

The Carters and the Phillipses now prepared for departure. Naomi was getting used to the unintentional spark Rick created whenever he kissed her goodbye (the man had no clue). She believed Leslie made similar ground in that respect (she still flushed, but less than before). But Naomi now noted Viv having a comparable effect on the men in their household. Viv dabbed Kevin's and Trevor's chests as she kissed their cheeks, and Naomi observed both men send fleeting flirty looks at Viv (although Trevor's bordered hungry desire).

Parties weren't her thing, and sleeping hadn't been a consistent thing since Tyson died, but she'd attended and had fun at a New Year's party, a charity ball, and an after-party. Parties had become her new thing—at least for a month. She'd had that one night during the Christmas break where she slept five hours—but nights like those were few. She'd been awake since two-something yesterday morning, prepping and dancing and socializing and eating and being a banana... Perhaps over three hours of sleep awaited.

It was daylight, but the drawn blackout drapes made that hard to tell.

Kevin lay beside her, arm curling her middle, snoring softly: sleeping soundly after another good (albeit slower) round of sex. His nude body, warm and hard (and soft in certain places), pressed against her with a lean familiarity she'd missed but was still getting used to. He had to work Sunday, so, given yesterday's festivities rolling into today, the rest of today would be all about the lazy-leisurely (read: no *working*).

Her yesterday's banana had ripened, was eaten, the peel discarded. Today, she was green again (allowing the process to start anew). Kevin would still advise her against working during social activities, but after explaining her "banana" metaphor to him, she reckoned he better appreciated how her life's work...worked.

The enticing scent of his Black Orchid around her, Naomi stared into space and listened to Kevin breathe, feeling his breaths against her hair. She was in that state where she could drift-off or fall wide awake.

She replayed many of the highlights from last night into this morning, reviewing for anything missed the first time (nope), determining whether she was end-of-day satisfied (yes).

A bit of group therapy extreme played out over the course of ten hours or so, but she believed Cecily, Louise, and Tim were all steps closer to getting well—or would be soon: Monday for Louise; Tuesday for Timothy; Tuesday, Thursday (and beyond) for Cecily.

Cecily Jamison Cooper, however, was Naomi's primary concern.

Cecily's aura didn't flicker at the ball, so Naomi didn't know if those planes of gray changed in status to another color. Even without aura information, it was clear Cecily was in some state of transition. Whether that transition was from dark to light or vice versa...

Cecily likely wasn't aware of how much she helped herself from going over the edge. Her long walks, the morning runs, the friendly interactions with the people at JAH Technologies, the spa days Joshua provided for his employees: all were tiny, beneficial influences that only augmented Naomi's treatment approach from her end of things.

She wasn't supposed to (and blah, blah, blah), but if she could use her therapeutic alliance with Cecily against Oscar, she was so inclined. Naomi considered it a resistance move on Cecily's behalf. The therapist-patient relationship was unique. Patients shared their innermost thoughts and feelings with the one person making no demands on them. Once therapists connect with patients in a respectful way, it created a heightened significance for both parties. The boundaries blended and softened sometimes, but this alliance could also impact other relationships in the lives of both doctor and patient. For said patient, life can seem mighty dull after spilling their guts to *the one person* who really listens. Conversely, for doctors, there is a level of "come down" after receiving pseudo-worship from a patient. Naomi didn't do pedestals (she was too short to even get up there) or high horses (same problem), so she had no concerns about that last.

Naomi respected the dangers of the therapeutic alliance (she covered them in her terms-and-conditions prelim during session one with a patient), but she also recognized its benefits. As far as she was concerned, the therapeutic alliance was a tool, and despite advice to the contrary, its use against third parties (third parties unfavorably impacting a patient's mental maladies) was warranted.

During the last few sessions, she checked to see if Cecily talked only to her. It was important Cecily share some of what happened in treatment with someone other than her. Not Oscar, but maybe Chelsea or Marcus, or her brothers. This "Janyce" person sounded like an option initially, but Naomi now doubted it (she didn't get a good enough vibe from her). So far, Cecily said she shared some of what they discussed in therapy with Kyle and Chelsea: good. Documentation of her social interactions outside of treatment was key to also documenting mental progression or regression.

And Joshua Hall?

Naomi's gut told her he was Cecily's happily ever after (and she was his). But there was work to do before getting to that. She knew Cecily wanted to "clean house" first: pack up all those suitcases and boxes full of PTSD and NAS drama...and set them outside for bulk pickup.

Chapter Fifteen

A Lesson Twice Learned

*H*e *made you ask permission before going on your run. If this isn't a new low...*

Cecily kicked things into a higher gear, speeding her pace uphill, attempting to kill any further thought.

She liked the dark and the cold and the solitude, liked the coolness from sweat on her brow and the icy fullness in her chest with each intake of breath. It was dark at four forty-one in the morning, but she ran her second-favorite route with a new intensity born out of several things.

What're you running from?

Headphones filled with musical encouragement, Cecily darted up the hill, maintaining a running-in-place jog at the top before going right instead of left and creating a new run route to add to her list of four. She liked odd numbers better, anyway. She approached the highway, catching glimpses of the neon-green reflective panels on her running jacket gleaming in her lower peripheral vision, not caring if the bright strips cautioned anyone behind a steering wheel of her presence.

What are you running away from?

Cecily crossed the four-lane street, head down, moving swiftly toward a new housing development.

Everything.

She passed the softly lit model home perched at the front in a sprint carrying her several blocks past it. Sidewalks and streets were paved, but there were only two new homes this far into the development. Cecily ran to the end of the developed part and stopped before the dirt hills and construction vehicles, bending over to catch her breath.

Running was good for her health, but this type of running, this *savage* running, tested that theory—and she couldn't self-administer CPR.

Standing upright and still winded, ignoring the twinge in her side, she pulled a tissue from her pocket and blew her nose. It wasn't yet forty degrees, but it felt a comfortable seventy inside her running gear. Cold outside but warm inside: her life in a nutshell. Checking out the lay of the paved land, Cecily resumed her run, "Just Ask the Lonely" by the Four Tops helping her keep the pace. She'd added Naomi's suggested song to her playlist, but it hadn't played yet. She looked forward to it blasting into her ears—sort of.

Some things are easier said than done, Naomi. Singing it and doing it? Two different things.

Cecily rounded the cul-de-sac, thinking about Janyce's comment at the ball about Joshua. Not knowing who he was, Janyce leaned close to her at their table and discreetly pointed Josh out, acknowledging he was new to the ball,...telling her he was rather fine. Cecily nodded politely (giving nothing away), and Janyce then turned to Karen Missenden, pointing Josh out to her. She'd already gone on for several minutes about that guy at Naomi's table, as if someone appointed her honorary charity ball critic.

Janyce had put the whole brooch fiasco behind her, but Cecily couldn't now (seven times seven was forty-nine). Yet she still didn't know how to handle it.

She didn't know how to handle...a myriad of things.

Cecily couldn't decide how to map her new route (worried over creating a route too long), couldn't decide about getting to JAH Tech on time or a little late (Josh wouldn't mind either way), and then there was the matter of pitching in to help get the second site in shape. She grew uneasy as she trotted, not wanting to overthink any of it but not wanting to pick wrong. Picking wrong could go so bad.

Oscar and Janyce berating her second-guessing echoed, and so, deciding not to decide (for now), Cecily simply ran. She left the new development and turned left, facing traffic as she ran along the shoulder toward the park a mile down.

Tired of missing her children, she'd spent the weekend with them and her grandchild. Chelsea was a junior at Bowie State, living in a townhome off-campus, but with her roommate away, the four of them hung out at Chelsea's after a day of shopping and catching a movie.

Marcus impressed her more and more whenever she watched him with little Roland. Marcus was young but a responsible father, good with his son. She was the same age Marcus was when she'd had him, but the maturity level of her generation at that age was much different. She liked to think she and big Roland left a footprint or two on how little Roland was being raised. Marcus was in love with little Roland's mother, Leila, and she with him, but both agreed: marriage was a ways off; Leila wanted to finish her degree at Howard, and Marcus wanted to change jobs, find something related to his degree in biology (from Florida A&M). Good for them.

Chelsea, too, had her head on straight, doing the working-while-schooling thing successfully. Cecily hadn't heard about a boyfriend (or girlfriend) and wondered if the rape hindered Chelsea from forming intimate attachments. A lot of sorrow, unhappiness, and...issues can take place behind those got-it-going-on smiles Chelsea wore. Although Chelsea reassured her she was okay, Cecily entertained having her sit with Naomi just to be sure.

Cecily reported the news about their uncle, and both were thrilled.

Oscar texted several times for status updates on her whereabouts and activities while with them. Cecily responded to each one to appear as if she had a life requiring much cellphone interaction with the nonexistent people in her circle, but Marcus's eye-rolling and Chelsea's annoyed sighs every time her phone chimed told Cecily her children weren't fooled. Oscar ended up calling, and Marcus adamantly told her not to answer. Her children were close. Their bond (from hating Oscar, from being victimized two years ago) gave them a unity Cecily envied, craved, and was proud of. They were her children, but when it came to Oscar, she was on the outside looking in. Marcus and Chelsea lived nearby, but the Oscar situation rendered them far away. Chelsea had been more tolerant of Oscar than Marcus had at one time, but that changed as she aged. Chelsea said she could spend the night with her; she didn't have to go back if she didn't want to. Cecily didn't want to. But she went back.

What're you running from?

From misery, loneliness, and melancholy. From fear, joylessness, constant wariness, and disturbing memories. Running from acknowledging Oscar somehow kills her flowers at home (he's the only common denominator, and seven times seven is forty-nine). From the old Cecily, who knew better and now made her feel ashamed. Running from a mother...who, when she was living, wasn't much different from her current husband. Brooches couldn't make it all better. And where was that brooch now?

The headlights of oncoming traffic grew blurry with her tears, but her pace didn't slow. Savage running had its perks. Physical exhaustion would offer nothing but comforting escape.

She suddenly felt unprotected, naked, unshielded from some phantom barrage of vindictive venom combined with some dangerous deviousness coming out of nowhere to keep her from running, moving forward. She'd never had an episode in the middle of the street...

Where're you going?

She knew that, too, but she'd let her darting feet answer that.

Cecily meditated and wrestled spiritual matters. She slowed her run to a fast jog, wondering why she, as but an imperfect human, was supposed to have all this compassion and understanding for others making mistakes against her, but God, the Perfect Non-human, didn't seem to be sending down any Divine compassion and understanding her way, instead, piling on the trauma and drama and gloom. Prayer and reflection and "being still" so far yielded nothing but more of the same. Sure, there were blessings of sporadic joy, but she wanted, needed, some of that joy to exist at home rather than not, to balance things out. She believed if she and Oscar could get things back to how they were in the beginning, she'd achieve that balance she longed for—and be better able to deal with...the rest of it. Long past tired of suffering, she was overdue for some perseverance. But God wasn't—

Her eyes registered seeing the Exxon sign, but her brain delayed processing that information (being deep in meditative spiritual challenge and contemplation), so her stride hiccupped as she approached it. Traffic increased with people beginning their day, but the gas station was empty. The station was open, but no one needed a fill-up just yet.

She didn't see a payphone booth and so slowed her jog to a walking-trot, keeping her eyes peeled as she headed past the pumps for the convenience store. What happened was two years ago. Use of pay-phones was on the decline. Who was to say she'd even—?

There wasn't a booth, but two payphones were affixed along the store's outer wall. Her stomach twisted uncomfortably with a weird certainty as she experienced a false déjà vu. Cecily went inside and purchased a bottle of orange-flavored Gatorade.

Nineteen minutes later, she entered her house through the garage access, sweaty and uncomfortable with the house's heat adding to the heat from her revved body. She needed to stretch but didn't feel like it (she didn't feel like doing much of anything since the charity ball).

Cecily put her leftover Gatorade in the refrigerator, hearing traces of that porn video coming from the basement again. Dawn barely broke the horizon, and already he was into the seedier side of things. It was porn because the woman (familiar?) made little sound while the men grunted and groaned and puffed, saying very vulgar, pornographic stuff to her (familiar?). In the before, Cecily didn't mind a little porn some-times, but Oscar's taste for it was too much on the violent, misogynistic side, which made sense (but shouldn't have). She grabbed a yogurt, sick to her stomach with the unwanted familiarity of that video. Famil-iar...and revolting.

What is love, Cecily?

She went to the top of the basement stairs, accepting the numbness descending whenever she knew he watched *that* video. "I'm back!"

"...Good. That eye appointment is today, right?"

Cecily cringed. "Yes." He wanted those contacts back in her eyes. She didn't have a backup pair of them, and Oscar was pissed about it when they got home after the ball, telling her he "couldn't get it up to fuck her" without them in, that she needed something to "make the rest of it" attractive. He'd squeezed her arm, pushed her to the bed in frustration, and left the bedroom. She'd thought that was the end of it—until he mounted her from behind in the middle of the night, fisting her hair and pushing her head into the pillow roughly, telling her she'd better have them back in ASAP. He climaxed and then punched her buttocks hard for emphasis.

She'd showered afterward, worrying about how she would face Nao-mi, and then remembered her doctor would give her an official excuse next session—but she couldn't wait until then. After showering, she called the Bat-phone. Naomi would have the note from the ophthalmologist ready this afternoon. She didn't want to lie, but she didn't want to wear those contacts anymore, and she didn't see reasoning with Oscar as an option. He wasn't satisfied with her having lost one, but her going in to get new ones and then coming back with notification from a doctor (whom Oscar generally distrusted) who prohibited her wearing them, would go over better than if she'd outright told him her eyes were bothering her. Some things she'd learned about his personality weren't the best, but she had to use whatever she could to her advantage.

"Get two pairs this time."

Cecily heard the warning in his tone (losing them wouldn't be a good excuse next time) and nodded despite his inability to see her. "Right." She turned for the stairs, wanting to get out of her running gear and get a game plan for going to JAH Tech later. They were doing something for Hadji for his birthday around lunchtime, so she wanted to get there in time to help. She hadn't spoken with Joshua since the charity ball; for the first time in four years, she was nervous about going in to work—and wondered if she should leave JAH Tech altogether.

She was nude, in the bathroom moving her bowels before her shower (she hated when her system wanted to work after she showered), when she heard Oscar in their bedroom. She froze, deeply dreading him opening the door on her. This was no way to live, but it was her life. Cecily hurried the process along, hoping to be in the shower if he barged in. He'd recently caught her similarly indisposed as she prepared for the ball the other night (she still felt some residual way about that).

Fortunately, she was in the shower when Oscar opened the door. "Hurry up, Cesspool. Trying to get out of here myself." He closed the door. He'd been calling her Cecil or Cesspool much more often since his last session with Naomi, and Cecily knew he did it more to symbolically give Naomi the finger. The only plus (if there was one to be had from being called out of your name) was she was becoming numb to hearing it, no longer saddening or having hurt feelings behind it the way she would weeks ago.

What is love, Cecily?

She didn't have time for internal philosophical exploration, didn't know what important lesson waited behind it, and didn't feel like learning anything right now, anyway. Whatever lesson awaited can stay a lesson unlearned for now. Finished her shower, she kept her hair in curlers while moisturizing. Robe on, she entered their bedroom.

Cecily immediately breathed the foulness of his flatulence (practically filling the room). She ignored it as taught, but she was concerned more than nasally offended this time, worrying Oscar was having gastrointestinal problems on top of his heart issues. And as her husband stood at his chest of drawers, sweating and rubbing his midsection with a mild wince of either irritation or pain, her worry only increased.

"How was your appointment with Doctor Halim?" She sat on her side of the bed, still undecided about her attire for the day. She also looked around their bedroom on the sly, checking for weapons (belts, charging cords, etc.), and feeling sick about the need to anticipate random attacks in her home. Cecily wanted to ask him how they could get back to how it was initially but feared an echo of silence from him as answer.

He shrugged. "Same ol' shit. Sees some improvement in my heart test or pulmonary function something or other." He waved a dismissive hand. "Should've been there; you understand his gobbledygook. But I guess other shit was more important."

That wasn't fair. "Oscar, I made the appointment, and then you switched it, saying nothing to me until after."

He looked at her. "What? I'm not mad. Just thought you'd be more on top of it. I switched it, yeah, but you're a smart-ass." He shrugged again and turned back to his chest. "Figured you did some appointment confirmation shit or something."

"You rescheduled your appointment for a time while I was in session with Naomi."

He scoffed. "There it is right there. Everything revolves around you. Now my heart problems hafta take a backseat to your PTSD bullshit."

Cecily secretly pinched herself, wanting to wake up from this almost-nightmare. She swallowed the hurt of those words (her PTSD wasn't bull) and redirected in a way she hoped would begin turning the clock back. "Why don't you come to my next one?" She didn't want him there, but she did because, if she was going to get better, she needed a happy marriage to help with that. Naomi didn't care for Oscar, but Cecily also knew her doctor would support whatever she needed. If she needed Naomi to add a little marriage counseling to the trauma counseling, Naomi would do that for her.

Oscar slammed his drawer shut, startling her. "Are you nuts?! I'm not going back to that shit!" He scoffed, giving her a nasty look with a shake of his head. "Yeah, you must be nuts suggesting that craziness." He turned to his closet, mumbling, "Your country hick-ass needs to be fifty-one-fiftied for real," before disappearing inside it.

She was from the South but far from "country," and "hick" was a racist insult he'd called her before, believing it wasn't racist because he was Black, too. Fighting tears, Cecily took deep breaths instead. She closed her eyes, taking slow, deep breaths, and praying for some relief, for some *better* lasting longer than minutes here and there.

What is love?

Having gathered herself, she reached for her book on her nightstand, but it wasn't there.

Cecily frowned. She'd listened to some Nina and then read a chapter of Octavia Butler's *Parable of the Sower* last night before retiring (noting how little has changed since its publication). She checked the floor in front of her nightstand (sometimes she dropped her book there before turning over), but it wasn't there, either. Cecily started to ask Oscar if he'd seen it, moved it, but changed her mind. She stood, examining her bedroom slowly, carefully, still going over the last part of her evening to determine whether she'd made a different move regarding the book and just didn't remember. Cecily walked over to the sitting area: it was on the ottoman. She liked to read in the sitting area but hadn't last night. Had she? Cecily approached their walk-in closets. "Oscar?" She heard him sigh but ignored it.

Oscar stood in his closet doorway. "Yeah?"

"Did...Did you move my book?"

His curious frown was more sneer than anything, looking more like the "Mr. Hyde" she secretly called him. "No, Cecil. The PTSD may be some bullshit, but something sure the hell is wrong with you. Stop asking me if I've moved this or seen that. I've got my own shit, sweetheart. Okay? Big, health-scare shit. Don't really have the time to be worrying about your book or your folder or your lotions and towels." He scoffed and went back into his closet. "Give me a break."

She was the one needing a massive break. Cecily turned back toward their bed and stopped. Her bookmark was on the floor by Oscar's nightstand. She stared at it long and hard before smirking softly. She picked up her bookmark, placed it back in its holding space in her novel, and put her book inside her nightstand drawer.

"What're you still doing here?" He was still in his closet, but his tone was lighter, friendlier.

And Cecily responded to that lighter, friendlier tone instantly. "It's still early…" She smiled hesitantly toward his closet. Maybe she'd been too self-involved lately, being a worrywart over every little thing, giving her husband reason to believe she was unstable. He had little family, and the family he had stayed away more than embraced him. That hurt him, even if Oscar wouldn't admit it. Cecily wanted him to see they were in this (whatever *this* was) together—because her family stayed away, too.

Oscar poked his head out with a grin, and Cecily almost fainted, because she hadn't seen many upturns of his lips—except when he was making jokes at her expense. "Yeah, but by now, you're closer to flying out the door."

The grin was genuine because it was in his eyes, and Cecily made quick effort to relax and respond to that true grin. She grinned back. "Just taking my time for a change."

"Good thing you're working just for the hell of it: bosses don't take kindly to employees playing hooky." He smiled and winked, and Cecily sat on the bed instead of fainting.

She returned a flirty smirk (like it was seven years ago). "I'm going in, just later." This was what she needed from him. More of this…that didn't leave her feeling worthless, ugly, and alone.

Oscar's scoff was playful. "Slacker."

Cecily giggled, grasping for the slice of happy. "You can't talk." Her stomach knotted, and her giggle died instantly; she meant it as a joke, all in fun, but life with him taught her that picking wrong (even words) can go so bad. She looked at him, the familiar wariness returning.

"Yes, I can." He nodded toward their bathroom. "'S why I need to get in there. Got an interview today." He returned to his closet, but Cecily detected no animosity from him.

He'd said nothing about it, but she was happy for him. Her grin returned. "Wear the gray suit."

"Fine. You get those contacts back in."

There was insult and threat in his response, but it was also commingled with humor—and somehow easier to accept.

Twenty-three minutes later, he was ready to go. Cecily looked him over as he stood in front of her dresser, looking in the mirror. The pants were too long, but he looked nice: interview ready.

He sighed and walked toward her. "A'ight. Wish me luck."

"Luck." When he pressed his lips to hers and eased his (minty) tongue into her mouth, she surprised herself by keeping her eyes open as they kissed. She registered the surprise in his eyes before his dark-brown eyes became a hard glee, reminding her how creepy it was to be kissing and staring eye-to-eye so closely. He slipped a hand inside her robe and gripped a breast, not massaging sensually but gripping with a touch of malice—reminding her of that porn video. When he pulled back, she contained a shiver of revulsion, knowing she wouldn't open her eyes while kissing him anymore. "Still don't want to give me any details?"

He released her flesh and pulled his hand away, shaking his head. "Nah. If it doesn't go well..."

"I understand. I think you'll do fine. You have experience in many areas of work, Oscar." She suddenly wondered why they never gave each other *cute* nicknames. "That's a benefit having 'book-smarts' doesn't touch."

"Thanks, Cecily."

She startled internally at hearing her name warm and proper from his lips. "Sure. I love you." No, it wasn't the kind she needed to thrive, but it was a love. Wasn't it?

He turned away, heading out. "Yeah, I know. Same here."

Maybe not.

Oscar had been out of the house a good fifteen minutes when, thinking about her brother, Cecily went into the smallest bedroom housing rows of white, rectangular boxes filled with pages and pages of colorful panels of storytelling (pages sealed in protective sleeves). Comic books were such an escape for her as a kid. She grinned, remembering how she and Larimore would spend hours in the basement of their home back in Cleveland, poring over new and old issues. She'd always been neater about her books than him, but that was boys for you. Several of the boxes held Marcus's comics, too. She went to a stack of boxes nearer the closet—those were the older issues. She needed to get to work, but the comics called. Although labeled, she knew the contents of each box almost by rote. Cecily chuckled and opened the top box for a walk down memory lane—Naomi style. She flipped through issues, just looking and reminiscing...

She looked forward to sitting down with little Roland, teaching the basics about mint-condition, CGC gradings, golden age and silver age comics, number ones, and—

Anger.

That was it, and that was all it was.

It wasn't mixed with any uncertainty or anxiety or any of those other emotions that kept her second-guessing everything, kept her from feeling anything fully.

Oh, she felt all of it now.

Every bit of the anger and...and...*outrage* moving through her now was unencumbered. They were just books (and all that), but they were *her* books and *her* memories and her legacy to pass on.

Everything in this room was *before him*.

Cecily rifled through more issues, her breath short and hostile. The angry heat moving through her made her sweat (she'd have to shower again), but she didn't care. This was...too far.

Seven.

Seven number one, first print, CGC-9.5 issues were gone. Issues worth hundreds (if not thousands) of dollars. But it wasn't about the money. It wasn't even remotely about the money.

Why would it be? She had plenty.

Cecily sat on the floor, unable to do much else for long minutes.

And then, she got up.

She *was* a smart-ass. A smart-ass woman with two degrees, and seven times seven was forty-nine. Cecily went to the basement without hesitation, looking for what was hers.

Her search of the other rooms in the basement turned up nothing, and Cecily now went through the folders and drawers of his desk, and her heart sank. Her books were gone, sold over a period of years. The evidence lay in those multiple sheets of papers from eBay detailing the sales.

What is love, Cecily?

She got her phone and took pictures of the papers before putting everything back as she'd found it. Heartbroken, she turned to go back upstairs when her foot kicked something which shot through the opened door of the utility room. Cecily saw the glint of silver disappear down the sump-pump hole and sighed. She didn't need any plumbing issues arising on top of everything else, so she donned a pair of cleaning gloves and entered the utility room. Cecily lowered to her knees, hoping to retrieve whatever she kicked down there. The sump-pump cover was loose...

Turns out, the comic book sales hadn't gone too far after all.

What is love, Cecily?

Not this.

Numb, Cecily again took pictures and put everything as she'd found it. She then went upstairs...for the bottle of vodka.

Two drinks and a shower later (she didn't even call Naomi), Cecily entered JAH Technologies, Inc. with a smile for Rhonda. She didn't feel like being here (she and Joshua had unresolved issues brewing), but she couldn't be where she lived right now, either (absolutely not). But here was a hundred times better than there. Besides, they were doing something for Hadji's birthday—she wanted to be a part of that. "Hey, Rhonda."

Rhonda smiled but didn't look up as she continued typing. "Hi, Missus Brooks. You missed it: signed up five new clients this morning." She glanced at her with a sweet smirk. "Don't even know why you came to work. Mister Hall's shutting down for Hadji's little birthday thing. Said, instead of closing for a couple hours today, he planned to reopen tomorrow." Rhonda turned to her. "Could've saved your g— Whoa. You look nice! I mean, you usually look nice, but," she looked her up and down with friendly appreciation, "this is more on the *hot* side."

Cecily shrugged, ready to head for her office in the back. "Thank you." It was a back-office type of day, no question. The vodka was for numbing, but she also needed something to lift her spirits; she used clothing in her closet accordingly. "As you said: today is Hadji's birthday thing. I want to help set up and everything, so...that's my calling today."

Rhonda stopped typing and stood, her black hair twisted atop her head, her beige blouse and black skirt as tight as ever. "You okay?"

"I'm fine." Cecily pointed toward the rear as she walked. "Buzz me when we're ready to decorate." She pointed toward the table with brochures and other promotional materials. "I'd like to titivate over there especially."

Rhonda, her eyes careful and concerned as she gazed back, nodded. "Will do. Everyone's here. Ms. Allen said she wouldn't bring Hadji and his friends till around quarter-to-one. We have time."

Cecily nodded and slowly headed for her office, registering Rhonda's words through an icy-numbness. She heard the Hall men talking in Workroom Three as she neared it.

"—even let Momma call you that!"

The men chuckled together, and Cecily smiled to herself in response to hearing their cheerfulness.

"I know. What can I say...?" was Josh's reply, sounding like he wore a blushing smile.

Cecily paused outside her office, still able to hear everything.

"She's perfect for you, Dad, if, well, you know..."

Joshua sighed. "I agree, Smeek."

So, there was someone in Josh's life. Someone the boys liked for their father. She didn't know the obstacle, but she hoped it worked out just the same. She was too numb to have hurt feelings or be jealous about it. Whatever it was "brewing" was likely all in her imagination. Cecily smiled, happy for her friend.

"If...If you love her like that, Dad..." Malcolm sounded a breath. "I don't know..."

He loved her? Okay.

"That why you went stag to the ball?" Brad sounded so concerned; he was a sweetie.

Cecily stepped into her office and closed the door, not hearing Joshua's answer. If he was into some woman, but the obstacle kept her from joining him at the ball, of course he came stag. She sat at her desk, wondering what it was she'd been assigning to Joshua's actions lately. Joshua was honorable. She knew that like she knew seven times seven was forty-nine. He wasn't a lead-them-on type of man. Although she couldn't be led on (she was married and unavailable to him), they still had a certain attraction. The idea she was so hungry for genuine like and affection from a man, so hungry to have a something other than what

Oscar offered, that she saw and read things in Joshua's words and looks at her that weren't there, settled inside her, and it was okay; she was still happy for him.

Cecily opened her desk drawer, grinning at the gift inside. They were having a small gathering for Hadji's birthday, but she hadn't been able to give Josh his birthday gift yet.

She'd give him his gift...and give him her notice.

Because, with all her "happy for him" finding love and being icy-numb to hurt feelings or jealousy in this moment, that other part of her, that *truer part* of her, would thaw, allowing the real—and she couldn't be around Josh when it did.

Wouldn't have mattered anyway, kid. Joshua wouldn't want you...not if he knew the whole deal with you, that is.

Simply put, this wasn't her day. Her winter of discontent dragged on.

She hadn't had many good days since losing Roland and fewer to nil after events two years ago. But today, this day, made any of her worst episodey days pale in comparison.

But she would not cry.

She would not call Naomi.

She would not...pray.

Cecily turned on her computer and lost herself in the numbers.

Oscar texted, then called.

Marcus and Chelsea would've been proud—maybe even Naomi.

The time flew by.

They were well into the swing of things by two o'clock: shop closed, music playing overhead, Hadji and two of his friends having the run of a specially cleaned-out Workroom Three. Josh, Malcolm, and Brad (who came down from Lincoln University especially for this day) set up video games and toys in the enormous room, spoiling Hadji (and his buddies) for doing nothing more than turning nine. It was a half-day at their school, so today was perfect.

The adults socialized and dined in Workroom Four, directly across from where Hadji and company giggled and played their young hearts out. The doors to both rooms were wide open, providing unobstructed view of the boys' shenanigans. Ms. Allen was warmer than she'd been during previous encounters: mildly protective over Hadji and defensive about her foster care for him (or lack thereof, as far as Cecily and Josh were concerned). Today she smiled and joked with Rhonda more readily.

Cecily still felt Hadji lacked the care and supervision he needed, because of Ms. Allen's age (67) and her other...interests. From what Cecily observed over the last eighteen months, the lady provided Hadji a place to rest his head at night and maybe a hot meal or two, but they'd determined she was mainly in it for the stipend. Cecily secretly worried about the booty Hadji would leave with (the toys and clothes). Ms. Allen seemed nice. But Cecily had had enough of *seems nice* to last her two lifetimes.

She resisted thinking about her discoveries at home. She didn't want to bring the crew down vis-à-vis her mood; this was a celebration.

Cecily used a knife and fork on her buffalo wings, unable to resist grinning at seeing Josh mimic her by using a knife and fork on his, signaling his sons to do the same. Malcolm and Brad dined extra daintily, dabbing the corners of their mouths for her teasing amusement. Cecily poked her tongue at Josh, he made a face back, and it was very much like the earlier part of the day never happened. Although since he first saw her when she came out to help decorate, it seemed like that.

Josh didn't bother her while she was in her office working; he had a thing for respecting someone in their zone. But when she stepped out into the front to help decorate, he stared at her as if seeing her for the first time, wearing this unusual smile on his face she couldn't interpret. Brad gave her the biggest smile attached to this big compliment about her appearance, and Cecily blushed her thanks.

She and Josh said their hellos (Cecily maintaining the icy-numbness necessary) and went on with decorating for Hadji's party. But she noticed, as the hours passed, either he was looking at her, or she was looking at him, or they were looking at each other, and now Cecily didn't know what the heck was going on because their looks at each other (in all honesty) had nothing casual about them. Anyone paying any real attention would see it (Naomi). But the problem was, she was comfortable with it, comfortable *in it*, as if old-Cecily swirled and bobbed her head to the surface, reminding her of the woman she used to be, making the icy-numbness recede (if only briefly). It wasn't about Oscar and being married, but everything about being comfortable in her own skin again.

What is love, Cecily?

The man looked good, too. He'd chosen to forgo his twists in favor of the kinky afro (saying something about he was too old to be wearing twists now). She had to admit, the unkempt 'fro looked hotter, sexier on him: and now the Cavalier goatee was growing back in—making things complicated.

One week's notice should be acceptable.

They dined on chicken wings and salads, enjoying the relaxed atmosphere. Peabo's "Reaching for the Sky" came on, and Josh didn't do a good job of not looking at her while it played. She was looking at him (obviously) to know he was looking at her, so, given what she'd overheard in Workroom Three this morning, she didn't know what was going on. Why *did* he come stag to the ball? It couldn't have been about her; he didn't know she'd be there. What was the obstacle? And what was it the woman he loved called him that even ex-wife, Angela, couldn't get away with? Probably some mushy nickname (something she didn't have with Oscar). Monitoring Hadji and his cohorts, Cecily ate her food and laughed and talked with everyone, those questions circling the back of her mind.

Her cellphone beeped and vibrated and chimed a few more times. She responded to all but Oscar...and Janyce.

Joshua went to the front for a brief period. When he returned, he handed her a courier envelope.

Cecily raised a quizzical eyebrow at him.

Josh shrugged. "My app notified something was being delivered. I accepted. It's for you." He wore jeans and a throwback #20 Frank Robinson, Baltimore Orioles jersey instead of his usual work attire (Naomi would've been pleased). His 46 looked 30-something, no joke.

Cecily accepted the package, doing her best to keep calm. "Excuse me..." She returned to her office.

When she opened the envelope, she sighed with relief and chuckled with the same: the note from the ophthalmologist. Cecily read it: yep, she was medically required to be free from using contact lenses for three months (Dr. Cading said so) to help deter an infection due to protein buildup on the lenses. Three months sounded like a lifetime. With all the other awful developments of her day, she'd completely forgotten about the hazel-contacts issue. Naomi was the best—and Cecily thanked God for her.

Doctor's note safely tucked away, she returned to the festivities to find Josh and Hadji embroiled in a clicking-clacking duel in some video game Cecily knew nothing about. She leaned against the doorjamb of Workroom Four and watched while Rhonda flirted and joked with Malcolm and Brad behind her. When Cecily laughed at Hadji's celebration dance over some victory, Joshua turned to her with that smile she couldn't yet interpret.

Josh stared at her for weird seconds before handing his game-controller to Hadji's friend, "AJ." "Here, man. Take over for me." He looked at her. "I know this is all about the fun. But can I talk to you for a minute, Cecily? Work-related."

The second syllable of her name always rolled from his lips in such a caring almost-whisper. "Sure, okay."

He led the way to the front of the shop, scents of dewy green leaves, blackberry, and mandarin from his Polo-Purple in his wake.

She stopped by the copier. "What's up?"

"Couple things, actually."

"Okay."

He cleared his throat. "First, this isn't work-related, but needs to be said. It's about our interaction at the ball..."

Cecily tensed as her heart dropped. This was it. They were friends; he wanted to tell her about the new woman in his life, that he was in love with whomever she was. "Okay..."

"I want to apologize, if, at the ball, I made you feel in any way uncomfortable or—"

"It was fine, Josh. Honestly." She didn't expect an apology before his big reveal, but that was sweet of him. She braced for part two.

He grinned. "Cool. Okay, now..." He lifted his laptop from her desk. "I've narrowed down a few marketing firms that might suit our needs..." He brought up whatever it was on his computer he wanted to show her.

Cecily blinked. Did she blank-out for some seconds and miss him telling her a new woman was in his life? No.

Josh waved her closer. "Come across these in your research...?"

She moved closer and stood next to him, peering at his screen. He had two she'd added to her list. She nodded and pointed to those names on the screen matching her list. "These two."

"Good. We're on the same page."

"Not the first time. Won't be the last."

He closed the application and turned off his laptop. "Say that again."

Cecily sounded a hushed laugh. "No. My accent is not for your amusement, Mister Hall."

He wore that uninterpretable smile again. "Where're you from?"

"I think the question is: where're *you* from?"

His smile changed from the uninterpretable one to something more mischievous. "Wait for it..."

She smiled at him, waiting for it, and then they chimed "Cleveland!" together, warm chuckles following their inside joke.

When their chuckles died, instead of licking him all over, Cecily turned to her desk and picked up the candles for Hadji's cake. "We'd better wind this down..."

"True. But I do have something else to tell you, Cecily." He was serious.

Now, here it comes...

"Or rather, show you."

Show? That didn't compute. She certainly didn't want to *see* him being in love with some woman. Putting the candles down, she frowned.

Josh remained solemn. He reached for her wrist and tapped it, but Cecily recognized him starting to take her hand in his. "Come with me..." He turned.

Cecily followed.

Josh bypassed the party fun for the security room. He held the door open for her, to a room not much bigger than a broom closet.

Cecily stepped inside, and Josh stepped inside with her, closing the door behind them. He wasn't the type, so he wasn't inclined toward any hanky-panky (neither was she), but with his subdued demeanor, Cecily grew anxious. "What is it, Josh?"

His eyes calmly settled on hers. "I'm going to show you. Let me bring it up, okay?"

She nodded, her stomach hurting.

Josh faced the panel of controls and screens and pushed a few buttons. "Look..." He pointed to a screen, blank at first...before livening with an image.

Cecily leaned closer and watched. Watched and wondered just how much of this day remained.

Oscar was on-screen, chatting with Joshua, giving that smile she recognized as false and conniving. Joshua went to the back...and Oscar rearranged things on her desk before sitting in the reception area nearer the front and enjoying a twisted doughnut. With the whole scissors-and-highlighter fiasco still fresh, she said nothing about seeing her knickknacks rearranged (moving her framed giraffe pic really hurt), but it bothered her. She watched Josh return, handing a sealed package to Oscar along with some JAH Tech promo.

"And then this, Cecily,...which made no sense to me..." He brought up another screen, and Cecily turned her attention there.

This one was from an outdoor security camera around the corner. Whatever that was Joshua handed Oscar, Cecily now watched him dump everything in the trash before getting in his car and pulling off.

Josh stopped the video.

He said nothing, and Cecily couldn't speak for the shame of it all.

Josh was a brilliant man, insightful. He didn't need her to explain, tell him anything: that video spoke volumes about her marriage—and she was ashamed. Nauseated, she wondered why she didn't consider: Oscar never married before her. "I'm sorry, Josh. Truly."

He touched her arm. "Hey, now. You didn't do anything. Don't be so sensit—"

She snatched away from him, looking into his eyes and breathing shakily. "Don't say that to me, Joshua. Don't— *Never* say that to me again!" She was losing her mind right before him, but she couldn't help that; the chaotic tumult of emotions she'd experienced since starting her run this morning left her raw.

He didn't anger in response, didn't become defensive. Josh nodded, his eyes registering a calm understanding that grounded her. "Okay. Can...? What...? What do you need, Cecily?" He sounded like Naomi.

Her needs weren't ever a priority, but right now, God help her; she needed his arms around her. Because if he didn't hold her, she was going headfirst into an episode—one she didn't believe she'd come back from.

It's all wrapped up in there together, Cecily, is what Naomi said.

Instead of speaking, she curled her arms around him and put her head on his shoulder. That was all, and it would do. When his arms reciprocated, she closed her eyes and wept, listening to the party activity outside the door while breathing the sage and thyme in his Polo-Purple.

Josh didn't rush her, waiting for her to break contact. Quiet minutes later, Cecily pulled back. "The 'security guard' forgot to check for security cameras."

"Huh?" He handed her his handkerchief.

"Thank you." The handkerchief smelled like him. Cecily wiped her eyes and blew her nose, clearing her head. She then shrugged and shook her head. "Nothing. Oscar used to be a security guard."

Josh held her gaze for a few beats and then snickered.

She snickered with him and nodded; it was funny.

Josh rubbed her upper arm. "You okay? You probably tire of hearing that question, but I don't know how else—"

"It's okay, Josh." She nodded. "I'm better, yes. Thank you."

"Cake and ice cream, then? Or we can watch the video again for a few more laughs." Still rubbing her arm, he wore the cutest smirk.

Cecily laughed. Josh was being facetious, which struck her funny (as she knew he intended). The laughter felt good, liberating.

His laughter died before hers. When her chuckles subsided, he offered a semi-smile. "Ready?"

She took a deep breath, nodded, and handed him his now-snotty handkerchief, which he accepted and pocketed without hesitation.

Something about that mattered to her.

A half-hour later, she forked a piece of yellow buttercream birthday cake and watched Hadji open his last gift. She'd helped him open and tidy all but this last: it was small; so he could manage. Every time she eyed Josh, he appeared just as excited as Hadji with every reveal. Josh's head of hair was off-limits; Cecily took every opportunity to ruffle Hadji's as she shared in his joy.

"Thought you were left-handed, honey..." Ms. Allen sent a confused smile at her right hand holding her fork.

Malcolm walked around the table holding a trash bag, discarding plates and cups into it. "She's ambidextrous, ma'am. Either hand suits her fine."

Ms. Allen smiled and nodded, still appearing befuddled at his explanation.

Hadji had several new pairs of pants, shirts, socks, new shoes, a few books, two remote-control cars, and other fun things, but Cecily and Joshua saved this last gift for the finale. Hadji pulled the paper off and jumped up, laughing and showing his friends what had him so excited: a starry-sky projection nightlight and alarm clock with all kinds of special effects he could activate. He'd been showing an interest in outer space, so the gift tied-in to that. Without prompt, he ran to Joshua and hugged him. "Thanks, Mister Joshua!"

Josh laughed and kissed Hadji's forehead, a distinct light in his eyes for the boy. "You're welcome, buddy."

Hadji turned away from Josh, and Cecily's heart warmed as he headed for her. "Thank you, Miss Cecily!" He wrapped arms around her, pressing his slight frame against her, smelling of chicken, boy-sweat, and lotion, and Cecily hugged him tight. "You're so welcome, Hayden." She pulled back and looked into his big brown eyes. "Gonna set it up tonight?"

Hadji turned to Ms. Allen, who nodded what appeared grudgingly. He turned back to her, grinning hard. "Yes!"

Cecily kissed his nose. "Good."

Brad held the box, turning it over and reading about the features. "This is sweet, Hadj. Had something like this when I was little, but this is nicer!" He handed it back to Hadji, who passed it to an impatient AJ wanting to see it.

Rhonda blushed and Cecily sensed Rhonda's preference shifting toward the youngest Hall (although she'd still *do* the eldest one).

With JAH Tech being closed for the day, another half-hour later, only she and Josh occupied the place. The shop was closed for business, but she worked in the front with him, she at her desk, him at Terrence's old desk. Cecily wasn't in any hurry to get home. She didn't want to go home at all, and once Josh left, she had no problem making a pallet in her back office.

Josh, however, didn't seem in any hurry to get home, either. "How's Larimore doing? He good?" He didn't look up from his laptop.

"He's good, Josh. Thank you." Cecily cheesed hard.

He looked at her with raised eyebrow. "What?"

She shook her head. "Nothing. Good news about my brother. Possibly. But I don't want to jinx it."

"I got you. Glad he's good."

"Me, too."

"Marcus and Chelsea are...early twenties, right?"

Cecily nodded at him, curious. "Yeah. Why?"

He jolted a shoulder. "I don't know. Nothing. Might be cool for them to hang out with my knuckleheads sometimes, if the vibe was right."

That would make leaving JAH a moot point, but he wasn't aware of that plan. She bent her lips in considering agreement. "Never thought of that. They're levelheaded kids: vibe shouldn't be funky at all."

He went back to focusing on his screen. "Finished selecting the paint for the new shop. Maybe that could bring them together..." He smirked at his screen.

"Uh-huh. You're just trying to get more free labor. No!" She laughed, but that was only to tamp down the anxiety. Given the day's events, she shouldn't have cared at all, but she stressed about participating in the new site cleanup (messing up her hair, pissing Oscar off). But more than that, she stressed over not taking part—because she wanted to participate and didn't want to disappoint Josh.

None of that came through her laughter (of course), so Josh joined in with his chuckle. "Am not."

"Either that, or you're just pressed to see me in jeans and my hair ponytailed-up or pulled back." Since moving up here, she couldn't remember the last time she'd done either with her hair. Curled and styled always, by either her stylist or herself: so, maybe not for the last six or so years.

He grew serious. "I'll take door number two, please."

Now she grew serious. "Why, Josh?"

"Just want to see you relaxed, Cecily. That's all."

"I'm relaxed now." *With you.*

He ran his eyes over her in that male way, but wasn't offensive about it. "I get that. But—" He shook his head. "I don't know. Never mind."

"No, tell me, Josh."

"I'd just like to see you a little less...'perfect,' that's all."

Her feelings weren't hurt, but they were, or something in between. She turned back to her monitor. "I'm far from perfect, Josh."

"I— I didn't mean— I just..." He whispered, "Damn," and sighed. "I'm sorry, Cecily. I was complimenting you."

She knew that, but she was doing it again: being overly sensitive (the thing she told Joshua never to say to her). She sighed. "I know. My bad. But let's leave 'perfection' with the perfectionists."

He grinned. "Deal."

They went quiet, resuming their tasks while muzak played above them.

"...Sometimes we're so busy being perfect, maybe we miss doing what God wants us to do, missing our true calling."

Cecily looked over at him. He explored and expressed more things spiritually in these last weeks with her than she ever remembered from him before.

Josh winked. "Believes, but doesn't know."

"Agnostic theist." She smiled at him. "A work in progress."

He smiled back. "As are we all. Do tell."

"For someone so practical-minded, I'm seeing more of an idealistic leaning coming from you, sir."

He turned back to his work, that hard-to-read smile on his face. "All in the company I keep, madam."

"So, osmosis?"

He didn't answer.

"From me?"

His answer, again, was no answer, and Cecily was touched. "Well, you're welcome."

He smiled at his screen. "Yes, thank you."

"That what the poetry book's for?" When he looked at her, she used her eyes to mean the book of poetry poking out of his leather bag.

He shook his head with a grin. "Sorry, babes, can't give you credit for that one. I like poetry; getting more into checking out works with a Parnassian flare."

"I see." She knew he liked poetry, and both were huge fans of Edgar Allan Poe's stuff; they'd recently explored the intricacies of his "Alone."

Josh scoffed. "Should give a copy to Rhonda. Give her something to do besides fribble her days away in idle pleasure."

She had to call him on that. "That's not true, Joshua. If it were, she wouldn't still be working here."

He sounded a conceding sigh. "You're right. My bad."

"You see potential in her. I can tell. Just give her some guidance, Josh. Or, better yet, have Malcolm or Brad do it..." She let that last linger with meaning. Josh would get it.

Sure enough, he raised an eyebrow. "Seriously?"

Cecily nodded.

"*Both* my boys?" Men could be so cute.

Wondering how his tongue tasted, she nodded again.

He returned a frowning-smirk. "Where've I been?"

Cecily twitched a shoulder in a shrug. "Working, planning,...avoiding a lot of fribble."

Now his smirk was sarcastic. "Cute. But you've been doing the same, although for a very exiguous salary. How is it you've got the scoop? I know Rhonda didn't share that."

"I'm a woman."

His gaze at her changed on the quick, and she realized the conversation she overheard earlier was about her. She saw it.

Did people give three-day's notice? Because now, she may have to leave JAH Tech for a different reason altogether. Right?

She changed the subject. "Got a joke for ya."

"You? A joke for me?" He assumed a kingly posture. "Proceed, Jester. But be funny...on pain of death."

Cecily curtsied in her chair. "Okay. Now,...how do you prepare for a party in outer space?"

He gave it some thought. "...No idea."

"You planet." Cecily giggled. "Get it? Plan for it. Outer space. You planet: P-L-A-N-E-T?"

Her Joshua held a straight face for solid seconds before tossing his head back and giving up the laugh.

She laughed with him.

Their laughter died, and he shook his head at her. "It would take you to have a joke about planning and organizing—something you're particularly good at."

"It is one of my favorites." Cecily hadn't been able to give him his gift yet (the timing was never right); now was as good a time as any.

"I don't know why we're listening to this muzak when the shop's closed. We can listen to whatever we want." He favored her with an inquiring gaze. "Jazzy-bluesy compilation?"

"Sure. And..."

Josh returned a questioning grin. "What?" He went to the music player.

"Hadji isn't the only one opening gifts today." Couldn't he see how relaxed she was? How...*herself* she was?

What is love, Cecily?

"Oh wow. Okay. Cool!" He laughed then, just this blushing chortle, making her want to—

She headed for her office in the back. "Back in a sec..."

Minutes later, he stood before her, mouth open, staring into the opened box, jazzy-bluesy playing from above.

"Well, say *something*."

"I... This..." He was tickled with his gift: one of Duncan's first yo-yos from the 1930s. It was wooden and painted black, red, and cream (perhaps white once), still in good condition.

She was tickled, too, happy her gift was the hit she expected. "I'm going to need some more consonants and vowels; a noun, verb, or adjective of some kind..."

He looked at her with absolute joy, and Cecily saw the kiss coming. Josh moved close to kiss her cheek in thanks, and she purposely turned to him, catching his lips.

The brief kiss sent a bolt of heat between her legs. "Sorry 'bout that."

Joshua chuckled low but not mockingly. "Are you, Cecily? Didn't feel like you were sorry." His honest smile was warm, nonjudgmental.

So true: that kiss didn't feel anywhere near being sorry for. She lowered her gaze, trying to get a grip on a rush of different emotions.

"Hey, Cecily. It was just a kiss."

Cecily looked up at him. "Was it, Josh?"

"...We're going to say 'yes,' because saying 'no' opens doors that must stay closed. So,...it was just a kiss." He held his yo-yo up and smiled (Cecily wanted to stick her tongue in that tiny gap on the left). "Thank you for this. It's so cool."

Thoughts of the charity ball filled her head. "You didn't have a date at the ball."

He looked perplexed, giving a balancing-scales motion with his hands. "Yo-yos...? Going stag to the charity ball...?" He shook his head and lowered his hands. "Sorry. Not getting the connection." He smirked sweetly at her, and Cecily wanted his clothes off.

She stared at him.

"What?"

"I want to ask you something, so out of line and none of my business." Joshua gazed back with honest eyes, another smirk. "I'm listening."

Sexual images of Joshua surfaced, and she was so flustered, her tongue wouldn't move at first. "How... I'm— I mean... What...?"

He put a hand to her arm. "Come on; let's sit." He gestured toward the reception counter, and Cecily tipped her head in approval. He sat on one side; she sat on the other. "Now, just ask me, Cecily. I'll tell you." He rested fingers of reassurance across the back of her hand.

Breathing more calmly with his touch, she swallowed. "What do you do for...? Shit. I can't ask this." She lowered her head, the question burning her tongue.

"You rarely curse, Cecily."

"Sorry."

"Why're you apologizing?"

"I know you're not religious, but I don't want to offend."

"Well, we both know my position on that. But, being a believer, I don't believe God cares about a 'curse' word, Cecily. Now, if trying to offend or harm someone verbally, that's different."

"It is."

"But, with you cursing, if the question affects you that much, seems you'd best ask it—if only to help yourself feel better."

"I— I can't, Josh."

There was a long pause: Joshua gazing at her, she, finding everything in that shop to look at but him.

"You want to know what I do for, or rather, how I satisfy my sexual urges."

Still unable to look at him, she nodded.

"Unh-unh. You want to ask me something like that—you have to look me in the eye at least."

That was true. Cecily lifted her head and looked into his eyes, wanting to kiss him. "Yes, that's what I want to know. You're not gay, Josh. And I can tell you're not involved with anyone. Which baffles me because you're so..." She looked away, shaking her head.

Josh leaned closer. "I'm 'so'...?"

She turned back to him. "I don't understand why a man who is as funny, smart, attractive, caring, responsible, and, well...utterly adorable as you, isn't attached. You're a man; I know you have needs." Women had needs, too...

He held her gaze with a soft smile. She thought he was the cutest thing (and there was just something about that scar-line in his mustache). "I used to see a female friend of mine..."

"Kristin."

"Yes. And, you know what a lay-don't-stay is...?"

Pangs of jealousy surfacing, Cecily nodded.

He shrugged. "Well, so, yeah."

His discomfort pleased her.

"But, well, she started seeing someone several months ago, so I begged off...out of respect. Let her do her committed thing." He shrugged again.

"Why didn't you two pursue a relationship?"

"A relationship in its truest sense wouldn't have been viable."

"Okay, that's *her*." Mackenzie came to mind. "But what about some-one else? I mean—"

"I want viability, Cecily. Sustainability. Not just availability."

"Oh. So..."

That hint of smirking-smile returned. "So,...what have I been doing these past months—without a woman's 'comfort'?"

She focused on the items behind him while bobbing her head.

"Cecily."

She coasted her gaze to him, loving how he says her name. "Yes."

Joshua spoke low. "Well, as you've noted, I'm not seeing anyone... And no, I'm not gay. Nor am I into escorts. You also noted I'm a man...with needs. So, what do you think I do?"

Cecily flushed.

"Come on. We're adults. You have this question. I'm letting you know you already have the answer. What do I do, Cecily?"

"...You jerk off." She whispered it, glancing toward the windows and the descending dusk.

Josh smiled that soft smile again. "Yes, Cecily. I jerk off."

Hearing Joshua say those words, coupled with heated images of him in action, Cecily grew dizzy. They shouldn't be talking about this. They shouldn't. But...

She put her head in her hands.

"Cecily?"

"I'm okay."

"Anything else?" Traces of Polo-Purple drifted her way.

She lifted her head, her eyes searching his. "Kind of."

"Go 'head."

Her level of comfort about their conversation increased with the passing seconds. "What do you think about when you...?"

His knowing grin held a bit of blush. "Well, it's obvious *what* I think about, but there's a *whom* before the 'what.' I think about a woman, Cecily. So, whom do you think I think about? ...You already have the answer to that, too. But I think it's best left unsaid. Don't you?"

"Josh..."

He stood. "Best left *unsaid*, Cecily. But I'll tell you this..."

She waited.

"With *that* woman, a relationship would be very viable."

Cecily nodded the truth of his words; it would be.

"So...'completely adorable,' huh?"

Cecily sat taller. "I think so. Yes." She borderline attacked him with the words.

Josh reared back. "Well, okay. Don't hit me."

Their chuckle was brief.

"Well, thank you for that. And..." He lifted his yo-yo and looked at her, his eyes serious, although he smiled. "Thanks so much again for this."

Nina Simone's "Sugar in My Bowl" played in the background; Cecily rose and approached him.

The sultry but cautious way he watched her awakened parts of her she thought dead. Standing before him, Cecily breathed in his Polo-Purple and placed fingers to his lips, touching the scar in his mustache, and fighting the desire to do so much more than touch him. She was in all kinds of improper territory.

But why did it feel like she wasn't?

She kissed him, allowing her lips to press against his for good seconds, raising a hand to his hair and enjoying its soft, kinky texture. Pecking his lips again, she used every fiber of her being to resist tasting his tongue, because his lips were warmly inviting, and his mustache echoed masculinity.

And in that moment, if Joshua were a different type of man to so much as guide her toward that ocean of full impropriety, she would've dove headfirst into that ocean, swimming freely (freestyle or breaststroke or backstroke, or all of them), and laid with him.

But her Joshua was honorable; he wasn't one of those men. He put just enough of his honor to the side to let her guide this moment, however. Her insides cramped deliciously with need from the pressure of his lips as he returned the sensual peck, kissing her back. His breath was quasi-sweet with remnant hints of cake and ice cream, and Cecily knew that if she tried to taste his tongue, he would stop her. But Joshua was also a giving man; he allowed her access to his lips, letting her say *when* and *how far* without so much as a hand on her. For a time too short, his lips were hers.

When they parted, she smiled at him, trembling. "You're welcome."

"You're trembling, Cecily."

"Was that 'just a kiss,' Josh?"

"You know the answer to that already, too. But I'm— I'm trying to keep doors *closed* here, Cecily."

Cecily held his warm gaze.

He wore a smile of pondering reflection. "You know,...this woman,...that I think about?"

She looked up at him, nodding, still trembling some.

"She...She does things, with no clue what she's doing to you, oblivious to how she's affecting you..." Josh looked away before bringing his eyes back to hers. His eyes held her captive. He cupped her cheek, and her trembles ceased. "And what's so insanely hot about her is...she really, *truly*...has no...idea."

Their gazes connected, and Cecily saw possibilities and daydreams coming to life.

"And I want to kiss her, I do. Kiss her and...love her. Want her as my wife, so she can feel and know my love for her. I want her lips on mine as I entwine my tongue with hers. Touch her where she aches for me to touch her, so when I finally slide inside her, it feels like coming home after a long, tiring, *trying* journey. And the woman will come, Cecily. Her climax will be so... She'll look at me as I work her and come harder than she ever remembers. And I will kiss her as I let go inside her." Joshua lowered his hand and stepped back. "She's lovely, Cecily. That's all. Inside and out." His gaze trailed over her.

Cecily wanted him. Wanted his tongue, his penis, that kinky 'fro in her passion-filled fist, and everything else.

Josh smiled, cleared his throat. He shook his head. "Anyway. ...I better go." He headed toward the back offices. "Maybe I've said too much. But we're adults, just talking, hypothesizing. So, there it is."

Her next words barreled forth, bumping into one another. "Why do you let me call you 'Josh'? You don't like 'Josh'..."

He stopped and turned to her with a smile unreadable but wholly benevolent. "Why do you keep asking questions you already have the answers to?" Josh went to his office but didn't close the door, didn't shut her out.

Cecily sat, thinking about the whole of this day, the tragic revelations and the pleasing ones, about her exchanges with Josh throughout the day. About the theme of a lesson most important.

As if on cue, "The Closer I Get to You" came on, and she listened to it during her rumination, knowing the song played overhead where Josh was; that they listened together while apart. When the song ended, she used the remote to stop the player, needing no further punctuation to the evening and allowing the silence to give her thoughts the room they needed.

Cecily came out of her reverie, her heart a little lighter, her mind heavier with thoughts of what to do next, and, honestly, she was hornier than she'd ever been since Roland. She was tired, too: mentally, physically, spiritually—but mostly, emotionally.

She couldn't stay here, though; that was out. And going home wasn't happening, either. A quality hotel sounded perfect: the solitude, the...freedom. Being charitable to herself, Cecily called and made a reservation. She called Chelsea and then texted her husband. She headed for Josh's office to tell him she was leaving. It was so quiet as she approached his door.

He sat at his desk, head bowed at his hands, lips moving. Cecily halted and backed up some. He was praying. Her Joshua explored more of the theist side of his agnosticism, while she leaned more and more toward the agnostic than Gnostic side of her spiritual self these days, remaining a believer but becoming less of a knower. Cecily stayed where she was, waiting, hearing bits of whispered words coming her way, hearing her name a few times. She didn't want to interrupt.

What is love, Cecily?

When she sensed he was finished, she tipped back to the front, pausing in the archway separating the shop zones. She called back to him. "That's it for me, Josh! See you tomorrow."

"Hold up."

Cecily turned to gather her things.

She soon sensed him behind her. "Wanna walk you to your car."

As always, of course. "That's fine."

While walking to her car, they said little, both cautious but respectful of that earlier exchange.

He opened her door for her, and Cecily, unable to help herself, kissed his stubbly cheek as she moved to sit in the driver's seat. She looked up at him, giving a nod toward the car door Josh held open for her. "Well, you can close *this* door. Those other doors..." she shook her head, "I'm not so sure." She surprised herself at her bold statement and the innuendo, but then, she meant every word. She wasn't sure those figurative doors Joshua was trying to keep closed would stay closed—not if she continued working with him. Cecily looked up at him.

His smiling-smirk in reply carried its own innuendo. "Let's deal with one door at a time. Be safe, Cecily. Good night." He closed her car door gently but securely and stepped back, waiting for her to pull off.

Given all she'd learned today and Oscar's probable annoyance from her minimal contact with him and her telling him she wouldn't be home tonight, she was glad she drove her 1967 Deville, her "Devin," to work instead of the Q70. Boxes of her comics (the oldest ones) were in the trunk (as were a few changes of clothes and the notes in her sock). Devin was a classic car, but he had modern features (including modifications to reduce CO_2 emissions): the car audio system was current and topnotch.

Windows down to allow the thirty-nine-degree night to help cool her still hot-and-horny (for only Joshua), Cecily programmed two songs to repeat: an L.T.D. music theme. She listened to "Stranger" and "Holding On" alternately, driving but heading nowhere in particular. "Holding On" was on that slip of paper Naomi handed her, and Cecily now gave the lyrics the attention Naomi thought they deserved. She drove around, jamming and listening, reflecting and grooving.

What is love, Cecily?

It was laughter, and communication, and grace, and charity. Love was friendship and laughter and understanding and confiding and appreciation and a refuge. It was disagreement without viciousness. Relaxed. Intense. Reciprocated. Did she say laughter? Love was protection. It was...safety.

Today, so many aspects of love reflected a lesson twice learned (what it was, what it most certainly was not)—in the spate of a few hours.

Cecily pulled in front of the Omni Shoreham Hotel in DC, mentally rehearsing drafts for resignation letters to Joshua.

She checked-in, still pondering the day's lessons in Love.

While watching an engrossing documentary on Sam Cooke (so amazingly talented), it occurred to her what lesson she learned most.

Love denied rested at the crux of her pain.

Chapter Sixteen

An Unexpected Visit

H e didn't think he had enough pills yet, but he may have to go with what he had and pray on it.

Something the fuck was changing—and not for the better. He could *feel* the shit.

Oscar took alternating swigs of Corona or his baking-soda-and-water mixture. He'd been drinking baking soda and water like crazy the last few days, but it wasn't doing the job for his heartburn anymore. The heartburn was worsening or something; he couldn't shake it. Fucking Halim was a quack. They all were.

He thought faking having that interview for appearance's sake would rate some cool points with his wife, make her believe he'd conformed like the rest of the punks. But if he'd gotten the points, he couldn't tell. Cecily was...different.

It started that same damn day. He'd texted for her status several times, called several times: nothing. Janyce bitched and moaned about Cecily not communicating with her, either, and that was the kicker. He didn't know what the fuck was going on, but as soon as she got home that night, he'd planned to remind her, *emphatically*, what the fuck *should be* going on in his house.

But she didn't come home.

That was three days ago.

She was with her bitch-slit daughter, Chelsea. She'd had surgery or some shit, and Cecily was staying with her for a few days. He still tried texting her for a status on her daily activities, and Cecily started replying again, but her texts were short, almost...dismissive. And she still didn't pick up to talk. He wished he'd gone Janyce's *Mission Impossible* route and put some secret trace-shit on Cecily's phone. Fuck.

Now that he thought about it, maybe it started before then. Right around the charity ball? He couldn't be sure because it was such a weird thing. She was the same in some ways but different in these tiny ways that had him thinking Naomi showed Cecily that secret door, but she hadn't walked through it yet.

For one thing, he noticed Cecily wasn't bugging him about affection anymore. She'd been on that tip hard for a while, but now... For another, her kisses were different. The same, but...different. He got off on watching as a woman kissed him, enjoyed seeing her eyes closed; it confirmed she was doing that woman-thing of being all into it, confirmed she was under his spell. But when Cecily stared at him as they kissed last time, he was excited and then...nervous about it, too. Why'd she do that?

Oscar scoffed, brooding about Cecily while watching a rerun of *Adam-12*. He tried watching some CNN, but turned after a few minutes. Damn the world's problems: it wasn't his fault, and he couldn't do shit about any of it, anyway. He didn't even care about recycling: Cecily was determined to save Earth.

Running a hand over his now-hairless face, Oscar switched to an episode of *Match Game*. Dickey Dawson was at it again: always getting picked for the big-money matchup and kissing the lady contestants.

He didn't mean to shave everything off last night, but he was so mad at Cecily for staying away; he took the razor to his face. He believed Cecily liked the goatee—*So there, bitch.*

Damn, he was horny (heartburn and all).

He couldn't get into Gene Rayburn and company; his thoughts were on what to do about his wife. Suddenly inspired, he grabbed his cellphone and called Winton, telling him he'd best get him a bottle of some serious pain or sleep meds—if he wanted to get paid. He hung up, feeling better, wondering what would be best to camouflage the taste when he made Cecily's smoothie. He'll see what the internet says.

Oscar texted Cecily for the third time, refusing to admit the truth: he missed her. Because when his cellphone chimed less than a minute later, it was her—and he experienced a weird excitement that had him rejecting the smoothie idea. She texted she was stopping by the house in a few. There was something he didn't like about *stopping by*, but he'd deal with that once he saw her. He spit in his spittoon (needed emptying) and turned the television off to get a shower and spruce up, now annoyed with himself for shaving.

Twenty minutes later (after switching around the contents in two of her dresser drawers), he sat in the family room instead of his man-cave in the basement, watching some home and garden show (Cecily liked those). The show was on; he wasn't watching, but appearances were everything. Odie liked those DIY shows, too. So did Otis. Those two worked together, refurbishing some rooms in Odessa's house. He could've helped, but they never asked, so fuck 'em.

Oh, how he wanted to show them up, get them together and brag about how he had deep enough pockets to attend the big charity ball—and they didn't. Those two never attempted to reschedule that lunch with him; they could forget having a free lunch on him now.

With the sound of the garage door opening, Oscar stood and then sat in one swift motion, and that pissed him off; she was fucking with his inner workings, how he operated—and that was not how this worked.

Rubbing his chest (the heartburn lessened), he took a settling breath. He planned to not say shit; she'd better be the one doing some talking, some fucking explaining. And if she didn't? Well, he just didn't know.

When she entered the house, his plan almost went out the window as soon as he saw her. Cecily was pretty, on the fine side, so he was extra glad to see her. He still didn't plan to say much, but he didn't think he wanted to hear an explanation, either. Still, he checked for the little things that would tell him what he needed to know. She'd styled her hair perfectly, as he'd demanded since day one. Good. She cast her eyes downward in a nervous, submissive way. Even better.

Holding a small plastic bag, she glanced his way and went to the refrigerator. "Hey." She placed fresh flowers on the kitchen table. He couldn't wait to water them.

He didn't respond, instead turning back to *Keep It or Sell It* (or something like that) on HGTV, with the lady decorator and the man real-estate agent.

She put something in the fridge. "You hungry?"

Okay, okay. Shit sounded proper; she was putting the focus back where it belonged. Still, he didn't reply. He wasn't saying shit, not even to ask about that daughter of hers, until he was ready.

Cecily sighed, but it wasn't her worried sigh; it sounded more like...an irritated one.

The fuck?

The phone rang as he tried determining whether to punch her in the arm, stomach, or lower back. Maybe a tittie.

"I'll get it..." She picked up in the kitchen. "Hello...?"

Oscar pretended to watch the couple decide if they liked the lady's redecorating enough to stay in their house or if they were jumping ship with real-estate dude, but he paid attention to Cecily's end of the conversation as she put those stupid flowers in a vase.

His stomach knotted: she was talking to his daughter, Keisha. He didn't attempt to connect with his daughter and was fine with that, but Cecily, soon as she knew about Keisha, tried her *Brady Bunch* way to keep the lines of communication open. Oscar let Cecily have at it; he could be a good father through her efforts. So far, from listening, he gathered she was coming back to the States soon. So the fuck what.

Cecily said something about her loser jailbird brother, and Oscar tuned that right on out; she was such a punk. But then he heard her say something about Larimore having a degree in engineering. Interesting; so he was a smart loser. Oscar scoffed. She probably told him that already, but he never paid attention to shit about her brothers, didn't care past knowing they existed. Kyle didn't like him, and the feeling was more than fucking mutual. Name and address were all he needed—especially when time came for notification about Cecily.

Should get him a White girl next. Training one should be easy-peasy.

She closed the conversation with some Pollyanna drivel about getting together when Keisha returned and then hung up.

"What was that about?" He wasn't interested in building a relationship with Keisha, but she was his, not Cecily's; he wanted the details. He got up and joined her in the kitchen, going to the refrigerator to see what she'd added. When she didn't answer right away, he looked at her.

Cecily stared at him with this faint frown, and he could see she didn't like his clean-shaven look. She shrugged as she checked her mail. "Just a woman in flux. She's had her fill of Germany for now. Wants to return to the US before starting a family." She shrugged again and sighed an uppity sigh he imagined snooty Kyle making. "Keisha's experiencing a bit of ennui over there, I guess."

"Don't start that shit."

"It means boredom."

He hated when she talked down to him. Oscar closed the refrigerator and stepped toward her, seeing the fear in her eyes and the dip of her shoulders, which he liked, but it was brief (and he didn't like that). "I know what it means." He didn't know until she said it, but fuck her. He reached out, gripping where that knife-scar was on her abdomen.

Tears leapt in her eyes, but he saw defiance mixed in with reaction to the pain. "Fancy words don't make you fancy. But those contacts would make you worth looking at, at least. When will they be ready?"

She stared at him, almost glaring, but didn't answer.

He pinched tighter, trying to make that old scar split open if he could. Anger over the loneliness in that house without her over the last three days pulsed through him.

The low scream pleased him, and he let her go, opening the fridge for one of those subs she brought. "When?"

"Not for three months."

Oscar turned back. "What?"

Tears streaming, she handed him a piece of paper from her purse.

He sensed her wanting to rub and soothe where he hurt her, but she didn't. Oscar read, skipping the medical gobbledygook, looking for sentences he understood. When he read the part about a three-month restriction from wearing the contacts, he balled the paper and threw it at her. "Fine." It was. It irritated him, but three months from now wouldn't matter. "Will just be harder to get it up for you, that's all—especially with those splotches back across your face."

She swallowed, sniffed, and reached for a napkin, blowing her nose.

"So, you back now? Ready to focus on something other than yourself? How's Chelsea?" He could give a shit about Chelsea but wanted to know when Cecily was going to stop playing nursemaid.

"She—"

The doorbell rang.

"Get in there and clean your face. I'll get the door. And I want chicken wings for dinner." Making her eat chicken wings with her hands was just the punishment she needed. He didn't know who she thought she was while away these last few days, but she was home now, goddammit. He planned to punch a tittie later. His dick jerked with the thought.

She hurried into the powder room, a hand over her mouth.

Oscar opened the door, peering at some tall (maybe six feet), beefy-looking dude. He was brown like Cecily, with a beard and a complicated tattoo alongside his neck. Hands in the pockets of his heavy wool coat, he wore a wool hat (down over his ears), navy sports jacket with gray slacks, and a white shirt. Oscar frowned. "Can I help you, bruh?"

"Yes. Cecily home?"

Oscar saw red. "Scuse me?! I'm her husband. Who the fuck're you?!"

Asshole pulled a hand from his pocket and checked his fingernails. "I know who you are, Oscar. Is my sister home?" He turned brown eyes back to him, gazing calmly, and Oscar saw the resemblance around the eyes and nose.

"Moe! Oh my God!" Cecily pushed past him and out the door, all but tackling her brother as she hugged him. "Oh, my God! They really did it!" She kissed his cheek, still hugging him tight. "It's wonderful!"

Oscar stared as they laughed together. He wanted to tell Larimore he could let his wife go now, but cut him some slack. "Oh! Okay. Yeah! An unexpected visit, but it's good to see you, man! Heard a lot about you. It's cold as shit out here. Come on in!"

When Cecily finally decided to surgically remove herself from Larimore's butthole, Oscar opened the storm door wider and extended a hand to his ex-con ass.

Both ignored his outstretched hand and walked past it, entering his house with more sibling chuckles.

In the foyer, Cecily helped Larimore with his coat and hat, repeating, "Oh my God!" so happily, Oscar thought she'd piss herself before they got to the rest of the house. He wondered if there was some incestuosity between them.

He trailed behind as Cecily took Larimore on a mini tour of his house, catching him up since they last talked, Oscar guessed. She didn't even look at him as they headed into the basement, didn't get his permission to go down, and Oscar couldn't wait for jailbird to be gone so he could recalibrate his wife.

Back on the main floor, they approached the kitchen. Cecily gazed at her brother, wearing this smirk of mystery. "And now, the pièce de résistance..."

Larimore chuckled. "Okay..."

Cecily opened the garage access door. "Ta-da!"

"Whoa! Seriously!" Larimore laughed and stepped down into their garage, walking over to the Deville. "Cee-Cee, this is major goodness, man! Damn!" He walked around the car, staring wide-eyed while nodding his appreciation.

"I know."

Larimore paused and arched his eyebrows at his sister. "By yourself?"

Shoulders back with a satisfied smile, Cecily nodded. "Just me, Moe. Well, tiny bit of help from the guys at the shop, but yeah."

Larimore grinned as he ran his eyes over the vehicle. When he looked at Oscar, his grin dropped. "Can you excuse us, man? Wanna talk to my sister privately, if you don't mind."

That was the first time they acknowledged he was even in the damn house, so yeah, he minded. He alternated his gaze at them as they gazed back: seeing Larimore didn't like him, seeing Cecily...didn't like him so much right now, either. "Yeah, okay. I'll just be—"

Larimore turned to Cecily, dismissing him. "I see you've got some nice setups on the dash..." He opened the driver's door and got in.

Cecily went around to the passenger side, but she glanced his way before getting in; so that was something.

Oscar went inside. In the family room, he heard strains of music by L.T.D. coming from the garage, trying his best not to obsess about their conversation and not doing a very good job. Maybe they were getting snooty Kyle on the phone...

About ten minutes later, they came back in. "So, you're staying for dinner, Moe. I'll hear no more about it."

Fuck.

Larimore sat on the sofa. "No arguments from me. Wanna see if you can still burn."

"Get him something to drink, Cesspool." Larimore needed to see who ran this ship. "Hurry up."

Cecily winced as if struck, sending a worried look Larimore's way when she should've sent it his. "Sorry."

Oscar couldn't get a read on jailbird, but Larimore watched his sister for quiet seconds. "Water's good, Cee-Cee. Thanks."

Cecily smiled at her brother. "Coming right up."

"Yeah, she can handle water, man. Keep things as simple as possible with that one: she confuses easy." Oscar sat back in his recliner. "So, how's it feel to be out, man? Great, I imagine."

Larimore eyed him with the same calm seconds he applied while gazing at Cecily moments ago. He semi-nodded. "Yeah, it's 'great.'"

"Used to be a security guard myself. So, you know, I have some experience with law enforcement, the prison system."

"Really."

"Oh yeah. Coulda made detective, but well, for all intense purposes, all that's mute now."

"I see."

Oscar didn't like that one-word response shit. What the fuck was that about? He changed the channel on the television, switching to CNN with a sigh. "Let's see what's happening with the world-at-large here..." He wiped his brow with a paper towel, feeling that fullness in his chest. Halim said his tests were good, but Oscar didn't see how.

"You hot?" Larimore frowned, his eyes on him wiping his face. He had a stud in his left earlobe. That was such a punk-ass move. Left earlobe, right earlobe: whatever—*women* wore earrings, not men. Winton wore a punk-ass earring, too.

"Nah. Just sweat a lot. Overactive glands or something."

Larimore nodded as Cecily brought the water. "Thanks, Cee-Cee."

Oscar cut in: "Now, bring my spittoon up before you sit down, Cecil. Thing's damn-near overflowing. Use the powder room instead of the basement bath." Cecily hated emptying his spittoon (her frown of disgust said it all), but sometimes he made her empty it to bring her ass down sometimes, remind her how things worked.

Larimore kept eyes on his sister.

Cecily hesitated (telling him shit was still different with her), but she half-smiled at him and then looked at her brother. "Be right back...?"

"Of course." Dude suddenly didn't speak more than two words at a time.

Cecily went downstairs and returned, going into the powder room with his spittoon and flushing the contents down the toilet. She returned his container to the basement and came back. "Need to go upstairs for a second..." She headed for the stairs.

"Take your time," Larimore said. At least that was three words.

The brother didn't make small talk while they watched television and waited for Cecily, which was okay with him. Oscar popped a mint.

Cecily returned with another bag she took to the garage, mumbling, "Some stuff for Chelsea." He wondered if she noticed he changed shit around in her dresser drawers.

Shortly after, they sat in the family room talking, but Oscar didn't like how Larimore watched everything so closely, being all quiet and shit...and only really talking to Cecily. The way he was acting, he wondered if Cecily blabbed to Larimore about what he'd said about him.

Cecily stood. "Okay. I want to get to the grocery store, get some items for dinner tonight." She spoke to Larimore: "You'll be okay?"

The brother nodded and stood, too. "I'll be fine. Have some man-to-man chitchat with Oscar while you're gone. But I want to see my niece and nephews when you get back."

Cecily grinned up at her brother. "I can't believe this."

Larimore kissed her cheek. "Believe it, Cee-Cee."

"Want a Twinkie?"

Larimore laughed. "Nah. Had one earlier. They don't taste the same."

"True. Okay. Back in a few," Cecily said. She patted her brother's arm and headed for the door.

Oscar stared at the television, not seeing it. "Be careful. Love you." He added that as a message to the jailbird: Cecily was his. Once Larimore heard Cecily say it back, everything should be pretty fucking clear from then on out.

Appearances were everything.

The garage door opened and closed. Minutes later, the Deville started. Cecily hadn't said it back, and Oscar clutched the armrest, scowling at the television. He went to the kitchen. "Sure, you just want water? We have beer."

Larimore entered the kitchen, too. "Water's fine. I'm good."

"Well, maybe I'll have one th—"

Larimore was on him, gripping his throat while backing him to the wall. Oscar's head banged against it hard. "Fuck, man! What—?"

"Shut up." Larimore's eyes roamed his face. His lip curled into a snarl and then relaxed. He shook his head, his brown eyes sending a jailbird-crazed stare. "My sister...is so unhappy...so...*miserable* in here with you. I can taste it." His grip tightened. "The taste is sour and bitter, so *foul*, man. I can't stand it. Can't stand *you*." He sent his fierce gaze through Oscar's eyes into the back of his head. "You want to extricate yourself from her life, bruh. I'm telling you. Extricate yourself."

Oscar gawked at him, trying to breathe, trying to keep his chest calm. What the fuck was "ekstrakate"? All the jailbird had was one-word answers at first; now he was showing off with words from that dictionary he had plenty time to read while locked up.

"That means *remove*, since you're looking at me funny. You think motherfuckers from jail can't speak correctly, can't communicate in anything but grunts and Ebonic-colloquialisms?"

Oscar just wanted him out. Wanted him to let his throat go and get the fuck out. He'll deal with Cecily about all this shit. Oh, yeah.

Larimore scoffed. He smelled of one of those colognes Cecily tried getting him to wear. "Anyway, get the fuck out. Extricate and leave Cee-Cee alone." He curled that lip into a snarl again. "And you don't have long to do it. Make up some shit. Just leave and allow her to file for divorce—*uncontested*. I don't care how you do it. My sister will be perfectly fine, better for it, regardless." He looked around them, around the kitchen and family room, into the workout room, and then focused his jailbird-crazy glare again. "But you'll do it. Because if you don't,...*I'll* extricate you. You know where I've been. I know people—and I can use Kyle's money to get shit done. Kyle can't stand your ass, either. So, it won't be me handling shit..." He looked him over, his nose wrinkling with aggravated distaste and assurance. "Although I could." Oscar saw confirmation of that in Larimore's eyes—because the jailbird-crazy in them was now gone.

The grip on his throat loosened, and Oscar took that time for gulps of air. He checked for the cordless phone's whereabouts, so he could get this crazy motherfucker on a siren-escorted ride back to lockup.

Larimore then looked him over again, smirking with disgust. "Probably have a Napoleon complex, too. ...You're a piece of shit, man. A disease of anger and disappointment. The Grinch personified. I can see it. ...And I know you're hurting Cee-Cee: mentally, emotionally, probably physically..."

Oscar recognized the situation he was in; he needed to get this convict calmed, get him to see his side. But first, he needed to know how he'd been betrayed. "What...? What'd she say?"

Larimore shook his head, the snarl back. "She didn't say shit. *You* just did." He leaned close, their noses touching, his breath warm and smelling of chewing gum. "*Extricate* yourself. She's too good for you, I promise. You've got to go." His grip tightened again, tighter than before. "I'll go back for my sister, man. *Trust* me."

Oscar trusted him, experienced the truth with the pressure building in his head, with the air not reaching his lungs. This couldn't be happening. Where was the phone?! He spotted it behind the vase of Cecily's stupid flowers. But would he be able to get to it? Shit.

"*Extricate* yourself...or have it done for you." Larimore loosened his grip, and Oscar couldn't help the tears of relief and joy accompanying the fresh air flowing into his lungs again. "Yeah. Cry. I'm sure my sister's done her share of crying because of you." Larimore began lowering his hand, but then gripped Oscar's throat again. Not tightly as before, but enough. "And if anything, *anything*, happens to my sister? I'm coming for your ass. Believe it. I told you: I don't have a problem going back to prison for Cee-Cee. Even if it's after you've extricated yourself. You've taken years off her life as it is. So, even if Cecily dies of old-age and natural causes, I'm still coming for your ass, still resting the blame at your feet. So, your best bet is to hope she outlives you."

"How could you even think that way, man? I love your sister."

Instead of answering, Larimore smirked. He released his throat and patted his head like he was a fucking dog. "Wasn't even close to nice meeting you. Tell Cecily I had to run, but I'll call her tonight. Staying in the DMV for the foreseeable, so I'll be getting together with my sister on the regular." He smiled, his teeth straight and white (for an ex-con), but so up-close, his canines looked big-bad-wolfish. "You know what? Matter of fact, *I'll* tell her the rest of that myself." After another glare of warning (and assurance of consequences), he turned away and walked toward the foyer.

Wiping his tears barehanded, Oscar listened to Larimore get his hat and coat from the closet (the motherfucker had the nerve to be whistling). He had a headache like shit now. But he didn't move for fear of reminding the asshole of some more shit maybe he forgot to say and making him turn back.

"FYI, you're saying it wrong: it's *moot*, man, not 'mute.' M-o-o-t. And the phrase is 'all *intents and purposes*,' bruh: *four* words, not three."

The front door opened. "*Extricate*. Look it up. And those mints aren't working." Larimore closed the door behind him.

Oscar waited a few minutes before going to the pantry for the bottle of Excedrin. He downed three pills with an entire bottle of Corona, gulping it down in one sitting.

After his belch, he grabbed the cordless phone but didn't use it.

Oscar returned to his recliner. Phone still gripped in one hand, he turned to ESPN for the background noise (wishing it was time for shows with judges named Judy). He tilted his head back and closed his eyes, slowly feeling better.

He was smarter than most people, extremely logical. Didn't have a degree yet to prove it, but he was. That life insurance was taken out on Cecily years ago: a cool $2.5 million insurance payout waited to be collected. The policy being so old wouldn't have them thinking it was the motive. With that amount of money, he could move around the country. Larimore would never find him; jailbirds had travel restrictions.

Cecily texted: she wouldn't be coming back; Chelsea was having some complications or some shit. She apologized, asking him to tell Larimore for her.

Oscar texted back as if all was fine and dandy, even telling her he wished Chelsea a speedy recovery. Plan C was moving full speed ahead.

He'd wait a day or two. See what Winton comes up with. Then, if all looked good, he'd contact Cecily, telling her he felt they were drifting apart or some shit, that he wanted another chance to make things better. She'd come. Seven years with her assured him of that.

And when she did, before they began talking about the future, he'd get a last bit of pussy from her, then offer a nice, cold smoothie to smooth things over...

Oscar chuckled at his pun.

Shit may have been a little different now. Cecily may have changed in some ways, but so what?

He had it all under control.

Seeing it all play out, Oscar grinned as he went for his special solution to kill Cecily's flowers.

Chapter Seventeen

Smoke and Mirrors

N aomi sat at her desk in her professional office, staring at the
wooden Rod of Asclepius piece Viv made for her, contemplating
the fallout from the charity ball.

Monday's session with Louise Nguyễn-Collins went as expected,
with the first twenty minutes comprising nothing but more of Louise's
Rick-Phillips obsessions. Naomi didn't realize there was anything more
to be said, but Louise didn't repeat herself once. Her neurosis over that
man was deep (to the trained ear) and scary (to the untrained one).
Naomi spent the last forty minutes of the session doing her best to guide
Louise away from the deep-and-scary.

After reading more of *Go Tell It on the Mountain* at Garden Meadows,
her session Tuesday morning with Tim Collins was better, a lot less
deep-and-scary. Still, he had neuroses over Rick and Viv, warranting
attention.

Naomi set her eyeglasses on the desk and rubbed her eyes using her
thumb and index finger.

The couple would see Dr. McNichol beginning next week—and
hopefully, soon, taking big gulps of air in the prudencesphere.

Two down from the charity ball. One to go (although this last wasn't
a one-and-done case).

She performed phone counsel with Cecily for Tuesday's session, but
Cecily would arrive soon for a face-to-face. If all went as planned,
this session was going to be intense. Even after this session's results
(whatever they may be), it wouldn't surprise Naomi if Cecily continued
fighting the truth, using denial as a defense mechanism.

Denial was the easiest to use when dealing with uncomfortable life events. Denial usually transitioned to acceptance at some point. But for patients needing therapy, that transition took much longer or was obstructed by other defense mechanisms interfering with mental and emotional progress. Cecily prefers to deny the control Oscar has, prefers to minimize the level of his meanness toward her. The charity ball showed some steps toward acceptance, but regression in the days since was always possible.

One nugget of good news: Cecily staying at the Omni for the last few days with no plans to sleep in her home. She'd find out more when Cecily arrived for her session, but Cecily having opportunity to decompress from a session alone and without Oscar's NAS interference could only help things move faster. Cecily still needed therapy for PTSD, but the NAS was so intertwined, Naomi wanted Cecily to combat that first.

To do that, Cecily had to go back to the night of the home invasion (and the related and subsequent PTSD).

A delicate dance of the macabre.

Intimidation, fear, bullying, passive-aggressive tactics, and subterfuge were all at work in the toxic atmosphere of a relationship swirling under narcissistic abuse syndrome. But Naomi considered the complex factor of shame to be the critical component. Any abuse reflects a failure in a relationship, and a victim's inability to protect themselves from it leads to shame. Long-term abuse creates a defaming imprint on the victim's personality.

With NAS (compared with the "gaslighter" who withholds information from the victim to keep them unbalanced), victims withhold details about the abuse they suffer. The secrecy gives them a sense of control over what's happening. Still, Cecily has shown signs of being tired of covering for Oscar and withholding information about what's going on in her marriage from those who would represent her support system. This weariness is her true personality fighting back. But the shame she feels over being a victim also leads to the defense mechanisms she uses, which unintentionally enables the NAS to continue.

Naomi ruminated, sending her contemplative gaze out the window while leisurely cleaning the lenses of her eyeglasses.

Considering the abundant compounding developments at the charity ball, time was of the essence regarding the home invasion at the Brooks home two years ago. Naomi's theories were nothing without Cecily's memories to confirm them.

Treatment for Cecily's PTSD has included a psychoanalytical-cocktail of cognitive-behavioral therapy and family therapy. Oscar's role created a plethora of conflict. So far, Cecily didn't want to include Chelsea or Marcus. As far as meds: a low dosage of benzodiazepines for anxiety (which Naomi sensed Cecily just wanted on standby). Although an option, Naomi didn't even entertain incorporating any EDMR. The Eye Movement Desensitization and Reprocessing utilized CBT and rhythmic hand taps to "unlock" the brain's processing (often interrupted during traumatic stress), but Naomi didn't think it necessary.

Naomi set her glasses back on.

Given plans for today's session, she sensed a breakthrough waiting.

Although she believed Cecily made considerable progress, her recovery needed to include some awareness education on the characteristics and effects of narcissistic abuse. She felt a mini-class on NAS was in order, but she hadn't been able to circle back.

Cecily fell prey to Oscar's mental machinations while still mourning losing Roland. Okay. So, under normal circumstances, Cecily's personality didn't lend itself to falling prey again—especially after Naomi provided details on recognizing it. Cecily surviving it without fully succumbing in many detrimental ways, was a testament to her perseverance and strength and was prime example of the resilience of the human spirit. She was proud of Cecily. Although it should be, breaking the NAS cycle wouldn't be cut-and-dried; this delicate dance of the macabre required some deft maneuvering on Cecily's behalf.

Naomi believed she'd get it done.

Cecily's mind depended on it. Maybe even...her life.

Henney-tea in hand, Naomi stood at the ready upon hearing Veronica greeting Cecily.

It was February, but instead of hearts and little cupids floating around, her office was in full Christmas regalia: a pine tree decked to the Yuletide-nines sat in one corner, gingerbread squares stacked on a plate on her desk, more poinsettias, some holly, and a small microwave with bacon cooked almost to burning sat in another corner. Fake blood dotted tosses of fabric about the seating. Naomi didn't go as far as adding urine, but she had a replica of that keychain made; the one she saw at the ball and as described by Cecily weeks ago. Yeah, she'd been busy.

The door opened, and Cecily entered, wearing a surprising ensemble of jeans and a Delta State sweatshirt. Her hair, however, was still hairdresser-perfect. Naturally, she paused and surveyed her office.

Naomi didn't expect Cecily to collapse into the throes of PTSD (she'd made considerable progress), but Naomi didn't expect Cecily's response, either: a smiling-smirk.

Cecily looked at her, still smirking while smiling, but Naomi recognized anxiety creeping into her eyes and posture.

"I have the Drifters' 'White Christmas' on pause. Plus, some other 'conversation starters.' ...But only if you're ready, Cecily."

Her patient lifted her hand and the small bag it held. "Guess it's show-and-tell day. I have my notes on everything."

Unrequested but that was fine; she'd blocked the day for Cecily.

"I know you didn't ask me to bring this, but, as you know, things have happened since the ball, and I just want to share what's in here."

Naomi held her gaze. "Do we even need—?"

Cecily shook her head. "No. Thank you for all this, but it isn't necessary. I know what happened to me. I know...*who* happened to me. Okay? Like I said: it's been several days of revelation." Her gaze turned pleading but angry. "But I've made vows. ...I want to forgive. ...I think. Forgive and make it work. ...I think."

Naomi heard how much she didn't want to do either of those, but Cecily had to get there. "So, let's make today a potpourri day. The rest of the day is yours, so use as little or as much of that time as you need."

Cecily gave a semi-smile. "What *I* need."

"I realize that's a concept seven-years foreign, but yes: *your* needs are the focus here."

Cecily returned a cautious headshake. "Naomi..."

"We'll get there. Where do you want to start?"

"I...I don't want a plan."

"Random discussion it is." Naomi sipped her Henney-tea and gestured at the seating. "If you'll pardon the bloody fabrics..."

Her patient uttered a brief, sardonic laugh. She rested a few of Naomi's props across the arm before sitting on the loveseat.

Naomi gestured at her desk. "Can I interest you in any refreshment: gingerbread, burned bacon...?"

Cecily Edana Jamison reclined against the loveseat, howling with laughter—then dropped to the floor, curled into a ball and screaming.

Trained to expect the unexpected, Naomi put her tea down and lowered to the floor with Cecily as she had that session before Christmas. Cecily hadn't succumbed to a PTSD occurrence in her office since then, but the manifestation was similar: Naomi believed Cecily's cowering on the floor mirrored her circumstances two Christmases ago. "It is *now*, Cecily. Daylight in *February*. Naomi's office. Morning."

Eyes tight, Cecily trembled and rocked on the floor, voicing multiple phrases from different people that night. The vulgar words and phrases spewing from docile Cecily's mouth (words and phrases used referencing the naked, beaten, and bleeding woman lying on the floor in front of a Christmas tree two years ago) might have shocked a layperson, but Naomi was far from shocked. She continued offering Cecily the grounding litany of current time and place, now also interspersed with a question or two. "What was in the closet?"

Cecily shook her head fast and hard: she didn't want to discuss the closet. She uttered these masculine grunts mixed in with more vulgarity: the sounds those men made while raping her.

Cecily started crying, whispering Marcus's name with a moan of mourning; she believed him dead. She cried harder, apologizing to Chelsea because she couldn't get to her.

On the floor with Cecily (but keeping her distance), Naomi now listened to her praying.

Cecily then mentioned metallics, iron, and The Gingerbread Man.

Something about an Exxon station? Naomi made mental note: she'd ask about that connection later.

"It is *now*, Cecily. Daylight in *February*. Naomi's office. *Morning*. Focus on any names, Cecily."

Instead of listing names, Cecily sang. She sang parts of "White Christmas" by the Drifters, not at all off-key, but with a loneliness and raw despair conveying how broken and bloodied she was on that floor two years ago. Cecily's pain was palpable; Naomi winced.

Cecily went silent. And then, eyes tight, still trembling but no longer rocking, she rattled off activities—and this time, Naomi reared back, eyes wide. In a detached tone, Cecily instructed herself to: deactivate alarm, leave duct tape on dining room table, separate everybody.

Silence echoed once again.

"It is *now*, Cecily. Daylight in *February*. Naomi's office. *Morning.*"

Cecily's eyes fluttered open. She stared, wayward breathing settling.

Naomi pulled an accent pillow from the sofa and edged it in Cecily's direction. When her patient reached for it and hugged the pillow close, Naomi knew she was back with her.

Cecily stared ahead. "I know why this happened to me."

"But, for the life of you, you have no idea why this happened to you."

Cecily's eyes found Naomi's and stayed there, brimming with misgiving as she nodded. "For the longest time, I believed some bad omen followed me, that some...some *weakness* in my person sent that misery my way by some cosmic default. After it happened, I was stuck on wanting to know why *me*, you know?"

"I do. It's a natural human response."

Cecily shrugged but remained on the floor, hugging the pillow. "I would never, ever wish what happened to me on someone else. But part of that wondering *why* it happened, was trying to get a fix on what I could've done to prevent it—"

"You can't p—"

"I know. But...," Cecily sat up, "you try to work that out for yourself."

"Sure." Naomi sat up with her, noting the mild flare-up of rosacea. With all that's happened, it was likely stress-induced.

"And now I can stop blaming myself. Because there's a *whom* to be punished for what happened."

"Several 'whoms.'"

Cecily closed her eyes. "This sucks, Naomi."

"Raw eggs. I know. But you want to get to the other side."

She opened her eyes, her gaze steady but fearful. "And it's all wrapped up in there together."

"It is, Cecily, yes." Naomi adjusted her posture on the floor, sitting back against the sofa. "What was in the closet?"

Frowning, Cecily stiffened and hugged the pillow. She shook her head. "Not sure. Nothing. ...One of their jackets or something."

She was pushing away that memory, lying about it. "Cecily, I understand your desire to avoid that hurtful memory. I get it; it's only natural. You've allowed so many other hurtful ones to push through. But numbing yourself to this one, pushing that memory into the recesses of your mind... It will only allow PTSD symptoms to worsen. Eventually, whatever it is you're wanting to shut out will return—maybe with a vengeance. Neither of us wants that. Work with me, Cecily. Let's both get the power and control back...with you."

Cecily stared at her. Finally, she shifted her posture to sit straighter against the loveseat and nodded.

"Cool. Now, you already have the memory front-and-center but don't want it to pass your lips."

Cecily's nod held a painful sadness.

"Okay. Slow and steady. Not the whole thing unless you want to give it, and we can stop whenever you're ready, but *try*; that's all I ask."

"I got you."

Naomi assessed their positions on the floor. "Think I should conduct all my sessions like this?"

Cecily's laughter in response was short of shrill. "Maybe!" She laughed some more, the shrillness element decreasing.

Naomi smiled, waiting for Cecily's laughter to subside.

Her patient began rising from the floor to sit on the loveseat. "The knife they stabbed me with came from the closet. Come on..."

"So much for 'slow and steady.'" Naomi rose and reached for her tea before sitting in her counsel chair.

"I know. Everything's just so crazy for me right now. I didn't want you to 'process' me. It's better if—"

"If it's random potpourri today."

"Yeah. I'm sor—" She stopped her apology with a grin.

"Very good. ...And I don't 'process' people."

Cecily's smile was broad. "True. But I couldn't find a better way to—"

"Yeah, yeah, heard it all before."

They chuckled together, Naomi waiting for the next random topic on Cecily's mind. She'd had the PTSD occurrence; freed key memories and internalized them. It was best they move away from the home invasion—and reevaluate if necessary. Some therapists would press for further exploration, would *process*. Naomi wasn't one of those doctors.

Random potpourri session work today was ideal—because oftentimes "random" wasn't so random after all.

Cecily fiddled with the pillow fringe. "He says *I'm* critical, but he's the critical one."

No need to identify who *he* was.

Cecily turned her attention to the bookcase. She frowned. "Didn't use to be, though. He had a good heart, was positive..." Her frown deepened. "But then, his sensitivity chip went missing; sympathy and support from him became this...this..." Cecily sighed, "constant antagonism and disdain for everything I did." She turned back to Naomi. "I tried talking to him about how things were changing. Tried keeping us on that good track. I still try. But all I'd get back, *all* I get back, is him twisting my words or trivializing them." She chuckled, not kindly. "Or, I'd get nothing back: just him staring at me as if I were a child who should know better."

Cecily didn't want an ordered plan for this session; she wanted a potpourri of topics flowing at random. But, because her patient's internal-self battled for control again, the source of that internal conflict would make today's session pretty centralized.

"Geez, Naomi: the fear, the sadness. The periods of being unable to move for—" Cecily gazed at her. "Always anxious. *Always.* And then sometimes being so numb—"

Naomi didn't interrupt or attempt to finish Cecily's sentences: Cecily was moving through a modified breakthrough—about her marriage—not the PTSD suffered after the home invasion.

Cecily sounded this sighing-hiccup of both relief and distress. "Days...*Days* I thought would be good ones...wouldn't be. I miss Roland." That random confession was a good one.

Naomi remained silent, offering support without words...and noting there was still no stutter (hadn't been one for weeks now).

She lifted her hands with another shrug and headshake. "Guess it's not that bad. I'm...I'm reading too much into things, being paranoid. It's how I can get someti—"

"Stop, Cecily. Don't do that. That's Oscar talking."

Cecily stared at her fingers fiddling with the fringe. "...And Janyce."

Interesting, but it made sense. Naomi wasn't sure there was malice behind Janyce's; she likely made similar statements out of attempts to be supportive. "Can I tell you a story?"

Cecily nodded without looking up.

Naomi sipped her tea and began. "This is a tale about Jamison Doe and Brooks Doe: two very different people who believed they were identical twins. They ignored Jamison being decades older, having been around long before Brooks showed up. And while they wanted to be identical, they just weren't. Jamison was sharp, witty, fun-loving, and decisive, while Brooks, although just as sharp and intelligent, barely laughed, was a worrywart, and took forever making simple decisions. The girls married, and those marriages only emphasized how different they were. Jamison's marriage, while not perfect, was a partnership mixing trust, love, and friendly cooperation to grow their lives and family together. But Brooks's marriage..." Naomi shook her head with a tsk. "It suffered after the first year together, filled with many one-sided compromises, fragmentation, and deception. Brooks could never win an argument and was often humiliated; her values, needs, and beliefs pushed to the side in favor of the husband's. Brooks lost a lot of her autonomy. Jamison did her best to help Brooks, still tries to help her, but..." Naomi shook her head again (no tsk). "Problem is, they still believe they're identical."

Cecily didn't look up. "And the moral of the story is...?"

Naomi didn't answer.

Her patient nodded at her fingers working the pillow fringe. She looked up. "I made vows."

"Detective Saunders have any updates on the case?" This redirection was a plant question: get her patient thinking about justice for herself.

Cecily shook her head. "I...I don't even ask anymore. It's not that I don't care. Just..." She shrugged. "But now..." She poured some water and took a long swig.

Mission accomplished. Naomi held in a smile. "So, how's work? Any recent spa days?" In Tuesday's phone counsel, Cecily hinted at a new wrinkle between her and Joshua, such that Cecily entertained leaving her job. Cecily didn't go into detail, but Naomi sensed this extra complication, this "wrinkle," was beneficial, not detrimental. Naomi calmed her patient down, convincing her not to make any rash decisions, to which Cecily agreed.

Cecily set her cup down and looked at her. "I'm taking a few days off again. Need to—"

"Take a break to regroup. Gotcha."

"Yeah. ...Haven't been to the spa in a while, though. Why do you ask? What's so special about the spa days?"

"Well, with those spa days, Joshua's helping without realizing it. Muscle relaxation and deep breathing, in tandem with the body massages and aromatherapy, is conducive to reducing anxiety...and anger."

"Oh."

"Does Oscar bake?"

"Boy, you're taking 'random potpourri' to the hilt, aren't you?" Cecily's smile was warm.

"Does he?"

"Never." Her eyes widened with something Naomi attributed to recognition, a lightbulb going off. Now her eyes narrowed. "He *never* bakes. ...Except once." She went quiet, her expression pondering.

Naomi indulged Cecily's introspection, having something else special she wanted to use for the session.

"What's your compass, Naomi? Where're you pointing, spiritually?"

"All directions."

Cecily pushed a smile up one-half her face.

Naomi chuckled. "I combine concepts of religions and classic philosophers; the parts that feel right, feel...*Godly* to me. Keeping in mind that it's all pointing to the same Absolute."

Cecily stared at her a few seconds before giving a slow, thoughtful nod. "Makes sense. ...Josh is agnostic." Sounded like she was, too—now.

"Theist or atheist?"

"Oh, definitely theist." Naomi all but heard her add: *like me.*

Silence followed.

Cecily looked around her office, focusing on the different Christmassy home-invasion symbols Naomi set up. Naomi had to admit, although festive, her office was quite somber—even with the twinkling Christmas lights on the tree. "How'd I get here...?"

Yes, that was the question. "Lie back, Cecily."

Cecily put on this smirking-grin. "*That* cliché? Seriously?" Her demeanor had this casual, witty friendliness Naomi recognized as truer than not.

"And close your eyes. How's that?"

Chuckling, Cecily reclined—and closed her eyes.

"Deep breaths."

Cecily nodded and breathed deeply.

Naomi reached over to the recorder on the table and pressed *Play*.

Seconds later, Cecily startled at hearing Oscar's voice, her own voice, and Naomi's, as she listened to playback from the sessions with Oscar.

Naomi watched Cecily's facial expressions change (eyes closed), moving through different reactions to what she listened to (sans Oscar's presence and, thus, his influence). There were times, during parts of the sessions focused on recall of the home invasion, that Cecily shook her head in response to things Oscar said about the event, and that was Naomi's whole point of the exercise.

Naomi edited the sessions, eliminating the periods of silence, but it was still a good half-hour before she pressed *Stop*. She watched Cecily take slow, even breaths. When she opened her eyes, tears fell. "God, can't I stop crying about it for *once*?!"

"You're no crybaby, Cecily. Emotional tears have purpose. Don't trip."

Cecily stared at the ceiling. She wiped her eyes with a chuckle. "'Don't trip.' Coming from you, that's comical." She sat up and finger-combed her hair, setting it right again with a trace of mania about it that (sadly) was ingrained. She gestured toward the recorder. "I sound so...pitiful."

Again, Naomi recognized she now interacted with the truer Cecily. The days alone at the Omni Shoreham Hotel already began working small wonder. "Not 'pitiful,' Cecily."

"Larimore's out." She smiled a little-girl smile.

"You told me. He's looking to stay local...?"

"Yes. Kyle's coming in a couple weeks. I'm so looking forward to it."

"I can tell." Naomi gestured at the bag on the center table: the bag with the notes. "Still want to explore what's in there?"

Cecily shook her head, looking stricken. "I'm— I need more time, I guess." She echoed a heavy sigh. "I don't know what to do."

"You made vows."

Her patient nodded. "And I'm still alive. It was 'unsuccessful,'" Cecily spoke that quote with bitter, hurtful disgust, but then tried to brighten how she sounded. "So, there's still hope. Right?" The newer Cecily pushed through more now.

Naomi stood. "Come with me..." She went to the closet and looked back at Cecily, waving her over.

Cecily soon stood beside her, staring at the closed door. "What?"

Naomi opened the closet door, revealing a full-length mirror attached to the back. She inched away until only Cecily's reflection remained in the mirror. Naomi returned to her chair, leaving Cecily at the mirror alone. "Let the smoke clear while you gaze in that mirror, Cecily. Take your time. See yourself."

Naomi didn't know if Cecily ever "saw" herself in that mirror, but it was a good ten minutes before her patient stepped away from it. She sat and looked out the window, blindly reaching for the accent pillow she often used for emotional comfort. The minutes passed. "...There's an explanation, Naomi. A reason for him having that stuff. Maybe he's waiting for the right time to turn it in to the police." The truer Cecily winced at the stupidity of that statement, but the newer Cecily fought just as hard. She shook her head, her gaze outside. "He wouldn't, Naomi. I'm good to him, Doctor Alexander. He wouldn't do that to me. Oscar's not the type of man to do something so..." She was in full-mode defense mechanism: denial.

It had nothing to do with her being good to him—and Oscar *was* that type of man. Naomi saw a similar realization and belief of that in Cecily's eyes. But the implications of what they were discussing (but not voicing) proved difficult for Cecily to reconcile and accept. Denial helped contravene the codes of reality the id adhered to.

People were born with natural, built-in defense mechanisms they employed subconsciously throughout their lives. It helped one cope with life's traumas on an unconscious scale. Cecily didn't show any signs of infantile regression (thank God), but there was still some cognitive dissonance and denial rationalization happening. She's built these defense mechanisms over the last six-plus years to counter the wounds of Oscar's relationship abandonment and rejection. Cecily didn't manifest infantile maladaptive behavior, but the minimal trauma bonding between them still worked to Oscar's advantage.

Twenty-one minutes later, Naomi sat at her desk, staring at her laptop screen, unsure how to document the session.

Kevin was cooking dinner tonight. Naomi had the day off, Kevin didn't, and since neither felt like going out yesterday, by default, she was grocery shopping for the ingredients for his planned Ghanaian dish. Kevin wanted some hwentea spice to add a nutmeggy-spicy kick to the stew; the challenge was upon her—because the store he relied on for his ingredients was out of hwentea.

She'd tried two stores with no results. It was a cold thirty-nine de-grees; three strikes, and Kevin was out (of luck). Feeling hopeful, she drove her silver X5 to this village of shops representing various cultures on the outskirts of northwest DC, near the Maryland line.

Standing in the spice aisle of Ethiopian Tagine, Naomi selected the smallest container of hwentea and heard a familiar voice in the next aisle (featuring unique stone-ground grains).

"Yes, Marcus, they have it. Picking it up now." It was Cecily.

Naomi eased in the direction of her voice. When she reached the grain aisle, Cecily was already off the phone and headed to the front. Naomi caught up and tapped her shoulder. "What's cooking?"

Cecily startled but turned with a big smile. "What in the world?! Hi!"

Eleven minutes later, culinary purchases in hand, they sat in a Star-bucks, each sipping servings of chai tea latte while Cecily caught her up on events since their last session. Naomi learned Cecily still hadn't returned to JAH Technologies, Inc. but planned to return midweek. She and Joshua were on good terms and talked every day, the "wrinkle" downplayed. Naomi knew she liked that Joshua, for good reason; he was a very understanding man. Cecily checked out of the Omni and now stayed with Marcus, under the guise that Marcus's place was bigger and that Chelsea was recouping there with Cecily's help. Chelsea was fine and in her own home near Bowie State's campus, but Cecily had to do what she had to do. Naomi wasn't mad at her.

Cecily sipped and looked around the café. "I'll have to return in the next day or so, though; it's been a week. Oscar's been patient, supportive, but..." She didn't sound like she trusted that patience and support at all.

"Have Larimore go back with you."

Cecily nodded, her lips bent with consideration of that before she shrugged and shook her head. "It's probably better if I go alone. Moe is no Oscar fan, and they've already had one run-in. Moe didn't tell me the details, but I know my brother—especially when it concerns me—and he's just been released, so..."

Naomi was no Oscar fan, either, so she liked hearing that, liked this Larimore. "Why 'Moe'?"

"Three Stooges. When he was little, he was sorta mean; too often, tried bossing Kyle and me around. Plus, people calling him 'Lari*mo*.'"

Two notes of a chuckle left Naomi's lips. "Okay."

"Yeah..." Cecily dressed casually in a becoming black sweater with peacock-blue slacks, and although she had a heavy coat, she again didn't have hat nor scarf.

"Where's your hat, Cecily? Scarf and gloves? It's freezing." Naomi touched her own gloves resting on the table.

Cecily looked away. "...I watched it again."

Naomi was good; her patient needn't clarify. Cecily watched the movie *Gaslight* again. Kyle gave her a copy years ago, but Cecily had rejected the implication. Naomi's mention of the movie at the charity ball prompted a similar response. "Is that still not what this is?"

After long seconds, Cecily turned to her. "You tell me."

And so, an impromptu session was upon them.

Patients often wanted therapy entailing answers and instructions on how to proceed; they didn't enjoy exploring root causes, too impatient for it. Naomi, however, considered Cecily's case especially pressing.

Some chase-cutting was fine. "From what I've observed in your sessions, with and without Oscar, your marriage is an example of Narcissistic Abuse Syndrome, Cecily, or NAS for short. Using the common vernacular: *gaslighting*. In these relationships, out of an ego-driven need to bend them to their will, the narcissistic partner uses different techniques to subtly harass their unknowing partner mentally and emotionally, occasionally physically. Although certain traits make some people easier targets for it than others, there is no classic profile of the victim. Anyone can become a victim of NAS, regardless of age, education level, gender. It's not restricted to marriages, either: it can be between siblings, coworkers, friends, between parents and children..."

Cecily made an odd expression at that last, solidifying Naomi's belief Cecily experienced some narcissistic abuse in the relationship with her mother. She checked her watch.

"Have to go?"

"No, no. The day is mine. I...I want to do this."

Naomi surveyed the place: Starbucks was busy. She regarded Cecily. "This isn't very private. Doctor-patient—"

"These people don't know us and aren't paying attention. We can be discreet." Her gaze intensified. "We're here. I want to do this."

Naomi nodded; her day was wide-open, too. "Okay. Still, let's try to find something less centralized..."

Cecily grinned. "Let's."

They found a table less central to the busy.

Cecily adjusted her seat. "There. This is good. So, finish telling me."

Naomi cleared her throat. She then spoke low but enough for Cecily to hear. "Okay. Your circumstances for finding yourself with NAS are key to your situation because your inner personality wouldn't normally be susceptible. But hereafter, you must avoid possibility of re-victimization because, as it happens, Oscar has primed you for future entrapment."

Cecily gasped, and Naomi stopped herself from adding: if she didn't end up with Joshua (who didn't have the outward traits indicating taking narcissistic advantage of her). Anyone *else* too soon after Oscar would leave her vulnerable.

Cecily stared into her cup. "...But it's been good at times. Or...really good at first..." She sighed, shaking her head with sad reflection. "Until it's not..." Cecily's eyes found Naomi's. "And it's 'not' at the weirdest times, to where I can never get a handle on—can't understand...what I do wrong to bring out that meanness so...*often*."

"Well, yeah." But Cecily was searching for answers Oscar didn't even have, because narcissists didn't need any specifics: vague and implied threats to their egos, to their sense of control, were enough.

"Oscar holds such rancor. I think it's having wasted away his twenties and thirties instead of going the route his sister and brother did."

Naomi shrugged. "Possibly a factor."

"He...He has such extremes in behavior: highs and lows making him overreact to trivial things. He'll get pissed over something small, but his weird sense of humor will have him belly-laughing over things that aren't funny at all." She frowned, rolling her eyes with an irritation that was good to see. "Oscar has serious mythomaniac tendencies, too. And he has this strange preoccupation with product sizes and prices..." She turned away, muttering toward the registers: "I don't know why he's so concerned; he doesn't pay for anything."

Naomi bit her bottom lip.

"He's a spitter, too. Not that distance thing guys do, hawk-spitting, but, ugh! he sits around spitting into containers..." Her eyes darted around the café, focusing with annoyance on the men present. "And he farts using no type of—" Cecily put her head to her hand with a deep sigh of frustration.

Naomi filled in "manners" for her. Much like Louise going on about the many things she adored about Rick Phillips, Cecily now riffed on quite the opposite about her husband, opening up about some unpleasant things she endured.

"He has the nerve to insult *my* mothering skills when he and Keisha have the most unfilial relationship I've ever seen. God!" Cecily looked up from her hand, her brown-not-hazel eyes piercing. "And he's been calling me 'Cecil' or 'Cesspool' more since you told him not to do it in your office. Although he tries to perpetrate like he's using them as terms of endearment, they're insults in and of themselves: 'Cecil' because he says I'm masculine, not feminine... And 'Cesspool'..." She scoffed. "Well, that doesn't need explanation, does it?"

"You're all lady, Cecily. You...You wouldn't have that 'wrinkle' with Joshua if you weren't feminine."

Cecily blushed but then waved a hand dismissively, settling more into her truer, stronger self. She leaned on the table, speaking in a conspiratorial tone. "But what he's not getting is: using those names more is only making me immune to having my feelings hurt when he does it." She sat back. "It's a small thing."

"But big."

Cecily nodded and picked up her cup. "Round nine: *Cecily*—not Mister Hyde." Her eyes turned cautious, embarrassed. She used the moniker with ease, with familiarity as if with regularity, and now looked at Naomi as if caught doing something wrong.

Naomi wasn't shocked or bothered and so smirked and sipped her chai tea latte accordingly, and Cecily relaxed at seeing her response.

Cecily sipped her chai, setting the cup down with a sigh and curious frown. "How is that couple from your table: the 'Lady Blue' couple?"

Naomi grinned, as mention of those two made her do often. "They're fine."

"They're *gorgeous,* is what they are. Children?"

"Girl, twelve. Two-year-old son."

Cecily nodded appreciatively. "More of the same, no doubt."

Naomi chuckled in answer.

"How old are they? How long have they been married?" She sounded pressed for the information, but not in a nosy way.

Naomi looked at her.

"I know. It's just something about them."

"She's forty-two. He's forty. Married eighteen years."

"*Really?* Thought they were much younger."

"Good for them."

Cecily grinned. "I know, right?" Another question filled her eyes, but she hesitated posing it. "If you don't mind me asking, what's your friend's name?"

Naomi didn't mind. "Kevin."

"He's handsome."

"No argument here."

Cecily smiled but grew serious, staring into her now half-empty cup. "...What do you think about emotional infidelity, Naomi? Or about fantasizing about someone, not your spouse; how you're not supposed to even think about another person *in that way...?*"

"Well, they're called 'fantasies' for a reason—and it's all in your mind. Emotional 'infidelity,' too, happens within the conscience; if you're in love with someone and nobody knows it but you, and God, of course, who's to say? It's not something anyone can know about unless you reveal it. Anent the sexes, the bias is organic: women get more hyped over their partner having feelings for someone else. In contrast, men focus on the traditional meaning of infidelity, based on the territorial violation of the sex act and another man having what's 'his.' Emotional infidelity is 'new' relative to history; people making a basic concept more complicated—because human beings are complicated, I guess. Ultimately, it's a judgmental thing: of people wanting to get inside your head, attempting to control something they can't. I say, keep it to your-

self, work through it, and move toward resolution—whatever that is."
She shrugged. "But that's just me." Thoughts of Louise surfaced. "Now,
if you're *fixating*, that's something else altogether."

Cecily nodded thoughtfully.

"Regarding sexual fantasies..." Naomi hesitated. Being a private person was an understatement, but Cecily needed something intangible
from this discussion. Naomi didn't mind sharing if it would help.

Cecily leaned forward with lifted brow, waiting, and Naomi saw
the hunger and pleading for information; it allowed her to plunge
ahead. "I'm going to share something with you. There's a man I'm close
friends with—like family. He's gorgeous, Cecily. I mean, you-can-hard-
ly-breathe-he's-so-fine gorgeous."

"Finer than *'Lady Blue' dude at your table?*" She sounded incredulous.
Cecily shook her head. "Whew, Lord!"

Naomi smiled inside at hearing confirmation ranking Rick an eleven
was valid.

"And he probably knows it, too."

Naomi shook her head. "No. That's the thing. This man, as sexy and
fine as he is, is wholly unaware, wholly unassuming; he couldn't care less
about his looks. And he's *good* people, Cecily. I can't stress that enough:
sweet, funny, caring, generous, good heart..."

"Sounds too good to be true."

"He's not perfect. Of course not. But, well, he gives perfection a run
for its money." Naomi looked at Cecily pointedly. "There *are* people
in the world who fall into such a category. That's a *good thing*, Cecily.
Keeps the good-v-evil scales tipping favorably."

Cecily smiled her agreement, comic-book fan that she was. "True."

"Anyway, he's married, considers me a sister. But sometimes, *sometimes*, I still fantasize having a good twenty-five minutes with him."

Cecily chuckled with a scoff. "You mean a good *five* minutes, don't
you? And if he's as gorgeous as you say, he likely can't...you know..." she
looked around sheepishly, "...fuck." She straightened her posture.

"So, you think: the hotter the looks, the colder the sheets."

Cecily nodded with a grin of appreciation. "I like that one. Something
like that, yeah."

"Well, truthfully speaking, three to five minutes of intercourse is
within normal range. I'm talking about the actual friction of penis inside

vagina, not 'making love.' Jokes about a man lasting only minutes only perpetuate the myth that intercourse should last for extremely long periods. A man with exceptional control can last longer than five minutes, stretching it past ten, but not always."

"Because that part's really about procreation."

"Yes. Sex has become about 'making love,' but it's *mating*—just like with lower animals. Sex has evolved for humans, but the basic scientific mechanics remain: friction of penis in vagina stimulates ejaculation; Mister Sperm might meet Miss Egg, and if so, forty weeks later..."

Cecily chuckled.

"Of course, there's also friction of the penis with other things, but we'll leave that wherever it is."

Cecily giggled with a nod. "Right."

"Friction in the vaginal passage can also become uncomfortable when it goes too long—without lubrication. And five minutes is longer than we think. Try holding your breath underwater for five minutes. Mind you: brain damage can begin after only *three* minutes without oxygen."

Cecily sipped her tea. "Point made. Never thought of it like that."

Naomi grinned; she liked Cecily.

"So, back to your 'crush.' *Twenty-five* minutes?" Cecily's eyes held disbelief, but Naomi also saw excitement at being able to talk freely.

Naomi nodded. "Now, I'm referring to 'making love,' and, trust me: twenty-five minutes, Cecily. This man, he's...attentive. He's...*talented*—because he gets what the female enjoys about physical contact with the male. He's good, and I mean, *extraordinarily good* in the feathers—before he even gets to the mating part of things...and he's one of those with that *exceptional control* I mentioned, able to make it last."

Cecily returned this appraising look, again revealing more of the real Cecily. "And how do *you* know?"

"I'm close with his wife, too. And, let's be clear: *she* can throw down in the bedroom as well, leaving her husband breathless. She doesn't give play-by-play, but she shares enough. They've been married nearly twenty years, and just looking at them, you know it's still on and poppin' in their bedroom. But now, please understand, Kevin's *very good*."

Cecily raised an eyebrow. "And we're not talking about the Lady Blue couple from your table?" They were, but thankfully, Cecily continued without waiting for reply. "Because you could tell with them."

Naomi nodded, not wanting to reveal they were talking about the same people.

"Between you and me? I know I wouldn't mind a few good minutes with *him*. With his looks, you'd think the bed must be a *glacier*! But watching him with his wife, just looking at them together: you can tell she gets plugged right."

Naomi reared back with warm surprise. "Cecily!"

"Sorry. I'm just saying. He's..." Cecily grunted softly, then shrugged with this reflective, admiring-flirty-yet-bashful smile.

Naomi resisted chuckling; Rick was causing problems with women he didn't even know. "What about Joshua?"

The blush in response was fierce. "Well, yes. Josh is..."

"So, there's nothing wrong with a little fantasy, Cecily. We all do it."

After a pause, Cecily chuckled, holding her cup at her mouth. "What?"

Cecily sipped. "Nothing. Just...'good in the feathers'..."

"An old-time expression, I know, but—"

"No. I like it. It's classy to me."

"Thanks. I try." Cecily's snicker prompted Naomi's next question. "So, who makes you laugh, Cecily? Besides me, that is. Who makes you just holler, it's so funny?"

"You ask the most out-of-nowhere questions."

"They're not, really. Who makes you laugh?"

Cecily solidified her gaze. "Laughter isn't something I've been persistently familiar with in a long time, but..." An eyelid flutter, however, suggested someone came to mind for those times she did laugh. Cecily started to answer but desisted. She shrugged. "Different people."

"Joshua?"

Cecily nodded.

"Okay. Laughter is good for the soul—no matter the source. Are you in love with him?"

It took good seconds, but Cecily tilted her head in the affirmative. "Slept with him?"

"No. I wouldn't do that. I've..." Her brow furrowed with internal uneasiness. "I've thought about him that way, though."

"The 'fantasizing.'"

Smirking, Cecily nodded, putting her cup down.

"Is Joshua in love with you?"

Cecily hesitated.

"If you know, you *know*, Cecily. Don't be afraid...or ashamed of it. Does he love you, too?"

"Yes. Very deeply, I think."

"Do you want to be with Oscar?" Kill-shot question.

Cecily scoffed. "We haven't been *together* in years, Naomi. Not from an emotionally connected standpoint. But we made vows."

"So you keep stressing. Cecily, 'for worse' doesn't mean sacrificing your well-being, your *essence*. It means you agree to stick together when times are hard, and hell, that's still only if you can. But a 'for worse' created on purpose because of mistreatment and ill-will?" Naomi shook her head. "I don't believe that's what God intended marriage to be about. From a spiritual perspective, that makes little sense to me."

Cecily nodded, looking less uncomfortable, but somber.

"Those vows must go *both ways*, Cecily. Both ways. Oscar isn't honoring you, cherishing you—other than cherishing what you represent and provide materially. His 'keeping' manifests as keeping you down. Oscar continues to geld you mentally, emotionally, for his narcissistic reasons, but also to gain your gelt, Cecily."

Cecily scoffed, nostrils flared. "Yeah, but Odessa's told me he maligns me and my wealth to her and Otis every chance he gets."

That sounded about right. "He displays an insouciance toward you that's tragic. If Oscar isn't abiding by his vows...?"

Cecily's gaze remained steady, but she didn't respond.

Naomi changed course. "Joshua's a cutie."

Cecily brightened. "Oh, yes. He's from Cleveland, too." That seemed an *out-of-nowhere* comment.

"Did you know each other, then? Run in the same circles?"

Cecily giggled as she shook her head and reached for her cup. "Cleveland, *Ohio*." She laughed then, just cracked up at something Naomi determined was a personal joke between her and Mr. Hall. Naomi contained her own chuckle watching her patient as Cecily's laughter died. "Am I just drawn to Josh because of the unhappiness in my marriage? Would any man look desirable compared to Oscar?"

Naomi sent her gaze around Starbucks. "Well, look around. You're still unhappy in your marriage. Ready to start a new life with any of the men in here? And, truthfully, Oscar isn't a bad-looking man by any stretch. Do any of these men make Oscar look like...a cesspool?"

Cecily smirked.

"Your boss could very well not be right for you. But the heart and mind *know*, Cecily. The *spirit* knows. *You* know."

A smile teased around Cecily's lips. "Anyway, Josh doesn't say he's my boss. He says he just owns the shop—I run it. So, it's more like we're—"

"Partners." Naomi smiled, noting the significance of her regularly using "Josh."

Cecily nodded shyly.

"And there's been nothing sexual between you."

"Well, I sorta kissed him, a peck to his lips..."

"I said, *sex*, Cecily. You know: tongues thrashing; his erection or your breasts exposed; five, maybe seven minutes of *mating*...?"

Cecily offered a smirking-grin before shaking her head. "Then, no. It's all gut emotion and sense of connection and attraction, but..." She exhaled and pressed her lips together.

"Go 'head. Let it out."

"...But I want him, Naomi. I do. I want to lie with him and do things I haven't thought about since Roland. Then, too, I want to sit with him and talk and hold him and care for him and grow together with him...and...and *laugh* with him. The thing is, I feel it coming back my way. We've been friends four years, the amative feelings between us steadily growing."

"Without the complication or *enhancer*, if you will, of sex."

Cecily's brown eyes widened with appreciative wonder. "Yes."

"I see. Well, find Cecily. Have a heart-to-heart with her. She'll break it down, tell you what you need to know—what you really want."

"Huh? *I'm* Cecily."

Naomi raised an eyebrow. "Are you?"

Long seconds ticked by. They listened to people in pockets of conversation around the café until realization dawned in Cecily's eyes. "No. I haven't been consistently myself, consistently *me*...in years." Cecily looked at her. "Is...Is that why you've been focusing so much on my past? Getting into stuff about me *before* I moved up here?"

Naomi let her gaze answer for her.

Cecily nodded. Her gaze then intensified, but she said nothing.

"What is it?"

"I don't know. Can I ask something personal?"

"Go 'head."

Cecily's eyes widened in surprise at Naomi's immediate response.

Naomi curved her upper lip in humor. "Ask your question."

"Do...Do you close your eyes when you kiss Kevin?"

The question was odd, but Naomi liked odd and out-of-nowhere. "I do. And on the few occasions I've opened my eyes while kissing him, Kevin's eyes were closed; so he closes his when we kiss. Why?"

Cecily shook her head with a shrug. "Just asking."

She wasn't just asking, but Naomi let it go; let Cecily work out whatever that piece was on her own. She checked her watch and then texted Kevin, letting him know she had his spices for dinner tonight.

"What does it mean when people close their eyes?"

"Different things: part reflex, part emotion, part learned. Some don't close their eyes during a deep kiss."

Cecily leaned closer. "And what does *that* mean?"

"Depends on the person, so I can't say for sure."

"It's creepy." Cecily sat back. She held her now-empty cup, fiddling with it. "...Do you know, in a short thirty minutes, I can go from relaxed happiness to anxious despair? I'm not talking about my PTSD episodes."

Naomi presumed she referred to the time between leaving work and arriving home. "Sometimes, there is nothing but a fine line between despair and happiness."

Cecily stared at Naomi. "And a fine line between love and hate."

Naomi smirked. "You said it, not me."

"Isn't that a song, or movie, or...?"

"Both, but it's 'thin,' not 'fine': 'A *Thin* Line Between Love and Hate.' I'm partial to the song, but to each his own."

Cecily stared off. "Fine lines..."

Naomi watched her think.

Cecily turned to her. "Naomi, why do men need us to tell them their penises are big? I mean, it's like a lie we're indirectly forced to tell."

Naomi raised an eyebrow. "Talk about 'out-of-nowhere'..."

Cecily chuckled, but barely. She waited.

"It cuts ice with a man's esteem and confidence. Apart from your A-list porn stars, the average male erection is between five and six inches. That's it. There are some over six inches, certainly. But that 'eight-inches-and-over' category...," Naomi swallowed (with thoughts of her 'brother'), "that's more the exception to the rule, not the norm. Most men are comfortable with their erection size, but some need to tether to the illusion they're hung like a horse. Just go with it, Cecily. Suggesting or implying Oscar has a large erection helps him feel better about himself—and there's nothing wrong with helping someone feel better about themselves. You are among millions." She considered her intimate encounters with Kevin. Her man worked with a strong seven, but he never prompted her for overt size declarations during their lovemaking. That wasn't her style, anyway, so yay.

More ideas for her clinical study surfaced.

"I guess." Cecily looked away. Closing her eyes, she sighed. "God, what I wouldn't give for—"

"An orgasm? Or rather, a *male-assisted* orgasm—an MAO."

"At this rate, all it would take is a long, warm hug of sincere affection."

"Affection encourages sensory sensitivity and physical intimacy; something you haven't had since Roland—not in its truest form. The heart and mind, the *spirit*, Cecily: they're craving it. People need people." She watched Cecily's profile. "...Speaking of affection, as an extension of some form of love, I've observed that Oscar doesn't express his love for you with sincerity. He doesn't say the words, *I love you*, and what he says is devoid of emotion and lacks eye contact. That's him. By contrast, you can express it using the words with some emotion and eye contact. Still, I must ask: Do you love him, Cecily? We know what I'm talking about here."

The shouldn't-have-been-there hesitation stretched into additional seconds.

"Nuff said."

"So, what do I do?"

"If you're stuck on the 'made vows' aspect, you're devoting yourself to Oscar, despite all you've learned. Okay. First, as we're talking about affection and sex: stop faking orgasms. Guide him regarding your arousal prompts. Teach him how to bring you off—without bruising his ego and thus causing more stress for yourself." She'd hold-off discussing masturbation for later.

"He doesn't care."

Saying that sentence aloud should have brought all kinds of messages home, but multiple influences were at play here. Naomi wanted to tell Cecily her efforts would be for naught, but couldn't.

Cecily stared outside. "And I don't need to fake orgasms, Naomi. Oscar doesn't require nor encourage my participation," she tucked her upper lip in with furrowed brow, "just mounts me and..."

Naomi knew her next (pitiful and painful) words and said them for her: "'Does his bidness.'" That expression was doubtless an old one (going back centuries)—but nothing classy about it (or use of the word, *mount*).

Cecily's shame-filled nod echoed something worse than pitiful. Still staring outside, she now shook her head. "It does no good to push or complain."

"But sometimes you must, Cecily. So, second, which is really *first*: address how he mistreats you. Address...what he *did*." Her annoyance, impatience, and incredulity began conflating into anger, and she wished for some Henney or Belvi. Restriction on her role in helping get that crime solved pissed her off, too.

"You're so upset with me, Naomi. I hear it. But people are inherently good. You know that. Even Oscar."

"But not about *all* things, Cecily. Anomalies exist for a reason. And the 'upset' you hear is not with you." Needing to step away for a second, Naomi stood. "Ordering another. You?"

Cecily nodded.

Naomi went to the register and ordered two chai tea lattes, feeling calmer when she returned. She placed Cecily's cup in front of her. "Here you go."

"Tell me more about NAS."

Naomi looked at her.

"Please. Just cut to the chase."

"Posthaste?" Naomi offered a sideways smile.

Cecily nodded but didn't smile back.

Naomi sat. She sipped, eyes on her patient. She gestured at Cecily's cup, encouraging her to do the same. "Let's everyone gather ourselves and our thoughts before I begin."

Nodding, Cecily used both hands to lift her cup to her mouth. Holding her cup poised, she stared out the window, sipping and gathering herself, her thoughts.

"Ready?"

Only the slightest movement of Cecily's head indicated affirmation. She held her cup (one finger stroking its exterior), sipping while staring out the window.

Oscar's first attempt on Cecily's life failed. Cecily knew about it now but remained all, vows-made-and-forgiveness. Noble. But Oscar wasn't done, and Naomi knew it. They didn't have the time for Cecily to come around and "get it" or figure everything out on her own. Cecily was 79 percent there: good enough. Naomi could get that 21 percent accomplished.

She began: "Occurrences of NAS don't have to be extreme to have severe consequences. Narcissistic abusers work subtly, using their words and actions with a bit of psychological warfare legerdemain to upset your perceptions of things, challenge your memories, erode your confidence—in yourself and your surroundings. Passive-aggressive tactics play a part, too. They may use phrases like: 'Don't be so sensitive'; 'It's all in your head' or 'imagination'; 'What is wrong with you?'; among others. It's not beyond the realm of a narcissistic abuser to do things like move items around, then deny any such thing happ—"

Cecily gasped into her cup but kept focus on the view outdoors.

Naomi continued. "To echo your point about people being inherently good: good people are also less suspicious, unable or possibly unwilling to entertain the notion of someone doing such devious, volatile things—because they can't imagine themselves doing it. Wearing these 'Pollyanna' blinders makes it easier for an abuser to cruise along undetected for years."

"Like me."

"Yes."

"...I'm jaded now, listening to this."

"Good for you."

Cecily smirked into her cup, eyes toward the window. "Go on."

"Although appearing erratic, the narcissistic abuser's approach is consistent and relentless because their victim's subsequent dependence on them for approval and assurance does nothing more than feed the abuser's ego. Once in the throes of NAS, a victim spends considerable time second-guessing everything."

Cecily gasped again.

"*But*, Cecily...I get the impression you don't do as much of it at work. You're much more on top of your game at JAH Technologies. Am I right?"

Cecily bobbed her head.

"No one goes searching for such a situation."

Brows furrowed, Cecily sipped. "So how...?"

"Pretense...and biochemistry."

"I'm listening."

"When—"

"And you can just substitute 'Oscar' and 'you' accordingly, Doctor Alexander." Cecily continued gazing out the window.

Naomi trusted Cecily would hold that listening pose until she finished her exposition. "When you two started dating, you both put your best foot forward—it's only natural. Except, in Oscar's case, it wasn't natural. His presentation was all smoke and mirrors, the only goal: to lure you in, have you 'in love.' And then he finds out how wealthy you are."

"Unreal." She then whispered, "Mendacious bastard."

"Top-o'-the-line. You said he had mythomaniac tendencies; he likely employed them to create a nice full-of-life world for you. With your own needs suffering, he had you hooked fast. Part of the excitement of falling in love comes from biochemical changes in the body. The endorphins released during this period are like a drug. That honeymoon stage is addictive; it's understandable to crave it constantly, want it to last. You were no exception. You became emotionally hooked on Oscar—the source of that 'high.'"

"Okay."

"You're experiencing something similar with Joshua."

"...But it's genuine. The 'smoke' would've cleared, the mirror reflecting the truth about him by now."

"It's genuine, yes."

Cecily nodded. "Continue."

"So, you and Oscar were doing your 'in love' thang, being independent individuals forming a couple—at *first*. But a narcissist, Oscar, needs that dependency, that control over you, to maintain a different type of endorphin-high he craved to build and sustain his ego. The script flips. It begins with critical comments about your attire, cooking, sexual inadequacies. Then it becomes a twisted version of narcissistic focus:

you must not love him because you're only worried about yourself and not giving what he needs."

Cecily's grip on her cup tightened.

"You soon became a shadow of your former self. Continuous existence under Oscar's tyranny of being controlled, battered, physically and emotionally, being subjected to his erratic rages; you're mentally drained, Cecily. Making simple decisions is a challenge. Your dignity suffers—as well as your sense of *safety*." Naomi paused.

"We've talked about feeling safe, yes."

"In *all* the ways."

"And I've lost my power of 'No.'"

"I believe you're finding it again, but mostly, yes."

Cecily nodded, her eyes directed toward the activity outside, but reading as both angry and sad. The anger would be what tipped the scales.

Naomi continued. "I'm sure you most times feel you can't do anything right around him. What's worse, you began doubting your own mind. Navigating this day after day, offered only one outlet: depression. Under his constant chastising and humiliation tactics, in time, you surrender your authentic potential, giving up who you are, your power of 'No,' to keep the peace. You're asking permission to do trivial things, begin accepting gross violations of your privacy as fine and dandy. You find your opinions...must match his. All...while your memories and perceptions are being messed with."

"Jesus, Naomi."

"Like I've been perched on your shoulder the whole time."

She gazed outside, rubbing a spot on her lower midsection.

"Physical abuse is merely used as reinforcement; the real fun is with the mental and emotional abuse. Believe it or not, it's established a bond between you."

That's when the tear fell.

"You're in the throes of NAS, but even then, you still have the sense of whom you used to be, Cecily. This dependent personality you have now is foreign despite the seeming acclimation. You still know that somewhere inside is this person fun-loving, confident, relaxed—a person *stronger*. Your middle name's 'Edana,' for crying out loud."

"Fiery, zealous." She sniffed.

"Precisely. But Oscar has trained you, yes, *trained* you, like one of Pavlov's dogs, to be someone other than your true self. Essentially, you've been de-Cecily-ized."

Cecily uttered a tiny chuckle at that, but her eyes were wet, and the chuckle was so sad. She cleared her throat and wiped the tear as she sat straighter. "So, why me? What sign did I have on my forehead?"

"As I mentioned, your true personality wouldn't have been receptive to his play. Oscar didn't meet the 'real' Cecily, for lack of a better expression. The real you would have kicked you off his radar. But he happened to meet you while you were still deep in mourning over Roland. Two teens needing a father, so you believed. You three had just moved, getting that new start in a new state."

"Classic vulnerability."

That impressed Naomi. "Pretty much. Plus, as strong as you are, you still have a bit of Pollyanna about you. You *care*. People like Oscar thrive on those who are empathetic, kind—because you're already inclined to put up with their foolishness for nothing but to make them feel better."

"Like the 'big dick' thing."

Naomi held in a chuckle. "Sure."

"...Narcissistic Abuse Syndrome. Gaslighting." The words fell from her lips in a reflective whisper.

"Yes. Narcissism has degrees and plays out in relationships in ways subtle and overt, but I call them all ROBs."

Cecily frowned toward the outdoors. "Why 'Rob'?"

"Whatever the degree, narcissists are Real Obnoxious Bastards."

Cecily cackled with a nod (a splash of latte spilling), causing heads to turn their way. "Oh, yes." She plucked a napkin from the table and blew her nose.

Naomi sat back, pleased.

"If...If I could just get us back to how we were in the beginning, Naomi. Get him well, and then get us *back* to that...that 'sweet' time."

Naomi almost choked, spraying the table with droplets of chai latte. "What?!" Their discussion had been relatively quiet within the busy café, but that response was louder. Cecily didn't sound 79 percent there (and Naomi thought she'd edged her closer to 90 percent by now). She shouldn't have been surprised by Cecily's emotional waffle, but it threw her; it did.

"I know, Naomi. *I know*. But I don't want to just throw away my marriage. Even with what I now know. Even with...Joshua." She still talked to the window, but her eyes pleaded understanding.

Naomi didn't have it. She reached for a napkin, shaking her head as she wiped the latte splotches. "You say you and Oscar need to get back to how things were *in the beginning*... Well, Cecily, you two *are* at how things were initially—because Oscar was this same person then, too. Any success you have returning to an amiable period between you will be short-lived. I *promise* you. The *sweet time* is over, Cecily. It's TLTB. Oscar's done with that part."

That made Cecily turn eyes to her. "'Done'?"

"*Done.* Your well of narcissistic supply is dry, Cecily. He's ready to move on. But not without your money. That would still provide the status, possessions, and bragging rights he craves. It's the only reason he married you."

Cecily's eyes widened, but not with shock, with...recognition. She turned back to the window.

Naomi hoped like hell she was over 79 percent there now.

"So, it's too late and too bad for the 'sweet time' to return, huh? TLTB?"

"I'd say, more too late than too bad, but yes."

Cecily faced the window, but Naomi sensed her woeful smirk.

"He...He killed someone once and got away with it."

Naomi laughed. She couldn't help it. "Really?! He said that?!"

Cecily looked at her, confused and feelings hurt.

When her laughter died, Naomi steadied her gaze on her patient. "Well, think about that, Cecily. Think hard. Unless done in the heat of some moment, killing someone and 'getting away with it' takes *work*. There's cleanup and covering up, and *disposal* to do. He doesn't even want to do the work necessary to maintain a marriage. Come on, Cecily. The operative word here is *work*. Does it seem like Oscar has done anything, *anything* more than all he's ever done?"

She turned away again. "...Not until me."

"And even then, he paid someone instead of doing it himself."

Cecily winced.

Naomi wasn't sorry. Instead of going for the jugular, she went for the "carrot" artery. "I've listened to you adopt social comparison as a defense mechanism in therapy. It's where you make light of your situation by comparing it to others in much worse scenarios."

"Oh."

"While people *are* suffering through a myriad of possibly worse situations, no amount of abuse is okay, Cecily, however 'mild' it is. *None.* No, Oscar hasn't broken your nose or arm. But he's trying to break your *mind*, Cecily, your spirit. And shit, Cecily, he tried to kill you. I know I should be speaking to you in a more imprecise way, *guiding* you but not telling you. I know, but..." But she was no longer interested in Robin-Hood's-Barn tactics; she didn't much like that part of treating people. Naomi took a quiet but deep breath. She needed to be careful. She was making the mistake of putting herself in Cecily's shoes, wanting Cecily to make the same choices she would. Her empathetic intelligence began easing beyond the professional boundaries; she had to rein it in.

"It's okay, Naomi."

Naomi shook her head with a soft scoff. "No, it isn't, Cecily. It's many things. 'Okay' isn't one of them."

She had planned this part of the therapy for closer to the end, but serendipity left them together here and, most importantly, again without Oscar. The closing piece Naomi had planned as part of her therapy approach for Cecily involved a bit of Solution-Focused Therapy. It was essential to work on the potential causes of a patient's problems, so Naomi didn't bypass it (as many solution-focused therapists did). Rather, after exposing root causes for Cecily's issues, she wanted to move her toward solving and stepping out of the mental-incapacitation box she'd put herself in.

Cecily's awareness of her husband's machinations was clearer, but a few pointed questions directed at Cecily while they sat at this table could work wonders. *Alternatives:* Cecily needed to work toward *that* as she overcame the effects of PTSD. Adding SFT onto combined CBT wasn't cookie-cutter, but Naomi didn't do cookie-cutter. With the condensed SFT session, her questions wouldn't be typical (they couldn't be), so Naomi would go about it her way. She'd pursued the Exception and Scaling approaches. Now, it was time for a Miracle...

Exception questions explored when a patient was least stressed: *I am a nutcase, except when...* Scaling questions helped a patient apply objective measurement to their level of healing, as when a doctor asks to rate pain on a scale of zero to ten: *I'd say my level of nutcase hovers around seven...* But now, the Miracle question supposes the perfect world—and asks the patient to ruminate what that would be like in terms of their mental well-being. There was no set way to ask any SFT category questions; as much imagination had to go into forming the questions as, hopefully, a patient's thought-out answer.

"I'm sorry. I said I wanted this, asked you to cut to the chase, and still, I'm acting fickle, acting unlike myself. I know what you would do, Naomi. I...I know what any person learning the things I have in these last days would do. I'm sorry."

"No, Cecily. *I'm* the one sorry. I crossed a line, and I extend my apologies. What *I* would do, or anyone *else* would do, isn't important. This is about you. Only you."

Cecily lowered her head to her hand.

"Hold that pose. Close your eyes. I'm about to...'process' you."

Cecily kept her head lowered, eyes closed and shielded by the hand supporting her head. She giggled. "Okay."

"Okay, now: you and me? We're going total fantasy with this."

Naomi watched Cecily's curious frown behind her hand. "Right..."

"Let's say real magic existed. I'm talking Harry Potter, Dumbledore, Hogwarts, muggles, quidditch, the whole bit."

Grinning, Cecily nodded, eyes closed.

"By some very real wizardry hocus-pocus, a magical, magic miracle happened while you were sleeping, erasing all remnants of Voldemort and his wicked spell of PTSD, home invasions, and NAS relationships. When you awaken, you and your life are totally on point, all problems and anxieties swept away."

"Got you."

"You there? Awake in On-Point Land?"

"I am."

"Okay. Live it, breathe it..." Naomi waited. "...Now, give me a few deets on what that first day is like for you."

Cecily did. She started her day with a run. There was a smoothie for breakfast before heading off to work. Something about Little Roland and Marcus and Chelsea. About Nina Simone, James Brown, and Peabo Bryson (she mentioned Peabo's "Reaching for the Sky" and "Let the

Feeling Flow" specifically). About reviewing financial reports and having lunch in a quiet bistro. There was Joshua, "Hadji" (no idea who that was), and Devin (her 1967 Deville). She walked her dogs, Paris and Madrid. She drank Earl Grey tea, went to the spa, had a nature walk, bought fresh flowers, read a book in the park, had peach sorbet, and overall had one of the fullest "days" Naomi ever envisioned for anyone. Cecily used up all twenty-four hours—and didn't mention Oscar.

Cecily finished speaking but held the pose, head in hand, eyes closed, for long seconds before looking at Naomi with a grin. "So, yeah."

"Sounds busy," Naomi jested. She withheld saying anything about not mentioning Oscar.

Cecily sighed as if retiring at the end of that busy-full day. "I know, right?" She smiled, her thoughts still somewhere in On-Point Land.

"Now, for next session, I want you to tell me the wizardry hocus-pocus, magical, magic miracle or spell it would take to make that happen."

Cecily's eyes lost some joy, which meant she knew the answer already; she just didn't want to face it. "Naomi..."

"Next session." Naomi paused. "And consider having Marcus or Chelsea attend. Not the next session, necessarily. Whenever you feel ready. But consider it."

"Already have. I will. Soon." Her gaze sobered. "Think I want you to talk to Chelsea, anyway. She seems fine..."

"Operative word: *seems*."

"Yes."

"Okay. Good. Your children are a branch of your support system you avoid using—but because of the NAS side of things, not the home-invasion PTSD."

Cecily stared at her with probing, semi-awed eyes. "You're a tiny woman, but that hawkshaw brain of yours..."

Naomi shrugged. "It's what I do for a living." She leaned closer to Cecily. "But use them, Cecily. They can relate to the intrusive imagery, the emotional numbing, the hyper-vigilance..."

"Am...? ...My PTSD isn't only from what happened two years ago, is it? ...You've said it's all wrapped up in there together."

"No, it isn't just from the home invasion. You're working a double-whammy, sweetie."

Cecily offered a tiny sardonic grin.

"Speaking of the home invasion..."

Cecily stiffened.

"Breathe..."

After a few deep breaths, she looked calmer. "What about it?"

"Couple things. Whom didn't you tell the shape of what? ...And do you know a Winton Hollis?"

Cecily's initial expression had Naomi thinking they would be on the floor of the Starbucks any second, but then Cecily's expression changed, looking *harder* (and the opposite of losing it). Almost a minute passed before she spoke. "My brooch: the one my mother gave me for high school graduation."

"Right. Made of opal and diamonds...and shaped like a teacup."

Cecily nodded slowly, eyes still angry or something. "I never told Janyce the shape—or the stones making it. All I *ever* said about it was that it was special, expensive, and a gift from my mother. The kids knew about it, of course, and Oscar knew after I reported it to the police..." Her glare intensified. "But whatever memories or perceptions Oscar may have messed with, *I did not tell Janyce details about my brooch.*"

"Yes, ma'am."

Cecily started smiling in response, but then her face crumpled with confused sadness, and another tear trailed. "It's possible Oscar said something, but it's so unlikely. But Janyce mentioned the shape while we were at lunch a while back. ...And she had it at the ball."

"Well, damn."

Cecily wiped the tear. "Exactly."

"And Winton Hollis?"

Cecily's expression shifted into fearful seriousness. "How do you know that name?"

Naomi told her.

When she finished, Cecily trembled. "I...I don't know him like that. He's more—"

"An acquaintance of Oscar's."

Trembling, Cecily nodded. "...Do you believe in aliens, in beings other than us?"

Naomi embraced the odd and out-of-nowhere. "Spiritual compass?"

Cecily nodded (still trembling).

"Well, who are we, as humans, to think God broke the mold with *us*?" Naomi issued a scoffing shrug. "It's a belief rooted in vanity."

Cecily turned back to the window. "God isn't answering my prayers, isn't listening. I pray for others. I do. I know She has many more important matters to address, but..." She looked pained, disappointed.

"God has already given you what you need to overcome this situation, Cecily. Look inside yourself. Look at who you are as a woman, a person, and identify those positive aspects of your personality and character makeup that are best useful to answering your prayers and changing course for the better in your life, achieving your dreams. Those qualities are your gifts from God; to help you do the things you need and want to do. You get what I'm saying?"

"I do."

"Prayer isn't solely about asking for things: 'Let this be the winning number,' 'Make him tall, dark, and handsome, Lord,' 'Just make my father well.' To me, prayer is a quiet time to commune...and listen."

Cecily shifted eyes to her, disbelieving. "God 'talks' to you?"

"Not in a Moses-burning-bush type way, no. I'm speaking strictly of feeling a spiritual *soundness*—and it doesn't happen all the time. Sometimes prayer yields little more than talking to myself in my head."

Cecily's grin was mild. "That makes sense."

"All I'm saying is, our talents, our gifts, are tools to answer our prayers, meet our goals. Some things are beyond our talents and gifts, yes. I'm talking about those things under our control that we experience frustration with. We're so busy whining and complaining and crying about how the dream isn't coming true, we don't use what we have to make it come true. If a woman's bitching and moaning about not having a man, but all she can do or see is how the men, who do come into her life, aren't making her 'list,' instead of using her positive traits to nurture a relationship, well, she'll continue to have that single-life to show for it—because her 'list-making' frame of mind is, alternatively, crossing her off some potential mate's figurative list; it goes both ways."

Cecily traced the rim of her cup with a finger. "I get that, sure."

Naomi continued: "Same with wealth. Other than by lottery or inheritance, it takes work. It takes figuring out how to use a God-given talent to make a better financial life for yourself, whether in computer science or farming. Recovering from an illness takes the talents and gifts of others trained, but still. We are of God, so we have what we need: collectively and individually."

"And there are still no guarantees."

"Guarantees mean no learning, no room for growth. Not that we must be learning and growing twenty-four-seven; a guarantee here-and-there works for me."

"Same here. So, use my gifts...?"

"'As every man hath received the Gift, even so minister the same one to another, as good stewards of the manifold grace of God.' First Peter, chapter four, verse ten. And while that 'Gift' is knowing God, I like to add some human flavor, using 'Gift' also to mean God's blessings of our individual talents, and using those to honor God, lift ourselves, achieve dreams. All kinds of good stuff like that there."

Cecily semi-grinned with her nod, and Naomi allowed her time to absorb. "...You know the Bible."

"Not like you mean."

"I wish I was more boisterous, more evangelical with my—"

"It isn't necessary to be loud and touting, Cecily. I'm far from either. God didn't make us all the same, to do the same things. For some, it's about showing by example. Remember the Beatitudes from the Sermon on the Mount: Blessed are the meek..."

"For they shall inherit the earth."

"Yes. Being boisterous isn't required to extend your spiritual message. To me, being meek and humble as you extend love and compassion to others without care for personal gain or notoriety is more important."

Cecily scoffed. "With what we're doing to this planet, inheriting the 'earth' isn't the promise it used to be."

Both women chuckled, Naomi believing Cecily had a point.

"...Still forgiving everything?"

"I want to try, Naomi, yes." She sat back in her chair, attempting to calm her trembling. "Isn't that what Jesus would do? To use your advice: it's just common sense—and all that."

"Well, common sense...isn't all that common."

Cecily laughed at her serious derivative quote of Voltaire, giving herself seconds of hearty escape from the gravity of their discussion. What remained of their chai lattes was now cold. "That was good."

"Hadn't heard it before, I take it."

Cecily shook her head. "But still, isn't it: what Jesus would do?"

"You're stuck on Jesus being God. Focus on the Jesus-was-human part."

Cecily sipped her cold chai latte. "True."

"I'm saying, if you can't ask 'What Would Jesus Do?', the Jesus-was-God part, try asking: What Would Anyone with Common Sense Do?"

"The Jesus-was-human part." There was a hint of Cecily wanting to laugh again.

Naomi nodded. "Humans attribute human emotion and response to God, when God is...*God*—and beyond the human experience. It's a fallacy in human worship ideologies. We can't really speak for God, although we believe we do. What we do know? In the simplest, common-sense terms echoing from the prudencesphere...?"

Cecily smirked.

"As learned through human history: we were created, beatific creation is better than vile destruction, love better than hate. We die."

Her patient nodded soberly. "...But if I forgive Oscar and keep my marriage together. With you keeping me aware of things to stay on top of not being his victim,...we can make it work."

"Are you hearing yourself, Cecily? Why would you want to go back into that intentionally? Why would you want to use your education about NAS to help yourself *endure* it?" Naomi, again, had to calm herself; she encroached that professional line again. Talk about your delicate dances.

Cecily turned away (feelings hurt). "...No one else would want me."

"That's Oscar talking. And after all we've said about Joshua today, I know you know better. You're insulating, making excuses, using defense mechanisms all over the place. Tell me again, the definition of insanity."

"...I know."

Nothing left to say. Naomi switched subjects. "Where's the stutter?"

Cecily looked as if trapped, and then she shrugged. "The old Cecily put a stop to that nonsense, I guess."

"You mean, the *real* Cecily."

"The real me, yes."

"Okay. But what's the deal?"

"I...I did it to keep him off my case."

"Because it makes you sound weak, intimidated, which, weirdly, makes him feel better about himself."

Cecily pitched a low but firm: "Correct."

"So, what made you stop?"

"Tired of remembering to do it. Tired...of doing it, period."

"Good for you. Take whatever minor victories you can. Win enough of those, and you'll win the war. Positive declarations coupled with baby steps toward resolution help us conquer many fears. This way, the subconscious takes in our conscious efforts—and baby steps are much less intimidating than giant, grownup ones."

"I hear you. He hasn't mentioned not hearing it, though. So, maybe it was all for nothing."

"Or maybe he's *done*, Cecily. Doesn't care about that stuff anymore."

"And by 'done,' you mean...?"

Naomi just looked at her. "I mean: men break into a family's home during the Christmas holiday..."

Cecily shook her head, not wanting to believe the worst (even when she had proof), swirling in some "inherently-good" bullshit.

Naomi switched topics. "Do you have a picture of Roland on you?"

Cecily stared, wide-eyed. "How'd...?"

"Just a hunch. Can I see it?"

Cecily reached for her bag. "I always keep it close, but these last few days, I've been able to keep it in my purse."

Naomi raised her brows.

"Oscar goes through my purse sometimes, steals from me." Her words were low, full of embarrassment (and trace fear) as she opened her Chanel bag. "I'm just realizing that in recent weeks, but yeah."

It was all Naomi could do not to get up and leave. She'd heard enough about his craziness, unwilling to sit and listen anymore to Cecily entertaining living with it, trying to "make it work."

Cecily handed her the picture, a gentle smile of loss and warm memory on her face. "This is him..."

As soon as she saw it, Naomi took a low breath. Roland and Joshua could've been brothers. Joshua was a little darker, a little leaner. Joshua had prettier eyes and overall was more handsome than Roland, but in terms of basic features, the two men looked similar, looked Cecily's type. Smiling, Naomi handed the picture back without comment.

Cecily's cellphone rang, and Cecily's glance her way said it was Oscar. Naomi kept a straight face; it was no use warning against answering.

Cecily pushed the answer button on her cell. "Hello?" She glanced her way again. "I know. Yes..." Cecily sent Naomi a look of apology in excusing herself from the table and stepped away, head lowered, talking just as low as she maneuvered around other Starbucks patrons.

Naomi people-watched while sipping cold chai latte, wondering if any hint of color began permeating Cecily's aura—and what that color was. She had her inklings (based on the True-Cecily traits she's glimpsed these weeks), but auras were such capricious phenomena—and the NAS-Cecily still reigned (for now).

Minutes later, Cecily returned, wearing a hesitant smile. "See, Naomi? This may be one of your anomalies. He said he misses me, misses 'us.' Oscar wants to get things back on track..." She sat (her hesitant smile less hesitant). "And I have a 'date' with him at the house to begin talking it out." She sounded hopeful, excited, dedicated to the inherently good.

Naomi, however (derived from some flash of truth offshoot), didn't have a good feeling at all. "I see." Her tongue weighed three pounds.

Cecily prepared for departure. "Don't forget: you're supposed to refer me to one of your business-marketing contacts for JAH Tech."

"I'm on top of it."

Cecily beamed. "Good. Thanks *so much* for everything. I know you think it wasn't worth it and you wasted your time, but you didn't, Doctor Alexander. I learned a great deal. See you Tuesday, okay?"

"Tuesday."

Cecily left.

Driving home, with Kevin's hwentea seasoning resting on the passenger seat, Naomi listened to Grieg's Piano Concerto in A minor, Op. 16, her mind on Cecily and their discussion.

They finally assembled the puzzle at that table. However, Cecily still had enough residual dependent personality disorder, enough residual NAS effects to break the puzzle apart and only keep the pieces assembled that kept her from going over the edge, kept her from accepting the *truth*. It was possible the true Cecily would be pushed further into the recesses. Naomi hoped against it, but that was how these things worked more often than not—sometimes it took several rounds of dead-horse-beating for the message to hit home (the heart and soul), and healing and progress moved fast forward.

Naomi just hoped Cecily lived long enough to see it.

Chapter Eighteen

Giving the Devil His Due

C ecily stood in the second-largest bedroom of Marcus's three-bed-room townhome, stuffing her dirty laundry into the bag on the bed. It was laundry she planned to take home for her "date" with Oscar tomorrow (because Marcus's washer was on the blink).

She chewed her upper lip as she stuffed, noting her sweaty palms and the tension in her shoulders: nerves. Cecily didn't understand being nervous; it wasn't that good, excited restlessness.

She was bad-omen-like...nervous.

That should tell you something. Listen to your gut.

Cecily sighed. "You sound like Naomi."

That's not a bad thing.

Sighing harder with self-irritation, she set the items for the cleaners at the foot of the bed. She had over a week's worth of laundry to take care of.

The day she discovered the worst things you could discover about a person, she called Chelsea to conspire with her on a reason for not going home, and then she stayed at the Omni for a few nights. The last few nights, Chelsea was still "sick," but now the recuperation from the didn't-happen surgery was here at Marcus's.

She didn't like lying but believed it was best that day (and for days after). Believed...her life depended on it.

And you still feel that way. Think about that. Doesn't sound very safe.

Cecily turned on some sports-talk radio to drown herself out, wanting to hear voices other than her own.

She listened to radio hosts debate selections for the upcoming NBA All-Star game for maybe three minutes before her thoughts drifted. She checked the clock: Marcus and Leila should be back with Little Roland in a couple hours for dinner. Chelsea was coming over, and Larimore (who lived in Marcus's basement for the time being but was also out of the house, doing his work-release gig) would join for dinner, too. Hanging out with Moe had been a blast. His presence reminded her of old memories as they created new ones. She didn't probe Moe about his run-in with Oscar, sensing it was best for all involved. Cecily smiled; she looked forward to the family sitting around the dining room tonight, laughing, dining, chatting, and teasing,...being a family. The only pieces missing were Kyle, Glenda, and her two nieces, but they were coming up by month's end.

And Oscar...? Didn't mention him as part of your family gatherings.

No, she didn't, and she didn't know where he fit in with it all, either.

Finished organizing her laundry, Cecily sat on her bed and grabbed the latest National Geographic from the empty side of it. It had been such a *peaceful* week, such a...*Cecily week.*

Yes, that summed it. Such a *true*-Cecily week. She'd sipped tea and ran and read and researched and napped and analyzed figures and taken walks and meditated and listened to music and locked doors and window-shopped and...lived something close to that wizardry hocus-pocus, post-Voldemort, on-point day Naomi theorized—and the irritating and embarrassing red blemishes across her cheeks and nose had faded.

She had an episode the other night when Marcus came in late; something about hearing the beep of the alarm in the dark (which didn't happen two years ago) sent her cowering, but she survived it fine.

That Starbucks session with Naomi was intense, funny, honest, and...scary. She believed she let Dr. Alexander down, but she wanted to give Oscar a chance to fix things; she wanted to try. Forgive and try. There was nothing wrong with that. She was glad Naomi would continue seeing her; she wouldn't be able to "forgive and try" without her.

He sold your comic books!

Cecily flipped a page, not having read it.

Oscar selling her books angered her more than that other thing. It did. She at first believed that *other* thing surpassed him taking her comics, but after days of processing it all, the comic-book thing angered her more and more. People wouldn't get that, but to her, stealing and selling her comics was just...worse. Consequently, she'd be storing all her comics here until she made new arrangements. She and Oscar would talk about it all, however. Tomorrow, they would sit down, and she'd tell him the things she'd discovered. She'd listen to his explanations, tell him what she needed—and give her husband and marriage a chance.

Her phone chimed. Cecily looked to find Janyce texting again.

She put the phone down without responding.

Oscar. Janyce. Oscar's buddy, Winton Hollis. She could only deal with one tragic disappointment at a time. Oscar was her husband, so he had priority by default. But she'd talk to Janyce. Eventually. Maybe.

"Well, good morning! Haven't seen you since the ball." Carson "Hank" Mabry leaned and kissed her cheek, smelling of burned wood; he'd been cleaning the fireplace—and it wasn't even nine o'clock yet.

"Hi, Hank. Janyce home?" *Eventually. Maybe.* arrived this morning. She awoke, wanting to get it over with, put it behind her, and try to move forward—and get back what was hers.

Seven times seven was forty-nine.

Hank shook his ash-smudged head. "Stepped out to pick us up some breakfast. Should be back in a few." His deep voice belonged on radio or voice-over commercials. He opened the door wider for her to enter. "Come on. Let's call h—"

"No. No, I can wait. Janyce isn't one to dawdle." Cecily stood in the foyer, removing her coat before holding it in front of her.

Hank smiled. Six feet and peanut-brown, he had a strong nose, but small ears emphasized by his fade haircut. His pencil mustache highlighted his thin lips, giving the lower part of his face a dastardly look, but Hank was one of the nicest, sweetest men she knew. "That's Janyce." He gestured toward the family room. "Getting an early start on the fireplace..." he gestured at himself: jeans and KISS T-shirt smudged with soot, "as you can see. But you're home, Cecily, so..." Hank shrugged and turned away, leaving his home open to her, and Cecily knew he was oblivious to the goings-on between his wife and Oscar.

"Thanks, Hank. I'll circulate, see what new décor items she's—"

Hank laughed. "You know your girl. Living room and powder room have some new stuff. Dining room, too. Probably some other stuff, but that's what I've recognized." He was out of sight now; Cecily soon heard the clink and bonk of fireplace tools and wood.

With this opportunity upon her, she wanted to go to their *bedroom*, but wasn't sure how to make that plausible. She was welcomed and all, but she didn't think she had run of the place. First stop: the living room.

Cecily noted the new chaise, wondering what they did with the "old" one they purchased new last year. Janyce bought a new picture for the wall behind the sofa. The small piano near the bay window was new. Cecily sauntered toward the dining room, hearing Hank swear after a tool hit the hearth.

She recognized the tiny box on the two-toned curved buffet in the areaway connecting the living and dining rooms, but still did a double take. Cecily released a soft gasp of surprise, a rush of relief and anger mixing and coursing through her. "Please be in there. Please be in there..."

Holding the black velvet box, she knew instantly. Her opal and diamond teacup brooch was weighty: the jewelry was inside. Cecily closed her eyes, thanking her Lord (with Whom she still had a tenuous relationship), and pocketed her property, fighting the urge to cry.

Seven times seven was forty-nine.

Unable to move for seconds with the joy of having her brooch back, Cecily heard someone enter the kitchen, heard Hank laughing and talking. She was too absorbed in the joy to pay full attention, but when Janyce entered the dining room, the joy switched to rage, and Cecily moved toward the source. She saw but didn't see Janyce's smile in greeting contort into confused shock, morph into fear, and then pain. But it all happened so fast (and her left hand now hurt like the dickens). Through her tears, she saw Janyce bent over, covering her face with both hands. Her ears received Janyce's sobs of pain and wail of confusion. Cecily heard Hank swear again for a brand new reason, heard his footsteps as he approached to investigate his wife's cry. Despite it all, Cecily leaned close to her former friend. "I'd say it's Janyce with a 'Y' instead of an 'I,' because you're not *nice*!"

"What the—?!" Hank's bass boomed, but he gaped at her with such surprise, the anger vanished into utter confusion. "Cecily?! What—?!" He bent toward his sobbing wife, helping her sit in a dining room chair.

"You deserve better, Hank. Trust me." Cecily held her hand to contain the ache and headed for the foyer. "She has some sort of spy software on your phone. It's fine if you like that kind of thing, but I thought you should know!" She left the Mabry home and started Devin.

Tears streaming, hyperventilating, hand throbbing, she parked in her driveway and waited, needing to get herself together and freshen her face before sitting with Oscar for their date. She doubted the Mabrys would call or come over. Not for a while. Confrontations weren't their style. Cecily put her brooch in the glove box.

God, her hand hurt.

When the garage door lifted, Cecily realized she'd waited in the car too long. Oscar now stood in the garage's entryway to the kitchen, waving her inside. His being bald was fine, but she didn't like him having no facial hair; that would be one thing she'd need from him once "negotiations" started.

And no more "Cecil" or "Cesspool"; no more hitting or pinching; no more "whore heels"; no more moving things around on her; no more barging into the bathroom on her; no more insults or silent threats or freeze-outs or...murder plots.

She took a deep breath, feeling more hopeful and less nervous than yesterday. Maybe that outlet with Janyce helped. "Here goes..." She reached for her laundry and then changed her mind; she'd bring it in later. Cecily left the car and approached her waiting husband.

"You don't want to drive it in?"

There was something about his smile she didn't like; perhaps because no hair surrounded his lips. Cecily shook her head. "No big deal. Maybe later." She walked the path alongside his metallic-boysenberry Maxima and entered through the door Oscar held open for her.

Huh?

He'd never ever, ever, *ever* held a door open for her, even in the sweet beginning time of their relationship, so her antennae should've been up. Instead, she chalked it up to him wanting to mend fences. He'd done it this once, he could do it again; she'd add *holding a door open sometimes* to her negotiations list.

"Hi." He pressed the button on the wall, lowering the garage door.

He reeked of Aramis, reminding her of things she'd best forget. Add it to the list. "Hi, Oscar." She held her hand, thinking maybe she'd fractured something because it still throbbed.

He focused on her hand as she entered. "What'd you do?"

"Sprained it or something. Need an icepack."

He stared at her, and she couldn't place the look he gave her. "Don't be nervous, now."

"I'm not."

Oscar closed the door. "I'm just saying: you know how you can get."

"I'm not nervous, Oscar." Cecily gazed around the kitchen, open-mouthed over the carton of eggs, slices of cooked bacon, and ingredients for fruit smoothies stationed throughout. She looked at him.

Her husband shrugged, wearing this grin bordering a sneer, and Cecily tensed. "Wanted to get off on the right foot here..."

She'd had her smoothie for breakfast after her run, so she wasn't hungry, but she appreciated him trying; she'd indulge him and have a second breakfast. With a headshake, she patted her stomach. "Not hungry-hungry just yet. You haven't done the eggs yet, so can we wait a bit? Talk some first?" She noticed her flowers: some dead, some dying...

His expression registered mild disappointment, which was understandable, but also a more-than-mild anger, giving her pause. He hunched a sulky shoulder. "If that's what you want..."

Cecily stiffened, recognizing the passive-aggressive response as she never had before the Starbucks session with Naomi. Force of habit, she started to back down from her original decision and give in to him, but some of this mending had to start with reclaiming some of her true self. "Cool." She turned for their family room, proud of herself.

"So, you're 'big woman' now since you've been out of the house? Been talking to your girlfriends and getting all pumped-up to talk it out with me?" He sounded like his old self, snide and petulant.

And...we're back.

So much for those first five minutes. It occurred to her: he had yet to ask how Chelsea was, that he didn't know her well enough to know she didn't have girlfriends up here other than (formerly) Janyce. This was going to be harder than a simple matter of list exchanging. "No, Oscar. Just don't want anything right now." She sat on the sofa, being careful not to joggle her hand. The television was on but muted.

"But why?"

She turned to him, liking him in the gray polo shirt and black jeans, but needing him to have a mustache or something (she'd even take those Muttonchops). "Oscar, I didn't know it was a breakfast date. You said you missed me, that you sensed us drifting apart. I agree. You wanted to get together and talk, and that's fine; it's why I'm here. But I had breakfast after my run this morning, and I'm not all that hungry. It's nothing against you. I'll have something shortly."

"It's 'why you're here'? What the fuck does that mean?" His lip curled into that familiar part-grin, part-sneer. The one she never knew what to make of because she never knew what she'd get from it. The look that didn't always mean a hurt.

Cecily hugged her coat tighter, feeling like a visitor in her own home (that she paid for, not him). "I'm just saying—"

"You know what? Never mind," Oscar sighed. "Don't worry about it. We're getting off on the wrong foot."

That was true. Cecily quasi-smiled with a nod. "We are."

He approached and stopped beside her, gesturing at her hand holding her other hand under her coat. "Thought you were gonna ice it?"

"In a few."

"We didn't even hug each other."

Huh?

Cecily stood and hugged her husband; he'd lost a pound or two. She shifted to peck his lips in additional greeting, but he pulled her close, pushing his tongue into her mouth, pressing fast-forward as usual. But this time, Cecily pulled back. The taste of an Altoid breath mint lingered from his poky tongue in her mouth. "Oscar..."

"Sorry. I just missed you. I'll check myself."

But she saw the infuriation moving through him. "Okay. Let's sit and talk as planned."

He wiped his brow, his shirt now ringed with sweat in some places. What in the world? "You're right. Need to sit, talk, and figure this shit out... Then get to those smoothies."

"What is the deal with the smoothies?"

"Researched online for a recipe I think you'll like. Guess I should've said it was a breakfast-thing. But I went to the trouble; least you can do is have one with me."

"I will, Oscar. I appreciate you thinking of me."

He nodded and sat next to her, wincing and rubbing his chest. He glanced her way from the corner of his eye. "Don't reach for your phone again: probably the onion rings I had this morning."

"So, you shouldn't be hungry, either."

"Way early in the morning: couldn't sleep without you here, so..."

That sounded like a crock of bull, but he was doing what guys do: saying the right things to make her feel better. He was trying. She'd take it. "So, what do you want to talk about first?" Looking at him straight on was difficult; the lack of facial hair bugged her royally. Go figure.

Does Oscar bake...?

Cecily ignored the intruding thought, sending Naomi's voice away, sending away the implications behind the question.

Oscar shrugged and sat back. "I don't know. Let's watch some TV together or something. Do some normal crap before getting all legal and shit with contract negotiations to avoid you leaving me." He aimed the remote and unmuted the television. Bob Eubanks hosted *Card Sharks.*

She hadn't seen it awhile, but she liked *Card Sharks*; guessing percentages and probabilities appealed to the numbers-girl in her.

While Oscar fussed at the contestants about their poll-percentage guesses, her thoughts wavered. Maybe she needed more time away, but as with Janyce, she just wanted to move forward. She needed help overcoming the episodes, and Naomi advised against doing it alone. Once she left her sessions, she needed someone...to counter.

Does Oscar bake?

Is the bitch dead?

She froze and bit her tongue with a painful grunt, that memory pushing through from the recesses of her...everything. "Mmh!"

Oscar looked at her, annoyed, before curiosity took its place. "What's with you?"

Hearing his voice solidified the memory, and she couldn't speak. She shook her head at him. Something slithery and episodey began coursing through her, but this wasn't the usual anxiety-ridden, despair-laden, scary, choking, air-zapping feeling.

This episode sensation held a new power and force; one she feared.

Cecily tried to focus on Bob and the poll-taking and the higher-lower card guessing, but too many things rushed through her mind in this combo image and distorted-dialogue montage-marathon, whizzing but slowing then doing something else altogether with the increase in her blood pressure and heart rate.

She remembered the first time he called her out her name (both names, both times) and the associated hurt (all the times thereafter). She remembered things about Janyce and Naomi and Joshua. But Oscar filled her head: some of the "sweet time" Oscar, but mostly...Mr. Hyde. She had a fresh pinch-bruise on her abdomen, around the scar where that knife went in, had a near-faded bruise on her lower back from that belt buckle he administered—after saying that awful thing about her and Roland's brain cancer that still coiled inside her with sorrow and outrage. There were pictures on her phone: of eBay statements for comics sold, of things in a lockbox—especially a blood-smeared To Do list. That was her blood. She knew it. And he sometimes relived what happened to her...because they'd recorded it.

Cecily shivered. They needed to do this date-thing another time. She didn't feel good.

Well, no, that wasn't it, either, but...

Her hand throbbed, but that lived in the backdrop of everything else.

"Speaking of legal shit, I noticed the life insurance papers expired. I'm sure you have the updated ones tucked somewhere." He stretched with a yawn beside her, sending a sickening whiff of Aramis her way. "I'll get the smoothies started while you go get 'em."

Cecily stared at the television, seeing but not seeing Jim Perry work the *$ale of the Century* (she liked him better on *Card Sharks*), suddenly wondering when Oscar's seasonal gig ended. He was home all the time again, for weeks now, but seasonal gigs carried through January to handle overflow activity post-Christmas. It was February now, but Oscar had been home since she came home from the hospital after that episode before Christmas.

Does Oscar bake?

She had news for him, too: the life insurance lapsed last November, and the grace period had passed. The premiums increased after Oscar's fiftieth birthday last summer, and she'd had a moment of true-Cecily clarity during the Thanksgiving holiday when she didn't pay the premium. A past-due notice came, but that was around when she went to the hospital after...Oscar baked gingerbread for her.

Cecily watched Jim Perry smile as the announcer described the details of a "brand new" 1983 Buick. "There isn't a new policy term; it lapsed back in November."

"Great. I've already sliced the strawberries for the smoo—"

Oscar grunted and swore, and then her hand sharpened with pain on beat with the side of her face exploding with similar agony. A rush of pressure came from the side, and she hit the floor under a barrage of his expletives. She kicked out and fought back, trying to get him off her, shocked they were fighting in the middle of the family room.

"You bitch!"

Is the bitch dead?

Cecily did her best to knee his nuts; she did. But his hands were around her throat now, and he slammed her head to the hardwood floor, causing a pain echoing memories of something hitting the back of her head two years ago. "You're not smarter, you hick whore! See this?! This is where listening to Naomi has gotten you! Think you're leaving me?! What about *my* plans?!!"

She stared up at him, trying to breathe but somehow not caring if she didn't anymore, seeing someone far worse than Mr. Hyde, seeing...*everything* now.

He slammed her head again. "You greedy bitch! Want it all for y—!"

He let out a gulping-wheezing gasp, eyes widening and face crumpling simultaneously, with this wince she'd never seen from him before. He released her, clutching his arm and chest, chest and then arm, as if trying to get at the source of something. "Ughdfnlmh! Cesspool!" He fell off her, still wincing and gasping and clutching.

Gasping and coughing herself, Cecily backed away with a hurried scoot using her hands, feet, and rear. She propped against the sofa.

"Call nine-one-dfmouhdfg—!" Oscar stared toward the ceiling fan as if angry with it, tears leaking as he made another unintelligible sound.

Her throat and hand and head and face hurt.

Her husband, the man who pinched her and belt-buckled her and insulted her and deceived her daily, gurgle-grunted his agony. His cellphone was on the floor, a few feet away: within reach if not for the acute pain claiming him.

Her cellphone was within reach: visible under the sofa. Or, she could get up, use the landline phone, and perform CPR until help arrived.

Cecily didn't move, witnessing the devil...being given his due.

Oscar's gasping and clutching and wincing stopped. He stared at the ceiling fan, no longer angry, no longer seeing it.

Somehow, minutes disappeared. Richard Dawson conducted the "dollar values are doubled" challenge on *Family Feud.*

Eyes on the devil lying in state, aching left hand resting in her lap, Cecily reached out, blindly feeling for the remote control. She turned the television off.

She sat on the family room floor, sometimes looking at her dead husband, other times not. At one point, she almost laughed aloud, considering the certainty of him not growing any facial hair now.

Minutes later, she had a headache, but her face and throat hurt less. Her hand, however, offered no reprieve. Cecily turned to a dead Oscar and crawled close, leaning over him and trying not to gag from the potent Aramis. She discharged an anger-fueled whisper to his corpse: "Baking that gingerbread was the *best thing* you could've done—because you sent me to Naomi!"

She half-expected him to turn his gaze from the ceiling fan and scowl at her in hostile response.

Cecily rose slowly. She headed for the kitchen, an episode different from a PTSD occurrence, surfacing again. "Guess you forgot about signing that postnup. I did have presence of mind enough back then to do that. You also signed for POA and EOE to be given to Kyle."

She went to the freezer, retrieved a frozen blue-gel pack from the door, and placed it on her excruciating hand. She walked the kitchen, casually returning smoothie ingredients to the refrigerator, icing her left hand in between.

The quiet was so soothing.

He'd planned a veggie-fruit concoction, but there was a small packet of white powder underneath the bag of kale greens. Suspicious, she used a paper towel to put the tiny bag inside another larger freezer bag. She'll give it to Naomi; maybe her medical background could shed light.

The phone rang.

Cecily finished straightening the kitchen.

No more "Cecil" or "Cesspool." No more hitting or pinching. No more "whore heels." No more moving things around on her. No more barging into the bathroom on her. No more stealing or selling her comics. No more insults or silent threats or freeze-outs, or...murder plots.

No more killing her flowers.

Who makes you laugh?

Kitchen straightened, Cecily donned gloves and went to the basement and the sump pump, bringing the lockbox up. She set it on the floor by his chair, tossing the key on the coffee table. She could use a cup of Earl Grey—but not here.

Cecily went upstairs for a few more changes of clothes. While up there, she took a couple Advil, then freshened and checked her face and neck. She secured an icepack to the "Janyce" hand with an ace bandage.

After gathering her coat and purse (now with that white-powder packet inside), Cecily turned the television back on and left.

It hovered forty degrees, but Cecily drove Devin top down, blasting "Smile" by Lyfe Jennings on repeat and loving the people's curious frowns. She wondered if Naomi was familiar with the track.

She pulled into the back lot of JAH Technologies, Incorporated, and entered through the back, holding a bouquet of fresh flowers.

"Hey, Malcolm. Glad you're early. Wanna get those servers back—"

"Not Malcolm." She stood in the doorway of Workroom Three.

Who makes you laugh?

Josh turned to her, sipping his breakfast concoction (which now edged toward being a brunch one). He grinned. "Wasn't expecting you until Wednesday at le— What happened to your hand?" The grin morphed into concern. He wore gray stonewashed jeans with a navy-and-white striped dress shirt and dark gray vest; an ensemble with refreshing appeal.

Hearing Rhonda up front on the telephone, Cecily moved further into the workroom. "I punched Janyce."

He stood. "Okay. What do you need?"

That question, the way he kept asking it, said everything. She moved closer to him. "That evening, when we were being adults, just talking, hypothesizing, I remember what you said about loving that woman. What you want to do to her, with her, for her? How...How the sex would be..." She moved closer and put the flowers down, breathing the pine, lavender, and roses in his classic Polo.

His concern shifted to confusion again. "Cecily, what—?"

She lifted her uninjured hand to cup his cheek. "Is it me, Josh? I'm asking another question I already have the answer to, but I need to hear the answer, not suppose it. Is it *me*?"

When she traced her thumb across the hair over his lip, he closed his eyes with a soft sigh. "Yes." His gaze then gripped hers. "I love you, Cecily, yes: unequivocally."

Cecily gazed into his eyes of molasses, seeing the depth of sincerity.

Allowing the reciprocal feelings to surface and claim her, she leaned close and pressed her lips to his for solid seconds. But when she attempted something deeper, he guided her back, shaking his head.

"You make me laugh, Joshua. You are my refuge. Do you trust me?"

He nodded, still looking confused and concerned. "Unequivocally. What's wrong?"

"Courier dropped off a big box, Mister Hall. Bring it to the back?"

Holding her gaze, Josh sent his voice toward the door, addressing Rhonda. "No. It's fine. Malcolm'll get it, Rhonda, thanks."

"No problem."

Josh guided her hand down from his face. "Need to talk?"

"I do, yes."

Minutes later, they were in his office, door closed. She sat in his chair at his desk. He positioned in front but next to her with a part-standing-lean-sit against his desk.

Another thirty minutes later, she was relieved of the story of the last seven years of her life, in a narrative containing bits of Naomi's explanation for some of it, which was sometimes accompanied by tears. Still, the cathartic experience gripped her—and she left no stone unturned for Josh as she recapped her abusive years with Oscar. She told him about pinches and belts and punches and insults and whore heels and stealing and...murder plots. She told him about Janyce. About everything—including what happened at her house over an hour ago. She even lowered the collar of her shirt to show the fading remnants of Oscar's hands at her throat.

When she finished, there was only a beat of silence. Josh looked at her, his eyes angry, serious, but also loving and concerned. "Okay. What do you need?"

"You're angry."

"Of course, I'm angry. How do you expect me to react to hearing such vicious knavery...upon someone I care about?" He looked away. "A part of me wishes he wasn't dead."

Hurt overtook surprise at his words. "Why?"

He turned to her; his molasses irises stony with displeasure. "Because I wouldn't have minded...doing the honors myself."

Nodding, Cecily stood, telling him what she needed. "I need a hug."

Joshua stood and pulled her close, his arms enfolding her with a warm comfort that was still friendship platonic, but she would take what she could get because the hug, as neutral as it was, still aroused her. She pulled back some, running her gaze over his comely face before settling on his mouth and that scar that tantalized and seduced...

Josh's lips moved, pulling her from daydreams. "We shouldn't, Cecily. Oscar's dead. Okay. Still, take your time in the aftermath of that."

Cecily stared at him, hearing the sanity of that, his encouraging support. Heard him say Oscar was dead with a non-judging calmness reinforcing he had her back regardless, but a part of her was still hurt. She shook her head. "You wouldn't want me, anyway, Josh. I have too many issues. Too much baggage." She looked everywhere but at him, fighting new tears as he held her.

"...And I'm baggage claim, Cecily. Your personal, private baggage claim." He mumbled, "Shit" again, this time with resignation, and then his lips were on hers.

She became aware of so many things at once: the implied strength from his drawing her closer; the nice, tingly pressure of her breasts into his chest; the hand around and behind her waist now gripping with an intensity far from platonic; of his tongue (tasting fruitily of his breakfast concoction), dancing with hers; of the healthy heaviness of his soft naps in her fist (finally!); ...of his erection pressing a masculine point against her, confirming just how long he's been into her.

Enjoying their kiss but unable to help herself, she parted her lids and peeked: his eyes were closed.

She'd wanted desperately to get to the other side of the horror, whatever relief that meant.

This was the other side.

When they parted, Josh whispered, "Shit" again. But Cecily heard nothing but compliment over their kiss in it, and her heart leapt.

She smiled.

He blushed.

"I'm safe with you, Joshua. *All* the meanings."

He had no clue what she was talking about (his expression said so), but he nodded. "Well, yeah."

She kissed him again, claiming a little more happiness before dealing with her husband lying dead in her family room.

When they parted this time, he rubbed her back. "How do you want to handle the 'discovery'?"

Oh, he truly had her back! He asked no conscience or eyebrow-raising questions about her choices with any of it.

"I'm calling my doctor. Then I'll return to the house, walk in, and call nine-one-one..."

"Need me to do anything?"

"...Wait here for me?" She relished feeling his erection softening.

He pecked her lips tenderly. "That's a given."

Seven people.

That was it, and it sounded about right.

Cecily stood graveside, staring at the shiny, solid hardwood casket, vaguely taking in the minister's scriptural recitation.

Seven people attended Oscar's graveside service: Walter and Nancy Brooks, Odessa Brooks Friesen, Otis Brooks, Keisha Naughton, Naomi Alexander, and herself. Oscar's three nieces and two nephews weren't in attendance. Marcus and Chelsea were okay with coming to support her, but Cecily let them off the hook, not wanting to force that pretense on them.

The Mabrys didn't come; Janyce knew better.

After punching Janyce, Cecily now wore soft finger splints on the two middle fingers of her left hand; there was a hairline fracture along the inside of her ring finger. She could have extended Hank the option to attend, but none of it was worth the hassle. Besides, with that lockbox "discovered" near Oscar's body, the Mabrys (at least one) would be preoccupied with Detective Saunders's reinvigorated investigation into the home invasion—and his pursuit of determining their role in it.

They arrested Winton Hollis two days ago.

Except for herself and Naomi, the faces of those in attendance were stiff and unforgiving, and Cecily pitied her dead husband.

Briefly.

Mr. and Mrs. Brooks were in their 70s; it seemed too cold to sit in those folding chairs, but those stoic expressions hinted at nothing but an annoyed impatience. Florida was a long way away, and they looked ready to get back. Oscar's features had favored his mother. Odessa looked more like Walter. Otis was a good mix.

The minister now offered some generic commentary about life and death as eulogy. Cecily provided what positive traits she could to the funeral home for the obit; she heard snippets in the minister's words.

Her mind wandered. She looked forward to springtime and wearing her new chambray dresses. Cecily liked chambray dresses, but those in her closet now were from a time...before; she'd be donating those.

"Let us pray..." the minister said.

Cecily bowed her head. "...Amen."

The minister (tall, light-brown, overweight but strong nose) shook hands with Oscar's parents, then came over to her, sympathy coming through his eyeglasses as he extended his hand. "Missus Brooks..." He grasped her hand with both of his. "The Lord—"

"Thank you, Minister Johnson." It struck her: she was a widow.

Again.

The minister stepped away. The Brooks family all approached, each hugging her, and Cecily sensed them being relieved for her.

"Don't be a stranger, Cecily. We'd still like you to come around: holidays, family gatherings..." Odessa smiled at her, her church hat a presentation all its own. She favored her father but didn't look manly. Her light complexion looked paler against the bleak February day.

Otis stepped up beside his sister. He was browner than Oscar and Odessa but leaner, his face friendlier somehow. "Yes, Cecily. Family activities, community events: we'd like to see you after this. Please try."

Keisha nodded, teary despite the estrangement with her dad. She had Oscar's eyes and mouth.

With a glance at Naomi (talking to Oscar's parents), Cecily nodded. "I'll try." She didn't know how hard, but she would try.

Odessa kissed her cheek. "Good. In the meantime, take care of yourself. We're going to get on a plane, make sure our parents are situated in Fort Myers. Keisha's agreed to stay with them. They're pretty self-sufficient, but having her there will be good." She kissed her again.

Otis kissed her cheek.

Keisha kissed her cheek and hugged her.

Cecily watched the family walk to their car, Naomi standing with her. Cecily waved as they drove away.

"...That tie is broken. Do nothing you don't *truly* want to."

A sigh of relief surfaced, but Cecily swallowed it, along with the urge to laugh her head off. "Thank you for being here."

Her doctor touched her elbow in parting. "See you Tuesday. Laugh when you get in your car, not out here."

Stunned, Cecily watched the tiny woman who saved her life walk to her metallic-blue BMW sedan.

Alone before Oscar's grave, Cecily walked to her car but didn't get in and laugh. She retrieved the wrapped flowers from the footwell behind the passenger seat and returned to Oscar's now-lowered casket.

These were the weeks-old flowers from the vase at home: a bouquet of petals and stems now dead, rotting and slimy, and fetid with decay.

Cecily stepped closer and peered down.

"...Here's to you, 'Home Skillet.'" She tossed the bouquet onto his casket and walked away.

Back in the Infinity Q70, her stomach still hurting after minutes of laughing so long and hard, Cecily tossed her church hat onto the backseat before pulling her hair back into a high ponytail.

She turned on Johnny Nash's "I Can See Clearly Now," made sure it was on repeat, and pulled off.

A month later, March and Old Man Winter were having it out, but March began showing the upper-hand, sending temperatures into the low fifties.

Cecily pressed the entry code on the access keypad at the rear of JAH Technologies, Incorporated, and stepped inside. "Cecily here. Hey."

Malcolm poked his head out of Workroom One. "Hi, Missus Brooks. Dad's up front with Rhonda." He came over to her with a blushing-smile revealing his excitement over recent developments, happy for his father's happiness. He hugged her, and when she pulled back, a question lingered behind his eyes.

Cecily grinned, curious. "Yes?"

"Well,... would you have a problem with Brad and me calling you...'Moms'? You know, after you and Dad...?" He shrugged, looking uncomfortable now. "I mean, it's not—"

"That will be *fine*, Malcolm. I have no problem with that at all. ...Thank you for wanting to."

Malcolm kissed her cheek. "Just all makes sense, man. It fits."

"Okay." She embraced the giddiness bubbling inside, her spine tingling in much the opposite way it used to (in recent years).

Rhonda emerged from the ladies' room, drying her hands. "Hey, Missus Brooks."

Cecily giggled as Malcolm shrugged. "Oh." He grinned. "Well, just Dad's up front then." He returned to Workroom One.

Rhonda headed to the front. "Yeah. Needed a potty break, and he didn't want to leave the front empty..." Those heels seemed narrower, higher. Goodness. "I'll let him know you're here, Missus Brooks."

Missus Brooks had long soured, but she didn't have much longer. Oscar's death certificate arrived weeks ago. "Okay. I'll be in my office."

It wasn't long before her fiancé stepped inside her office. "Hey." Josh still wore the clothes from being at the second shop earlier: paint splotches dotted his T-shirt and jeans. "May not want to kiss me right now. Need to step into the shower real quick..."

Cecily lifted her left hand, showing her extremity, now splint-free.

He smiled; that tiny space on the left just delightful. "They removed it?! Cool!"

She wiggled her ring finger, now devoid of that other wedding ring—and ready for the new one. Keisha could have her and Oscar's rings if she wanted: get whatever she could for them.

He chuckled. "Ooh-hoo! Just in time, too!" With spring upon them, the pollen count was higher today; his allergies were flaring up.

"I know. Come here. Close the door."

Her soon-to-be husband grinned as he closed her door.

Cecily met him halfway and wrapped him up, sending her tongue all in his mouth and making him chuckle with it. He did smell like he'd been cleaning and painting and sweating, but she couldn't have cared less. She put both hands to his hair, running her splint-free hands over those soft naps with glee.

Their kiss soon grew hotter. In moments, he was hard, and she was ready. But, as he'd been doing since forever, Josh broke their kiss, pulling back with a masculine gasp of arousal. "Look, *you*."

"What?" She brought their bodies close again, that hardness below his waist making her crazy.

"You *know* what." He checked his watch. "Are we seeing the new action-flick or that horror Chelsea and Malcolm have been talking about?"

This subject change (something they both needed to excel at recently) had a different, sexy flavor. "I wanna see the horror joint. Already checked for showtimes." The idea of turning her face into his shoulder during the creepy parts titillated. "You take an antihistamine?"

He nodded, then a half-smile slowly formed. "Mardia finished yet?"

"Almost. Your house was so guy-bare, she practically had a blank canvas to work with."

"But you're sure putting a stop to that." His smile was part-smirk.

Cecily pecked his lips. "Yes, I am." She was moving in with him, and he gave her free rein to redecorate his six-bedroom colonial on Neale-Hurston Drive in Bethesda, making it blended-family-ready.

In the meantime, she still lived at Marcus's townhouse with Larimore. Marcus and Little Roland now lived in the house she once shared with Oscar (where Marcus lived as a teen). Moe would live alone in the townhouse in the coming weeks. She'd paid both houses off. Her brother was working as part of his release; he could afford upkeep and taxes on the townhouse.

Cecily sent a hand down between their bodies, feeling on what she wanted.

Josh's eyelids fluttered with his moan.

"We are good and grown. Why're you torturing me, making me wait?"

He eased her hand off his hardness. "It'll be worth it."

"I'm sure. But it's been four years already." It was true; this union with Joshua had been four years in the making—not the six weeks since Oscar's death.

"True. So, another four days shouldn't be a problem."

She smirked at him, just happy. She wasn't all healed (several recent sessions with Naomi revealed that), but she was on a good road—an excellent road.

"Sure you're okay with a JOP ceremony?"

"Yes. It's perfect, Josh. I've done a big wedding with Roland. I'd sooner forget the medium-sized family-and-friends gathering for my marriage to Oscar. Something small, intimate, with the people who matter most around us: *that's* ideal."

"Reminiscent of the three bears: with the big, medium, small…" Josh grinned, looking a little worn out. He still had a lot going on—and not just with JAH Tech now. Months ago, she couldn't massage his shoulders or rub his head to comfort him. But she could now.

She rubbed the back of his neck, massaging gently. "I wish Naomi could come."

He sighed and rolled his neck, appreciating her fingering attention. "I know. But she's RSVP'd to our reception in a few weeks."

"There is that, yes." She had a lot going on, too: the legal proceedings regarding the home invasion were underway. Winton Hollis rolled on everybody; four guilty-plea appearances were scheduled over the next few months. Legal teams conducted most of the interaction, leaving her, Chelsea, and Marcus out of it, but it still brought many things back, bothered her on many levels. Thank goodness for Josh…and Doctor Alexander.

He pecked her lips. "Got a joke for you."

She grinned at him, taking her massage to his shoulders. "Okay."

"I apologize in advance if it offends, but it seems harmless to me."

Cecily liked some "offensive" jokes, too. "I'm all ears."

"Okay. Now, 'god' spelled backward is 'dog,' right?"

"Uh-huh."

Joshua smirked for effect. "So, does that mean the Lord is my German Shepherd?"

She massaged his shoulders, holding a straight face for as long as she could, and then cracked up, not the least offended.

Josh laughed with her and then tongued her quickly. "Need to shower..." He turned away, a low chuckle still echoing from him.

Cecily popped his butt. "And on the quick: movie starts in an hour."

Chapter Nineteen

Reaching for the Sky, An Ear to the Ground

S pringtime bouquets of Anemones, Eremurus, Daffodils, Dusty Miller, and Hyacinth filled the room.

Also present: seven people (not including the judge).

That was it, and it was all right.

Chelsea, Marcus, Malcolm, Brad ("Smeek"), Little Roland, Joshua, and herself: that was the wedding party.

Marcus and Malcolm were signed witnesses, Chelsea and Brad took pictures, and her grandson was a lively joy. Her ceremony wasn't long, but Joshua ensured it included two songs. "Here Comes the Sun" by Nina Simone played before the exchange of vows and pronouncement, and then they danced to "Reaching for the Sky" by Peabo Bryson.

Her wedding party then joined Larimore, Leila, and Rhonda for celebration with dinner at Legal Seafoods in Crystal City. Kyle, his family, and Josh's sister, Dimitra, were coming to the reception in a few weeks.

And now, she was alone with her husband in their newly decorated main bedroom, the moment of consummation upon them.

Four days ago, she was all over Joshua, at the office, at the movies, frustrated to the point of being mildly annoyed with him for imposing the mini embargo. She hadn't seen him for two days (more of Josh's bright idea), so with that navy pinstriped suit on (the navy tie knotted to perfection), that unkempt 'fro freshly lined, and the whole damn thing, her husband looked good enough to eat.

But she couldn't move, frozen with some blushing-bride fright that shouldn't have existed—since this was her third time at bat.

What a difference four days make.

She wanted to see that centaur tattoo up close and personal. Had been dreaming about it.

She couldn't move.

"I love your hair, Cecily. I know I've said it a few times, but I do." He wore a gentle smile; a perfect gentleman as he awaited approval to proceed to what they both longed for.

"Thank you." She liked her hair, too. She cut her hair out of Oscar-defiance, having nothing to do with Joshua. Still, after she had it cut, although pleased with the short, spiked pixie she'd considered since seeing Dr. Alexander for the first time, she had second thoughts with worry about Joshua's reaction. When she walked into the courthouse, his look at her said it all—all positive. He'd complimented her haircut times since.

"Nervous?"

"I am. I know. I'm sorr—"

"Don't do that, sweetie. It's okay. Wanna just strip, go to sleep?"

She shook her head.

His faint smile stirred something inside her, had her wanting more—of what she came for. He pulled out his cellphone. "Okay, look... Listen to this..."

She enjoyed seeing the glint of her wedding band on his left finger. She checked her left hand, smiling at his wedding rings on her finger. Moments later, James Brown's "Out of Sight" drifted into the room and then connected to the speaker on her nightstand, the music louder. Cecily grinned at him. "Okay..."

Her husband grinned back, then began singing to her, about her, doing a bit of James and making her feel more comfortable, helping her to relax—somewhat.

When the song ended, he stopped the music. "That help any?"

"Some."

He moved close and kissed her cheek, taking her hand in his. The mango and pepper in that glorious Polo Double Black carried its own enticing message. "Want to undress...each other?"

The thought of it generated some heat. "I'd like that."

Josh nodded and led her by the hand toward their bed.

Cecily stepped out of her heels. She started with his tie, and he finished with her bra, and between the tender tongue-kisses, soft caresses, and slow striptease, the hot foreplay had her anticipating intimacy with him. Her lapis-blue dress lay in an indistinct heap at her feet, her bra and lace panties on top. He'd felt her breasts through her clothing but hadn't seen them—more of his bright idea. Self-conscious, she covered them with her hands, keeping her gaze way above his waist.

"What're you doing?" His tone held benevolent concern, not anger.

"These aren't the breasts of a twenty-four-year-old, Josh. They're not pointing at the ceiling."

"I want to see you, Cecily. Take your hands down."

Cecily hesitated, staring at one of the art pieces on her dresser, sensing him looking her over.

Joshua lowered her hands, and she froze again with him gazing at her breasts. He fondled both before lowering and mouthing a nipple. "Oh, yes..." He massaged one breast while sucking the other, and Cecily couldn't help the gasping moan that escaped. Josh switched-off on her breasts, moving to suck the other while squeezing the one his mouth just vacated. He inched a hand behind, caressing her back and butt.

Both breasts swelled, the nipples hard and tingling. Cecily sighed a wavering breath, need for him building well now.

Josh lifted away and looked at her, thumbing a wet nipple. "From your response, they still work like a twenty-four-year-old's."

Cecily blushed with her attention now below his waist. She flushed excitement at seeing Joshua's erection: molasses-brown and bigger than Oscar (and maybe Roland) on sight; she'd know better once they got to the good stuff. There was a slight curve to it, giving his erection some character, the veins more prominent near the head. She couldn't have been more pleasantly surprised.

"Do I come across as shallow to you, Cecily?"

Cecily met his eyes and shook her head. "You know you don't."

His nod was slow while still running that teasing thumb over her nipple. "I didn't marry your breasts, Cecily. I married *you*." He cupped the other breast and caressed it, making her moan. "But for the record, your breasts are soft yet firm and supple to me. No, they don't 'point at the ceiling' like a twenty-four-year-old's..."

Cecily wanted to re-cover her breasts, but he had them at his mercy, so she was both hot and embarrassed. She lowered her head. "Right."

"But you aren't *twenty-four*, Cecily. And neither am I." He eased a hand back to her butt and caressed it. "Mm... They're still pert and perky, though, sweetheart. Just fine, girl..." He lowered to mouth one nipple while using his free hand to still play with the first. His squeezes to her rear grew nastier as he moaned his arousal.

Cecily stiffened again—this time with absolute pleasure.

Josh lifted from her nipple and stood, sliding his hands over her body before pulling them away. "But feel this..." He placed her hand on his erection. "I'm responding like you're twenty-four. Isn't that what matters most?"

She gave him a demure semi-smile and caressed his length, the heat within making her stroke his erection with womanly purpose.

Joshua closed his eyes with a low grunt. "And uh, no twenty-four-year-old is gonna move her hand over me *like that*." He looked at her. "I love you."

"I love you."

"Can we do this? ...*Please, baby?*" His wince of desire was part-jest.

Cecily giggled and nodded, unable to remember the last time the simple anticipation of sex happened so sweetly for her.

Josh turned, lowering the covers, and Cecily wanted to bite that centaur-with-yellow-rose tattoo rippling with the movement of his upper back. Damn! He turned back with a ladies-first gesture. "After you..."

He ran a hand down her back and over her bottom as she climbed in. His grunts of approval quelled more of her anxiety. She settled in supine, still feeling like a teen losing her virginity, but it was all good.

Her husband climbed in, looking down at her.

She smiled up at him. "Mister Hall."

Josh grinned back but then closed his eyes with emotion. "Missus Hall...*finally*." He lowered his mouth to hers. His lips were warm, his tongue patient and tasting of the Sprite he had earlier. He kissed her and played with her breasts, sometimes lowering his hand to trace along the nasty scar on her midsection, where that knife went in, making the skin there flutter and tremble under his exploring yet caring fingers. He paused, hovering his lips over hers, "Your Guerlain Samsara, Cecily. Shit....," and then his tongue was in her mouth again.

His fingers inched toward her sex, and she tensed.

Joshua broke their kiss. "We can wait, Cecily."

She shook her head with force, nervousness shifting into frustration. "I don't want to *wait anymore*, Joshua. I've been waiting. And waiting..."

Josh grinned. "Okay." He resumed their kiss, and when his hand approached her sex this time, she gradually opened for him.

She shut her eyes tight, now self-conscious about how wet she was. Despite all the anxiety, her body was ready for intimacy with him.

He broke their kiss again. "Hey."

Cecily opened her eyes.

"Married twice before, but you're still a blushing bride. I could not be more honored." He stroked her opening. "You're very wet, Cecily."

She bit her upper lip, her embarrassment unending. "I know. Sorry."

Joshua breathed a slow, rumbly chortle.

She looked away.

"Cecily. Being ready for me to enter you is not something you should apologize to me for...*ever*."

Cecily covered her mouth with a giggle.

"That's better. Hey, Missus Hall..."

She gazed up at him.

He resumed fingering her. "Yeah... That's right. Look right here..." He took her higher, his hard body brushing against her with his movement.

The heat doing its proper thing with her, she grabbed his hand and embraced the carnal pleasure, grinding against his moving fingers, guiding them, faster and faster, until her climax ripped through her with a nearly ten-years-dead strangeness: strange but not new (and so good). She panted, heart pounding as she gazed at the ceiling.

He kissed her cheek. "I love you, Cecily."

Mortified all over again, she covered her face with a hand. "That was so embarrassing."

"No, it wasn't. Shh... Just *come down*, Cecily. Don't think so much. ...Can I ask something?"

She nodded behind her palm.

"Did...Did you ever work any out for yourself?"

The answer to that (as he could tell from that desperate display) likely required additional sessions on that yellow sofa. She whispered: "Not when I was with him, no."

"...Interesting, but okay." He kissed her neck, caressed her waist. "Just relax, sweetie."

Instead of relaxing, Cecily turned onto her side, reaching behind for his erection to insert him that way.

He put a hand to hers, stopping her. "Cecily, what're you doing?"

"Just trying to give you yours—"

He guided her to lie supine under him. "What's the rush? I'm forty-six, Cecily, not sixteen. I know how to take it slow. We'll get to that."

"Yeah, but..."

"You think I can't hang?"

She shrugged. It had nothing to do with his abilities, but she couldn't express the new worry moving through her.

"My hard-on isn't going anywhere, Cecily. *I want you.*"

Cecily stared at a painting of Negro League players on the far wall; she couldn't look him in the eye.

He traced a finger over her breasts. "...Was Roland attentive? Was it good with him?"

She hesitated.

"It's okay, Cecily. I won't be offended."

Remembering sex with her first husband, she nodded.

"And Oscar?"

Now he was asking a question he already had the answer to. Cecily shook her head.

"Did you ever fantasize about sex with me?"

She shifted her gaze to the items on his armoire, his finger-trace over her breasts and her scar getting things started again. "Much more than I ever should have."

"And was it more like when you were with Roland...or Oscar?" His somewhat nasal voice was lower, all buttery and entrancing.

"Roland."

"Then why're you treating me as if I'm Oscar?"

His question broke her heart. "I'm sorry, Joshua." Tearing, she slapped the mattress. "He's dead and gone. And he's still—"

"No, he isn't, but you're letting him."

Cecily held Joshua's gaze. "...Please send Oscar away."

Her husband grinned with a gentle nod. "I'll do my best." He kissed her, caressing her body and getting her worked up again.

Her womanly aggression taking over, she moved her hands over Josh in ways she (instinctively) knew excited him, and her husband's breathing changed as they tongued with increasing passion. With Oscar, he made her feel inadequate; not liking any of her moves, the experiences one-sided—to Oscar's benefit. In this bed with Joshua now, everything was to both their benefit, and it was time to get to the good stuff, time to get what she came for. She pulled back. "Husband."

Her husband nodded and shifted position. Bracing between her legs, he entered her.

She closed her eyes with the sensation, knowing she made some expression. She didn't fully remember Roland's dimensions anymore, but Oscar's erection was narrower; Joshua's was longer, thicker. Her shaky breaths pulsed with arousal, not anxiety.

"Cecily?" He continued a gentle thrust. "Is it uncomfortable? Do you want me to stop?"

She couldn't answer right away. Josh felt terrific—and it *was* like coming home after a long, trying journey. She remembered good sex...and this was it.

He spoke to her while continuing that deliciously slow, deep thrust. "Cecily, if it's unpleasant, you gotta say something *now*. Because this is good to me, and soon it'll be difficult for me to just 'stop,' so..."

Cecily looked at him, impressed with his ability to talk while doing what he was doing. "You're bigger."

He blushed. "Well, aren't you the little ego-booster?"

She cupped his cheek and moved with him, her long-buried instincts kicking in. "Just being honest."

He closed his eyes with a faint sigh. "And...your honesty...is boosting...my ego."

Cecily closed her eyes, too, and kicked things into high gear. Although not yet near another orgasm, she went into porn-star mode for him, saying all kinds of dirty stuff and grabbing his muscles, moaning as if she had climaxed.

To her surprise, Josh paused, waiting inside her.

She opened her eyes. "What's wrong?"

"You didn't come, Cecily."

Cecily blinked at him for several seconds in awe.

"You're used to faking orgasms...or not."

Cecily nodded the sad truth of that, hearing Naomi in her head.

Josh resumed a slow thrust. "I know what a woman's orgasm feels like. So, if you think dirty words, acting wild, and giving fake moans will fool me, you're mistaken. Now, concentrate on what's happening between us, between your legs, Cecily. Do I feel good?"

She closed her eyes again, focusing on the sensation between her legs. His penis felt fantastic, making her hot and flustered. Her nipples vibrated against the muscles of his chest. She looked at him. "Yes."

"Sex is for the male *and* female, Cecily. I don't mind...dirty-talk, but it's gotta be *genuine*; that's what's hot to me. If it's good,...but you want to...quietly moan through it, I...like that, too, okay?"

His ability to talk low while still working his erection inside her left Cecily undone with feeling for him. "Okay."

In her memories, she thought Roland could do the same. But this wasn't about Roland.

Joshua's brown eyes probed hers. His breathing was stilted with his arousal, but he didn't huff and puff at her (like someone who shan't be named). "Remember what I said to you?"

She nodded, the heat between her thighs growing.

Josh closed his eyes. "Good. Now, let me send Osc—"

A real climax very near now, Cecily grabbed into his hair. "Enough talking." She trailed her other hand down his back to his butt and ground against him with feeling, making Josh open his eyes and gaze down at her with aroused approval and wonder. He thrust harder and faster, and she matched his rhythm, her eyes on his. "Oh...Joshua..."

Lost in the joy of his hard body on hers, of his Polo Double Black all around her as he kept up such good work in her passage, the pleasure thundered through her with a force that scared her, making her call his name again. "Joshua!" And as she watched her husband, gazed into his understanding eyes filled with passion for her, Cecily didn't think she could love him more.

Josh growled low and lowered his mouth to hers. His kiss changed to match his impending release, becoming more demanding, but still loving. When he climaxed inside her, Joshua moaned into her throat with his kiss: as he onetime said he would, when they were adults just talking, hypothesizing, that night after Hadji's birthday party.

Quiet minutes later, they lay (Cecily's head on his chest). "Josh...?"

"Mm-hmmm...?"

"Oh, you're not asleep."

"I'm getting there." He sounded it, too.

"Most times, Oscar conked right out. He didn't—"

"Cecily...?"

She heard the light warning. "Sorry. I don't—"

He rubbed her arm. "Shh... It's natural to make comparisons, but—"

Cecily sat up. "What is *wrong* with me?! There is no comparison." She filled her gaze at Josh with intense love. "There is no comparison, Joshua. *None.* I won't do that again."

He quasi-smiled. "Thank you."

She leaned down and kissed him, bringing fingers up to his lip to touch the scar there; Joshua was where she lived and breathed.

When she pulled back, he wore a shrewd, inquiring grin. "So, let's see... I'll hear 'Josh' when everything's regular, and 'Joshua' when you're serious..."

Cecily lay her head back on his chest. "Uh-huh."

"Or when I'm making you climax—which is pretty serious biz, too."

She smiled to herself (she had to). "That, uh, yeah; that about sizes it up." She giggled. "And if it's extra, super-dupery serious, you'll hear 'Joshua *Ambrose.*' So, you may hear that, too,...when it's good to me."

Josh made them more comfortable. "I can live with that."

They drifted off...

She didn't think once about showering.

Cecily opened her eyes first, listening to his soft snoring.

She froze again, lying next to Josh, but this differed from the fright from before. This time, she froze with certainty, with feeling things were *right*. She'd taken a sad detour after Roland passed, but her path was clear now, and she was in a good place, the *right* place.

She was near two months without Oscar's criticism, his daily belittling. If Josh messed up and she called him on it, he didn't get unduly defensive or vindictive (as Oscar would). Josh didn't have the erratic extremes in mood, didn't get angry over trivial stuff—or have such a weird sense of humor where he laughed at things not remotely funny to most. These last weeks, she'd resolved (the few) conflicts with Josh much more to her liking—without fear of random retaliation from him.

She shouldn't be lying next to Joshua, comparing him to her second husband, but she wasn't all healed yet, and Josh already acknowledged her tendency to make comparisons would be natural (although there was no comparison). However, she did not intend to continue such actions counterproductive to her marriage to Josh; Naomi would be the key there. With Josh, she'll be reaching for the sky.

Josh sighed and turned over, facing away from her and resting partway on his stomach—giving her full view of his Iota Phi Theta tattoo: the centaur with the yellow rose in its mouth.

The contrast in colors against the smooth but contoured canvas of his dark skin enticed her; Cecily couldn't resist reaching for her man's back. She trailed fingers over his tattoo, getting the finer details of it, and then kissed and nibbled it.

"Mm..."

"You like?" Cecily gently used her teeth on that tattoo, one hand pushing into Josh's hair, the other reaching around the front of his body and below his waist. She groaned with the heat of him in her hand. Fondling him so intimately, kissing on him and smelling him and rubbing her body against all his male goodness, had all her female parts firing with memory of what good sex and this quiet *closeness* felt like: her breasts swelled and tingled; those dippy, trembly sensations fluttered in her middle with emotion for him;...and that unique vibration of arousal kicked-off down below. "I know I do. Shit."

Chuckling, her husband turned over, sending the covers off them. "Pardon my tumescence."

Cecily climbed atop him in a straddle. "You mean, *enjoy* your tumescence, don't you?" She didn't give him time to answer. Kissing him with intensity, she teased her tongue along the sliver of gap on the left side of his mouth, and her tongue on his teeth like that was so special; so many times, she'd wanted to do this to him.

The insecurities of round one vanished. Round two was hers.

Joshua broke their kiss.

"Something wrong?"

His smile assured. "Oh, it's very right. I...have something for you."

"I didn't know we were getting each other gifts."

"We weren't." Josh kissed her nose and eased her off him before he left the bed, his erection bobbing well. He went to his armoire and opened it, retrieving a small, champagne-colored gift bag. He approached the bed, and Cecily couldn't keep her eyes from below his waist. When she found his eyes again, he grinned at her with flirt and extended the bag toward her. "For you..."

A breezy warmth filling her chest, she shifted to her knees and accepted the bag. "Thank you." She removed the tissue paper and reached in, feeling something small, soft. Cecily sent her husband a curious frown as she pulled the item from the bag. She smiled and gasped and teared-up at once: a giraffe Beanie Baby. "Oh, Josh!" She loved giraffes; they were so regal and unique. Such calm and unassuming animals; they fascinated her. She didn't collect them, but they were her favorite animal. She wondered why Oscar ignored knowing that, wondered when, if ever, she mentioned it to Joshua, then decided none of that mattered.

"Gonna name it?" His smile at her was full of heat...and love. He also looked as if he'd already given a name some thought.

"I see you have one in mind."

Josh grinned. "How about...Upya?"

She gazed at his handsome face, at that inviting scar in his mustache, waiting for the explanation.

"It's Swahili, for *renewal.*"

She loved it, loved him. "That's his name." She would keep Upya close, in her purse, or near her bed—a reminder of Josh and the lovesome place she'd landed after...that other stuff. Cecily placed Upya back in the bag. She reached for Josh, guiding him back into bed with her. "I love you, Joshua. It's about to get real."

He smiled, those molasses irises twinkling as he reclined under her. His smile soon changed to something full of desire, making her crazy with feeling. What now seemed forever ago, in one of their earlier sessions, Naomi had asked if she was more aurally or visually stimulated concerning sex. Sadly, she couldn't recall then, but here with her husband, she could answer: visually. And her husband possessed many visual cues to stimulate her interest in getting naked with him.

She straddled him and reclaimed his mouth, then began inching toward his erection, inserting him as she rose over his body. She massaged her breasts and locked eyes with him, pleased as Josh's grips to her hips and licks to his lips showed his excitement watching her.

A hand to Josh's torso, she began a gentle bounce on his stiff flesh.

He grunted with pleasure. "Reclaiming your inner self, sweetheart?"

"Yes, dammit." Cecily threw her head back. He felt so good; yes, sex was for the female, too!

She bounced and swirled on him for good minutes, more concerned with reaching her own approaching orgasm than being focused on his.

"Damn, Cecily!" He gripped her hips tighter with a single deep thrust, sending a long, heavy sigh into the room with his release.

Making him climax reasserted her confidence in her femininity, her skills, but delight in that triumph would have to wait; she was so close to her own gratification.

Cecily rushed toward the joy, knowing her husband would go down soon, that the friction would be uncomfortable for him. Gazing at the slow-spinning blades of their ceiling fan, she smilingly whispered, "Joshua Ambrose," with an orgasm spreading like wildfire through her loins.

Josh grunted. "Your contractions feel good, Cecily."

She breathed, "I love you," into the space above her.

Joshua sent his hands all over her, soothing where he touched. "I love you, too. Relax on me, sweetie." He guided her down to him, "Come on," pulling the covers back over them.

Her face in the crook of his neck, she breathed the coffee, rich woods, and nutmeg in his Polo Double Black, coming down in his arms...until she knew no more.

Again, her eyes opened before his. She checked the digital clock on his nightstand: 2:19 a.m.

Cecily gingerly lifted from his warm body. She was ready to shower and wanted to take one with him, but she let him sleep. Perhaps she was a bit more wired than he.

Josh breathed a sleepy moan with a rub to his chest and quick grab to his genitals as he positioned more comfortably, moaning deeper with what Cecily accepted as complete satisfaction—because she heard her name in a drowsy but loving murmur from his lips.

Blushing, she air-kissed him and turned for their en suite.

The hot shower soothed, revitalized. She stood in front of her vanity, using one of Josh's all-natural shea body butters to moisturize with (more of her Guerlain Samsara ready to put on for him) when there was a knock on the door. "Cecily?"

The way he said her name...

She hadn't locked the door, but he knocked and awaited response from her. So much had changed in a matter of months; it was hard to wrap her mind around. She hesitated but a second. "It's open, sweetie."

He cracked the door open. "Why didn't you wake me? I would've loved to join."

She waved him into their bathroom, wanting to see all of him. "I wanted you to join but let you sleep."

He opened the door wider, crossing the threshold, presenting a bit of molasses male wonder—at 46. "Oh..." Josh's gaze trailed her nude body head-to-toe with nothing but desire. "Cecily..."

Cecily saw everything coming from him was positive and she wanted to receive it, but Oscar told her she had nothing anybody wanted to look at so often; a part of her believed it. She used her hands to shield her lady-parts. Her robe hung behind the door. "I'm sorry. Let me just—"

"No. Don't be sorry. Can you do me a favor?"

She lowered her hands and nodded, figuring his request was for her to stop covering, stop...*cowering* from him.

"I'd like you to try to break that habit of apologizing so much. You can't be sorry for *everything*—it's not healthy."

He was right, of course; it wasn't healthy. Naomi had already said as much. But her doctor also told her she'd been "trained." Habitual apologizing wasn't a part of the true Cecily but a part of the NAS Cecily: an "old" version of herself that was still relatively new. She resisted her initial inclination to offer another apology (and retreat into herself further). "You're right. I'll try."

Josh resumed looking her over in that male way, making her feel a complete woman again. He grunted and moved toward her, his penis closer to her than the rest of him. This man could definitely *hang*. "Damn, Cecily. I'm..."

She didn't get to hear the rest of it. Her husband let her experience the emotion behind his words instead, making the chilly slate tiles forming their bathroom floor one of the hottest spots to be—without turning on the in-floor warmer.

Nineteen minutes later, they lay tangled on their slate floor, breathless and satisfied once again, wrapped in nothing but each other, the need to hit the switch for the in-floor warmer returning.

"Joshua?"

"Yes'm?"

Grinning, she kissed all that soft, kinky hair atop his head; he didn't look close to balding (not that she cared if he did). "What was your plan...if Oscar hadn't died?"

The seconds stretched before he hugged her closer, licking a nipple. "...I don't know. I was already trying to get over you, Cecily, but I didn't want to stop working together, end such a multidimensional partnership. True confession: I went to the ball, anticipating meeting someone to help me get over you."

"Oh, really."

"Yeah, but then I saw you there, sweetheart, talked with you,...danced with you—and that plan went out the window, or was at least derailed for the moment."

She chuckled (and blushed).

"After that," he sighed, "everything was just..."

"Harder. ...Like this floor."

They laughed together, their bodies rubbing with new but warm familiarity.

Josh licked her nipple again. "Yeah, something like that. Come on. Take another shower—with *me*, this time. Then let's go downstairs and find some nourishment; I'm starving."

Sounded like a good plan, but no one moved.

They ended up napping on their bathroom floor instead.

Headquarters for JAH Technologies Incorporated was closed, but the shop was full of people.

Josh wanted their reception at one of the smaller banquet halls in the area, but the shop was best: it was roomy enough for the small gathering they had planned—and it was where their story began.

Cecily stood by her former front desk (now devoid of anything of hers; the desk now belonged to new tech employee, Gail), sipping champagne, alternately watching her husband socialize and her doctor do a very-toned-down version of the same.

Dr. Alexander was with one-half of that Lady Blue couple from her table: Viv Phillips. Viv's husband, Rick, was coming later: he was the marketing contact Naomi mentioned. When Naomi inquired about bringing them to the reception party for a quick meet, Cecily thought it was perfect.

Everyone that mattered was here, dressed casually for the affair: her children, Little Roland, Leila, Josh's children, her siblings (and their families), Josh's sister and husband, Naomi and one of her plus-two, the photographer, a few key business clients.

She considered inviting Oscar's family but then took Naomi's advice, acknowledging her tie with them was broken, and she wasn't forcing anything that would have made her uncomfortable.

She was now Cecily Edana Jamison Hall. "Brooks" was gone (of course), but "Cooper" was gone, too. Nothing against Roland (she loved him dearly), but her children were adults now, and she was starting a new life.

Her name was also now on the JAH Tech legal documents. None of her money at first, just her name. In Josh's view, he wasn't a part of her life then, wasn't instrumental in her attaining that wealth, but she was very instrumental in the success of JAH Technologies—she belonged on everything.

Josh never so much as suggested, but Cecily put his name on her stuff, too, and still invested major dollars in JAH Tech's bottom line; if her name was on it, so could her money be. It was their friendship and their marriage and their business and their life together; she wanted everything exactly the way it was. Black Love.

Besides, he delivered delicious dick. She was all-in with his fine ass.

Cecily sipped and laughed and watched her husband, getting hot for him—yet again. Yeah, she was a nasty little something these last weeks, her mouth and hands and other parts just all over Josh, trying to catch up on over seven years of good love missed—and using her husband's good love and sexy body to do it. Her mouth on him... Yeah, she'd been reacquainting herself with many a skill long underused—now with desirous purpose. And Joshua was a most happy recipient. Her libido was such, she'd even reinstated a version of Whore-Heels: *her* version, where the enjoyment flowed on both sides.

Sex imbued with emotion: extra-good.

As if she'd sent him some telepathic message, Josh winked at her.

Cecily winked back. She should mingle with their guests, but she enjoyed watching everyone having a good time. The music was popping, there was food aplenty, the drink flowing. They'd opened workrooms one and two for overflow, and the under-30 crowd made the most of that space.

Naomi and Viv chatted with Dimitra (and husband, Nelson). Cecily watched as her doctor excused herself and approached, wearing straight-leg jeans and a cute Baltimore Harbor lady-tee. "Enjoying yourself?"

Cecily chuckled and sipped. "As hostess, I should be asking you that."

"I am. Good music: lots of James Brown..." She raised her old-fashioned containing three fingerfuls of Hennessy on the rocks. "Good drink."

Cecily lifted her now half-empty flute of champagne. "I agree, and I'm glad. Josh is a big JB fan, yeah. Sorry Kevin couldn't make it."

"Yeah. He had to work, bless his heart. But I'm taking a plate home for him; show him some video from tonight. It'll be like he was here."

"Good." Cecily, however, sensed this was more than casual check-in as Naomi watched the party activity. Cecily waited. Naomi wasn't an easy read, so she didn't know what was on her mind, but something lingered.

"...You had an easy out, Cecily. And by 'easy,' I don't mean—"

"I know what you mean. I know, Doctor Alexander. I did."

Her doctor (such a petite person) watched the people. "People in similar situations don't necessarily have that sudden 'out' happen for them in their relationships; they continue to deal. So, what if he hadn't died, Cecily?"

"You mean, if *I* hadn't died from that overdose-smoothie of his?"

Her doctor frowned with anger. "Yes, if that, too."

Cecily watched the reception activity, her mind's eye conjuring snippets from her marriage to Oscar—and that little bag of white powder under the kale. "I...I believe he was a misogamist misogynist."

"Sounds nail-on-the-head to me."

Cecily scoffed. This wasn't something they discussed in therapy. Cecily didn't speak for several minutes, considering the question posed. She wouldn't be with Joshua, of course, but Naomi wasn't talking about the obvious. "I agree Oscar's death was an 'out' of sorts, but then, I was also making little steps then, too."

"True."

She appreciated hearing Naomi agree; she needed confirmation that her steps weren't just her opinion. "I know I talked a lot about 'goodness' and 'forgiveness,' but inside, Naomi, I had already started leaving Oscar in little ways, so it wasn't an 'out' like that; the little ways would've led to some big break—whatever the outcome." More snapshots of her life with Oscar whizzed through her mind. "Spending years of my life trying to do everything to please him, keep him happy and *off* me. ...And he *still* tried to kill me—*twice*." She swallowed the hurt behind those words and embraced the power now back with her. "No, Naomi. My 'out' was coming, regardless."

Naomi nodded. "Okay. Well, I suggest you continue reading and researching about NAS. There are also forums you may find useful for sharing information. I can recommend another doctor, someone specializing in trauma work, or maybe a somatic psychotherapist. We'll continue our thing, of cour—"

"Thank *God*."

Naomi smirked. "But those can be additional steps as part of your treatment recipe."

"I'll...I'll consider it." And she would. Naomi was vital to continuing her healthier mental journey, but she'd keep her ear to the ground regarding options for supplementing her doctor's valuable guidance. From now on, she'd keep an ear to the ground in more ways than one—just paying attention.

"That's all I ask. So, Janyce got two years for conspiracy, huh?"

Cecily took a bigger sip of her champagne; she would need another drink if Naomi kept this up. "Yes. They cut her a break for calling the police."

"Mm. Okay. Honeymoon?"

Now they were talking. "New Orleans next month. Neither of us have been. There's sure to be some festival going on: that's how NOLA rolls." She chuckled, looking forward to whatever they would be up to on Bourbon Street or the French Quarter.

Her doctor chuckled with her. "Good for you, Missus Hall." Naomi's eyes grew piercing, perceptive. "How's that compass?"

Cecily pondered her spiritual status. "I believe. Always will."

"But the *knowing*..." Naomi's eyes packed complete understanding, "not so much."

She nodded, peaceful resolution filling her. "It's a compass I share with Josh—and it's the most comfortable I've felt with God in a long time."

Dr. Alexander cheesed her response, sending her glass toward her in a toast. "Cool. Here's to a long and happy married life."

Cecily clinked her glass to Naomi's with a postscript. "Here's to being...*safe*." They said, "In all the ways!" together, laughing but very serious.

Naomi touched her arm in a gesture saying she was happy for her and headed away, rejoining Viv and Dimitra.

Cecily drained her glass (happy for herself, too) as Josh joined her.

He kissed her cheek. "Another?"

She shook her head. "Better not. I'm horny enough as it is."

Her husband moved closer, their hips touching, and put his hand to her rear, the fingers grazing with an arousing feel-up over her skinny jeans. "So hot for it, Cecily; the dam has burst..."

Cecily focused as best she could on the people, her eyelids fluttering. "It has." She was hungry for him constantly, and his thorough ability to meet her needs didn't help (although it *really* did).

"Yay, me, or rather...*us*." His hand left her body too soon. "Damn, you have a nice ass, girl." His voice was doing that entrancing, buttery thing.

She looked at him, the slight bump-and-curve in his nose from being broken once (which contributed to its strength), turning her on. "Shut up. Unless you're ready to go back to one of our offices, shut up."

He leaned close again, a hand curling around her waist. "I'm game. That faint Mississippian accent of yours does something to me."

Cecily quivered inside. "Change the subject, Josh."

His chuckle was so sexy and sweet to her ears. "Okay, okay. Looking forward to having the house to yourself next weekend?"

Brad had crossed recently and was now an Iota, like his father and brother. Josh planned a getaway weekend with his boys, getting together with other Iota fraternity fathers and sons for some fraternity-legacy bonding. They were leaving Friday morning and returning Saturday night, so it was only two days and one night she'd have to herself, but it was just enough. They were still newlyweds, so it was just enough; she would still miss him. "Can't wait."

"Oh! Thanks a lot!" He laughed, and she laughed, too. "Come on..." He took her hand, and they went to socialize with their guests.

In nine minutes of chitchat, Cecily determined, not only was Viv Phillips model-gorgeous, capable of capturing the attention (and affections) of every man in the room without trying, but she was also friendly, intelligent, funny, and so *nice*. Viv's "casual" looked more fancy-funky with the bootcut-flare jeans and white cotton top bordered on the hem and sleeves by a sheer floral design. She'd parted her headful of chestnut hair off-center and styled it with side-swept long layers: very feminine.

"I love your spiky-pixie, Cecily. I vacillate over cutting mine..." Viv gazed at her hair, nodding with admiration, and Cecily wondered if she wore contact lenses to make her irises so crazy-dark like that.

Cecily touched her 'do (still liking the cut herself) and gestured at Naomi. "My inspiration. ...I may let it grow back in the fall." Saying it aloud, she loved the simple idea of having the option.

She and Josh talked with Naomi and Viv a few minutes more, when Viv smiled toward the entrance.

Malcolm held the door open, talking to a man who could only be Rick Phillips. While chatting with Malcolm, he stood in the doorway scanning the place, smiling upon seeing his wife, who waved him over. Cecily understood he was coming from work: tie loosened at the neck, top button of his dress shirt undone. He wore a black pinstriped suit, white dress shirt, and a necktie with gray, white, and black horizontal stripes giving keen direction-contrast to the dark-gray vertical pinstripes.

Rick greeted his wife before acknowledging anyone else, and Cecily liked that. He kissed Viv's temple. "Hey."

Viv cupped his cheek and pecked his lips. "...Tired?"

Rick nodded with a slight grin. "Little bit."

Cecily watched Viv caress Rick's head, the back of his neck, and across his shoulders, thinking about how she did the same for her Joshua. Continuing to massage the back of his neck, Viv brought Rick's forehead to hers. She pecked his lips tenderly. "Yeah, somebody's sleepy, too."

Rick closed his eyes with a sigh, meaning Viv was correct. Cecily couldn't help looking them over with approbation. This was the "Lady Blue" couple from the charity ball. Oh yeah: God was indeed showing off when She created *these two*. And then had the nerve to bring all that beauty together—to make more of it. The couple exchanged pecks as Viv massaged Rick, relaxing her husband. "Thanks, Viv. Hello."

"Hey, you." Viv kissed him with a delicate sample of tongue and pulled back, looking up at him. "Better?"

Rick nodded, sighing, "Much." Up close, Cecily noted his suit was by Everett Hall.

It was like they considered the other thirty-plus people not in the room, and Cecily found it touching. Taking Josh's hand, Cecily noted Naomi waiting patiently, as if used to the way the couple interacted.

Rick interlocked his hand with Viv's and turned to them. He leaned to peck Naomi's cheek. "Sup, Sis."

Naomi smirked at him. "What're we going to do with you?"

Rick shrugged, returning a perplexed smirk her way. "I just got here. What'd I do?"

Her doctor shook her head at him with a grin. "Nothing. I want to introduce you to your hosts. Rick, this is Joshua and Cecily Hall. Joshua and Cecily, this is Rick Phillips."

Josh released her hand and smiled, extending his hand to Rick. "Nice meeting you. Thanks for your time." The men shook, adding a power-handshake embrace that surprised and pleased her; maybe it was some male vibe communicating that the other was solid folk.

"No problem. Glad to do it. Love the music choices in here, too."

She was totally into her Joshua; even so, she ran another women-only gaze over Rick. He was almost unnaturally good-looking. The cinnamon-brown skin was smooth and even, his nose angular and strong. Strong didn't mean obtrusive or big; it simply meant one with pleasing character, implying internal strength. It was her thing. Rick's facial hair shadowed in with late evening approaching, but didn't obscure the deep cleft in his chin. His dark-brown hair, longer than when she saw him at the ball, had flecks of copper and gray in the tapered waves at his temples. His eyes (with long, thick lashes and irises an interesting and unusual golden-reddish color) were impossible to ignore. Rick's irises were a pyre, a quiet scorching.

Cecily glanced at Viv, trying to see if Viv took offense. Viv's warm smile, with a hint of knowing-smirk, let her know she didn't. She may have even been used to women gazing at her husband so.

Josh gestured at her. "My wife, Cecily..."

Rick turned to her with a smile and extended his hand. "Hi, Cecily."

"Hi, Rick. Thanks for coming." Looking up at him as she smiled (he seemed even taller up close), Cecily tamped down her feminine impulse, making it a point not to run her eyes over the rest of him.

From just his smile, Cecily determined: Rick cared nothing about his striking looks, that he took no stock in his physical appearance. Some handsome men smiled at you and greeted as if they knew and conceitedly accepted they looked good; as if your hello reflected a confirming compliment coming back to them. Not Rick. Although he had every aesthetic reason to be as conceited as he wanted, his eyes and smile were about nothing but her in their exchange.

Rick thumbed toward the windows. "Whose sixty-seven Deville is that parked outside?" His eyes alighted with men-only appreciation.

She relished being the answer to his question as Josh grinned at her.

Rick's smile at her brightened, revealing a dimple in his left cheek (goodness!). "*È una bella macchina*, Cecily. Truly."

Oh, yeah: sumptuous. Cecily smiled back, knowing he said something nice about her car in Italian. "I think so, too. Thank you."

Rick turned to Naomi. "So, Viv and I good to join you Tuesday?"

Naomi looked up at Rick with one of those expressions Cecily again found hard to interpret; the woman wasn't an easy read. "Yes. Meet me at the center after you drop the kids off."

Rick smiled, adding a curt nod. "Bet." He looked at his wife, reclaiming her hand. "I'm kinda looking forward to it. You?"

Viv nodded, giving him this blushing yet flirtatious smile; her husband turned her on just talking to her. Cecily observed, fascinated, wondering if she'd still have the same with Josh after almost twenty years of marriage.

Joshua leaned toward them. "Looking forward to...?"

"Sis does volunteer work on Tuesdays," Rick explained with a slow, supernal smile. "My wife and I want to do something similar."

"Sounds decent, man." The way Josh took her hand again, Cecily imagined he was considering doing more charitable work. "And 'Sis'?"

Rick's expression changed, the smile fading some. His gaze at Joshua clouded, giving the impression he thought Joshua bordered being nosy. She could see and tell he was a congenial man, and Naomi told her he was good people, but in that brief look at Joshua, she also saw: Rick wasn't a man to be tried or trifled with, either; he suffered few fools. Viv's rub to Rick's arm offered credence.

Rick nodded and grinned, gesturing toward Naomi. "Yeah, she's like a sister to me."

And with that, Cecily knew: Rick *was* the subject of Naomi's fantasies. She could see him becoming a subject in hers.

Cecily turned to Naomi, sending her a knowing-smirk.

Naomi winked back.

Rick turned to Viv. "Missus Davenport texted. She's good to watch Al and RJ until nine." He'd knotted his necktie in a fashion Cecily hadn't seen before, going beyond the Simple, Four-in-Hand, Kelvin, Windsor, or Pratt. This knot was more adventurous with an appealing presentation of tucked folds and flaps.

"Yeah, she sent me the same. That's fine: we'll be home by then. I brought a change of clothes for you..." Viv looked her husband over and then at the rest of the party attendees before looking at Rick again with a funny smirk. She reached for the black garment bag draped across the back of a nearby chair and handed it to him. "You're standing out from the crowd here."

Rick poked his tongue at Viv and shifted his attention to Josh, transferring the bag to carry it over his right shoulder. "Men's room, man?" With his left hand, he released the single buttoning of his suit jacket, and Cecily had to admit, there was something low-key sexy about the way he did it.

"You look okay to me, bruh, but uh..." Josh pointed toward the rear of the shop. "Second from the last door on the left."

They talked maybe a minute or two after Rick returned (jeans, porkpie hat, chukka boots, and loose-fit button-down) when Naomi checked her watch. "If you're going to talk marketing..."

"Right, Naomi." Josh turned to Cecily with a grin. "Want to do this in your office or mine?" That scar in his mustache twitched (making her twitch, too).

She pecked his lips. "Yours is fine. Come on." Cecily looked at Rick and Viv. "Follow us..."

Over ten minutes, Cecily listened to her husband provide a high overview of what JAH Technologies was about. There was tech-talk about applications, ATX, BIOS, client servers, defragmentation, SATAs, protocols, architectures, LANs, mappings, partitions, and other tech jargon that made Cecily's eyes glaze over.

Rick turned to Viv, tilting the brim of his hat. "Why aren't you chiming in here?"

Viv shrugged, giving a smiling smirk.

Josh bent his head toward Viv, eyebrow raised. "You know about this stuff?"

Rick nudged his wife, and Viv shrugged again. "A little, I guess."

Cecily wasn't fooled. They talked some about families and outside interests up front, but not careers so much, since Josh's was obvious, and Rick was present because of his. Now Cecily was curious. "What do you do for a living, Viv?"

Viv's gaze at Rick was indecipherable. "...I'm a systems analyst."

"So, you know what I'm talking about without me having to dumb it down, huh?"

Rick kissed Viv's cheek. "Yup. Extensively."

Viv sent Rick another look Cecily couldn't decipher, but it was wholly loving, wholly seductive.

Rick returned his wife's look, but he blushed some, and Cecily noticed a rather flattering flaw: a raised scar curved over the top of his right ear. She enjoyed watching them, amazed they still had such sexual tension between them after being married so many years. And Lord, she loved Joshua so much, but she understood Naomi's dilemma, too. Cecily found she did hold her breath sometimes when looking at Rick; he was *that* handsome. Cecily also admitted, if she had a onetime opportunity to explore any inkling for another persuasion, Viv would be her "freebie."

Cecily smiled at Rick and kissed Josh's cheek. "Our little techies."

Rick leaned close to Viv and paused, his lips a breath from hers, his eyes focused on Viv's. "Yup."

Viv smirked at him, even as he kissed her lips. When he pulled back, Viv semi-rolled her eyes with a headshake. "Anyway, we're here for *your* expertise, Mister." She poked Rick's ribs in fun. "Not mine."

There seemed to be a quick conversation between them without speaking, carrying a trace of heated spark, before Rick hugged Viv and she kissed his cheek.

Josh looked around at them. "So, we have two techies, a badass numbers-girl, and a marketing guru. Hmm..."

Readjusting his porkpie, Rick shook his head. "I'm no 'guru,' man." But Cecily could tell, without him having opened his mouth yet about marketing, he was better than good at what he did for a living. "But let's talk some preliminaries based on what you've shared..."

Rick then explained what he considered potential marketing steps to employ for JAH Tech. Cecily's eyes didn't glaze over, not exactly, but Rick expanded way beyond those pages she'd printed, with talk of branding, KPIs, golden ratios, targeting, programmatic advertising, and psychographics, plus some other concepts (*word vectors,* anyone?) letting them know that man knew his stuff: "guru" may not have been much exaggeration. When he talked about the social-media aspects, Cecily exchanged a look with Josh: Rhonda would be ideal.

Josh interrupted with a grin. "Excuse me, man, but where—?"

"He's from Virginia, parents from Georgia and Alabama. That's what you hear." Viv grinned back.

Josh uttered a chuckle. "Thanks."

Viv nodded, gesturing toward Rick and Cecily. "We're their 'techies,' but they're our 'drawlers.'"

Joshua pointed at Viv with a small laugh. "There you go!"

Rick rolled his eyes upward playfully before providing additional bits of potential marketing strategy.

Viv interjected her views based on her technical background, and Cecily noted that once he learned about Viv's technology background, Joshua became animated toward her, smiled at her more. She was cool with it; she smiled at Rick more, too (if for no other reason than to have his beautiful smile come back at her in response).

Truthfully, it surprised her Joshua entertained including someone other than herself; he wasn't much of a *team* person. Cecily said as much to him.

Josh jounced his shoulders. "I have a team, Cecily: one comprised close-cuff. That approach hasn't hurt hitherto..."

"But Josh, you still attempt to do most of it yourself. Allow others to take the reins..."

Her husband gestured to those present (as example of her words).

Cecily shook her head. "Okay, sweetie."

Rick cleared his throat. "I can see both sides. There's no 'I' in 'team,' but if you want something done..."

Joshua A. Hall hollered with laughter. "My man!" He extended Rick props with a power-handshake, and they all laughed.

"Poppa's Got a Brand-New Bag" came on, playing on low through the speakers overhead, and no one hesitated breaking out in dance. Rick and Viv hand-danced to parts of it, and then the ladies got a kick out of watching their men doing the Jerk, Twist, Mashed-Potato, the Fly, and the Monkey.

When Joe's "Beautiful" followed, Joshua pulled her close for a slower dance, and Rick did the same with Viv.

Cecily realized she and Josh likely wouldn't interact with the couple in such a social and casual setting again, which saddened her. When she moved here, she lost contact with many of her girlfriends in Mississippi. She now understood that under Oscar's NAS, the desire was to keep her isolated as much as possible, so she only befriended Janyce—for that to turn out the way it did. Cecily moved her body with Joshua's, shifting her thoughts to happier things as she watched the other couple dancing.

"The Closer I Get to You" floated into the room, and Cecily watched Rick hold Viv tighter (just as Josh's arms tightened around her). The couple pecked lips, and their embrace changed, their grind intensifying.

Eyes closed, Rick and Viv were in their own world again (like at the charity ball). Seems this song held special meaning for them, too.

Watching Mr. and Mrs. Phillips, seeing their love, the depth of their connection, she looked forward to having the same thing with Joshua one day. They weren't quite at the level of the younger Phillipses with their love and devotion, but it was just a matter of time.

It was also hard not to conjure Naomi's words about Rick's lovemaking skills as she watched the couple. Good for Viv. Cecily held in a smile: both she and Viv lucked out in *that* department—her Joshua laid it down, too. Still, she mimicked Viv, touching Joshua the way Viv touched Rick as they danced, and the song was over too soon for Cecily.

Song ended, she and Josh watched Rick and Viv kiss, just taking them in and getting warm for each other themselves. The couple didn't tongue-down (although Cecily recognized periods Viv may have wanted to), but the gentle tonguing and soft pecks still translated hot. Josh took her hand, his thoughts in line with hers, and leaned close, offering her a tender taste of his cake-and-wine-tinged tongue.

When all the kissing ended, Rick looked at them and cleared his throat. "So, what were we saying?"

They laughed together, and Cecily said a small internal prayer of praise and thanks.

Rick did a double take toward Joshua's desk. He walked over to it, picking up one of Josh's yo-yos. "I throw, too, man. You mind?"

"Knock yourself out." Josh was ten again as he moved to join Rick, pulling a second yo-yo from a desk drawer.

She and Viv stood together and watched their husbands go on about yo-yo moves and trivia, both "walking dogs" or doing elevators or rocking babies as they talked it up. She shared a few wives-only looks and comments with Viv, feeling like an old-head with Josh instead of a newlywed; it was one of the most grounding experiences.

Rick's eyes lit up again at seeing Josh's Negro Leagues jacket, and the men shifted topics, getting into a brief discussion of the Homestead Grays, the Kansas City Monarchs. Josh considered Babe Ruth the "White" Josh Gibson, and Rick talked about James "Cool Papa" Bell's legendary speed, mythically having once scored home from first on a sacrifice bunt. Josh and Rick talked: John Jordan "Buck" O'Neil; Martin Dihigo ("El Maestro"); pitcher, Satchel Paige; Ray Dandridge; Willie

Wells; and, of course, Andrew "Rube" Foster, who started it all. Josh mentioned a few first basemen, and Rick believed Lou Gehrig could be considered the "White" Buck Leonard—and Josh agreed.

Josh shook his head. "All that's left now: a bunch of 'what-ifs,' man."

Rick re-examined the back of Josh's jacket. "Yeah, those players: contenders for being true legends, having mythical talent lost in the memories of those who witnessed many of those games, but none of it confirmed in any true record-keeping." He released a low but lengthy whistle. "What if they'd been allowed to play against the key White players of their era?"

"Uh, fellas, they did play them sometimes—and won the higher percentage of games. There's that." Viv grinned at the men.

They talked awhile longer, getting to know each other, and ending with Josh and Rick setting up something more formal for the next week. Josh was sold, apparently, no longer interested in running through the list of other candidates. Which was fine: she was sold, too.

Before leaving, Rick hugged her, smelling wonderfully of Hugo Boss, traces of cedarwood, rum, spearmint, jasmine, and pine needles wafting around her. He rocked that porkpie hat, too. "Take care, Cecily."

"I will. See you next week."

Viv hugged her goodbye as well. "Best wishes to you, Cecily." She looked at Joshua. "And *congratulations* to you, sir."

"Don't I know it. Thanks, Viv."

Holding Viv's hand, Rick gave Josh a parting power-handshake with his free one. "A'ight, man. Stay up."

They left, and she and Josh stared after them. Reggae music played quietly overhead.

"...So, what'd you think?"

Josh returned a musing nod. "The chemistry we saw between them at the charity ball is real—and even more intense in person. I like them."

"Me, too. ...What'd you think about Viv?"

"Same thing you think about Rick."

Cecily turned to her husband, embarrassed.

Josh gazed back, eyes calm. "Hey, if we can't even admit other people are attractive, we're doomed, Cecily. Viv's beautiful. Smart. Sexy. Witty. But I don't want Viv instead of you. You're those things, too. Do you want Rick instead of me?"

Cecily shook her head, her eyes on the door whence they parted. "Rick is quite uh... I mean, yeah, he's very..."

Josh chuckled. "Listen to you: you can't even talk."

She blushed at the truth of that, but then grew serious. "Maybe. But no, Joshua, I don't want him instead of you. You're quite handsome and sexy yourself. I'm in love with you."

"Good to know." A smirk curled his lips. "But now, if we were all freely attending a Swingers Party..."

Cecily laughed. "Oh, yes!"

He pecked her lips with a chuckle, taking her hand. "Uh-huh. Same here. Come on. Let's rejoin our party."

Naomi, Rick, and Viv hadn't left yet, still talking and laughing (now with Larimore, Kyle, and Leila), and Cecily was glad to see them hang around. No one knew who Naomi was to her except Joshua, Marcus, and Chelsea. She'd asked Naomi more than once if her attendance and socializing was a therapist violation of some sort, but Naomi redirected topic and never answered, apparently not caring if it was or wasn't. Something about that made her doctor even more appealing.

The reggae set flowed from the speakers, people "winding" to Desmond Dekker's "Israelites." There was dancing up front and in the overflow rooms, people eating and joking or in loud but pleasant debate—celebrating and happy for her and Josh's union. The small but intimate gathering of people was what she'd envisaged.

Hand-in-hand, she and Josh worked the room, but Cecily's mind often wandered to being alone with Josh at home later, going through those gifts on the sales counter—maybe making love among them.

Upya was in her purse.

Rhonda approached. "Sorry to interrupt, guys, but you should come to the back: Hadji's here..." She looked concerned, alarming Cecily.

Josh gripped her hand tighter (alarmed as well). "Okay."

They pardoned themselves and walked with Rhonda to the back. "He's in your office, Missus Hall." Rhonda patted her shoulder and detoured into an overflow room.

She and Josh paused outside her closed office door.

Josh looked at her with worry, inquiry, and anger. "Cecily..."

Cecily pecked his lips. "Yes? What is it, Josh?"

He shook his head. "Nothing. Just come on..." He opened the door.

Hayden Joshua Leeds sat in a chair by the rear window, holding a cup of punch from the party. He was nine now, but looked so small in that chair. Hadji looked up at them as they stepped inside. He smiled and came over to them. "Hi, guys!"

Cecily bent down for a hug. Hadji never smelled dirty, not ever,...but he did now. He wore old clothes and none of the new stuff he received months ago. They invited Ms. Allen and Hadji to the reception, and the woman RSVP'd "two," but it seemed they would be a no-show. Cecily rubbed the little boy's head. "Hi, Hayden. What's going on, sweetie? Where's Ms. Allen?"

Josh lowered to a squat, hands clasped in front of him. "Hey, buddy. You hungry?" He smiled, but Cecily read the frustrated anger.

Hadji nodded, and Cecily opened and closed her left hand, shaking it to relieve the tension of irritation. She now knew what her husband wanted to say before they entered her office. "Come here, sweetie. There's a change of clothes in here... Want to put something else on?"

Nodding, Hadji stared at Josh. "I'm sorry, Mister Joshua, but—"

Josh shushed him. "No apologies, little man. Get those clothes from Miss Cecily. You know where the bathroom is. Get cleaned up. Hang out in my office, okay? Someone will bring you a plate."

The little boy's nod and grin were pitifully hesitant, and Cecily wanted to punch something or someone (Ms. Allen).

Hadji accepted the clothing with a stronger grin. "Thank you." He practically ran from her office, his gait typical of boys his age.

Josh went to the door. "Smeek!?"

Cecily sensed Brad come closer. "Yeah, Dad?"

"Fix Hadji a plate for me, okay? Seafood, pasta salad, fruit. No deviled eggs, though: he's allergic. Take it to my office."

"Got you."

Josh closed the door but didn't turn to her. "Cecily..."

"The answer is 'yes,' Joshua. I'm answering a question you haven't even posed yet."

He faced her. "Really?"

Cecily nodded. "You've been dancing around it since that little boy began coming around. And now we're a couple: part one of that dream floating around the recesses of your mind."

Josh stared at her, nodding. "Thank you. I love you." He regarded the closed door, then her. "We may not get 'im."

"That's one way to look at it." She walked over to him and cupped his cheek. "I'll do glass half-*full*. You know, reach for the sky—because I love you, too."

Her husband smiled hard and pulled her close, turning and backing her to the door, and then his tongue was in her mouth. When he pulled back, his eyes danced. "Something more to have together. *Our* son..."

Cecily nodded, seeing the hopeful joy in Josh's eyes and receiving some of it by osmosis. "It's been a long time since either of us has had a grade-schooler to mind after."

"At least ten years."

"At least."

"Think we're too old?" He held her close, a hand on her rear, the other caressing her back.

"No. He isn't a newborn, but we have a lot to think about, talk about. Parenting approaches, for example."

"Yeah. We're getting back in the swing with little Roland: relearning or readopting proper discipline methods."

Her breasts tingled and her nipples hardened with the way he held her, and she wondered if Josh noticed. "True. We'll keep it old-school for sure, but we'll also keep an ear to the ground for alternative approaches to discipline we can try." She and Josh reaching for the sky while keeping an ear to the ground sounded like a plan for a life together.

"Yeah, okay. I like." Josh tilted his head. "How do you discipline your pet rock?"

"What? Why would I discip—?" She grinned at her husband. "How?"

"...You hit rock bottom."

The corniest ones were always the funniest to her.

Back at the front, they resumed being the guests of honor. Times they saw Hadji and little Roland together, Josh would nudge her with a grin.

The cleaning crew arrived, and Josh invited them to join for some food and a last song before getting to work. He put on "Night Train" by James Brown, and everyone hollered approval. Cecily danced with

Josh, laughing at watching Rick pump his fist for Richmond, Virginia, and Naomi raise her hand with a shout-out for Baltimore, Maryland. Brad, Viv, and Mike (from next door) all gave props when "Philadelphia" was called (Brad wearing another Eagles jersey).

It was supposed to be the last song of the night, but Cecily went over to the player, searching for one more. Her husband tilted his head back with a laughing-chuckle as "Boogie Shoes" bounced into the shop. He came and swooped her up, and they commenced jamming to K.C. and his Sunshine Band, everyone partying hard to the popular beat.

Their reception couldn't have ended better.

Hours later, after securing permission from Ms. Allen for Hadji to spend the night at their house, she and Josh were alone in their locked bedroom, the wedding gifts piled on their dining room table downstairs.

Cecily lay naked atop her husband, whose clothing situation matched hers. He'd just finished eating her, making her climax; now, she wanted more. Josh's erection (poking her pleasantly in different places as she moved atop him) was ready to give her more. She pecked his lips. "I'm the only girl in the house, what with Malcolm, Brad, Marcus, little Roland, and Hadji spread out in the other bedrooms..."

Josh caressed her butt; he'd had a hand (or two) back there regularly this evening. "Mm... We wanted Marcus and little Roland here as company for Hadji; the ratio will change over the next few days."

"You know whom we forgot to invite?"

Eyes closed, Josh shook his head. "Whom?"

"Mackenzie."

"I guess."

"You realize she hasn't been to the shop since finding out we were together..." She watched Josh's expression change as he considered it.

He didn't open his eyes. "Think you're right." He shrugged. "Probably changed her route or whatever. Not my problem." His hold on her rear turned very suggestive. "Yours, either. I've got something else needing your attention..." Josh lifted and claimed her mouth as he rolled them into a new position.

Chapter Twenty

Intellectual Smorgasbord

S unday dinner was over, and now a serving tray full of tiny peanut-butter-and-honey sandwich hors d'oeuvres rested on the island counter, courtesy of Leslie.

"Got any sardines to go with those?" Rick smiled and went to the cabinet in search of.

All but Viv issued Rick varied groans of disgust. Standing around her kitchen, Kevin, Leslie, Trevor, Joy, and Brendan sent Rick frowns of grossed-out confusion. Naomi just wore a frown of grossed-out.

Viv wore a semi-smile of non-confusion and not-surprised.

Naomi wasn't confused or surprised, either (she'd heard about his preference for sardines on the side of his PB&J sandwiches), but hearing his request made it all real, made it all...yech! "Ugh, Rick." But she had sardines on hand—specifically for her "little brother."

Rick turned to her with a smile as he opened a cabinet and chuckled at seeing the others looking at him. "Well, dag! If it's all that, I don't *have* to have 'em. But, you know, I figure it's winners' choice..."

They looked around at each other and shrugged consensus on the point: Rick and Viv won the game of Twister.

With RJ upstairs sleeping and Alna, Zenobia, and the Giles's 10-year-old daughter, Bria, in the basement hanging out, the adults indulged in some gameplay. They spread three Twister boards throughout her great room. Rick, Viv, Joy, Brendan, Leslie, and Trevor played while she and Kevin monitored, taking turns spinning and calling out the moves. Each couple had their own Twister gameboard, and it surprised everyone when the youngest fell first. However, the older couples held their precarious positions while still heckling Leslie and Trevor in fun. Joy and Brendan toppled next, leaving Mr. and Mrs. Phillips the last couple "standing."

To celebrate, Rick was having sardines with his PB&Hs. Maybe.

Joy tossed a paper towel in the trash. "You're right, Rick. You guys won. Have at it."

Rick closed the cabinet. "You know what? I've had my veggies today: Viv made me drink them this morning. Even ate that pesto asparagus for RJ's benefit during dinner. Not bad, but still...*blech*! But now it's time for *fun*-eating, doggonit." He smiled at Leslie, pointing at the tray of sandwiches. "Les, would you mind wrapping a few of those up for me, please? I'll doggie-bag those and have a slice of that cake you baked."

Leslie baked a six-layer chocolate cake with toasted peanut butter ganache filling and malted chocolate frosting; this, too, with a particular someone in the room in mind. Rick would have his peanut butter one way or the other.

The lighting in the kitchen highlighted the fire-like hues of Rick's irises as he gazed at Leslie, and Naomi was sure Rick could have said, *Stay in this kitchen and bake seven more cakes, Les,* and Leslie would've been fine with it. And that manicured beard scruff helped matters not. Leslie cheesed back: "Sure thing."

Naomi headed for the cake container. "Kev, grab the Keurig, please. Les, after you wrap some triangles for Rick, bring some K-cups."

"I'll get the K-cups and mugs, Naomi. Some plates." Viv turned toward the cabinet behind her for the task.

Naomi nodded. "Cool. Okay: cake and hot beverage of choice in the great room, everyone."

Various songs played on low volume from the music player in the entertainment center. Only three couples remained (Brendan, Joy, and Bria left soon after having some cake). Viv checked on RJ: still sleeping. Alna and Zenobia had the basement and all its kid-friendly amenities to themselves; they only came up for refreshment.

Rick returned from the powder room, and Viv smiled his way from her spot in the lounge chair. "Hey, sexy boy..."

Blushing, Rick went to his wife and sat on the floor, settling between Viv's legs again. "What were we talking about?"

Sitting next to Naomi on the settee, Kevin sipped his mountain blend. "We were talking about the 'taboo' of being left-handed, and you and Naomi were explaining about how words like 'gauche,' which means 'left' in French, have more negative connotations here in the US because 'gauche' here means lacking grace, being unsophisticated etcetera. Naomi was saying something about 'sinister' being traditionally used to describe things on the 'left'..."

Rick winked at her; Naomi winked back. Rick reached for his mug of chai-maple cider. "And that's all we lefties have to say about that. Glad you were paying attention, Kevin."

Trevor guffawed, and all eyes glanced his way. He sat near Leslie on the leather chaise lounge with Leslie occupying the foot. "Sorry, that was just funny."

Viv played in Rick's hair. It was late April now, springtime upon them after that bleak and unfriendly winter, and Rick's hair had long grown out of the Dark Caesar haircut from the charity ball. Naomi's hair, too, was much longer than her close-cropped usual, now styled into a medium-short length tapered cut. Viv sometimes hugged her husband from over his shoulders or rubbed his head; she sometimes leaned over and kissed his cheek as they socialized. "No worries. Trevor. To each his own."

Trevor nodded and ran a hand over his face. He blushed hard, but only Naomi realized that.

Naomi sipped her India-spiced chai tea spruced with Hennessy X.O. "Question: How much of oneself should one give up for a relationship?"

Fingers to Rick's hair, Viv shrugged. "Well, I think most people, in the beginning, give up or downplay aspects of their personality for the sake of *starting* a relationship. When it's kicking off, you're vulnerable and insecure about everything anyway, so you 'hide' what you think isn't great about yourself."

Leslie leaned forward. "So, when do they get to see the real you?"

"It happens over time." Kevin crossed an ankle over his knee. He took a few hours out of his day yesterday to join Rick's mentorship session with transitioning convicted juveniles, presenting information on careers in forensic science.

"That's when you see any points of compatibility...or not," Rick stated.

Naomi lifted a hand. "So, how much of yourself do you give up?"

"For me? None. I mean, Rick and I are good together, but we're not perfect. Perfection is boring. So, we work with or around each other's 'shortcomings,' I guess, but we don't 'give up' those pieces of ourselves for the other—we wouldn't be our true selves then."

Leslie sipped her french toast coffee. "For example?"

Rick frowned at her. "Nosy, aren't we?"

Leslie looked embarrassed.

Rick's frown shifted into a smile. "Just messin' with you." He tilted his head back, gazing at Viv upside-down. "Go 'head, Lady Blue."

"For example, I'm not overly sentimental about stuff, but Rick can be. I like a little romantic fuss here and there, but don't overdo the candle-light-dinner thing, or it's a turnoff for me. Rick gets that. Just the same, I let Ricky see when I'm being sentimental about the small stuff—because that's important to him. If Rick gave up his sentimentality and allowed my non-sentimentality, if you will, to run things, he would be unhappy. Flipped? I'd be unhappy if I gave up my non-sentimentality and allowed Rick to shower me with mush every day."

A bag of Skittles popped into Naomi's head.

Leslie offered a grinning-smirk. "And then there's the charity ball."

Viv blushed. "Yes, and then there was the charity ball. I was very sentimental and emotional. I let Ricky see everything that night."

Rick moved his eyebrows Groucho-Marx style at the double meaning, and those who could see him laughed.

Viv leaned over Rick. "What'd you do?" She kissed his cheek before giving his head a playful push.

"Seriously though, has it always been like this between you?" Leslie put her cup down.

Rick's and Viv's eyes changed with varying emotions over some seconds, and then they nodded.

"Even with everything else, yes."

Trevor frowned at Viv. "'Everything else'?"

Naomi turned to him. "Mind your business."

Trevor swallowed, looking contrite. "My bad."

Viv sighed with a delicate smile. "...Meeting Rick years ago at that economics lecture was such a foudroyant encounter."

Rick rolled his eyes with a kind smirk at his wife's use of words. "'Foudroyant.' Simply put, it was way beyond the normal boy-meets-girl gig right from the beginning. Some cosmic shit, scuse my French, kicked-off like crazy when we met. It did."

"And the sex?" Trevor's eyes bugged.

Leslie pushed his arm. "Now *he's* the one being nosy." She sucked her teeth, shaking her head in jest. "And in such typical fashion."

Rick tilted his head backward to Viv. The couple smiled at each other. When their eyes swept over everyone again, they shrugged, wearing false expressions of bored-mediocrity, responding together: "It's a'ight."

Laughter all around.

Viv resumed playing in Rick's hair. "Nah, it's pretty amazing. Rick is amenable to my mood. He'll be the tuxedo-wearing romancer or the wife-beater and jeans hood-boy when I need it, or even somewhere in between. ...Mister Phillips...?"

Rick tilted his head back, eyeing her upside-down. "Hey, as long as I'm getting the pussy, I don't care how it's going down."

"Hey!" Viv bit her lip, popping Rick's shoulder in fun.

Rick smiled at Viv before looking at everyone else. "And Viv can be the shy schoolgirl, the sexy diva, the corner whore, the loving wife...or a combination, depending on *my* mood."

Viv blushed and pushed his head again.

Trevor left the chaise, leaning toward Rick for a high-five. "Ha! Yeah!" He apparently felt a male-bonding moment at hand.

Rick glanced at Kevin but didn't leave Trevor hanging. Naomi surmised Rick considered the timing inappropriate (the handshake and laugh about sex with women was most times reserved for men-only occasions), but understanding Trevor was young, he gave the young man his high-five handshake—sans that stupid laugh (like Trevor). Maybe it was a lesson Rick would later teach.

Kevin wore an amused grin as Trevor high-fived him, too. "We do have those, you know." He sat back.

Leslie tilted her head. "We who? Has what?"

"Men. Sexual moods," Kevin said. "We don't always want the quick-and-dirty-corner-whore experience."

"We know that, Kev."

Kevin sent her a calm, saddle-brown gaze. "*You* know that, *now*."

It went quiet a beat.

Naomi's gaze was just as calm. "Long as I know it, that's the important thing. So why—?"

Rick extended his hands toward them, waving. "Kids, kids... You agree. So, chill. Back to topic."

Leslie cleared her throat. "Uh, yeah, and like, *quickly*, please."

Viv rocked back with a short but airy laugh.

Leslie looked at Viv. "Right? I don't wanna hear about them having—"

Naomi interrupted her daughter. "We got it, Les. Thank you!"

Kevin snickered.

"You were saying, Viv? About giving up yourself in a relationship?" Naomi gestured for her to continue.

"I just think people naturally downplay parts of themselves; it's part of the compromise of being in a relationship. But no one should lose who they are for the sake of one."

"In the end, it's about finding a balance." Kevin turned to her. "I know you hate middle-of-the-road generalities, but sometimes they apply, Naomi."

Smirking, Naomi shook her head. "I know they do, Kev." She spoke to Viv: "Now, that's fine for personality traits, but what about your values and morals?"

Rick answered: "Viv and I lucked out on that one. Same book, same page. Viv and I have different religious backgrounds and had different approaches regarding religion and spirituality—"

Naomi raised an eyebrow. "'Had'?"

Rick and Viv returned long looks, responding together: "*Had.*"

Naomi nodded. "Hmmm... Okay, cool. Go 'head, Rick." Of course, now she was intrigued regarding how the couple approached spiritual matters. Was Rick still Catholic?

"We had different religious backgrounds but the same core values, so we lucked out. But, and I'm playing a little *Tattletales* here, I'd say, Viv would say, you never give up your morals and values for a relationship. And I agree with her." Rick tilted his head backward. "Honey?"

Viv wrinkled her brow. "'Honey'? You *are* doing *Tattletales*. Next, you'll be referring to raw-mounting as 'making whoopee.'" She sent her gaze around. "But we'd win money for our rooting section because that is what I would say."

"The blue rooting section," Rick put in.

Viv scoffed with a smirk. "No, the *yellow* section."

Rick grinned at Naomi, and they responded together. "Of course."

The older adults chuckled.

Trevor looked around at them. "'*Tattletales*'?"

Leslie waved him off. "Let it go, T. Over-forty crowd."

"Oh. A'ight."

Rick tilted back to Viv: the couple kissed upside-down. Viv trailed a hand over his Adam's apple before easing it down his chest.

When her hand headed lower, Rick grabbed her wrist, chuckling before speaking against Viv's waiting mouth. "What're you doing?"

Viv smiled against Rick's mouth. "Reaching."

"Uh-huh." Holding Viv's wrist to keep her from reaching further, Rick resumed their kiss.

Viv continued running a hand over Rick's chin or his Adam's apple, and her touches to his Adam's apple elicited moans from him: his Adam's apple was an erogenous zone.

"What's that thing y'all say: 'Kisses don't lie'?" Leslie intoned. "Well, there's a lot of *truth-telling* going on over there."

Tonguing gently, the couple murmured, "Mm-*hmm*!" together.

All chuckled except Rick and Viv (preoccupied).

Their kiss ended, and Rick looked up at her. "All the way, Viv."

"Mm... You spoil me, boy. All the way, sweetie." Viv then looked at everyone with a blush. "Sorry about that. There're just moments when—"

Kevin put a hand up. "Don't apologize. It's healthy to see. Too often, we adopt the view an older couple showing some PDA is being childish and immature. Why showing affection, even with sexual overtones, is supposed to be limited to people under the age of thirty, I don't know. I've seen some that can be obnoxious, excessive with it, but you guys are low-key and tasteful with yours." In Kevin's comment, Naomi thought she heard his desire for her to be more expressive sometimes.

Trevor grinned. "'Low-key,' but *hot*: like at the end of the charity ball. Whew!"

"Trevor!" Leslie nudged his leg.

"What?"

Kevin laughed. "Yeah, that, too."

Leslie smirked. "Hmph, watching you two sometimes can make anybody wanna—"

"Leslie!" No parent delighted in thinking of their children as sexual beings—even when said children were adults.

"Sorry. I'm just saying..."

Kevin smiled at Leslie. "Well, just like you didn't want to hear about your mother and me having s—"

Leslie covered her ears. "La-la-la...!"

Everyone hollered.

Viv hugged Rick over his shoulders, placing her cheek on his.

Leslie lowered her hands from over her ears, smirking at Kevin and Naomi.

Naomi shook her head at her daughter, then turned to Viv. "Might have to modify your statement, though, Viv. Because—"

Viv sat up. "Because I'm openly showing all kinds of emotion and love for Ricky these days. Especially since..."

Naomi finished for her. "Since he's been home."

Viv uttered a wispy "Yes."

Rick interlocked their hands. "Viv's still private with it, Naomi. It's around close friends and family. She's not regularly tonguing me down in the middle of the mall or anything. Not that I'd mind if she did."

Viv disengaged her hand to caress Rick's head. She smiled but then grew solemn.

Naomi smiled at Viv. "Life events can change a person, Viv. You're in unfamiliar territory. Just go with it. Are you giving up anything?"

"No. I'm embracing." She hugged her husband and kissed his temple. "Life is short."

Leslie clapped once. "Nuff said."

Rick kissed Viv's draping arm. "I'm not giving up anything, either. But all this kissing and caressing me is getting distracting."

More laughter all around as Viv pushed his head again. "That's enough, Richard."

"I forget his name's 'Richard.'" Trevor forked more of his cake.

It grew quiet. Rick turned to Viv. "Now's as good a time as any."

Viv nodded and pecked his lips.

Leslie scooted forward. "What's up, you two?"

Rick and Viv settled gazes on Naomi.

Naomi gazed back. "Yes...?"

Rick cleared his throat. "We'd like you to be guardian for Al and RJ."

"Aww..." Leslie reclaimed her cup.

Kevin shook his head. "Uh-oh."

Naomi swiped at him with a smirk. "Stop it."

Leslie turned to Rick and Viv. "What about Louise? I thought she was Alna's godmother."

"She is." Viv left it at that.

As did everyone else.

Tim and Louise Collins continued sessions with Dr. McNichol, but Naomi didn't pursue information regarding their progress (if any).

Naomi alternated peering into the eyes of Rick and Viv Phillips. Naomi didn't do "friends," but these two people were...family. They, without trying, brought a happiness to her life that was hard to explain. The seconds passed. Rick's and Viv's gazes didn't waver from Naomi's.

Leslie grew impatient. "Ma...?"

"She's answered us already, Les." Rick nodded at Naomi.

Viv caressed Rick's head. "Thank you, Naomi."

Leslie put a hand on her hip. "Okay, so now you're doing the whole 'talking-without-speaking' thing, too, Ma?"

Naomi kept her eyes on the couple (smiling knowingly at her). "Only in this instance, Les."

Trevor scoffed. "Yeah. That one was easy. Rick and Viv have entire dialogue exchanges without speaking a word and shit."

Leslie popped Trevor's arm. "Trevor!"

"Sorry, my bad." He glanced at Naomi.

Naomi stared at Trevor. "Accepted." She turned back to the Phillipses. "I'm honored."

The couple smiled, then Rick viewed Viv upside-down. "See? Done."

Viv nodded back. "Done." She looked at Naomi. "We were hoping you'd say yes. So,...the papers are drawn but not signed."

Naomi smiled at them with affection. "Just give me the date and time to sit with your lawyer. I'll be there."

Viv grinned, warming Naomi's heart. Rick smiled his appreciation, the unintended sexiness of his smile warming Naomi in other places.

She placed a hand on Kevin's leg. "While we're at this place, I have a request for you two, too."

Viv's brows dented. *"Both* of us?"

Naomi grinned.

Rick gave his curt nod. "Shoot."

Naomi regarded the couple for some seconds. "I'd like you two to serve as facilitators for my upcoming sex study."

Rick's expression was unreadable. "Okay. What're we 'facilitating'?"

Viv chuckled and rubbed Rick's head, but her black eyes asked the same question.

"Part of the study involves group discussion, and I want laypersons for this, not doctors. Viv, I'd like you to lead the women's groups, facilitate a session or three—"

Trevor punched the air with exaggerated disappointment. "Aw, dag!" He grinned broadly, his infatuation with Viv more transparent than ever.

Leslie's eyes chilled with jealousy before warming with friendship.

Rick gazed at Trevor, his eyes registering a flare of irritation before he semi-smiled.

Viv frowned at Trevor, unaware until that moment the young man had a thing for her.

Leslie turned to him. "Shut up. You're not even in the study."

"I know. I'm just saying..." Trevor's gaze at Viv changed with several meanings within seconds.

Kevin scoffed. "Unfortunately, it's quite clear what you're saying. *Chill*, young man." That was the closest Kevin had come to reprimanding anyone in Naomi's presence. He did it with subdued style, which appealed to her, generating interest in receiving an MAO from him later.

Trevor detected Kevin's displeasure. "My bad." He checked Rick, apprehension cloaking his expression.

Rick's focus on Trevor was steady, echoing Kevin's sentiment. Many a man would've made rude and obnoxious attempts to warn Trevor from a misstep (Oscar Brooks came to mind (may he rest in peace)), but Rick wasn't one of those men. Without words, Rick issued Trevor his boundary.

Trevor nodded his apology and acceptance of the boundary. It was a men-only exchange that could've played out differently.

Naomi cleared her throat to emphasize and ease the tension, making everyone laugh. "And, of course, Rick: I'd like you to do the same with the men's groups."

Leslie laughed too hard. "Too *bad*, ladies." The comment, while sincere, was in direct comeback to Trevor's response about Viv.

Young love: oh boy.

Rick lowered his eyes and cleared his throat; he blushed.

Viv shook her head with a sweet smirk (also knowing Rick's response).

"You won't be the only facilitators, and you have more than a year to think it over: the group sessions are toward the end of the study. ...Before all that though, I have stuff to do: design the experiment, write the abstract, identify variables, determine if I'm double-blinding for aphrodisiacs, carry out observations, measurement, interpret the findings—"

"Okay, Ma. We get it: the study will take some time."

Viv reached for her mug of tea. "Married couples?"

"I'll have LGBTQ-plus participants, and I'll need a representative sample of not-marrieds, but for your sessions, yes."

It went quiet, all eyes on Mr. and Mrs. Phillips. The two swapped glances, doing that conversation-without-words thing.

Trevor sloped his grin. "There they go."

Kevin's rumble of a chuckle followed.

"We don't need a year to answer, Sis."

"Sure we will, Naomi," Viv affirmed.

Rick gestured to his wife and himself with this playful smirk. "Now, if we're divorced or—"

Viv popped the back of Rick's head in fun, but Leslie jerked back and sounded this soft gasp of despair, showing the severity of her feelings over such an event.

Rick turned to Leslie, his playful smirk gone. "Just kidding, Les."

"I know. It was just—" Leslie shook her head and lowered it.

Rick started rising to go to her, but Naomi shook her head at him just as Viv restrained him by his shoulders. Rick looked back at Viv, who shook her head subtly at him, too.

He settled back into his wife and looked at Trevor, signaling him to comfort Leslie.

Trevor shifted closer to Leslie, curling an arm around her shoulder. "You okay?" He kissed her cheek.

Leslie lifted her head with a sigh. "Yeah. Sorry about that. Turning a light moment into something dark and heavy."

Kevin leaned forward. "*Your* bad?" Naomi continuously got a kick out of Kevin's struggles with specific vernacular, but this one he had right; good for him.

Leslie giggled. "Yeah."

Rick and Viv looked concerned but uncomfortable; seeing how much Leslie revered them had to be unsettling.

"Oh!" Viv leaned over to her bag. She reached in and retrieved a DVD. "Trevor, hand this to Naomi, would you?"

Naomi accepted the DVD, brows furrowed until she read the label. She grinned. "Finally!"

Kevin leaned close, trying to see. "And, so...?"

Viv answered. "It's a home video from our wedding reception."

Naomi smiled. "Thanks." She was excited about watching a much-younger Rick singing gospel with his dad and brother and assorted male relatives.

Rick frowned. "What you wanna see *that* for?"

Viv popped her husband playfully again. "Mind your business."

Rick lifted his hands in mock-defense. "My bad."

Everyone hollered and semi-dispersed, rising and getting re-ups of refreshment or putting mugs or plates away. Soon, one of the cutest little boys Naomi had ever seen bounded into her great room, well-rested and wanting his mother (for a change). Viv changed him and gave him a snack of sliced roasted chicken (left over from dinner), tangerine slices, and milk, and then RJ was semi-over his mother and was all about his father. His adenoidectomy went well, but Naomi remembered that being a harrowing week for his parents. And although Viv changed him, potty-training seemed to be underway, because, at one point, RJ grabbed the front of his pants while pulling his father's fingers, telling him, "Pee-Pee." According to Viv, they'd started having him wear big-boy underwear for a few hours at home.

The rainy afternoon passed, ignored by those hanging out and having fun at Naomi's.

"Say Yes" by Floetry came on (more of Leslie's playlist influence). Viv sat in the recliner, into the song with eyes closed, head gently swaying as she mouthed the words, just grooving. Rick had RJ on his lap, on the sofa, watching his wife with this hard-to-interpret expression. Naomi observed them, sensing an exchange brewing. Three-quarters of the way through Floetry's songful plea, Viv opened her eyes. She looked over at her husband, and Rick mouthed "Yes," to her, holding his wife's gaze. Viv air-kissed him and resumed grooving, eyes closed.

With the way she abruptly excused herself and went into the kitchen, Leslie witnessed the exchange, too.

Chuckling to herself, Naomi stood. "If you all will excuse me..." She sent Kevin a look to reassure him she was okay. She then headed for her office, listening to Alna joking with her father.

It was still early but getting late; the Phillips family would leave soon. Naomi entered her office, greeted by J.S. Bach's (music-only) Cantata No. 208: "Sheep May Safely Graze."

Her thoughts went to Cecily Hall, who now "safely grazed" in the pasture of her marriage to Joshua. The "wolf" was gone. Cecily no longer lived with someone whose perceived benevolence toward her was (in reality) false, broken by the non-physical violence of deceit and treachery. Gaslighting fed into the pathological behavior of a NAS perpetrator and represented one of the vilest characteristics of someone with a narcissistic personality disorder. But Cecily triumphed over it.

At their wedding reception, Cecily's aura flickered for her: the commingled red and blue energies of magenta. Naomi believed those initial planes of gray represented a transition from light to dark—and back again before resolving, settling into something more accurate. She hadn't seen Joshua's aura and didn't have to; seeing them together said more than enough about the strength of their jibe.

Naomi sat at her desk, thumbing through Cecily's file. Cecily's turnaround didn't surprise her: NAS victims were quite resilient. And marrying a man whose love and benevolence was full and ripe and overflowing and...*unbroken*, also went a long way toward boosting resiliency.

She'd seen her fair share of reactions and responses to mental revelations and personal eye-openers. Some became angry; others felt guilty. There was shock sometimes, or sadness, utter disbelief, to quiet introspection. And these reactions elicited an array of physical responses: from fatigue and abreaction to panic attacks and eating disorders.

Invariably, however, there was an irrefutable expression of *relief* with the revelation. You're relieved to see what's behind the curtain (finally), but what happens *after* that reveal:...a myriad of responses.

Cecily's response to her revelation about NAS and her marriage to Oscar had been most surprising of all—and Naomi put little past anyone. Cecily was kind-hearted and compassionate, caring, a bit Pollyanna about some things. But every dog has his day. And sometimes victims...have their turn.

Her patient never said as much, and she didn't have to, but Naomi knew Cecily watched Oscar dying—and did nothing to help him. And through session observations, Naomi determined Cecily felt no guilt or shame over that decision, keeping it to herself: discretion being the better part of valor.

Naomi grabbed Friday's newspapers and tossed them in the recycle-bin; she finished getting her psychoanalytical profile of the nation and the world-at-large yesterday.

Joshua was joining them for Tuesday's session, to be included intermittently in sessions going forward. Joshua knew the entire story, from one ghastly detail of the Oscar-Cecily relationship to the next. Naomi sensed he also knew how his wife "resolved" her issue—and his support for Cecily remained steadfast.

As with Rick and Viv, Joshua and Cecily worked within similar spiritual arenas now; all four were comfortable in levels of agnostic theism, with Viv's and Joshua's compasses pointing in that direction much sooner than their respective spouse's. However, Naomi believed each of them had minute degrees of *knowing* within their spiritual consciousness (and not just believing). Embracing both perspectives, knowing and not knowing, helped maintain a gratifying balance.

Cecily also took her advice and joined a PTSD support group to supplement session help related to the home invasion. Naomi would also continue to treat Cecily for the NAS—and any grief over Oscar's death she may be suppressing. And after sitting with Chelsea, Naomi reassured Cecily her daughter was okay. Chelsea wasn't afraid of connecting emotionally. She was just being very selective—prudent for a 20-year-old.

Naomi turned for the bottle of Belvedere on her credenza and poured two fingerfuls into an old-fashioned. She knocked it back, her thoughts (weirdly) on asking Viv how Patrice and Garrett were doing and then on possible names for her gun. She didn't know why the gun-naming proved so difficult. Thoughts of Tyson and Jassiel surfaced, and Naomi poured and drained another fingerful before rejoining the group. Between her cup of "Henney-spruced" coffee and the fingerfuls of Belvi, she had a tiny buzz.

She returned to the delicious aroma of pipe tobacco smoke: a warm, mildly sweet, burning-floral scent permeating her great room. Rick stood by the window. He drew from his Savinelli Venere rusticated half-bent Canadian: his gift from Kevin, which he kept at her house for convenience. He'd christened this pipe "Kalimba Story." Although it was sweetly aromatic, Rick never smelled like pipe tobacco except when smoking—his fragrance was always fresh, carrying traces of whatever cologne he wore.

With noise, music, and conversation around him, Rick appeared introspective, lost in reflective thought as he exhaled smoke through his nostrils while taking in her painting by Thomas Hart Benton (Benton was White but controversial—and why she liked him). He quietly sang some of "I'm Coming Home" as it played, harmonizing with the Swan Silvertones, and the low volume allowed hearing how good he sounded.

He was secretly taking guitar lessons, hoping to play a few bars for Viv's birthday in August. Naomi foresaw a scenario of Rick playing for Viv while holding that pipe between his teeth... Good for Viv.

RJ came up from the basement, grabbed his bag of Duplo Blocks, and dragged it toward the basement until Trevor jumped up to help him.

Naomi heard someone in the kitchen. Hearing Alna and Zenobia fussing at RJ from downstairs and having everyone else visually accounted for, the only one missing was Viv. Naomi made a detour.

"Hey, lady."

Viv closed the refrigerator, bottle of water in hand. "Hey. We'll be pulling out shortly."

"*I* understand. RJ, however, may have something to say: he just dragged his Duplos downstairs..."

Viv rolled her eyes upward with a sigh. "Good thing it's just family. This won't be pretty."

Naomi chuckled. "Can I ask you something?"

"No." But Viv's expression contradicted her curt response. "*Past that*, Naomi. Come on now."

"Right. Well,...does Rick ask, need, or want you to tell him he has a large erection? You know, during intimacy?"

"This for your study?"

"Not necessarily." It had more to do with her Starbucks session with Cecily.

Viv shook her head as she sipped some water and recapped her bottle. "Well,...he doesn't *ask* or prompt me for that, so no, he doesn't *need* to hear it, I guess." She looked at Naomi with a blushing expression full of reflection. "Girl, the first time we mixed it up, I couldn't help giving that man my unsolicited opinion of his joystick."

"Okay."

"But no, Rick's one of those who's fine working with what he's got. He's very humble or, rather, oblivious about that, too. He doesn't refer to his size, and he doesn't need, want, or ask to hear me tell him he has a big dick." Viv shrugged. "I sometimes let him know anyway, shit. Partly because it's a hot part of our interplay, and partly because, well,...it's true."

With a kind smirk (and fighting images of a nine-inch erection), Naomi nodded. "I see."

"Does Kevin?"

"He's more into...expressing how much he likes what we're doing."

"Hmm... Now, I'm just going to ask, no preamble. Kevin's fifty: Can he still hang?"

"Yes. Quite well."

"Good for you."

It was.

A burst of male laughter came from the great room; Rick saying, "Sex, love, and money, baby! It's all God, so it's all good!" as the laughter rolled.

Naomi exchanged a look with Viv. They shrugged with nods, responding "True talk" together, and then their laughter blended with that in the great room.

"Anything else?"

Naomi shook her head. "That's all for now. There's plenty to go over in the next couple years. Come on."

As they headed for the front exit, Rick pushed the swinging door open and popped his head in. "Ready, Viv?"

"Yes. Don't forget your hors d'oeuvres."

Rick headed for the fridge. "Oh yes. We can enjoy them while we watch the show tonight, baby." Naomi heard how much he loved hanging out with his wife, how much he enjoyed Viv's company.

"As long as the sardines are on a *separate* plate, near wherever *you're* sitting, that's fine." Viv watched her husband standing before the opened refrigerator. Naomi realized their brief discussion about erection size had Viv's thoughts elsewhere, having nothing to do with enjoying peanut-butter-and-honey snacks in front of the television. Viv bit her bottom lip.

Yep.

Chuckling, Rick reached into the fridge. "Okay, Lady Blue."

"C'mere."

Naomi stepped back some; Viv was in a specific frame of mind.

The way Rick cleared his throat, he detected it, too. He set the wrapped sandwiches on the counter and approached his wife, wearing a gentle smirk. "How can—?"

Viv's lips cut his question off.

"Get 'im, Viv."

Rick paused their kiss. "Yes. Get me, Viv. Please *get* me."

Smiling with no hint of blush, Viv sent a hand to Rick's hair and tongued him tenderly for quiet seconds. When she pulled back, Rick released this tiny gasp in the seconds it took his eyes to open. Viv held his gaze until Rick nodded agreement he'd been fully gotten and was owned. Viv turned to her. "And that's a wrap for us, Naomi. Next time, you guys come to our house for a small kickback. Bring it to 'The Bard.'"

Naomi returned a smirking-grin (they'd all nicknamed Rick and Viv's house "The Bard"). "Sounds good. Don't forget, the four of us, dinner at Ben's Chili Bowl on Thursday. And we have those tickets to The Birchmere..."

Viv pointed her way. "I remembered."

Naomi turned to her brother. "You okay, Rick?"

Rick inched back from Viv, nodding trance-like, and Naomi believed he'd stopped to ponder life. He cleared his throat again, but Naomi couldn't decipher; Viv knew better what his throat-clearings meant. "Yeah, I'm good. Let's go."

Viv winked at her. "The Black-woman mystique. The end."

Naomi hollered, making Rick and Viv laugh, too.

RJ indeed gave Alna a hard time and didn't want to come upstairs when it was time to go. But then Rick exited the powder room and paused at the top of the basement stairs. Two mellow-baritone sentences later (sentences tinged with some authoritative bass), RJ was upstairs, teary-eyed and lip poking but quiet, putting his Duplo Blocks in the corner of the great room where they belonged.

Forty-seven minutes later, she and Kevin had the house to themselves. They hung out in the great room awhile, playing Scrabble, but were now enjoying time in her upper-level library, reading while listening to classical music as a light rain pattered against the windows.

She'd relocated "Kofi" (her Sankofa bird figurine) from the mantel in the great room. It now rested on a bookshelf in the library, sharing the space with only a few volumes. As Kevin presented it to her on a Friday, Naomi considered that its "bornday," and so, its name was Kofi.

She still hesitated embracing Kofi altogether, and she knew the reasons why, but when those reasons would no longer be reasons...only time would tell.

Kevin sipped his beer, rereading Richard Wright's memoir *Black Boy*.

Naomi worked, reviewing and charting notes from profile summaries for her upcoming sessions while sipping iced water. They talked some in between, creating an enjoyable period of relaxation.

But will you marry again?

Sunday dinner was hours ago: stomachs rumbled.

Kevin fixed her with a look, his eyeglass frames glinting. He closed his book. "Wanna share a roasted chicken sandwich with lettuce and tomato?"

"Yes, please."

He leaned close, pressing his soft lips to hers, and then headed two floors down to the kitchen.

Naomi went back to prepping for patients, but inevitably, her thoughts swirled around Cecily, Viv, Oscar, and Rick (and Joshua), about the impact of love and the role of intellect. One uses an entire intellectual smorgasbord of resources to navigate the discord and embrace the concord of relationships.

"Fuck 'em if they can't take a joke."

Naomi smiled with memory of Viv's words at the charity ball.

The Phillips marriage reflected a *tested* love, having endured the pain of child-loss and infidelity, having suffered the heartbreak of court proceedings and Rick's imprisonment. They've grieved through the trial of separation—all of which strengthened their friendship more than anything, thus, making their love stronger, more profound.

Love and the heart were abstract yet literal concepts coexisting with one's soul—and Viv didn't want to go forward without him, knowing it would lead to that *someplace lonely and unhappy.* Viv's intellect and the intellect of others had her going another way after learning what Rick did. Intellectually, Viv reasoned that leaving him was best. But her heart wouldn't let that true love go; the stars would be forever unaligned. As far as Viv was concerned, it was a matter of fuck 'em if their intellectual minds couldn't take what her heart was telling her to do.

Cecily, an intelligent, college-educated woman, was "reduced" by her life with Oscar. She compromised her emotional intellect on numerous fronts, such that she couldn't see Oscar for who he was (a misogamist misogynist—and narcissistic, at that), and she lost touch with her innate personality traits that otherwise would've helped her. Cecily had tested love, too. Not to determine how much she would suffer (as with Rick and Viv), but to bring to light what she *wouldn't* suffer for love. And she almost missed it. With talk of *inherently good* and *forgiveness,* she almost suffered...to the death. Although Cecily knew better intellectually, Oscar's emotional dominance kept her craving a love and emotional fulfillment gone missing since Roland died. But to get that love...there was a price—of which she could never pay because Oscar's love was a concept unattainable—even to him.

Our intellectual beliefs don't always match how we must live our personal lives.

She stared at Kofi as she listened to Kevin returning with their late-evening snack, believing their love held a pleasant blend of guidance by intellect and emotion.

Okay, intellectually, spiritually, emotionally, whatever: Will you marry again?

Naomi smiled as Kevin entered the library, hoping the question never came up.

But she knew him. It would come up.

And...?!

Kevin set her plate (with her half of sandwich and a sliver of Leslie's cake) on the table. "Added some cake for that sweet-tooth sure to follow, my Sankofa Bird, but just a taste for you because you'll say it's getting late." He held his plate in hand: same sized serving of sandwich but a larger piece of cake—because his newfound love of sweets mattered not the time.

Naomi set her papers aside and dug in. "You know me so well."

And he did.

Intellectually speaking.

Chapter Twenty-One

Epilogue

C ecily stood and clapped while Josh aimed the video camera at the stage, smiling ear-to-ear.

Smells of pine, holly, and gingerbread wafted around her from the decorations and the refreshment table, but they didn't faze her. Dr. Naomi Alexander made sure of that. She still had Bat-phone privileges, but it hadn't been necessary for a long time.

She missed her—for reasons not tied to therapy.

A line of children in colorful costumes held hands on a stage alive with Christmas themes from around the world and then took a bow. The curtain closed to a round of applause and shouts.

"You got him?" She tugged her husband's suit at the elbow.

Josh chuckled, lowering the camera from his eye. "I got 'im, baby. Couldn't help but get all of them." Smirking, he sent that line in his mustache close to her lips for a peck.

She had years of marriage to Joshua behind her, but standing in this auditorium with him, nothing felt staid and very much like they were in a time warp, reliving that newlywed stage repeatedly.

She and Josh Hall were meant to be.

Rick Phillips's marketing expertise and guidance indeed helped carry JAH Technologies Incorporated to the next level: four shops open around the DMV, with a fifth scheduled to open in New Jersey for Josh's 50th birthday next month. Malcolm and Smeek were in the final stages of preliminary plans for shop six in Bedford Heights. They'd all been working full tilt to make things happen; she'd never been so crazily, happily busy with numbers before in her life.

But now, the Christmas holiday was upon them; they were taking a much-deserved break. And what better way to kick off Christmas than a play featuring the burgeoning talents of—

The force from a giant hug against her interrupted her thoughts. "Ma? Dad? Did you like it?!" Hayden Joshua Hall beamed at them, eyes wide and hopeful and excited. Turning 13 next month, he was a seventh grader in middle school. His lean body already showed inclinations toward fulfilling the athletic build his form now suggested—even in his Costa Rican costume. The area above his lip seemed to darken with each passing day, but Hadji was a good kid, in no hurry to grow up (although the young ladies calling their house or texting him wanted to accelerate his schedule). Those big, milk-chocolate irises melted her heart.

She had big plans for those milestone birthdays coming next month.

Cecily hugged her son back and caressed his head. "I did, Hadji. You did a wonderful Costa Rican Christmas." She kissed his face all over, making him laugh.

Hadji turned to Josh. "Dad?"

"I liked it fine, man. I'm glad they used your ideas." Josh hugged his son, kissing the top of his head. "But come on. Go change and make sure you and Ethan are clear to leave. Got a lot to do before heading to the ski resort tomorrow."

"Snow-tubing! Yes!" Smiling hard, Hadji gave his father some dap before dashing away.

Josh stared after him, chuckling, and Cecily kept eyes on her husband. He shook his head, eyes still on Hadji. "How...How could you give up parental rights to such a *good* kid?" That wasn't his first time asking that question, likely wouldn't be his last.

Her answer, too, echoed past responses to that question. "It's better knowing you're not cut out to be a parent and give away those rights, than not to be a parent but hold on to those rights out of some faulty sense of pride."

He looked at her. His polished fade had considerably more gray hairs now, but it didn't age him; it just made him look hotter to Cecily (and the man could still hang like the dickens). "We did good?"

Cecily took his hand and kissed him with a dip of tongue. "We did."

"...Ready to be my little snow-bunny?"

She blushed, looking forward to them hanging at the resort with Rick and Viv (and Alna and RJ) and then to snuggling with Josh in their cabin after being out in the snow, sipping cocoa or cups of Earl Grey. Yes, in recent years, she's experienced winters...of *much* content. "We'll see."

His eyes of molasses told her he loved her, but he smirked. "Where're you from?"

Cecily smirked back, gritting on him with playful attitude. "Where *you* from?"

They still told jokes to each other under penalty of death, but this private joke had a unique history.

Cecily looked in his eyes, waiting a longer beat than usual: long enough for them to fall deeper in love. She smiled at her husband just as that tiny space between his left incisor and cuspid appeared with his.

"Cleveland!" they said together, and the ensuing laughter was as pure and sweet...as everything else between them.

Author's Postscript

Domestic violence is sometimes carried out quietly, insidiously—as with Narcissistic Abuse Syndrome. The slightest suspicion regarding domestic violence (in any form) requires a phone call to The National Domestic Violence Hotline: 1-800-799-7233 (1-800-422-4453).

And so, my dear Bodacious Bibliophile:

- Did you enjoy the story?

- Did I illustrate Cecily and Oscar's troubled marriage well? How about the simmering heat between coworkers Cecily and Joshua?

- This work was two books in one. How'd you like the follow-up storyline involving Rick and Viv? Was the charity ball fun?

- Did you like Naomi's approach to this case?

Reviews Help Authors Telling Good Stories!

Word-of-mouth makes a huge difference for authors trying to attract readers. If you enjoyed the story, let others know with a review on Amazon, Goodreads, B&N, etc., or a shout-out on social media. A review at sfpowell.com works, too! If you enjoyed *Broken Benevolence*, please leave a review.

As always, I appreciate your support.

Sign-up on my email list for more book-series fun, and connect with me via social media (author.sfpowell).

Up next: *Gracious Bitterness*, in which Naomi provides family counseling. Four sisters: a history of betrayals and one too many secrets.